SHIPS AND MEN

THE COMPLETE EPIC

H. BED
SHIPS A

ORD-JONES

ND MEN

THE COMPLETE EPIC

Illustrated by
FREDERIC ANDERSON
GEORGE AVISON
JOHN RICHARD FLANAGAN
LEYLAND R. GUSTAVSON
ROBERT L. LAMBDIN
ARTHUR LYTELL
ALEX RAYMOND
ALFRED SIMPKIN
YNGVE E. SODERBERG
HARVE STEIN

ALTUS PRESS ~ 2019

Published by Altus Press

Visit altuspress.com for more books like this.

"Ships and Men" originally appeared in the January 1937–November 1939 issues of *Blue Book* magazine.
"A Large-Output Writer Talks" originally appeared in the July 1926 issue of *Writer's Digest* magazine.

THANKS TO
Digges La Touche and Janice Roberts

CONTENTS

DEEP-WATER PIONEER 1

THE FIRST SAIL 9

THE MOTHER REEF 18

NILE SKIPPER 28

ASTARTE SAILS TO WAR 37

THE FACE THAT LAUNCHED A THOUSAND SHIPS 46

THE WIDOW'S SON 57

WORK OF THE DEAD 66

THE THINGS THAT ARE CÆSAR'S 75

CLEOPATRA'S BEADS 85

THE SILENCE OF THE SEA 94

SON OF THE DRAGON KING 106

THE MAN WHO RULED THE WORLD 119

THE DEAD STRIKE BACK 129

A GIRL LIKE A SWORD 139

GOOD NIGHT TO ALL THE WORLD 150

PRINCESS OF CALICUT 159

FOR GLORY AND THE MAIN! 171

WE MUST FIGURE ON DEATH 180

FLYING DUTCHMAN 189

ROGUE'S YARN 198

CORSAIR OF CANADA 206

SATAN SAILS THE SHIP 218

HERO IN DEFEAT 227

LONG TOM O' DEVON 234

HANGING JOHNNY 243

BLACK CARGO 254

THE FIRST CLIPPER 265

SKIPPER OF THE GREYHOUND 274

MEN OF THE RIVER 284

STORMALONG 294

THE YELLOW SHIP 305

DEATH GAVE HIM HIS CHANCE 316

TRAMPS OF THE SEA 326

A LARGE-OUTPUT WRITER TALKS by J.R. Johnston 336

DEEP-WATER PIONEER

The San Marino shipyard was a lazy, sun-warm place, of steaming mud-flats, with every sort of old craft keeled along the shores or rotting in the creek. Away from all this backwash, the yards themselves hummed busily, while a blimp droned overhead with advertising banners displayed; across the hills, the towers of Los Angeles glittered in the blue California sky.

A number of old mariners hung about the place, inactive skippers gamming of an afternoon, or loafing in the shade. I met some queer characters here, and all of them ready and anxious to talk.

On this afternoon, as I came to the oily, dirty creek, I encountered Cap'n Powers, who in an interval of silence after a few minutes of desultory talk, took his pipe from his mouth and pointed with it to the creek.

"There's the first original sailor-man, matey!" said he. "Clap your peepers on him. Got real human sense, he has!"

Looking closely at the water, I perceived a large stick floating on the sluggish stream; on the stick was perched a grasshopper. Nothing more. Yet, as Cap'n Powers talked on, it loomed significant.

The straggling grass-growth along the edge of the creek took on shape and size to my reflective gaze. It waved heavily, in great tree-fern fronds, curled with winter's cold. The water itself changed, widened out, splotched with ice-cakes.

The floating stick grew before my eyes; it became a log, with a huge brownish splotch clinging to it. No grasshopper now, but a man. A queer man. The very look of him, like the look of those tree-ferns, carried me back and back across the centuries and ages into the bitter glacial days, the days of little three-toed horses, and ice-caps over the world. There was nothing strange in either an insect or a man floating on a bit of wood; but it did arouse one singular and exciting question which hammered for answer:

How did he get there?

For reply, look at Shorty the outcast, sitting alone and forlorn among the rocks, contemplating his unlovely image in a frigid pool, and wondering where his next meal was coming from. Shorty was stubby, wide-shouldered, with a most ingratiating grin, and next to nothing in the way of garments; for which lack his shaggy hair made amends.

Shorty was not admiring the scenery, by a good deal. He had been all but killed as a heretic—and an enemy of society by his own people, the Fish-eaters, who lived among the huddled rocks of a narrow-necked promontory far down the icy lake....

Chief Bignose had spent a year domesticating and training a wild dog, until the beast stood night watch on the long, narrow promontory. Only a fortnight back, the dog had saved the village from an attack by the Cave Folk. Shorty, anhungered and revolting against the fish and mussels, grubs and weeds of the communal pot, killed the big dog and ate him at two sittings.

So Shorty was stoned. He took refuge in the icy waters and managed to save his life by scant margin. Now, outcast, he sat unarmed and bare-handed, looking at the lake with its occasional islets of glacial ice. He had survived one encounter with this ice and water, and was not anxious for another.

small stature, now thrilled to the scent of blood and the lure of a woman at the same time—it was enough to turn a pygmy into a very hero!

What a woman! A wild girl, of the Cave Folk, with bronze-colored hair that hung to her hips. It was clean fine hair, not matted like that of the Fish-eaters; nor was her body shaggy like theirs, but covered with a lovely reddish fuzz that allowed its alluring outlines to be clearly perceived.

She was no slouch, either, but active as a man. Shorty comprehended that she was cutting up and dressing a roe deer, holding a long implement in her hand—one of those white bone knives the Cave Folk used. Shorty could see the use of the thing now; it was far better than the flints of his own people. But why the devil was this Cave-girl off on her own? Was she another outcast like himself?

"She's a beauty!" he muttered. "And worth while, if she can bring down a deer with that long knife of hers! With her brains and mine, two of us could live better and more cheaply than one. But I want some of that venison."

His mouth watered at thought of the high-flavored taste of Chief Bignose's pet. He peered into the blue-green pool, and then went on to other pools, hoping for the sight of a fish, but in vain. And then, across the narrow end of the lake to which he had come, drifted a sudden and enticing scent. He rose erect, wrinkling his flat nose.

Rigid, Shorty turned his shaggy bearded head, testing the wind. Yes, nose had told truth! Blood; the scent was beyond mistake. Fresh meat was being skinned or cut up. And just across this narrow arm of the lake! Shorty cupped his hands to shut out the dazzling sheen of sun on ice and water, and began to search carefully among the trees on the opposite shore.

A movement caught his eye, and again. He fastened on the spot. Then he stiffened incredulously—and froze with excitement, at what he saw. A woman! His breath came quick and fast. His eyes glittered. Shorty, disdained by the village girls because of his

True; food came first. The gnawing in his empty belly was intensified by the smell and sight of food. He measured the distance across the lake arm, and shivered. In the warm season it was not so bad, but just now the lake shore held massed snow, and the water held chunks of ice; and his feet were bruised and torn. If he went around, she would take to flight long ere he could reach her. But if he went straight at the job, she would have to leave some of the meat, at least.

With a grunt and another shiver of dread, Shorty went at the shore, clambered over ice and snow and driftwood, and reached the water. At the first touch of it, his body-hair curled from the numbing shock. He took a deep breath and plunged.

It was bitter, piercing to the very marrow. He struck out doggedly, heading straight for the opposite shore. He must have that meat or die; hang the girl! Meat meant life.

There was power and a tremendous vitality in this stubby frame of his. He progressed rapidly and furiously for a hundred yards, hurling himself through the bitter water with a savage intentness upon his goal. Then, without warning, a pain like the stab of a flint knife constricted his belly, empty of food this long while. Cramps seized his legs and arms; his eyes, frantic and bloodshot, rolled with dumb agony.

He could not draw breath to cry out. He was helpless, his lungs seeming to give way and collapse, a giant's hammer pounding at his temples. Then came a very miracle from the gods.

A wool-white cloud of mist, borne on the wings of a sweeping icy squall, swept down the narrow lake arm. The fantastic thing leaped straight for him and upon him; the water heaved around; a ripple of wavelets struck him; a drifting mass of icy particles hit him and skittered around. With the swishing blast of the squall came the rumble of subdued thunder, which faded and passed away among the peaks. And upon the thunder, a voice:

"Fight! *Fight!* I'll help you!"

The gods had spoken! Shorty, gnawing his blue lips to blood, struggled with new and frantic life. His hands kept him up as they nailed the water, but the numbing chill had crept into his heart, and the cramps were agonizing. Yet the gods had spoken!

No gods, had he known it, but the woman there beside her kill, watching him, shrieking at him as the squall struck and passed above him, leaving him still struggling in the water. Redfur of the Cave Folk, screaming her impulsive, eager encouragement at this man alone. Seeing him stricken, then swept by the squall and still adrift, her first exultant laughter passed into admiration.

Clutching the long bone knife, arms bloodied to the elbow, she stood at the water's edge, breasts heaving, hair flying, eyes blazing. This man was fighting the universal enemy, the gods of mountain, sky and water; deep instinct sent her to help this fellow-animal.

Like all her mountain folk, she hated and feared the water. She called out to the man, again and again. He renewed his feeble struggles, only to go under. Anger upburst within her. She waded out into the lake knee-deep, shook her knife, cursed the water, the glaciers, the snow-locked peaks. Suddenly a new and deeper cry broke from her lips, a cry that reached and rang across to the drowning figure:

"Behind you! Look behind you, man!"

Shorty, half-frozen and nearly helpless, twisted his head in sharp quick fear, only to see that the huge shape close upon him was no enemy, but part of a waterlogged tree, broken off and adrift, barely showing above the water. His clawing fingers reached for it, clutched at it, caught and held.

Sobbing out sharp breaths, he rested and then pulled himself to it, stretching out full length. He waved a hand at the woman; she shook her knife in response, a wild and exultant gesture. Shorty grinned. The cramps were leaving him now. Those mighty shoulders of his had drawn him to safety, but he was chilled through, and very numb. The biting wind struck him, knife-like.

He lifted his head, blinking at the shore. The woman was waving her arms at him, swinging them; she came knee-deep into the water again, pawing at it, slapping it, shouting at him. Shorty wondered if she was stark crazy. Scowling, he heard her shout to do the same thing.

Puzzled, he put out an arm and imitated her action, though unable to see any sense in it. Freezing as it was, the water was still warmer than the air, and for an instant felt good to his hand. He dipped in the other hand to get the same pleasant effect, paddling and thrusting.

Suddenly he realized that this motion of his arms made the log move.

It burst upon him full force, momentarily stunning him with the comprehension. Why, the woman had brains! He could move the thing, make it swim; and frantically he fell to work, with all his furious intensity of strength.

Blood resumed its circulation, and feeling returned to his numbed body. He waved at the woman and uttered a yelp of delight. He was moving the log, propelling it toward shore—very slowly, but surely. And the fresh raw meat was there, reaching out to him, inviting him!

His whole store of energy went into the job: flailing away like a madman, he gradually moved the log inshore until he could glimpse the bottom. Then he flopped off, gasped as he came into the water again, staggered shoreward. His eyes clouded, and he collapsed as he neared the snow-bound beach, Redfur, whimpering eagerly, dashed out and caught him, dragged him ashore, helped him past the ice to the bare ground.

Shorty was utterly exhausted. The hands of Redfur seized him; he tried to fight her off and could not. He stood swaying, until he realized that she was trying to help and guide him. More dead than alive, he stumbled on among the trees, while she pushed and shoved and dragged. Twice he went down, but she pummeled him until he came staggering up again in anger. Then he fell, and remembered nothing more....

When he wakened again, Shorty the outcast found the morning sun tinting mountain peaks and glaciers with a roseate glow. The smell of wood-smoke was in his nostrils; the smell of cooking meat aroused him. He found a rabbit-skin robe about him, and drew it closer. He was warm and joyous, despite his empty belly.

Fire, food, a woman! He had everything. Dimly he recalled how she had rubbed him, fed him, shoved him down into dreamless slumber.... He spoke sharply:

"Woman! *Woman!*"

No answer. He sniffed the air; no sign of her that way. He flung off the robe and sat up. He was lying in a shallow little cave, a fire outside it. Nothing here to indicate another presence. He leaped up and strode outside.

Fire embers among stones, a rude clay pot holding cooked meat; nothing else. The trees, dark and dismal, hemmed him in." The woman had gone. He cursed his heavy slumber. Gone! Then he had no woman after all, damn it! But she had left the meat. He started for it—and halted abruptly, his animal senses suddenly alert.

A slight sound reached him. He glanced around for a weapon, found none, then crouched at one side of the cave mouth, listening. Something was there among the trees of the slope. Ah! The woman! She came suddenly into full sight. A small deer was flung over her shoulder; in the girdle about her hips Was the long bone knife. Shorty felt a wild, ecstatic glow take hold of him.

He stepped out into the open. The deer fell; the bone knife flashed out; then she recognized him and relaxed. Shorty grinned, and his grin was a thing to like at first sight.

"Who are you?" he grunted. "Cave Folk?"

"No; I've left them, I'm alone," she said. "Redfur."

Shorty

"Good name, Redfur. Suits you. I'm Shorty—got kicked out because I don't like fish. I'm on my own. Redfur, you're all right!"

He came to her, caught hold of her, put his arm about her shoulders and looked into her face. His arm tightened—then she twisted free, fetching him a sound clip that knocked him sprawling.

He leaped erect, met her angry defiance With a snarl, and balanced for the leap. She had drawn her bone knife and was poised to meet him, a flame of anger in her eyes. Shorty was on the very point of springing, when he rocked back suddenly on his heels. Fear and terror froze him. The hulking, shambling thing behind her, following the scent of fresh blood—a bear, just out of winter hibernation, ravenously hungry, still soft-pawed but enormous.

"Look out!" Shorty found voice. "Old man of the caves! Jump for it! Grab the tree-branch above you. Then throw me the knife. Quick!"

A ruse on his part? Redfur darted one quick glance over her shoulder, and saw the beast, rolling forward and almost upon her. With one cry she was in the air, leaping for the limb overhead, springing upward with frantic velocity. She caught the branch, twisted her lithe body, swung up astride the limb. The huge beast reared up underneath, pawing at her, growling and slavering.

Then, whirling, the bear blinked at Shorty and went for him.

Redfur had dropped the bone knife, but Shorty could not reach it in time. He had the cave behind him, and ho refuge except flight; but Shorty was not the man to run for it and leave meat and woman behind. He dodged the first vicious swing and backswing of those huge paws. A claw caught and ripped his shoulder. No running for it, now! That apparently clumsy creature could run down any man.

Dodging, ducking, sent sprawling by a swipe of the huge paw, Shorty reeled over and was up again. He had the knife now, and the shambling beast had him, was hard upon him, was reaching for him. He lunged desperately, sank the long splinter-like bone to the very grip in the fur and skin and flesh of the throat. Then he went down and knew himself lost....

With this, something happened—a tremendous crash. Shorty somehow scrambled aside, squirmed clear. Redfur was out of the tree, had picked up a huge rock and smashed it home; now she was poising another, a fifty-pound jagged knot of rock. It drove home to the skull of the great brute and did its work. Shorty darted in, freed the bone knife, drove it again into the toppled carcass, and leaped away with agility from the flailing, dying paws.

Panting, he stared at Redfur in wild exultation. With skull crushed and throat pierced, a bear lay dead, an old man of the caves! Usually it took wild dogs and a dozen hunters to subdue one of these beasts.

"You and I—ha! We are good," said Shorty in delight.

"We are good," Redfur cried, her eyes ablaze.

"We go together. You are my woman, Redfur!" And he waved the reddened bone knife at her. He saw a change come into her face. Her mouth flew open; the blood ebbed from her cheeks; her excited eyes distended.

"Then prove it," she exclaimed. "Look!"

Shorty turned and saw them—two of them, Cave Folk, huge hairy men, padding down the slope among the trees, heading for them: one with knotted club the other with spear ready.

"After me—they've come after me!" gasped Redfur. "I ran away from them—"

Her words died in sudden stark fear. But Shorty braced himself, a snarl on his lips. His traditional enemies, were these Cave Folk, who raided the Fish-eaters and carried off girls and women. Bone knife against club and flint-tipped spear? So be it. This sliver of bone in his hand was a joyful thing.

Redfur

The two great hairy men came running straight in, yelping With eagerness, weapons poised. Shorty stood motionless, wary, alert. Spear came first; thrusting for him, darting at him to transfix his body. He twisted quickly, crashed into the man behind it as he evaded the stroke, and the long bone knife lunged upward, driving home with savage force. The little wide-shouldered man was a sudden demon, ducking the club that swung for him, squirming away from the dying man, to plunge at the second for full tilt.

That second giant slipped in the bear's blood, and Shorty had him in a flash, drove the long knife through his throat, jerked it loose, sprang away. The two of them were sprawled there; and a wild, fierce laugh broke from the killer.

"Proved it, Redfur!" he shouted joyously, and caught her long hair. "My woman!"

She whimpered and clung to him. Then she broke away, stood with hair astream, head flung back, breasts quivering, and pointed upward. Shorty

The woman was down, half-senseless; the hair giant, about to pick her up, wheeled as the little man drove for him. His club swung.

a thing or two—bringing back a woman and a knife like this! I said you had brains. Come along, then."

They moved—halted, looked at each other, then at the shore, where boulders broke the snow and ice. No log here, no fallen tree. It was gone.

"Find another!" she cried sharply. "Look—"

Shorty glanced back, and growled. The pack, indeed! Moving figures, outspread among the trees; the eager, excited tongues of half-wild dogs. One figure, dog leashed close, ahead of the others, was leaping and slithering along with the animal.

looked. There above the cave on the ledge, another of the Cave Folk, who uttered a loud yell and then stood, waiting, staring down.

"My people—all of them! With dogs, to run me down!" Redfur cried out. "Too many for us, Shorty. Wait!"

She darted into the cave and came out again, the robe of rabbit-skins over her shoulder. A robe, at such a moment? From Shorty broke a laugh.

"To the forest?" he exclaimed.

She dissented.

"The dogs—no! They would run us down. There is only one way. Come!"

Shorty was very far from comprehension, but he knew well enough that to face that pack of Cave Folk, with their wild dogs, were sheer folly. To run from them were useless. This woman had brains, so he fell in beside her and saved his breath. What a woman she was! Pride swelled within him as he eyed her lithe bronze body, her blazing eyes, her firm loveliness.

The lake glittered before them, and the shore of the arm that Shorty remembered from last night. If she had grabbed up the fur robe, he had snatched meat from her clay pot. He tore at it with his teeth, gave her part of it, and came to a halt.

"Well?"

"The tree," she gasped out. "We must go in the water."

"Ha!" Shorty leaped exultant to the idea. "To my people, yes! Kick me out, will they? I'll show them

Redfur had darted away, running desperately along the snow and rocks that fringed the lake-edge, and Shorty darted after. She leaped from boulder to boulder like a wild chamois, but Shorty found himself failing. He had done yeoman's work this day; he was battered and ripped; his feet left red stains in the snow.

Glancing back, he saw that hairy giant with his leashed wild dog coming with great bounds, holding a long splay-ended club in his free hand and swinging it like a toy. Shorty lowered his shaggy head and stumbled forward. He squinted ahead among the jagged boulders where Redfur had disappeared; they were larger here, jutting masses of rock. He lifted his hoarse voice and called.

Then he had his answer. He came into sight of her, perched on a great boulder, all agleam in the clean hot sunlight like a bronze goddess, against the blue of the water. She waved to him, called him on, and Shorty plunged forward.

He pounded down to the boulder; she slipped from it, and pointed to a great broken tree, one end fastened in the snow, the other adrift.

"Hurry! It's too big for me to move—I tried it."

Together they bent to the task, grunting, shoving, breaking the tree loose. It cracked clear of the snow and ice; it moved.... Then lifted a sudden wild yell from behind. The man and the slavering dog were upon them.

Redfur wheeled and stood with teeth bared, a cornered animal. Shorty whipped out the bone knife, had a glimpse of that hairy giant leaping forward, was aware of the dog loosed and hurtling at his throat. He stabbed ineffectually; the weight of the animal knocked him backward. Hairy arm helped; the shaggy beard saved his throat and caught the gleaming teeth. They rolled together in the snow, claws and nails at work, teeth slashing—then the bone knife slid home.

Shorty lurched to his feet, glaring.

The woman was down, half senseless, the hairy giant about to pick her up in one hand and fling her body over his shoulder. He wheeled about as the little wide-shouldered man drove for him. His club swung; but Redfur awakened. She bit and clawed savagely, so that the huge Cave-man dropped her.

Shorty dodged the clumsy sweep of the club, and struck. The knife plunged into the bulging chest. The giant's free hand fetched him a buffet that knocked him headlong, sending him sliding and sprawling ten feet away, with blood running from ears and nostrils. But when he scrambled up, Shorty saw that great hairy figure collapsed beside the dead dog—snarling, and plucking feebly at the bone knife still fast in the wound.

Redfur exclaimed: "We could burn a hollow place—then we wouldn't worry about falling off." Shorty hugged her. "I said you had brains!" he cried exultantly.

Then Redfur, catching up the fallen splay-bladed club, swung it once and settled what her mate had begun. She spat at the dead thing and freed the bone knife, and caught Shorty in her arms as he came staggering back.

"Good! You're good, Shorty!" she gasped out. "Quick, now—"

They bent to the log again. He took the club from her and used it as a lever, and the huge fallen tree was afloat. One protruding branch remained. With the club, Shorty smashed this off. The tree was long dead—pithy, it floated light.

A baying of dogs, a wild outburst of voices—the pursuit was swift and close upon them. Redfur scrambled onto the log, and Shorty pushed at it, shoving it out, sending it away with one thrust of his powerful shoulders. He waded out after it. A spear went past his shoulder. He planted his feet deep, set the club against the log, Shoved mightily again—then flung himself after.

Club still in hand, he caught the end of the surging, drifting log, and after a moment hauled himself up. Redfur, jubilant, was standing erect and jeering back at the Cave Folk. These, in utter blank amazement, fringed the shore, staring, cursing, bellowing threats. Some of them fell to work heaving stones; but already the log was drifting well out.

Shorty jeered and cursed, capered, shook the club, and finally dropped with joyous exhaustion. Safe!

Bloody and battered, he grinned at Redfur, and she broke into an excited laugh.

"Your people—suppose they kick us out?"

"Let 'em try!" said Shorty with a grin, and touched his club. "Just let 'em try, Redfur! They're a pack of rabbits. Any man who can kill bears and Cave-men can master the lot of them; especially with you to help. Woman, you've got brains!"

"So have you." And she laughed again, happily. "But we'll never get there just by floating in the lake. Shall we use our hands?"

Shorty frowned. He picked up the splay-bladed club and tapped the log; solid and wide, this log; a little tippy, but safe enough. He reached the club down into the water and then again, to see how the club floated.

"Shorty!" exclaimed Redfur suddenly. "Do that again!"

"Huh? Do what?" he grunted, staring at her.

"*That!* With the club, in the water."

Shorty dipped the club; and then was aware that the log moved a little to the thrust. Surprise leaped in his face; a quick, eager laugh broke from Redfur. Once again; the log surged ahead a little.

"It's like a hand, Shorty!" the woman cried. "You move it back, push against the water, and we move forward!"

Like a hand indeed. Pleased as a buck deer with a new set of antlers, Shorty flailed away. The log moved and moved. The ripples and the ice-chunks stirred past them and fell slowly behind.

The daylight died; the cold stars came out. Imperceptibly, but steadily, the log now was creeping across the wide lake. They would get across by morning; Shorty looked forward with grim intentness to the meeting with his own folk again.

Redfur, who had been taking her turn with the club-paddle, joined him in the middle of the log; they huddled together for warmth. Redfur scooped at the rough bark with her hand.

"Look—we could do that!" she exclaimed. "We could put fire on it and burn a hollow place to lie. Then we wouldn't worry about falling off."

Shorty hugged her tightly. "I said you had brains!" he cried exultantly.

The first boat, the first paddle, had been found.

*A sharp mill-whistle, blasting five-o'clock closing-*time, jerked me out of my musings in the past, recalled me to the shipyard and the oily, dirty creek. The stick still floated there, around and around, with the insect clinging to it.

Old Cap'n Powers, who had fallen fast asleep in the warm sunlight, straightened up with a jerk. He eyed me guiltily, and fumbled for his lost pipe.

"Hey? What was that you was talking about?" he demanded. "Oh, sure; that there hoppergrass on the stick—the first original sailor-man! But here's a queer thing, matey: It ain't what he does when he gets on the stick and begins to navigate, that sticks in my gizzard. The question is, how did he come to get on that there stick in the first place, and shove out from shore? And if you ask me, I'll bet you a dollar ag'in' a Mexican cent, that there's a lady grasshopper in it some place!"

And thinking of Redfur of the Cave Folk, I knew that Cap'n Powers was dead right.

THE FIRST SAIL

Perhaps you remember the furor in the newspapers and magazines over the award of last year's Grand Prix to an unknown Chicago artist? You must have read about the storm of censure that broke over Kleman's head when his picture was hung, and about his tragic death, and about the Grand Prix being awarded him. You must have seen the reproductions of his prize painting, "The Shell," and the wide controversy that raged over its symbolism.

First, let me recall the picture to you: A strangely provocative canvas, misty, with striking projections into the light and mysterious fadings into the dark. A single figure on the seashore, fingering a shell; another shell floating in the water. A figure askew, humpbacked, with wistful savage features and wide eyes—so strange an expression on that face as it stares up, that the beholder gasps, and looks again.

So much for the canvas. Now for the man and his story. I am the only man in the world who knows the truth about Kleman's death....

I was wandering one day among the vast sand-dunes south and east of Chicago, near the Michigan State line, when I came on the man and his easel. It was a quiet, secluded spot—one of those rare little retreats that trippers have not yet found and stripped of its ground-pine and wild loveliness.

Kleman looked up with a savage scowl as I approached. Then he changed to an expression of grudging tolerance; we had met the previous week at the studio of Broch, the Viennese muralist, on the North Side.

He grunted reluctant admission now to his charmed circle, and I looked at the work before him.

It was "The Shell," still unfinished, yet breathtaking in its powerful planes and marvelous surfaces; a nebulous thing defying all art, yet gripping at the soul.

I was, of course, blind to the figure of Kleman himself—that broken, twisted figure, one shoulder higher than the other, chin puckered into the chest, which left him solitary among mankind. I gazed at his canvas, and blurted out what came into my head.

"Hm! The poor benighted savage doesn't make a portrait of his Deity; in fact, he doesn't know what his Deity looks like. He sees God in clouds and hears Him in the wind. Congratulations, Kleman. Thanks be, I'm no art-critic. This is worth seeing."

Those chance words drove straight home. Kleman's apparent ferocity was all a mask. Inwardly he was the gentlest and kindliest of men. Now he fairly beamed at me.

"Good God! A man who understands my picture!"

"Far from it," I said thoughtfully. "I doubt if anyone could really understand it; but it's well worth the effort. I never in my life—well, very seldom—saw such a thing. You've done others?"

"Daubs." He waved his hand. "This is *the* picture, for me."

A long time we talked. He was waiting to capture the swirl of twilight along the shore. He loved this spot. He had come to the dunes for years past, to sit and dream here. I noticed an odd thing. The misty vagueness of his canvas was very like the high uncertain drift of Chicago's smoke across the lake. When I mentioned this, he beamed again. We were friends....

that the dead tree-branch on the shore had the touch of an infernal Dürer, he laughed excitedly and patted my arm.

"Wonderful! I took it from one of Dürer's devils. Nobody seems to know it, but the church at Fairford, in England, has stained glass windows that a buccaneer captured and brought home and installed there in 1493. The most glorious devils you ever saw, and all from the very hand of Albrecht Dürer! Yes. That is my tree-branch. And the twisted man! How I know him! He has talked to me, I tell you. That sad, wistful, struggling face, the face of birth and death and triumph—you see it! And the world will see it, my friend. I too will find the ecstasy of creation, of conquest and comprehension and compensation, as he found it, this queer old Humpy of mine, who lived in the fogs when the world was young, and the island people were cruel as the people there in Chicago across the lake—"

They were very cruel, these island folk in the youth of the world; barbarically cruel and crude and fierce, clad in skins, believing that the deities of earth and sea were devils to be propitiated with bloody sacrifice.

They voyaged about in dugouts, logs of trees hollowed out, with as many as a dozen paddlers; huge, ungainly, unwieldy things that sometimes blew out to sea and were lost. In these they looted one another and the mainland, savagely.

Amid this welter of barbarism slowly emerged Humpy. Chin sunk, one shoulder high, a twisted foot: a man accursed. His father was the great chief, and therefore he lived, but not as these others lived. Humpy was very powerful in the arms, a strong swimmer, but not like the others in the face any more than in the body. He had wide, luminous eyes and a wide, strong mouth; and he was very gentle with the old folks; he did not believe in knocking them on the head when they grew feeble.

I came back to the same place on recurrent days. We sat and talked for long hours. Kleman was sensitive about his misshapen figure; but by the law of compensation, it had given him some far, deep quality most men lack. An accident in boyhood had broken his life and welded it again at strange tangents.

There was an eerie, faintly macabre something about him, about his picture. After a time I came to comprehend it, in a way; and the feeling took possession of me with greater power as time went on. Kleman talked freely enough about some things, merely hinted at others. I had to grope for much of what I discovered.

He had lived with this picture for years. No great work of art bursts suddenly into being; it is the fruit of slow sap and patient pruning. Kleman had a most amazing fund of knowledge, too. When I remarked

He did not believe in the devils, either, but talked strangely about a lovely sea-foam girl who whispered to him at times in the night, and came to him when he was down by the shore and the tide was out. She was a goddess, he said. This raised much laughter. Because of his twisted body, he had nothing to do with the women, and they despised him and hated him. He spent much of his time alone, either in a small dugout or off on the mainland shore.

Once he tried to make the wind carry his dugout along, by raising a screen of hides that caught the wind. It worked for a time, and others imitated him; but a gust caught all the unwieldy craft and overturned them. Humpy swam five miles and was safe; seventeen others were drowned or eaten by sharks, and this made all the people hate Humpy more than ever. Often, after this, he tried to make a sail carry his dugout, but had no luck with it.

Then came the time when the devils tossed up the sea in a great wave that swept many people away. The sacrifice of Humpy was demanded, but his father was the chief, and despite some doubts, saved him. Soon after this, his father and some other men, in two of the largest craft, were swept out to sea and lost in a storm.

Then the island folk came to take him, to sacrifice him to the devils. He fled from them, with his bow and his dugout and some food. Two arrows found him, but not mortally; he reached the mainland alive, and they lost him.

Humpy discovered a cave near the shore, and settled down there, a man accursed....

A strange happiness came to him here. He was no longer harried and hunted and hated. The mainland people thought he was some strange god who had come out of the sea to bring them luck. They fetched offerings of food and skins to his cave, and he was gentle with them, and cured some of them who were hurt or sick. But ever his heart turned toward his own people, and the indolent islands scattered along the blue horizon.

Humpy lived in curious fashion, these days. He had no need to kill the wild creatures for food; instead, he made friends with them, so that the mainland folk were all the more certain that he was a god of some kind. Even the savage beasts avoided him, or looked at him with lazy glowering eyes, standing silent as he talked to them. His gentleness and his power were astonishing, for it had no weakness; he did not fear to kill sharks by sticking double-pointed sticks in their jaws as they clutched for him.

He was much in the sea, over the long reefs at low tide, sitting for hours by the rush of waves and the spindrift in the sunlight, by the long bursting rollers in the moonlight. Voices came to him out of the waves. The sea-foam girl was there often, in the sparkle of the water.

He could see her; he could talk with her. Sometimes, in a heart-wrenching agony of desire, he would rush into the long waves and seek her beyond the white surf. Frequently, when a great billow swept in and reared up full thirty feet for the curving burst, he would see her in the foaming sun-struck whiteness. But he could never find her.

And then, one day when he was lazying down by the cove, came the shell, and the sweet secret voice of her, murmuring into his brain from the vasty deep beyond.

"Why not, why not?" it said, in the reverberant mistiness of the white surf. "Why not you, if it? If it, why not you?"

If it—why not he, indeed?

He wakened, sprang up, went down ankle-deep into the swirling water. A shell was there, like the others on the beach; but this was floating in the water. He fancied that the slim white fingers of the sea-foam girl had reached out to put it there as she spoke to his brain. A curl of the receding wave showed her face for an instant—a lovely face, radiant and comforting, looking back to him with love and tenderness ere it vanished. He was awed; his heart was near to bursting. He wanted to go leaping down into the water and find her. But there was the shell.

Others of them, large and small; but this one was afloat. He stared down at it. Pointed at one end, rounded at the other, half-decked. It floated, swerved about his feet. He reached out his hand to it.'

"If it, why not you? Why not?"

The words came again, tenderly reaching to him out of the white foam, wakening something in him, bringing comprehension to him. Why not, indeed! He put the shell in the water again. From the shore, he picked up another of the same sort, but larger. He stood fingering it.

A blaze lighted in his eyes. He lifted up his face, stared into the sunlight and the spindrift; his wide eyes held all the glory of the dawn, of wakening life, of understanding. It was the moment, the supreme moment of vision, of grasping brain and hammering pulses, of unseen things and forces surging from within.

"Sea-foam girl!" he shouted at the surf, and waved an arm wildly. "I hear you! I understand!"

But did he, indeed? With the shell, he hastened back to the shore and took his sharp hardwood fire-drill. Carefully he went to work on the shell until he had broken a tiny hole in the half-deck. Into this he thrust a slender twig, and with the twig transfixed a leaf. He took the shell down to the water again and set it afloat. The wind caught the leaf, sent the shell hither and thither.

Humpy clapped his hands, then turned about and went running and leaping back to his own home, shouting in his deep rich voice like a madman. But he was very sane. It was only the ecstasy of comprehension, of vision, that gripped him. The voice of the sea-foam girl had wakened the brain in him.

"If it, why not you?" The words came to him out of the white foam. Why not, indeed? "Sea-foam girl!" he shouted. "I understand!"

During long days he labored away in ecstatic fury, now failing, now winning as he learned from failure. He peeled saplings and bent them, and lashed them together with gut strands, until he had a framework rudely shaped like the shell. Over this he stretched skins, sewing them together with gut. When the thing was finished, he lifted it down to the water, shoved it out, and clambered in; it sank in two minutes, for the water poured in through the seams.

He talked again with the sea-foam girl that night, sitting beside the shore and groaning, listening, lost in despondent hopelessness. But a whisper came to him in the dawn; the mist, curling about the shore trees, showed a slim white shape that grew upon him with outreaching hand as though to touch him. He stumbled toward it, clutching at the air, and the sea-foam girl lessened and was gone.

"The wood in the fire!" he heard her voice.

What it meant, he knew not. He came back to his fire and looked at the wood. A resinous sap was exuding with the heat. He touched it, burned his fingers, sucked them, found them sticky. Her voice whispered again to him. Frowning, he collected some of the sap and smeared it on the seams of his boat. It hardened; it was impervious to water! Shouting, he ran to collect more of the resinous pine, and in a few hours had all the seams calked and water-tight. Now, he discovered, the boat floated.

More days of anxious, eager experiments followed. At length the pole was made secure, and to it a skin sail was hung. Then you might have seen Humpy, in wild joy, sailing forth, steering with his paddle while the skin boat skimmed over the water. True, it was a wabbly and uncertain thing, and it would only go as the wind pushed it, so that he had to paddle home again; but—*it sailed!*

The very next day, finding the wind fair, he started forth to make the blue islands on the horizon. He got no more than a hundred yards, for he started at low tide, and just beyond the surf ran on a submerged reef. It cut the bottom out of his boat; the craft went down from under him, and he had to swim ashore.

He emerged laughing, then shook the water off him and stood a-drip, staring out at the sunken reef, his brows knotted. He lifted both arms.

"Not yet, sea-foam girl!" he cried. "Now I understand! You wanted me to build a boat so that I might come to you, so that you might clutch me down in some far dim place, to join you! Well, wait a little. Wait till I have built a good boat, and then I'll come to you, across the horizon."

He fell to work again, building a stouter and larger craft....

Now happened an unkind thing. A flat calm fell upon the sea, and in this calm the island people came in their dugouts to raid the mainland, stealing women and killing men, burning and plundering. The havoc they caused was sore, and they went home to the islands with huge booty.

But the mainland folk, such as were left in these parts, took it into their heads that Humpy had brought this ruin upon them. Instead of regarding him as a god, now they came to stone him. Because his bow was strong and his arrows far-reaching, they dared not come nigh him, but stood afar off with threats and jeers; nor could he win them from this hatred. Certain of their hunters slunk in the thickets to waylay him, also.

The poor twisted man, who hated none, clung to his cave and his work by the shore, with grief and loneliness upon him. He was despised and cast out by all men, an accursed creature without hope or future. In all the world, he had only this: his vision of the sea-foam girl, and the boat she had given him to make.

He spent hours by the shore, communing with her, finding solace and consolation in her loveliness and her tender eyes. She would come in the mists, in the driving spume from off the reefs, or in the depths of deep green pools he would see her face. The pine trees overhanging the shore would carry her voice to him; strange things would waken in his brain.

A comber lifted her higher and higher; in the curling crest of the burst, she was there, arms outflung—alive, alive!

And all the while, his work went forward, the new boat that he was building taking slow but sure shape, larger and firmer than the first.

The boat became his vision, his life. Over each detail he would commune with the sea-foam girl, the only creature in the world who had tenderness for him. His outward fierceness frightened away the hunters who slunk through the trees. All these folk now left him quite alone, and he was glad.

More and more, his heart turned to his own

people, out there on the islands, for the sea-foam girl whispered to him about them, and he longed for the reefs and pools and the islands he had known as a boy. He would give his own people all the secrets of his boat, be would teach them the mastery of the waters; then they would realize that this twisted body of his had produced something after all.

More—he would lift the sea-foam girl to a proud place as their goddess; would do away with all their devils and bloody worship of evil things. Farther and higher lifted his vision of the future. His people would see it too, when they realized what this boat would do, would mean to them! They would enshrine the sea-foam girl; and he, the disdained and malformed outcast, would become their benefactor and ruler. And through the years, as the sea-foam girl whispered to him, her secret lover and friend, more and more secrets would be evolved, wonderful creations without end.

"Aphrodite!" Standing waist-deep in the water, he called out to her as the high spindrift hung in the air, and made a glorious rainbow bridge in the sunlight. "Aphrodite Anadyomene! Love, born of the sea-foam—this is my name for you, beloved! By this name shall you be known forever among men!"

His boat floated at last. Now he labored getting a mast in place; and having learned from his first one, he made a yard across the mast, the better to stretch his hide sail. When all was done, he tried it out cautiously, carefully. Steering with his paddle, hauling in on the thong made fast to the bottom of the sail, or letting out again, he could even handle the craft to some extent, and its possibilities grew upon him. It was incomparably superior to his first boat.

In exuberant, heart-pounding delight, he waited for an offshore wind that would sweep him out to the islands on the horizon. Forgotten was his askew shape, all his handicaps. His people would welcome him, would welcome this boat with awe and wonder; the past was wiped out, the future would make amends!

Storm came, instead of favoring wind: a three-day gale that drove in furiously upon the coast. And on the first night, while it was gathering force, a strange thing happened.

Humpy had crept out upon the rocks of the cove, where the spume flew high in the night. He had built up his fire on shore, as he frequently did at such times, for then the ruddy reflection lighted the spray-filled air and the spouting crests, just enough to let the sea-foam girl appear sometimes in flashing glimpses.

He crouched among the rocks, enjoying the salt sea-spray, shouting aloud to Anadyomene as the breakers smote and burst. He fancied her there, all white and shining and ruddy-gold of hair; he talked with her, felt her voice beat in upon his brain and waken it.

Then, suddenly, in the momentary back-rush of the breakers, he saw her figure clear and distant against a dark blotch. He leaped upright. A comber came driving in, lifted her higher and higher. In the curling crest of the burst, she was there, arms outflung, alive, alive!

Humpy went into that mad swirl of bursting waters with one leap, and battled it. The dark blotch, a tangle of wreckage lashed together, logs and paddles, had smashed and broken asunder—but she was there, she was safe, she was clinging to him. The wonder of it lent him furious strength, and his long arms beat back to the rocks, and he drew her before the firelight.

All white and slim and ruddy gold of hair, his vision came to life, Anadyomene come to his arms! In the radiance, blood flecked her body here and there as she lay with closed eyes, breathing faintly. Humpy worked over her. He heaped skins upon her, warmed her, saw her at length open her eyes and look up at him. And then she smiled, and touched him with her hand, and closed her eyes again.

His heart was full to bursting at the smile, at the touch. It was the tenderness of his sea-foam girl made flesh—the one creature who loved him, who shrank not at the sight of him, nor derided him with jeers. She had come out of the storm to him.... Would she go away again?

He watched, unwinking, until the day came, with gray scud of cloud, and the increased whooping of the gale at full splendor of power.

She was still there. She wakened to warmth and fire and food in the cave. Not until now had he dared to touch her wounded flesh, lest he waken her and she flee back to the foam in the darkness. But now, in the daylight, she was real and no dream!

"Anadyomene!" he said, his voice like a caress, his wide luminous eyes filled with all the longing of his heart.

While he probed her hurts and bandaged them, his massive gnarled fingers were soft and gentle as down. She gazed into his eyes and lay smiling as he worked, watching him. Perhaps this sea-foam girl thought him, too, some deity of the mainland shore, very ugly and kindly and compassionate.

Some vague consciousness, at least, of his singular power over all wild things must have possessed her, something of the queer feeling that the beasts had for him, so that they trembled and caressed his hand—for she, too, trembled a little as she lay there watching.

When he had finished, when he held food and broth to her lips, when he wiped the white hard salt from her skin and from the gossamer-spun red-gold of her dried hair, she smiled again, and held her hand against his cheek, and spoke.

Her voice was low and penetrating, the same voice that had come to him from the sounding sea and the whispering trees; but he could not understand her words, nor she his. No matter; it was a small thing. Tears came into his eyes and glittered on his cheeks, at her touch; tears of happiness, of sheer soul-ecstasy.

"Anadyomene!" burst from him. Then his head fell forward.

The storm mounted. All this day, and all the next, that wild gale swooped on the coasts, and the thundering surf hammered and battered on the reefs, while the two of them lay close, here in the cave mouth. Two more days passed, ere the tossing seas quieted and the wind came fair for the islands on the horizon.

The poor twisted man was a new creature these days, lighted from within by such a glory as transfigured him, so that there was a flame in his face and a glow in his wide eyes, and magic in his voice.

Humpy worshiped the goddess and loved her, and she him, very gently and tenderly as though he were a child. They could not comprehend each other's speech, but she assented to all that he said, and smiled, so that his heart was warm and content. By gestures, he told her of his people out there in the islands, and how he was now able to take them not only the gift of the sea-foam goddess, but herself as well; and if Anadyomene did not get his meaning, she smiled none the less.

Evening came—the seas were down, and Humpy knew that with the dawn the offshore wind would be here to take him to the islands. His boat was ready for the trip, tested and sure; he had a skin of drinking-water, and food enough, to put in. In less than a day, if the wind held, he would reach his own folk again.

He told her of it that night.

"Sunrise will see us off, Anadyomene! Sunrise, and you and I together. Will it make you happy, beloved, to have the worship of my people?"

She smiled and assented, and touched his brown hard arm with her fingers.

There was a very high, still tide that night; the moon was out full and strong and round. The tide crept in silently, with no smashing surf. In the vibrant moon-glow, phosphorescence rippled and twinkled about the reefs.

"Strange things out there tonight," said Humpy, looking across the water. "On high tides like this, the deep creatures come out after storms, and crawl to the reefs. Things with a lot of arms, searching trapped fish in the pool. Stay away from the shore at times like this, beloved."

Anadyomene smiled and nodded, and her hand touched his cheek caressingly.

Late in the night, or early in the morning, Humpy wakened to chill air. He heard the voice of Anadyomene, calling him, but very far away and faint. He started up, felt for her beside him, and found nothing.

The moon was wan and westering. But there was light enough. He called to her, and heard her voice again, for the last time; it came from seaward. He ran out of the cave, and there in the white sand found her tracks, and followed them down to the shore, where the tide was ebbing out now. A little faint, far sound of her voice, and nothing more. She was gone—gone, back to the sea-foam whence she had come.

Humpy stood there stupefied for a long time, looking out at the curling, changing phosphorescent lights in the water. Desolation and loss were upon him. Gone! Then he shook himself suddenly. She had gone, yes! Gone out to the islands to await his coming. She would join him there, would come to him again, when his people had made him welcome. He stretched out his arms and called:

"Tomorrow, Anadyomene!"

The breeze came up with dawn. Eagerly, lustily, he got the boat out into the water, loaded everything aboard, pushed out and clambered in. The skin sail took the wind, bellied out, and to the thrust of his steering paddle the boat skimmed the long slow waves.

Humpy roared out joyous songs as the wind swept him. His boat was good; the wind was fair and full, he was homeward bound, homeward! And Anadyomene would meet him there in the splendor of the spindrift, in the curling thrust of surf—she, the goddess whom his people would adore and worship! She had gone back to the sea in order to meet him out there at the horizon!

The wind held. Morning passed, and the islands were growing now, blocking that long sword-sweep of the horizon line. Fresher grew the wind, and the boat danced on merrily, answering to every twist of the sail, every paddle-thrust and swerve. Humpy was overjoyed by the way she handled.

Squinting at the old well-known islands as they grew, he steered down between them to make for the chief village of his people, a long and deeply sheltered cove. The afternoon drew on. In every wave-crest, each white swirl that marked hidden reefs, Humpy looked for the sea-foam girl to rise and greet him. He saw her not. Later she would come, perhaps when night had drawn down the sky.

Eagerly, he turned his thoughts to the meeting with his own people. As he came in between the islands, conch-shells were being blown, smoke-signals were going up. He had been seen from afar.

And now the deep harbor opened, and a dozen dugouts were being paddled forth to the meeting. He clawed at his sail, and bit in with his paddle, and came sweeping down upon them. He waved an arm exultantly. There were men he knew, chiefs and warriors at the paddles. They recognized him.

"Humpy!"

The yells were shrill and high, with a fierce deep note that boded no joyful greeting. Humpy, his eyes ablaze, waved his paddle and let the hide sail go flapping, and drifted down toward the dugouts. They had spread out before him. He stood up, now, in his boat—and lifted his voice joyfully:

"People! I bring you a gift from the sea-foam goddess! Look at this boat. With boats like this, you can master all the islands, all the seas and coasts! With this sail—"

A long, shrill yell rose up and drowned his words.

"Yah! We've heard that story before!" shouted one of the chiefs. "And because we listened to you and used sails, seventeen men died in the grip of the sea devils! —Let him have it!"

An arrow glittered on the sunlight, then another. There was a twanging of bows....

Humpy stood there, clinging to his peeled pole of a mast. Surprise and dismayed astonishment were frozen in his face. He clutched with one hand at the long shafts that thudded into his twisted body, and then he slowly sank to his knees, so that his head overhung the gun-wale of his leaning boat. He tried to speak, but at first only blood came from his lips.

"Anadyomene!" The word burst from him. He looked down into the sun-struck radiant water, and he saw her face there, saw her rising from the depths, her arms outstretched to him in sorrow and tenderness and glad greeting.

"Anadyomene!" he said again, and then his head fell forward.

The dugouts gathered around, cautiously, and came closer. With amazement the island folk looked on this strange craft. Those among them who were the best seamen, comprehended it vaguely, and seized upon it with swift eagerness. And ere many days had passed, they were at work building other such boats.

But Humpy, poor twisted man, had found his sea-foam goddess at last.

This was the story that I had from Kleman the hunchbacked painter, in his quiet little cove among the Michigan sand-dunes. Not in so many words; you understand, but in gropings and comprehensions of gradual progress. The story that lay behind that painting of his, that obsessed and thwarted life of his.

"You haven't put Anadyomene in the canvas, though," I said. He looked up at me, his eyes dilated and luminous.

"But I have!" he said in a low voice. "She is there, my friend; but you must have the eyes of Humpy if you would see her."

Something in his voice made me shiver.

His picture was finished and sent in, and I neither saw nor heard anything from him for some time. Then, when it was rumored that his picture was one of those being considered for the Grand Prix, the howls began to burst. How that canvas was derided! It encountered a storm of criticism from all quarters—and yet the power of it was not denied.

One morning I got a scrawled postcard in the mail. It read:

> *What did I tell you? Only the eyes of Humpy could discern Anadyomene. Always the dream fails.*
>
> *—K.*

And when I opened the morning paper, I was greeted by his picture, and the story of his suicide.

Two days later, his picture was awarded the Grand Prix. Kleman, who like the poor twisted man of his obsession had already found his Anadyomene, must have laughed when he heard of it.

THE MOTHER REEF

The moon hung low across the sea that night, as we sat by our driftwood fire.

Out across the Palawan reefs the surf was rolling and muttering, creating dim white streamers of phosphorescence that eddied into the lagoon. Up on the higher shores behind us were other fires; other tourists, who were doing the Philippines on more active schedule, were feasting, indulging in song and dancing, buying knickknacks and curios.

But we sat here by the water, away from all that: Myers of the Constabulary; and old Karlak, Moro of the Moros, who had served ten years in the force and had twice been on long visits to America, before returning to his native village and the fish-nets and the long boats; and I was the third.

Some of the boats lay out there before us, rocking gently under the stars. Off to our left, on the shore, was the rotting carcass of the great boat Karlak had been showing us—one of the last of the famous old Malay stitched boats, of full schooner size, a sea-going craft.

"I've heard tell," said Myers reflectively, "that boats of this kind, stitched together, date from very ancient times, and mark one of the chief developments in the art of ship-building. Too bad, Karlak, that you don't happen to know who first thought up that kind of a boat, and why! Must have been one of your people."

"It was," Karlak said simply. "And I do know."

"What?" I exclaimed. "You mean you have some legend about it?"

Karlak grinned and spat.

"Not legend, but facts," he said, and looked out to sea as he squatted on his hams, his old, lined face a mass of shrewd wrinkles. "It was a man out there on the big mother of the reefs, that lies just over the horizon. And it happened a very long time ago, in the ancient days when all my people were idolaters, before the Prophet of Allah had told the world of the true God, may his name be blessed! This man bore the same name that I bear today, but he was young, and I am old."

"Young enough," said Myers slyly. "I hear that there was a new son born in your house last month."

The words drew a chuckle from Karlak.

"Allah is good, Allah is great," he rejoined complacently. "This was long ago; it was even before the time when yellow barbarians of China traded with these coasts. Only once or twice had these infidels ever been seen by my people, yet at long intervals they had come out of the sea, and they knew these islands."

He fell silent for a time, staring now into the embers of the fire, and I thought he was listening to the faint laughter and the music that drifted down from the village behind. But no. He was listening to the reef-music, as the long endless rollers burst upon the coral. And far greater was the sound out there on the mother of the reefs across the horizon, the long coral islets that broke the sea-surge sweeping in from uncounted leagues, where at low tide were vast expanses of pools and exposed reef.

In those pools, in the now shallowed lagoons, huge treasure lay trapped at each low tide—treasure of fish and shell and octopus. Strange things drifted up to the mother of the reefs, too, across the trackless ocean. That was why Karlak and his dozen men were out there, so far from the islands, in search of these treasures. Out there in the big hollowed-tree canoe Karlak had built from one huge log, fitted with sail and outrigger and with ample cargo space for the spoils of the sea.

Karlak, *panjiran* or sea-going chief of the tribe, had found a rich harvest and his ungainly craft was deeply laden. But, despite the risk of delayed departure, for two hours he and his men had been staring out at this queer vessel that rode the tidal currents along the reef. A huge ship, to his eyes; a monstrous thing, with bulging lattice-like sails, with no crew in sight, steering an aimless course and yet ever drawing closer to the opening in the reef. Then fell the calm, with the sea like a burnished shield under the hot sun. The strange, huge ship hung listless.

Quick! It was their chance! He snapped swift word at his men. They leaped to the great canoe, and running it out, seized paddles and headed for the channel. Icol, war chief of the village, was with him, taking the stroke paddle. As the canoe emerged from the reef, every eye was turned on the ship in momentary paralysis of fear and vivid curiosity. She was not two hundred yards away, unmoving, deserted.

"A trap!" yelped Icol. "A trap of the water devils! Leave her alone."

"She's falling to pieces," said another of the *orang laut.* Sea people have quick eyes. "Battered and smashed. Planks hanging loose. She's not a log, but many logs!"

Karlak stood erect, a lithe, handsome bronze figure who might have been the god of the reefs in person. Many logs indeed! That huge ship was built of hewn logs, of planks innumerable cut from logs. Her idle sails were of woven matting. But she was falling apart; there were huge gaps in her bulwarks, her bows were split, there was no sign of life aboard her.

"Lay in the paddles!" ordered Karlak abruptly, catching a riffle on the water. "Offshore breeze coming up. Step the mast!"

The men leaped to obey, getting the mast stepped, laying the square carang, a light but tough woven sail, ready. Karlak stood by the steering paddle; one man to the tacks, four to the halyards. Icol and the others grasped spears and knives.

"Look, *besar!*" cried one of the men, excitedly. "A golden woman devil!"

Hearts leaped, eyes strained; Karlak felt his pulses hammer. A figure was crawling up the inclined poop deck of the ship—a lithe, golden, half-clad figure, a woman, lifting arms and waving frantically, a vision of shapely loveliness. The men gaped, until the voice of Icol blared at them in new warning.

"A trap, a trap! Warriors are ready behind those bulwarks, while we make sick-dog's eyes at the woman devil—flee, I tell you! Wake up, Karlak!"

"I am *datu,* not you," grunted Karlak. "I give orders—but you're right. Up with the sail!"

They had the breeze now. The sail went up; Karlak swung his weight on the oar, the canoe whipped around. The brails were let go, the sheets hauled aft, and like a racer the great canoe went hissing and foaming away.

But Karlak looked back. The yellow woman still stood there, though her arms had fallen. Karlak fancied that tears were streaming down her cheeks; slowly she dropped, a dejected, beaten figure that sent a pang through him. Devil or not, trap or not—what a woman! Then she was gone from sight behind the bulwarks, and the canoe rushed through the seas toward the islands over the horizon. The ship did not follow. The men breathed freely again. Karlak cursed the squat, powerful figure of Icol in the bow, and looked back again and again, but in vain.

Before the breeze, the ship drifted farther away from the reef again.

Under the shattered and broken bulwark, the yellow woman sat in collapse; tears were indeed glittering on her cheeks, tears of weakness, of utter despair. In all that long stretch of reefs, with its trees and lagoons and glittering white coral strands, she had seen no living creature except these men; and now they were gone....

At the moment, Ming Chu was far from being the "Glorious Pearl" her name bespoke. Her dulled eyes looked along the hot decks. Here lay what remained of her brawny crew of yellow seamen, dead or dying of bubonic plague, the black death. Her father had gone long days ago. Yu the Tiger, that powerful seaman and adventurer who served as mate, had skipped out with the small boat two nights ago. She was alone with the dead and stricken.

Until the breeze failed, she had hoped to get through an opening in the reef. This hope was gone now. The light offshore breeze was beating the shattered hulk farther from the reefs.

For a long while she sat, despondent, hopeless, resigned; then feeble voices roused her. She staggered up, gave each of the helpless yellow men a bit of the precious water remaining; then she went to the rail and stared. That canoe with its brown sail had long since vanished. Ming Chu, who had spent most of her life at sea with her father, knew the meaning of the ominous purple cloud lifting in the sky, spreading up from the horizon to the east. Afternoon was passing. The storm would burst ere sunset. There was nothing to do but accept this final blow of fate.

Weak, wearied to nothing, haggard for want of sleep, Ming Chu went to the helm and lashed it. She could not lower the sails; she cut them down, then made them fast. Off to the west was the long reef, smoking under the lash of long ground swells. She sank down, covered herself decently, and awaited death, as night and storm approached.

Death came, from the sea; the dreaded *baguio,* the black squall of the islands. The storm-devils tore at the laboring, shattered ship, already soggy with water in her hold. The twisting, agonized hulk snapped the lashings of the steering oar; a giant comber pooped her as she broached to, tons of water flooding aboard out of the darkness and driving her helpless toward the reefs once more. Weak thin screams shrilled on the blast. The decks were swept bare of dead and dying.

Ming Chu moaned weakly. If Yu the Tiger were here, there might still be some hope. Although she hated that wild adventurer with all her heart, he was strong in the will to live and in any crisis fierce and swift as the tiger for whom he was named. But Yu was gone, the Coast of Flowers was far away, death was close.

Another tremendous wave hissed over the doomed craft. Ming Chu was knocked to the deck, but, half-senseless, managed to wedge herself between a mooring bitt and the poop bulwarks. The tremendous cannonading of the surf on coral boomed even above the whining shriek of the wind; two leeward giant geysers of spume shot skyward, and then a scream burst from Ming Chu as the hulk dropped and dropped, only to heave up again on the great-grandfather of all combers. With a million wind-devils lending impetus, the hoary-crested wave picked up the hulk and hurled it.

The coral reefs plucked up with eager fingers, but the foaming white sea-horses lashed back, tore triumphantly over the barrier, and spent themselves hissing on a sandbar, a thousand yards to leeward. And with them, the hulk, dropping to pieces under the hammering, smashed into the sand, little more than a heap of wreckage.

The men gaped, until Icol blared at them in warning: "A trap! Warriors are behind those bulwarks, while we make sick-dog's eyes at the woman devil! Flee, I tell you!"

So the night wore on, and the squall passed, and dawn came hot and white.

The sunlight wakened Ming Chu. She sat up, bleeding and battered, and stared wildly around. Then she realized that she was stark naked, stripped clean by the sea. To any woman of her race, this was the depth of shame; she hastily crawled among the wreckage that strewed the whole lagoon shore, while the white sandfleas popped out of the coral sand in all directions. A torn strip of matting from a sail wrapped about her body, she made it fast with a cord, then took stock of things.

Here was the hulk, little more than a framework; the entire beach was a mere raffle of planks, spars, all sorts of litter. The big ship was actually fallen apart. Yet it had been built as well as the yellow people knew how, the planks fastened with crude bronze clamps and bolts, and tied in place with shrunken bamboos. Little these had availed against the stress of hammering waves, the strain of cargo. The brittle bronze had snapped or slipped, the split bamboo had burst. Well enough for rivers, even for coasting voyages, but not for the deep far sea.

Water! Ming Chu was afire with thirst. She searched the wreckage frantically but vainly. Burst casks and jars, hampers of rice and dried fish swept to nothing. Not a morsel of food, not a drop of fresh water. Everything of metal had gone into the bed of the lagoon. Something bulked under a pile of planks, and she tore them off in spasmodic hope, only to turn away listlessly when she disclosed her father's chest. She knew too well what was in that chest. The bow and the arrows her father prized so greatly, wrapped in waterproof coverings, and with them the images of her gods. Small use to her here, either weapons or gods!

The sun mounted higher over a fairly serene sea. The sky was cloudless and innocent as a baby's eyes; but the reef was hot, and the white coral sand, reflecting the blinding rays, radiated like a gridiron. Ming Chu felt the tortures of thirst.

She looked at the reef, the trees, the thickets; useless to search. If water were here, this place would be inhabited; but it was empty of life. She studied her father's chart. She had been here with him two years ago. Five leagues off to the southwest should be the Island of Spotted Snakes, while the Island of Giant Lizards lay due east, nearly as far. Out of sight from here. And the largest of all the islands, that of Renegades, was a bit farther; a place of fierce men, of large native towns, of gainful trade. But she had no boat. Yu the adventurer, the strong, burly master of his own destiny, had taken boat and water and chart—everything. Would have taken her too, had he not thought her down with the sickness of death.

Wearily, she turned and started toward the pandanus scrub that fringed the trees. At least, she must make the search; there was always a slim chance of finding water somewhere.

Half an hour later, on the other side of the reef, she stared dejectedly out at the vast expanse of jagged coral pools and rock, exposed at low tide far beyond the mother reef itself. No water. No living thing. No food.

"Ming Chu! The Glorious Pearl—or her spirit!"

The words pierced her, brought her around. There, half emerged from the brush and staring at her, was the powerful figure of Yu, bronze sword in hand, his slant eyes drugged with sleep and dazed by sunlight.

"Yu!" Her thickened tongue almost refused duty. "Yu! Cowardly dog! Son of a turtle that you are.... Water! Water!"

The Tiger lowered his blade. "Alive! You are no spirit!" he muttered. "Water? I have none. I have nothing but the boat. It was on the shore; the water, the food, was all spoiled—"

Ming Chu slumped hopelessly, then gathered herself.

"We are both dead people and shall soon drink our fill from the Nine Springs of Eternity, so enmity is a foolish thing. You have the boat? Then we can still make the islands—"

A joyous blaring laugh broke from the Tiger. His bold eyes had kindled. Now he moved suddenly, and with a leap was beside her, grasping her arms.

"Aye, the islands, you and I!" he cried. "You're my woman now—"

She fought against him with an upsurge of vicious fury. Abruptly, his grasp loosened, he went lax, he stood staring past her. She turned. Silently, a shape of gleaming bronze had come upon them—Karlak, who stood poised, in his hand the knife that denoted his rank; the *balarao,* the throwing knife, with its balanced hilt of rough gold and shark-skin.

"Drop it!" cried Karlak, and the Tiger unclasped the sword he had whipped out. "Leave the woman alone, yellow devil; she is mine. I am Karlak, *panjiran* of the Dusur people."

Snarling, yet aware of menace in the brush around, Yu stood motionless. Ming Chu stared at the bronze shape of Karlak.

"K'uei! Beneficent Dragon!" she croaked. "Water, water!"

"It is coming," said Karlak. He strode toward her, an arrow-straight figure of smooth muscle; then halted, touched forehead and heart, and smiled. From his bulging breech-clout of python-skin he pulled out a length of scarlet grass cloth. This was his own *bahag,* a combination sarong and covering against the night mist that no native went without.

He shook out the cloth and held it up, draped it about her shoulders, and she comprehended his wordless gesture. Then he turned.

"Tubig! Water for the woman and for this yellow devil."

Other men were around, but it was Icol the warrior who brought a joint of cane and unstoppered it, and held it to the lips of Ming Chu. She gripped at it, drank greedily but carefully, and lowered it again. Icol handed it to Yu the Tiger. Those two men exchanged a quick, comprehending look, and Yu drank.

Karlak had watched them with a frown; now he gave sharp, abrupt orders. The whole party started across the reef to where the ship had been wrecked. Explanations were simple. The lingua franca of all these islands was known to Yu and Ming Chu, as to all traders from the Flowery Land.

Heading for home, Karlak's craft had been caught by that sudden sharp blow, and he, nothing loath, ran before it, back for the reef. And this morning, with patience of hunters, they had tracked down Yu the Tiger and the golden woman as well. And Karlak knew he had to deal with Icol the warrior, over that woman. The men would take no sides in a private matter.

Evening saw all hands in camp near the wreckage of the ship, which had been explored in vain for plunder. When Ming Chu claimed the chest, Karlak gave it to her unopened, whereat Icol scowled and spat oaths. If plunder lacked, bits of bronze and other useful things were plentiful. The big canoe was brought around into the lagoon, and so was the Tiger's small boat, with its oar and sail of matting. All this while, Yu had kept his head and held his peace; he was crafty, this adventurer. He had been

places. He had dealt with such island men as these before now.

In the westering sunlight, Karlak took Ming Chu to the beached framework of the ship. His tawny eyes reflected strange glints of fire as he bade her tell him how such a craft was made. Using the small boat to illustrate her point, she explained the split bamboo withes, the bronze clamps, the hewing of great planks from logs. Karlak and his people had soft iron, but no bronze, and any tools aboard the ship had been lost. But he could see, quickly enough, how futile had been such means of fastening a great ship together against the endless hammering thrust of the sea. And it was easy to comprehend the massive framework of this ship.

They talked of themselves, too; and later that night, when as now, the Malay folk loved to talk about the fires, while the surf pounded on the reef, Karlak heard of her father, of this unlucky voyage, of the Tiger. His heart kindled to the silken loveliness of her; and Glorious Pearl, looking upon this bronze god of the reef, felt the liver turn to water within her. She admitted the fact. Karlak, who had no understanding of the Chinese phrase thus translated, burst into laughter and took her to the tent he had erected near the wreck, from one of her own matting sails.

The *orang laut* stared after the two of them, red grins wreathing their faces. Icol also stared, gripping at the knife in his girdle, his broad, flat features atwist with rage. When he glanced at the yellow man, the prisoner, he met the bold, quick eyes of the Tiger fastened upon him. In that look, an unspoken question was asked and answered. Then Icol rose. His lean brown hand flicked the hilt of his *barong,* and a smile came to his lips, as though the touch of the knife had brought it.

Karlak came back alone. "The golden woman is mine," he said bluntly. "Everybody to sleep, for we have work tomorrow. Bind the yellow devil, and to sleep."

More work than he knew, or dreamed!

That night there was a new moon, a crescent moon, that glimmered for a while and dipped under the horizon. After its passing, the warrior Icol rose very quietly and loosed the bonds of the captive Tiger, and well away from the camp, they conferred together for a long time, squatting in the sand and talking. They went side by side and looked at the great outrigger canoe, drawn up above high-water mark, still holding its huge load of fish plundered from the reef pools.

"It is too much for us," said Icol. "Take the small one. But first—"

They laughed softly, and from the fires Icol brought embers, which he laid under the canoe amidships, and put other wood on the embers.

"The woman is mine, remember," the Tiger said after a time, when they had made ready the small boat, putting water and food in it. "To you the *balarao,* the golden-hilted knife of the chief, but to me the woman. Later, when we sell her, we divide the price."

"Agreed," said Icol. "And all this gold of yours, we divide also."

Now passed some little time. From the shelter of Ming Chu came slight sounds, a gasp, and silence. Under the stars, the Tiger came striding down to where the small boat lay, the woman's figure in his arms; she was bound and gagged. He set her in the sand, and laughed in her ear.

"Glorious Pearl, you are the Tiger's woman now!" he breathed exultantly. "These fools take the bronze fittings to be gold; this squat barbarian is tempted by it, and we go to people he knows. Perhaps we return here—who can tell? Be happy, Ming Chu, for you're the Tiger's bride. We'll put you aboard when he comes, with the golden knife of this chief he is killing—"

Karlak wakened suddenly. There was an interval in the booming of the surf; in it, the sand crunched under naked heel. He looked up and saw a figure against the stars. In the same instant, he writhed aside, rolled over, clutched his throwing-knife as he came up—all one movement, the startled swiftness of a wild animal in his instinctive motion.

Icol missed the blow of his six-pound *barong.* The sharp soft iron blade went *whick* into the coral sand. Then Karlak, with a yell, was leaping at him. Icol turned and ran for it, glanced back, saw Karlak poised. Desperately, frantically, he leaped aside. The throwing-knife whistled where he had been. Next instant, he was plunging for the boat. And the Tiger, with a growl of sheer fury, had to give up his prey—it was choice between woman and life, and he took life.

Karlak stumbled over the bound figure, paused to cut it free, saw the small boat slithering out across the lagoon for the reef passage, her sail up and bulging.

His men came running, yelling, spears streaking the night, but the boat was safely away. With one accord, they jumped for the big outrigger—and then stood stupefied, staring at the two parts of it. The craft had been eaten asunder by the fire. Even to patch it up was impossible.

The taunting laugh of Icol drifted from the water. "We'll be back, friends!" And the growl of Yu the Tiger added a curse to the prophecy.

Karlak, with the woman beside him and his men respectfully squatting before him, faced the dawn and the hard future. Icol's mother was of the Balinbing pirate folk; the two would go and bring those fierce slavers upon them, eager for Dusur blood. It would not be quickly done, but it would be done.

"We have food and water in plenty," said Karlak, once dismay was past. "Without a boat, we cannot get home; therefore, I shall provide a boat—such a boat as no man of the Dusur has ever seen! But I must talk with the gods."

That was logical. Karlak went alone into the darkness to seek speech with the gods. He squatted beside the bulk of the wreck's framework. Ming Chu had told him what the Tiger had said, and how Icol took the bronze to be gold; well, so had the others. He himself half believed it to be gold, despite the woman's words.

This great ship of the yellow folk—if any man could build such a ship that would be seaworthy and strong, he would have the world at his feet! Karlak was no dim groping savage, but of a race that did things. The framework bulked above him in the starlight. It was heavy enough; it could be pegged, to make it stouter. But those planks—his brain went searching among the handicrafts of his people. No tools here. Plenty of cane on the reef, yes, rattan of all sorts.

He touched the matting sail-remnants. Queer woven stuff, this matting! Nothing like as strong and resilient as rattan—ah! By the gods! He leaped up in a blaze, then sank down again. It could be done, but there were no tools. How to bore holes? He stared up at the dawn-hints in the sky. A scrap of talk from the men drifted over to him.

"I still have the scars from the bites of those accursed *anay.* I saw some here on the reef, too—the little devils are everywhere."

The *anay!* Fantastic, yes; but better than boring holes with bits of the bronze. The planks would not be weakened. It might work, it might work! Karlak came to his feet again, his excitement whipping up. He stalked over to the fire.

"Men!" His voice blared at them, wakened the yellow woman from her doze. The firelight struck on him, brought out all his vivid eagerness. "The ship is here. We have the frame; with wooden pegs we can strengthen it, repair it. You have heard how the women of the Balinbings make the little boats those people use on the rivers? We shall make this great ship again in the same way. Use these planks and timbers. Cut down that queer poop—"

"We have none of this golden metal, we cannot work it," said a man.

"Fool! We need no metal. I have just told you. Stitch the ship together! Stitch it, from stem to stern and back again, with rattan. Out, and gather the green cane! And we need help from the *anay*—from those very ant-people you were just cursing. Out with the dawn, and hunt for them! Ants, plenty of them; bujuco and rattan, plenty of it! The ship's keel is unbroken, the timbers are good, but the wood is like iron."

Iron indeed, this wood—hard red teak, all of it, even the planks. Too hard for soft iron to pierce.

With the dawn, Karlak set his men to work, and Ming Chu flung herself into the task with him. She had seen many a ship built, but not in this strange fashion.

The planks were laid out in separate piles, sound and broken. By cutting down the lines of the ship, there were enough and to spare. Cordage and sails, everything was salvaged and drawn high, and the framework laid out above high water, and pegged stoutly.

Then, watching as the holes were bored, Ming Chu shrieked with laughter. Many of the *anay,* those giant white boring ants, had been collected, and the *orang laut* knew how to handle them. A Malay would grasp an ant carefully, take a small shell in the other hand, and dropping the ant into the shell, clap it quickly on the plank.

The furious ant, turning from the hard shell, would bore through the teak wood. As it emerged triumphant on the other side, it would be caught and set to work again. Ming Chu insisted on trying this novel tool, and was so severely bitten that she writhed in agony on the hot sand—and tried no more.

The outer timbers were seized to the framework, most of the stringers and strakes being sound

enough; the ship had been hammered apart rather than smashed. The tough bujuco, stripped of its poisonous thorns, and rattan soaked in water until pliable, did the work.

And, as the ship grew, with everyone toiling from dawn to dark and after, the Dusur chief and the Glorious Pearl drew closer, though there was no time for love. To the woman, he was a never-ending amazement, totally unlike her own people as he was. Karlak had no lucky or unlucky days, but his ingenuity met and conquered each problem that arose. To Karlak, this golden creature was woman, yes, and she set his spirit in a flame; but for the present he treated her exactly as one of his own men, though he talked often with her.

And all this while she kept the chest that had been her father's, prayed sometimes to the gold and vermilion gods, and said nothing of the weapons therein.

The ship grew, to the amazement of those men, grew until the shapely hull was all complete. There were no coconuts here on the mother reef, but their sail and mats were of coconut fiber; this they worked into tow for caulking, and used tree-resin with powdered shell for the outer caulking. Once back at home, this could be greatly bettered with beeswax and other products, but all they cared about now was getting home.

Then came the great day when they rolled the ship down into the water and saw her afloat. Save for needed repairs, the steering-oars of the original craft had come through well enough, the spars and sails and cordage were worked over. They were at work in the dawn, stepping the masts, when one of the men who had been up among the trees came tearing down with wild yells.

"Balinbing! The slave-hunters!"

He dashed in among them with report. Two giant proas or war canoes were in sight, far northward, but evidently working down along the reefs. Karlak cursed under his breath.

"So Icol has brought the pirate folk down on us, eh? Look alive, men!" he shouted. "They're searching the lagoons. They'll not get here before mid-afternoon, if then. Off and out of here before they come! Stake everything on our ship!"

For the two masts, the original sails had been worked over—no job to boast about, true; but these dozen men were working only for the short voyage home. Once there, Karlak knew that he could refashion this ship to his heart's desire.

Once there? That was the terror of it. The men muttered as they worked. Old Talut, chief paddler, shook his head gravely. Karlak flew at the business in hand with furious energy, but Ming Chu read his face aright.

"What is it?" she asked. "What is so wrong?"

"Us!" Karlak laughed bitterly. He swept a hand toward the pitifully few weapons piled on the sand, spears and knives. "Can we hope to fight those warriors, a dozen of us? No. The only chance lies in the size of our ship."

"And the way it handles," said she. "I know it, Beneficent Dragon; I can handle it. Let me have the steering-oar, with one man to help. You give the orders."

He nodded, and went back to work.

Already her chest was aboard, with her gods and the bundle beside them. The ship's original decking, though sadly in need of repair, was good enough for their purpose. With the masts stepped, the rigging and sails in place, all was ready a little past noon. But the man sent to watch from the trees brought in bad news. The two giant proas, outrigger craft, were close.

"Let's go!" ordered Karlak. "I'll look to the sails—you to the helm, Ming Chu!"

The passage through the reef was easy to see, with the sun overhead and behind. There was a steady wind; as the sails bellied out and the ship moved, Karlak uttered a wild cry of exultant joy, and his men echoed it. A screaming snarl broke from Talut, in the bows. He pointed; and, as the reef opened up and they stood out, the two proas appeared, racing down. One glance told Karlak that they had the legs of him.

"All hands, for quick work!" blared his voice. "Hard alee, there! Quick with it, woman!"

Ming Chu and the man with her put the helm hard over. The ship swung into the wind, hung for an instant with her sails booming, then filled smartly away on the larboard tack. One huge proa, not unlike the *vinta* of later days, with a great spread of sail, and another canoe, smaller, but crowded with men, under paddles alone. Karlak sized up matters swiftly, and swung toward Ming Chu.

"Head for the smaller one—smash her!" he shouted.

She waved her hand in assent. A tangle of cordage, as something gave way; Karlak leaped to help with the work. All well again, and the ship holding true. A thrill went through Karlak at the feel of her, at her resilient response, though without ballast she rode high and light. What he would do with this ship, if he lived!

They were two hundred yards from the paddled proa, drawing closer with each moment. The larger craft was behind them, tearing down at racing speed, conch-shells blowing and men yelling. Closer and closer now—a yell from Karlak, and the helm was swung, as the sheets were eased off. The ship wore sharply and plunged at the proa.

The stroke missed. Those paddlers knew their business. They avoided that sweeping death by a yard, and sent a hail of arrows aboard the ship—then they were astern and out of it, with the larger craft charging down past them, overhauling the ship at a rapid clip.

Karlak looked at this craft—its huge spread of sail, its enormous outrigger sweeping the combers, its crowd of men; and he knew himself lost. He could not run, he had not men enough to fight. She was coming up fast, men were standing ready with lines and grapnels. Talut touched his arm and spoke grimly.

"Look! At her steering-oars."

Karlak nodded. Icol was there, and behind him the Tiger, Yu, and one of the Balinbing chieftains. A line was thrown, and another. Arrows hailed in upon the doomed men of the Dusur tribe. Three of them were down, others were wounded. The two craft were side by side, the lines were fast—

Karlak leaped to cut the lines, hacked one free. Already half a dozen men were clambering aboard; his own men met them hand to hand. Another line aft—he darted to it, and severed it. Then he heard the twang of a bowstring, and looked up.

Ming Chu stood there, a great curving bow in

her hand, a long shaft notched; the string twanged again. A frightful yell burst from Icol as the shaft went through him. The Balinbing chieftain was down. Ming Chu loosed the twanging string once more, and the Tiger, Yu himself, that bold adventurer, plunged forward among the pirates and was lost to sight.

And, the last line parted, the huge proa sheered away wildly, amid yells of dismay from her crew, while aboard the ship the few boarders were met with spear and knife. Karlak found himself with six men left alive, and the ship clear. He leaped to the side of Ming Chu; she was shouting at him:

"Look! With that outrigger, she's helpless if we take her to leeward—"

"For the love of the gods!" cried Karlak, laughing excitedly. "Haven't you done enough, woman? No! Let her go. We've only half a dozen men left—we've beaten them off, we've whipped them, your shafts have killed their leaders—enough for this time, my woman! Enough, until next time comes!"

Her eyes widened upon him. The bow fell from her hands; she caught at him suddenly, touched the long arrow that was through his thigh.

"Oh! Beneficent Dragon—you're hurt, you're wounded—"

Old Talut, bloody but still sound, came darting to take over the helm, and grinned widely, as the ship ran up the dark waves toward home, and the enemy fell behind.

"Next time!" he grunted. "Aye! And next time we'll take toll of those devils!"

Next time indeed, and for many a year to come, and across the purple seas to Borneo and Celebes, on to the far mountains of Asia—the sturdy resilient ships of the islanders took toll for many a century and more.

As we sat there by the dying fire, Karlak told me how this toll was taken, of yellow man, Dyak, white man. Then his head lowered, and through the shuddering booming of the surf his voice was all but hushed.

"And now the old days are gone," he said. "And we of these islands are no longer Americans; we have our own government, our own republic—*hai!* By Allah, we shall see about that! There is nothing but trouble and fear and war to seek from the future. The old days are best. The old days are ever the best—"

Myers, of the Constabulary, looked at me, and wrinkled up his nose in a grimace.

"Anyhow," he said awkwardly, "that's one hell of a good yarn of the old days, Karlak, and the first stitched ship! Was that chap your ancestor?"

Karlak lifted his head. "My name speaks," he said with dignity; and we had our answer.

NILE SKIPPER

O*ur steamer was getting into Rangoon.* I stood at the rail, taking "home movies" of the Burmese fishing craft, a strange solitary Chinese junk, and all the queer river-life of the Irrawaddy delta, when the chief steward came along and halted.

"There's something you seldom see nowadays." And he pointed to an ungainly boat coming down the river. She was propelled by long oars, but she carried an odd sort of double mast, shaped like the letter "A."

"A real old-time Burmese junk," the chief steward replied to my query. "The type that has sailed this river for hundreds of years, for centuries past counting, and is pretty near extinct today."

"Obviously, a craft peculiar to this river," I remarked.

At this, the chief steward grinned and produced a photograph.

"I thought some of you would spring that remark on me!... Here, look."

His photograph showed a ship model, exactly like this Burmese junk. The same double mast, the same overhang of prow and stern, with steering-oars at one side of the stern.

"That," said he, "is a model from an Egyptian tomb of five thousand years ago."

"What?" I exclaimed in surprise. "Exactly similar to this Burmese junk?"

"In every detail. The Irrawaddy, my son, is like the Nile: the current flows one way; the prevailing wind blows the other. Take a good look at that photo, and let me have it back later. I'm on a call to the bridge." He dashed off....

Five thousand years ago? Khufu had been king in Egypt then, he whom the Greeks named Cheops. A legendary golden figure, seldom or never seen by these workers in the shipyard below Memphis; and only then a tiny dot amid throngs of priests and nobles and slaves. To these workers, the authority of the Pharaoh was represented wholly by their immediate overlord, the thin and saturnine Enuser, chief of naval construction.

The comings and goings of Enuser were unhappy occasions, and luckily rare. Borne on his palanquin, attended by secretaries and nobles and slaves, the eagle-eyed, cruel-lipped lord would get his monthly reports, issue clipped orders to the overseers, and then men would be lashed to death or mayhap rewarded. Even the captains of the Nile ships, free men, bronzed hearty fellows, stood in fear of Enuser, for they too were beneath his authority, and when things went ill, they felt his displeasure.

Things were going ill enough now, and over the shipyards arose the sound of men groaning, and the whistling of knotted whips. Enuser was in a white rage born of his own fear, since upon him had descended the threatening anger of the Pharaoh. He had left his palanquin, was talking furiously with the overseers, and at one side waited the captains who were about to catch his wrath.

"It's intolerable!" he snapped at the overseers. "The chief priests and architects complain that we don't deliver sufficient stone from the quarries—and whose fault is it? You all know that the Pharaoh is building this pyramid at Gizeh, that the labor and material is eating the heart out of the country, and that if the granite supply fails the whole work is delayed."

"Lord, is it our fault?" spoke up the chief overseer. "Look. The boats are large and well built, all is done according to regulation—"

"And last month a good fifty of them disappeared coming down from the quarries," Enuser snapped. "The month previous, thirty-five sank or went ashore. What is worse, on the way upriver a dozen were lost and the others were so slow in reaching the quarries that the whole system was thrown out of order."

"That, lord, is not due to the construction," said the chief overseer sturdily. "We supply the boats. We've added two thousand workers to the shipyards since that pyramid was begun; we turn out double the former number of craft. There our responsibility ends. If the captains and pilots can't deliver the stone or handle their ships, it is not to our account."

This was plausible enough, and a hum of approbation rose from the mass of overseers. But, from the throng of pilots and captains waiting, who now saw the gaze of Enuser turned on them with the threat of approaching wrath, stepped out one Nefer, youngest of the captains.

He was bronzed and smiling, a resolute, handsome fellow; and as became a free man, made no obeisance to Enuser.

"Lord, the argument is good but the facts are otherwise," said he boldly. "If you'll honor me by listening, I can show you where the fault lies."

"Have the gods inspired you, then?" sneered Enuser.

"They have, lord," Nefer replied calmly. "Also, I know my trade. I have pilot's license for the entire river, and captain's ticket to boot. I have piloted above the cataracts and in the Nile delta. I have helped construct ships. In other words, lord, I know my business inside and out as a seaman should."

Enuser noted the confident carriage of the man, the eager, assured eye, the air of authority. His guile returned to him, and he banished his sneer.

"I listen," he said quietly. "Where lies the fault?"

"Not in these overseers," Nefer rejoined. "They do honest work; there's no fault in the yards. Not in their product, either. Not in the labor concerned. Not in the pilots and captains, all of whom know their job and have good crews. But look, lord—look at the basin there, and you'll see the fault."

Enuser, for all his cruelty and deep craft, was a man of brains who overlooked nothing. He turned. In the canal basin at one side lay a number of nearly completed ships of the largest size. Enuser joined the young captain and approached the basin, walking among the piles of huge beams, each stamped with bird and sun and serpent, the mark of Khufu the Pharaoh. Nefer stopped and pointed to the nearest ship, whose mast was being stepped. A plain, old-fashioned, solid mast, with broadsquare sail-yard.

"There is the fault," said he. "These boats were designed a thousand years ago, lord. They are built today as they came down to us, broad-beamed, pegged together, heavy of stern and bow, with a mast solidly stepped. They were designed to carry slaves and corn and produce and trading-goods—not stone from the quarries. Even with fifty slaves at the oars, they are most difficult to handle when full laden. The fault lies in the design of these boats, and nowhere else."

At this, men gasped. It was the rankest heresy. Construction of all kinds, all architecture, carving, design, was done according to the strictest form of conventionalized art.

"Careful!" said Enuser sternly. "These are the designs of our fathers, approved by the high priests, laid down by law. Perhaps the devil Typhon has inspired you, rather than the gods."

Nefer laughed. "Not so, but from my voyages up far beyond the cataracts, where men use other craft than ours, I have learned. At least, my lord, listen to me. You know well that our boats go upstream with the wind, though it does not always serve their stubby masts and low square sails. They are designed for cargoes, not for lumps of stone which weigh heavily but take small room. Now look at this."

He stooped, and in the dust drew with his finger the outline of a boat, while Enuser frowned down with careful gaze. Enuser was actually ready to grasp at any straw. The previous night his brother, one of the chief priests of the sun-god, Ra, had slipped him word that unless he got busy there would be a shakeup that might land him in a chain-gang.

"Here is a boat, long and narrow," and Nefer pointed to the enormous overhang of bow and stern, "which can make the landings without smashing up, as ours so often do. So far as weight of cargo goes, it can handle as much as our two-hundred-cubit keels. The straight, high sides will give thirty oars to a side, double our present strength. But most of all—look at this double mast!"

He indicated the high bipod mast.

"That will carry a lofty sail to catch the higher currents of wind," he went on. "Each foot is fitted into grooves, so that when not in use it can be taken down and won't be in the way. Such a boat will handle like a charm, my lord! It will have twice the speed of our present bumboats," he added with contempt. "And six men with oars on the right quarter will control her perfectly."

"Hm!" said Enuser. His quick brain grasped the conception at once. "If you presented such a scheme to the chief architect, you'd be flogged to death for heresy."

Nefer grinned. "But if *you* presented it through the priests of Ra, as a direct inspiration from the sun-god—eh? It might mean a step in rank, even a seat on the board of engineers. For you, of course."

"And for you?" Enuser glanced around, to make sure no one had overheard.

"Well,"—Nefer chuckled softly,—"if you should happen to vacate your present post, I'd be very glad to become chief of naval construction."

"Agreed," said Enuser abruptly. "Suppose I give you full authority to construct two of these boats, a requisition on whatever workmen and supplies you need—how soon could you produce them for tests?"

"In a month's time. Say, two days before the feast of the Nile god."

Enuser summoned a scribe and dictated rapidly. As he took the reed pen and bent over the sheet of papyrus to sign, he darted one swift, terrible glance at Nefer.

"Failure means that you are flayed alive," he said curtly.

"Agreed, my lord."

That afternoon Nefer moved among the swarming thousands in the shipyard, picking master carpenters, shipwrights, crews, material. He chose a secluded basin for the work, sketched out preliminary designs, and ere sunset was satisfied that the morrow would see the job under way.

Then, with sunset, he turned to something else.

Bathed and freshly clad, the last lingering daylight found him sauntering among the vast crowds that sought the quays and landings of the river for relief from the oppressive heat. The Nile was tending toward its new flood, but the feast of the annual inundation was still a month distant, and all Memphis emptied itself along the river to seek the evening coolness there.

For any who might not be seen together, there was greater seclusion and protection here amid the crowd than in any corner of massive temple or palace. Slaves were filling water jars, hawkers of wine and food moved about, and on the stone stairs fringing the quays were multitudes at their washing or bathing.

Dusk descended. Nefer came to a certain spot on the quay and waited there, staring at the river where a few boats of nobles or princes passed up and down, hurling boomerangs or shooting arrows at drifting marks where the daylight died, with snatches of music and song coming from the larger craft. In their place, his wandering vision beheld a longer, stranger boat, whose lofty sail would catch the upper breezes that scarce stirred the water surface.

"So the sailor takes his holiday in watching the river!" said a soft voice.

Nefer stirred. At his elbow stood a figure, hidden under the robe of a woman of the artisan class—a slender girlish figure, a face half glimpsed that was alive with eagerness and rich youth, an olive face of beauty and glowing flame.

"Ah, Tera!" he exclaimed joyfully, and put out his hand to hers. "I heard that the court had gone upriver to the summer palaces, and I feared the chief scribe had taken his family along."

"We go tomorrow, Nefer," she replied. "But

Enuser. I dread those sharp, cruel eyes of his, that agile and unscrupulous brain! Did you ever hear the story about the wharf at Tanis, and how Enuser became chief of construction?"

"Hm!" grunted Nefer. "I've heard some hints at the captains' mess, but nobody speaks too openly about it. Didn't some chap design that wharf, and Enuser take the credit for it?"

"Yes," she said. "And the man died very suddenly. Oh, I'm afraid for you, my dear! You shouldn't be associated with that man—you shouldn't trust him!"

"I don't," said Nefer. "But in this case, there's nothing obscure. The matter is open; the tests will take place openly, before the board of engineers. I'm not turning over plans that he can steal."

breathe not my father's name nor mine, for the love of heaven! It would ruin us both."

"Not now, my dear," he said, with his quick, eager laugh. "I've news for you! A month hence, I'll be chief of naval construction—a job that carries nobility with it, a fat salary, a palace on the river, and will let me seek the chief scribe openly and demand his daughter in marriage!"

"Nefer! Are you mad?" she gasped. "You know well that Enuser holds the place. You know that if he dreams of aught between us, you'll be dropped into the Nile with a knife between your shoulders some night. Only today he was talking with my father and me, hinting at some great fortune about to befall him, and trying to get a decision out of me. If I don't want to marry him, my father won't force it—but Enuser can use his influence with the priests."

"Time enough to worry about Lord Enuser when the moment comes," said Nefer. "Listen, my dear, listen to what happened this morning!"

He told her rapidly what had occurred at the shipyard, and with sweeping brush painted his glowing vision of accomplishment and reward. When he had finished, his hand could feel the shiver that passed through her.

"Ah, my Nefer, my beloved of Ra!" she said softly. "You're quick and bold, frank and ardent; but you don't know these palace folk as I do! And I know

"Perhaps; but life is such a big thing, Nefer, and it can fly through such a tiny hole, no bigger than a dagger-blade!" she said. "I'll not see you again until the festival. But if I get any news, if anything comes up, I'll send you word. Trust anyone who carries my own scarab—you know it well."

"Aye," said he. "And don't worry about Enuser. Why not give your answer at once and get rid of him?"

"Better play him along. If he brings pressure to bear from the priests of Ra, and you know his brother is one of them, my father would have to give in. It's an open secret that Snefru, the keeper of the royal strong-room, was treacherously dealt with by them last year. The chief scribe would be an even easier victim. Of course, once you're made a noble and have a real position—"

"Everything's different, then!" Nefer laughed, and pressed his lips to the girl's hand. "Thanks, my dear; I understand. And I'll play safe with that rascal, I promise you!"

The girl turned away, with a little sigh of dread and regret. He was so confident, so sure of himself! Such a man would make the easiest sort of a victim for the keen cruel eyes of Enuser to gloat upon. And there was no use trying to make Nefer realize it.

With the next day, Nefer settled to his new job. Tera had departed, the court had departed; and Enuser also had departed with the court. The chief of naval construction was an important man, as needs must be since the office carried with it a title of nobility.

Day by day, the two ships grew, with a rapidity that was astonishing. Nefer made a number of rough sketches and drawings for the various portions of the work, merely for use of the artisans. He acted as his own overseer, giving detailed and explicit instructions by word of mouth alone.

When, one day, a caldron of pitch overturned and burst into flames that came near causing a disastrous conflagration, and in course of this the sketches he had made were reported destroyed, Nefer merely shrugged. This made no difference whatever to him. In his own room he worked late into the night over secret plans of his own, so that each morning he came to the task with every last detail in his head. And the two ships grew.

They were not of great size, barely a hundred cubits indeed, but plenty large for testing under working conditions. The tremendous overhang of bow and stern caused some of the old hands to shake their heads ominously, as did the new-fangled notion of an A-shaped bipod mast and its high yard. The linen sail made according to Nefer's demand was lofty and thick; the hull of pegged timbers was strengthened and padded both inside and out by stout lotos stalks woven together.

As the weeks passed and work continued, other innovations were noted. As in the old ships, the bow platform remained; the bowman with his sounding pole was indispensable. But under this, and again in the stern, a massive bollard was built into the deck, for which Nefer gave no explanation.

With his absolute authority, he visited the rope-walk and there gave orders for two massive cables such as had never been seen in the world. As thick as a man's waist, made of twisted hide, they were enormous and unreasonable things, beyond any conceivable use. When they arrived, he had them placed in a hut, with a number of heavy forked sticks; then they were forgotten....

Two weeks passed. The third was nearly completed when, one afternoon, a Nubian slave sought him out as he directed the work, and showed him the scarab that bore the name of Tera. He walked apart with the Nubian.

"You have a message?"

"Yes, Lord Nefer. The noble Lord Enuser has presented the Pharaoh himself, having the approval of the priests of Ra and the board of engineers, with the sketches and designs of a new type of ship for bringing stone downriver from the quarries. This ship is of his own making and was inspired by the gods."

Nefer clenched his hands, stood for a long moment motionless, in stupefaction. Warned he had been, yet the thing was a blow that sapped him to the very marrow. No doubt informed by spies of the progress of the work, Enuser was taking full credit. What was more, that flaming caldron of pitch had been no accident; the plans and sketches had not been destroyed; instead, they had been conveyed secretly to the crafty chief of naval construction.

"Come to me at my lodging tonight," said Nefer to the Nubian; and the black departed with obeisance.

That afternoon, Nefer gave careful directions to his chief overseer. The two ships had been launched and floated before him in the basin. Their details were now complete; there remained only to finish the work and assemble the various parts that remained, such as mast and cordage and oars. This would take a week at most.

Nefer gave his orders as to each and every finishing touch. He was no longer the laughing, eager-eyed man he had been, but was grave and thoughtful, as though he had aged ten years in a few hours. In all truth, he saw that death was very close to him. Spies were at work. Enuser had presented those sketches as his own designs. And to the Pharaoh himself! Clearly as he had foreseen the magnitude of his invention, Nefer now for the first time realized how great it really was.

Two thousand years, these clumsy old-style ships had plied the Nile, year after year, life after life, century after century, unchanging. How long would these new-style ships of his endure? It was past realization. Uncounted generations and dynasties. Perhaps as long as the Nile endured. And for this Enuser would be honored and rewarded and made immortal—perhaps.

Nefer smiled grimly.

The cymbals clashed; the work-day was ended, and the thousands poured from the shipyards. He himself went to his own lodgings, where he found the Nubian slave waiting. He beckoned the black into his room, took a slim roll of papyrus from its

"Enuser lied," said the Pharaoh. "He lied. He thought to steal from another man's brain and labor. Quick, Enuser! Your defense?"

The black slid away like an eel. Almost before the curtain had fallen, into the room strode a captain of guards.

"Nefer, captain of the river, you are under arrest," he snapped.

"For what cause?"

"Ask the Pharaoh, who orders. We but obey."

The men came in; and Nefer, bound, was led away among the spears—away to the dungeons of the Pharaoh and the priests of the sun-god Ra.

And there the days passed for him, in filth and darkness and sickening heat. He needed no explanation. Enuser had found the new type of ship so promising in its vast importance, had found himself so well equipped with the rough sketches and the nearly finished ships, that he had acted with ruthless precision. Only one man could give him the lie; with that man out of the way his road to fame and greatness was clear.

And if by any mischance the new ship failed, the actual inventor would be flayed alive. Not a pleasant prospect; but the possibility kept Nefer from a quick death.

Thinking of these matters as he lay in his dungeon, Nefer still smiled grimly. Two things Lord Enuser overlooked: love, and seamanship.

hiding-place in the brick wall, and gave it to the Nubian.

"Take this to the Lady Tera your mistress," he said, and gave the slave money. "Now for the message that must go with it—"

He spoke rapidly, low-voiced, curt, explicit. The sharp-witted black missed not a word. Nefer had nearly finished when, outside, he caught a clash of grounded spears and a harsh voice asking after him. Swift premonition seized upon him. He jerked aside a curtain.

"Quick!" he told the Nubian. "The back way—run for it!"

Now the Nile was coming to flood once more in its annual miracle of fertility. The court returned to Memphis for the yearly festival, and Enuser was commanded to make test of his new ship on the daily widening river, before the board of engineers and the Pharaoh himself.

There was something of roughness in this Rhufu who sat upon the throne of Egypt; he had character, as must have a ruler who could have built a pyramid greater than all those of the preceding three dynasties that had ruled the land. Because Enuser had brought this affair to his attention, and because the board of engineers viewed the new type of ship as a development of the greatest importance, he commanded the test to be viewed from his own galley.

They were hard-bitten, skeptical men, these engineers; great nobles and princes as became their achievement, but not chosen from the court. They were picked for their ability, and from the hewing of an obelisk to the planning of a temple, they ran the business with a hard hand and a shrewd eye.

So, with Enuser in their midst, they saluted the Pharaoh on his golden throne, with ostrich-feather fans to shade him from the sun, and the galley stood out. Before them moved the new ship, one of the twain Enuser had chosen for the trial, with a crack river captain aboard, a picked crew of oarsmen, their blades glittering in the sunlight.

Under the oars, the ship handled like magic, now coming close for inspection, now sweeping about the royal galley in circles. Then she ran far down the river and her sail was hoisted, and with the wind fair abaft she came bowling up against the current with a bone in her teeth.

Suddenly confusion was observed aboard her. Exclamations broke out from the engineers. Khufu himself leaned forward intently.

"By the disk of Ra!" he cried. "Look! Look! Those overhanging ends are dipping—she is rising in the center!"

"Hogging it, by the gods!" said one, of the board, who had worked his way up from common seaman. "Hogging it!"

So she was, indeed; buckling upward amidships, the huge overhang of bow and stern being unsupported by the water and dropping down. Hastily the sail was taken off her.

"What's this, Enuser?" exclaimed one of the board. "No correction for such a fault?"

Livid, Enuser saluted the Pharaoh. Another of the board spoke out.

"And what are those bollards for, bow and stern? They have a reason, Enuser?"

"Aye, my lord," said the hawk-beaked man. "For spare cables, indeed. And with a fair load of stone in her bottom, she'll behave aright. She was not designed to sail empty."

"By the gods, she sails upriver empty and down under the oars, full laden! Or that's her purpose, indeed," was the tart response.

"Beloved of Ra,"—and Enuser, desperate, saluted

"I'm afraid for you, my dear!" said Tera.

Khufu again,—"let this test be repeated tomorrow with the second ship I have built. Perchance there is some flaw in this first vessel, perchance the design has not been followed aright."

"Granted," said Khufu promptly. "After the way she handles under oars alone, she's well worth careful testing. But it looks to me as if that queer mast and the high sail are too much for her."

"Humph!" grunted one of the naval engineers to his neighbor. "Any fool of a seaman could tell she wouldn't swim with that overhang. Why blame the new-fangled mast?"

An unexpected silence caught the words and wafted them to the Pharaoh, and all those men fell into stark consternation. But Khufu's black eyes twinkled at the speaker.

"Right, my lord; what should a mere son of Ra know of your trade? It is you doers of the word who have made Egypt what she is, and may I be damned if I don't love you for that hearty tongue of yours! Back to the palace. We'll have in those singers and dancers from the lower country and make a night of it."

So the royal galley put about for the Memphis wharves again....

That night came torches to the cell where Nefer lay, and the bronze grille rattled as the bolts were shot. Bidding the guards to remain to outside, Enuser stepped into the cell, bearing a lamp, and threw the light on the unshaven, filthy, naked figure of the prisoner. The shadow of his old laugh broke from Nefer.

"Ha! My lord Enuser come to visit me! Welcome, noble chief of construction! Or are you now a member of the board of engineers—no?"

A snarl contorted the thin-lipped face with its glittering eyes.

"No jests, Nefer. I have come to draw you from this cell."

"Indeed? Then the tests must have been held. And the ship failed. Eh? She hogged it, as seamen say; but you're no seaman, Enuser."

Furious anger and comprehension flashed over the thin hawk-face.

"So! You knew she would fail—is that it?"

"Precisely," Nefer made cool retort. "Who designed the Tanis wharf for which you got the credit, Enuser? Do you think I was fool enough to put all my secrets in your itching palm? Not much! And the ship failed—ha! She failed!"

Enuser denied nothing, made no protests.

"The second ship is to be tested tomorrow," he said curtly. "Can you keep her from buckling in the center?"

"Of course I can; but you can't," said Nefer. "You got no sketch of that with the others that were stolen. You got no finished design of the ship. And you thought a knife would stop my mouth, eh? Once you succeeded, I was to disappear."

"What's done is done," Enuser rejoined. "Liberty and wealth for your secret, Nefer. What's your price? Can we come to agreement?"

"Perhaps," said Nefer. "Are you willing to keep the bargain we made?"

"Aye, gladly, and repay you with wealth beside."

"Then swear it, by Ra, by the gods of the upper world and of the lower world! Swear it by the head of Osiris, by the hand of Isis!"

The eyes of Enuser glittered sharply. He took the oath, and it was a great oath; swearing to keep the former bargain, should the morrow's test succeed.

"Let me out of here, place me in command once more, and I'll handle that ship tomorrow myself," said Nefer, "And, lest you forget your oath, she'll not be made ready until the very time that she leaves the yards for the test. Agreed?"

"Agreed," said Enuser.

So Nefer was set at liberty, to get rid of the prison-smell ere morning if he could. But later that night, in the palace of Enuser by the river, three men stood before the chief of naval construction. They looked at the wealth piled on the table—the gold, the scarabs, the garments, the rings and amulets—and greed convulsed their brown faces, and they listened right willingly to the words of Enuser.

These three were the overseer of the rowers and two pilots, from the picked crew of the test ship.

"Agreed, then," said Enuser. "This wealth is yours; and further, you shall have good positions under me. Remember, do nothing until the tests are finished and the new ship returns to the yards. Before she enters the shipyards again, fall upon him and kill him."

"And if there are questions from the police, lord?" asked the overseer.

"Then I will make answer. Did not this man cause the first ship to fail today by departing from my plans for her construction? I have placed him in command of the other. He will do the work aright, under pain of death; therefore, see that he dies anyway."

It was agreed; the three departed.

When Ra was in mid-heaven and a light wind was blowing up the Nile, the royal galley set forth again to witness the second test, with Enuser and the board of engineers grouped about the throne of the Pharaoh.

Now, Khufu was no puppet. As heir to the throne, he had been initiated into all the mysteries. The theories of architecture and of design were all his, and while he practised no engineering, he had studied every branch of the art. Because of this he was causing that enormous pyramid to be built at Gizeh, and with his own hands had drawn some part of the plans.

A flush of confidence tinted the lean features of Enuser when that long, swift ship came dancing upriver, high linen sail aloft and drawing. Then down came the sail. The mast was lowered until it rested on its supports. The oars flashed out, and Nefer, standing on the stern platform beside the overseer with his whip, put the ship through her paces.

Again the mast went up, and the sail broke out from the yard. The ship heeled, took the wind, ran before it nobly, with never a sign of hogging.

"Order her closer," said Khufu, and he signed to a trumpeter, who blew a blast, while a signal-man repeated the signal.

As the new ship drew in, from the engineers broke murmurs of astonishment. Now they could see that an enormous cable or truss made of twisted leather thongs ran the full length of her. From the forward bollard, where the individual thongs were made fast, to that in the stern, ran this huge truss. It was upheld by massive forked beams which put sufficient strain upon it to withstand three hundred tons' pressure.

"Clever work, Enuser!" exclaimed the Pharaoh. "Yesterday you showed us how the ship would buckle if left alone; today you show us your ingenuity in overcoming this defect. Is not Enuser worthy a place on the board, my lords?"

There arose murmurs of assent. But Khufu, smiling a little, crooked a finger at the captain of his galley.

"Order that ship alongside. I desire to speak with her captain."

Voices blared over the water. While Enuser watched, a shadowy frown in his eyes, the new ship crept alongside, a line was thrown, buffers were put out, and then Nefer leaped lightly aboard the royal galley and came aft.

He fell on his face before the son of Ra.

"Stand up," ordered Khufu, and Nefer did so, bronzed and stalwart. From about his neck, the Pharaoh took a massive necklace of wrought gold and stones, and the captain of his guards handed it to Nefer. "You handled the new ship well; it is my pleasure to reward your service. My lords,"—and he glanced at the ranks of the board of engineers,—"you agree that the designer of this new ship deserves a place among you?"

There was a murmur of assent once more. Nefer stood silent; until the Son of Ra addressed him directly, he could not speak. But his pulses hammered.

"My Lord Enuser,"—and Khufu took from a scribe a small roll of papyrus,—"can you inform me what this paper contains?"

"I, beloved of Ra?" exclaimed the surprised Enuser, staring on the roll. "How should I know what is contained in a scroll I have never seen before?"

"Then you have not seen it? Look well, Enuser!"

Troubled, perplexed, Enuser scowled at the roll and shook his head?

"Never, beloved of Ra."

"So!" Khufu leaned back and held up the roll. "And you, Nefer, captain of the river—know you what this roll contains, which was given me last night by the daughter of the chief scribe?"

Nefer saluted. "Beloved of Ra, it contains detailed plans for this new ship which I invented, with calculations as to the thickness of the truss necessary for ships of different sizes, and the weight of stone cargo each may carry."

"Give this roll to the board of engineers," said Khufu to his guard captain. "Let them determine whether this man speaks the truth."

Pale and yet more pale stood Enuser, glimpsing now the frightful trap into which he had fallen; sweat stood out on his livid face, and his lips twitched. The board of engineers crowded about the unrolled papyrus. Murmurs of astonishment broke from them. One after another verified the words of Nefer.

"Beloved of Ra, he spoke the truth!" exclaimed the chief engineer.

"And Enuser lied," said the Pharaoh, a sudden flash in his eyes. "He lied. He thought to steal from another man's brain and labor. Quick, Enuser! Your defense?"

Enuser tried to speak, but his voice failed. His stunned senses could summon up no plausible tale.

Khufu signed to the guard captain. "Slay him."

So it was done, there in the white sunlight; and across the bulwark of the galley spread the dark stain. It was like the crimson stain of betel-nut juice, spat out by Burmese rowers as their craft came down the Irrawaddy and drew in beneath the counter of the steamship at whose rail I stood, staring and dreaming of other days.

The chief steward came bustling up to me, and took back the photograph I still held in my hand.

"Funny thing about it all is," he observed, "that this bipod mast idea was used on the British dreadnaughts, which only goes to show—"

What it went to show, I did not learn; for I was staring over the water and thinking of the new member of that ancient board of engineers, and the ships which brought stone down the Nile for a good four thousand years.

ASTARTE SAILS TO WAR

In even the best of weather, bizarre things can happen on Hollywood Boulevard. But given a foggy, misty night, you just never can tell. Here are some of the queerest people on earth, some of the most astonishing names and occupations ever gathered into one spot.

It was most devilish foggy on this evening, and I was cursing other drivers as I felt my slow and cautious way. I was far from the lights of Vine Street, and I was lost. That is, I had no idea just where I was, for every landmark was obliterated. Also my head was full of the odd story that had broken in the evening papers, about a Chinese woman who claimed lineal descent from "Chinese" Gordon, and who lived here. She was typical of the queer things that leak out from Hollywood's bypaths.

And then it happened, despite all my care and slow pace.

Something moved directly into my path. There was the flash of a white face, and then a quick shrill cry. I jammed on the brakes, tore open the door, and jumped out to extricate a man's figure, prostrate under the bumper. To my vast relief, he came to his feet.

"No, no, I guess I'm not hurt," he said. "I didn't see you coming. You didn't hit me; I slipped, trying to get out of the way. Good thing you stopped quick, though!"

Mindful of ambulance-chasers and damage-suits, I urged him into the car, offering to take him wherever he might be bound. He was clutching a bulky package, and after momentary protest, he climbed in.

"It's not far," he said; "I'm going to my workshop. Turn right next corner and go four blocks up the hill. Mighty decent of you to do this. You'd better come in with me, and we'll mix a hot toddy to keep out the cold."

"I could do with it," was my response. "What kind of a workshop is it?"

"Oh, I do models for studio sets," he said. "Right now we're working on ships for the naval spectacle that Colossal is doing. I come down evenings and lay out the work for my men to do next day."

"Are you the one who made St. Paul's Roman galley a two-master?" I asked with deep guile.

He emitted a snort, "Huh! Not likely. Just because a bunch of landlubbers translated a word wrong, I wouldn't put a mainsail where a spritsail should be. That's like the French word *misaine*—it means *foresail* or *foremast;* but most of these birds call it the 'mizzen' and think they've done something good.... Well, here we are: where the light's burning.

The man interested me by this time.

We turned into a drive, left the car, and presently I found myself in an amazing room. My host (so nearly my victim) was a thin, wide-shouldered man of perhaps forty, a very pleasant fellow who gave his name as Keble.

Around the place were miniature models of anything and everything, from the White House to a Chinese junk. Most of them dealt with ships, of every kind. As Keble said, the movie method of wrecking a miniature ship had given him a constant job, and he had built up a very good business. What was more, most of his ships were fitted with miniature figures, lifelike and beautifully made.

Keble mixed a hot drink, which was gratefully

received, and then opened up the bulky parcel he had been carrying.

"You almost gummed up the works, he said with a smile, as he exposed the model of a long-decked ship with one mast. "This is Astarte's ship, one of the most important steps in the history of naval construction: and if you'd wiped out the lady and her Phœnician ship together, it'd have been a tragedy!"

"Phœnician?" I said, examining the model and the tiny figures aboard it. "But those ships had a ram in the bow—"

"Oh, you're thinking of the big Tyrian traders of a thousand years later," be broke in. "The ships that voyaged to the Tin Islands and out into the Atlantic! This is the vessel of the great Phœnician migration from the Persian Gulf, up through the Red Sea, and on across to the shores of Palestine."

"Where Astarte was certainly a goddess," I said.

"Sure. But these Phœnicians came from Assyria, and carried Assyrian gods along; then their great heroes became gods—people like Astarte and Melkarth. Maybe it would interest you to read the working script of this thing. It has a good deal of the dialogue in, too, and shows what this one studio is trying to do in their pictures.

He refilled the glasses, and handed me a bulky script.

With a grimace, I turned over the pages carelessly, until my eye was caught by a phrase, then by a scene. If you have witnessed that remarkable picture, which I believe was released sometime since, you'll remember the scene: It was after the migrating host of the Phœnicians had got well on their way and had halted before reaching the Red Sea; the scene where the spies came in, the spies who had been sent a year ahead. You remember, no doubt, how the two ships bearing the spies came in among the fleet of the Phœnicians, and were brought up to the armed camp and received by the lordly old prophet Melkarth.

Here for months the migrating host had been camped, awaiting this news, repairing their old ships, building new ones. It was an impressive scene, as the old prophet and his daughter Astarte, who were rulers of this people, heard the stories of what lay ahead, while the throngs massed around their tent and the flare of countless torches picked up the sea of faces with keen highlights.

The first spy had come the longest way.

"Lord," he said, after saluting the prophet, "as you saw in a dream before I departed, so was the truth. I went to the end of the Red Sea, then by lakes across a desert land to a farther and greater sea. And there I came to the place revealed to you, the place called Sidon. It is a large island close to the coast and easily defended; some of our people are settled there now, and will welcome the host."

"Will it contain these thousands?" Melkarth gestured toward the throng.

"Easily, lord, and as many again. There is no lack of good water. From what I gathered by talk with Egyptians, a mighty city in this place would control the whole commerce of this farther sea. Our people already there say that these lands are not deserts, such as the lands hereabouts, but very fertile and thickly peopled. I have brought maps and all directions."

This report was good, but less good were the others. The Egyptians, whose ships controlled the Red Sea, had heard of this migratory wave approaching from the east, and were determined to halt it. They slew Phœnicians without mercy, wherever found. They had built many ships to stop the seaward passage. At this, Astarte spoke up and questioned the man.

"Ships of the same kind, or of new kinds?"

"Lady, there is but one kind of ship," said the man, wondering. He did not know what had been transpiring, here in the camp, since he had been long gone. "The same ships the Egyptians always use, and that we use."

Astarte, smiling a little, drew back behind the seat of her father Melkarth. She was a tall and stately woman, still very young, and of such beauty that men's hearts burned in them to look upon her; but she looked twice at none of them.

Here in the host of her people lay her heart. Men voyaging afar had brought back word of that farther sea beyond the sunset, a blue and lovely sea with islands and fertile lands, and freedom. So, by her doing, the prophet Melkarth had aroused his folk to escape from the Assyrian lash, to follow the sea which they knew and loved, to seek past Egypt for this farther sea and the mighty potential commerce it would afford. Old was Melkarth, indeed, but mighty in brain and in thew still, though guided largely by this beautiful young daughter of his, and by her vision.

This vision was one for all the Phœnician race, a vision of freedom and greatness; in it her whole heart and soul were bound up. And of this host, whose

thousands had been picked for the first wave that would end in conquest or disaster, Astarte was the chosen leader. The captains obeyed her as they did Melkarth her father.

That same night one of these captains sought her out, as she made her nightly round to make certain the guards on the camp and the shore, where the ships were updrawn, were vigilant. Ithobal, he of the hawk nose and fierce bold eyes, was mightiest and oldest of the captains, though not yet forty. This was a young men's war; the prophet Melkarth was the only gray head in the entire host.

Ithobal joined Astarte as she stood looking out over the sea, and they spoke together of the various reports from the spies. Then he laughed softly.

"You're a shrewd woman, Astarte. You know that I love you?"

"What of it?" she replied. "I love no one."

"But you do—this host. I've watched your methods," Ithobal said quietly. "I know how for years you've talked with captains and pilots and strangers, how this dream of leading our people to a new free home has taken hold of you. I know how you've worked on your father, inspiring his visions and prophecies. I know how you talked with that wanderer who had been to the farther sea, and how his stories inspired your father's prophecy of a place called Sidon—"

"Be careful, Ithobal!" she struck in, menace in her throat.

Ithobal laughed again.

"Nonsense! I say, you're shrewd, and you're great! Your heart is bound up with our people and their migration. But now we're heading straight to destruction. The Egyptians will show no mercy. We have families, flocks, herds, goods, stores of food and water, loaded aboard our ships. Their fighting-ships will destroy us. And this notion you have of building new ships—well, it's no go. I've been looking at these new ships of yours."

"And what?" she demanded, as he paused.

"Death-traps for honest seamen. One of those solid Egyptian ships can smash 'em like paper," he said bluntly. "The first reverse will mean trouble for you. Already there's some talk about a man being needed to command this fleet, in case anything happens to Melkarth."

She laughed softly.

"I'm building twelve ships, Ithobal; and they're nearly done," said she. "And as you say, I've caused this migration of our people. When this host of ours has settled securely at Sidon, others of our people will come flocking, until we occupy all those coasts on the farther sea. These twelve ships of mine will be like this one chosen host—merely a beginning. I am busy with such things; and your petty brain is busy with desire for marriage. You can dream of nothing else."

Ithobal stifled an oath. "So you're dealing with great things, eh? And what about that yellow-haired Greek halfbreed you've made a ship-captain—that fellow Hiram? He's building your new ships; why? He's becoming a great man among us; why? Perhaps because he has a way with the women, eh? Even with a prophet's daughter."

"Poor Ithobal!" she said mockingly. "You think you can goad me to anger? Not a bit of it. You're a valuable man, a splendid captain; we need you. In fact, I'm making the morning to break camp and sail on into the Red Sea. But I'm not marrying you."

"Who knows?" he said, passion hoarse in his throat. "You may do worse than that, Astarte, ere you do better. By the god Bel, I'm going to have you for my wife if I must wreck the whole enterprise to get you!"

Her laughter mocked him again. "What? With two wives at home? No, no, Ithobal! Go and get your orders ready. The fleet breaks camp and sails in three days, and you command it. Get scout-ships out at dawn to cruise ahead. And we take no flocks and herds with us. We slaughter them before sailing."

She was gone, leaving him standing there in shocked amazement and dismay. Slaughter the flocks and herds? Why, the people would rebel at the very thought!

But they did not.

Now, Astarte dealt thus with Ithobal by reason of her shrewdness and deep guile in all mailers. She knew well that if she flew into anger against him, a large part of the host would acclaim him as leader, and she might be forced into marriage. This she did not want; therefore she made him leader of the whole host, loaded responsibility and trouble on his shoulders, and gave him hot and fast work to do. Also, she was looking ahead to the meeting with the Egyptians.

To break camp and get all those two hundred ships loaded and off in three days, after camping here for long months, was a man's job. Ithobal managed it, working day and night at the task. The sheep and cattle and camels were slaughtered here, as the prophet Melkarth commanded; there were sacrifices to Bel the god; the ships were put into the water; and by the fourth morning the whole fleet was off into the Red Sea—all save Astarte and those who remained here with her.

Chief of them was Hiram, the half-Greek captain who was building her new ships. These were nearly finished; with them stayed their crews.

A strange man, this Hiram. Young, yellow of hair and blue of eyes, filled with a wild vital energy, a flaming eagerness. From the start he had grasped her idea in building these ships; and he had carried on the work with a fierce and unflagging enthusiasm that accomplished wonders.

Melkarth had gone with the host. Astarte, in the late morning, left her tent and came down to the shore, when the work was going forward, a scant fifteen hundred men left laboring, the crews of these twelve ships. They differed from all the other ships, which were of the standard model borrowed from the Egyptian. Most of them were already in the water and being rigged.

"The last two will be launched today!" cried Hiram, when Astarte cant to where he directed the labor. Stripped to the waist, darkly bronzed by the Arabian sun, he was of a different type from the other red-skinned men—their very name, indeed, came from their reddened skins. His blue eyes smote her like a sword of steel.

"Look, Astarte!" He swept one hand out at the floating craft. "Provisions and ballast going in; and tonight the new sails and rigging. And all your idea!"

"But your work," said she gently. Suddenly, as she met his gaze, the words of Ithobal returned to her mind. A trace of color mounted into her cheeks; her eyes warmed. Then she went on, more coldly than usual, as though to deny any personal feeling. "Have you tried the new sail?"

"No," said Hiram. "Too cursed busy, Lady Astarte. If we get these two last ships into the water today, well have to sweat blood; but we'll do it. And before sunset, if you like, we can try out one of the finished craft."

She nodded and passed on, to superintend the work of rigging the launched ships. For this rigging was her own idea.

Not hers alone, however. Many a long night had she spent in talk with grizzled sea-captains, listening to theories of rigging and oar-banks and hulls. And once, up the Tigris, she had experimented with just such a new type of sail on a small boat, and had found it worked admirably. Yet no one had listened to her. Only now, with the host on the move, was she free to do as she desired; the captains, men like Ithobal,

Twelve ships here, ten captains, with Hiram and herself. When the sun verged toward the west, she called the ten and they went aboard the ship she had chosen for her own. A hundred men flocked aboard to handle ropes and oars. Hiram came, fresh-bathed and vigorous as though he had not labored since daybreak, and they drove out the ship, oars aflash. There was a light wind, so that presently the sail was loosed, and then the captains gasped.

All other ships they knew used the cumbersome Egyptian oblong sail with its enormous boom, curved up at the ends like the horns of an ox, and its spread of topping lifts. Here was no boom. Here was a yard, which could be swung, and a huge square sail that trailed upward to the yard when not in use. The sail could he handled with the yard, so that when it was braced aslant, the ship would head half into the wind's eye, which other ships would not do.

And how she tore through the water! Men stood stoutly at the two steering-oars,—one to either side the stern,—immense oars whose butts reached up ten feet above the deck, then came down in a forked prong, by which they could be manipulated easily. Under oars alone the ship was a marvel of speed and handling. When it was headed back, Hiram came into the high stern where Astarte stood.

"You've won, you've won the world!" he said with a rush of words. "It's past belief, Astarte! There's speed in length, as you argued. This long, shallow hull lifts easily, and answers to the oars or sail like a witch. Its very lightness is an aid, too. Marvelous! But if one of those heavy Egyptian craft ever smashes into us!"

"I don't intend that one shall," she replied, smiling.

"Then warn the captains well," said Hiram. "I was in some doubt about this new thin planking, nailed on instead of being heavily pegged to solid braces; but it certainly answers!"

He looked at the ship; then he turned and looked at her for a long moment.

"You're a goddess in very truth," he said, his blue eyes regarding her with admiration and impetuous

were too busy with their own affairs to gainsay her wishes and her experiments.

Yet now and again, as she ordered the men who stepped masts and sent up the long yards, she turned and sent thoughtful glances at the yellow-haired man directing the work ashore. Something stirred within her. What a living flame he was! And in him was none of Ithobal's fierce guile. He was all seaman, all frank and open, able to do the work of ten; and the men, she noted, served him gladly, willingly.

Abruptly it came to her how she had all along depended on this man Hiram, how he had encouraged and fed her dreams, how he had whipped them into substance and form. Until now, she had not realized his weight. She saw him for the first time as a personality, as a man; and the sight was startling.

Shielded by a canvas canopy from the white-hot sun, Astarte remained all day at the work, changing and correcting a hundred minor details. These vessels, hastily built, constructed out of old and worn-out ships, would serve the need; but some day, she thought, and the vision kindled in her brain, she would build entirely new ships, incorporating still further advances. Some day, when that far unknown land was won, and the town of Sidon became a city!

affection. "The most beautiful of all women, the wisest, the most wonderful!"

Then the captains came crowding up, and they were no longer alone.

These men had beheld a marvel; and seamen all, they took hold with right eager hearts. Two days, three, passed by, an inferno of labor by day and night shifts. Men worked until they dropped, under hot sun or by flaring torches: others look their place; the task went on.

Astarte, meanwhile, drilled her captains, seeing clearly that success or failure hung upon the handling of these ships. She devoted every spare moment to this; and the captains gained but little sleep, being responsible to her for the outfitting as well. The high bulwarks had to be fitted with shield-racks so that shields could be hung along the rails. Weapons and provisions had to be stowed. The tackle had to be adjusted, and men trained to the ropes. The hides of the slaughtered cattle had to be stretched along the upper sides of the ships and heavily greased. Signals had to be arranged and studied. The details were endless.

"We must begone," she said abruptly.

Then, suddenly, everything broke with a rush. One of the small dispatch-boats came tearing back from the fleet under all oars. The whole Egyptian force had been sighted—full fifty and more fighting-ships. Ithobal, halting the host, had made a four-day truce with them. It would expire before Astarte could possibly catch up with Ithobal.

She questioned the messengers there on the snore, while her captains listened.

"Did he do as I commanded—did he move all the women and families and bulky loads aboard half the ships, to leave the others free for fighting?"

"No, lady," replied the skipper of the dispatch-boat. "He ordered the women to arm with the men: if it came to fighting, all hands would thus do better."

"Fool, *fool!*" she cried out, in a white heat of anger. "In those crowded ships the Egyptians will raven like wolves in a sheepfold! Aboard, aboard, everyone! Blow the trumpets! Captains, remember the signals. To the ships!"

Trumpets sounded; cymbals clanged. Within half an hour the ships were moving out, following the lead of Astarte. And how they moved! There was a light following wind that filled the sails; but with a hundred and fifty men to each ship, the oars were manned likewise, with no lack of fresh shifts to take the ash from weary hands. In an hour's time the fast dispatch-boat, which had started with them, was hull-down astern. Such speed was a revelation.

The northeast monsoon was blowing, and the tremendous currents of water flowing into the Red Sea were on full force, greatly increasing their speed. With veteran pilots who knew all the far-flung coral reefs, Astarte had no fear of hidden dangers. When darkness drew down, instead of landing for the night as was the invariable rule, she drove on into the north.

Morning dawned, and wore on until noon. The pilots stood incredulous; three days' sailing, they said, had already been covered. Astarte, on the high platform in the stern, suddenly leaped erect. Sails on the horizon! A trumpet from Hiram's ship confirmed the fact. The fleets were in sight!

A dispatch-boat came toiling down the sea, oars aflash in the sunlight. Astarte ran alongside and heard the news shouted out. It was enough to blanch her cheeks and make the men look at one another, aghast.

"Truce ended—Egyptians are attacking. A score of ships already destroyed or beached. Melkarth the prophet is dead—"

Melkarth dead! Astarte turned to her sailing master. "Unfurl the canvas. Out oars give way, together! Break out the arms!"

The ship plunged forward afresh, the others in her wake.

The captains took oaths to serve her.

Arms, spears and arrows, no more were brought forth. Armor was donned: in the stern, Astarte stood awaiting her armor, when one of the men came bearing a hide bundle and laid it before her.

"Lady," he said, Hiram the captain bade me bring you this gift from him, before battle, saying that himself had made it in the forge."

Astarte opened the hide, and found a light but strong shirt of overlapping iron plates, each one curiously worked and highly polished; and with this, a glorious mantle dyed in the royal scarlet such as the Assyrian kings wore, a scarlet dye taken from shellfish in a secret manner. Then she remembered that Hiram was a cunning worker in metals; and that he had once told her he, and he alone, knew the secret of this shellfish dye. She put on the mail-coat, and over it the scarlet mantle, so that all her men let rise a wild shout of admiration and delight. Two men leaped up with their shields to guard her, and the ship drove on with foam under its forefoot.

But now all the battle lay outspread ahead, ships seeming to cover the whole sea and it was a bitter sight to Phœnician eyes. To the right lay the Arabian coast, mountains running up into the sky from a short reach of shore. All the host had broken and scattered. Some part of the ships had run ashore for shelter; others were huddled in groups; and like wolves indeed, the Egyptian ships ravaged among them.

Crowded, hampered by families and goods, the Phœnicians could neither fight nor run. The Egyptian ships smashed in among them and poured forth hordes of warriors who slew to repletion. Many and many a ship floated idly, red with blood; and seeing this, Astarte motioned to her trumpeters and told them what signal to give.

The brazen notes sounded. They were repeated and passed on from Hiram's ship, which lay close, and so to the others. Hearing the signal, the twelve vessels sheered off and broke into pairs.

Seeing these newcomers, certain of the Egyptian ships headed out from the slaughter to meet them. One, larger than the others, bore straight for the ship of Astarte. She waved her arm at Hiram, who, from his own high stern platform, waved response. The two headed for the great Egyptian.

"Take in sail!" shouted Astarte.

A dozen men clambered aloft to the yard.

The sail was brailed up. The oars flashed to quicker stroke. The Egyptian steered between the ship of Astarte and that of Hiram; rather, they rushed upon her from either side, their men sheltered behind the shield-wall. Close and closer, until from the massed throngs aboard the Egyptian came arrow and stones, and the air was filled with death.

Then, as the Egyptian was all but between the two, Astarte gave the word. The bowmen leaped up. Into those massed warriors poured hail upon hail of shafts, from either side, as the two Phœnicians ran her length. They left her half crippled, her oars all in disorder, for the next two ships to finish; and, themselves scarce hurt, darted upon the next Egyptian.

Ship after ship of those wolves was disabled and left for other Phœnicians to grapple and clear. In vain did the Egyptians try to avoid the flashing stroke of those fast, new ships; they were too heavy and clumsy. In vain did they rain spears and arrows; they themselves were exposed and helpless, but Astarte's men had the shield-wall along either side for protection, and vast quantities of arrows.

They tried to ram. One succeeded, and the Phœnician was smashed like an eggshell; but one alone. The others maneuvered clear, and stayed clear, struck their deadly blow and flashed on. It was a new system of fighting, due wholly to the ships which carried it out; and now Ithobal burst forth from the fugitive huddle, and with what craft he could hastily muster, fell upon the rear of the Egyptians.

No mercy was there, for Astarte dared risk no second encounter. When the Egyptians turned and fled, she was after them. More of their ships fell back, crippled, to be laid aboard by Ithobal and swept bare. Out of all their mighty fleet, scarce a dozen ships won clear across the horizon that night.

But Astarte came back to her people, where the host was drawn up on shore, and to the funeral pyre of the prophet Melkarth. And with her came Hiram.

It was a night of mourning, of flaming torches, of vast booty, of Egyptian ships captured and brought in. All these things Astarte left to her captains and remained secluded with her dead father, until he and the other dead were burned on the long pyres at sunrise.

Then, with her armor laid off, but still wearing that glorious cloak of royal scarlet, she called her captains together. All the people hailed her as their leader, in place of her father; but she passed into the council of the captains, and laid before them strips of parchment on which were drawn lines and markings.

"We must embark and begone," she said abruptly. "Now is the time, before the Egyptians can gather armies and fresh ships to stop us. Look! Here are maps, snowing our course, which the pilots have prepared with me. We go to the head of this Red Sea, and on through salt lakes until the ships can go on no farther. Then we take these new ships of mine, which are light; they can be hauled across the sand on rollers until we reach the farther sea. The host must trudge afoot."

Hearing this, the captains burst into wild acclaim, and took oaths to serve her as they had served Melkarth the prophet. Lists of the dead, of the captives, of the plunder, were brought forward, but Astarte suddenly interrupted, her eyes gazing about the huge tent:

"I ordered all the captains to assemble. They are not all here. Where is Hiram?"

One looked at another; but Ithobal smiled darkly, and Astarte noted the smile, fleeting as it was. Men went to seek, and presently one came running, with a knife that was all red with blood. Pale as death, Astarte listened.

"Lady!" said the messenger. "The captain Hiram was just now found in his tent. He had been stabbed, in the night, and is dead."

"Lady! The captain Hiram came ashore last night and was working at the Egyptian ships, clearing them of dead. He was just now found in his tent. He had been stabbed, in the night, and is dead."

Astarte took the knife—then dropped it suddenly so that it fell, and looked at the blood on her fingers. Then her eyes lifted, and met the gaze of Ithobal.

"Your doing, Ithobal!" she said in slow, still voice. "This is a knife that my father gave you before we left Assyria. You dare not lie!"

"Neither dare nor would," and Ithobal stepped out boldly. "Aye, lady, I slew him. And now listen to me, Astarte! I am not alone—"

Had she let him speak his will, matters would have been different, for he was deep in guile and had a multitude of the host to back his purposes. But none of his friends were here among the captains in the lent.

Swift as light, Astarte caught a spear from the ground and flung it, and the spear smote Ithobal where neck and arm come together; and he lay dead. She lifted her arms to the stupefied captains.

"You, who took oath to me! Am I your leader or not?"

"*You,* Astarte!" they cried, giving tongue swiftly. "*You,* Astarte!"

"Then depart and say that I have slain Ithobal,

and tell why. And if there are any who like it not, seize them and bring them before me."

They looked upon her in her anguished wrath, and departed hastily to do her will. And as they went, another messenger came stumbling, panting out his swift words to her.

"Lady! He—Hiram—is not dead, as they thought—"

Then might have been seen a strange sight. Through the vast tumult of the camp a woman running, heedless and blazing-eyed, white-lipped, intent upon one sole aim—a woman after whom all stared in wild, startled recognition, a woman careless of the pealing shouts lifting her name from all quarters of the host....

That was all.

I took a deep breath and laid down the script, and met the quick eyes of my host. He read my expression and laughed softly.

"What an ending to it—eh? Suggests everything, leaves everything unsaid; yes, I like that ending! It sends you away with an upthrust, a lift. It's great! But I suppose some sap will put another end to it and show her holding the wounded Hiram in her arms for a fade-out."

Which, if you recall the picture, is exactly what some sap did. But nothing could spoil the vision of that woman, who became the hero-goddess of a people after her city of Sidon waxed great—Astarte!

THE FACE THAT LAUNCHED A THOUSAND SHIPS

Two *small boys were sailing toy boats* in the civic fountain of Beverly Hills, and a fuzzy old man was watching them in keen delight.

They had no earthly business doing it; but the traffic officer had a blind eye for them, and it was a lark. The two boys were whooping it up joyously, arguing and almost fighting over their boats. One of the toy craft wallowed around; the other cut the water cleanly. I sat down beside the fuzzy old fellow, who had wisps of gray hair sticking out from under his battered hat, and a keen shrewd eye like that of Will Rogers.

"Y'know," he said to me with the easy familiarity of idle men, "those kids are worth watching. That red-haired one has built a good craft. Knows his business. The other one don't. He's like the old Greeks. He ain't learned yet."

"The old Greeks," I said, "knew something about ships."

"Nope; you mean, they learned something." He wagged his head, and begged a cigarette, and lit it with appreciation. "Away back in them early days they were split up into little kingdoms. They had cranky, poorly made ships that went to pieces in a seaway; couldn't stand the strain. Traders came to them. They didn't go places."

"You seem to know a lot about it," I observed.

He nodded shrewdly. "I do. Two or three generations before the Trojan war, a bunch of Greeks settled over in Asia Minor and built a city called Troy. Contacts showed 'em how to build the proper kind of a ship; they were like that red-headed kid there. The Greeks back home had never learned the trick. They were like that other kid yonder."

He pointed to the fountain, with a knowing wink.

"One o' those Greek kingdoms was a little place called Sparta," he said. "I been there. A lot of these here Greek cafe boys come from there today. The king lived in a town called Therapne, twenty-five miles up the Eurotas River, quite a jag from the sea. This here king, Menelaos, had a shipyard. He used to go jaunting around in his ships in fair weather; but they wouldn't stand the strain of any blow."

"Was he a friend of yours?" I inquired with mild sarcasm.

The fuzzy old rascal winked at me again. "Yeah.... He was good-looking but a futile sort of a bird; and his wife was right sick of her bargain. Well, there was a ship from Troy that dropped in, and brought company. The sailing-master was a fellow named Skopas, and his boss was a gay sprig whose dad was the king, back in Troy. He was quite a sport, this here Paris was; but he had something on the ball, at that. Old Skopas, he killed a lot of time around the shipyard; and since he sort of ran things for Paris and had a weather eye for trouble, he knew all right why young Paris was hanging around here instead of picking up and going somewhere else. And one day when they were walking together from the shipyard up to the palace, he cut loose. Funny old rascal, this Skopas was—"

Funny old rascal indeed, and the very image of this fellow on the bench beside me. He walked with a lurch, he had the same wisps of gray hair over his hard, weather-beaten countenance; and he laid down the law to the blue-eyed laughing Paris as they walked up through the hot white sunlight.

His words were neither polite nor decent, for he had a rough tongue. Paris, who loved the old seadog, merely laughed again at warnings.

"You'll laugh out of the other side of your mouth," said Skopas, "if this here Menelaos puts a spear through your gizzard some day. Everybody's talking about it. You mooning around with this dame—"

"You mind your respect to the Lady Helen," struck in Paris.

"Yah!" gibed Skopas. "I ain't stuck on her, even if you are. And we've got just forty men, remember, which don't amount to much when you think of all these Greeks around here. What's more, we're a long ways from our ship, down at the ocean; and even if we had the ship here, these Greeks would be too many for us. Don't you go to start anything, Alec."

"And don't you go to calling me Alec," snapped Paris. "Just because I was called Alexander when I was a kid, doesn't mean anything now. Forget it. And never mind about these Greeks, either. They're shipbuilders, but they don't know anything about ships. I've a notion to show 'em something."

"You'd better not," said old Skopas. "Show these Greeks anything, and they'll beat you at it. They don't like us Trojans anyhow. One of these days they'll crack a belaying-pin over your head if you don't stay away from the shipyard."

"Mind your own business," said Paris shortly. "I'll send you down the river to get the ship ready for sea, if you don't tauten your jaw-tackle."

"The ship's ready," Skopas retorted. "I've sent word to the men to keep her in shape to skip out any time."

Paris gave him a sharp look. "What makes you think we'll skip out?"

"Huh! If we don't, we're liable to be carried out," said Skopas sourly. "I know when weather's brewing, if you don't. And you'd better quit your bragging about the walls of Troy. It don't set good with these fellows. They build walls like they do ships."

There was some justice in the observation. The palace, imposing as it was, had been built of cut stone blocks fitted together. Yet it was a glittering, showy place, gay with Cretan and Egyptian weaves, the long halls gleaming with gold. A wealthy man was Menelaos, who believed that precious metals and handsome weapons were for use and display, not for sticking away in chests and hoarding.

Greece was wealthy too. The traders of all the world came here—Tyrians, Cretans and Egyptians; so that the Greeks had no urge to go forth themselves. Yet in the eyes of the visitors, this quiet, humdrum back-country with its rather crude structures was something of a joke.

The forty Trojans, camped close to their ship near the mouth of the Eurotas, swaggered among the gaping rustics with tall tales of the windy plains and pine-clad mountains of Troy, and the huge commerce that poured in there from all quarters. At first the Greeks drank in the stories greedily; then they came to resent such talk.

They resented other things too. These foreign seamen had a way with them when it came to the women. They were a blustering, gusty, high-handed lot, all of them: men of the world, who laughed at the country bumpkins in the Spartan villages. The girls thought them magnificent, and so indeed they were.

*At the Therapne palace, however, Paris was ex*tremely popular. He was no braggart. With his crisp yellow hair, blue eyes and infectious laugh, with his great address at all sports, with his perfumes and fine clothes and silver tongue, he was an instant favorite.

Much of his time was spent with Helen the queen, for Menelaos was often away looking after his herds and farms. A stodgy, canny sort, he entertained the visitor royally and went on about his business as usual, while Paris filled the women's ears with talk about Troy town and its wonders. And as shrewd old Skopas foresaw, such a business could have but one ending, very human and natural withal.

And when Paris himself was aware of this, it was too late.

Anyone would have fallen in love with Helen: half of Greece had courted her until she made the mistake of marrying Menelaos. She was tall and lovely past words; and the very heart of a man melted with longing and sharp pain when her eyes were turned upon him; she was wise, moreover, brave and clearsighted in all things.

Realization came to them suddenly one day. Paris sat with her in the lush grass beside the river, watching her women playing at ball. He was talking of Troy, and a slow sigh came from her.

"Oh, I long to see these far places!" she said softly. "I'd love to watch these strange ships and people. But what good is longing?"

"Longing?" repeated Paris. "It's the greatest and bitterest and most beautiful and most universal of human feelings, my dear Helen. Longing after something—that's what makes the world go forward! To conquer the unattainable—why, that's ambition worth while!"

"For a man, yes," she said, and smiled into his eyes. "But for a woman—"

"The same." And he laughed gayly. "Your very name shows it: *Helen the Taker!* Taker of men, of beauty, of tribute due you! Why, my dear, I'd lay all Troy town at your feet—"

He checked himself abruptly, but it had been said. Their eyes met in silence; the sharp laughing cries of the girls at play came to them; and from somewhere near by, the tootling pipes of a shepherd. Paris touched her white fingers.

"Well, there it is," he said abruptly. "Take Troy, then; you can have it. Everybody in the place would be at your feet. Even that dour, upright brother of mine, Hector—yes."

"Don't be foolish, my dear Alec," she said softly; but she had gone white to the lips. He looked up sharply.

"Who told you that name of mine?"

"Skopas," she said, and colored again. "We were talking about you the other day. That old rascal loves you. And—"

Silence again. Her white fingers quivered to his touch, then twined suddenly about his shoulder.

"By the gods!" said he in a low tense voice. "It's true! What I've felt, what I've dreamed—it's true. Say it is!"

"No, no!" She drew her hand away. A shaky laugh came from her lovely lips. "Why, even if you gave me all Troy, I couldn't keep it! Menelaos and his brother and all Greece would—"

"Greece? Bah! Look at those ships of yours!" he exclaimed hotly, eagerly. "They couldn't sail that far. And look at those walls of ours! You know, we used to build like you folks. Back when my grandfather was king, two fellows showed up and showed us how to use cement, and you ought to see the walls they put up around the city! Why, those walls could keep out the whole of Greece, honest! I've heard tell that my grandfather did 'em in one night, and then gave it out that a couple of gods had built the walls and disappeared. That was like the old man. He was a tough one, he was."

He caught her hand again, gazed into her eyes, his face ablaze.

"I'll always love you," he said quickly, abruptly. "It's out; why hide it? I'll give you the world—all of it! And you love me. I can feel it."

"Yes," she said under her breath. "Yes. That's true, Alec. I like the name better than Paris. But it's so useless! What can we do about it? Nothing. I'm no common woman, my dear."

"You're the most glorious woman in the world," he said brokenly, then drew away from her as the girls, laughing and panting, came from their play. No more chance now for private talk.

That night Paris, out under the stars, was striding up and down, trying to see some light on the affair, when he was aware of a dark cloaked shape behind him. It was Skopas, who chuckled at his instinctive gesture.

"Hand to sword, Paris? Too late. I saw your looks, and hers, at supper. So you wouldn't run for it, eh? All right, my boy, I'm with you. Say the word, and I'll bring up some of our men from the ship, and we'll bump off that pompous Menelaos—"

"Stow your jaw!" snapped Paris. "You fool, he's my friend, my host!"

"Which didn't prevent your falling in love with his wife. Well, blame the gods for that; but when you're on a lee shore, watch your helm! What's to come of it?"

"Damned if I know, Skopas," said Paris with a groan. "What do you suggest?"

"Go back to Troy tomorrow."

"I will not."

"Then face the music," said Skopas coolly. "Sure you aren't fooling yourself? Just a bit of passion, or do you want to be hitched for life?"

"It's the real thing, Skopas," Paris rejoined in a low voice.

"I believe you. Still, she's no common wench; she's not the girl to do any cheating," the old seadog commented, "This thing is going to raise hell; but all Trojans stick together, so write your own ticket and we're with you. What's it to be?"

"I don't know," said Paris helplessly. "Wait and see; I'll have a talk with her in the morning."

"I can tell you one thing," Skopas rejoined. "If she ever steps inside the gate of Troy, she'll own the place. Another man's wife or not—boy, what a woman she is! Your dad wouldn't have a word to say, I bet."

"Shut up and go to bed," snapped Paris impatiently. "I'll fight this thing out somehow myself."

The Abduction of Helen

And stooping, he drew with his finger in the dust.

"There y'are: A stout six-foot walk from stem to stern, braced to every cross-timber. Then your ship's a solid thing, and can stand the waves."

"But such a walk is above the rowers' benches!" protested the foreman.

"Of course it is, you fool!" cried Paris angrily. "For the officers and crew to use in fighting; for the overseers to use in keeping the slaves at work!"

"Well, we're not slaves, and we don't use 'em at the oars, and we don't care to have any godless Trojans come along and call us fools," said one of the designers hotly. "What's good enough for our fathers will serve us—"

"And go to pieces on you as on them," Paris cut in. "That solid walk serves as an additional brace for your mast, also. If you built a ship like this, your imitation seamen might get somewhere in the world."

"You mean, she will," said Skopas, and then vanished hurriedly, as Paris aimed a blow at his head....

Next morning Paris found that Helen had gone into town with her husband to hear various lawsuits. Menelaos was the lawgiver; but the lawyers and people had more faith in Helen's judgment, which was indeed exceptional.... So Paris went down to the shipyard and lent a hand in the building of the king's new galley, but he was in no good humor.

Stripped and sweating, he flung himself into the work, and presently lost patience with it all.

"When you get the thing finished, you'll have nothing," he snapped at the foreman and draftsmen. "She won't stand the strain and stress of a ten-mile wind."

"The timbers are strong, My Lord," the foreman said. "Look at those cross-pieces! Good solid oak, every one."

"The whole thing's out of kilter," Paris rejoined. "Why, she gives and shakes like a snake in motion! Your keel's not strong enough, and you need a brace from for'ard to aft to keep her from shaking to pieces. Like that on Tyrian ships, or on my own ship. Look here—"

One thing led to another: words came to blows, and the pack of them went for Paris with anything handy. He laid out first one, then another, and was in the thick of a fine hot scrimmage when spearmen came running, and King Menelaos himself appeared on the scene. His spearmen rounded up the ship-workers, and he ordered them given fifty lashes each. Then Paris came forward, wiping the sweat and blood from his eyes.

"Don't do that, Menelaos," he cried out. "It was all my own fault. I prodded 'em into the scrap, and there's no harm done."

Menelaos, black-browed and angry, eyed him up and down.

"Hang me if you don't look like the god Phœbus himself! Well, I'll have no guest of mine insulted. Not if he were a common thief instead of a prince. Hospitality is the first law of the hearth, as you know well."

"The fault was all mine," said Paris. "I'll go along with them and take what they get, if you're so cursed set on a flogging."

"Don't be a fool," said Menelaos, and signed to his spearmen. "All right; let 'em off. Paris, I want to have a word or two with you tonight. I'm off to look over a pair of horses that a merchant from Argolis has brought to town, and I may not be back early this afternoon. When I return, give me a few minutes."

"Gladly," said Paris. The two of them were eye to eye for a moment; and in this moment, Paris saw that the king knew. Then Menelaos went his way, to harness a fresh team to his chariot and be off to town again.

Paris went down to the river, had a swim, and afterward fell asleep. When he woke up, Skopas was sitting beside him with a basket of lunch and some wine.

"You've certainly played the devil this morning," said Skopas grimly. "Forgot all about eating, huh? Here, pitch into this grub. And this is the best Chian wine you ever sampled. Save some for me."

"What are you so grumpy about?" Paris demanded, as he eagerly seized the food.

"Weather brewing and a high sea running offshore." Skopas cocked an eye at the sky, which was fair enough. "By tomorrow night, we're going to have one hell of a blow if I'm any judge. Rain's coming out of the west. Well, you've started a lot of talk, in spite of my warnings. I told you not to teach these Greeks anything about ship-building."

"By the gods!" said he in a low tense voice. "It's true—what I've dreamed—true! Say it is!"

"Huh! Nobody could teach those fools anything," grumbled Paris.

"Sure. That's what you think. Just the same, they drank it all in; and I hear they're going to work right away at a ship along proper lines."

"What's that to me? Or you?"

Skopas scratched his fuzzy chin. "I dunno. It may be a lot, later on. By the way, Lady Helen said she'd be in the back garden, if you'd care to see her."

Paris leaped up. "Why didn't you say so in the first place?"

"What's the rush, anyhow? She'll keep. I've laid out that second-best suit of armor you brought along. Better use it if you get in a pinch, for the other one looks better, but wouldn't stop a blunt wooden spear."

"Huh?" And Paris eyed him keenly. "What are you driving at?"

"Breakers ahead and plenty of 'em, my boy."

"Then you pull out of here," ordered Paris. "Take one of the small-boats and go downriver to the ship. Overhaul the tackle and have the men ready to go aboard at a moment's notice."

"I sent down a message yesterday to that effect." And Skopas grinned.

"Go yourself, and go now, and have everything shipshape."

"All right, all right," grumbled the other. "About tomorrow morning it's going to be blowing great guns—a good time to run, all right. None of these Greek ships can take it on the chin the way we can."

"I'm not running, you idiot," snapped Paris, and started for the palace.

Just the same, he knew that Skopas was a wise old man; and when he sought the private back garden, he was scowling in uneasy thought. For Menelaos knew. No doubt about it.

Helen greeted him with a friendly smile and a quiet gesture that held him off.

"Have you thought about it?" she asked.

"About nothing else, confound it!" Paris looked at her for a moment, then burst out: "My dear, my dear, let's have it straight out with him! He knows; I could read it in his face. He wants to see me tonight."

"See him, and leave," she said quietly.

His eyes blazed. "I will not! When I go, you go with me. That's final."

The rose-leaf color slowly ebbed out of her face.

"The easy thing to do—yes. But I can't do it, Alec my dear; and I can't slink away; and—and there's just nothing else for it than to do the hard thing. Live my own life, be true to him, hold you locked in my heart forever, and keep silent."

"Now, listen to me, Helen," Paris broke in. "I love you, and you love me. I don't take any stock in high nobility and self-sacrificing and so forth. We've got our lives to live, my dear. You're the biggest thing in the world to me, and always will be. I'm not infatuated with you; I love you! Do you know what that means?"

"I know what that means, since meeting you," she said, looking at him steadily.

"Then I'll face the issue tonight, and face it squarely," said Paris. "If he wants to fight it out, well and good."

"He's no fighter," she replied, her eyes thoughtful. "My dear, it's an impossible situation. I'll give up everything—home, friends, honor—to go with you. But I'll not sneak out and away. There's something you don't know. We had a dispute this morning; that's why he left the law-courts early. He didn't like the way I settled a case. He got furious, and stalked out."

"What of it?" And Paris uttered a curt laugh.

"He'll kill us both; don't you see?" she urged gently. "I don't want you to die, my dear. He'd call in fifty men and have you killed."

"A guest—killed?"

"A thief killed, yes," she said. "The man changes his mind from hour to hour. You can depend on nothing he says. Alec.... Now listen to me! I'm not worth it. Give up all thought of me, and go your way, and forget me—"

"I will not," said he again, and meant it to the bottom of his soul; and she saw that he meant it. She leaned back on the stone seat, and her hands fell in her lap.

"Will you go with me to Troy—for life?" he asked calmly and steadily.

"If I can take my pride with me, yes," she replied. "But you see that it's not possible, otherwise. And to go with his consent, is impossible. There's no way out."

"There's always a way out," said Paris. "The only trouble is to find it."

Fear lightened in her eyes. "Don't look for it, my dear," she said, her voice like low vibrant music. "Don't look for it! I know the man. It means death. And I want you to live."

"By the gods, I intend to live!" swore Paris, and laughed gayly, lightly. He held out his hand to her. "An oath! If you can go with his consent, you go?"

"I go," she said, and gripped his hand for an instant. But when he would have come closer, when the swift blaze in his eyes warned her, she shook her head. "No, my dear, no. I am still his wife."

Paris turned and left her.

Not until the afternoon was run, and dinner was being set up in the long hall, did Menelaos return. And Paris, all this while, sat with his own thoughts, cursing the impulse that had made him send Skopas away. He needed that man's wit and guile this night, as never before.

He knew Menelaos well, knew him like a book, and feared him. No great warrior, and in many ways of thought a petty fellow, but filled with a pompous pride, an ear to what people might say, and hence a crafty man. Stubborn weaklings are ever crafty; and Paris knew that he might well stumble into some snare this night.

"That poor half-witted sister of mine said some great evil would come of this cruise," he muttered. "True, Cassandra is always croaking, and nobody pays any attention to her; but it would be awkward if my funeral proved her right this time! And my good host Menelaos is a slippery one. Hospitality, eh? He'd prate of anything, and deny it next minute. Oh, why the devil does a wonderful girl like her always take up with some sap such as he is?"

He cast an eye on the armor that Skopas had laid out, and then went in to dinner, wishing vainly that he had a few of his Trojan seadogs along. A sense of foreboding, of oppression, had come upon him; only the smile of Helen dispelled it, as he joined her and the king.

Menelaos was courteous; but there was a glitter in his eye and an acid touch to his words. The captains and courtiers at the lower table were more silent than usual too. Paris fancied that they eyed him appraisingly, as men eye some noble ox destined to the altar of sacrifice. It was an oppressive night, with thunderclouds massing high, and a shrill keen moaning of wind among the trees, yet no wind here beneath them. Skopas had been right about a storm coming up fast.

When the meal was over, Menelaos cleared the hall, sent away the wine-bearers, and the three of them were alone. He bent his dark brows on his guest.

"I hear you don't think much of our Greek ships, Paris."

"Candidly, my dear Menelaos, they're not worth a good deep-sea oath." And Paris laughed a little, as he met those glowering eyes. "Of course, they're all right for coasting operations and trips among the islands—"

"But our women are more to Trojan taste, eh?" broke in Menelaos. "Those men of yours have been raising merry hell down at the coast. And just how far do you and my wife think the duties of hospitality should extend? Or will you try to lie out of it, my fine popinjay?"

The steady gaze of Paris did not flicker, although Helen went white as death.

"You don't seem to know your wife very well, Menelaos," he returned coolly. "And I don't lie—unless it's really necessary. If you mean to insinuate that I'm in love with Helen, that's quite true. Everyone who knows her, I think, loves her."

Menelaos flushed darkly.

"I've watched the two of you!" And his voice was harsh. "You've slunk into my house and made love to my wife—"

"No, no, Menelaos," struck in Paris, with his gay smile. "I've won your wife's love. There's no use your acting like some Bœotian hill-billy and raving about vengeance and so forth; look at the matter sensibly. You couldn't hold her, and I can. Now, what's to be done about it? I'm perfectly willing to meet you with spear and sword, if you care to settle matters that way—"

Menelaos grunted, and met the questioning gaze of his wife.

"Is this true?" he rapped out. "Do you actually love this fellow?"

"You're well aware that I ceased to love you quite a while back," she replied evenly, "—ever since I found out about that girl from Miletos. It's no surprise to you, so don't affect airs about it. As for Paris—yes. I do love him."

The king took a deep breath. His anger was a cold, still flame, not a raging fury.

"The gods know," he said slowly, "that I've stood your contempt and lack of love long enough. Not to mention the way you cut in on my position. Why, you're more king here than I am! You, with your giving judgment in the courts—"

"I've always been loyal to you, Menelaos," she said quietly.

"That's just it; you're so damned pure and noble!" he cried, white about the nostrils. "I'm sick of the sight of you! You're no wife to me, no wife of mine. If you want to go with this blasted foreigner, go and welcome! Disgrace yourself, disgrace me and my family, become a thing scorned in the eyes of the world! Go, then!"

Quick as a flash, Helen stood up before him, and took from her arm the great ring of beaten gold that symbolized her wifely estate. She flung it on the board. Gone was her poised calm; and in her face was such a glory, such a blaze of living exaltation, that the two men stared at her as at some goddess.

"Free!" she cried out, her voice ringing down the hall. "I am free! Now you have indeed spoken the truth, Menelaos, and exposed your whole dark unkind heart and soul. Well, I take you at your word."

"And I." Paris rose, and extended his hand to her very gallantly. But Menelaos started up with a swift cry.

"No, no! You can't do this, Helen—you can't do this to me, disgrace me—"

She turned to him, with cold scorn.

"You have set me free—"

The stabbing knife pricked at him; desperately he fended it off.

"I didn't mean it!" The cords stood out on his temples; a break came into his voice; his dark eyes were wide and anguished. "Can't you see? You're more beautiful than ever before; you're the most glorious creature in the world—"

"As you told the girl from Miletos," she rejoined acidly. Then she turned again to Paris, and smiled into his eyes, those deep violet eyes of hers like great stars. Menelaos cried out gasping, incoherent words; but her lips moved a little, and Paris caught the low-breathed sound.

"In the back garden—as soon as you can come."

Then she was gone from them, gone quickly and eagerly, while Menelaos cursed in his black-curled beard.

Paris gave him a look.

"You'll excuse me, I trust? Perhaps you'll even have a chariot harnessed, to take us as far as my ship? It would be very good of you. And I've enjoyed the visit very much, I assure you."

Menelaos lifted his head.

"I'll have a chariot harnessed at once," he said in a dull voice. "At once."

Paris strode out of the great hall to his own room. This had a window that opened on the large garden, whence the little back garden could be gained. Hastily he buckled on his corselet and felt for sword and spear. A cold sweat of fear was upon him—not fear of the king, but fear of the unknown. Somewhere, he knew, guile was at work.

And he was right. Scarcely had he bared his sword, when feet sounded outside his door, and there was a clash of arms in the passage. He reached out to his light, doused it, and with a leap was at the window. Another leap, and he was out—out, and in the very arms of half a dozen men. A yell shrilled up.

"We've got him!"

Paris leaped again, twisted himself sidewise. With naked sword for his only shield, he thrust with the spear—a terrible weapon in his hand. A man screamed; and freeing the long bronze point, he thrust again. Another guard was running up with a torch, and the nickering light showed Paris that he was ringed in. A spear flew for him, but he dodged it with lightning agility and sent his point home to a brown Greek throat, and twisted aside from two rushing figures.

Suddenly there was a blinding crackle of light as the heavens split open. In the glare, Paris saw himself hemmed in, surrounded by a score of spearmen, others coming on the run. Then the searing, deafening peal of thunder, upon an intense blackness that paralyzed every person—except one.

*It was his chance. He seized it, death-fear spur*ring him. Two steps, and he went up into the air, clear up above the foremost figures and over them—over them and down. His spear struck a shield; his left hand drove in the sword-point. Through them now, away from them all, running like a deer, while their shouts rose vainly, confused.

He came to the low wall, the back garden close ahead. Another lightning-flash ran across the sky. A guard directly before him; no chance to evade. The man's spear drove straight at him, smashed at his corselet, struck him squarely and was embedded in the metal. Paris whipped his own spear through and through that man, whose scream was lost in the thunder-roll. Then, freeing himself of corselet and embedded spear, Paris was over the wall at a leap.

Torches were flitting everywhere.... Bruised, breathless, he groped in the darkness, found the hands of the woman who awaited him, and drew her

close. He could feel the hammering of her heart as he held her. Now her voice sobbed at his ear.

"My fault, my fault! I could not resist taking him at his word—and he has trapped us, my dear. There was murder in his heart. Now we cannot reach the stables—"

"The stables be hanged," he broke in. "The river's just below. Over the wall and down to the water, take one of those boats on the shore, and be off! We can make it."

She shivered against him. "Alec, I'm afraid! Of him."

"So am I, my dear. All the more reason to fight it out to the end."

"But you don't understand. I think he intended all the time to murder you; but now it's worse. He hates me for having taken him at his word. He'll deny that to everyone. He'll try to disgrace me; he'll say that I just ran away with you. He'll kill us both if he can. He's always thinking about what people will say—"

"I don't give a damn what people will say," said Paris with a short laugh. "I know that all Troy will be at your feet!"

"Troy! That's just it; don't you see? Why was he away all afternoon? Why did horsemen go riding out before dinner? Your men, your ship, Paris!"

He understood, and cold sharp dread pierced him like a knife. If his men had been attacked and killed, or laid by the heels, if his ship were seized—then he was a lost man indeed. And this woman in his arms was doomed. Then he rallied.

"Bah! Wait and see. Trust old Skopas; he's too sharp to be caught like a rat in a trap. Come along, now."

No more lightning, luckily, although there was a thunder-roll over the horizon, and the wind was whining in the high trees. Torches were everywhere, and a babel of tongues; spearmen were searching the grounds, the palace, the stables.

Down the slope toward the river and the boat-landing the two of them hurried. As they neared the landing, a gasp broke from Helen; she caught his arm, checked him. Voices ahead.

"Guards!" she breathed.

"Aye," said Paris quietly. "A couple of men, no more, apparently. Go right ahead. One of the boats and a paddle—your job. Can you do it?"

"Yes," she said, and her voice was calm. For an instant he held her close, and their lips met. The first kiss, the first touch, here under the stormy sky, with death ahead and behind.

"Who's there? Who comes?" rang out the challenge.

"The Lady Helen," she replied, and went straight to the landing. Two spearmen were there in the obscurity. They drew back, startled and confused by her appearance. Then one whipped around.

"Look out, Agias! Here he is!"

Paris was into them with a rush. Only his sword left now, a short slender blade of keen-edged bronze. Lightning rippled along the horizon, revealing all three figures distinctly.

Paris felt the spear-point touch his breast, felt the warm blood spurt—then his blade drove in. One man cried out and crashed away. The other leaped in, missed his spear-stroke, dropped the weapon, jerked out a knife, and grappled. Paris felt himself all but helpless, crushed against this mailed figure. The deep voice bayed out warning and alarm. From somewhere along the shore, two other men came running, torches bobbing and smoking in their hands.

The stabbing knife pricked at him, and desperately he fended it off. The red light of the torches lit the scene. Paris, in frenzied dismay, saw that Helen had been unable to shove out the heavy boat; it would not budge. Lost! The two spearmen with torches were close.

His sword-hilt smashed up, bore back the fellow who gripped him; a second blow, crushing in the sweating bearded face. His weapon came free, and he drove in the point, writhing aside as one of the two spears flicked out at him.

Then something sang in the torchlight, sang and thudded. One man pitched forward; the other whirled around and dropped his spear and torch, and plucked with both hands at his throat, where the shaft of an arrow stood out. In the darkness, a shape surged on the water, the voice of Skopas sounded.

"Come aboard, Cap'n! Quick about it. Lucky this Cretan archer of ours was along. Hey, Cap'n! Where are you?"

Somehow Paris fell into the boat, the arm of Helen supporting him. Skopas and half a dozen men at the oars, sent the boat spurting away down the current.

"Hurt, boy?" said Skopas, leaning over the wounded figure.

"Nothing to worry about." And Paris, gasping, sat up. "Safe, Helen?"

"Quiet, my dear, quiet—don't move!" she said, busily at work. "I've got to bandage this wound in your chest."

"Damn the wound! You, Skopas!" Paris exclaimed swiftly. "What's happened? You haven't had time to get to the ship and back—what brought these men here?"

"Death," came the dry, harsh voice of the sailing-master. "Lucky thing I had ordered the ship moored out from shore! The Greeks jumped our men early this afternoon, all of a sudden. Killed about half of

The Flight of Helen

'em, took the camp, burned it. About fifteen got out to the ship; they can hold it. These boys got away to the river, found this boat, and started up after us. I met 'em and turned back with 'em, and here we are. The men aboard the ship will wait for news of us. If we get down there before the storm breaks and makes the ship run for it, well and good. If not, we won't see Troy again, my lad."

A joyous laugh broke from Paris.

"We'll make it, we'll make it!" he cried. "And once out to sea, these Greeks won't dare follow us. Luck's with us!"

"Maybe you think so," the old seadog grunted. "But what's to come after? Ten to one we'll have half Greece knocking at the gates of Troy; they'll never forgive you for getting away with their queen. Your fault, blast you! I warned you not to teach those fellows how to build ships—I warned you! If you'd kept your mouth shut, they wouldn't be able to do much with their ratty little craft. But you've showed 'em how, you've taught 'em the trick, and they'll have something to come and get."

"Aye, something worth while!" And Paris laughed

softly, happily, gayly, as he gripped the warm fingers of Helen in the darkness, and the boat surged down the rippling stream toward the waiting ship and the open sea and Troy.

Before my eyes the wrinkled, whimsical features of Skopas took form and shape. They were those of the fuzzy old man sitting beside me on the bench. Twilight had come; the sun was gone. The two boys playing with their boats had disappeared. I came back to reality, roused up, and came stiffly to my feet.

"Well, you can bet that was the way of it," said the old fellow. "Them Greeks learned to build ships, and started off to lick Troy, and done it."

"I don't know but that you're right," I rejoined slowly. "Anyhow, the theory is interesting—"

"Theory, hell!" said the fuzzy old man. "I was there, I tell you! I seen the whole thing. Say, if you got another of them cigarettes to spare, I'd sort of like to take it back with me."

"Sure," and I proffered my case. "Back where?"

"Back to the old soldiers' hospital, over the hill yonder. I slid out when the guards weren't looking, and I got to be back if I want any supper. Much obliged, friend. See you again sometime."

And he drifted away in the dusk, leaving me to wonder.

THE WIDOW'S SON

"Hiram, the Widow's Son—"

The words flashed out at me as I passed a dingy little shop in a back street of Avignon, the City of the Popes, a city of dust and death and towering ruins. The last place in the world, you would say, where one might find a roaring lusty sea-tale for the plucking.

Yet it was on those ramparts above that the exiled Richelieu planned his re-conquest of power. In the pleasant little hotel down below, lingered singular anecdotes of Bonaparte.... Queer romantic things could be sensed in the very air of Avignon, as one looked out across the river bottoms at the abruptly shattered old bridge and the massive tower of masonry rising into the sky, where Popes had ruled....

I turned and peered into the window of the dingy little shop again. Here were all kinds of junk: old jewelry, would-be antiques, colored prints, pathetic faded worthless relics of past generations. And printed in English words on a tag-end of old paper lying in the window:

"Hiram, the widow's son—"

Pushing open the green-painted door, I went into the shop. It was as dingy as the window. An old man with yellow-gray hair and a hooked nose inspected me. He had a wild and wandering eye.

"That paper in the window," I said. "Just what is it?"

"It is not what you think," he responded, and paused to take a pinch of snuff.

Strange words, those, jerking me up sharp. How the devil did this old man know what I thought? He peered at me and cackled a laugh.

"It's a paper to bring good luck," said he. "Handed down in the family. I put it in the window, and men stop to ask about it—men like you, tourists, Americans. What should they know of the widow's son? No more than I know myself. All that was long ago, and it is a story of my people, not of yours. You are no seafaring man."

His people? But I had many friends among his people, said I, and we talked desultorily, until he took another pinch of snuff, slowly shaking his head.

"The story is not in the Talmud," he said. "We hand things down from generation to generation, as the Moors in Morocco hand down the keys of the houses their ancestors left in Spain. Things, or ideas. Some generation seizes upon them and uses them. A woman whispers to her son; and in fullness of time he remembers and makes use of her whisperings, and perhaps changes the face of the earth and the story of nations. If I told you the story of the widow's son, and the great tin ship, and how the blood ran down her decks—what would you do with it?"

"At least, I might understand it," I said. This pleased him.

"But the story goes back, far back," he said, blinking at me with that wild eye. "Back to the time of King David, and Solomon his son, when Hiram was not yet king in Tyre, and the commerce of great Tyre was growing by leaps and bounds. Her colonies were reaching out, for those Phœnicians were fine seamen, and their captains held jealously guarded secrets passed down in their families."

"Yes," I said. "They were the first to use the stars in navigation."

The wild eye lit up. "Ah! Then you do know something about it!"

"Was this Hiram who figures in your shop-window, the king of Tyre?"

"No, no." The old man cackled with amusement. "The name was common in those days, when young King Solomon sat on the throne and had not yet grown great. The widow's son, this Hiram was called; his father had died before he was born. But his mother knew all the wisdom of ancient days, passed down in the family—wisdom of the sea, of the children of Abraham, of work in metals, wisdom of commerce and practical affairs. Ideas, handed down—"

By his gestures, his words, his strange intangible force of character, this old Provençal Jew conveyed an impression of singular deep wisdom poured into the heart of a youth, there in a corner of the blazing city of Tyre where the waves ringed the whole place and the sea-winds blew down the narrow streets.

A woman dark and sorrowful and lovely, whispering into the brain of her son those fancies and traditions, those ideas and inventions, those dreams of what might be if a way were only found, as the months and the years passed.

His father? He knew not, nor asked; men cared little in those days. There was no stigma in his title of the widow's son. If she were from the city of the Jews, as some said, all who knew her respected her; if Hiram's father were also from that city, no one knew. Her heart was intent upon his taking the seafaring road, and if she spoke sometimes of Jerusalem and its god, she had some good reason for not returning there nor urging him to go. He fancied that his father had been one David, from things she said, but this was a common name among that people.

And ever as Hiram grew, the city waxed greater, galleys and commerce pouring in from Greece and Egypt, Carthage and Sicily, caravans going out into the Eastern deserts and coming back again, until Tyre reeled with wealth and power and golden vistas. Young Hiram worked in the shipyards, learned to draft construction, and when he had his growth was apprenticed as gentleman officer.

He was bound over to old Captain Adoniram the hawk-nosed, who was taking a new galley out to Carthage and the isles in the spring. But before spring arrived, two things happened.

First, word came from Jerusalem that the old king, David, was dead at last, and in his place, rocking upon unsteady throne, sat one Solomon. In those days the widow mourned greatly, though Hiram knew not why; then came the second thing, and caused his own mourning. For his mother, the widow, died.

Before passing, she gave her son a broken half-shekel of Jerusalem, an old coin struck by the first king, Saul. The broken coin was strung upon a cord.

"Some day," she said, gasping out her life, "when you have greatest need for the help of man, let this come to the eyes of King Solomon. Say to him that Hiram, the widow's son—sends—sends—"

To the young man, bowed in grief, the death-stopped words meant little. Jerusalem was but a name to him, a far inland place. If his mother were perhaps of the house of David the king, if his father had been some valorous man in that court, if her story held some odd secret of destiny that linked itself with this new king, Solomon, the youth's eyes could not visualize nor grasp it. A puny little city back in the hills, fierce warriors who worshiped an unknown god—what were they to Tyre the glorious? Here was life, here was destiny!

So, when the spring came and the gales were done, Hiram went abroad with that hawk-nosed old skipper, Adoniram, whose great rule of life was that a thing be done right or not at all. Most of your old shellbacks have some such fetish, which rules them hard, and Adoniram preached at all times this dictum of his.

Only one of all this ship's company was ever to see Tyre again.

Adoniram did not lay up his ship at night, as most seamen did in those days. He drove on and on, knowing the secrets of the stars and how to steer by them. Hiram knew these secrets also, and learned more.

From the start, however, the voyage went ill. By the time that they reached Carthage, there was but little cargo in the hold; and at Carthage, a tiny place, the merchants had been cleaned out by some Cretan traders. So Adoniram went on, clear to the Balearic Isles at the end of the world. A year had passed; ill luck dogged them still. At the Balearics, however, they found store of strange metals, bright tin and soft lead, which had come from some unknown land far to the west. Adoniram resolved to find that land.

"If we come back empty-handed we get the sack," he said.

So the ship was revictualed, and when the crew had had their fill of wine and women, they put forth once more. Through the Strait of Gibraltar and on around Spain they nosed, looting here and raiding there, trading when the chance offered, and the word of the Tin Isles came ever clearer to them.

In the long night watches, as he paced the deck beside Adoniram, Hiram came to open his heart to the grim old man. He spoke of the things handed down, and of the ideas that were his own.

"Our ships are good enough for voyaging to the isles of Greece and even to Carthage and the Balearics," he would say. "But they're not stout enough for such seas as these, for such long cruises. We need ships bigger in the beam, ships that can fight like the Greek ships and trade like our own; fighting-ships with cargo space."

Adoniram said little, but asked cunning questions that drew Hiram into talk of construction and how it might be improved. The other officers flouted such ideas, but Hiram took small heed of their jokes and jeers.

In the end they came to the misty islands where tin and lead were found, and here they loaded the ship deep, after scraping her bottom of weed, and set about for home with a wondrous rich cargo.

By this time, near two years had passed. What with sickness and fighting, the crew had shrunk to a scant eighty. The officers had changed also; Hiram was second mate now, a tall and powerful man, so shrewd of wit and arm that none could meet him with weapons. Adoniram was gray and grim, wasting with some sickness.

They crept back toward the coasts of Spain through tempest and hurricane. Then the grandfather of all gales smote them out of the west and north; dismasted, foundering, the first officer swept overboard with five other men, Adoniram none the less got his splintered hulk to a cove of the coast and there beached her, cargo intact.

"One lesson learned," said he grimly. "Not to take this voyage in winter!"

Barbarians swooped down to loot the sea-spoil, but after one taste of Phœnician weapons, they judged friendship the better part; then barter was opened, and the Iberians helped the castaways build a village of huts, gave them women in marriage, aided them in all things.

Adoniram, looking over the ship with Hiram, found her ruined; her back was broken. There was nothing for it but to build an entirely new vessel, or rot in Iberia.

"And while we're doing it," said the old grim seadog, "we'll do it right. Build the ship of your dreams, Hiram."

They fell to work, men of all trades being in the crew, and the Iberians lending eager help. It was the labor of months, but time meant nothing to Hiram, and little to any of them, save only old Adoniram, who had but scant time left....

With the help of the old hulk, a new one arose as the weeks and months fled; a massive-beamed ship of Spanish oak, fighting-ship and cargo-ship in one, according to the plans Hiram drew up. She went swiftly on to completion, once the main task was done, for they wasted scant time on ornamentation or frills.

But Adoniram lay on his last bed.

"For every new ship built, an old skipper passes, they say," and he smiled at Hiram. Then he touched a roll of sheepskin that lay beside him. "Here's your commission as master, young 'un; it'll hold legal. There's few go out apprentice and return master, but it'll be three years and more since we left Tyre ere you raise the island city again. You'll do. And remember, when you come to stow cargo, do it right!"

They buried the old skipper there by the sea.

None disputed Hiram in his command. He had grown very masterful, powerful beyond most men, skilled and cunning in all ways and equal to any emergency. When the ship was floated and tested, he alone held the steering-oar which three other men could scarce manage, and the tests were good. His heart swelled to the joy of the keel under him—keel of his designing, finer than any keel that swam the seas, better suited for the work of Tyre.

Amidships was built an altar of stone to Eshmun, the chief god of Tyre, and when the cargo had been stowed away, with jars and skins of water, sacrifices were made to the god while Hiram looked on. He took small part in such things, for the widow had whispered to him of another deity, and her words lingered with him.

Summer at last, of the third year. He took aboard the men and their families, and shipped Iberian slingers and archers for fighting-men, and so sailed forth from Spain for the long voyage home.

Safe through the straits, he laid course for the Balearics, and there watered and revictualed. Carthage? Not he; too many Sidonian pirates in those waters. A straight course for Tyre, with a stop at Cyprus if need be.

The winds bade them fair, and the smoking cone of Aetna rose into the sky to steer them past Sicily. On the day they sighted the cone and lost it again, two men fell sick and died suddenly in the night. Hiram put in to shore, where there was a Greek colony a-building, and here took on fresh food and water. While they lay moored, other men fell sick, and the sickness spread among the women and children. An old man from Tyre, long stranded in this place, begged passage home again, and Hiram gave it him, and took him aboard.

That night the Greek colonists came with torches

and spears, and bade Hiram leave or suffer burning, because of the sickness he had brought. So he cast off and stood out into the wine-dark sea, and the wind was fair. He thought little of the sickness spreading among his men.

The old Tyrian came to him as he stood by the tiller that night.

"Here is a curious thing, Captain Hiram," said he, mumbling his words. "When I was a young man in the inland trade, I went up to Jerusalem where David was king, and did good business with him too. A full two hundred per cent profit. And, by the gods, you are as like to him as two peas! I could swear in truth that you were that Jewish king come to life."

Hiram laughed. "Dead men rise up never," said he. "And who is king there now?"

"Solomon, and like to be the greatest of his line; and Hiram the Wise rules Tyre and has made alliance with him. Eh, eh!" The old man coughed. "I like not the sickness in this ship."

No wonder he misliked it, for by morning he had caught it, and ere sunset was dead.

The days passed. Despair and frightful terror fell

upon all the company. No sacrifice availed; the sickness spread. The children died quickly. The women and the Iberian slingers offered no resistance. They too died, and the Tyrian seamen, tough and hardy men, began to perish.

Gone was all their laughter and exultation. Some god had cast this plague upon them; they bowed their heads and died. As the crew thinned, Hiram headed for Crete—but winds blew him off that course and he had too few men left to tend the canvas. He drove on toward Tyre, a gaunt and spectral man,

When the Jewish officer came before his king, he asked to speak privately with Solomon.

worn with weariness.

The time came when he was alone, with three others. The dead had gone overside. These four moved about like ghosts; but Hiram, whom the sickness had not touched, was as good as any half-dozen. Luckily, the wind held fair, the seas rose not.

Now the last three men sickened, and lay dead, and the wind fell. Hiram put the bodies into the sea, and dropped on the deck, and slept the sun around. When he came to himself, voices were in his ears. He started up, and found his arms and legs bound with cords, and men aboard the ship.

The dead calm continued, but alongside, her oars still dragging, lay a Sidonian trader. Her captain and two other men came and stared at Hiram, their dark fierce faces alight with the treasures they had found below.

"What, pirates of Sidon?" said Hiram. "Loose me. Put me some men aboard. If you tamper with a vessel of Tyre and a captain of Tyre, you'll have trouble!"

"Hearken to the lion's growl, Cap'n Jabal," said one, and they broke into laughter. "Trembling in your boots, ain't you?"

"Aye, sweating with fear." And Captain Jabal eyed Hiram shrewdly. "Stout as an ox, this fellow is. He'll bring a fat price in the Cyprus market. Captain of Tyre, eh? Well, I'll take the name of Hiram myself, and the ship to boot, and her papers will be in order."

They all laughed again at this jest, but Hiram said nothing. Sidonian slavers and pirate-traders; he was taken, and his ship was lost, and he would be sold into slavery at Cyprus. There was, he felt, no use wasting words.

Captain Jabal stooped over him, plucked at the thong about his neck, and eyed the broken shekel, then dropped it with a laugh.

"A Jewish love-token, eh? We'll leave it to him, for luck. All right, boys! Clap a score of men aboard here; I'll take her over myself. You, Azazel, take charge of our ship and keep company. If separated, we meet at Cyprus. And stay! Fetch aboard that image of Moloch and set it up over this altar—the gods have been too good for us to forget them."

"True enough," said one of the others. "Moloch is more to the point than this accursed Tyrian god Eshmun."

"There's no luck in laying your tongue to any god, you fool," snapped Jabal, the Sidonian captain. "And Eshmun was a god of our own people once—wasn't Tyre founded by us? Bring Moloch aboard, and that puling Greek girl we picked up in Chios, and do the thing right. We'll sell everything in Cyprus, and no questions asked, and every one of us a rich, man for life. We can well spare a girl, to make our luck hold."

Hiram was picked up and dropped abaft the deckhouse. There he lay, silent, and saw a small image of the god Moloch brought aboard from the Sidonian ship, and set up over the altar. A Greek girl, a child evidently abducted for slavery, was dragged aboard and laid screaming over the stones, and Captain Jabal cut her throat and prayed to Moloch as the blood spurted.

Seeing this, Hiram heaved at the cords binding him, but they were new and strong, thongs of bullock hide, and not even his great muscles could burst them.

The two ships headed together for Cyprus.

That night came wind, and fierce gusty squalls swooping down. The great ship rode steady and serene, but the Sidonian galley was lost to sight, and daybreak showed no sign of her. Whereat Captain Jabal laughed heartily.

"If she doesn't make Cyprus, so much the more for us all!" said he.

Dawn came gray and lowering. When it came to feeding Hiram, Cap'n Jabal looked on with mocking words. He had found all the accounts of the cargo, and the ship's papers transferred from the wrecked vessel, and he jeered gayly as Hiram ate his fill.

"Captain of Tyre, eh? Well, I'm Hiram myself—Cap'n Hiram, you dog! And I've got everything to prove it. Enjoy yourself and have a nice passage, you rascal; soon enough you'll be set to earning your keep."

The course was set to the south steadily, away from danger of encountering any Tyrian galleys, but clouds covered the sky and when evening came there were no stars. Instead, rain came down in sharp abrupt squalls, incessant downpours that soaked everything, including the naked man who lay abaft the deckhouse, under the steering-platform on the poop. That the ship had been swept far from her course for Cyprus, Hiram could well believe; but not even he could tell where she was or whither heading, though he thought that with morning the skies would be clear again and the gale past. Now, if ever, he must act.

"Jahveh!" he muttered, peering with salt-rimmed eyes at the cloaked skies.

His mother's whisperings came back to him. In time of stress, when aid he most needed, the broken shekel; in time when no man might help him, something else. Call, she had said, upon the god of her own people—when no other god would help, Jahveh would hear his heart's cry. He had indistinct memories of things she had said, besides, about his own father who had thus cried to Jahveh and had been helped, not once but many times. One David, a common name among the Jews.

"Jahveh!" muttered Hiram, as he lay there. "Never until now has the time come; in Spain, in the far isles, in the plague, was time for the help of men. Now it is past, and there is none to help. Give ear, Jahveh! Perhaps You have small need of a worshiper, but I have great need of *You* in this hour."

But no god came from the sodden skies to help him. Only a fresh squall of rain swept down, drenching him afresh.

Then, suddenly, he realized that the wet and slippery hide thongs about his arms must stretch with their condition. He swelled and hardened his muscles; the thongs stretched. With a gasp in his heart, he put forth all his strength and worked at them.

Midnight was well past before his arms came free. His legs clear, he lay in silence; it was a long time before the circulation was restored in hands and feet. Jahveh's doing? Perhaps, and perhaps not.

"Let the issue decide," thought he grimly. "The credit goes to Jahveh, and I go with it, if the impossible happens. For, if no god stands at my side, I

cannot overcome these men."

With early morning hours, the clouds swept away and stars came out pale and thin. Captain Jabal left the after cabin and mounted to the platform above, to plot the stars and see where he was, and to lay his course. Then, so quietly that he made no sound, Hiram rose and went into that after cabin, which had once been his own.

He needed no light for his purpose, going straight to the chests slung along the bulkhead wall. They had been smashed open, but the contents were intact. From his own chest he took a shirt of cunningly meshed iron rings, and a sword that Adoniram had given him, well tempered and keen.

He donned the shirt, girded on the sword. In another chest, protected from salt and weather, were the slings of the Iberians, with chosen pebbles and rounded pellets of lead. Those slingers, during the long months in Spain, had taught him all their art. He chose a sling, filled a pouch with stones and lead bullets, then went back to the deck.

The day was breaking; the first red fingers of the sun were streaking scarlet flames across the eastern sky. Captain Jabal, who in his cruel way was a devout man, ordered the steersmen to lash the huge oars in the stern, then summoned all hands to the 'midships altar, there to offer thanks to Moloch and Baal.

A black cock was fetched from the pen. As the first level rays of the sun struck across the waters, the cock was killed and its blood sprinkled on the stones. And suddenly a cry burst from one of the Sidonians.

"It is the god Baal himself—look! Look!"

They all swung around, gaping. On the poop platform, between the two massive steering-oars, stood Hiram. His sling was in hand; and the level sun-rays glittered from his mail coat, and the sound of his grim laughter came down the deck to them.

"A god who seeks better sacrifice than a crowing cock," said he, and whirled his sling, and loosed it.

The leaden slug took Captain Jabal between the eyes and crushed in his head, so that he fell forward across the altar and lay dead. Swiftly, Hiram set another bullet in the sling, whirled and loosed it, and then another, each to the mark.

Now they recognized him for whom he was, and between fear and anger fell into sharp action, some rushing for arms, others running aft to get at him. Two more men died ere they reached the quarterdeck ladder. Then a spear flew through the air, and a second after it. Hiram evaded the one and caught the other.

"Thanks, Sidonian," said he—and he thrust down with the spear at a man on the ladder.

When it was cleared, even more men lay dead, and Hiram hurled the bleeding spear and transfixed a man who was climbing aloft with bow and arrows. That man screamed, and plunged into the water alongside.

Now, whipping out his sword, Hiram leaped to the deck below and flung himself on the Sidonians. Some turned and fled, some stood against him with weapons, one or two caught his feet and prayed for mercy; but all died. When one does a thing, Captain Adoniram had said, one must do it right or prove a fool.

The sun was strong and high when the last of those Sidonians crossed the threshold of hell. Hiram rid himself of the mail-shirt, and bound up his wounds, which were not deep. Then, after washing himself, he went to the steering-platform and changed the course, and set the sails to suit. He judged that the ship had overshot Cyprus, so he headed straight into the east to make the coast of Phœnicia, the wind being fair and steady.

The corpses he flung overboard, but he could not wash the decks, or the crimsoned altar. Once more he was alone aboard the ship.

The day passed, and then another, and ever the wind rushed him along eastward. On the third afternoon, he raised purple shadows above the eastern horizon, and made shift to brail up the canvas and slacken speed. All night he drove on, and sunrise showed him the barren hills of the land close ahead. A little to the south he descried fishing craft, and then made out a hill with a white city sprawled below it.

Not Tyre, certainly. No great place, indeed; however, the authority of Tyre must be acknowledged here, so he had come to journey's end. Unshipping one of the massive steering-oars, with the other he headed the ship southward.

The city came closer. No harbor, but a breakwater, and small galleys drawn up on shore. The great ship swam in, ever closer. A fishing-craft swooped by, and to the men Hiram called his name and rank.

Ashore grew wonder and vivid curiosity. By his recent marriage with Pharaoh's daughter, King Solomon had gained Egyptian outposts, widening his borders and by arrangement with King Hiram of Tyre, held joint authority here in the city of Jaffa, which put the southern trade route in his hand and gave him an outlet to the sea. One Saul, who ruled here for the Jews, was summoned forth by the Tyrian governor to see the strange sight.

"A ship such as never was seen, with all its decks bedewed and splashed with blood, and only one naked man aboard—look at her!"

Men came running. "A boat came in! The man says he is Cap'n Hiram of Tyre!"

Tyrian and Jew watched while the sails fell, and from the bow of his ship the lone naked man let fall a great weight poised there, so that his ship was anchored. Then, in vivid curiosity, they went out in the governor's galley.

Hiram welcomed them. At sight of him, the Jew emitted one startled gasp and came up to him with a question.

Hiram laughed wearily.

"Whence came I? Why, perhaps from the east, or the west, or beyond the world's end—what's it to you?"

"Hm! You look uncommonly like a man I once knew," said Saul, muttering in his beard.

The Tyrian governor intervened.

"Enough of this, Saul! You, Hiram, whether captain or no by authority of Tyre, will consider yourself and your ship at the disposal of King Hiram. This is no affair of yours, Saul; the man looks like a Jew, but the new law confiscating all ships of thirty ton or over to the use of King Hiram—"

"Confiscate my ship?" blazed out Hiram suddenly. Weary and worn as he was for lack of sleep and rest, he fired up on the instant. "Confiscate a ship that will change commercial history and open a new era to shipping—I'll see you damned first! What's this about King Solomon?" and he whirled on the Jewish commander. "He has authority here?"

"Enough," said Saul dryly.

Hiram plucked from his naked breast the broken coin that hung there. He thrust it at the Jewish officer.

"Take this. See that it comes to King Solomon himself—I appeal to him, do you understand? Tell him that Hiram, the widow's son, sends—sends to him—"

He staggered as he spoke. The Tyrian governor, who was not a bad sort, and who was anxious to keep on friendly terms with the Jews, intervened. There would be no trouble about it. Saul could put some men aboard and await a response from Jerusalem. If this fellow spoke the truth—

"It is in my mind that he does," said Saul, eying the broken coin and then the face of Hiram. "In fact, I'll take the message to Jerusalem myself; I have to go up there to attend court day after tomorrow."

So it was arranged, and Hiram turned into his bunk and slept like a dead man.

When the Jewish officer came before his king, he asked to speak privately with Solomon; and the latter took him out into the scant, scrawny garden of the rocky hill palace, and heard his story. King Solomon whistled softly at hearing it, and fingered the broken coin.

"I have the other half of this coin," said he.

"I thought you might," said Saul, and met his eye. "To be frank about it, Solomon, I've heard a story or two—"

"Don't be frank," said the King quickly. "It's a bad habit, Saul. Let us suppose a case.... Do you think that this fellow Hiram, who looks so much like my father David, could have any erratic ideas about it? That is to say, about his birth?"

"No," returned Saul. "I spoke with him before he went to sleep. He thinks this ship of his will do wonders, and that other ships like it will hold the commerce of the seas. His mother left him this coin. She's dead. By the way, he says Jehoveh helped him and he wants to join the church."

King Solomon fingered his bushy black beard, and then smiled a little.

"Give that fellow anything he wants, but keep him out of Jerusalem," said he, at length. "Ships, eh? If he has something good in ships, I can use him. Now that we have Jaffa for a port, I'm aiming to go in for shipping myself. Good! We'll give this Hiram a commission to build us a navy. I'll send up to Tyre and get King Hiram to take a fifty per cent interest in it, and he may copy these new ships if they're worth while. Let this Hiram, the widow's son, draw on the treasury up to ten talents for personal expenses. The cargo of his big ship, as I understand it, goes to Tyre. Good. I'll have the letters made out at once—"

The King laughed softly.

His laughter died away with the sunlight, and became the cackling mirth of an old man in a dingy

Avignon shop. He had come to the end of his story, and now was chuckling delightedly.

"Just what does your story imply about this Hiram?" I asked him. "That he, to put it frankly, was a brother or half-brother to Solomon?"

"Take the great king's advice, my friend," said the old man, wagging his finger at me. "Take the great king's advice—and never put things frankly. So you will never be embarrassed."

After a time I went out of the shop, and as I left, directed a glance at the window. The paper was still there, with its strange words:

"Hiram, the widow's son—"

What secret those words hid, or whether the curious traditional story really had given me the origin of the great Phœnician trading and fighting ships that held the commerce not only of King Solomon but of the ancient world—I did not know. For the mists of time had closed down upon all reality.

Hiram caught the spear. "Thanks, Sidonian," said he—and he thrust down at a man on the ladder.

WORK OF THE DEAD

There are certain towns in the world through which most of us, to our loss, rush in order to get somewhere else. I like to linger in these places—Dover, Havre, Plymouth, Las Vegas in New Mexico, San Pedro, Pass Christian, to name a few. One turns up curious things in such places, especially if they be seaport towns.

No seaport is Brantford, on the Canada shore, but a dingy, calm, old-world solace to the nerves, with sweeping great trees in every street-vista, prim and precise as is most of eastern Canada to the American eye. It has a quaintness, a flavor of romance all its own, with its very name eloquent of Joseph Brant and colonial days.

Tucked away on a side street with a huge sugar-maple burgeoning before its entrance, I found a shop where a little old man sat among curious things. Not all old men are wise, but this one was. He had probing, twinkling eyes, and he kept rarely silent as I looked at old prints and Mohawk relics, Georgian silver and Victorian knickknacks. He was good at silence, a sure sign of wisdom.

I came back again and again, broke through his silence by degrees, and unearthed some real treasures from his stock. Come to find out, he had once been a college professor, back in New Brunswick, but had fallen upon evil days. His people had all been shipbuilders "down East." He knew ships, up, down and across.

On the last day of my stay in town, I dropped into his shop and he brought forth a package wrapped in old yellowed newspapers. I noted, as he unwrapped them, that the newspapers were all dated in the year 1916. He laid bare the model of a ship—a queer ship. It had been built with beautiful precision in every detail.

"Hello!" I exclaimed. "That's something like! A Greek trireme, isn't it?"

"Right the first time," said he, with a nod of satisfaction. "A great link in the evolution of ships as they are today. The trireme—that wrote half the history of Greece in water, scattered colonies and civilization everywhere, whipped the Persians and changed the history of the world."

"Where'd you get this model?"

"It was made by my favorite pupil—a genius," he said slowly. "We worked out each detail together, he and I; from deduction, from new discoveries, from what is definitely known, from pictures on Greek vases, and so on."

I fingered the beautiful thing.

"Nobody knows how the trireme started, or who invented it?" I asked.

"Yes; that's a matter of definite record," said he, and launched into careful talk, gradually warming up to his subject. "It was invented about 700 B.C. by a citizen of Corinth named Aminocles. Up to that time, Corinth was just a small but promising city. She had founded a couple of colonies, Syracuse and Corcyra, and was at war with Corcyra. She was rather helpless, for the Corcyrans were seamen, and as yet the Corinthians were not."

I thought back to my half-forgotten Greek history.

"Corinth was ruled by a president and council, wasn't it?"

He was pleased to find that I was not a complete ignoramus.

"Exactly; she had plenty of money, a large growing trade, and was heading for the highway of destiny," he said. "This Aminocles was a trader, a seaman himself, a remarkable character. You know, those Greeks were rather barbarous at the time. They were writing history, and they wrote it in blood."

He hesitated and fell silent, frowning a little.

I studied the model, taking in more of its details. It was a perfect gem. Three banks of oars it displayed—hence the name *trireme.*

I waited. Something was coming; I could sense it.

Not in the big cities of the world are the curious things of history written. In a little town no larger than Brantford, I had looked upon the ring of Saladin, had heard the story of Saladin's armor, which is entirely authentic and exists to this day—one of the treasures of history, unguessed by the world.

"Do you know anything about this Aminocles chap?" I prompted at last.

"Yes. He owned a couple of trading ships—big ones for those days, with fifty oars and a mast nearly amidships. But he was working on new ideas, on a new form of ship; something hitherto unheard of. And Corinth laughed at him, said he was crazy, jeered at him.

"He got in bad with the priests of Poseidon, if you don't mind my using a bit of slang," and the old man chuckled. "Poseidon was the god of the sea, you know. This Aminocles had small reverence for the gods. So we find, one morning, his bloody dagger lying on the altar of Poseidon, and a fine scene in progress."

He told me about it as though he had been there, with the blue sky of Greece overhead and the sunlight blazing down across the high white altar of the sea-god. The glittering waves of the gulf were outspread below the city, running off over the horizon.

But here at hand, all was rich with the pouring sunlight. The bloody dagger lay like a crimson smear on the white altar. And, standing by the altar, was Aminocles himself. He faced the angry priest of Poseidon, and the staring throng of citizens who had gathered around to see and to listen.

"There's a gift to the gods for you!" rang his voice, sonorous and ironical. "A real sacrifice of blood to Poseidon! In the darkness of night, men came out of the sea and slew my slaves and would have slain me. They went back to their boat and fled, taking their dead with them. And I still live."

The angry bearded priest answered him furiously.

"You have no respect for Poseidon. You scoff openly at the god and his power, and you pay him no tribute. You are now building a ship without making sacrifice to the god. Can you wonder that he sent men to slay you?"

"He made a poor job of it!"—and Aminocles laughed harshly. He was a tall, wide-shouldered man, with crisp yellow hair and blue eyes like ice. "Perhaps it was not the god, but the priest, who sent those killers—eh? Yes, I defy the power of Poseidon, and my ship defies it. She'll conquer the sea, all seas, for Corinth! So make the most of it, you snake-eyed priest!"

Here was defiance, sure enough, and men wondered that some monster did not come forth from the sea to catch and kill Aminocles for his blasphemy. He strode away and the crowd parted to let him through, some muttering at him, others praising his boldness. He might be a crazy inventor, but seamen liked him rarely, and he had a way of winning the love of men. But the sly priests of Poseidon liked him not.

He came into the slave-market and met his friend Persippas, who was his chief helper and assistant in the building of his new-fangled type of ship. A dark, keen man was Persippas, and these two were more like brothers than friends. Together they talked with the slave-dealers, buying here and there men who had skill in building ships, for Aminocles ever sought more workers on his new craft.

And then they came face to face with the Cretan woman, the girl with red-gold hair and ruddy skin, who was just exposed for sale. Aminocles stood and stared at her, and Persippas caught his breath at the sight of her; for such beauty had not been seen in Corinth.

But Aminocles spoke first, his voice lifting above the bids of the merchants and nobles with a roaring offer that made everyone gape. Upon this startled pause, the Cretan girl was knocked down to him, and he came to her and took her hand.

"What is your name?"

"Œnone, lord," she said, looking him in the eyes.

"You are free," said Aminocles; "for I cannot marry a slave, and it is in my mind to wed you, if friendship grows between us. Go to my house; Persippas, will you lead her thither? Then join me at the dockyard, for I must haste."

So he went his way to where the ship was building, a lordly man, very swift in all impulses, living eagerly and joying in life, so that strangers to Corinth thought him some god when they first saw him. Persippas, however, led Œnone away, and talked with her, and his dark eyes held a flame when he looked upon her face.

He came at last to the ship and rejoined Aminocles.

"She is a treasure, my friend," he said. "And fresh from Crete. She knows much of shipbuilding."

"That is not her affair, but mine," said Aminocles. "Now look! The thing that puzzled us is solved." He pointed to massive timbers, reaching from the lower to the upper deck, and inclined toward the stern at an angle of sixty-four degrees. "Each of these timbers supports three oarsmen's benches. It is very simple, like all great things."

"Perhaps," said Persippas. "But I still think the shock of the seas will knock the upper part of this huge hull to pieces. We shall see."

The ship grew with the days, grew to lines of the small model Aminocles had first made. Crowds of shipmen, citizens, sailors, gathered to watch and criticize as the tall sides arose and the ribs were covered and the decking laid in place. A higher and taller ship than any known to man before this—but would it work?

The ram, the bronze spike for ramming other ships, was in place. From stem to stern, Aminocles ran waling-pieces—lusty timbers set within the ribs for strength. The goose-neck rose high, carven and gilded. The three tiers of benches were set for the rowers; the two masts were stepped. The great ship was ready to launch.

But, in this time, other things had passed ashore.

Aminocles, in his simple and forthright manner, had freed Œnone, had given her place in his home, had found friendship ripening into love. He was driven night and day by the fury of construction; for the moment, his ship came first. Yet he was ever more deeply in love with this woman—as was half Corinth, for that matter.

The nobles, the students, the philosophers, came to talk with her and to admire her beauty and wisdom. She was ever very calm and serene and gracious, seeming far removed from human passion; that she was to be the wife of Aminocles was well understood. And he, busy each day in the shipyard by the shore, rejoiced that Corinth found her so supreme.

But before Persippas, that dark and keen and piercing man, came gradually to open a yawning gulf.

For, be Aminocles ever so kingly, so godlike in all his ways, his friend Persippas had the eye and heart

"There's a gift to the gods for you—a real sacrifice of blood to Poseidon!"

and wisdom of man, which was much more to the point in the practical affairs of life. It was Persippas who went to the priests of Poseidon, with warning that were Aminocles again molested by men from the sea, he himself would slay these priests; and he abated their hatred, for the moment, by sacrifices.

True as steel, never boasting, indeed speaking little, Persippas could get as much out of the workmen as could the impetuous and eager Aminocles. And, with as true eye to himself as to aught else, Persippas knew clearly enough that he, too, loved this Cretan woman; what was more, he knew that she loved him in return.

With Persippas, Œnone was no longer cold and serene. It was to him that she came with perplexities and troubles, until the bonds between them grew solid and enduring; yet most often it was of Aminocles that they talked.

"When I speak to him of ships," she said, her lovely eyes clouding, "he laughs and jests and will not be serious. He seems to hear what likes him best, and to be deaf to all else. Yet my father was chief naval architect to the king of Crete; and I am no fool."

"No; you are the most beautiful woman in the world," said Persippas quietly. "So beautiful that Aminocles looks upon you, and is blinded by love."

"And you?" she asked, smiling. He shrugged a little, and parried the question.

"By Zeus, I am not blind, at least! Well, I must go; the calking is my task, and it must get under way. We're approaching completion."

"And ruin," she said, looking at him strangely.

Persippas remembered that look, as he sought the shipyards. He knew how fine and true was this woman, how splendid and frank was his own friendship with Aminocles. He swore by all the gods that come what might, no word or act of his should sully this friendship and the trust Aminocles had in him.

When he had set the gangs of calkers to work and saw that things were going aright, he went into the ship. He found Aminocles stripped and at work with the rest, building the platforms for the two steering-oars in the stern. They drew aside and talked, and Aminocles asked what had become of the model trireme he had built.

"It's at your house," said Persippas. "Œnone was examining it. By the way, aren't you making a mistake by not talking construction with her? She knows a good deal about the business."

"Women know everything there is to know about everything!"—and laughing, Aminocles clapped him on the shoulder, "No, this is a seaman's job, old chap. I've seen her on the wall up yonder, every afternoon, watching the work and followed by a dozen gallants. She swallows all the nonsense Corinth yaps—"

"She'd give her life for you," said Persippas. "She wants only to help you."

"Aye. " Aminocles squinted down the deck, and nodded. "Right. But I want no repeating of all the knocks and the half-baked criticism that Corinth utters. These nobles and merchants don't know our business; and we do, Persippas. They're betting more and more heavily that this ship of mine won't stand the strain."

"And you've been, taking the bets until your whole fortune is tied up!"

"Well, haven't you?"

The two friends laughed together. Then Persippas sobered.

"I support you; not that I believe in you, mind! I don't think the ship's strong enough for the stress and strain."

"Oh, absurd!" Aminocles exclaimed. "Man, those waling-pieces—"

"Are inside the ribs. They'll stand up against outside shock, yes. But what about these tremendous beams which support the rowers' benches?"

"Who the devil told you that?" Aminocles asked quickly, with a sharp look. "Hm! I was worried about those beams myself. That's why I've double-braced them. So don't worry about inward stress. When will you have the calking finished?"

"End of the week."

"Good. Another week, and we'll have the Admiralty test out the ship—a three-day cruise down the Gulf and back, rowers and soldiers aboard."

So it was arranged; but the priests of Poseidon muttered that without sacrifices the sea-god would grant no good luck to this new ship.

She was launched, and floated bravely in the basin, towering above all other galleys, and dwarfing even the battered Phœnician traders of huge beam. And suddenly Corinth began to see this great ship with new eyes, with the eager eyes of Aminocles himself. The betting languished, the odds lessened. If she won the test, then indeed was a new era opened for Corinth, an era of conquest that would sweep the seas!

"I am afraid," said Œnone, as she talked with Persippas. Before them was the model that Aminocles had first built; she had begged it as a gift, and her finger touched it as they talked. "Did you give Aminocles the hint about the inner strain?"

"Told him flatly," said Persippas. "He had thought of the same thing; said he had double-braced all those beams."

She shook her head, then pointed. They were sitting in the hillside garden that overlooked the slope to the Gulf, where the whitecaps tossed in the sunlight. Below, in the harbor, lay the ship to which she had pointed.

"You see that Phœnician trader, Persippas? She has just come from Corcyra. I was talking with merchants who came in her—strange, furtive men. Corcyra is the bitter enemy of this city. Although, for her offspring, the war has gone badly."

"Yes?" Persippas knitted his black brows into a bar as he gazed upon her. "And what's in your mind?"

"I don't know," she admitted. "Aminocles laughs at vague warnings; but I must be vague. There are too many who hate him, who envy him."

"Envy doesn't mean hatred," Persippas said slowly. "His best friends might envy him, yet be true to him."

"Don't bandy words; you know what I mean," Œnone rejoined. "Watch over him."

"I shall."

"And I'm going on that test cruise with the ship."

"You? A ship's no place for a woman."

She laughed a little. "You talk like one of the city fathers. Now, there's something I want you to do for me."

"Anything," said Persippas. Just the one word; but it held so much that a slow touch of color mounted in her face, and silenced her. She looked into his eyes, and her color deepened.

"With one word—to put me to shame!" she murmured. "Oh, Persippas! You are too wise. You must not—you must not love me."

He clenched his lips for an instant, then made determined answer as he read her gaze.

"And you, Œnone—you must not love me."

They were strained and tense, both of them; a moment of unveiled eyes, of torn and hurting spirits, until suddenly Persippas lifted his head.

"Well?" he asked roughly. "What is it you want me to do?"

"Avert ruin," she said. "For his sake." She told him what to do, then, but he frowned over her words, not comprehending what she meant. Nor would she explain.

"Never mind; do all this, be ready, and let's see." She held out her hand to him.

Persippas looked at her slender, delicate fingers lying in his hard palm; he stooped, and kissed them. His heart pounded, his temples throbbed. She loved him, as he loved her. He knew it as though she had spoken the words.

Then, with a curt nod, he turned away and departed.

The ship was being fitted and finished. The Admiralty insisted that she be named after her builder, so she was given the name of Aminocles. In these short days, Corinth had swiftly caught up the vision of this man, so lately reviled as a crazed dreamer, until now the whole city was afire with his ideas.

No cargo-vessel was this trireme, but purely and simply a fighting-ship—the first naval unit. This novel conception set a spark to the imagination of the impulsive, fickle Corinthians. Already the council was talking of floating a war loan in order to build a hundred such triremes, a fighting-fleet which would be more than a mere collection of trading-ships—the first naval force in history.

That the test cruise would succeed, was taken as a matter of course. Aminocles was voted a seat in the council, a patent of nobility, special civic honors; suddenly he had become the most popular man in Corinth. He took it all in his carefree, splendid fashion, and went on working day and night over the ship.

A picked crew was put aboard and trained for the trial cruise, Persippas taking charge of this matter. So the work drew to an end, until even Aminocles could see no least detail that was undone. On the morrow, the cruise would begin.

That night, one of the priests of Poseidon came to the house of Aminocles, and talked with him and with Persippas. The sacrificial omens, said the priest darkly, were bad. The attitude of Aminocles was unfortunate. He must show proper respect to the sea-god and to the priests; he must provide large sacrifices for the morrow. At this, Aminocles laughed heartily.

"Bad omens, eh? You mean there's weather making. I know it myself, without any of your mumbo-jumbo; any seaman knows it. And this ship of mine will laugh at any weather, as I laugh at you. Sacrifices? Hell take you! Don't think you can rule me. You can't. Get out of here before I kick you out."

Splendid, headstrong, blind, this man of no guile. Persippas went out into the street with the furious priest of Poseidon, and halted him.

"Heed him not, priest, but listen to me—"

"Heed him not?" spat the angry priest. "Let him heed Poseidon! Aye, and that she-devil from Crete, that godless woman! It is she who has put such things into the man's head."

"Careful," said Persippas; and so sharp was his voice that it silenced the priest. "Listen to me. Forget what was said. At dawn, the sacrifices will arrive, in the name of Aminocles. Let all be done properly, with due respect to Poseidon and his priests."

A tactful man, Persippas, a shrewd and wise man. The priest grudgingly admitted as much, and allowed himself to be appeased. There was no weakness

"That godless woman has put things into his head!" spat the priest.

in this action on the part of Persippas, but deep wisdom; it was an effort to stave off trouble which would come at a bad moment if these priests chose to exert themselves.

He said nothing, of course, to Aminocles of what he had done. Inwardly, he had a new sharp fear. So the priests blamed Œnone, did they? That was bad. They were quite capable of anything. That evening, when he was alone with her for a little while, he told Œnone of what had passed, and of his fear. She smiled.

"My friend, thank you for the warning. But, if this trial cruise succeeds, these priests can do nothing. Aminocles will be the first man in Corinth, and Corinth the first city in the world."

"And you, the wife of Aminocles," said Persippas. For a long moment, her eyes met his, again with unuttered thoughts.

"Yes," she said quietly.

Morning brought a scud of gray cloud, tossing gray sea, and joyous laughter from Aminocles as the great ship prepared to sail, with members of the council, chief citizens, all who wished to go aboard her. Wait for calm weather? Not he! Let this be a test indeed! And if citizens got seasick let the gods help them!

The end of the matter was that most of the citizens hung back. Some of the council went, and many seamen from the waterfront, ship captains and such, together with the Admiralty board. Amid crowded walls, fanfares of trumpets, clashing cymbals, and wildly shouting throngs, the ship was loosed and went out into the Gulf under shortened sail.

She swam the waves nobly, beating out to sea while the great surges hammered and smashed at her. Such a ship had never been seen until now, and Aminocles alternated watches with Persippas in command.

With afternoon the oars were put out. The lower deck oars had leather bags that fitted about the tholes to make the oar-holes watertight, without interfering with the action of the oars. A wild, gusty fury of exultation possessing him, Aminocles drove her hard with oars and sail all that day and into the night, and she sprang never a leak.

When darkness came, the Admiralty board were more than satisfied.

"Enough, enough!" said they unanimously, between seasick groans. "Put about for Corinth!"

"Put about? Not I!" shouted Aminocles joyously. "Three days, said you; and three days it is. Storm? Let Poseidon do his worst! Let him hurl the whole vasty deep upon us, and this ship will still conquer him!"

Aminocles' voice lifted above the other bids with a roaring offer that made everyone gape. The Cretan girl was knocked down to him.

So it seemed, in all truth.

Morning brought still wilder seas, but the ship rode them easily. Now Œnone went with others about the ship, examining all below and aloft. Toward noon, she came to Persippas, who was on watch, and mounted into the stern beside him, and beckoned. He followed her down into the lee of the deck-house, for so wild and shrill was the wind that talk was impossible elsewhere.

There she spoke swiftly, and his bronzed face went white.

"Right," he said. "I'll waken him; he's asleep. Get under shelter."

He eyed the gray mountain-peaks and changed the course, setting the sails and running straight before the wind. Presently Aminocles came on deck with gusty oaths, and sought Persippas.

"What the devil made you change course? I ordered—"

"Never mind your orders," said Persippas. "Come with me."

Alone, the two of them went down into the creaking, groaning hold, atop the well-stowed ballast. There Persippas got a lamp alight, and took Aminocles the length of the ship, and showed him where the massy beams that supported the rowers' benches came together.

One after another; all the same story. One deep moan broke from Aminocles, but he said no word until the inspection was done. Then he stood, bracing himself against the ship's roll.

"So! It is failure," he muttered. "You warned me; she warned me. What a blind fool I was and am! Why, the accursed ship is splitting asunder!"

"She'll hold," said Persippas, "if we run for Corinth with the following wind. And you've not failed yet. Cheer up, man! Œnone has some plan. She predicted this. She had me arrange a remedy. True, the weight of these beams won't stand the stress of seaway, but there's a cure. We'd best talk with her at once. And let no one know of this."

Aminocles looked at him with bitter eyes, then dashed out the lamp.

"True friend," said his voice in the darkness. "Aye, true friend, Persippas! Sometimes there comes a moment of wakening to a man."

"What mean you?" exclaimed Persippas. "What are you driving at?"

"You take me for a blind laughing fool, and it's true enough. But a moment comes, always. I've seen you look at her, and her at you; I've read your hearts like your eyes."

Persippas went cold.

"What of it?" said he, and then was astonished to hear the ghost of that brave wild laugh, and to feel the hand of Aminocles clamp down on his shoulder.

"What of it, Persippas? Everything. True friend, true heart; both of you, true as steel! You're ten times the man I am, and that's the honest truth. D'ye think I'd have a wife that loves another? Not I, by the gods! It's been a bad moment all around—seeing one thing, saying another. This calamity and that hurt i' the heart. These beams splintering, this ship falling to pieces under us; and she loving you. Well, I love you too, old friend. Now let's get on deck and make the best of things, and somehow we'll beat the sea-god yet."

Their hands met and clenched hard for an instant.

All day they ran before the gale, with the sails blowing out into ribbons and new canvas blowing out, and finally a mere scrap to send them bowling ahead, so that they made no speed but had scant battering from the waves. In the cabin assigned her, Œnone sat toying with the trireme model which she had brought along, but there was no time for either Aminocles or Persippas to seek her out. When one of them left the deck, he dropped and slept, and rose to take the deck again. To bring that ship home safe, with no soul aboard suspecting that she was falling apart under them, was man's work.

The inner stress—that was the devil of it. No carpentry would avail to hold against it; no carpentry that Aminocles could devise would do the work. When evening rushed down the dark gray sea, and they bore on for Corinth, they had a word together.

"You've not seen Œnone?" asked Persippas. "She's kept below."

"No time." Aminocles wiped the salt from his curling yellow hair. "We're doing it; keep easing the ship off with every sea, and we'll manage it. But it's hell's own job. What a fool I was!"

"What a man you are!" Persippas exclaimed. "I don't know what's in her mind, either. She had me prepare huge cables; they're all ready, in the storehouse. Why, I don't know."

"Cables?" And Aminocles snorted. "What good is flaxen hemp when beams and nails won't hold? Well, take over; and the gods help us if we make the harbor and they don't have the flares alight to guide us in!"

It was the second watch of the night when the ruddy glimmer of the flares was descried. The ship was leaking badly now, wrenching asunder beneath them, but this very weight served to steady her. Persippas, who had the deck, went down himself to waken Aminocles with the good news of Corinth close.

He roused up his friend, then went to the cabin of Œnone. All was dark in the passage, for no lights could endure this tossing; but as he approached her cabin, Persippas collided with some one in the blackness. A startled oath. A blade bit at him. With a shout, Persippas grappled with the unseen man. They reeled to and fro, and the knife slashed again.

Then Persippas, wild with pain and fury, backheeled the man and they went to the deck in frantic unseen struggle; and ere Aminocles came running, Persippas had his own knife out and at work. That man died there. He was one of the crew.

"Hurt? There's blood on your arms," cried Aminocles, as he helped Persippas to rise. "Why, the man must have gone mad—"

Not mad, but caught almost in the act of his black murderous work. Together they found Œnone lying as she had been stabbed, her lovely eyes welcoming them, a faint murmur on her lips.

"New hemp!" she said. "Remember, Persippas—new hemp, as I told you. The water shrinks it, and—and then—"

That was all.

It was Aminocles who brought in the ship, as Persippas lay below beside the dead woman, his wounds bandaged. Aminocles, dazed and blinded by the shock and the grief that was upon him, aged twenty years in that night, yet bringing in the ship perfectly and seeing to all details, and shunning the roaring welcome of Corinth. The city had thought the ship lost, and all the people came with torches ablaze so that the water and the sky were ruddy.

But Aminocles came down into the cabin and barred the door, and stood staring at the dead woman and the bandaged man, and the model trireme that was on the deck. He set his lamp on the table, picked up the model, and frowned at it.

"Her gift," said Persippas. "Her gift to you, Aminocles. Are we in?"

Haggard of face, Aminocles nodded. "Aye, we're in," he said dully. "Her gift? True enough. She's dead, Persippas; the most beautiful woman in the world, and the wisest. She's dead. And she loved you."

"But her gift was to you," Persippas said gently.

Aminocles looked at the model again. "The cables; you see? All hell couldn't burst them. Look! She's twisted cords to show how. They follow the lines of the waling-pieces inside the ribs.... Hell take the ship!"

He suddenly flung the model into the corner, put his face into his hands, and sat there with silent tears trickling through his fingers.

In the days that followed, the ship was put into drydock. The great cables of new hemp, two of them, were fastened about her from stem to stern, then were twisted and made so strongly taut that they became a very part of her. And when she was put into the water again, the hemp shrank, until it was as though two iron bands were about the galley, holding her solid against all stress....

Through following years and centuries, the galleys of Corinth and of Greece, lordly triremes bound about with twin-cables that all hell could not burst, conquered the coasts and the islands, subdued the broad wine-dark seas, scorned and smashed the might of Persia, set the grip of the sea-god at naught, and wrote the name of Greece large in naval history.

Where the triremes went, also went the memory of a friendship strong as the twin cables that held the triremes together. Thus, when seamen came to set names to these cables, the one was called Aminocles and the other Persippas. These names endured until later days when men learned how to build ships that held without the binding hemp.

Such was the tale of the trireme.

Illusion vanished. I was back again in Brantford on the Canada shore, in the little dingy shop of the old man who had told the story. He sat with his chin sunk on his breast, forgetful of me.

I fingered the model again, touching the two binding cables, the finely carven wood, the minutely fashioned oars.

"What's your price on this?" I asked. "I'd like to buy it."

The old man stirred. He gathered up the heap of yellowed newspapers, dated twenty years ago, and shook his head.

"I'm afraid it's not for sale," he said gently. "You see, it was made by my favorite pupil—he was my son. That's his picture there, on the wall."

I turned and looked at the picture. A young man, a smiling boyish face, the uniform of the Canadian Highlanders, and under it the words:

Killed in Action. 1916.

THE THINGS THAT ARE CÆSAR'S

Rear Admiral Lucas, commanding the Pacific Coast squadron at San Diego, leaned over the luncheon table and roared with laughter.

"That's a new one!" he exclaimed. "Upon my word, that's a new one!"

"I beg your pardon, admiral." Little old Professor Boggs drew down his bushy brows and scowled. "It is not a joke. When I say that one of the oldest and most formidable of naval weapons, which actually wrote a great chapter in history, was a sickle, I am not joking."

The Admiral wiped away his tears of laughter.

"No offense, my dear chap," he said tolerantly. "But you must admit—"

"Admissions mean weakness. I admit nothing," shot back the Professor. "The sickle might even be called the basis of naval strategy."

The rest of us kept silent. What had begun as a mere discussion, had now settled into a duel between our famous guests. The Club has some queer fish at its weekly luncheons, and raises some singular discussions; but as the Admiral said, here was something new.

"A sickle!" repeated the Admiral, and chuckled. "A sickle as a naval weapon!"

"Precisely," snapped Professor Boggs. "I presume you never heard of Captain Jean Jacquet and his singularly beautiful wife?"

"I do not recall the names," confessed the Admiral. "It is quite possible that I have met the captain in question while I was in France—"

"Captain Jacquet lived two thousand years ago," the Professor said. At this, the Admiral waved his cigarette.

"Oh! In that case, I fear we never met. But you interest me, sir. What has this gentleman to do with sickles as naval weapons? Unless you mean that they were used by boarding parties, in place of swords and daggers, in some chance engagement."

"I do not. They were used, sir, in the first naval battle to be fought in the English Channel. Thanks to them, an entire nation was destroyed and the invasion and conquest of Britain by Julius Cæsar was made possible. Do I interest you still?"

"You do," said the Admiral frankly.

Indeed, Professor Boggs interested all of us with his apparently incredible thesis. We knew him to be a noted historian and scholar, and whatever he said was sure to be accurate. The newspaper men present scented a news story and pulled their chairs closer.

Boggs drew on the tablecloth a thumbnail sketch of the Breton coast.

"Here is the present Quiberon," he said. "I shall stick to present-day names in the story, to avoid confusion. This entire coast was held by the fierce and warlike Breton people, whom the Romans called the Veneti. Cæsar and his legions were camped on the Loire, building ships. It was hopeless to attack the Bretons, who could take to the sea in their huge ships, without naval craft to cut them off in retreat. This was the situation when Captain Jean Jacquet came home from the town of Painbœuf and found a Roman officer sitting in the parlor talking with his wife. You will see, gentlemen, that the story has some very modern angles." And Professor Boggs shot a glance at the grinning news hawks.

Modern angles indeed! The story was all modern angles as he presented it, and but for one thing might have happened today. That one thing was the character of Julius Cæsar, the most brilliant soldier and most arrant rascal Rome ever produced....

What with the war and the Roman occupation, money was rolling in and shipping was brisk, and Captain Jean Jacquet, thrifty Frenchman that he was, congratulated himself. He had just come down from Nantes with a barge-load of hides, seasoned timber and other supplies for the new Roman shipyards, and would get cash in hand on delivery. It was after dark when he got the barge tied up, and started home.

He was amazed by the progress made in the yards; these master shipwrights, imported from Marseilles, knew their business. Three weeks ago, when he had sailed upriver, hardly a keel was laid; now galleys were afloat and others crowded the ways. The same thing was happening at Brest, Rochelle and Rochefort, and Cæsar would soon have enough bottoms built to launch his attack against the Bretons. These Roman ship-men could assemble a fighting galley in twenty-four hours after the parts were laid out. They had everything—foundries, rope walks, carpenteries—and the immense yard was in a fury of industry even now, by night.

But Captain Jacquet laughed in his beard as he strode along. These Romans were due to get a surprise when they did attack. He knew the Breton seamen.

The early spring evening was overcast, with a sharp wind-driven drizzle pelting down. Despite this, the town was filled to overflowing. The narrow streets, flanked by squat and ugly stone buildings, were alive with swaggering, boisterous soldiery; the Seventh Legion was in town, pay in hand, and as usual was out to raise hell.

Drab balconies protruding over the muddy street displayed signs scrawled in Latin, protected lanterns lit dim doorways; flutes and Breton pipes resounded from the taverns. Here and there roaring fires were blazing away, surrounded by throngs of soldiers in leathern caps and surcoats, entertained by jugglers or street merchants, while ladies of the oldest profession plied their trade with gusto—a trade highly honorable in Roman eyes. Pay night was a big night for everyone, rain or not.

Captain Jacquet put all this behind him, came to his house on the outskirts of town, and walked in to find that his wife had company. A Roman officer, Captain Caius by name, and evidently a man of note.

"Jean! I'm so glad you came in time to meet Captain Caius!" cried Virginis Jacquet, after her first eager greeting. "I was downtown buying a roast, and some of those soldiers got fresh. Captain Caius came along and put them in their place, and escorted me home. He's very anxious to talk with you, too."

Captain Jean Jacquet clasped hands cordially with the Roman and insisted that he stay to dinner, and Caius accepted gladly. The two men talked while Virginis bustled about, laying the table. Singular and somewhat remarkable, these three persons on whom the destiny of nations were to depend.

Jacquet was bluff, bearded, wide-eyed, a huge-muscled giant known far and wide as the best captain on the coast and the finest pilot—and the strongest man. Beside him, the smooth-shaven Caius looked strangely slender. Yet Caius was tall, somewhat scanty of hair, with imperious dark gray eyes and high thin nostrils, and a most infectious smile. A charming fellow, this Roman.

About Virginis, the most beautiful woman in France, there was something cold and glorious, like moonlight. The glitter of her ash-blonde hair was marvelous; her blue eyes held a flame; she herself was like a cold flame of fire that stirred the hearts and souls of men. Jacquet worshiped her beyond words.

"D'you know this commander of yours?" asked Jacquet, as they sat down to dinner.

Caius laughed.

"Who, Cæsar? Yes; I'm on his staff. The worst scoundrel in Rome, between you and me. They say no woman's safe from him."

"I've heard as much," said Jacquet, with a frown. "But a fine soldier."

"Aye." Caius sobered. "The shadow of Cæsar is over everything, my friend; a man of parts, who knows everything, does everything, shrinks from nothing. He'll crush these Bretons like an egg held in his hand."

"Not he," said Jacquet confidently. "I know 'em, know their ships, their seamen. You boys will lick the tar out of them on land, and they'll take to their ships—and your puny little galleys won't be in it. Why, their ships are built of foot-square beams! And you haven't any pilots who know these waters, and the islands."

"Correct." Caius stretched out his long legs. "Cæsar has given me the job of getting a master

your monthly earnings—merely as a starter. Would it interest you?"

Jacquet stared at him for a moment, then met the eager, breathless gaze of his wife. He laid down his knife, wiped his mouth, and shook his head.

"Nope. You Romans look down your noses at anybody working for you. Take orders? Not me. I'm a free man, and stay one. I'm not a Breton; your money looks good to me, yes. But not your job, cap'n. I don't like all this war business. One more voyage, and I'm going up to Boulogne, where I've got an interest in a big Gaulish freighter. Virginis and I are going to Britain and settle down in peace and quiet—eh, my dear?"

Caius glanced at Virginis, and smiled.

"I suppose so," she said quietly.

"Roman peace is better than British peace," said Caius. "Besides, Cæsar is going to Britain himself—with his legions."

Captain Jacquet roared with laughter.

"Yes, he is! I tell you, even if he drives the Bretons off the mainland, they'll retire to the islands and keep the Channel controlled."

"No," said Caius. "Cæsar means to destroy them so they can't do this."

"Cæsar! Cæsar!" And the seaman grunted. "You talk as if he were some god. I tell you, he's a fool—a woman-chaser who's played in luck. I've heard the soldiers talk about him. I know his story. A sharp fellow, yes, but he's a fool to go up against the Bretons. They'll smash him and his ships."

"He may find a way to smash them," said Caius calmly.

"A way? Yes." Jacquet frowned and tugged at his beard. "I know a way; but you high and mighty Romans laugh at simple men. No offense, cap'n. You're different from most of them. If more of 'em were like you, Rome would be better liked in these parts."

"No offense meant, none taken,"—and Caius

pilot who knows every inch of the coast. I've tried half a dozen; they were all worthless braggarts, and they've been crucified to teach people that Cæsar means business."

"Life and death doesn't mean much to you Romans, does it?" said Jacquet.

"It means nothing," said Caius coolly. "We all die sooner or later. Cæsar himself shrugs at it. He's been something of an adventurer, you know; can use a sword with the best of us, but has learned to use his head instead. You should do the same."

"Me?" Jacquet looked up in surprise. "How do you mean?"

"You're too big a man to be in the petty business of making money." And the Roman's thin lip curled in scorn. "See here! I can offer you the job of master pilot with the fleet, at a salary of five times laughed. "Look here, would you like to take a look over the camp, up-river? If the weather clears tomorrow, I might take you up, both of you. Would it interest you, Mrs. Jacquet?"

"I'd love to go!" exclaimed Virginis. "I've heard so much about your camp—"

"Well, you go if you like," Captain Jacquet put in. "I must deliver cargo and check invoices most of the day."

So it was arranged, and Captain Caius departed. A splendid fellow, said Jean Jacquet. A thorough gentleman, agreed Virginis, and with most elegant manners.

Virginis went over the camp, on the morrow, with Captain Caius; he came for her in a military chariot and showed her a wonderful time. Cæsar was daily expected to arrive, and she was eager for a sight of that famous soldier.

Captain Jean Jacquet, during the ensuing days, went about his business and had small joy of it. Scarcely was his huge barge unloaded, than one of the newly launched galleys fouled her moorings and smashed her against the quay, crushing her whole port side. Furious at losing time when the lucrative river freighting was at its height, Jacquet filed claim against the military authorities.

The upshot was a beautiful riot, in which Captain Jacquet laid out half a dozen of the Seventh before a centurion brought up the military police.

He pressed the claim hotly. And once in the law business, he was soon in up to his neck and floundering, and wishing he could get out of it.

As Captain Caius had said, the name of Cæsar, the shadow of Cæsar, was everywhere. Stories of his incredible energy, his exploits, his personality, were on all lips; and plenty of these tales were not of the supper-table variety by a good deal. The legions were moving up, the Roman fleet promised to be ready soon; when Cæsar came, there would be a swift and smashing attack on the whole Breton country.

Not that there was any serenity in Painbœuf. The Bretons had treated the Roman envoys with contumely, the whole country was in a flame against the invaders, the coasts and rivers and towns swarmed with spies and pirates. Sabotage was in the very shipyards. Isolated Romans were murdered, foraging parties were attacked. When any of the Breton raiders were captured, crosses decorated the river front, but this had no effect. No Roman ships got through by sea, or could venture forth alone.

"If Cæsar were here," said the soldiers, "he'd finish off these rascals like he did the Miletan pirates. Where the devil is Cæsar, anyhow?"

Nobody knew. In the camp, said some, secluded and making his plans. Roistering with wine and women in Rochelle, said others. Traveling from town to town and personally seeing that the work went forward, according to some.

Captain Jean Jacquet had his troubles in court, since he was dealing with Roman citizens, and a Roman citizen got all the breaks. He had trouble at home, because Virginis was continually after him to take the job Captain Caius had offered; there was really no reason against it, except that the bluff, simple skipper was obstinate. However, he was too thoroughly in love with his wife to refuse her anything, and he began to see that he must give in sooner or later.

About this time one of the huge, massive Breton ships turreted like a castle, met three of the new Roman galleys coming up from Brest. The Romans attacked; two of their galleys were sunk trying to ram the Breton, and only one got away.

Captain Jacquet heard of this happening while he was sweating in court, and his frank remarks on Roman seamanship did his cause no good whatever. His temper was short.

When court was finally adjourned, he started for home in no pleasant mood. Captain Caius was throwing a party this evening in camp, and was sending a chariot for Jacquet and Virginis; it promised to be a gay affair. Caius had been away on official business for some days.

Captain Jacquet, heading for home to bathe and dress, ran into a crowd of legionnaries who had drunk unwisely and well. They began to make fun of his beard, and Jean Jacquet buffeted one of them half across the street. Two others fell upon him, and while he was handling these, some Loire barges came running from a tavern and mixed in the row, knives out and fists flying.

The upshot was a beautiful riot, in which Jacquet laid out half a dozen of the Seventh, before a centurion brought up the military police. Several of the bargees were cut down and Jacquet, knocked senseless with a spear butt, woke up in jail with a lengthy list of charges against him. As his cheerful jailers assured him, it meant slavery or crucifixion at the least.

An hour later, he was summarily ordered out with word that he was free. Captain Caius was waiting in the office, and waved a hand at him.

"My chariot's outside; pile in, and I'll be right there."

Jacquet lost no time in obeying. Caius followed at once and climbed in beside him, telling the charioteer to drive hellbent for camp.

"Your wife heard of this mixup, and told me," said Caius. "I've managed to get you out, and can arrange things with the procurator in the morning. Nothing like a little pull, cap'n! How's your head?"

"Still there, but with a bump on it," said Jean Jacquet ruefully. "See here, I've had no chance to change my clothes—"

"Nonsense! There are a couple of the staff, no more; we've got some Greek dancers and some grand wine," Caius exclaimed. "Who knows? Accidents often bring good luck, skipper. A philosopher named Crates happened to break his leg while he was in Rome, and got the whole city off in the pursuit of culture, until now we have more highbrows than Athens itself. You never can tell! By the way, I heard today that you're in some court squabble about your barge. What judge is handling it?"

"A fat lunkhead named Crassus, at military headquarters," said Jacquet.

Caius clapped him on the back. "As good as settled this minute! Crassus will do anything for me, anything; so forget the whole business and enjoy the evening. We've got a jar of the finest Falernian wine that ever came out of Italy, and you'll see some dancing that'll knock your eye out."

When they reached camp, dinner was awaiting them in the tent of Caius. Virginis was radiant over the release of her husband; never had Jean Jacquet seen her look lovelier. The two young officers who made up the party were of old Roman families, and Jean Jacquet found them thorough good fellows.

"Just to prove to you," said Caius behind his palm, "that there are other Romans of the right stripe, cap'n!"

Naturally, Jean Jacquet was grateful to this staff officer; the more he saw of Caius, the more he liked the man. During dinner, a number of officers on duty dropped in for orders or decisions; the high authority of Caius was plainly evident. So was his friendliness, and the peculiar charm of his character. He promised Jacquet that the claim regarding the barge would be settled in cash, on the morrow.

Captain Jacquet was not the man to pass up rare Falernian. By the time the Greek dancers finished their performance, he was feeling mellow. Virginis, who had been chatting with Caius, suddenly turned to him in quick excitement.

"Jean! Captain Caius says that Cæsar has offered a large reward to anyone who will devise some way of overcoming the Breton fleet. I know you have some scheme; you've mentioned it more than once. Why don't you try for the reward?"

"Easiest thing in the world, my dear,"—and Jacquet chuckled in his beard. "Sickles will do the trick."

"Sickles?" Caius caught him up swiftly. "What do you mean by that?"

Jacquet winked. "If I told you, the secret would be out. What's this you and Virginis were saying about Cæsar being here?"

"He's in camp now!" Virginis exclaimed, her eyes alight. "And Captain Caius is going to arrange things so we can see him, one of these days."

Caius filled the skipper's wine-cup anew.

"We'll all be busy now," he observed. "Busier than ever. Cæsar means to drive the Veneti into the sea."

"And then what?" Jacquet grinned. "They're seamen, those fellows. These garlicky lubbers you've imported from Marseilles can't even handle a galley in the basin without fouling barges. Once those Bretons are at sea, you'll not touch them. Their ships are massive, high-sided, castled. Your ships are too frail to ram—"

"Once our legionnaires get aboard, they'll put every Breton to the sword!" Caius broke in, a flush in his cheeks.

"Right. But they'll never board those Breton ships. And you've no pilots who know the waters." Captain Jacquet drained his cup and slammed it down. "You Romans are not so hot. You play hell in your courts with anyone who's not a Roman citizen, but you haven't any Roman citizens who can take a Breton ship or sail the Breton coast with a fleet."

Caius leaned forward intently. "But, Cap'n Jacquet, suppose we found such a man—and made him a Roman citizen?" he said softly. "Suppose I get Cæsar to send the Senate a recommendation to that effect? And on top of it, make this man master pilot of the fleet—one whose orders will be obeyed by every Roman skipper?"

Virginis caught her breath sharply. Jean Jacquet stared at the speaker. A Roman citizen! Why, that was an honor to be sought only by the greatest of men! A Roman citizen, with rights and dignity no other could touch, with the power of looking anyone else in the eye and telling him to go to hell—a Roman citizen!

"Eh?" said Jacquet, and his jaw fell for an instant. "Look here—you don't mean me, do you?"

"I mean you," said Caius sharply. "You're the man to serve the turn, Jacquet. You can do it. If I can make Cæsar agree—what do you say?"

"Done!" Jacquet exclaimed. "Done, by the gods! Jean Jacquet a Roman citizen! What do you think of it, my dear?"

"It's wonderful!" breathed Virginis, but her blue eyes went to Caius, not to her husband.

"And now," exclaimed Caius quickly, "what did you mean by mentioning a sickle?"

Jean Jacquet looked at him and grinned.

"That," he said, "is something I keep to myself, drunk or sober, till the time comes to make use of it. Otherwise, these Bretons would cheat me. And us Romans have to stick together, so let it be."

The gray eyes of Caius flashed slightly.

"If I report that to Cæsar," he said, "he'd have you crucified in a minute."

Then the wine showed, as Jean Jacquet snapped his fingers over the table.

"That for your Cæsar!" he exclaimed. "A carousing, woman-chasing aristocrat who has no honor, decency or pride; his very soldiers sing scandalous songs about him and give him nicknames that couldn't go through the mails. A good soldier, of course; but a cursed poor excuse for a gentleman, as we know gentlemen in France."

The thin nostrils of Caius had turned white. The two officers were staring at one another with bated breaths.

"Not so loud, my friend," said Caius warningly. "Cæsar has spies, you know, and tent walls are thin. Perhaps you do him wrong."

"Oh, he has his good side too,"—and Jacquet shrugged. "An energetic fellow, they say, always on the go. Crucify me? Nonsense; your Cæsar isn't a fool. Without me, he can't lick these Bretons. I heard today that one of their ships has just whipped three of the new galleys; did you hear about it? They're seamen. They know the coast and the islands—and you Romans can get no pilots worth a tinker's dam."

"*We* Romans, you should say, rather!" And Caius laughed. "Once you're a Roman citizen, you're safe from crucifixion, that's true. But there are other things."

"Please,"—Virginis leaned forward, pleadingly,—"I know Jean didn't mean to offend you by his talk about Cæsar."

"My dear lady,"—Caius turned to her with his charming smile,—"no apologies, I pray you! Cap'n Jacquet is dead right. This Cæsar of ours has no pride whatever; he'd let your honest husband stand on a housetop and curse him, so long as he was being well served and helped to win a victory. By the way, I hope to have you both meet Cæsar in a few days. I might arrange a luncheon, if you say the word."

"I'd love it!" Virginis exclaimed, her blue eyes eager. Caius nodded.

"Then we'll see. Cap'n Jacquet, I'll send a chariot for you at eight in the morning; we'll arrange a conference with some of the staff. How much time will you need to prepare to meet the Breton fleet?"

"Two days," said Jacquet.

"Eh? Very well. Tomorrow the army moves forward. The fleet will assemble at once—and if Cæsar beats the enemy by land, he'll depend on you to take care of their fleet."

"It's a bargain," said Captain Jean Jacquet. "But it'll be a matter of weeks before Cæsar walks over the Breton defenses."

He was right about that.

Two of the Roman galleys were sunk; only one got away.

In the morning, Caius sent for him and introduced him to the staff. Already the legions were on the march; the camp was all but deserted, the entire army had been hurled forward. And these Romans who met with Jacquet were more worried about the sea than the land. They did well to worry, said Jean Jacquet grimly.

"The Bretons have above two hundred ships—big ships," he told them. "Never mind the reports of your spies. I know the truth better than they. These are shallow-water ships, flat-bottomed, with high bows and sterns, solidly built of oak with foot-square timbers fastened by spikes. Their sails are of leather. Under this heavy top-hamper the craft are unwieldy, but massive and solid, practically impregnable."

"And what can you do about it?" asked one of the captains, Lepidus by name.

"Take them," and the eyes of Jacquet twinkled. "All I want is full authority."

"You have it,"—and Caius laid down a wax-faced tablet. "There's your authority, over the seal of Cæsar himself. And he has written asking a special decree from the Senate, making you a Roman citizen. Your claims, by the way, are settled; the paymaster has the money waiting for you. Your salary as master pilot begins today. Are you satisfied?"

"Aye," said Jacquet, beaming.

"Then we leave you in charge—we're off in ten minutes to join the army. Kindly give my regards to your charming wife; I regret that Cæsar has already departed, and we must postpone the luncheon date."

As the chariot bearing Jacquet back to town whirled him away, he caught a roar of laughter from the staff officers in the tent, but thought nothing of it.

Decimus Brutus commanded the fleet for Rome; he was a fine officer with whom jacquet could work admirably. And work he did, while the legions of Cæsar beat back the stubborn Bretons, town by town, driving them into the sea.

The fleet captains were picked men—some of them Romans, most of them Parthians from the far east. Jean Jacquet had models of the Breton craft built and rigged for them, he showed them how the lighter Roman galleys must adopt entirely new tactics; for against these massive ships built to breast the broad Atlantic, the usual ramming tactics were futile, the catapults and engines of the Roman ships were powerless.

And meantime, he had the armorers at work turning out sickles by the hundred, but to no man would he breathe a hint of his idea....

During these days and weeks he had small comfort of Virginis. Now and again a messenger came with greetings from Captain Caius, bringing rich gifts to them both; at such times she would be radiant, brilliant, eager. She talked much of how they must go to Rome, once Jean Jacquet had won great place for himself. But in general he divined a coldness in her, almost an unfriendliness; she had definitely changed.

It worried him, yet his bluff, frank spirit saw in her attitude only a passing indisposition. He, too, had changed in these days. His Roman citizenship was a certainty, and he was utterly delighted with it. He talked largely of "us Romans," he slapped soldiers and officers on the back, he strutted and posed like any actor; but so boyishly unaffected was his exuberance that no one resented it in the least, and the association of pilots of the Loire even made him honorary chairman.

"Why go to Rome?" he said one night, as he and Virginis sat at supper. "Better to stay here. Do you know how many Gauls are Roman citizens? None; I'm the only one. Here, I'm a great man, your place is among the first, my dear. In Rome, we'll be lost."

"What?" The blue eyes of Virginis flashed. "Not go to Rome? Jean, you're insane! Why, Rome's the center of the world! No telling what heights await you there—"

"I don't know," he broke in moodily. "Oh, I know you've set your heart on Rome, but I'm afraid of the place. It's too big. It's not our style. Cæsar, they say, often declares it's better to be the tops in a little village than the second man in Rome. He's right about it."

"Oh, Cæsar!" she exclaimed. "Cæsar! I'm sick of hearing the name. Well, if you don't go to Rome, I do—so think about that. We'll both go, and you'd better make up your mind to it."

"All right, my dear," and Jacquet grinned. "But first, we've got to lick these Bretons. Then, if Cæsar gets a triumph, we'll figure in it and you'll have your heart's desire."

It was next day that the messengers began to flood in.

Action! The Bretons were being driven into the sea. They were putting their wives and treasures aboard ship. Decimus Brutus strode into Jacquet's office with a letter just arrived.

"The fleet's assembling, cap'n," he said brusquely. "Here are orders—cut off the Breton fleet and destroy it. We must sail tonight. Ready?"

"Ready," said Jean Jacquet.

That night the fleet sailed, and Jean Jacquet with it, to meet the other squadrons. And if, next day, a cavalry escort left Painbœuf and took with it a woman of cold and glorious beauty like moonlight—how was Captain Jacquet to know of it?

"Ave, Cæsar! Hail, Cæsar!"

The rolling shout of the legions, camped on the eastern promontory of the Bay of Quiberon, lifted and thundered across a sunlit morning, upon a scene such as few men in the world's history had ever witnessed, or would witness again. Cæsar and his veterans were gazing down from the height upon destiny.

Below, in the sheltered expanse of the bay, rode two hundred and more great Breton ships, filling the whole vast sea scene. Massive ships, heavy leathern sails aloft to the breeze; each one covered bow and stern with raw bull-hides to keep off boarders. Huge turreted ships, standing well inside the shallows and islets, crowded with men.

And, coming up across the sunrise, the three hundred Roman galleys, sails stowed and oars flashing. Three divisions of them—one heading straight for the enemy, the others spreading off to close the way to any escape.

"Ave, Cæsar!"

From the oncoming galleys lifted that rolling shout toward the glitter on the headland, where Cæsar sat watching.

Captain Jean Jacquet, with Decimus Brutus at his side, led the shout from the flagship, as he led the vanguard into action. The orders had been simple. Each captain was to follow the flagship, avoid ramming, and then do exactly as the flagship did.

Jacquet sent his flashing-oared galley straight in through the shallows, on at the nearest Breton vessel. Catapults were loosed, arrows curved in air, trumpets blared brazen on the sunlight. Close in and closer,

"Sickles?" Caius caught him up. "What do you mean by that?"

oars were run out, the helm was put over hard a-starboard. The galley sheered away from the Breton ship—and the sharp sickle-blades cut through the standing rigging of the huge ship like twine.

As the galley shot away, the immense leathern sails of the Breton ship came slithering and tumbling down, covering the decks. The galley swept around to the other side of the stricken Breton. Again the long poles fingered up; down came the starboard standing rigging, with what sails remained—and the hooks held fast.

"Boarders, away!"

Upon the stunned and frantic Bretons above, spears and arrows played; ladders lifted, while the poles held fast the two ships. The killers went up—heavy-armed Romans, legionnaries, butchers who knew their work and did it. Once they won place on a Breton deck, only killing remained.

The other galleys swept in upon the dismayed Bretons, each captain with a chart of the shallows and reefs, each galley with dozens of the long poles and sickle-blades. Ship after ship was reduced to a helpless hulk.

The Bretons tried to run for it, but escape was cut off. And the fast-darting galleys drove in with shearing poles; once those blades did their work, the heavy leathern sails came toppling. Men died, yes. Here and there galleys were smashed and went down. But, as the long hours passed, the wide expanse of the bay became dotted with hulks, drifting helpless, while the legionary killers did their steady and relentless work.

Some few of the great ships worked away, but were sooner or later caught, crippled and taken.

The afternoon drew on, the sun went westering, and the long and frightful Breton agony ran its course....

That night, Decimus Brutus laid his flagship alongside the stone quay of the little port of Sarzeau, where torches and cressets smoked ruddily. Cæsar

while men died; then the voice of Captain Jacquet rang down the rowing benches.

"Oars—starboard! Stand by to ship. Ship!"

With machine-like precision, the starboard oars were run in. The galley was actually rubbing strakes with the high-walled Breton ship, dwarfed beside her impregnable walls.

Again Jacquet's voice rang forth.

"Hook-men to the starboard bulwarks. Get set!"

Men scrambled hastily along the bulwarks. In air rose long poles, each handled by six men, each pole having at the end a sharp, sicklershaped blade. Feeling above the Breton rail like giant fingers, the hooks fastened on to the shrouds of the towering ship.

"Bow men shove off!" shouted Jacquet. "Starboard oars stand by—stand by, all! Starboard helm—stand by to give way—'way together!"

The long poles were secured to the rowing benches with leather thongs. The galley was shoved clear, the was waiting there, and came aboard the moment the plank was down—a tall, imperious figure clad in senatorial toga, girdle negligently fastened. He greeted Brutus warmly.

"And this Captain Jacquet—where is he, Brutus?"

"Below. He'll not last long; he got an arrow through the body at the last ship we boarded."

"Take me to him."

Jean Jacquet opened his eyes and looked up. A smile touched his bearded lips.

"Caius!" he murmured. "Caius, give her—tell her—can't go to Rome now—"

Cæsar straightened up. He slipped off his toga and spread it over the dead figure, and turned to Brutus.

"Get me a toga—anything will do. This man receives burial as a Roman citizen. Now get rid of your armor and come along to a feast of victory. I want you to meet the most beautiful woman in all Gaul."

"So?" Brutus eyed Cæsar quizzically, then glanced down at the cloaked figure. "Hm! The gods are always kind to you, Julius. In this case, you've been saved a good bit of trouble, eh?"

The thin lips of Cæsar drew into a smile.

"Nonsense, Brutus! Tears for the dead, wine for the living; and if a lady wants to go to Rome, she'll go—one way or another. Get a move on! Do you want to keep me standing here naked all night?"

So was history written.

When Professor Boggs had finished his story, Rear Admiral Lucas regarded him frowningly, but with a twinkle in his eye.

"A most immoral tale, my dear sir!" he said with mock disapproval. "Do you insinuate that the great Cæsar gallivanted around with another man's wife?"

Professor Boggs fairly snorted.

"I have shown you, sir, that the sickle was a prime weapon of naval warfare, and it remained so for centuries. Do you admit it?"

"Oh, absolutely!" said the officer. "But you might have gone into a little more detail on—er—some other aspects of the matter."

Even an Admiral, as one of the newspaper men observed, is human.

CLEOPATRA'S BEADS

On *a bypath of the Nevada desert reaching up to Utah,* with naked sun-scalded rock on every hand and the only water in sight rank poison, was a car and trailer. I approached it painfully. My own car had boiled about dry and I needed water badly.

It was a Saturday morning.

Halting, I left the car and approached the battered trailer, with a hail. I was aware of music, but paid little heed, being absorbed in my own plight. To the door of the trailer came a massive hairy man, naked to the waist, tattooed blue and red all over his torso and arms.

"Can't talk now," he said jerkily, With a gesture of invitation. "Come in and set. Flagstad is singing *Isolde.*"

He disappeared.

I stooped and entered the trailer. A radio was going, and my host motioned in silence to a stool. I took it and sat staring around. Shelves, pictures, polished stones—and the deathless surging music of "Tristan," coming from the Metropolitan thousands of miles away!

Signs on the Wall proclaimed that I was in the abode of Mogollon Pete, the rockologist. At the moment, Pete was wholly and utterly absorbed in the magic of the "Liebestod." He sat silent, entranced, a flush in his hairy cheeks, staring at the radio until the music died and there followed the thunderous applause that was shaking an opera-house half across the world.

With an oath of irritation, he shut off the thing.

"Why the hell people got to clap when they hear music, I dunno," he growled. "Say, wasn't that swell? Waves, that's what it was—made you feel waves, made you see 'em curling and smashing under the bows of a boat, going back and coming on again like to tear your heart out. Huh? Sounds foolish, I guess."

"Wise," said I. "The most wonderful love-waves ever imagined."

"Love-waves?" Pete frowned. "I mean sea-waves. Me, I used to be a sailor; but I wanted to learn about rocks, so here I am in the desert. I dunno what them folks were singing about, but the music was sure great. Made me think of Cleopatra."

For the next hour or so I learned a lot about rocks—all kinds of rocks. Pete knew them right down to the ground, loved them, lived for them. He made a living by selling rocks he collected and polished.

Presently he took from a drawer a glorious queer-shaped opal.

"Found that just the other day and polished her, without cutting," said he. "Finest Nevada opal I ever did see—green on one side, red on the other. Cleopatra herself never did have a piece of gem-stone like that one—for all her pearls."

This was the second time that he had mentioned Cleopatra.

"How d'you know she hadn't?" I queried idly.

Mogollon Pete looked startled.

"Huh? I'd ought to know," he stated. "I was sailing-master for her and Mark, that time over on the Greek coast. You know, off Actium."

I looked up at him sharply. He was quite serious. Of course, I knew well that all desert rats were said to be cracked on some subject; but Mogollon Pete looked pretty well balanced.

"Just which Cleopatra do you mean?" I asked. "There were seven queens of that name, you know."

"More'n that," he calmly returned. "This was the seventh. I was back there about six years ago—just before I quit the sea. Looking over the ground, so to speak. Funny thing, too, how one little notion changed the whole history of the world."

"Little notion?" I echoed blankly.

"Yeah. Me saying to that there double-crossing Crispus what I'd do if I was Octavian. It was a durned good thing for me that I happened to do it, of course, but just the same it went kind of hard. I thought a lot of Mark, even if he had got to liquoring up pretty heavy. I'm bound to admit that when it came to taking a tip, Octavian was right on the spot. Yes sir, it was me that founded the Roman navy, just like that! They'd never had one before my time, you know; they just got a bunch of ships ready for a job, and then disbanded 'em. But Octavian started a regular navy."

It was not hard to see that I had run into a character. Whether Mogollon Pete took himself to be a sort of Wandering Jew or Flying Dutchman, I was not sure, but he was interesting. And mind you, he was dead serious about it.

"That particular sea-fight," I said slowly, "happens to be a specialty of mine. That is, the circumstances surrounding it. I've read up on it a lot. It certainly did change naval history! Up until then, fighting-ships were immense affairs, the bigger the better; Actium altered all that. And the course of history with it. But nobody knows exactly what happened, to make Mark Antony skip out as he did."

"Well, I know," said Mogollon Pete.

He opened up book-shelves hidden in the trailer walls. As you may guess, I was studying this brawny tattooed man rather closely. When I saw the sort of books he kept on hand, I had the key to his mental quirk—rather, the ostensible key. For these books dealt with all sorts of queer religions touching on the occult, the transmigration of souls and so forth. Obviously my host was some sort of crank who believed that he had lived before now.

But he was something more. When he started in to recount his story, he not only made it live, but he had his data correct. He knew his subject, when it came to this battle for the world.

"This Crispus was my chief signal officer," said Pete, sadly shaking his head. "A smart seaman, too; but the night before we sailed, he got cleaned out in a crap game. It was a big game, for the fleet was lousy with money. We had the loot of the whole Eastern world aboard—Mark had looted the temples, the treasuries, everything in sight, and all of us got ours. But Crispus got taken for his wad, and he skipped out and told Octavian how to lick us. Told him what I had said about it, the dirty so-and-so! But let me show you how we were fixed. Boy, we had things by the tail!"

Now you must take the story in his own words....

Here on this rocky coast of Greece were gathered all the forces of the known world, with empire staked on one turn of a card. Octavian, crafty and cold-blooded, the heir of Julius Cæsar, led the armies and fleet of Rome. Not much of a fleet, either. Chiefly Liburnian galleys with two banks of oars—biremes, we called 'em. A couple of hundred, all told.

We had Roman legions too, the legions that had followed Mark Antony for years and worshiped him. That army could have whipped Octavian without half trying, but the fleet was even better, and Mark had more confidence in the fleet. Cleopatra was on hand with sixty Egyptian galleys; the bulk of the ships, however, consisted of about a hundred of the most tremendous vessels that had ever walked the water.

They were regular floating cities, if you ask me. Why, some had up to forty banks of oars, and bathrooms, and a theater stage, and God knows what all. Engines of all kinds, too, for hurling stones and huge arrows and weights. Given a five-knot breeze, any one of those ships could smash through a whole fleet of biremes and never turn a hair. I was quartered aboard the *Thunderer,* Mark's flagship.

Mark was out to lick Rome, and Cleopatra was helping him. Between them, they had plundered everything in sight. Why, I've gone down below with Mark and seen the ballast brought up to pay the legions ashore—ballast of gold coin and silver bars! And when it came to girl slaves, and wine and rations, that fleet was living high. Mark was no miser. If we won, we had the plunder of Rome ahead; and if we lost, we'd not need what we had, so the sky was the limit those days.

I fouled hawsers with Crispus, this signal officer of mine, over a girl in the camp. Her father was Flavius, a centurion in one of the legions, and she was rightly named Flavia, but answered to Dimples. Her old man was a hard egg who had been in Gaul with Cæsar.

The Battle Fleet of Actium

"Pete, Flavius says we're going to get licked," Crispus told me one day. "He says the talk in the ranks is that Mark has lost his grip. And there's a lot of Roman money around. Some of the brass hats have sneaked out and joined Octavian."

"Good riddance!" said I. "A lot of bums sitting around drinking all day and spouting about their family connections! We're better off without 'em. Anyhow, the fleet's going to win this war, not the army."

"That's what Flavius thinks," says Crispus, giving me one of his impudent grins. "He figures that Dimples will be safer aboard the *Thunderer* than ashore—especially if she and I get spliced."

"Says which? Listen, that girl is going to marry me!"

"Not if I know it, Pete. You've been seen too often hanging around those Egyptian ships; your rep's ruined. So lay off Dimples."

Right then, we tangled. He pulled a knife on me, but I finally got him down, got my own knife out, and was just about to finish him when the door slams open, and in walks Mark himself. If he hadn't interfered then, he'd have been emperor of Rome.

"What the devil's this, Pete!" he exclaimed. "Two of my best officers fighting? What about?"

"Dimples, sir," I says, and he broke into a roar of laughter. So did all the officers with him. When he had heard what it was all about, he turned to Crispus.

"Cap'n Peter is your superior officer, young man," said he. "If he wants that girl, or a dozen like her, I'll see that he gets her. You run over to the slave-market and get a couple to your taste, and charge 'em to me."

Crispus went white. "Flavia loves me, sir! And I love her."

"Don't answer me back, or I'll have you crucified," says Mark. He had quite a hangover that morning, and was in an ugly mood. Then he swung around to me. "Pete, is there any chance of Octavian's fleet licking us?"

"Not with him in command, sir," I says. "If I had his fleet, I might do it, but—"

"Eh? You might? How so?"

"Well sir, these light, fast galleys of his are good. If I had 'em, I'd try and catch your fleet in a calm, when the big ships were about helpless. I'd break off the oars, ram in and out, use fire, and bust things up generally. It could be done. But only in a calm, mind you. With steerage-way on 'em, ten of our ships could whip the tar out of his whole fleet."

And Crispus heard me say it.

"Then we'll see to it there's no calm." And Mark laughed. "Besides, Octavian hasn't your head, Pete. I want you to go aboard the Queen's ship at six tonight with me. There's to be a council of war, and I may need you to answer questions."

I saluted, and he went out.

Crispus went ashore, and so did I. Going up to camp, I found Dimples and sat down to have a talk. Pretty soon she lit out on me for fair, when I mentioned her marrying me.

"Marry you?" she said. "I'd sooner drown."

"You'll get over that," I told her, "once we're settled down together, and you get used to me. Besides which, you've got nothing to say about it, Dimples. If you've got any fool notions about that fellow Crispus, forget 'em."

"He's a better man than you," she flashed out. I grinned at her. Give me a girl who has a temper, every time.

"But he'll come to a worse end, and pretty near did this morning. Where's your dad?"

"Over at the quartermaster's store."

I hunted up Captain Flavius. I stood pretty well with the centurion, and the two of us went over to the canteen and washed out our throats....

Mark Antony, drunk or sober, never forgot the men around him. He had already sent Flavius an order that Dimples was to marry me, and Flavius was willing enough.

"But don't expect miracles, Peter," he said. "That girl's got a will of her own; and let me tell you, she can raise hell. It's a caution what the young folks are coming to, these days. Why, back in my time—"

"Let things ride," I said. "Anyhow, right now it's against regulations to have women aboard ship. See what breaks. If Mark trusts to the fleet alone, your camp here will be the safest place for Dimples. Meantime, kick Crispus out if he comes around."

"You bet I will," the centurion replied. "It's bad enough to have a sailor for a son-in-law, let alone a wild young devil like him."

"What d'ye mean, sailor?" I says. "I'm flag-captain and sailing-master of the fleet, and that's a damned sight more than you, with a measly company of flat-feet under you! What we need is another drink."

"Two," says he, and we ordered them.

During the rest of the day, I was the busiest man in those parts. I had to check on the condition of every ship in the fleet and have everything at my tongue's end by night. There was a lot of sickness ashore, some of the legions being only at half strength, and I had a hunch that Mark would stick to the fleet for the fighting job.

Cleopatra's flagship was lying alongside the *Thunderer.* Promptly at four bells I went down the ladder to the galley with Mark and his chief officers. Being the end of August, the weather was hot as blazes.

The after deck of the galley had been cleared of everyone except Cleopatra, who received us there. She was all for business, and so was Mark; and we lost no time getting down to cases. There would be a feast later, and you could smell the roasts that were cooking, but first we had to settle things.

Naturally, I knew the queen pretty well, as any man in my position would. She was not so much for looks, being in her late thirties; but at that, she was mighty easy on the eyes, and she sure had everything there was to have on the ball. Neither I nor anyone else who knew her, could blame Mark a particle for preferring her to all of Rome. Boy, when that dame turned her lamps on you, something happened inside!

"What's your weather-report, Cap'n Peter?" says Mark to me.

"Blow coming up, sir," I replied. "Looks like a gale, tomorrow or next day."

"And that's what we need," he says. "In a blow, these ships of ours are steady as rocks. Give me a stiff breeze, and we'll win the world."

"Not me," said Cleopatra with a grimace. "I get seasick."

"Then you stay out of it. Peter! Condition of the fleet?"

"First class, sir. Can't answer for the Egyptian galleys. The other ships are every one of'em in shape for battle at an hour's notice."

"Good." Mark turned to the queen. "Now, Cleo, here's the lay of it," he says. "Two spies came in from Octavian's camp today. He's getting cold feet and wants to skip out. I know many of my officers have gone over to him, but that makes it all the worse. He's fully aware that we can whip him. Agrippa and some of his captains are trying to force him into battle; he doesn't like it."

"I had the same report from an Egyptian who was in his camp," said Cleopatra.

"Then, I say quit the army, take to the fleet, and move on him!" exclaimed Mark Antony quickly. "His fleet won't dare attack us. Day after tomorrow, at dawn, we embark, weigh anchor, and go after him. Do you agree?"

There was a flame in that man, when he was sober, that would carry any woman off her feet, or any man either. It was so agreed; and the council was ended then and there. Cleopatra called me over and gave me a string of beads off her own neck, Mark shoved a wine-cup at me; and inside of another fifteen minutes the dancing girls came along and things got hot. It was pretty near daylight when I clambered back aboard and somebody tucked me into my bunk.

*At noon I was up and going ashore, having sum*moned a council of all the fleet captains. We had no admirals in those days; I was the nearest thing to it. Nearly three hundred of us met in the camp theater.

"All shore-leave canceled at midnight tonight, and be ready to sail at dawn," I told them. Somebody objected that weather was coming on. "Exactly what we want. When it comes to fighting, I'll lead with the heavy ships, the rest of you follow and mop up. You all have your signal books. Crispus! Where's that damned signal officer?"

He was not in sight. Philocrates, who commanded the Egyptian galleys, took me to one side after the meeting. He seemed worried.

"Peter, the Queen insists that she goes with Mark Antony and the fleet. Now, if we have a blow, Lord knows what may happen! That woman can't stand the sea. She gets sick and loses her color, turns sea-green, and becomes wild. I tell you, it's cursed dangerous. Don't place dependence on our sixty galleys."

"All right, you follow us and play safe," I said, and that was that.

Half a dozen of us located Flavius and some more officers, and a big crap-game got under way. Crispus showed up, went into the game, and got cleaned out in no time at all.

"Luck at love, no luck at dice," says he, and walked off.

Along in the shank of the evening I went home with Flavius, meaning to have a talk with Dimples and settle things. She was gone. One of the slaves told us she had skipped out with Crispus about dusk. When we investigated further, we found they had left camp entirely. Crispus had deserted to the enemy.

"So help me, I'll have him crucified when we've licked Octavian!" Flavius threatened.

"You're not the only one," I said grimly. "Still, he's a smart lad. Let's find another drink or so."

When I went aboard at midnight, shore parties were coming out fast. Mark Antony was on the Queen's galley alongside, and I went down to report the desertion of Crispus and the obvious betrayal of our signal-books to the enemy. Mark roared with laughter when I told them about it.

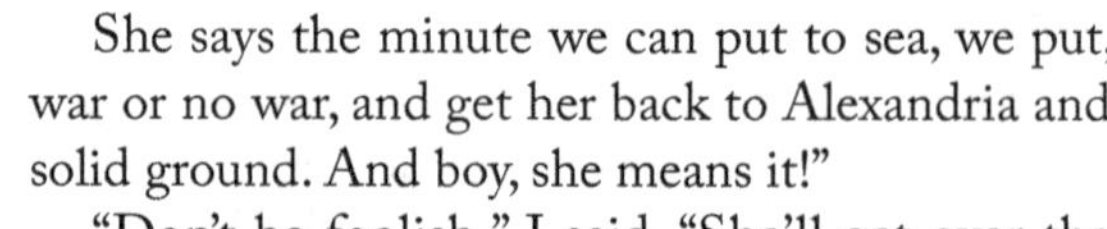

"Signals be hanged, Cap'n Peter!" said he. "We'll whip Octavian by fighting, not by signals. Here, have' some of this Falernian."

Cleopatra gave me a smile. "Where are those beads I gave you last night?"

"Right here." And I showed them, around my neck.... I still have 'em, to this day.

"They'll bring you luck," she says. "They came from the tomb of an ancient Pharaoh. Maybe I shouldn't have given them to you."

She refused to take them back, however. Mark said that when we took over Rome, I could take my pick of the senators' daughters for a wife, and that cheered me up a lot.

Promptly at dawn the fleet pulled out, with a stiff breeze freshening out of the north. Barely were we clear of the land, however, than it switched around, and by noon was blowing great guns out of the south, which was dead against us.

There was nothing we could do except wait for the wind to switch again, so we anchored in the lee of the Actium promontory. I laid our big ships well up inside the gulf, leaving the lighter vessels and the Egyptian contingent strung out toward the promontory. We had small, fast dispatch-boats at work among the fleet, and also spying on Octavian's fleet across the gulf.

And there we lay, pitching and tossing, four blessed days. It was the end of August, and this was the first of the equinoctial gales. Along on the third day, Mark and I got into one of the dispatch-boats and we went aboard Cleopatra's flagship. Mark went below to see her, and I stood in the lee of the deckhouse with Philocrates, her flag-captain.

"Is she laid out?" I asked. Philocrates wagged his head.

"Matey, she's pretty near dead, and no mistake. Ain't seen anyone so seasick since I can remember; and she's been keeping us on the jump with her notions.

She says the minute we can put to sea, we put, war or no war, and get her back to Alexandria and solid ground. And boy, she means it!"

"Don't be foolish," I said. "She'll get over the notion when the sea goes down."

"When that woman takes a notion, it takes for keeps," said Philocrates. "You know that priest of Isis we had aboard—that old duck with the cast in his eye? Well, he undertook to cure her seasickness, and didn't do it. He went over the side this morning with a knife in his gizzard. I bet you a cookie that Mark Antony comes on deck faster than he went below."

Sure enough, Mark came up looking flustered and angry, and we started back for the *Thunderer.*

"You're damn' lucky you lost your girl, Pete," he says to me. "Take a tip and leave the women ashore."

"This will be all blown out by tomorrow night, sir," I said; and he brightened up a bit.

Sure enough, by next night the wind was falling, but the sea was pretty high. The stars came out clear and fine, and I turned in.

It was getting along to four bells in the morning watch, when somebody yanked me out of my bunk, and I jumped for the deck. A dispatch-boat had just come alongside in the dawn—one of those watching the enemy fleet. It seemed that they were out and coming. Mark came on deck, heard the news, and rubbed his hands together delightedly.

"Fine!" says he. "Fine!"

"How come?" I said, pointing to the water. "Nothing fine about that."

Sure enough, a flat dead calm had fallen. There was not so much as a cat's-paw on the surface.

"What of it?" said Mark. "We have oars, haven't we? Out with 'em, Peter!"

Our trumpeter gave the signal, and it was repeated from ship to ship. Anchors were weighed, and the whole fleet slowly got under way. Before we were well started, another dispatch-boat came in with word that Octavian's whole fleet was not five miles off, and coming down fast with all oars double-banked.

And there we were, in a flat calm.

However, there was something about that fleet drawing out to sea in the sunrise that gripped you, made you forget everything else. The lighter ships and the Egyptian galleys kept the wings, and the solid ranks of our heavy ships moved out slowly and majestically, oars aflash, drums beating time for the rowers, cymbals clashing. Even her forty oar-banks could scarcely move the *Thunderer;* she towered above the sea like a castle. I kept the two dispatch-boats at hand, for messenger use.

With close to three hundred ships on the move, you can imagine the sight we presented. We were just off the cape, when the morning mists lifted a bit, and there was Octavian's fleet, within a mile and bearing down on us fast. Nearly all his ships were Liburnian biremes—long, fast ships, but so low in the water alongside our great hulks that the idea of their attacking us was rather ludicrous.

One of our biggest, the *Ajax,* was well in the van of the rest. The biremes came down for her; we could see her engines working, and she sent a huge stone aboard one Roman that smashed him like an eggshell. She went slap into another, rammed him, rode over him—and then something happened.

A bireme came in on each side of her, and drew in oars. They struck her massed oar-banks, smashed them, splintered them, and sheered off. Two more biremes dashed in beneath her sides; and when I saw black smoke drifting up in masses, I turned to Mark with a groan.

"Somebody's too blamed smart, sir," I said. "See that? We've got to stop it. Shall I signal the lighter ships to engage?"

"Do it," said he, and the signals went out.

Our wings circled around; the Egyptian galleys did their share; and the two fleets were engaged, ship to ship. Meantime the *Ajax* was afire and crippled, and some of the biremes were heading down for us.

Our engines went to work. We smashed two of the biremes. A third swept in and caught our whole port side as the oars flashed. Screams went up from below-decks; the oars splintered or dragged, but the starboard oars swung us around, and inside of a minute that bireme was drifting away with most of her crew dead or dying, under the hail of arrows and spears that we poured into her.

Rowers were shifted, new oars put out, and I signaled the battleships to form behind us, with the *Thunderer* for the apex of the triangle. This, for the moment, held off the enemy's attack.

This is all soon told, but took hours in the doing. Most of the morning was gone. Our lighter galleys were all engaged, but another of our big ships had followed the *Ajax* and was in flames. We were well outside the cape now, and there was a heavy, rolling swell. Suddenly Mark caught my arm.

"Look there! What's happening?"

I squinted seaward. Wind! No doubt of it. A breeze was coming up from the west; the water was darkening; and that sea, full of iron and clanging fury, was beginning to kick up again. Then a Scarlet red sail was loosened, bellied out, and I knew it for the royal galley of the Queen. It was drawing out of the fight.

We made out well enough at first: we fought them hour after hour; our sides were never scaled. None the less, our men died under an unceasing hail of arrows and stones.

Mark Antony let out an oath. "What's she doing, Peter?"

"Running," I said. "Philocrates was afraid of it. There go some more!"

Drawing out, indeed—ship after ship of the Egyptians pulled out of the tumult, as their canvas took the wind. They headed straight out and away to the south. With a curse of fury and dismay, Mark flung his cloak around him.

"Call in that dispatch-boat, Peter!" he yelped at me. "I'm going to bring her back.... Stow your jaw, blast you! Carry on here until I reach her."

The dispatch-boat ran in under our counter, Mark clambered down a ladder all by himself, and hardly a soul knew he was gone. I was simply too dumfounded to stop him. Bring her back? Not a chance of it. Why, the whole Egyptian contingent was on the run after her by this time, and the biremes were tearing in for us big fellows, and now there was merry hell to pay.

And all because that dame had got seasick with the swell.

It was about noon when this happened. The breeze was freshening out to seaward, but it died before reaching us, and there was not a thing we could do. Ship after ship came darting in to smash our oarbanks, and to save our men below and avert the chance of fire, I ordered the oars in and the lower ports closed.

Thus, we could give our entire attention to fighting, and we did it. I signaled the other captains to repeat what I had done, but few caught the signals. The whole Roman fleet was in around us by this time; it was every man for himself; and to their sorrow few of the others heeded my signals.

We made out well enough, at first. There was no way for firepots to be slung into us, with all ports closed; and from the advantage of our towering height, we sent Roman after Roman drifting away. Those who tried to board us, never got a man over the bulwarks. The biremes were too light to damage us much by ramming, and our engines kept up a storm of arrows and stones that did heavy damage.

Given mere steerage-way, we could have run through the whole Roman fleet. But, we were helpless to move. And those Romans were putting into play the very tactics I had thought up. No doubt whatever—that rascal Crispus had lost the day for us! *One by one our huge ships were crippled, as the* oars were rammed and splintered. True, the Romans lost heavily; but one by one our immense craft were set afire. None were captured, I will say for them. They fought to the finish and went down in flames.

The Egyptian galleys were clear over the horizon, and Mark Antony with them, by this time.

Our lighter ships were cleared or captured or ran for it. Those of us who remained in the battleships, knew the day was lost, but no quarter had been proclaimed; and none of us was anxious to decorate a cross to celebrate Octavian's victory.

Besides, there was still a chance. The breeze reached us at last, we shook out the canvas, and some of us got under way. Ship after ship was afire, however. That trick of using firepots was really what settled the use of big navy ships for good and all.

The Romans had engines, too. We had our spritmast shot away; and a half-ton chunk of rock came aboard and splintered our mainmast, and that finished the *Thunderer*, so far as motion was concerned.

It was a regular bit of tactics, as I soon saw. The biremes circled off any of our ships that had canvas up, and played their engines until the masts carried away, then closed in. Once those high oar-banks had been rammed and splintered, the ports were smashed open and the whole below-decks were in ruin, so it was no trick to hurl in firepots.

As the afternoon drew on, ship after ship smoked to heaven and then went hissing down. The whole sea was covered with smoke and wreckage and bodies of men by the thousand. Around the *Thunderer* were grouped a ring of biremes. We fought them hour after hour: our engines played; our bowmen and spearmen hailed death into them; our high sides were never scaled.

None the less, our men died under an unceasing hail of arrows and stones. I got a shaft in the ribs; and a stone smashed my helmet and laid me out for a while; but I was back in the fight presently. Meantime a bireme laid in under our stern, and her crew literally chopped a way into us, and set us afire.

Even so, we were the last to go down. The wind came up, toward sunset, and lifted the smoke to disclose blazing hulks everywhere. We were ablaze too, and could do nothing about it. We had not a score of men left on their feet when at last the Romans did lay us aboard, and came pouring up over the side, with the whole after end of the ship roaring up in flame.

Some of us were killed; some were taken with nets, like fish. I was netted and tied up, and taken aboard a bireme, so exhausted I fell asleep in my bonds.

And the *Thunderer* went down like all the rest—hulks ballasted with gold, crammed with all the treasure of the Eastern world! Lying there to this day, off Actium....

I woke up again to daylight. Morning had come, and soldiers were bustling me around; we were ashore. They were taking me before Octavian, they said, but little I cared what might happen. Somebody had looted my armor, and I had nothing left except that string of beads around my neck, which Cleopatra had said would bring me luck. Luck! A lot of luck it had brought me. For now Octavian would crucify me.

They hauled me to his tent and set me before him. A pale, crafty-eyed fellow he was.

"So you are Captain Peter, sailing-master of the rebel fleet!" said he. "Well, I owe you something."

"Then make it short," I said sourly. "And remember I'm a Roman citizen, so no flogging."

He smiled a little at this. Somebody moved behind him, and I looked up to see Crispus there. Crispus himself! And he was grinning at me. I straightened up and let him have it straight.

"You blasted this-and-that!" I said. "If it hadn't been for your double-crossing us, things would be different!"

"They might," said Octavian. "But things are as they are, my man. Aye, Crispus gave us an idea of what tactics to use, thanks to you. And that idea has saved your life, Captain Peter. It may do more for you. I'm going to build a standing navy for Rome, all biremes; no more big ships. I'm putting Crispus in command. He's spoken for you as his chief of staff, so to speak. Yes or no? Allegiance to me or not?"

I gulped hard. Then I met the grin of Crispus, and saw him nod to me; not a bad sort, he wasn't.

"Yes," I said. And that's all the story.

All the story? Well, that was all Mogollon Pete told me, as we sat there in the Nevada desert and watched the sunset light touch the rocks to fire. With a deep breath, I came back to realities again, and lit a cigarette.

"And," I said slowly, "you believe all this actually happened—to you?"

"It did," said Mogollon Pete earnestly. "And I've got the proof right here to show you."

He went to one of his drawers and took out a string of beads, and handed them to me. They were of glazed beads and glass. They were certainly Egyptian; I had some of the same kind that I got from the museum people in Cairo.

"That's the identical necklace Cleopatra gave me for luck," said he. "Glass was something wonderful back in those days, you know. Yes sir, she gave away her luck and no mistake! And yet, for all her wealth and glory and empire, she didn't have a jewel in the whole lot that could touch this here Nevada opal. Take a look at it."

That opal was a glorious thing. Hard to realize that it was nothing but a mass of silica and water that had once been like jelly! Opals are nothing else, if you stop to think of them that way.

In the sunset light, one side of it had a glowing greenish opalescence, the other side was all red fire.

"Think what a ring that would make!" said Mogollon Pete. "Of course, opals are mighty soft and shouldn't be used in rings; but they are, just the same. Or you could give it to your best girl."

By George! That reminded me that my wife, was waiting for me to come, up in the camp. I got up, and asked a question.

"Only fifty dollars," said Mogollon Pete. "And dirt cheap at the price."

I thought so myself—the story included. But the queer part of it was that his story was correct in every detail. And if you can figure that out, you are good.

THE SILENCE OF THE SEA

The report of First Officer Joseph Pertinax of the freighter Castor and Pollux, who investigated the loss of the Diana off the Maltese coast, is one of the most curious maritime documents in existence. Not for what it says, but for what it leaves unsaid.

Joe Pertinax deliberately suppressed many of the facts in the case. They were too incredible by far, even for a confidential report to the owners. Pertinax knew those owners; his uncle was one of them.

Had he submitted a report of the literal truth as he saw it, they would have eyed one another and asked what the devil was wrong with Pertinax. It would have finished his career with the line then and there. The actual story appears here for the first time, unabridged. As to believing it, you must decide that for yourself.

Whether you believe it or not, you will at least understand why those hard-headed ship-owners, who gave but small credence to table-tipping, to spirits or to miracles, would have been shocked by it, even horrified. And when you read the report that Chief Officer Pertinax did send in, you will comprehend why it was so much better than the whole truth....

There was no love lost between Pertinax and the skipper of the *Castor and Pollux.* Trouble really came to a head when Cap'n Stentor brought a shore-party out to look over the ship. She had been laid up here at Malta for some days with damages, the extent of which were not yet determined. Pertinax was shifting cargo in the main hold to get at the foot of the sprung mast, when the skipper came along and introduced him to the two ladies.

Joe Pertinax saw only one of them. When he shook hands with Lydia, the world flopped over for him, and was never the same world again. He vaguely understood that her brother ran a big trading concern ashore, which was owned by their invalid father, and that the skipper was putting over some deal with him. But nothing really mattered except those glowing black eyes and their laughing message, and the girl behind them.

Next thing Pertinax knew, he was being invited to dine ashore that evening with the family; the skipper was going too. Then he was taking Lydia over the ship. He was well aware of the sour look that the skipper sent after him, but gave not a hang for it.

Then, when the visitors went below with a stewardess to powder their noses, he found the skipper at his elbow, and a typhoon was blowing up. Captain Stentor was a slim, swarthy, handsome man; he had a way with him, and he stopped at nothing.

"Mister," he said, "you'd better stay in charge aboard here tonight."

"Yeah?" Pertinax met the angry black eyes with his usual cool smile. "Sorry, sir. The second's in charge tonight. I wouldn't pass up that dinner-party for the world."

"You heard me, Mister. Just because you're the owner's nephew—"

"Belay that stuff!" Pertinax's gray eyes were suddenly aflame. "Are you asking for a showdown?"

"I intend to have discipline upheld. You're taking orders from me, I think?"

Pertinax broke into a laugh, but his eyes were like sun-blazing ice.

"All right. You were dead drunk the whole way from Alexandria to Cyprus. At Nicosia we lost fifty passengers because police inspection showed the cabins weren't fit for animals, let alone humans; that was your responsibility. We're laid up here because you rammed us into that Greek coaster and damned near lost the ship. What discipline there is aboard this hooker is due to me, not to you. And you even ordered the second officer to falsify the log about it. If you want to go up before a board of inquiry, you stand a good chance of losing your ticket altogether."

A Roman freighter

Captain Stentor flushed darkly, then paled. All this was true; but he could deny it, and would. And he would be credited. As a captain in the Corn Line, he was practically above the law, so long as he delivered his cargo safely.

"I'm ordering you to stay aboard tonight, Mister," he said quietly.

"You can go plumb to hell!" said Pertinax. "You're master in name only; I'm doing the work. You've been stopping ashore ever since we dropped the hook, instead of attending to business. And I bet it wasn't Lydia who invited you to dinner, but her brother. Yes, you always did like the ladies; but you're not her stripe, Cap'n."

Stentor showed his white, hard teeth in a snarl.

"Joe, I've broken many a better man than you. Is she worth it?"

"I think she is," replied Pertinax. "Anyhow, I'm going to find out."

"Your funeral, then." And the skipper turned, as the visitors approached.

Pertinax, saying good-by to those flashing black eyes, felt the vivid animation of the girl tug at him like a sentient force; what a girl, what a girl! And she liked him. He could feel her friendliness.

He stared after them thoughtfully. There was nothing much ashore; her folks owned most of the place. Fishing-craft, coasters, warehouses, a small town, with the white villa of her family among green gardens. Going ashore tonight? You bet he was.

*Demetrius, the chief steward, came along, grin*ning. Old Demetrius never missed much; he and the first officer were friends, and understood each other.

"Some dame, Mister!" said he. "I heard some of your run-in with the Old Man. If you need any backing, the whole crew's with you. Affidavits may be worth having."

"Thanks." And Pertinax smiled. "He won't bother me."

"I ain't so sure; he's bad medicine," said the chief steward seriously. "Looks to me like a poor morning's work, Joe; but I can't blame you. Boy, what a dame! They tell me her old man just about owns the whole island, but is dying. Publius Trading Corporation, that's him. Say, you heard about the rumpus ashore last night?"

"No. Trouble?"

"Uh-huh. I said it meant trouble when we shipped those two priests of Isis at Alexandria. Every time a priest comes aboard ship, look out for squalls. Those two Egyptians are stopping ashore with the skipper, you know. Well, I hear some talk that last night they raised hell; I dunno the truth of it. I'm going ashore now to see about cabin stores, and I'll be back after lunch with details. You keep your eye open for those two Egyptians. They're pals of the Old Man, and they're sure hell on magic and suchlike."

Joe Pertinax shrugged, and went back to his inspection below. Yes, Captain Stentor was a bad enemy; his very position made him practically immune to attack; he could make things pretty tough for a chief officer he disliked. But what the hell! Lydia was worth it. The very thought of her, the memory of her face, was heart-warming.

In this year 62 A.D., Rome ruled the world, but all Italy depended on Africa for her food supplies. Hence the development of these huge corn-ships, which could carry above three hundred souls all told. They were the biggest and finest ships afloat.

Any skipper of the subsidized Corn Line was at the very top of his profession. He outranked even a naval captain; he had special privileges granted by the Senate, such as private speculation; and if he got his cargoes through safely, he could do what pleased him on the side.

Corn for Italy! Get the corn through at all costs of delay or life; so ran the orders. Never risk the precious cargo. Lay up for the whole winter, if need be, but get the corn through! Do anything the skipper pleased—but get the corn through, sooner or later.... And Cap'n Stentor always got it through.

Egyptians, priests of Isis—huh! Pertinax grimaced at thought of those two passengers, who were now stopping ashore with the skipper. Tall, shaven, cold-eyed men, masters of wizardry and magic; and if report said true, with a finger in all sorts of evil and swindling and graft.

This was the last voyage of the season. Already the winter gales were breaking. Once home, the *Castor and Pollux* would go out of commission until May. Why not come back here for the winter? There were worse places than this tight little island.

"Must be losing my grip," thought Pertinax angrily. "To fall for a dame just because she looks twice at me! Or to think a girl like that would fall for me!"

Still, most would look twice at Joe Pertinax, bronzed and ruddy, clear of eye, and a Roman citizen to boot—no small honor in those days. He had already passed his master's examination, and had his license; but he might wait years before he got a ship, even if his uncle was one of the owners. A master's berth in the Corn Line was something to dream about....

The chief steward was slow to return. But in mid-afternoon the local agent of the line came aboard. Finding Captain Stentor gone, he was furious.

"Damn it, if I owned this line, I'd give the skippers less leeway!" he snapped at Pertinax. "He's been at monkeyshines ashore, with those Egyptian priests. Those two birds threw a show last night—magic and hocus-pocus. Old Widow Flavia was trying to raise the spirits of her husband and son, who were drowned two years ago. Well sir, those Egyptians hooked her for all her money and scared her to death—yeah, to death! She died this morning from some kind of shock. The whole town's worked up about it. Priests of Isis, huh? I'd like to see every blasted Egyptian strung up."

"Those fellows stand pretty high, back in Egypt," Pertinax said.

"Well, the old gods are good enough for me," snorted the agent. "Look here: you know the *Diana?* She cleared from Alexandria two weeks ahead of you."

"Sure. Newest and best ship in the fleet. What about her?"

"That's what I want to know. The mail boat from Syracuse came in yesterday, and I had a letter from our agent there. The *Diana* has never showed up."

"That's nothing to worry about. Maybe she went to Italy direct."

"Nope. She took freight and passengers aboard at Myra, in Lycia, and hasn't been reported since. A Greek trader from Myra brought word of her to Syracuse. She took aboard a pack of prisoners and soldiers under Julius, a centurion of the Augustan Legion, with freight for Syracuse. The Greek reported some cursed bad weather off Crete, and the *Diana* may have caught it."

"That's no sign," replied Pertinax. "Cap'n Ariston is a careful old shellback, the best seaman in the fleet, and he has a top pilot, that chap Myron. Maybe he ran into some Cretan harbor to ride out the weather; it's up to the master's discretion, you know. The corn must come through safe."

"Maybe. But the centurion had charge of a religious maniac, some Jew who happened to be a Roman citizen, being taken to Rome for trial. One of this new religious sect they call Christians; this fellow's name was Paul. There's been a lot of talk about him. And that was sure bad luck for the *Diana.* Well, what's the report on your damage? A sou'wester is blowing up, and the dispatch-boat is getting off tonight ahead of it, with any mail for Syracuse and Italy. I'd like to get our report off."

"It's bad," said Pertinax. "Come along and see for yourself."

The *Castor and Pollux* was indeed badly off, with a smashed rudder, sprung mainmast, and so wrenched and strained that to chance the winter gales would be sheer folly.

"Wait till Cap'n Stentor sees those bulkheads!" said Pertinax. "I expect he'll decide to winter here and play safe."

"You don't look unhappy about it," commented the agent, and took his leave.

Unhappy? Chief Officer Pertinax was tickled pink, to put it bluntly, and set about stowing the ship more safely.

The big square mainsail, heavily embroidered with the figures of the heavenly twins *Castor and Pollux,* was stowed under tarpaulin. The staysail was broken out from the artemon, the highly steeved bowsprit mast; and under this canvas the pilot ran the huge ship to a more secure berth. Then, moored with hawsers, all was set to await the skipper's verdict. That he would decide to winter here, was a certainty.

"Old Man won't be aboard till tomorrow," said the chief steward, coming aboard near sunset. "Big wind blowing up. Publius is throwing a dinner-party tonight."

"I'm going," said Pertinax. "Got to shave and dress pretty quick."

"You going! Boy, you're showing class. But mind your step. Those priests of Isis have played merry hell. The town's pretty mad; also, it's scared stiff. They claim to be divine healers, magicians and what-not. Publius is going to have 'em heal his dad; the old boy is pretty near dead with dysentery and fever. And say! They got some of those Christians here. Ever see any?"

Pertinax shook his head. "Don't believe so. What are they like?"

"Look just like anybody else; you'd be surprised, after all the yarns we've heard about them eating babies and killing folks with magic and so forth. I guess the stories are exaggerated. What about shore-parties?"

Pertinax started; a deadly reptile was coiled by his foot…. Smiling grimly, the priest held up a hand.

"Second officer's in charge for the night. Ask him."

When Pertinax joined the dinner-party that evening,—it was an all-night affair,—a gale was howling over the island. He was astonished by the luxury of the villa, which was large and in the best Roman style. The company was a gay one, with numbers of the chief townsfolk present, and slaves to anticipate every desire. And the dinner was a marvel. As Publius said, it might not come up to Roman standards, but it was the best Malta could furnish.

This Publius, the host, was a young fellow of five-and-twenty, narrow in the eyes, pinched in the nostrils, a sharply disagreeable type, not at all the shrewd merchant type Joe Pertinax had anticipated meeting. A rich man's son who lacked proper ballast. Reclining on a couch beside that of Lydia, Pertinax looked across the festive board at Captain Stentor, to find the skipper smiling and amiable. So were the two Egyptian priests. All three were at their ease.

The chief officer used his eyes. When, later, he found himself alone with Lydia, he spoke thoughtfully.

"Strange house, strange man! A queer something about the place, the slaves; I don't know how to explain it. A feeling in the air. Your brother's not like you. He's not what I expected."

She was silent, looking at him, a touch of fear in her gaze. Then she broke out:

"How can you say such things? Are you a magician, like those Egyptians?"

"Eh?" Pertinax laughed suddenly. "Heaven forbid! I spoke before I thought. We're like old friends; I've known you all my life, somehow.... Forgive me!"

"I'm not angry, just surprised," she said in a low voice. "It's true. Poor Father has been ill, wasting away; nothing can cure him. The business is going to the dogs. Publius is obstinate, opinionated, afraid of himself and afraid to show it. He's been gambling in wheat futures—oh, if my father were only well again! Then you'd see things different around here. But he'll never leave his bed. These magicians say they can cure him. Useless! They're impostors."

Tears were in her eyes. Barriers were down; they talked together like comrades. The girl turned to his cheerful vigor, confided in him impulsively. Gambling in futures? Pertinax glimpsed the truth as they talked. Publius was sinking hard cash with Captain

"Oh, Oh," she gasped, "surely you cannot believe such wild stories!"

Stentor, gambling on the latter's knowledge of the grain trade—a sure thing, it appeared. Stentor had gripped the boy with his big talk, was playing him for a sucker, had the two priests of Isis at work. A soft business for the skipper!

"I'll help, yes," said Pertinax presently. "Wait and see; something will turn up. By the way, I hear you have some of that queer sect on your island. You know, the slave religion. They say the slaves are being armed, are going to revolt all over the Empire. This queer eastern cult that eats babies—Christians. Got any of 'em around? I'd like to see some of them."

Fear in her eyes, no doubt of it! She gasped a little.

"Oh, surely you cannot believe such things, such wild stories!"

Pertinax laughed. "Why not? I don't know much about 'em, for a fact; but I'm curious. Can you show me some of them?"

"Yes. Tomorrow, if you like. We must go back now—"

They rejoined the others. Later, when he was taking his leave, Pertinax encountered one of the two Egyptians. The surly priest halted him, looked intently at him.

"Careful, Mr. Pertinax! I can see strange things in your face; an aura of evil surrounds you. Bad influences! The stars are against you. For the next week or so you must be careful. Would you like your horoscope cast?"

"Not I!"—and Pertinax laughed. "I take no stock in frauds and their mummery, so good night to you."

He returned to the ship. The gale was sweeping

harder over the island; a good three-day blow, it promised to be….

With morning, Stentor came out to the ship, inspected her damages, and signed the entry in the log. He approved all Pertinax had done, and showed himself most friendly.

"Now, Joe, we mustn't have trouble," he said, his hand on the chief officer's shoulder. "You're a good seaman. I must have had a touch of dyspepsia yesterday. Let's forget all about it."

"Right, sir," responded Pertinax.

In the early afternoon he went ashore and met Lydia. The gale precluded sight-seeing; he went home with her, and there met her father. Once a fine, lordly man, the elder Publius was now no more than a wasted skeleton awaiting the touch of death.

Among the family slaves was an elderly Greek, a scholar who handled the firm's books. Lydia sent for him. After they had talked for a while, the Greek went back to the office. Pertinax was impressed by the man's intelligence, and said so.

"He's one of those Christians you mentioned," said the girl shortly.

"What! That man?" exclaimed Pertinax. "You're joking!" Then, as he met her gaze, he started with sudden comprehension. "My dear girl! You can't mean—"

She nodded gravely. "Yes. I also—one of that sect you despise."

"But I don't!" he rejoined in confusion. "That is—dammit, I didn't dream you could be—well, I don't know much about these Christians—"

"You don't." And her eyes warmed on him. "But I wish you did."

A slave summoned her to her father's bedside, and Pertinax took his leave in a strange tangle of emotions.

He was dumfounded. That this girl could belong to the strange new sect, which was said to comprise only the dregs of the underworld, was simply incredible. Yet she had admitted as much. She had walked suddenly into his life and heart; none the less, Joe Pertinax knew she was there to stay. And yet, to find that she belonged to this cult—well, it was pretty stiff!

Near the entrance to the villa, he came face to face with one of the priests of Isis. The shaven Egyptian lifted his staff, and in silence pointed to the ground. Looking down, Pertinax abruptly started back. A deadly reptile was there by his foot, a cobra, coiled and in the very act of striking.

Then the priest touched the snake with his staff. Before the very eyes of Pertinax the serpent collapsed and became a lump of inanimate stone. Smiling grimly, the priest held up a hand—and Joe Pertinax remembered nothing more.

Like a man a-dream, he went his way, moving mechanically; his eyes were like those of the staring dead. When he neared the docks, he encountered a throng of the island folk in high excitement. Their language was strange to him. He knew not what was going on. A sudden tumult broke around him, and knives were whipped out.

Men rushed about, jostling him; he lashed right and left with his fists to clear a passage. A knife sliced at him, not deeply but angrily. With a roar of fury, Pertinax caught a staff from the nearest man and laid about him. Bones were cracked; heads were broken; men went sprawling. Then a dozen of the ship's crew appeared. They charged to the rescue and bore Pertinax off to the ship. He was dazed; he could remember nothing; his whole upper left arm had been slit by the knife.

Captain Stentor bandaged the hurt. Certain leaders of the townsfolk came aboard, angrily demanding that Pertinax be punished; they said he had wantonly attacked them, and insisted upon a trial. Now, the only magistrate in the island was Publius, a justice of the peace, occupying the bench of his father. The skipper stood up before those men and laughed at them.

"You try an officer of mine, who's a Roman citizen? Not much. If any of your men die and it becomes a murder charge, Pertinax appeals to Cæsar and goes to Rome for trial. Clear out of here, and do it damned quick!"

The crew said admiringly that for once Cap'n Stentor acted like a man.

The skipper took Pertinax to his own cabin, called in two of the stewards, and slapped down a document before the chief officer.

"Sign this requisition of stores, Joe," said he.

Submissive, unquestioning, Pertinax signed, and the two men witnessed his signature. Scarcely was this done and the document put away, with a glitter in the dark eye of Captain Stentor, when there rose a tumult of voices on deck.

Here came young Publius himself, excited and in hot haste.

"Stentor! A shepherd just came in from the other side of the island with word that a big ship was wrecked there last night. Most or all of the ship's company were saved. A corn ship, they say. It must be the *Diana!*"

Stentor leaped up with an oath.

"The *Diana!* Then we've lost a pile of money, my lad. Here, wait!" He glanced at the expressionless Pertinax. "You hear that, Joe? How'd you like to go and draw up a report on the loss?"

"All right," said Pertinax blankly. Stentor swung around to Publius, talked under his breath for a moment, and winked.

"Pick a couple of townsmen to guide him—men you can rely on. Understand? We'll be rid of him for once and all."

So Pertinax, his arm in a sling, departed with two guides.

"Here's the confession that you yourself signed, regarding your culpability for the collision with that Greek trader. On board with him, men—and keep him locked up!"

Scarcely were the three of them beyond sight, of the town, when those two men whipped out knives and went for him. Clouded his mind might be, but the one-armed Pertinax was no sheep for the slaughter. He laid out one man with his staff, and the second dropped his knife and shrieked for mercy.

"All right. Lead on," said Pertinax in his dull, staring way.

Some hours later, Pertinax arrived at the scene of shipwreck, where the crew of the *Diana,* with her passengers and soldiers, were being cared for by the country folk. Pertinax was warmly greeted by the ship's officers, who knew him well.

Close to three hundred souls were here, and among them a man who was treated with singular respect by the others. Curious things were said of him. This was the Jewish prisoner Paul, in charge of Julius the centurion.

As Pertinax was making notes for his report, the centurion came to where he sat with Captain Ariston, and saluted him.

"Greetings," said Julius bluntly. "My prisoner demands speech with you."

"What does he want?" Pertinax said mechanically.

"He says you have need of him. Perhaps he means your hurt arm. He's a healer."

Pertinax stared up dully. Captain Ariston, elderly and broken, went apart with the centurion and spoke frowningly.

"Something wrong with Joe Pertinax. He doesn't seem drunk, but he's not himself. He doesn't seem to know how he got wounded. I don't understand it."

"It's not my affair." The centurion shrugged. "But we all know this Jew has made some remarkable predictions. Then there was that business of the snake who bit him last night but did him no harm. He's insistent on speaking with this man Pertinax."

"Then fetch him along, by all means."

The prisoner, who enjoyed complete freedom of action, was a tall, gaunt man, so remarkable in his sheer force of character as to dominate the whole group. He had brilliant and penetrating eyes under shaggy brows, and a face like a rock. He came to Pertinax, looked into his face for a moment, and touched his arm.

"Take off the bandage," he ordered.

Captain Ariston removed the bloodstained wrappings, and uttered a sharp exclamation. There was no wound, merely a closed scar. The gaunt Jew put out his hand and touched the eyes of Pertinax.

"Let the evil spirit come out of this man!" he said sonorously.

There was a moment of silence. Then Pertinax stirred. He stared around, leaped to his feet, and cried out sharply:

"Ariston! You here? Where are we—"

His voice died, surprise and bewilderment struggling in his face. As though wakening from dream, he had no comprehension of where he was, until the others explained matters. To the rest, it looked singularly as though he had really been drunk. Pertinax himself did not know what to think or say.

But once he had the situation in hand, he went ahead with his report, and presently the whole company set forth for town. As they went, Pertinax fell in with Paul and the centurion.

Paul questioned him about the town, about himself. All his mental cloud gone now, Pertinax fell into eager talk with this man, whose strange personal force and unbounded vigor was fascinating and astonishing. Paul eyed him grimly.

"Young man, I was sent to this place for you and for others," said he. "Rejoice not that the evil spirit is departed out of you, for another and more bitter trial is at hand."

His words were hard to comprehend. The centurion nudged Pertinax and told him to watch his step and not stir the Jew up to any religious talk, or the man would prate on by the hour.

When they drew near town, a huge crowd came out to meet the refugees. Captain Stentor and most of his ship's company were there, with Publius and townsfolk and guards. The first thing Pertinax knew, men had closed around him and he was under arrest.

"Arrest?" he cried indignantly. "On what charge? Hey, Cap'n Stentor! What's all this about?"

"Plenty," said the skipper. "Two of the townsmen are dying this moment from your blows. Further,"—and he showed a signed and witnessed document,—"here's the confession you yourself signed, regarding that matter of graft in the cabin-stores account, and your culpability for the collision with that Greek trader. On board with him, men, and keep him locked up."

Confession? Amazed and bewildered, Joe Pertinax was clapped into irons and taken aboard the ship. But the fact that his arm was unhurt caused much wonder.

That evening, the two priests of Isis sat in talk with Captain Stentor, in the house he had rented for the winter. All three of them were in high spirits. Publius had definitely engaged the two priests to cure his father, and the fee was a fat one, in advance. The skipper, who got a share of the "take," had engaged to give the priests his full protection, should aught go amiss with them.

"But how was my chief officer's wound healed?" he asked in perplexity. "And he's recovered from the spell you laid upon him. It's all due to that Syrian or Jew who came with the *Diana's* people. How did he do it?"

"Clever people, these Jews," said one of the priests. "But always nosing into other people's business. We must get rid of him."

Presently, after some talk, Captain Stentor went out to find Captain Ariston and his pilot Myron.

They were indignant with him for arresting Pertinax, until he said his say. Then they became thoughtful.

"Now," went on Stentor cheerfully, "the notes Joe Pertinax made for his report cast the full blame on you and your officers for the loss. You know what that means, boys. Loss of your tickets. No pension. A lay-off for good. And maybe a heavy fine. You dumped your cargo, and that means hell to pay. I clapped Pertinax in irons, so he won't talk; I've got plenty of charges against him. I'll see you through this."

"But how far will this island magistrate go?" demanded Cap'n Ariston.

"The limit," said Stentor. "Don't worry about him. He's fixed. And before the winter's out, I'll marry his sister. Pertinax will be broken; can't help that. And nobody cares about a Jew. Do you go through with it?"

"Guess we'll have to," said Cap'n Ariston, wagging his gray beard....

Aboard his ship, Pertinax sat talking with the chief steward Demetrius, and knew himself a lost man, without realizing how it had happened. Demetrius could give him small consolation.

"You were drunk, Joe, no doubt about it. First came that scrap ashore—two men dying from it now. Then you came aboard and signed that confession; no man in his right senses would have done it, but you did it. The skipper holds all the cards. I hate to admit it, but you're hooked."

"I tell you, I never had a drink!" Pertinax cried angrily. "I just don't recall a thing that happened. Last I remember is meeting one of those damned Egyptians, outside the villa of Publius. Everything else is vague and shadowy."

Demetrius eyed him dubiously. "Well, you sure acted drunk when you came aboard. Now the Old Man saddles you with his own graft, with negligence in that collision, and with responsibility for that row ashore. It means your ticket is gone, Joe. And on the way to make the shipwreck report, you attacked those two guides. Remember?"

"No," snapped Pertinax helplessly, and gave way to dour despair.

Next day, when Demetrius brought in his lunch, he slipped Pertinax a bit of papyrus, with a wink. It was a note from Lydia, short and to the point:

> *Cheer up. We're working for you. Paul says that in two days you'll be free.*

Pertinax snorted scornfully. Paul, indeed! He might have known Lydia would get in touch with that gaunt Jew, who seemed so highly regarded by these Christians. Well, the fellow might be a magician and a healer, but here were cold hard facts, not so easily sloughed off....

It was on this same afternoon that Publius, sitting as magistrate, summoned Julius the centurion before him. Captain Stentor laid forth a complaint, which was backed up by Captain Ariston and the officers of the *Diana.* Paul the Jew was accused of having caused the loss of the great corn ship by his wizardry and spells.

"Your prisoner, Julius," said the young magistrate, "is evidently a dangerous person. The statements of these ship officers all agree."

"Then they lie," said the centurion calmly. "Or it may be that you've caused them to lie. Had they heeded the advice of this man, the ship wouldn't have gone down."

"You're no seaman," Publius said. "You allow this prisoner at large. As magistrate, I won't have it. He's a public enemy, a Christian, a wizard. I want him kept in close confinement and in chains."

"What you want, and what an officer of Cæsar's may do, are two different things," replied the centurion with open scorn. "So they're trying to blame him for the shipwreck, eh? The rats can't do it. He'll not be chained; and if anything happens to him at your hands, I have plenty of soldiers to hold you to account, Publius."

"I think," said Captain Stentor, "that I have some authority here."

"I don't." The centurion turned on him. "You're a Corn Line skipper, huh? Well, by the gods, I'm a centurion of the Augustan Legion—and you can be damned!"

The hearing promised to grow interesting, when tumultuous shouts sounded from the street. Men came running. Into the courtroom stalked a figure which brought Publius out of his seat, all staring and slack-jawed. It was his father, Publius the elder, who came toward the magistrate's bench with an excited crowd following.

"Well, my son?" he said, smiling. "You see I'm cured. As well as ever, and all done in a moment! What's going on here?"

"Praised be the gods!" cried his son. "Then the Egyptians cured you!"

"Egyptians? Not much! Those two fools were

"Young man, I was sent to this place for you and for others," said Paul.

torturing me with their mummery when the Jew came in," said his father. "At the touch of his hand, I was healed. I believe that you're hearing some complaint against him? Well, I'll hear it myself. Your power is revoked. Turn over the bench to me."

Indeed, Publius seemed in perfect health once more, so that amazement and wonder fell upon all those in the courtroom. Taking his place on the bench, Publius the elder gave an order, and the crowd parted to let Paul come through.

The gaunt Jew nodded to the centurion, then fastened his penetrating gaze upon Captain Stentor.

"There is no need of a hearing," he said in his slightly accented Greek. "The first officer of the *Castor and Pollux* has investigated this shipwreck and will bear witness to the truth. This man here, who brings false testimony in all things, bears the seal of death in his face. Let him go, nor listen to his charges; for when the sun sets, he will be gathered to his fathers. Those who sin without law, shall also perish without law."

There fell a dread silence. Captain Stentor rose and tried to speak. A pallor stole into his swarthy features. He could utter no words. Under the undeviating gaze of the tall gaunt Jew, he suddenly turned and strode out of the courtroom.

Now came guards, bringing with them the two priests of Isis. Those dour men stalked in, grimly proud and scornful.

"Is there any charge against us?" one of them demanded.

"There is," said Publius. "I saw enough of your rascally doings while I lay sick and dying. You're fakers and grafters. You've extorted money from my son under false pretenses."

"The judge cannot be accuser, for that is the law," said one of the Egyptians scornfully. "Who, then, is it that accuses us?"

"I," spoke out the gaunt Jew, Paul. "I accuse you of spells and sorcery. Pertinax, chief officer of the *Castor and Pollux,* will bear witness against you, and will himself lay fresh accusation."

"And what of it?"

"Just this." Paul stretched forth his arm, pointing at them. "What you do for money, I do for love. What you do in the name of Isis and by power of the devil, I do in the name and by the power of God."

The magistrate Publius leaned forward, frowning.

"I do not quite comprehend," he said. "Paul, do you desire to lay charges against these men whom you accuse? Do you seek their punishment?"

Paul, grim and gaunt, regarded the two priests, and his deep eyes flamed.

"Such is not the faith I preach," said he slowly. "It is not I, but God, who requires punishment. The vast silence of the sea is the patience of God. Loose these men. Let them go their way and seek their own appointed destiny, for it comes not by my hand. Woe unto you, Egyptians! When you draw the knife, it shall be turned against you both!"

"A fine court, this, where a prisoner gives orders," one of the two priests said. They walked out, with no man hindering them.

Now, Captain Stentor had gone out to his own ship, and with him Captain Ariston and the officers of the *Diana,* in no little confusion and anger. Once in the cabin, Captain Stentor listened to them; he was white and shaken, a queer look in his eyes.

"You've made a fine mess of things, Stentor," said Captain Ariston. "You persuaded us to throw all blame on that Jew. Well, I didn't like it from the start. Something about that fellow it doesn't pay to monkey with. And now where are we? The centurion gives us the lie. The magistrate's father walks in and changes the whole set-up. This Jew suddenly towers over everyone in sight, and now—"

A groan broke from Cap'n Stentor. Sweat was standing out on his face.

"Forget it all, forget it!" he cried in a passionate burst of words. "I'm a sick man; my heart's been acting up. That accursed Jew told the truth. Somebody get me a doctor! Give up the whole thing. I tricked Pertinax into signing that confession. He didn't know what he was doing."

The skipper struggled to his feet. They stared at him, alarmed by his ghastly aspect.

"I confess the whole thing," he groaned bitterly. "Go shoulder your own blame, Ariston. That Jew has cursed me; I'm a dead man, I tell you, Clear out, and send me a doctor! Dismiss the charges, all of'em—"

He stumbled away into his own cabin and slammed the door. The officers of the *Diana* exchanged startled glances. Then Captain Ariston shrugged.

"All right, lads; come along. We were damned fools to try and shift the blame. We'll withdraw the charges and forget it."

So they went ashore, and on their way passed a boat that was bringing the two priests of Isis aboard the ship.

These Egyptians tried to see Stentor, but the skipper refused to admit them. For a space they talked together, angrily. Their entire scheme had come to naught because of the chief officer. The Jew mattered little, but this fellow Pertinax was dangerous.

"He's the nub of the whole business," said the older priest craftily. "This accursed skipper has lost his nerve; first thing we know, he'll set Pertinax free, and then the fat's in the fire. But we can still save the day. For our own sake, we must do it. Stentor undertook to get rid of him—and failed. But we will not fail!"

So the two priests of Isis came to their decision. One thing was sure in this world of uncertainty—a dead man can bear all blame, can carry anything charged against him, without any chance of back-talk.

One of the two priests went to the guard at the door of the chief officer's cabin, and fell into talk with that man. After a time the seaman stood stiff and wooden, like a man dead. Then the other priest came. They unbarred the cabin door and walked in.

Pertinax, loosely chained, came to his feet at sight of them. Their glittering eyes, their tensed, sweating features, gave him warning enough.

As one of the two began to lay a spell upon him, Pertinax knew that in another moment he would be hypnotized and helpless, as before. He flung himself furiously upon the two priests. Their knives flashed out; they took him between them.

But they dealt with no man bemused and wandering of wit. Joe Pertinax had seen knife-work in many a waterfront brawl. He tripped up one of the priests; he caught the other's knife-arm between his chained wrists. Reeling, staggering in a frantic death-grapple, the two antagonists stumbled across the priest who had fallen.

The Egyptian held in Pertinax's grip shrieked out—the knife of the fallen priest had gone up through his back, as he went down. But the tripped priest, writhing clear, snatched up the weapon of the dying man.

He flung himself on Pertinax and bore the chief officer back. The knife rose and fell, but missed its aim.

And as it missed, Pertinax caught the brown wrist in his two chained hands.

They clung, thus, for a long and desperate moment, face to sweating face. Suddenly Joe Pertinax brought up one chained leg. He whipped it clear over the head of the Egyptian, and then flung forth all his strength. His leg bent back the brown torso; his hands gripped the other man's wrist; their straining bodies were tangled like those of two intertwined snakes.

In this frightful wrench which had tore him apart, the Egyptian looked at the knife. Next instant Pertinax had the blade, and shoved it home, up into the brown straining throat.

It was then they came rushing in upon him, Demetrius and the others; and it was thus they found him. Captain Stentor had sent for him; the skipper was dying. They struck off his chains, and all bloody as he was, hurried him to the Captain's cabin.

"You—you're acting master, Joe," gasped the dying man, clutching at his heart. "I'm done for. Something gave way, here. I've confessed. Forgive me, lad—forgive me!"

"Aye," said Pertinax.

In the cold, clear sunlight of morning, Pertinax sat ashore talking with Lydia and her father Publius. Word had just come that the two men gravely hurt in the riot were recovering.

"Paul went to see them," said the girl, radiant, wide-eyed. "He put his hand on them and healed them, as he did you, Father. They confessed that my brother gave them money to start that riot and to kill Joe, here."

The magistrate's head was bent in chagrin and sorrow.

"Pertinax, you must prefer charges against my son. He conspired with Stentor and with those Egyptians. It is your duty and mine to see that he is duly punished."

Joe Pertinax shook his head, thoughtfully.

"Nope. Remember telling me what that Jew said in court—the vast silence of the sea is like the patience of God? You know, there's a lot of truth in that. Any seaman can appreciate it. There's something terrible and mystical in the silence of the sea. I wonder how a Jew came to think of such a thing?"

Then he roused, and broke into a whimsical smile.

"Forget the charges," he said. "Those against the Jew have collapsed. I'm in the clear myself. I don't want any punishing. You know, I'm hanged if I can see what to make of this whole business! If Paul has done these things, then he's some god. I just don't believe the yarns about him. They're too tall for me to swallow."

The girl was staring past him. Publius rose.

Joe Pertinax looked around and hastily jumped to his feet. The gaunt Jew was standing in the doorway, regarding them.

"Well, it's a fact. Since you heard me, I stick to it," blurted out Pertinax. "Come, be honest! You can't expect me to believe this nonsense. Either you're some kind of a god, or else you're not."

Paul looked at him for a moment, with a slow smile.

"In your present state of mind, young man, I can't expect you to show much sense at all," he said dryly. "And considering the cause, I don't particularly blame you, either; I was once young myself, strange as it may seem. —Publius, I want to talk with you! Come along, and give these young folks a chance to readjust the world as they'd have it."

The two departed.

Joe Pertinax gazed after them; then he swung around to Lydia.

"Well, can you beat that! Mind-reader, that's what he is. There's something about him that gets you."

"Then you do believe in him, Joe?"

"Upon my word, Lydia—whether I believe all the yarn or not, Rome certainly wouldn't believe it. Suppose we talk it over. We have a good three months in which to discuss it."

She smiled quickly, reading his eyes. "You do! In your heart, you know the truth—and you just won't admit it!"

Pertinax started to speak, only to check himself, as the voice of the gaunt Jew drifted to them from somewhere outside.

"Truth," it said, "is from heaven."

"There's your answer," Pertinax said softly, and touched the arm of the girl. "Your answer, Lydia, and mine. And now I'd better get that report on the *Diana* drawn up before—well, before I get to believing too much!"

Long centuries later, the report was exhumed, along with a mass of other documents from the Corn Line offices. It was brief:

> *The Diana, lost by hurricane off Malta, is a total loss. Due to seamanship of master and pilot, the crew and passengers all saved. Investigation shows no blame attached.*
>
> *J. Pertinax, Acting Master*
> *Castor and Pollux.*

But of the winter months in Malta, ere the great corn ship set forth for Rome, of the bride who sailed in her, of the gaunt prisoner and the centurion who escorted him—these things are to be sought elsewhere, and the tale thereof.

SON OF THE DRAGON KING

It happened in Canton last year, before ever an enemy bomb had wrought havoc and horror. Chinese friends were entertaining me. Sui Lo was a gorgeous young woman; she had a degree from Berkeley and another from Columbia, but tonight she masked her loveliness with Oriental robes, and acted as translator.

The dinner had lasted three hours. I think there were thirty-seven courses up to the time I lost count. Now we sat out in the garden under a full moon. We looked out across the Pearl River, with its city of water-dwellers who spent their whole lives in boats, to the Huangpo or Yellow Anchorage island. The moonlight was clear and intense.

My hosts were talking about the various kinds of junks, which are legion. Then a huge ghostly shape came drifting down the river, an ocean-going junk.

Sui Lo clapped her hands delightedly.

"What does it look like?" she cried.

"Like a squatting Pekinese dog," I said. At this, they all laughed.

"No," she replied. "Like a dragon! Because it looks like a dragon, and is made like a dragon; it has painted eyes and teeth."

"I thought the eyes were for junks to see with?"

"Oh, no," she said. "My people are not so silly. It was a night like this that the celestial fairy visited the young man Ming, and it was over yonder on that very island. He was the son of the Dragon King of the ocean."

"Is that some fairy story?" I asked.

She was actually shocked. A fairy story? Not a bit of it. An actual, true story of happenings in China's golden age, under the T'ang dynasty.

Back in those days the Yellow Anchorage island was entirely owned by the merchant Li King, greatest of all Canton merchants. He lived on the island, he lavished money on it, and because of its beautiful gardens, it was known as the Garden of Green Gems.

Li King was wise and tolerant, for wisdom and tolerance flourished then; the poet was greater than the soldier, and beauty was sought afar. Li King had no sons and but one daughter, who was named Pure Jade.

His ships were many; his trading enterprises were vast. It was in one of his ships that the priest Kien Cheng made his celebrated voyage to Japan, in 742 A.D. His diary of the trip is still in existence today....

To Li King, therefore, was brought the mysterious stranger, with two frightful sword-slashes in his body and nothing else, except a girdle of the most glorious green gem jade that the rich merchant had ever laid eyes upon. Green jade was then very little known, jade being all black or yellow or white.

The captain of a salt-carrier from the coast, who had brought the hurt man to Canton, took Li King to see the stranger.

"Honorable Li," the skipper reported, "we found him in a small boat, nearly dead. He has never recovered consciousness. From his delirious mutterings, we learned that his name must be Ming. Because of this jade girdle, he must be some great prince. Therefore, I ask what disposition shall be made of him ere he dies. It is not possible for him to recover from such wounds."

Li King observed the hurt man attentively. Young, vigorous, handsome, girded with an emperor's ransom; decidedly, no ordinary person. Racing pulse and high fever: a man doomed, if left to himself. Here on the Pearl River, Canton was sweltering in midsummer heat, but the island was cool and quiet.

"Carry him to the island," said Li King gravely. "I will place him in one of the summer pavilions. Perhaps Jung Miao can save his life. Leave the girdle with him, for it is his property. Was nothing else in his boat?"

"Only a broken knife of no value, venerable Li. Here it is."

A plain knife, the long, keen blade broken at the haft. Li King gave orders to have it welded and returned to Ming. Then he sent gifts to Jung Miao, the most accomplished healer in Canton, asking that he come and look over the patient.

Jung Miao was a man of forty, lean and cruel-eyed, with the three holes of his initiation as a Taoist priest burned into his shaven skull. Like all Taoists, he was a proficient magician, and some extremely dark and ugly stories were told about his magic works.

He came and examined the patient, and his eyes widened at sight of the jade girdle. On every other piece of jade making up the girdle was lightly graven a dragon; on each alternating piece, a phœnix, of exquisite carving.

"This is a wondrous thing, venerable Li," said he, with greedy gaze. "It is the famous girdle of Wang Chi, the scholar of ancient days; its owner has power over all spirits. The man will live, but his cure will be slow and arduous. Give me the girdle for my fee."

"The girdle is his to give, not mine," said Li King. "I will pay your fee."

Jung Miao did not like this reply, but agreed to take the case. After some time Li King was taken with the summer fever and had something else to think of than the stranger occupying the pavilion in a far corner of the island.

Yet—out of this beginning arose all the greatness of China by sea, and her towering commerce with the southern countries and the islands beyond.

*Upon a day, Ming opened his eyes and was con*scious—but so weak he could not move a finger. From where he lay he could look, on one side, across part of the Garden of Green Gems, and on the other side through the willows and across the river, teeming with water craft, to the city. He lay staring for a long time, until a moving object in the garden caught his eye. This was a girl in green robes, very graceful in every movement; her brows were delicately arched, and she was singing as she moved among the flowers. She paused beside the turquoise pond with its dotted lotus leaves and its dwarf trees, and then came close to the pavilion. Ming lifted his voice and addressed her.

"Are you a fairy goddess, and is this some place of the immortals who dwell in the Western Mountains?"

She started in alarm, then came into the pavilion and looked at him.

"Not so, honorable sir," she said. "I am Chong Yu, the daughter of Li King. You have been here many days. I am rejoiced that you have come to your senses."

"Pure Jade!" he said, repeating her name. "It is lovely, and you are lovely, and this is the loveliest place I have ever seen. How did I come here?"

"You were found in a boat," she said, and told him all of it.

"It is a fairy story," said he, smiling. "It is not real. I am in a dream and shall waken unhappily. While I am dreaming, will you sit down and tell me more about this place?"

"Yes. First tell me who you are."

"My unworthy name is Ming," he replied. "I am a seaman, a builder of ships. If you are indeed a fairy, then I am the son of the Dragon King of the Ocean."

He said this in jest, but before he could say more, sleep came upon him, his eyes closed, and he did not waken again until the next morning. By this time, Pure Jade had repeated his words to others, so that the slave girl who was attending him stood in great fear and awe of him. When he found that he was really supposed to be the son of the Dragon King, he laughed a little and let it go at that.

"But where is the fairy Pure Jade?" he asked. The slave girl went away to call her mistress.

Ming wondered at his luck, as he lay there. He was no fine gentleman of China; he had none of the education which was the basis of all aristocracy. He had not the faintest idea of his family. He had grown up among fishermen and pirates down the coast, and piracy was his whole life. Piracy, which involved seamanship, building of ships, handling them, fighting, holding his own. Survival of the fittest. Somewhere there must have been good blood in him, for it showed in his ways and looks.

Now he laughed as he lay here, and looked at the jade girdle set on a stand near his bed. Loot out of a north China ship—loot and a grand fight. This was all he could remember. Somehow he had won clear. And now he was in Canton, living out a fairy story!

Pure Jade came and sat near him, and talked, while her attendants played on musical instruments or sang songs. But Ming looked out over the crowded shipping. He saw there ships he knew well: Chinese coasters, river junks, salt junks from the south, ships from Po-se or the Malay coasts, from Java and Borneo and Siam. And it came into his mind there and then that he had a fortune in his hand for the taking, and all the gifts of destiny, if he played his cards aright.

The merchant Li King, very weak and wan from his fever, was carried in a litter through the gardens, and stopped to speak with Ming, the litter being placed beside Ming's bed. After the proper politeness, they spoke together of ships and trade, and the river-routes, and the far sea argosies.

"You have the wisdom of the great oceans," Li King said. "Before you leave here, son of the Dragon King, you must teach me some of it. I am not satisfied to be master of the rivers and canals. I seek new things."

Those words lingered with Ming—*"I seek new things."* He saw that this man was wise and far-sighted, used to vast enterprises, yet realizing that there were greater horizons for the finding.

*Talking with Pure Jade and others of the house*hold, Ming perceived for the first time the greatness of a peaceful and calm existence ruled by the head, not by the hand. And then one day Jung Miao came into his pavilion, dark and tall and smiling thinly upon him, like some figure from an evil dream.

"You will lie here a long time; but thanks to me, you will live," said he. "Tell me where you got this jade girdle."

"From the palace of my father, the Dragon King," said Ming.

"Indeed? Well, I have heard stories, queer stories," said the Taoist. "We will not discuss them now—later, when you are feeling stronger: Stories about pirates on the east coast, and one of their leaders who is supposed to be dead. Guard that jade girdle well; it is possessed of great magic powers. I am leaving you the powdered bones of ancient dragons. One dose each day, and fail not."

He went away, leaving Ming with the distinct impression of evil brewing. This Taoist knew or guessed the truth.

Pure Jade came repeatedly. Sometimes Ming played the flute as he lay, for this was his one accomplishment. Half jestingly, wondering that anyone could believe such things, he would describe the marvels of the Dragon King's palace beneath the ocean. At times he desired to tell the truth about this little joke, but memory of Jung Miao halted him, warned him. He might yet need friends.

"It is quite clear to me," said Chao. "Jung Miao keeps Ming in his power by means of medicines. There is some great evil force at work, but I cannot see its object."

He questioned Pure Jade about her father. *"I seek new things"*—the words haunted him somehow. She told him how Li King was eager for new enterprises, how his commerce reached afar.

"Tell your father," he said to her one day, "that if he will come to me tomorrow and talk awhile, I will reveal to him certain teachings and wisdom of the Dragon King my father."

All delight and eagerness, the girl departed. Ming looked up at the jade girdle on its mount, and smiled. He knew now what he would do with this wondrous jewel; he destined it for this girl, who had opened to him a new idea of life.

Li King came to the pavilion next day, walking weakly, supported by two servants. These arranged cushions for him beside the couch of Ming. Wine was brought, and a heating brazier, and the hot wine was poured into tiny cups of gray jade.

"To your health, venerable Li," said Ming, and drank. "Ah! That is good wine."

"It is the finest product of Shaohsing, but I fear it is poor stuff compared with what you get at home,"

Li rejoined politely. "My daughter tells me that you wish to impart to me certain wisdom of your father. I am unworthy of such an honor, but I will receive it with humble appreciation."

Ming pointed out to the river and its crowded shipping.

"Your barges and junks go everywhere in China, by the rivers and canals," he said. "But your seamen fear the ocean."

"That is true," said Li King. "We do as our ancestors did."

"You seek new things; I will show you the way," Ming replied. "Out there, I see ships from the southern islands, Malayan ships, Siamese ships and others. They come here to Canton, bringing trade. Why do not your ships go also to their countries, seeking their trade? Why should it come to you?"

"For the very reasons you have just uttered, in your wisdom," the merchant said. "Our ships are not big enough to withstand the ocean, our seamen are afraid of it. We do as our ancestors did."

"Yet you seek new things!" said Ming, and smiled. He thoroughly understood the oblique mind of the man before him, and knew that the only way to reach it was by an oblique method. "If I show you a way to seek commerce in these far countries, would you do it?"

"That depends on the way," evaded Li gravely, though his eyes sparkled at the prospect. "The Dragon King, my son, is very cruel to our poor ships."

"Right!" exclaimed the young man. "And why? Because they do not do him honor. Now, if I could show you how to travel on dragons, that would honor the Dragon King of the Ocean, and he would then favor you. Your ringers could reach to far countries, with his favor."

Li King caught his breath at this.

"Do you mean ships like dragons?" he asked.

"Exactly," agreed Ming. "Ships in the form of dragons, which I can show your master builders how to construct."

"Ah! But you will not be able to leave your couch for a long time!"

"Bring the men to me," said Ming. "Even a helpless cripple may be of some use in the world, perhaps. But venerable Li, does the prospect appeal to you?"

"Yes!" exclaimed the merchant eagerly. "Yes! It is like pleasant words heard in a dream. However, I warn you my master builders are practical men. In talking with them, you must be both practical and explicit."

"Leave that to me," Ming said. "If I convince them, will you build such a ship?"

"Not one, but fifty of them—a hundred!" exclaimed Li with energy, as his mind envisioned the possibilities. Then his caution returned. "This, however, must depend upon the master builders. I doubt whether they would understand the conception of building a dragon. Better to describe it as a ship. You and I alone will know that it is to be so built as to become acceptable to your venerable father the Dragon King."

"Right," said Ming, smiling slightly.

In the morning Li returned, bringing with him the three master builders of his shipyard. These greeted Ming respectfully.

"I desire your help," said Ming with the greatest tact, "in designing a ship so large that she can cross the ocean to the southern islands and yet be safe from the pirates of the eastern coasts."

"A ship of great size cannot withstand the shattering blows of ocean waves," said one of the three.

"That is true," Ming said. "Therefore the hull, for strength, should be divided into watertight compartments. And instead of using light wood, she should be built from the teak whose beams are used to hold up the roofs of houses and temples."

"A ship is fastened together with bolts or nails," objected a builder. "Nails will not hold in teak, because the wood is so hard; often it even blunts nails."

"You are right," assented Ming. "Therefore I suggest that the ship be trenailed or pegged together. This will lend elasticity and increase strength. The keel, middle keelson, side-stringers, reverse frames, ribs—everything should be fastened together by scarfing, fitting and joining. Thus no water will have a hole through which to creep."

The master builders conferred, and declared this to be feasible.

"Such a ship must have great cargo space," went on Ming. "She must be high in the stern and square in the bows, and high-sided so that pirates cannot board her easily. She must have a deep rudder and keel. This is possible?"

One of the builders grinned. "She'd look like a dog with its head down and its tail high!"

"Precisely! Or, let us say, like a dragon swimming on the water." And Ming cast a glance at Li King. "Such a dragon would frighten off all evil spirits and water devils. You could build such a ship?"

They questioned him regarding size and dimensions. He answered readily to all they asked, one of them noting down his replies and roughly sketching the craft. The three conferred again, and one made reply for all.

"Venerable elder brother, such a ship could certainly be built, but who could sail her? To handle such weight, she must have many sails. Off the coast, the winds are sudden and violent, and many sails cannot be taken in or loosed with rapidity."

"On the contrary!" Ming came to one elbow, leaned over, and traced with his finger in the dust to illustrate his words.

"The ship must have three masts, not one. Each mast with one sail like this. Here is a lug-sail, the most effective for sailing of all. It must be stiffened by battens, and bent both to the yard and the boom. It is kept to the mast by a hauling-parrel, and fitted with topping-lifts on both sides of the sail—thus. As you can see, in case of a squall it can be lowered on the instant, and is a handy rig without an equal. I suggest that you try out this rig with a craft on the river, before giving your decision."

The master builders, who were used only to the square matting sail of river craft, and who paid no attention to the rig of foreign ships, decided to accept this suggestion. Also, they wished to test the figures Ming had given on the dimensions, weight and displacement of a large ship built from teak.

They departed. A little later Pure Jade came to the pavilion in search of her father; but he had gone with the builders, and she remained for a few words with Ming. Alone together, speech failed them. The color in the girl's face, her downcast eyes, her modesty, heightened her beauty.

Ming was about to cast loose restraint and utter everything that was in his swelling heart, when a shadow fell across the threshold. In the entrance stood Jung Miao, looking sternly at them.

Pure Jade fell into confusion at being discovered thus alone with a young man, for this was contrary to all the Rites. She hastily withdrew. The Taoist came forward and grimly examined his patient.

"Very good," he said at last. "Take no more powdered bones of dragons. I have here an elixir made from the horns of snails dissolved in the blood of toads. Take one dose of this elixir every other day, and in a month from now you'll be on your feet."

"Venerable ancestor, your skill is superhuman," murmured Ming.

"True," said Jung Miao, a flash in his dark eyes. He sank down and spoke in a low voice. "You are dealing with one who has strange forces at his command, young man. If I am a friend, you will find me valuable. I am about to propose something to you which will bring us both vast wealth. First, let me convince you of my power. I am about to leave with you two guardians, spirits who serve me faithfully."

From his pouch he took two scraps of paper on which sacred characters were inscribed. He tossed

The first dragon ship

in the blood of victims. Thought of him brought agony. It was like some evil touch from the dark past.

"I see you recognize the name!" And Jung Miao smiled. "Tse Kin is in Canton. He came searching for a leader of his associates who was lost, a young man named Ming. With Ming departed all the luck of those pirates. Now they seek him, in order to make him their sole leader and chief. And it has occurred to me that, when this is done, these pirates and others might be assembled here in Canton, make a sudden outbreak, loot most of the city and be gone again to their home on the coast. Think it over, young man. There is no hurry. And do not speak of it to anyone, or these two guardians will slay you and all others in this place."

The two warriors clashed their armor to emphasize the words, and Jung Miao departed, smiling.

Ming lay in a cold sweat, trembling, a tumult of agitation in his spirit. All in a moment, his whole house of cards came tumbling down about him; he saw that a man cannot escape his past. His pleasant life here, his hopes of the future, his plans and dreams—all were shattered.

He stared up at the two guardians. When he spoke to them, they made no answer. They withdrew to the entrance and stood on either side of it, immobile, ominous, silent. From time to time he caught their fierce gaze fixed upon him.

Tse Kin here! Himself made leader of that wild pirate horde! At the very thought, repulsion seized on him; horror at the plan of the Taoist filled his heart and soul. His ambition, his entire life, had altered. The bare idea of his former existence was frightful to him.

Yet, looking at the matter squarely, he could see that Jung Miao had evolved a scheme whose awful simplicity spelled success. A few hundred pirates here in Canton, rising suddenly and swiftly against the authorities, could spread blood and fire through the

them to the floor. Before the very eyes of Ming, two full-armed warriors sprang up with clash of armor; one held an immense sword, the other a spear. At a word from Jung, the spearman thrust his weapon against the body of Ming so that the keen point scratched the skin; then he withdrew it.

"They obey me, and me alone," said the Taoist. "They shall remain with you. To other eyes they are invisible; but you know the truth, and see them clearly. Now tell me. Do you remember a man called Tse Kin?"

Ming started. Tse Kin—Purple Gold! This man had been one of the chief pirates in the band: an ambitious, crafty, viciously cruel fellow, whose name had been gained from his custom of dipping golden loot whole city, and be off with immense loot before any troops could so much as be brought to restore order.

In other days, he would have thrilled to the notion of such a *coup.* Now it palsied him. Li King, his generous benefactor; Pure Jade, whom he loved; this quiet, peaceful life, this exquisitely beautiful island—all these bathed in blood! Not to mention his own ambitions, his dreams of higher things, sent to ruin! A groan broke from him. Like an echo, came the clash of armor from the two guardians.

Later, when attendants came with food and refreshment, Ming watched with frenzied incredulity. The guardians assumed threatening postures, but the attendants did not so much as see those two figures. Jung Miao had spoken the truth. At the entrance of the pavilion were two little bronze dogs, representing the *fu*-dogs or companions of Buddha, and the two warriors stood beside these dogs, yet were, incredibly, unseen.

That night he took a dose of the elixir, but it did him small good, so worried and agonized was his mind. When Pure Jade came next day, with her attendants, she was struck by the change in him. He longed to make a clean breast of everything, but so wildly and fiercely did those warriors watch him, that he dared not. He spoke to Pure Jade of those guardians; he pointed them out to her, but she saw them not. However, his strange words, his altered looks, troubled her.

"I have here an elixir," said Jung Miao, "made from horns of snails dissolved in the blood of toads. Take it without fail."

Now, at the Spring of the Three Fairies, outside the city, lived the Buddhist monk Chao, a hermit of great age whose knowledge was universal. So revered was Chao for his austere life and good deeds that the Emperor had sent him a robe of honor. Pure Jade resolved to seek the advice and help of this famous man.

Accompanied by her two handmaids, she took gifts and went to the Spring of the Three Fairies. She found Chao sitting before his cave in contemplation, looking like an ancient bag of bones. She knelt politely before him and told about the guest in the garden pavilion, and what had taken place.

"Venerable sage, your unworthy daughter does not know what to think or do," she concluded. "His mind is affected. There are no warriors in the place. Deign, I pray you, give me the benefit of your wisdom and advice."

"It is quite clear to me," said Chao. "The priests of the Taoist faith sometimes subvert occult teachings to their own advantage. Jung Miao is notorious for this, although he is a clever healer. He keeps Ming in his power by means of medicines. There is some great evil force at work, but I cannot see its object."

"Can you advise me, venerable sage? Can you help me?"

"Yes," rejoined the hermit. "I advise you to steal this elixir and replace it with colored water. You saw no warriors there, but Ming could see them plainly. But did you observe anything unusual?"

"Only two bits of paper near the door."

"Good! It is part of Taoist magic to change scraps of paper to living creatures, in the eyes of those whom they delude." The sage reflected for a time, then his brow cleared. "I shall pray to Lord Buddha and to the Queen of the Western Mountains. The superior man should feel it a duty to lend full help against such creatures as this Jung Miao."

He talked for a while longer, and Pure Jade drank in his words eagerly. When she went home, her attendants easily stole the flask of elixir and threw away the contents, replacing it with water of similar color.

Li King and the master builders returned to interview Ming. The rig of his explaining had been carefully tried, and worked to perfection. The shipbuilders' guild had agreed to construct the ship of his dreams, and Li was footing the bills.

At any other time, Ming would have greeted this news with keen delight, but now he only threw despondent glances at the two armored guards, who remained invisible to his visitors, and assented without interest to what was said.

The master builders saluted him and departed. The merchant Li King remained for a private word with him.

"You are not well, my son," he said with solicitude. "I must summon Jung Miao to examine you. Now tell me something. You have described and given dimensions for this ship, which will look in general like a crouching dragon. Will this suffice to make it acceptable to your father, the Dragon King of the Ocean?"

Ming uttered a wild laugh.

"You will find it more seaworthy than any other known craft," he said. "But in order to make it look more like a dragon, you must paint large eyes on the bow. Do this, and the result will be excellent."*

But day and night, the position in which he found himself preyed on Ming's mind. Short of destroying himself, he could see no way in which he could save Canton and his benefactor from the evil schemes of Jung Miao. This keen anxiety brought fever back upon him, so that he had strange fancies and visions.

All his hopes of a glorious future were gone. He no longer dreamed of a great fleet of ships, able to withstand the ocean gales and carry the trade of Canton to all parts of the Yellow Seas; he had no joy in life, and concluded that for him there was no hope, save in death and a new reincarnation.

Then, in the bright sunlight of morning, a glorious figure came slipping down the sunbeams: A lovely girl, radiant as the day, clothed in gems and rare silks, and her face was the face of Pure Jade. As she passed them, the two guardians shrank aside, but she came straight to the couch, and smiled, and stooped to touch his hand.

"Moonlight is my name, and I have been sent to help and comfort you," she said. "Come, put your head in my arms and tell me all that worries you. The prayers of the sage Chao have reached heaven, and those of Pure Jade as well."

"But you are Pure Jade!" murmured the amazed Ming.

The fairy smiled.

"I have assumed her earthly form," she replied. "I wish you to tell me all that is in your mind, so that I may help you."

The two guardians clashed their armor, and bent threatening glances on Ming. But Moonlight sprang up quickly and touched the two bronze images of Lord Buddha's dogs. Instantly these sprang into life and flung themselves at the armed guardians, and chased the warriors from the pavilion.

Ming lay in the arms of the glorious being, and it seemed to him that he was in the arms of Pure Jade herself. A soothing peace stole through his fevered body; he was being anointed with a salve that allayed the inflammation of his wounds.

"This is po-tsan, the famous ointment of Fulin, in the far west of the world," said Moonlight. "It will heal and refresh you. What is your trouble?"

His brain still afire, Ming did not hesitate, but poured out to this celestial creature all his worry. He told of his early life, and how his jesting words about being the son of the Dragon King had been taken in earnest. He told of Jung Miao and what had passed between them, and of the ship that was now being built in the form of a dragon.

"I do not know what to do, and my brain is tortured," he concluded. "I cannot bring disaster upon those whom I have come to love. Yet I must do so, or else be handed over as a pirate, and lose everything here that I have gained. And I love Pure Jade with all my heart and soul."

"Does she love you?" questioned Moonlight.

"I do not know; at least, she looks kindly upon me."

Reaching under the couch, Moonlight drew forth the plain knife that had been in the boat with Ming, and was now welded and repaired. She thrust it under his covers.

"Take this. I must hide, for now Jung Miao is coming, and I wish to hear his evil counsels from his own lips."

She slipped behind a screen in the corner. Ming

**A fact. The usual statement that these painted eyes are for a junk "to see with," is an utter fallacy, unworthy of the Chinese intelligence.*

looked around; she was gone, and the bronze *fu*-dogs had returned to their places. The two warriors came back to the entrance, clashed their armor, and scowled ferociously, but Ming was no longer afraid of them.

Presently Jung Miao appeared. He was not alone this time. With him was a man who wore the blue robe of a scholar; but when Ming saw this man's face, he trembled, recognizing the features of Purple Gold, the pirate.

"I have brought a friend to see you," said Jung Miao.

Purple Gold dropped on his knees beside the couch, greeting Ming with delighted rejoicing, and accusing himself bitterly for having contributed to Ming's present condition.

"We have been deeply punished for our mistreatment of you," he said in shame. "Now that I find you alive, all is well again. You have been elected supreme chief of the pirate bands, under the title of Emperor of the Eastern Coast. As soon as you're able to be on your feet, I'll summon all our men to Canton, and with the help of this honest Taoist we'll get away with such loot as never was known."

"And what does Jung Miao get out of it?" asked Ming.

"A tenth part of all the plunder, and one hundred of the most beautiful slaves who are taken. By his magic, he will aid us in the enterprise."

"I do not wish to do this thing," said Ming bluntly. "My life here is pleasant, and I will not return to the pirates. Elect another chief."

"That is impossible," said the Taoist sternly. "Your name has banded them all together. Without you, they will do nothing. If you refuse, I will turn you over to the magistrates as a pirate, and you shall be publicly executed. Thus you will gain nothing at all."

Ming sighed. "That is true," he assented. "It is evident that I am in your power."

"One word to Li King, and he himself will have you executed," said Jung Miao. "It is much better to choose life and fortune. All men believe that you are the son of the Dragon King. When the moment comes to strike, fifty of your old pirate command will come here, pretending to be envoys from the Dragon King. Once they seize this island, all the shipping is at our mercy, and our men in the city will strike."

"Our men?" said Ming. "Then you intend to become a pirate leader? Very well. Today I am burning with fever and cannot think. Worthy Jung Miao, return tomorrow morning and we will make all arrangements. Leave Purple Gold here with me now, for an hour or two. I wish to talk over old times with him. It will quiet my fever."

"Very well," said the Taoist, and suddenly stamped his foot. There was a burst of smoke, and he was gone. Ming, whose eyes were glittering with fever, laughed aloud at this, and spoke.

"Come closer to me, Purple Gold. Closer still, so that we may speak softly together. Would you indeed force me to do what I do not desire?"

The disguised pirate came very close. "It is for your own best interests, Ming. Think of the slaughter and looting there will be in this city!"

"That is what I am thinking of," said Ming, and suddenly drew forth the knife from under the covers, and plunged it into Purple Gold's throat.

"Moonlight! Moonlight!" he cried; but there was no reply from the fairy. The two guardians clashed their armor and brandished their weapons. At this moment some of the attendants, hearing Ming cry aloud, came running. They halted, aghast, at seeing the bloody knife in his hand and the dead man stretched beside his couch. Ming looked at them with his fever-bright eyes, and spoke.

"Tell me quickly! Do you see two pieces of paper by the entrance? Bring them to me."

The breeze lifted those pieces of paper so that the attendants could scarcely catch them. But to the eyes of Ming, it seemed that those two warriors struggled to evade the clutching hands; however, they were quickly caught and thrust toward him. He drove at them with the knife, again and again.

To the attendants it appeared that he had gone mad, for he was slashing the bits of paper into fragments that blew away with the wind. Then Ming fell back on his pillows, laughing wildly.

The servants sought Li King, and brought him hurriedly. When the master appeared, Ming threw down the knife and spoke

"Venerable Li, this scholar came with Jung Miao and remained to talk with me. I recognized him as one of the leaders of the eastern coast pirates, and killed him. Have his body removed to the yamen of the magistrates where no doubt some of the river captains will recognize him and prove my words. It would be best to say nothing of the matter until this evening, however, and to keep my share in it a secret."

"Moonlight is my name—and I have been sent to help and comfort you," said the fairy.

The body of Purple Gold was removed; and Ming, exhausted from his fever, fell into a troubled sleep. When he wakened, the two guardians had disappeared, the day was almost done, and in the golden radiance of sunset he found the fairy Moonlight seated beside him, playing softly upon a lute.

"You have done well," she told him approvingly. "But there remains Jung Miao, who will not be easy to deal with."

"It is due entirely to your help and encouragement," said Ming. "How can I ever display my gratitude to you?"

"By presenting me with this lovely girdle," she said, indicating the jade girdle on its stand.

Ming sighed.

"I had intended this as a gift for Pure Jade," said he, "but I can refuse you nothing, celestial being. Take it; and since to me you have the appearance of Pure Jade herself, I beg you to remain a little while and endeavor to banish my fever, while I dream that it is her lovely voice beside me."

Moonlight smiled and assented to this request, and played the lute softly....

The day died. The stars came out, and the silver moon appeared in the sky, bathing the Garden of Green Gems in radiant fantasy. Hand in hand, the two alone in the pavilion watched the starry depths, until at last Ming breathed a prayer to the Moon Goddess, Chang-o.

"If it were only Pure Jade who sat thus beside me! Grant me this favor, Empress of the Heavens. Grant that she and I may be as the moonbeam and the moon, as the shadow and the substance, forever!"

"I will pray also for her happiness and yours," said Moonlight, and added her prayer to his....

The richest flowers must fade, the fairest hour must wane; and soon the moment came when Moonlight must depart. Ming clung to her slipping lingers, and begged her for advice and counsel.

"Very well, and you must obey it," she rejoined. "Never, to Pure Jade or anyone else, breathe a word of your past; never admit that you are not the son of the Dragon King. Even when tempted to confession, let your lips be sealed."

"But what if Jung Miao dooms me?" said Ming, troubled.

"I will whisper into the heart of Pure Jade, and she will save you." And Moonlight touched his forehead with her fingertips. "Sleep, worthiest of mortals! Waken refreshed and strong, that you may rise superior to the evil of Jung Miao!"

With morning, Ming wakened. He found the fever entirely gone from him, and new strength in his body.

He thought that the entire visit of Moonlight must have been some delirious fancy; but when he looked for the jade girdle, it was gone. Then he knew that she had indeed been real, a visitor from celestial realms.

Of this he had further proof almost at once, when two of the household servants came to bathe him and bring food. One of them cried aloud, and picked up an exquisite little bottle fashioned from coral, with a jade stopper, which stood at the far side of the summer pavilion.

"Look!" she cried in astonishment. "Here is the precious flagon of *po-tsan,* the wondrous ointment of Fulin that is the chief treasure of our master! If he finds it missing from his cabinet, we shall all be punished. Hurry and replace it!"

The other servant departed hurriedly. Ming understood that Moonlight must have removed it from the cabinet of Li King, with her invisible presence, in order to treat his wounds.

From the remaining attendant, he learned that Li King had been summoned to the city and had taken Pure Jade with him, for reasons unknown. There was excitement in Canton, for the notorious leader of a gang of pirates had been discovered and killed, and the magistrates were making strict investigation.

He had a brief moment of wondering delight, when one of the master builders came with diagrams for him to see, and word that the ship was progressing. There was praise for Ming's figures; already, said the master builder, these were seen to be exact and of great proportionate worth. At this, Ming smiled. Well they might be! He had spent many an hour working out this ship of his dreams, which would swim any sea and be easy to handle in any weather.

Scarcely had the ship-builder departed, however, when the blow fell.

There was a great outcry, and the garden was filled with running servants, with tumult and confusion. The astonished Ming, coming to one elbow, beheld files of yamen guards approaching, escorting the governor and the chief magistrate of Canton. As he stared, the soldiers surrounded his pavilion, the officials took their station in the entrance, and upon the scene stalked Jung Miao.

Then Li King and Pure Jade appeared, with an escort of guards. The governor recounted briefly how one Purple Gold, a known leader of the pirates, had been found dead the previous evening, and recognized by many who had seen him. Accusation had been laid against the miserable Ming, here present. The accuser was no other than Jung Miao. With this, the Taoist stepped out and spoke.

"This is the truth," he thundered. "It was I who killed this wretched pirate Purple Gold. Why? Because he came and sought my aid. He confessed to me who he was, and that this wounded man was his leader and chief; between them, they had schemed to bring many pirates to Canton and loot the city with great slaughter. This man, who pretends to be a son of the Dragon King of the Ocean, was to have a number of his men come, presumably as envoys from the Dragon King his father, and seize this island with everything in it. I killed the unhappy wretch. Now seize this creature before you and execute him!"

Ming listened, thunderstruck, to this accusation. He was almost on the point of confessing all, telling the story as it really was, and trusting that the governor would recognize the truth—but he remembered the advice of Moonlight.

Li King was now interrogated. The merchant implored mercy for his helpless guest, and spoke highly of his character and talents; he was forced to confess, however, that he had no actual knowledge whence Ming had come. The magistrate who was conducting the examination turned to Ming.

"You claim to be the son of the Dragon King. Have you any proof or witnesses?"

"No, venerable parent of the people," stammered Ming. He was bewildered, angered, confused. He knew not which way to turn. He caught a smile and a gesture of reassurance from Pure Jade; then the girl stepped forth and begged leave to address the governor. After some deliberation over such unheard-of presumption, the leave was granted.

"Venerable father and mother of the people," said Pure Jade, "last night when I had prayed to Lord Buddha and the gods, I dreamed that a celestial being came into my room and instructed me, saying that today there would be an interrogation here. I was told to visit the famous sage Chao, who lives as a holy hermit by the Spring of the Three Fairies, and to request him to come here and testify. I sought him this morning early, and he is here."

This speech caused the most intense surprise. When it was found that the venerable hermit, whom the Emperor himself held in honor, was indeed outside, he was ushered in with the greatest of respect. Looking like an old bag of bones, he saluted the magistrates, and then pointed with his staff to Jung Miao.

"Tell the honorable court," said he, "with what weapon you slew Purple Gold."

"With this very knife," replied the Taoist boldly, displaying a broad-bladed weapon. The sage smiled.

"Impossible. The gods have told me that the wretched creature was killed with a thin-bladed knife. Those who saw his wound can bear witness if this is so."

"It is so, venerable Chao," said the magistrate. "I myself saw the wound."

"Then," said the hermit, "who can produce the knife which caused the wound?"

"I!" cried out Ming, and brought the knife into sight. "Further, I killed the man here, in this very spot. The merchant Li had the body taken to the city and left at the yamen."

"That is true," said Li King gravely.

It was obvious that the Taoist had lied. However, he repeated his accusation against Ming, but the hermit intervened.

"Here you see a vile wretch, honorable magistrates, who himself plotted the thing he accuses another of plotting. He is worthy of instant death."

"But," asked the perplexed governor, "how are we to know that Ming is indeed the son of the Dragon King? If there were even one witness of weight who could testify to this, it would close the case."

"Then I can testify to it," said the sage Chao. "For last night my spirit was in the palace of the Dragon King, who spoke to me of this young man his son, and said that he had been sent here to confer many and great benefits upon this city and upon the whole empire."

In a voice of thunder, the governor ordered Jung Miao executed; and it was done. As may be inferred, the hermit Chao, whose spirit sojourned with the gods at night, received vast honor. Upon Ming the governor conferred rewards for having killed the evil pirate....

After a time Ming found himself alone in the pavilion. Then upon the silence came a footstep, and he looked up to see Pure Jade standing timidly before him. His eyes widened. Incredulous, he stared—for she was wearing the jade girdle.

"Pure Jade!" he exclaimed, pointing to it. "Where did you get that girdle?"

"I do not know," she said. "Last night I dreamed that a lovely celestial maiden had brought it to me as a gift. When I wakened this morning, it was there beside me. Did you choose that way of sending it to me, dear Ming?"

Ming lay back upon his pillows, utterly amazed. It was of course evident that Moonlight had taken the girdle to this sleeping girl. As he pondered, Pure Jade came and stood behind his couch. She touched his head with her fingertips, as Moonlight had done; and if there was in her eyes a smile of tenderness and amusement, Ming could not see it.

He could see and feel nothing except her presence. He caught her hand and held it, felt the gentle response of her fingers, and knew that all the future indeed lay golden and fair before him.

In that future, however, he never made any reference to his own past. That celestial creature Moonlight was very, very wise! And if there were any earthly explanation of his fever fancies, Pure Jade never mentioned the matter.

So ended the story, while the moon poured down silver radiance over the garden where we sat, and the river, and the crowded boats. My hosts asked how I liked the story. Sui Lo showed all her dimples as she smiled at me.

"Well, the girl was smart," I observed. "If you're anything like her, I can see how she put it over on Ming by pretending to be the fairy Moonlight—"

"Oh, now!" My hosts were shocked. So was the lovely girl beside me. "The fairy was a real person, you know!"

"And the magician was real too? And his magic?"

"No," said the young lady, with a wink she must have learned at Berkeley. "You can see Taoists priests pulling that sort of magic all the time. It's hypnotism. But the celestial creature—ah, we must believe, always, that the beautiful is real!"

"Thank God it sometimes is!" I said, and bowed to her, and then everybody laughed, and she blushed, and the dinner-party was over.

THE MAN WHO RULED THE WIND

A *small, chunky, roly-poly man was* descending the rope-and-wood ladder from the side of the factory ship, the "mother" whaler, to the deck of the "killer" ship below. He carried a bundle of clothes under his arm. No one else was in sight. Fog, drifting in from the Pacific, cloaked the harbor and eddied about the whalers.

I watched the man until he was close, then addressed him:

"Any objection if I look this killer over, Skipper?"

He turned—an apple-cheeked Norwegian, blue eyes shrewd and appraising.

"Why, no. I'm not skipper here, nor in the big one either. But as one old shellback to another, make yourself at home."

I strolled about the deck. It was the man who attracted me, not the ship. There's not much to see in these small craft, stripped as they are to the bare essentials of their smelly trade. After inspecting the ponderous mechanical harpoons secured alongside the fiddley bulkhead, I found my man again by the galley. He was seated on an upturned bucket with a tub of steaming clothes before him.

We smoked and fell into talk of ships and men. He was gunner on this ship; after a bit he mentioned that he had once been owner and master of a similar craft. I had guessed as much by the cut of his jib: scarred hands and an old-young face, an eye that could leap to decision in the flash of an instant.

"You're not the only master to have lost your ship," said I.

He laughed harshly.

"Lost her? She was burned from under me. And not by accident, matey."

"How so?"

"My wife's old man owned a fleet o' trawlers out of Kirkwall. I sailed master in the flagship until one day I shanghaied his daughter and married her. He came aboard and sacked me. I sailed into him and laid him out for inspection.... He could never forgive that. Later, when I had my own tub, he came aboard one night with his gang, and gave us a mainsail haul. Stripped the cabin, laid me out proper, and burned her. My wife's in Bergen now with the kids. Aint seen them in eleven months."

There in a few pithy sentences was an entire saga of the sea, the gist of a man's whole life. About the man, as he spoke, the fog swirled and thickened, while he sudsed the clothes around in the tub.

"Norwegian, aren't you?" I said. "Met quite a few in my time. I'd bet a weeviled hardtack that you're from the north, up around the Salten fiord district."

He stopped short and gave me a queer look from those blue eyes of his, and grunted.

"I guess you win, matey. Don't see how you knew it, though."

"I was thinking of an old story," I replied. The fog had put it into my mind, the gray vapor curling around him and weaving up the high side of the factory ship behind him. "And to make you fit into it rightly, your name should be Raud. Ever hear of him?"

He dropped the clothes in the tub and gave me another look and a nod.

"An unlucky name, where I come from," he said slowly. "Aye. You'd be thinking about Raud the

Unchristened, no doubt. Funny thing, how those old stories get handed down by the fire, of winter nights, century after century! You got it out of books, I guess, but I got it out of the old folks. I mind my grandmother spinning, and gabbling away as the wheel went around, telling me the story just like she got it from her own old folks, years back."

We talked it over, one of us putting in a snatch, and the other amplifying it—that old story of Raud the wizard, who could sail against the wind and command the fog and storm to do his bidding.

Between us, we made the yarn come pretty much alive, for this chap had a gift of putting flesh on dead bones, as though these people had lived only yesterday. The tub of clothes was forgotten. The two of us went back to a night far gone, close to a thousand years in the past, when fog curled around through the streets of Trondhjem and eddied about the hall of the King of Norway.

Into the King's hall that night there wandered a short man with blue eyes and red cheeks; he warmed himself at the fire and drank the King's ale. He wore a bearskin for a cloak and kept to himself and held his peace, but his bright eyes roved about the place continually, and dwelt most often on the King, at the high end of the hall.

Back in those days, kings won their right by the strong hand. Olaf, Triggvi's son, was the noblest man in all the north: Viking and rover, adventurer, soldier of fortune; a romantic and splendid figure with his ruddy flashing hair and beard, his stark eyes like ice. At his feet sat his great wolfhound Vig, growling and eying the steaming men in the hall with fierce eyes. At his right hand sat black-browed Bishop Sigurd, who was more warrior than cleric.

Of a sudden, King Olaf noticed the new figure by the huge fireplace, and asked the man who he was. The stranger hitched up the bearskin about his shoulders, looked up at the King and the bishop, and spoke humbly enough.

"Biorn is my name, and I am a merchant," said he. Biorn means *bear,* and King Olaf was quick to suspect mockery here. He spoke out swift and sharply. "Strange bears don't come into city halls, fellow."

"True, Lord," said the little man. "But to outland men like me, it is always interesting to see new things. And here I find the saying true, that good luck and good looks are brethren."

Olaf, despite the flattery, was somewhat angry.

"Are you minded to match wise sayings with me, Biorn?" he demanded.

"Not I, Lord," was the reply. "It is ill luck to match wits with the wisdom of the ancients," went on Biorn, "and a wandering man sets no store by himself in a king's hall."

Bishop Sigurd burst into hearty laughter.

"Ha, Olaf! The man has brains. What are you

doing in this place, Biorn?" The little man saluted the bishop reverently.

"I came to look upon the face of King Olaf. He has made all Norway into a Christian land, except one spot in the north. I was in that place not long ago, and came from curiosity to see what sort of man was this king, of whom such great tales are spread."

Now King Olaf bent his brows on the speaker, perceiving that this stranger was a sharp and cunning fellow.

"There is but one man in all Norway who flouts me," said he slowly, "and that is Raud the Unchristened, Raud the wizard, who sits north in the Salten fiord and prays to his heathen gods. Behind him are gathered the men of Halogaland under his foster-brother Thorir Hart; they have ships and men enough. Is this your meaning, Biorn?"

The little man in the bearskin cloak nodded.

"True, Lord. They say strange things of this Raud; that he can command the wind and fog and storms, that he can sail with or against the wind at will—"

"God save all here from such talk!" exclaimed Bishop Sigurd violently.

"Bah! It's no more than everybody says," put in the King. "When I catch this fellow Raud, I'll christen him with the sword-edge! Have you seen him, Biorn?"

"Yes, Lord. I wintered with him."

"Good! Tell me about him. What sort of man is he? How does he look?"

"He is ill-favored and huge, with a shaggy beard, and has a cast in one eye," said the little man. "He trades each year with the Orkneys, has gone there now with his great ship, and is very lucky in all he does."

"I'll change that," said the King with an oath. "What did he say about me?" The bright eyes of the little man probed up at the high seat of Olaf.

"I heard him say only one thing of you, Lord. That an ill deed ever brought ill luck."

Olaf flushed, for he had done ill deeds enough, and was a ruthless man.

"Says he so? Then I'll give him a better rede, and this is it: Sword's edge saves much talk. To the Orkneys, eh? And my ships are boun and ready for sea—hm! What about the ship you mentioned? Is it a fine one?"

"Finer and greater than any ever seen in Norway," the little man said. "She has a dragon prow, a sail all blue and white, and an altar to Thor on her after-deck."

"Then before hay harvest I'll put Thor into the sea and replace him with an altar to Christ!" swore Olaf the King. "And Raud the Unchristened will go with his false god."

"Ale words are ill words," said the little man impudently.

It was true that Olaf had been drinking deeply. At this open taunt, he let out a roar of anger, and shouted to his men down the hall to fetch this insolent stranger before him.

But even as he gave the order, there came a terrific gust of wind down the chimney. It blew a cloud of ashes from the fireplace out into the room. And when men ran up to seize Biorn, there was only a bearskin in a huddle, himself was gone.

"After him!" shouted Olaf in hot passion. "Find him, bring him back!"

Men seized weapons and ran out, but it was useless to seek the stranger, thick fog filling the streets. After a time a man came to the hall; he was a watchman from one of the ships in harbor. He said that a huge strange vessel had been seen; she had come and gone again, despite the fog and ill wind. King Olaf told him to describe that ship.

"We saw her close," said the man. "She had only four oars out and was all hung with shields. Her size was immense, and she was deeply stained and discolored, as though by long voyaging. Also, her mast was gone; she seemed to be storm-crippled."

Olaf started up out of his high seat.

"That was the ship of Raud the Unchristened!" he declared wrathfully. "The man who sat here in the hall and taunted me, was Raud himself. He's back from the Orkneys and is heading north. Sound horn! Up with you, Bishop Sigurd—out, every man, to the ships! I'll feed this wizard cross or sword before he gets home again!"

There was mustering and running, blowing of horns and a lift of voices: but men recalled that gusty wind down the chimney and the blowing of ashes, and when they came to the ships there was fog and wind together, which was unnatural. Here was evident sorcery, but Olaf was so eager to catch Raud that none dared gainsay him.

In half an hour his own ship, the *Crane,* followed by four other longships, headed out to sea. Barely was the harbor cleared, when the fog thinned and vanished and the stars glimmered overhead. Olaf, at the helm of the *Crane,* laughed deeply and spoke to Bishop Sigurd beside him.

"There's guile for you! The man slips into Trondhjem, taunts me to my face, and slips out again with a crippled ship—why? To draw us after him. He takes desperate chances—why? Because a trap is set and waiting. A sharp fellow, this Raud!"

The black-browed bishop scowled. "A trap, you say? How's that?"

"Thorir Hart of Halogaland is foster brother to this Raud, and has been gathering men and ships. D'ye see the light now?"

"I do not," said Bishop Sigurd. Olaf chuckled, and stooped to caress the ears of his hound Vig, who had come aboard with him.

"Raud thinks to lead us out to sea in chase of him. Then he'll bring us in among the northern islands, where Thorir Hart's ships will be wailing to catch us. Good! Instead, we'll lake the inside passage, get ahead of him, and when he reaches the islands he'll be the one to be nipped."

"Hm!" grunted the bishop uneasily. "What was it the little man said—ill luck to match wits with the wisdom of the ancients? Have a care, Olaf. We're dealing with wizards and warlocks, men who hold to the ancient gods."

"That's their ill luck," said Olaf, and cast his eye proudly along the deck.

The oars were stowed now. The sail, with its blood-red cross, bellied out in the wind. Starlight glittered on steel, as the eighty picked men of the crew furbished arms or stretched canvas storm-aprons, against the salt sea spume. So the *Crane* drove north on a course of Olaf's setting, the other four ships trailing him.

Meantime, Raud the Unchristened headed out to sea, with a two-day sail before him.

By morning, this little roly-poly man with sharp blue eyes realized that he had lost his wager, that the ships of Olaf the King had not come after him. Yet he held his course, for he could do nothing else now. Nor was he deceived in the matter.

This dragon-ship of his was a noble thing, a ship of thirty rowing-benches, with a gilded dragon's head at the prow, upcurving dragons tail for stern-post, and a fair blue-striped sail. Yet the ship was not so fair or noble to the eye as was Gudrun, the wife of Raud. She Was a tall, stately woman whose flaxen hair streamed in rich profusion. Raud had stolen her when he was on a raid in England and she was no more than a girl; it was said that she was a king's daughter.

Now she sailed with Raud, fought with him, guided him with wise counsel, but the men whispered there was no great love between them....

On the sunrise of the third day, they were coming in to the land again. Raud himself was at the helm when Gudrun brought him hot broth and fresh boiled herring.

"So they have not followed us," she said, while he ate. "What does that mean?"

Raud grinned at her. He was very cunning at guessing other men's minds.

"It means that Olaf was too sharp for me. He has headed north along the inner course and means to cut me off yonder, at the islands."

"Then we're heading into a trap," she said sharply.

"I can do nothing else," said Raud. "I must join Thorir Hart yonder. Therefore I must risk being caught by Olaf. If he is waiting, it is among the islands to the south of the cape, but Thorir Hart is waiting close under the cape. Thus, if I can pass Olaf, he may still come into our net."

The men were enjoying the warmth of the new-risen sun. The ship drew closer to the shore, savage and forbidding with its misty mountains, glittering glaciers and rocky headlands. Off to starboard lay the lesser isles where danger might lurk.

"Olaf is a bad enemy," Gudrun said slowly.

"So am I," said Raud the Unchristened, and laughed softly. "And all the worse, because men think me a wizard."

A sharp yelp from forward interrupted them.

"Sail ho! Off the starboard bow, putting out from the isles and the inner passage!"

Up leaped Raud, squinting into the sunrise light. A land mist half veiled the islands there, but above the mist glinted a speck of ruddy gold.

"The beak of a ship, gilded," said Raud. "A king's ship, beating out from the islands—here, Gudrun! Take the helm. If that is Olaf's ship, we're lost, for he's too sharp a man to be fooled. If it's one of his other ships, we may yet win."

He ran forward, his voice barking at the men.

"Douse sail, all hands! Douse sail, strike the mast. Break out the shipwreck canvas; arms ready!"

There was a rush and scurry, with every man knowing his post and his work. The vane and sail were lowered, the mast was struck and stowed in its chocks. The long pins were knocked out that held the gilded dragon's head and tail; they disappeared inboard. The glittering shields along the bulwarks vanished.

The ship was draped with clinging, lead-hued canvas. A few men were stationed here and there along the benches. A few oars were run out. They pulled raggedly, as fishermen weary after long night's labor. So it would seem at a distance.

At the helm stood Gudrun, gazing off to where the warship with its gilded prow and high sail was now emerging from the mist of the islands. Raud came back aft and took the helm from her, laughing a little.

"Olaf's ship carries a red cross on her sail. That's not his ship."

"He may be too smart for you yet," said Gudrun darkly.

"The game's not won till the board's cleared," Raud replied.

"They say Raud can sail with or against the wind at will."

Perhaps it was well that Raud the Unchristened was too absorbed in the enemy at this moment to pay his wife heed, for he was skilled at reading faces. And a strange look dwelt in her deep, eyes as she, too, watched the other ship. Olaf and Raud, Christian and pagan, seeking each to entrap the other to death and doom; the one quite ignorant of her existence, the other paying her little heed. Yet it might come to pass that a woman could entrap them both, if time and tide brought them into her net—

"Ha! By Odin, we win!" cried out Raud sharply.

True. The warship was wasting no time on that gray, awkward hulk so soggily forging through the water. She swung around; the sail was topped, the yard trimmed, and the longship turned in again among the islands. The men cheered and echoed Raud's laughter, but Gudrun eyed her husband, unsmiling.

"Perhaps Olaf is smarter than you deem him," she said.

Some of the men heard this, and lost their mirth. For all her glorious youth and beauty, they muttered that there was no great good in her. Tales were told of her doings in the Orkneys, and it was said that more than one man had come to his bane because of her. If Raud heard such things, he cared little. He was all for wealth and shrewd profit.

Now the dragon became itself again. The golden head and stern-post were restored, the canvas was pulled off, the benches were manned; under full swinging oar-stroke she stood in for the more northward islands, under the cape. Here should be lurking Thorir Hart with eight or ten stout ships of Halogaland.

Raud cocked an eye at the sky and sea. The wind was refreshing, a wrack of cloud was bearing down. This was the weather Raud liked. Ere night a wild gale would be blowing; but things would happen before darkness fell. A king would die in Norway, muttered Raud the Unchristened, and he himself would be scudding home again, laden with loot, to the boiling currents of the Salten fiord.

"A smoke!" went up a yell. "A smoke from the cape, Raud! The signal!"

All was well, then; more than well! Thorir Hart was here as promised, had descried him, must have descried Olaf's ships also, bearing north straight into the trap. With savage joy, Raud headed in between the outer isles, bare skerries of rock all around. Ahead and merging with the land lay the inner islands, as Raud steered for the inner sound.

Then, suddenly, he caught another yell from forward, a yell of dismay and warning; and from Gudrun beside him, a swift sharp laugh.

"Caught, Raud, caught! I told you he was no fool!"

The islands had opened, and Raud's blue eyes glittered on the revelation. Here was Olaf's great ship, the *Crane,* standing out from an inlet, to cut him off, her square sail with its blood-red cross bellying in the wind. Far behind her, but also coming into sight between the islands, were other longships.

Viking Dragon-ship

Raud might have turned to sea and fled, but this would have lost every hope of entrapping the King. And Raud was no man to shirk a fight, especially when he had a trick or two up his sleeve. His voice barked out eagerly:

"By Odin, he'll get his bellyful this trip—all hands alive! Break out the short mast. Oars! Stand by to bring inboard and secure—

A splendid, hard-bitten crew; small wonder that Raud the Unchristened was termed wizard and warlock. The oars were stowed. Up went a new mast, shorter than the former spar, with an odd triangular canvas furled about it. This was shaken out and peaked. With the wind dead abeam to starboard, the ship stood off on the starboard tack while the *Crane* came foaming down with a bone in her teeth, under both sail and oars.

Gudrun, steel-clad like a man, brought Raud his helm and mailcoat, and took the tiller while he donned them. The men were arming. Spears and arrows were being placed in readiness; now the King's men were to witness some wizardry that had teeth wherewith to bite.

"Stand by to tack!" Raud's voice blared out. "Man the sheets. Ready about!"

The dragon was leaping ahead close-hauled, at astounding speed. Raud gave her a good full, waited for the exact moment, and eased down the tiller.

"Boom amidships," came his order. "—Yarily, men! Smart with it!"

Keeping the sail drawing as long as possible, the men handling the boom hauled it amidships. The ship's head came through the wind. The men slacked off the weather sheet, cleated home the leeward sheet. The sail filled. Raud, his eyes gleaming, ordered the sheet hauled flatter aft. The dragon was now close-hauled on the port tack, sailing within four points of the wind's eye—sailing against the wind by sheer magic, it seemed to all who watched.

Gudrun stood with shield ready. Raud eyed the Crane: Again he had the dragon put on the starboard tack, then back to port. And with this, he was rushing straight for the king's ship as though intent on the one simple tactic known to these seamen—to lay the enemy ship aboard, grapple her, and come to sword-strokes.

Olaf altered his course a bit to starboard. This was precisely as Raud had figured. He laughed, and pressed the king's ship farther to leeward, as though intent upon ramming the *Crane.* The latter ship wore farther to starboard, and farther—and suddenly caught the wind dead abeam.

Then the *Crane* was rolling in the trough; Olaf was roaring furiously at his crew. The oars fell into confusion. The huge square sail was lifted by the wind and blown out to leeward. And here came Raud's dragon, close-hauled, flashing under the very stern of the proud King's ship. War-horns blared, bows twanged, spears flashed in the sunlight. They twanged and flashed again as the dragon fell off to starboard, hailing death on the decks of the *Crane* along the starboard quarter.

In the mad confusion and crisis, scarcely a shaft had made response. Now, suddenly, the massive bow of King Olaf hummed deeply. Through Gudrun's shield, through it and slapping into the tiller betwixt her and Raud, drove the King's arrow. Raud cackled a laugh, waved his hand, and sent the dragon off to windward in a smother of foam.

Off he went, straight in among the skerries and islands, with the wounded *Crane* frothing after her, with the other ships of the King dashing through the channels. They had Raud now, had cut off his escape, would drive him ashore and finish him! Long and loud laughed Raud as he watched them come.

Suddenly, dead ahead, the inner sound opened up. Raud's men vented a blare of exultation. Here came into sight the array of Thorir Hart—a dozen longships spurting forward, the trap laid and sprung!

This was the last laugh of Raud the Unchristened for many a day.

Olaf could have turned and run for it, but pride forbade. Besides, here was what he and his men knew best; cold steel against long odds. He had not warred over half the world to turn tail now to a few ships crammed with farmers. His war-horns blared, and the other four longships followed him, straight for the enemy.

There befell a fight which was short and sharp and terrible. Arrows and spears went fast to work; ships smashed in, axe and sword began to clang. The King and his picked fighting-men swept all before them. Three of the Halogalanders' vessels were cleared, and the others turned and made for the beach. A smother of mist came down in a wild howling squall of wind and cloud.

Out of the smother ran the dragon-ship of Raud, beating against the wind, evading those who tried to follow, slipping among the islands and then vanishing out to sea. Rank sorcery, said Bishop Sigurd!

But no others got away. They were beached, one by one, and Olaf's men came after them with hot steel. The king himself, with his wolfhound Vig, followed the blowing scarlet cloak of Thorir Hart up from the shore among the trees. No man in Norway could outrun Olaf, and at last Thorir Hart came to desperate stand.

The hound leaped for his throat. His sword sent Vig wounded and staggering, but the stroke left himself open. Olaf drove spear through and through the chieftain, and there died Thorir Hart with most of his followers.

Olaf called his men together swiftly, and with two of his ships following the *Crane,* drove northward despite wind and wrack. If the wind was good for Raud, it was bad for Olaf, but turn from his determination he would not. He kept Bishop Sigurd hard at work exorcising warlocks and witchcraft, and at last he came to the Salten fiord. Far inside the long fiord, on Godo Isle, lived Raud the Unchristened.

Getting at Raud, however, was another matter.

Long and narrow was the fiord, very large inside but with a narrow throat. At ebb tide and at flood, but especially at the ebb, the water made a wild millrace for miles out in the ocean, so that no ship could live in it. This wild rush of water could only be crossed during a few moments between the tides. The fiord could only be entered at the same time.

No man with Olaf knew the waters or the way of entry to the fiord. All this coast was empty and barren, and no pilot could be found. To make matters worse, Olaf arrived with a fine brisk wind, and clear sunlight, but in the fiord was a wild wrath of mist and fog and tempest. This endured day after day, and all Bishop Sigurd's exorcising did no good whatever. It was clear that Raud, as long as he had a mind to conjure up this weather, could hold them at bay.

King Olaf swore a great oath, beached his ships under the headland, and settled down to wait.

The third day they were there, a woman came riding down the shore on a horse. She was finely dressed, and so wondrous fair that men stood in awe of her. Now the *Crane* lay a little out from the beach, where King Olaf was swimming and playing games with Bishop Sigurd and certain of his forecastle men. The woman watched them for a while. Then the oars were put out and the players began to walk the long oars as the men rowed. But one of them, a tall naked golden man, juggled three knives in the air as he walked.

"It is in my mind," said the woman, "that no one in the world can do that play but Olaf Triggvi's son; and never has a lordlier man been seen in the world."

"That is true," said the men around her. "King Olaf is yonder, and with wits or sword or muscle, no man in Norway can equal him."

The woman smiled and said nothing. After a while the *Crane* came in. King Olaf, now dressed and wearing a scarlet mantle he had won in Constantinople, leaped ashore and saw the woman, and came up to her. He asked her who she was, and she smiled at him.

"My name is Gudrun. My thralls said they had seen ships here. I came to see whether we had to do with honest men or Vikings or traders."

"You seem to have no fear," said Olaf, his eye lingering upon her.

"Appearances are true," she said, laughing a little.

"Have you anyone who can take my ships into the fiord?" he demanded.

"I have not," said she. "But I might do it myself, if I had a mind thereto. I will come back tomorrow and bring a horse, and see if you can ride as well as you can swim."

With this she rode away, and King Olaf looked after her right joyfully.

As she promised, she returned on the morrow with a spare horse, King Olaf mounted and called Vig to ride with them, but the hound showed his teeth and would not. Men said this was a bad omen, but the King laughed and rode away with Gudrun.

"Tell me," said Olaf, as they rode. "Do you know where Raud the Wizard bides?"

"I do," she assented. "On Godo Isle, far up the fiord. A ship must row all day and night to reach there. His great dragon is hauled up and he has few men, for many were hurt in the south. Raud himself, I hear, lies abed with a sickness."

"If we get through into the fiord, could you guide me to Godo Isle?"

"I might, if I had a mind thereto," she said, and smiled at him. "But not for gold or silver would I do it."

On the next day and the next, Gudrun returned, and Olaf rode with her, though each day the hound

"My oath for yours, Olaf!" said Gudrun. Olaf swore the oath; and they kissed.

Vig curled his lips and sulked. Each day the King returned joyous to camp. It was clear to all men that she had cast a spell over him, but he would let no one speak ill of her, not even Bishop Sigurd. Each day the fog and tempest hung blacker over Salten fiord, and when men watched that wild race of the waters at the change of tide, they crossed themselves and said it was well that the ships were safely beached.

King Olaf thought that never had he seen so goodly or fair a woman as Gudrun. He was not strong in patience, and one day he would have had his will of her, but she struck him so stoutly that he loosed her and went staggering.

She laughed heartily.

"What! Olaf calls himself King of all Norway, yet cannot enter the Salten fiord? It seems to me that Raud the Unchristened must be the better man. And it does not like me to ride alone with one who does not seek me in marriage."

"By God, I will do that!" said Olaf, his eyes flashing. "If you will first accept christening at my hand, and lead me to where Raud bides."

"So said, so accepted," she made answer. "My oath for yours, Olaf!"

Olaf swore the oath, and they kissed and were very gladsome.

"Have your ships ready ere the morning tide," said she. "I will come then."

When the ebb tide was rushing out in the morning, the three ships were ready. Gudrun came riding, and was set aboard the *Crane,* and the hound Vig let out a dismal howl. Gudrun took the helm herself, with Olaf beside her, and let steer straight for the fiord entry, in the few moments between the tides. In the bow stood Bishop Sigurd, beside a Cross he had set up there, with all his Mass-array. He burned incense and said prayers, and the oars gave way full force, and the *Crane* drove straight for the heart of the fog and black storm.

As they advanced, it lessened before them, and the walls of the fiord appeared on either hand, and the other ships followed safely where Gudrun steered. On they went and on. Before the full force of the rushing flood was felt behind them, they were through the narrowest place and bearing for the open fiord ahead, though there was still some wind and fog against them. So, being through, they halted a while to give thanks, and then took to the oars again.

All that day and into the night they rowed, and so came to Godo Isle.

It was very late in the night when they came ashore, where the dragon-ship was drawn up under cover, and the stead of Raud the Unchristened lay beyond, all lightless. Gudrun showed the way to everything. The men landed, and Olaf spread them out around the stead so that none might escape.

Then he went to the doors and burst them in. A man who slept there was killed, and Olaf led his men into the hall, killing all they came upon. Raud was found in his bed, and was fast bound: then lights were brought, and Raud was haled forth before the King. Olaf had a spear in his hand, and he pricked Raud with it, and offered him life if he would accept baptism.

"Life is nothing to me," said Raud, looking at Gudrun and then at Olaf. After that he would say no word, and the King had him put to the torment.

"Tell me how you sail your ship against the wind, and with what magic," Olaf said, "and still I will spare your life."

Raud looked at him, and looked at Gudrun, and laughed shortly and would not speak. So he was put to death with little enough mercy.

Now Gudrun spoke to Olaf and reminded him of his oath. Just then two of the men came in from outside, dragging with them a thrall they had found hiding in the pigsty. The thrall howled for mercy, and flung himself at the feet of Gudrun, calling her by name.

Thus it came out that Gudrun was the wife of Raud the Unchristened. Olaf looked at her with an icy glare in his eyes. But she smiled.

"Your oath, Olaf!" said she.

"That was given to Gudrun the maid," said Olaf, "and not to the wife of Raud. It is in my mind that she who betrays one husband will betray two."

A wild scream broke from her as she met his eyes, but Olaf lifted his spear and drove it through her, so that she fell dead. With this, a foaming madness seized upon him, and in his fury he ordered the thrall slain, and sent out his followers to kill every man of Raud's force they might find alive in the island.

This was done; and meantime Olaf laid fire to the house and burned it down.

The dragon ship was run out into the water and saved, but all her gear was burned with the buildings. None the less, Olaf took her home to Trondhjem and fitted her out afresh. She was the fairest and greatest ship in all Norway, and he named her the *Short Dragon,* later building the *Long Dragon* that carried him to his death.

Such was the story that we built up together, as I sat talking with the whaling man while the mist curled around his blue eyes and red cheeks. We had lighted our pipes, and smoked as we talked. Whether the King or the rover or the woman in that story was the most to blame, I could not determine.

"And it doesn't matter," said my friend shrewdly. "The odd thing is how King Olaf cheated himself! He had the ship but not the ship's gear, and he killed everyone who might have told him the truth about it. For this Raud, of course, was no wizard. He had simply learned the art of tacking, of beating to windward—the greatest single step forward that ever happened in the history of the sea!"

"A queer tale and a bloody one," I commented. "Seafaring men were hard men in those days, eh?"

The whaler grunted. He looked at me and his eyes darkened. I knew he was thinking about his wife's old man out of Kirkwall, who had set him on his beam ends.

"Aye," he said. "Aye. And they still are, matey."

THE DEAD STRIKE BACK

If you hang around a certain club in Hollywood long enough, you'll run into writers and diplomats and foreign correspondents and clairvoyants and what-not. The monthly stage shows draw a lot of what-not, because anyone with an act is tickled pink to put it on at the club, in the hope it will catch a producer's eye and step into the screen. It has to be good, too....

One night a Dutchman with a broken nose and a wide grin and a title blew in with a couple of correspondents who introduced him all around. In no time at all he was popular. He had plenty of money, and he wanted to put on an act for the fun of it. Let us call him Jan Rubens and leave off his title.

He put on his act. It was a puppet-show, of all things, called "The Merchant of Venus," and it created a mild riot. Rubens gave a monologue as the show went on, and this helped the riot.

After the show we crowded about the bar, and Rubens held us spellbound. These puppets constituted his hobby; he did not go in for the usual sort of puppet-show either, but had all kinds of adjuncts.

"I like to teach something by the dolls," he said, beaming at everybody. "Every one of my acts teaches something, about men or history or whatever you like to name."

"One thing you can't teach about with puppets," I said, "is ships."

He chortled and waved his cigar.

"Hollanders, the greatest seamen in the world, not teach about ships? You make fun of me, my good friend. Of course I can. With puppets, too. Did you ever hear of the cog?"

Cog-wheel, cog in a wheel—yes, we had heard of cogs. Rubens beamed, chuckled, and puffed at his cigar. Not that kind of a cog at all, said he amiably.

"A long time ago, a very long time, you know," he said, gesturing with his cigar, "Bruges and its seaport, Sluys, were the centers of commerce for all western Europe, the way Venice was in the east. And in all the world nothing was known like Sluys, or Bruges either; the two were only seven miles apart in those days. Why, at brisk seasons seven and eight hundred ships a day cleared out of Sluys—a *day!*"

"Yeah," said somebody. "But what kind of ships?"

"Cogs, for the greater part," Rubens answered promptly. "The cog, my good friends, was a portly ship with a great square sail, and an enormously high forecastle and poop. It was not pretty. It was awkward; it was ungainly; it was a poor sailor: but it could carry a world of freight. It was the great cargo ship of northern Europe. King Edward of England embarked an army of fifty thousand in one day, men and horses—because he had cogs to ship them in. Well! Who started this cog? Where did it come from?"

"I'll bite," some one offered. "Who?"

"That is what my play will show you," said Rubens triumphantly. "Look! All the commerce of western Europe centered here. And off these coasts were the birds who preyed on that commerce—pirates: Moors and Genoese, English and German, these and others lay in wait. Well, well! Today Bruges is a city of the dead; but six hundred years ago it was to Europe what New York is to America. Shall we go and see? A private show, eh?"

We were all eager enough for another taste of his magic, and trooped into the club theater. His had been the last act of the evening, and all his apparatus was in place.

The lights were turned on, and the curtain was rung up. A dozen or more of us gathered in the front seats, and Rubens disappeared into his perch above the puppet-stage.

"This, my friends, is not like other plays," his voice came to us, sonorous and vibrant. "I tell you this as we go along, yes; but first there is a panorama. You must realize what sort of city this was, with its canals coming up from the seaport of Sluys, its harbor, its multitude of shipping! For it was a free and open port, open to all men alike on the sole condition of peace; and any man who might break this peace was straightway hanged."

The peculiar bronze timbre of the Dutchman's voice, no less than the expert manipulation of his puppets, was gripping. It had a hypnotic effect. Further, he had a sort of moving background and scenery that was new to us—panorama was perhaps the name for it, but it kept on the move through his entire show.

None of us cared about his cog at first; we did before he finished. Here was a wine of wizardry that thrilled us—not in the voice alone, or the moving, speaking puppets, but in the perfect timing of motion to the story that unfolded. Now the puppets spoke, now their master; he used a rolling monotone as subtle and as powerful as the throbbing background of kettledrums to music. Further, his scenery or panoramic setting was as exquisite in detail and lighting as could be desired.

Bruges in its olden glory flashed before us: The great Waterhalle astride the canal, where all ships were unloaded that came up from Sluys; the churches and streets, the vast bazaars of merchandise, the churches and streets and the taverns, famed for their excellence. The people too, all kinds of them, painted and puppets, who moved with a gabble of talk. Suddenly the scene halted before the rich counting-house of a great merchant, the greatest merchant in Bruges.

"*Bras-de-fer!* Iron-arm!" he said, a testy gray-beard with deep voice. "The most damned pirate in Christendom! Iron-arm, the accursed Norman—"

They were discussing piracies off the coast. The scene ran on: A road, carts, wagons; the great canal that ran down to Sluys. And here was Sluys itself, walled and moated and bursting with foreigners and merchandise, so that booths were put up outside the walls. But the eye passed on to the wondrous harbor of this town. If the town were marvelous with its people drawn from all nations and races, the harbor was an astounding sight.

Here lay so mighty a fleet that it seemed half the world must lie in leaguer before these walls. Up to the very walls, indeed, were ships; with the ebb tide they lay aground, careened over, in so soft and firm a bed of sand that they were as well off as though afloat.

Galleys from Italy and Spain, wine-ships from Bordeaux and the Garonne, sloops and busses from the German ports; pinks and flutes from the English coasts, whalers and decked galleys from Norway. And out beyond them all, by the sandbanks, a huge gray shape like nothing ever before seen on land or sea; a monstrous ship, ungainly and massively towering of stern and bow, all of a gray hue.

This misshapen wight had provoked the hilarity of seamen and townfolk alike. Crews lined the rails; burghers and merchants thronged the walls; boats went out and rowed about her, with mirth and comment and jest. From the French coast, it was said, though nothing so monstrous was known to any of the French pilots here. Her crew had stayed aboard; they spoke French, at least. Her master alone had gone ashore, with bales of goods. A bronzed, foreign-looking man with a patch over one eye and oddly assorted garments; but he spoke good Spanish and Flemish and French. Some said he had gone up to Bruges; others, that he was bartering in the town here. People thought less about him than about the monstrous ship out yonder; the *Gray Cockerel* she was named in French.

Captain Dubois had indeed gone on to Bruges, with his bales and a leather chest that rode ever close to him. Well ahead of him had sped tales of the *Gray Cockerel,* and there was talk of nothing else. Jests flew fast and wide; seamen from stout busses and swift handy galleys heaped derision on the ungainly thing. Some guttural German shipmaster found her name harsh on his tongue, and called her the *"cog."* The name stuck. It was ugly and blunt and awkward, like the ship herself. Amid gales of laughter, it spread over the city.

Coming into Bruges of an afternoon, Dubois went straight to the office of Messer Leonello the great merchant, near the Grand Place on the canal. In his youth, Messer Leonello had come out of Italy into

The master of the *Gray Cockerel*

Dubois entered, and the little chest was brought in. The merchant took one glance at the jewels and trinkets therein, and repressed a gasp. He took the paper Captain Dubois handed him, the list of goods aboard the *Gray Cockerel,* and stupefaction came upon him. Goods of the richest, from silk to cut Genoa velvet, in enormous quantities.

"This is no matter of hours, but of days," he said slowly. "Your goods must come ashore; we must bargain carefully. The town is so filled that you can get no inn-room. May I offer you accommodations in my own house? It will be an honor."

Dubois, with his queer silent laugh, accepted. Then he showed that his left arm was in a sling.

"The yard fell, killed a man, broke my arm," he said. "I may be a trouble to you—"

"I have servants," Messer Leonello said curtly. "They are yours."

So Dubois was lodged in the merchant's house, and the merchant's wife made him welcome. When his one eye fell upon the lovely Eva, it glittered, and a flush came into the dark thin cheeks; when he saw how her gaze touched upon her graybeard husband, he laughed in his silent way, and became very merry. That evening he told many a strange tale of foreign lands, and presented Eva with a little case in which were three enormous matched emeralds.

So courteous was his speech that the girl, stammering refusal, scarce knew how to decline. Messer Leonello bade her accept the gift, and his eyes glinted with avarice, as he thanked the good captain handsomely.

With morning, Dubois slept late, shaved and dressed carefully in new garments of fine gray wool, and finding the merchant gone to his office, talked with Eva. As they talked, he took the patch from his eye, showing a lean brown hawklike face.

"But your eye is sound!" she exclaimed; and he laughed heartily.

"Certainly it is. I made a vow to St. James of

Flanders. He was a citizen now, and a burgher, and had a Flemish name; but men still called him Messer Leonello. He had a thin gray beard, an eye like steel, and was a most vigorous and hearty man. He was, indeed, newly married; and if there were any softness in his heart, which men doubted, it went toward his wife.

Captain Dubois saluted the clerks courteously and brought in his bales and his chest. Messer Leonello came forth, greeted him, and eyed the bales aslant.

"I don't buy cloth by the ell," he said harshly.

Dubois laughed a little.

"Indeed? These are mere samples for your convenience. Perhaps you'll buy jewels by the yard? The leather chest may accommodate you, good messer."

One of the clerks whispered. Oh, the master of the cog, eh? The gaze of Messer Leonello swept his visitor curiously; then he bowed with gravity.

"Will you come into my private office?"

Compostello that during a whole year I would wear an eye-patch, unless I were alone with the most beautiful woman in the world. This is the first time the patch has been removed, dear lady."

She blushed, but showed no anger, and Dubois talked on. Without the patch, he was an eager, handsome man, very gay and of a blithe heart; no mere trader, indeed, but a man of high knightly air and bearing, with all the magic of the wide world at his tongue's end. When he departed for the counting-house, she was in a glow, and her deep blue eyes were all set on wonder and delight; but when the eye-patch was on again, Dubois was a very different person in looks and manner.

Unloading the cog, getting the goods up to the city, was a slow business. No man save port officials was allowed aboard the cog; nor did any of her crew come ashore. Master's orders, they said to the lighter-men, and that was an end to it. They seemed to hold Captain Dubois in stern respect and awe. They were a hard lot, too, the stories ran: men of all nations, apparently, weaponed and armed even while at their work.

Then, after the goods came up to Messer Leonello's warehouses, they had to be examined and appraised; and the little leather chest of gems and trinkets made slow business in itself. Dubois was unhurried. He spent much time with the merchant, and more time with Dame Eva, so that her eyes came to light up when he appeared, and color grew in her cheeks at his word.

As for Dubois, what had begun in pleasant gallantry grew into most deadly earnest. Pity for this lovely girl, tied to an unloved graybeard of iron heart, passed into something deeper as he came to know her better. She had a radiance and a quiet tender bravery that drew his admiration and compelled his respect. Too, she had a delicate clear soul untouched by any stain, so that her blue eyes looked out upon the world with sunny faith, like the eyes of an angel who sees no evil, or refuses to recognize it.

Dubois loved her, and knew that he loved her, and shrank back aghast. He knew, also, the dark and terrible depths of his own evil heart, and this was torment unutterable. For him there was no redemption on this earth—and none beyond, when he reflected on the matter....

Now, there were two English archers carousing in a tavern of Bruges—Long Wat and Tom o' Devon. They had served a year under the Count of Flanders, and had started home with full pockets; but the lasses of Bruges and the good Spanish wine tempted them to fall from grace, and the fall was not by any means light.

Upon a day, they saw Captain Dubois walking with Messer Leonello, and blinked. Long Wat nudged Tom in the ribs; and Tom o' Devon nodded and stared. When they were a trifle sobered, Long Wat made inquiries here and there. Being very blunt and honest men, master bowmen both, they came early one morning to the counting-house and asked private speech with Messer Leonello, and were taken into his office and the door closed. They nudged one another; and Long Wat, fingering his hat, took up the word.

"Master, two years ago we sailed from Southampton with Sir John Calverly's company in many small craft; and a storm came up, and pirates fell upon us. They laid our craft aboard, and the chief of those pirates was one they called Bras-de-fer, or Iron-arm, because one arm ended in a hook of iron. He fought like a devil, and killed good Sir John with a foul blow; and we took oath that if we lived, we would some day put a shaft through that villain. Our other craft rallied, and he drew off, and we're alive; and by our Lady, he's here in this city and calls himself Captain Dubois and is your friend; so we came to give you warning of him."

Messer Leonello's shaggy gray brows drew into a line over his keen eyes.

"How do you know this man is Iron-arm?"

"He looks like him," said Long Wat. "Dressed different, but has a profile not to be missed twice, a high nose and a twist to his lip, and his left arm in a sling to hide the iron spike he wears instead of a hand."

"You're honest men," said Messer Leonello slowly; and he laid out gold. "Here's a rose noble for each of you, with my thanks. Let me know where you may be found, in case your evidence is needed against this rascal."

They complied. "But mind," said Long Wat, "we've sworn to put a shaft through him for the memory of good Sir John; so if it comes to weapons, give us the first chance."

To which Messer Leonello assented very gladly.

Instead of laying information against his guest, he had a very curious conversation with Captain Dubois in the privacy of his office, that same day. The great amount of rich goods coming ashore from the cog, no less than the quantity of jewels, came to a figure higher than any one merchant could handle, he said; therefore he had formed a syndicate of merchants to take care of these goods.

"My colleagues," he went on, "think it odd that you should own so vast stores of goods, instead of handling them on consignment for English merchants. It has even been hinted that you might be acting for some one else—perhaps for sea marauders."

"What?" exclaimed Dubois. "You suggest that I might be acting for pirates, that these goods might have been gained by base piracy? Well, well—and would that make any difference to the purchase of them?"

"No," said Messer Leonello. "But it might cause a discount for cash—eh? And it might lead to future business of a mutually profitable nature."

"I see that we understand one another," said Dubois, with a thin smile. "Suppose that some enterprising captain of freebooters, with several galleys to swell his business, collected large quantities of plunder and fetched them to Sluys—let us say, twice a year. The facts of the matter wouldn't be generally known, of course."

"Naturally," said the merchant, his avid eyes keen. "Nor could his piratical galleys show up with the goods. But this odd ship of yours might do so. In such case, what's to prevent other pirates from pouncing on this ship of yours and seizing the plunder?"

Captain Dubois chuckled. "Why, the ship herself! I built her, planned her, put her into the water, for just such a purpose. With the size of her, she has incredible cargo-space. With the enormous poop and forecastle and thick bulwarks, she overtops any galley made; they can't pour men aboard her. With a stout crew, a catapult in the bows, and a mangonel aft, she can fight off a dozen pirate galleys. D'ye see?"

Messer Leonello stared at him, and clutched with thin fingers at the table.

"By the saints! I see more than that," he said slowly. "Why should not I send out such trading-ships myself, which are proof against pirate galleys?"

Captain Dubois laughed. "You'd have to build 'em. Who'd do it for you? Not I. Not your Flemish shipyards. It'd take them years to make the experiments, the plans, the model ships, to figure strains and stresses, weight and displacement. It took me years to make her." He slapped the merchant on the shoulder and turned to the door. "No, no, my good friend! The secret of the *Gray Cockerel* is mine, and is safe with me."

Messer Leonello sighed. "You're right. Don't forget, the port captain of Sluys is dining with us tonight. *Au revoir!*"

Left alone, however, the merchant fingered his thin gray beard, with eyes that were very bright and fiercely calculating and eager. Ships reasonably safe from sea-marauders spelled fortune for a merchant, if one but had a model on which to build such ships. What was more, an astute man who went about obtaining that model in the right way, might well find a more immediate fortune within his grasp. And it was clear why no one was allowed aboard the Gray Cockerel: Captain Dubois wanted no shipyard men prying into his secrets and obtaining measurements of his ship.

"But," said Messer Leonello softly, "there's always a way! In fact, there are usually several ways."

He sent a clerk on an errand, and the clerk brought back Long Wat, reasonably sober, who sat in talk with Messer Leonello for a long time, and at length drew a long face.

"By Our Lady, messer, you read me a tough riddle! The laws are strict, and devilish severe; any man who bares weapon or looses shaft in Sluys harbor is straightway hanged, and no talk about it. That Captain of Sluys is no man to tempt, either."

"No; but he's my very good friend." And the Italian smiled slowly. "Suppose you get your dozen men together and select the proper boat. Here's money, to make everything ready. Then await word from me. There's no hurry, remember. The right moment may be slow in coming; when it comes, don't fail me or you'll, repent it."

"No danger, messer!" said Long Wat, and departed joyfully.

"How do you know this man is Iron-arm?"

That evening the Captain of Sluys, who had been aboard the cog as his duty demanded, complimented Captain Dubois highly. Never had he seen so stout a ship, quoth he, nor so well manned. Indeed, her outward looks of awkwardness belied her inner excellence. Messer Leonello said little, but his quick eyes darted and lingered shrewdly; a stab of color came into his gray cheeks when he surprised occasional glances between Captain Dubois and his lovely wife.

Dame Eva had a strong desire to see that ship, and so had Messer Leonello, who craved that they might go aboard her.

"Why, so you shall!" said Dubois heartily. "Later, when the freight's out and the water and stores shipped, and she's been made all clean and fresh to behold, we'll go aboard her, and my hospitality may repay a fraction of yours."

"It may indeed," said the merchant with his dark smile. "And I'm sure, my dear Eva, you'll have great pleasure of the visit."

The bartering and bargaining went on, day after day; the rich goods were gradually disposed of; the jewels sank lower in the leather chest, and in their place grew hard round money and bills upon bankers and merchants abroad. Until, as Messer Leonello said with a jesting laugh, the *Gray Cockerel* would prove an empty prize, but a rich one, for any pirates who might master her.

"If any could, they're welcome!" Dubois replied cheerfully.

In these days, he tried to see little of Eva, but could not; and they were greatly together. The love between them became deeper and firmer, though he fought against this also.

"I must tell you this," he said to her one day, desperation in his eyes. "It has come to frankness between us; I love you, but you are another man's wife. I love you, yet I respect you with all my heart and soul. And you must not think twice of me, for I am no good man. I am the opposite, a pirate and a thief and a recreant knight."

She looked at him, and smiled.

"I do not think people are ever fit and ready for heaven each day of their lives," she said gently. "What of it? So much the greater chance for repentance and for good works. I could not love any evil man; and if I hold you in regard, it is because I know you are not evil now. The past is of no account."

"It is of great account," he said hoarsely. "Do you know the story of Iron-arm the pirate? He was once a Norman knight, but he went from better to worse—"

She smiled again. "If you were Bras-de-fer himself, what is that to me? Because I loved him, he would be no longer Iron-arm, but himself once again. No, my dear, don't try to shake our friendship down. This is the one beautiful thing that has ever come into my life. I say no ill of my husband; but my marriage was a matter of buying and selling, and not of joyous happiness. As I think you know well, I would not dishonor either my husband or my love; thus, for the little while you are here, let life be beautiful."

Dubois questioned himself, how would this thing end. She, in her innocence, thought she could be wed to one man and love another, in all goodness. Perhaps she could, being little short of an angel; but it was otherwise with men. Suppose he wakened her from this childish and immature dream-life of hers—suppose he carried her away in the Gray Cockerel. Would this flower-woman droop and fade, or wax strong and blooming?

"By my soul," said he, looking into her eyes, "you are right about it. If the man you love was ever a pirate and a rogue, he is so no more; I swear it! The wealth he has thus won goes to his men, and they go their ways. He'll have none of it, and none of them, henceforth. Instead, there are ways of honesty and good emprise open to him. With this ship of his, he can do great things, for your husband has shown him the way."

Her eyes were starry and very beautiful to see, as she put out her hand to him.

"My dear, I understand; and you make me very happy," she said softly. Dubois pressed her fingers. Then, hearing a step outside, he clapped the patch on his eye.

"By God, I'll open all of life to you, and make you more than happy!" he said quickly.

And yet he knew he could not. He knew that if he yielded to this temptation, the best part of their love would be smashed and broken.

Messer Leonello came in, and smiled upon them thinly, noting the glorious starry eyes of Dame Eva and the alert gayety of Captain Dubois. Presently he went his way again without comment; it was not in his nature to believe that love could exist, without being a criminal love. Eva somehow sensed this.

"I'm afraid!" she said, lifting startled gaze to Dubois. "He suspects something; he has a horrible way of knowing things without being told. And he'd never understand."

"No, he'd never understand," echoed Captain Dubois with a grim smile. "But we've done no wrong, my dear, and we'll do no wrong under this roof, so be of good cheer. He doesn't suspect anything—how should he? Forget it."

Dubois struggled with himself, but could reach no decision. His own future seemed clear: He would sail the *Gray Cockerel* and make an honest living with her, and a fortune to boot; that is, if Eva sailed with him. If she sailed not, then devil take the future! But he must seize her away, carry her off, cause an irrevocable break.

At times it looked simple and logical. Other times, the prospect was impossible; he was afraid for her; and the thought of hurting her, even for the moment, was intolerably tormenting. Yet he must come to it, for the day of his departure was drawing close. The traffic in goods and jewels was about done.

During this while, he had not neglected occasional visits to the cog. His men were well content to stay aboard; carouse would come soon enough elsewhere. Secretly, he had one of the cabins made ready for a lady, sending aboard rich silks and gear that was honestly bought. He could not do otherwise, if Eva was to use it. But he had no suspicion that every move he made was watched and reported to Messer Leonello....

Upon a sparkling summer's day the accounts were settled, and evening saw all finished. With next morning, Dubois was departing; and with noon Messer Leonello and Dame Eva would come aboard, to view the cog and to enjoy his hospitality ere she sailed.

On press of business, the merchant went out that evening, and Dubois saw his lady alone, for the last time. He looked into her eyes and almost did his heart fail him; for he had made his decision now.

"It will not be easy to sail the seas honestly, and alone," he said. "They're too wide for a lonely man, my dear, or for a lonely future."

She smiled a little. "What's easy is not worth while. You need no help; you have all strength within you. Yet it will be hard to think of you—"

Her voice failed, and her eyes fell.

"Why, then, sail with me, always!" said Dubois huskily.

"I will, my dear," she said, not dreaming that he meant his words literally, or that decision tore his heart. "I will, always; you'll have my prayers; you'll have me near you—the best of me, while the worst of me stays here with duty."

Captain Dubois turned away, and put the eye-patch in place again.

With morning, the merchant and Eva saw him off. Messer Leonello pressed his hand warmly, promising to follow to Sluys within an hour and to come aboard in his own barge, that would take them back to shore again.

"You'll have to take your ship outside the port," he went on, "or else you'll not be able to sail later against the tide. Do so; it won't trouble us, for there's no sea running today. And another thing! It is said that the good wishes of men about to take the sea, bring good luck. I'm sending with you a cask of Italian wine from my own cellar, as a gift to your men. Let them drink to my health, and that of my lady, and drink well, so that when we come aboard, all hands will be merry."

For this kindness, Captain Dubois thanked him with right good heart, and so departed....

When they two were about to follow, Messer Leonello smiled upon Eva and bade her wear the three great emeralds Captain Dubois had given her.

"It would do him honor thus to show his gift," said he. "And I beg you, put on that new sarcenet-trimmed dress which so richly sets off your beauty."

So she did. All the way to Sluys, Messer Leonello beamed upon her, and never since their wedding-day had she known him so kindly and intent upon her pleasure.

When they came to the port, the Captain of Sluys met them, and spoke apart shortly with Messer Leonello, and then escorted them to the merchant's wharf houses. Here at the landing-stairs waited a barge, which Messer Leonello had rented, with a dozen men at the long sweeps. Long Wat had the stroke, with Tom o' Devon behind him; and the others were Englishmen also, straight-eyed, hard-bitten master bowmen. At their feet, over the bottom of the barge, a large tarpaulin was laid.

Eva settled herself on soft cushions, under the gilded canopy in the stern. Messer Leonello, beside her, took the tiller, and the barge swept out with oars dipping.

Wide as the harbor was in those days, before it was silted up, the merchant had no little trouble avoiding the ships, so thickly did they lie on every hand, by the hundred; a forest of masts pierced the sky; and as the tide was on the ebb, the outer sandbanks were solid with careening hulls. To the girl, all this was a marvel to behold—strange men and foreign tongues, ships from half Europe, even two galleys filled with Moorish men from Seville, their dark faces alight with mirth and gayety.

On and on the barge threaded its way, coming at length to open water. There, outside the bounds of the port, the cog was at anchor. The gray enormous mass of her was gayly decked with flags and pennons; as they approached, Messer Leonello eyed her with sharp and calculating gaze—the huge square stern, high-crowned with poop, the high side bulwarks, the rising tall forecastle. Ugly, awkward, uncouth—but what a ship wherewith to set all the pirates of the world at naught!

Her ladder was out, and Dubois waved them welcome as they came in under the high side. Two of the rowers made fast the ladder; and laughing at the adventure, Dame Eva fought her way upward. Dubois caught her two hands, lifted her, and swung her in to the deck below; though he had but one arm for the work, it was enough.

And if their lips met for an instant, there in the sunlight, Messer Leonello could not know of it as he jerkily toiled his way upward.

Dubois met him gayly.

"Will your barge return for you, or wait? If the latter, let the men come up."

"Nay, let the rogues stay," said the merchant. "They have their orders, and are well enough off."

"As you like. We've just broached your cask."

The crew, grouped in the waist about the open cask of wine, shouted lusty greeting. Messer Leonello surveyed them narrowly; a hard lot, a bad lot, by their looks. They were quaffing the good Italian wine right heartily.

"Will you come to the poop for the view?" asked

"Take that for good Sir Hugh!" yelled Tom o'Devon. "The dead strike back!"

Captain Dubois. The merchant assented, but the girl laughed and shook her head, as she eyed the high ladders.

"I'm still out of breath from the climb," she responded. "Let me wait here, I beg!"

Dubois shrugged, and accompanied the merchant to the poop, pointing out to him the various features of the cog. Dubois' arm was still in its sling, the patch still over his eye.

When they came down, Dame Eva was among the group of sailors, one of whom was just taking back a huge silver flagon from her hand. Laughing, her eyes sparkling, she turned to Dubois.

"I was joining in the toast to your health, good captain; but I could not drink the half of that huge flagon. My dear husband, I didn't know you had such glorious wine in the cellar! It's magnificent."

"No, *no!*" A hoarse cry broke from Messer Leonello, as he thrust forward. "No! It's impossible—you didn't drink of that wine—"

"Bah! Why not?" Dubois laughed heartily. "Wine never did anyone harm. But come along and see the cabins; the table's laid, and my cooks are busy in the stern cabin."

"Eh?" Messer Leonello, in sudden agitation, swung on him. "I'd like to see the cabin you've furnished for a lady, yes!"

"For a lady?" Dubois eyed him narrowly. "What mean you?"

"Rumor, gossip—God knows!" The Italian turned away. He cast one terrible and inexplicable look at his wife, and wiped sweat from his face, though the sea air was cool enough. "What's done is done, and there's no help for it."

"Say you so?" Dubois laughed harshly, moving aft toward the poop entrance. "If I had a mind, now, I could carry you and your good lady away to sea and hold you both to ransom—eh? What could you do about that, Messer Leonello, and how cure it?"

"Easily enough," said the Italian, throwing a glance forward. There was confusion among the men there; one of them had fallen; the others were grouped about him.

"What? How, then?" And Dubois laughed again, clapping him on the shoulder. "Come, man! How to save yourself from villainous hands?"

"Why, like this!" So speaking, Messer Leonello put a whistle to his lips, and blew a long shrill blast.

Dubois stared at him curiously. Some of the men swung around, looking. Others were crying out, a sudden fear in their voices. Another of the men had pitched forward as though drunk. Messer Leonello went to his wife, and took her hands, and looked into her eyes. His face was gray and drawn. His own eyes were filled with a strange agony.

"God forgive me, and you, my dear!" he said quietly. "I had not intended this; it is too late. Once that wine passed your lips, there was no help for it, indeed. Give me your pardon, I beseech you—"

She shrank a little, not comprehending, but terrorized by the look in his face. Other of the men were bawling out something; they were staggering, clutching at their throats, lifting their voices frantically. Captain Dubois, in wild alarm and perplexity, stared at them, then broke into a run and started for them. Midway, he whipped around, as men came over the rail.

For at that whistle-blast, the rowers in the boat had leaped into life. The tarpaulin was jerked away, to reveal long yew bows and quivered arrows. Long Wat, snatching up a bow, deftly strung it, caught up shafts, and leaped for the ladder, with Tom o' Devon at his heels and the rest trailing.

They came over the bulwark. Some of them leaped to the deck; some stood there on the bulwark, notching their shafts. The voice of Long Wat blared forth shrilly:

"For Sir Hugh! Here, ye damned dogs, the dead strike back at ye!"

The bowstring twanged and hummed. Captain Dubois groaned deeply, and caught at the clothyard shaft, driven to the very goose-feathers through his body. He staggered back against the farther bulwark, and another bowstring twanged, and the second shaft went through his body and pinned him to the oaken bulwark.

"Take that for good Sir Hugh!" yelled Tom o' Devon. *"The dead strike back!"*

No one heard, or cared, that Eva had uttered one screaming cry of grief, and breaking from her husband, rushed across the deck to Dubois. For now men died fast.

"Poisoned! The wine was poisoned!" Too late the cry, too late the swift snatching at arms. Long shafts were hurtling, fast as those dozen bowmen could notch shaft and let fly; hurtling and whistling death across the decks at the staggering, yelling crew.

Some few of these, despite wine and shafts, darted forward. A few men came running from the rear cabins. They died, most of them, as they came. Two or three reached the group of bowmen; and swords flashed, and knives bit; and two of those Englishmen rolled in the scuppers. That was all. Death twanged and whistled until there were no marks left, and the crew of the *Gray Cockerel* lay stretched about the wine-cask or sprawled on the red decks.

Messer Leonello moved to where Captain Dubois hung pinned to the bulwark with eyes already glazing, the black patch gone now. He looked down at his wife; she had fallen to the deck, quivering as those fallen men had quivered about the wine-cask. Then he spat into the face of the dying Dubois, and spoke with a snarl of hatred.

"Thrice-damned dog! Even so, she's better off than gone overseas with you and leaving me shamed. Take the blame to your own soul, for I wash my hands of it."

"Judas!" said Dubois, very faintly.

*His eyes flew open. He made a sudden, spas*modic effort, and tore his arm free of the sling. Steel glittered; the spike he wore in place of hand drove out, squarely to the breast of Messer Leonello. And with that one last effort, he died.

The Italian staggered. That sharp, hard thrust had torn his mantle away, revealing the chain-mail beneath. Unhurt, he gathered the mantle around him, turned to meet the wondering Englishmen, who knew not how his wife had died; and his gaze lifted along the decks. He caught sight of a barge approaching, and a smile touched his bearded lips.

"Ready, men! The Captain of Sluys is coming aboard, and you're outside the harbor bounds and in no danger," said he. "And mind, there's reward enough for the killing of these pirates to send you all back to England rich men: You did well."

Long Wat met his gaze, looked down at the sweet dead face on the deck, and looked up again with a low oath.

"I'm not so sure of that," said he. "But our vow's fulfilled, and plague on your money!"

The lights went up. A stage, the puppet-show, the beaming features of the broken-nosed Dutchman—we all of us came suddenly and awkwardly back to the present, and to where, we were.

"And that was the beginning of the cog, the great cargo craft of northern Europe!" said Rubens, as he joined us. "Messer Leonello founded a trading company, built ships, died a man of tremendous wealth and power—"

"And went to hell, if your story's true," said somebody with an oath.

It was a tribute; and Rubens took it as such. The utter mastery of his little show had left us all shaken. Still, there was one point that remained vague.

"Rubens! One thing I didn't get: Did Dubois intend to run away with the girl or not? What decision had he reached?"

Murmurs of assent showed that others had the same doubt. Rubens beamed around at us, and chuckled softly.

"My good friends, I thank you; this is a compliment to my art, and I am very proud of it. You see, gentlemen, all great art leaves something to be desired. Frustration, the agony of the heroic soul, is the theme of great epics. This little epic of mine brings to life the people of a past day and age; it teaches you something about ships, maybe, and it leaves you asking a question."

"Well, answer it!" I blurted. "Did Dubois intend to carry off the girl?"

Rubens spread his hands wide in an eloquent gesture.

"My dear sir—I do not know. History and legend fail to say. You must answer that question yourself, after the dictate of your own heart. The show is over; shall we have a little drink all around—just a tiny drink?"

A GIRL LIKE A SWORD

S*omebody had tried to put something over* on Inspector Rosch, and he was really angry. You would not have thought that a gentle, spectacled, gray-haired Customs official who had the smile of a benignant cherub could make the fur fly; but Inspector Rosch made it fly all over Port Huron and parts of Michigan adjacent.

Then he returned to his interrupted talk with me.

"Where was I?" he demanded. "Oh, yes! Pirates, lateen rig, history—the funny thing about history is that it hasn't a darned bit of interest unless you get the human side of it. Right?"

"Dead right, Inspector," I assented. "I wish I had your knowledge of ships, too. But you mentioned the lateen rig and its origin."

"Yes." He rubbed his chin and looked across the river at the Canadian shore, and the new bridge that had done away with the old ferry. "Yes. That got its start with a chap who was in a bad jam. One of the knights of St. John, who held Rhodes and made it their business to fight the Moslem pirates."

"Hold on," I said cautiously. "The lateen rig started away back before then. And those knights of St. John used galleys entirely. No sails at all. Just oars."

He chuckled. "Your story is where human interest lies, isn't it? A man may invent a thing, and a lot of folks use it, and nothing comes of it until some one comes along and grabs the works and introduces it in a big way. True?"

"Sometimes," I admitted, still cautiously; it doesn't pay to be too cocksure with any government man. "But let's keep the record straight. Those knights were swell fighters and left a big mark on history; still, they were vowed to celibacy. Where's your human interest in that?"

"Right there, maybe," said he. "Boy, when a monk falls in love, you've got one hell of a human-interest story to follow up!"

"These knights weren't monks," I objected; and he nodded.

"They were vowed to celibacy, though. They were drawn from the eight chief nations of Christendom at the time; they all came of great families. Each nation had its own college or home at Rhodes, but they usually worked together for the Order, regardless."

"Where'd you learn so much about it?" I asked curiously. "And what has it to do with the lateen rig? The Arabs really took over that rig from the Egyptians."

"Sure; but the fighting ships of the Mediterranean were galleys just the same," he rejoined. "You know, my folks used to be French. The name was St. Roche originally, until one of them came over with Lafayette and settled here! He fetched along a lot of old family papers and such truck, and I've dug some queer things out of those documents. One was about the lateen rig, and that old ancestor of mine was in one bad fix, by the looks of it. I can't stand here gabbing all day, so if you'd like to look the yarn over, I'll send it along. You can use it if you want."

I told Inspector Rosch I'd be tickled pink to get his ancestor's yarn, and went my way. He sent it to me, all right. And when I dipped into it, so help me, I thought at first he had gypped me. Story? Human interest? Celibacy? Lateen rig? Where was it all?

Nothing here but a storm-lashed islet in a driving sea.

The picture of it grew upon me. A steep, rocky islet, so sharply jutting out of the water that a goat could not climb it. A man could; men had, for atop the rock was a thick-walled castle of reddish stone. Hence the name of Castelrosso. Below was an excellently protected little harbor in which two naked galleys were rocking. On the storm-wrecked horizon lay the mountains of Asia Minor. On the rocky shores of the islet, wreckage was strewn. A ship had struck and gone to smash there. But on the whole islet, not a living soul was visible—at first.

Then a figure grew, coming from a postern gate of that castle apparently deserted. This was a man who wore no armor; a belt closed the mantle of the Order, black with a white cross, showing he was one of the knights. Alone, he came down to the rocky wreckage-strewn shore and stared at the tossing débris there. He was a young man, but his face was haggard and curiously drawn.

A faint, gasping voice reached him. He stirred, started into life, and suddenly plunged down thigh-deep in the water below. A tossing mass of spars and timbers drove in at him; amid it was a human figure, hand outstretched. The man seized the hand; in two minutes he had drawn to safety the sole survivor of this wreck: a woman, shivering and spent, wearing a scarlet silken robe that clung to her body—a young woman, with rich masses of black-blue hair that fell in wet ringlets about her waist and knees.

"Courage! Not hurt? Climb, then!" He supported her with stout arm and cheering words, and helped her up the steep rock. Occasional glimpses showed that no other living thing had come ashore. Twice she nearly collapsed, but they made the little entrance and went on into the castle.

A deathly place, a ghastly place, with nothing alive in the walls, yet with evidences of abundant life all around. They passed through the courtyard, up a stairs, and the knight led her to a room.

"Rest," he said. "Dry clothes are here in plenty. I'll bring you food and wine. Do you understand?"

She gave him a wanly flashing smile and replied in his own French.

"Certainly. You are very good. You are not alone here?"

"I am alone," said the knight, and withdrew. His voice echoed from the empty walls with mournful cadence; the words seemed to linger and hang in the air.

After a time he came back with a tray, knocked, and entered at her word. She was lying on the bed, heaped over with blankets; her scarlet robe lay wet on the floor. Her black hair was spread out over the pillows like a cloud, her extended arms were bare to the shoulder, but a laugh sat in her eyes and warm color in her cheeks, and Pierre St. Roche saw that she was beautiful and had a straight, firm gaze.

"You're a knight of St. John!" she exclaimed. "What place is this?"

"Castelrosso Island," he replied. "I am Pierre St. Roche, Knight Commander of the Order. I command the garrison here; the island belongs to Rhodes."

"Where is your garrison?" she asked.

"Dead," he replied, and set down the tray. "I'll leave you this—"

"No; don't go. I don't want to sleep. I'm quite all right," she said. "A little wine is all I need. St. Roche! Weren't you at Cyprus last year with the Grand Master?"

"Yes." He poured wine and held it to her lips, smiling a little as she drank. Never, he thought, had he seen so lovely a thing as this girl; she was no more than a girl. "And your name, lady?"

As she met his gaze, a tide of color came into her cheeks.

"Eleanor," she said in a low voice. "More than this, I do not wish to tell you; nor do I wish to lie to you, Sir Pierre. Will you be satisfied with the one word?"

"While it bears a smile, yes,"—and laughing, he sat beside her. "There's nothing I can do for you, really?"

"Nothing, thanks; I'll get up and dress presently. It's afternoon. Did you say all your garrison is dead?"

"All," he assented. "Forty knights, retainers, slaves—all. I buried the last a week ago. A Pisan galley stopped for water, and left us the plague in exchange. When a galley from Rhodes will arrive, I do not know. Luckily, we have no lack of anything here."

He wondered how she would take it. The plague—dread word! The plague had swept the whole world, these last fifty years. Death in the sea might have been easier. For an instant her cheeks blanched; then she smiled, and put her hand in his, and her voice was steady and unafraid.

"Good! You have a recruit. I think you yourself are in bitter need of rest; go and sleep. I'll watch, and waken you at sunset."

He saw that she meant her words. And in his fine, strong features she read relief. She comprehended that he had been on watch night and day, lest either friend or enemy show up.

"Eleanor! That is a queen's name," said he, and kissed her fingers. "At sunset." He went out, stumbling with utter exhaustion.

A few hours sleep made vast difference. He was himself again, alert, ten years younger; his body, hardened to bear the weight of armor, was a ripple of corded sinew. And he found her, for lack of any woman's gear in the place, garbed in the surcoat and doublet of one of the dead knights; but these garments could not hide the lovely warm lines of her body, and her face was like a flower. The straight, true eyes of her kindled a flame in him which he could not and would not conceal.

What was more to the point, he found a cooked meal ready; and this, after a week and more of moldy cheese and bread, was no less than a miracle....

Thus began what, for Pierre St. Roche, was the most joyous time of all his life. Not because he was alone with a beautiful girl in a place of death; but because this girl had within her a spirit that was a blazing force, and because she loved him. Of this he was sure all too soon, and of himself as well.

That she was no vagrant demoiselle he knew at once. Things slipped out; besides, she had authority, and there was the fine high goodness of her. A girl like a sword, to be reverenced and kept from all stain and held in knightly honor; so he held her, indeed. They were alone in the company of the dead, and love ripened fast between them.

She talked much of herself, not at all of her life or station. She showed him a wide girdle that had been under her robe when she came ashore. It had many little pockets, and each held precious stones of great price, all manner of them, so that Roche stood aghast.

"It is a fortune!" he said in awe, and she laughed at his expression, and swept up the stones carelessly.

"No doubt. What is that to a knight vowed to a simple life and celibacy?"

But not to chastity. Simplicity, celibacy, warfare against the infidel, poverty, yes; yet they were not monks, these knights of the white cross. Roche put the thought sternly away from him. Still, they were alone within the wide compass of sea and sky, and love grew upon them.

And there was the eternal peril to quicken emotion. Any Moorish, Egyptian or Turkish corsair that dared take a chance would find them and the castle at its mercy. Indeed, on the fourth day of her presence here, a sail broke the horizon. Roche dashed off for his armor, and when he regained the walls found a new person there. Leather coat and chain-mail, black hair sheared short by sword-edge, dark sun-browned face no more telltale than the blurred figure. He stared.

"I'd not dream you were the most beautiful woman in the world—or a woman at all!"

"Safer so, perhaps," said she. "I'll keep the costume. And the ship?"

He squinted at the sea. "Veering off. A Moor, by her sail; she'll not tempt our galleys, after all. Little she knows! Safer so, you say; afraid of me, are you?"

"Afraid of you?" She came close to him and looked

into his face, her dark eyes more lovely and eloquent than any words. "No, my dear, not of you!"

Roche trembled, and touched her hand. Suddenly he took her in his arms and kissed her on the lips, and she did not say no to that. Then he loosed her.

"I'll not do that again," said he, but did it; then after a little, drew away from her again.

"By God, I will not," he said, and did not. However, there was no hurt in speaking of love, and this they did very frankly and tenderly, looking out upon the sky and sea. Each of them joyed in the other, and their hands clasped and their bodies drew close, but before their lips met, Roche stood up.

"An oath is an oath, and though I love you with all my heart, I will not kiss you again, my dear. Perhaps, indeed, because I do love you."

She agreed with him, though no doubt sorely against her will, and they came to speak of other matters. Roche talked of Rhodes, of the knights there, of his cruises against the Moors. And looking down at the empty naked galleys in the little harbor below, he shook his head, frowning.

"Look at them! Oars alone, with slaves rowing them; and the corsairs, who had both sails and oars, ever hold the advantage of us. Here, come with me. I want to show you something."

The horizon was clear now, the ship gone. He caught her hand and led her down into a room below. Here, upon a small block of wood, was mounted a tiny arrangement of mast, sails and ropes.

"Do you know anything about ships, Eleanor?"

"A little." Her dark eyes danced. "All my life has been lived with them."

"Good! As you know, the galleys of the Order use oars alone, no sails; so do all war-galleys. But Moorish and Egyptian corsairs use sails as well. They have the speed of us, and often they escape us, with their big lateen sails. Now it is in my mind that if we had a fighting galley with canvas, as well as oars, we'd be able to smite the infidel hip and thigh."

"Obviously. The galleys of Venice use sails, however."

Roche grimaced. "Yes; square sails, like the old Roman ships. Clumsy, unhandy; the lateen holds a better wind and is quicker in stays. A corsair can sail rings around any Venetian. Now, here's a rig I've worked out for use with our galleys—"

He showed her the working of the miniature rig, how the lines ran, how the high lateen would catch light winds, could swing now here, now there, how the imaginary galley could outsail heavier craft, portly cogs or dromonds with their great square sails.

"It's absurd that this rig should be left to heathen infidels to use," he concluded frowningly.

The girl's eyes flashed.

"Right! Why should it be, then? Why not make use of it?"

"The Grand Master orders, we obey. He is a very gentle knight, but elderly. What, says he, make use of sails when we have Moorish slaves to handle oars? Never been heard of and never will be in his time. And that's the answer."

"Poor Pierre!" she said softly, and her fingers found his. "Never mind, my dear; there will come a day, I promise you! Is this thing the desire of your heart?"

"It's one of two, and you're the other," he said. "And there's no hope of either."

"You might be absolved of your vows and leave the order."

"How support a wife, then? Besides, it could only be done at the request of a king or a great man, or of the Grand Master; I've no influence. No, my heart; I must love you all my life. And if as I think you are some noble lady of Cyprus, so much the worse for us. The king and others of the Lusignan family, who own all that island, are very jealous and proud, and would never consent that one of their great ladies should marry a poor and humble knight."

"That is true," she said, and her face was troubled. Then it cleared. "But if we love each other, my dear, does it matter if we ever marry?"

"To be honest about it, yes. It matters a good deal," Roche said.

She laughed and pressed his arm.

"Good! I agree with you. We may find a way; now let's see about supper."

Another day descended upon them, and another; the sea was empty, and the blue mountains of Armenia hung upon the horizon, and they were alone.

A bitter man was Pierre St. Roche in these days. A happy man in the moment, yet bitter at thought of the long years ahead, and the hopeless future. He had no powerful friends in the Order. His command of this islet fortress was by way of punishment, because he had cried out against the luxury and small regard for their vows which possessed so many of the knights at Rhodes. And now, as though by ironic fate, love had come into his life and a wild desire to escape from those vows; but he could not.

Yet he, and Eleanor who loved him, were too high of soul and too knightly bred to seek any way out that might besmirch love and honor.

Then, abruptly, came the end. A sail broke the horizon, and another vessel; a galley of the Order escorting some merchant here to Castelrosso. Roche shouted aloud and ran for his armor. When he came forth, all in mail from head to foot, he met with Eleanor and stared again at her. She had found nondescript garments and some stain to darken her face yet more. She did not seem a woman at all.

"You must not tell them my name, or that I am a woman," she exclaimed.

"I cannot lie," he said simply.

"No need. Listen! I was being sent by my family to marry a lord whom I had never seen." She spoke rapidly, breathlessly. "Now let the ship be accounted lost and all in her; let my family think me dead. You see? You don't know who I am, Pierre; you've only my word for it. Excellent! I tell you that I'm Jean Guiri, a merchant of Cyprus; and that ends it. I have jewels and therefore am wealthy—"

He plunged thigh-deep into the water, and in two minutes had drawn to safety the sole survivor of the wreck.

"But good God, girl!" cried Roche, looking at her from tormented eyes. "Where will you go? It means that we must part."

"Yes," she said, with tears springing to her cheeks. "Trust in God, my dear."

The two ships came in. One was a ship of the Order, with forty knights aboard, and the other was a Venetian galley bound to Crete. This great and wealthy island was owned by Venice and was her richest possession.

The Venetian was anxious to be on her way, and readily gave passage to Jean Guiri. So well had the girl disguised her figure, that her sex was not suspected. Roche parted from her with a handclasp and kept the torture of his heart secret. When he came back to his own room, he found his block of wood and the model of his rigging vanished entirely; he guessed she might have taken it as a memento of him, but cared not. Nothing mattered to him now.

Worse was to come. The galley landed what knights and slaves it could spare, and sped back for Rhodes to send other ships with a new garrison. Roche, talking that night with the knights who remained to help keep the fortress, heard them discussing the wreck of the ship from Cyprus. Jean Guiri had given the name of that ship.

"This will be sore news for the Lusignan family," said one. "On board that ship was the king's daughter. She was going to the Morea, to be married to the Count of Modica. And now she is lost, and her wealth with her."

"What was her name?" asked another.

"The Lady Eleanor," the first replied. "I met her in Cyprus a year or so ago, and she was the flower of all that family, and the loveliest of women."

Pierre St. Roche knew then with whom he had been dealing, and choked down a groan. Now, even had other things been equal, she was more removed from him than ever. And she was gone into the world, and lost to him.

He fell into a brooding melancholy from which nothing could stir him. This passed into a fever; and when the ships came with the new garrison, he was taken back to Rhodes for treatment, a very sick man.

Here, after some weeks, he began a slow recovery, but there was no joy in him. The general opinion was that he was oppressed by thought of all those gentlemen who had died at Castelrosso, he alone surviving; but the matter was much worse. Upon Roche had settled the conviction that he was marked out by destiny for misfortune, that he was accursed, that whatever he touched would turn to grief and loss and death. So firmly did this notion lay hold upon him that it became a fixed idea in his mind, and he had no interest in anything, and talked of entering some religious order....

One day a Venetian trading-ship came into the harbor. Her master, who was a supple Greek seaman, sought an audience with the Grand Master and obtained it readily.

"I hear in the town," said he, "that Sir Pierre St. Roche is grievously ill. Once I owed my life and freedom to this noble knight; two years ago he captured a Moorish corsair in which I was a slave at the oars. Now I may repay his kindness. I am bound for Acre to trade with the Arabs there, and we have aboard a skilled physician of great fame. Let this knight, I pray you, go with us that our physician may heal him."

"Willingly would I grant him leave," said the Grand Master, "and though his illness is more of mind than body, the voyage might benefit him. However, this is for Sir Pierre himself to say."

He summoned Roche, who looked at the Greek, and said he did not know the man. What he did, however, was all one to him; he accepted leave, indifferently, and sent for his armor, and with evening went aboard the Venetian. When the anchor was up and the galley standing out of the harbor, the Greek took him to one of the cabins.

"The physician will see you, Lord," said he.

"Indeed?" Roche shrugged. "I saw cannon on the deck, and your crew have the look of soldiers rather than seamen."

"They are soldiers, Lord," said the Greek. "Twenty Catalan crossbowmen and thirty seamen who are trained men at arms. And we have fifty slaves for the oars."

"But these sails, this rigging?" In the gathering dusk, Roche frowned up at the spars and canvas. "By heavens, where did you outfit this ship? If this is not

Messer Mocenigo, the Venetian.

my own rigging, the sails and, ropes that I planned myself—hah! Answer me!"

"The ship is owned by this same physician, Lord." The Greek threw open the cabin door. "He is awaiting you."

Roche went into the cabin. A man rose to greet him; a man who uttered a low choked cry and clung suddenly to him, a man whose soft rich voice pierced into his soul, whose eyes brought comprehension to him, whose embrace set him to trembling. No man indeed, but the maid Eleanor! Roche sank down beside her and gripped her hands.

"Oh, this is madness, my dear, madness!" he said, and groaned. "I know who you are; Dame Eleanor of Cyprus is accounted dead. You have let your family think—"

"Plague take my family!" she exclaimed. "I've little to love them for; I've everything to love you for, Pierre. If they knew I was alive, they'd sell me off to some noble in wedlock. You've been ill, I hear—ah, my dear one, I'll make you well again!"

"No, no, you must not tempt me!" he cried hoarsely. "Now that I've seen you, now that I've held you in my arms, know you still love me, I'm well again and strong, and life is a different thing. Put the ship back—"

She laughed. "But you don't understand! This is your own ship, the galley which you dreamed, rigged with the sails and ropes you had on your little model! I've been in Crete all this time; no one suspected I was not Jean Guiri, a man, a merchant. The Venetians sold me this galley, I had her rigged and armed, I bought slaves, I hired archers and fighting men. She's yours, you understand? Now take her and seek the infidel corsairs, and put your great idea to the proof! Here is one of your heart's desires come true."

"And you did this!" muttered Roche, overwhelmed with it all, when once he fully understood the matter. "You— But how? It must have cost a fortune!"

She laughed again. Her joyous, eager laughter was a brave thing to hear.

"I *had* a fortune; those gems—you remember them. Now none are left, and the outcome is in your hands. Seek plunder from the Moors, or we all starve!"

When Roche heard this, his admiration and love and wonder passed all bounds, and the heart quickened in him. Then it faltered again.

"It is no use," he said gloomily. "No luck will come of it. Whether I forget my vows and become a recreant knight and go off to the world's end with you, or whether I hold to honor, I am accursed in either case. Put me on shore and leave me, I warn you."

"Don't be a fool," she said quickly. "I'm not here to argue. I've staked everything on you, on your love, on your ability; and I don't intend you shall fail me. The Grand Master gave you leave of absence. Make the most of it! Remember, aboard this ship I'm not a woman but a man. Now, what you need is a drink, a square meal, and a long sleep; and you shall have them, and wake up captain of your own dream-ship."

So he did, though even in the morning sunlight it all seemed a vision unreal. None the less, Roche took heart, forgot his misgivings, and donned his armor that day for the first time in long weeks.

The ship, his ship! Bought for him with her love, her faith, her wits, her jewels; humility touched him with the thought, and a surge of savage resolve that he would be worthy of her. He found the crew good enough, the Catalan cross-bowmen superb, and he drilled them according to his liking, working them at the ropes and the little cannon day after day. To the slaves at the oars he gave wine instead of whips, so that they put out their strength gladly for him.

But the sea remained empty.

The days passed. Roche headed for the Greek islands, where the corsairs were wont to raid for slaves and lay in wait for Byzantine galleys; Moors they saw none. Provisions were running low. The Catalans began to murmur about ill luck. It was true they had cruised for weeks and sighted no one. Questions of pay arose; the Lady Eleanor had no more money. Her jewels had all been sold. And Roche, who had a guilty feeling about the whole affair, scanned the seas with his mouth adroop at the corners and the old sense of misfortune bearing him down.

"I tell you, whatever I touch will come to evil destiny!" he said fiercely to the girl, his eyes clouded and somber.

"Nonsense! We can put in at Candia and mortgage the ship," she returned.

He shook his head. "It's no use."

"At least, you have your strength again!"

He eyed her gloomily. Before he could speak, the Greek master knocked hastily, and came into the cabin on the word, his eyes rolling.

"Guns! Flashes of guns on the horizon, Lord! Ships at work there—"

Roche leaped up, and darted on deck. It was true. A calm, almost windless sea, and across the horizon the flashes of guns. The oars were put out.

All that night they rowed on, until with dawn sprang up a fine steady wind and the weary slaves rested. The guns still flashed, and now could be heard plainly enough. Short deep-throated culverins, like those the galley herself carried. But with the dawn, they ceased.

The red dawn streaked across the sky, and the ships came clear. Here was a great galley of Venice, dismasted and crippled, and about her lay three Moorish craft, pouring their men aboard her, the Venetians still holding their deck with flash of steel. The corsairs poured back into their own craft, the three put out, and leaving their helpless prey for the moment, they came driving with oars and sail at the approaching galley.

Roche was in full armor, the mantle of the Order belted over his Milan mail. Jean Guiri stood by him clad in steel cap and chain-mail. He took the helm from the Greek. His voice rang down the deck; it was his moment, the moment of which he had dreamed.

"Catalans! To the starboard rail. Stand by the lines and take cover, seamen; gunners ready! All oars inboard."

He had the wind of them; this was what he needed most. The three corsairs spread out to lay him aboard, crews massed, the drums sounding, and yells to Allah rending the sky. They drew in to catch him, grapnels ready, arrows already pattering.

His voice lifted again; he swung the tiller. Sharp-darting, the galley wheeled and evaded those three, whose bow-guns were already spouting smoke and flame. Wheeled on, leaned steeply to the thrusting wind, suddenly drove at the nearest of them, and swept in upon her as she desperately came about. Struck her larboard oar-bank and tore along it, shattering her oars, throwing her into confusion while her tumbled rowers shrieked. Sudden the guns banged out. The Catalans rose and loosed their deadly quarrels at short range into the crowded mass of Moors, loosed again and again.

Then the galley wheeled and was off, leaving one of those corsairs crippled in oars and her mast down, and bore straight for the other two. There came rush after rush, while she wheeled and luffed and evaded, only to swoop in again with deadly aim and pour death into one of the two, then into the other.

Not unscathed this time. From the guns of the corsairs, stones hurtled across her decks and struck down men, arrows pelted aboard, and scarlet rivulets went trickling into her scuppers. The Greek master fell, a shaft through his throat. Jean Guiri took his place at the tiller, leaning on it as Roche commanded.

He had the heels of them and kept the wind of them, darting now here, now there, the lateen sail and the jib forward handling her as though by magic. They had the same canvas, but not that of his devising; and the crossbow bolts smote them sore, and as the galley wheeled and wheeled, her guns vomited into them and swept their decks.

Roche bore into the fray; that broad blade of his sheared through chain-mail and turban. Behind him the Catalans fought like devils.

"No bolts left for the crossbows, Pierre!" shouted Jean Guiri, brown features white and strained, woman's eyes wide and set. The Catalans, most of them, had laid aside their arbalests and were taking to sword and shield. Roche nodded. As he did so, one of the corsairs fired her guns. A lead slug smashed into his helmet and sent him headlong on the deck.

Jean Guiri leaped to aid him, and got him up, dizzy and shaken. In this moment the tiller swung untended; a moment of disaster. One of the corsairs smashed full into her bows and flung grapnels, and scimitars flashed across her rail. The other, momentarily disabled, got out oars to creep up astern.

The battle-cry of the Order pealed up. Roche, his heavy sword swinging, bore into the fray. Sword and sling and arrow left his clanking figure unscathed, but that broad blade of his sheared through chain-mail and turban. The attack was met and held and checked. Behind him, the Catalans fought like devils, and the seamen drove into the fray, casting the Arabs back to their own decks and following after. Certain of these seamen bore axes, and suddenly the mast of the corsair toppled and crashed down.

"Back!" shouted Roche, and headed his men back aboard, casting off the grapnels. Barely in time, too; the other corsair was coming up under her stern. Just in the nick, she veered away; the lateen sail swung to the wind, and was clear.

Two of the Moors lay crippled now. Roche, unheeding the rain of arrows that poured in upon him, aimed for the third corsair; he was doing the hunting now, grimly determined. Desperately the Moor evaded, but could not escape. At last Roche had his prey, luffed sharply and drove for her, seamen handling the lines expertly. This time he crashed along her starboard bank of oars, splintering them, smashing them.

"Let loose the slaves!" he shouted, and promised freedom to all those who fought for him. They yelled like madmen. Already he was bearing back, coming alongside that third corsair again. Grapnels were flung. They caught, they held. And now Roche headed his own men over to her blood-slippery decks, and hewed his way through the Moors until their captain fell under his sword. Then, with yells of despair, they surrendered.

Wounded here and there, blood running from under his armor, Roche leaned on his sword and panted forth orders. The Christian slaves chained to the benches of the corsair were freed. Most of them leaped for weapons and followed him back, aboard his own ship. No lack of men now!

The grapnels were loosed. He bore down upon one of the two cripples and laid it aboard, and was over on the Moor's decks when a shrill, high yell from Jean Guiri gave him warning. The second cripple was heading in, oars aflash, and it was too late to evade. She smashed into the bows of his ship with cruel force and her men poured over.

Now befell the grimmest fight of all. Each of the Moorish champions tried to bring down that steel-clad figure whose mantle had been ripped away and whose massive sword swung in tireless hands of death. Bring him down they could not, but one by one went down themselves before him. The freed slaves, Moor and Christian, fought like devils behind him, and those who remained of his own men.

So in the end one ship was cleared, and then the other, until the Moors chose slavery rather than steel, and flung down their arms. Then Roche found Jean Guiri at his side, screaming something. Exhausted, he put up the vizor of his helmet.

"But if we love each other, my dear, does it matter?" she asked. "To be honest about it, yes. It matters a good deal," Roche said.

"The ship, the galley! She's sinking, Pierre—her bows were crushed—"

Barely able to stand, utterly spent, Roche took the blow helplessly. It was true. His galley was sagging, was filling fast, her bows smashed in. For his men, engaged in making the victory secure, all was wild exultation, but for him, defeat. Wearily, he put off his helmet. Jean Guiri helped him doff his armor, and bound up his half-dozen wounds.

"We've won, and we've lost everything," he said. "Three corsairs taken, yes; but our own galley gone."

"But she proved your ideas, Pierre!"

He laughed bitterly. "At the cost of everything. Our men gone, our ship gone. What good are these corsair hulks, these Moorish slaves, to us? None. I told you there was no luck in loving me, in anything I did. There is a curse upon me, and it is the end."

He sank down upon the deck, leaned back against the bulwarks, and stared before him with eyes dulled and lifeless. The weakness of complete exhaustion had him in its hold. His eyes closed and he passed into unconsciousness.

The Venetian ship drew down, and men from her came aboard in a small boat.

When Roche came to himself, he was in the richly dight cabin of the corsair. Jean Guiri was gone now. Beside him was Eleanor, all disguise flung aside, pouring wine between his lips. He wakened, drank gratefully, and felt warmth flood into him. A third person was here, a grave, keen-eyed man clad in the sober garb of Venice.

"Pierre!" exclaimed the girl. "This is Messer Carlo Mocenigo of Venice—"

"Who owes you life and liberty, noble knight," said the Venetian, smiling. His eyes went from one to the other of them, probing, questing, comprehending. Roche nodded and let his chin fall on his chest.

"It is nothing," he said dully. "You have won much. I have lost everything. You owe me no thanks."

"Still, I desire to speak with you in all courtesy," Mocenigo said. "How you fought those Moors was a marvel. Never have I seen a galley so handled, or one so rigged as to accomplish miracles."

"And you never will again," said Roche bitterly, and came to his feet. "Good signor, if you would talk, then talk with this gentle lady, who has also lost much. I must ask you to excuse me and charge me with no discourtesy; I need the fresh air, and am in no mood to talk."

He went out on deck and paced up and down the red planks, speaking to no one. He had won a victory, yes, and a bitter one. Now he knew, more than ever, that life held nothing for him and for this woman who loved him. He regretted sharply that he had not died in this fight. There was nothing left for him, or her!

Of a sudden he halted his stride, and his brows drew down. He saw Mocenigo before him, and was angry.

"You still press me?" he exclaimed.

"Yes." The Venetian smiled gravely. "You have lost a ship, sir knight, but you have, perhaps, gained a hundred ships, or five hundred."

"Eh?" Roche looked hard at him. "What d'you mean?"

"Why, just this: Venice needs you; come and take charge of the Arsenal, and provide us with war-galleys that will handle as speedily and neatly as this ship of yours handled. With such ships, Venice will sweep Genoa off the sea! Can you do it?"

"No," said Roche, though his pulses hammered. "I am vowed to the Order, signor, and could not do this without being released from my vows."

Mocenigo's lips twisted slightly.

"Aye? Released—for Venice, or for other reasons?"

"It is impossible," Roche said curtly. "I have no influence, no wealth."

"Venice has wealth for you, and influence for others," Mocenigo said. "Listen! This is a business proposition, sir knight. Will you come to Venice with me? Yes or no. I'll guarantee your release from the vows of the Order, and full charge of the Arsenal."

Roche stared at him a moment, then grunted skeptically.

"And what's your guarantee worth? How do I know you have any influence?"

"I should have," said Mocenigo. "I'm one of the Council of Ten, and my uncle happens to be the Doge. Yes or no?"

The Lady Eleanor had come up to them, listening.

"Yes," she said briskly, and took the arm of the astounded Roche. "Yes, my Lord, a thousand times yes! Eh, Pierre?"

It was already said. And when Mocenigo turned to his boat, she shook Roche by the arm and looked up into his face with wide starry eyes.

"My brother is Cardinal de Lusignan, and my father's the King of Cyprus," she said softly and gayly, "but you're the only living soul who will ever know it, my dear. Are you satisfied with your evil future, and properly ashamed, and very humble?"

Roche laughed, as though a weight had fallen from his heart, and kissed her.

"I'm humble, for all my life long, before you," he said.

So there was the story, as I got it from the old documents of Inspector Rosch. Next time I was in Port Huron, I had a chat with him about it all. The curious thing was, that there was really something in the story, for I had discovered that about this time Venice did change over the rig of her galleys, and swept the seas with them. When I asked the Inspector about that point, he laughed.

"Well," he said, "I've got the best possible proof that it's all true, although I didn't mention the fact. You see, I'm the proof."

"You?" I said, puzzled. He chuckled softly.

"Yep, me! You see, this Pierre St. Roche was the last of the family—and I've got the genealogy to prove it."

I got the point after a minute.

"You mean, he married the girl!"

"Just that," said Inspector Rosch.

GOOD NIGHT TO ALL THE WORLD

Bill Joyce flipped the landing net expertly and eased the big pike into the boat, then hitched up his sweater and beamed.

"Four pounds if it's an ounce," said he. "That's the kind of a wall-eye to land! Now we've got a four-mile row home, so hop to it."

"And what'll you be doing?" I inquired sarcastically.

"Trolling," he said, "and talking. That's the best thing I do."

With a grunt, I put out the oars. Bill Joyce, broad and stocky, looked like a football player for all his grizzled hairs, and so he was. He did not look or act like a college professor, but he was that too, and a few things more. He must have read my mind, for he gave me a grin.

"Even a college professor may have something on the ball," he observed genially. "Ever hear of a Norwegian cat?"

"No, but I saw a Siamese in town yesterday."

He chuckled. "This is a ship, not a feline. Single mast well for'ard in the eyes of the boat, with a lugsail and bowlines; the craft itself double-ended like a Viking ship. Hasn't been in use for three hundred years or so, but did a great thing once. By the way, you write stories, and stories have got to deal with heroes, so you ought to be an expert. What's your notion of a hero, anyhow?"

I cocked a wary eye at Bill.

"Might be anyone or anything. Might be a little old woman who drags a man around by the hair; might be a stalwart buck with two guns and notches on 'em; might be an office clerk who slugs the cop on the corner—"

"Aw, lay off," struck in Bill. "I'm serious. What's your real idea of a hero?"

"Let's say, the soldier of fortune—sometimes. What's yours?"

"All right. I'd say, the feller who sets out to lick the world and who gets licked, and who knows he's licked and yet hangs on and keeps his chin up, and finally crawls out with the world by the tail."

"You sound like a football pep-talk."

"Football, hell!" grunted Bill Joyce, who runs to very unacademic language at times. "I was thinking," he went on, "of Cap'n Jens Munck."

"Never heard of the gent."

"You wouldn't, with your mind on movie heroes. This was a bird who licked everything there was to lick—world, flesh and the devil, and death to boot, and the North Atlantic for good measure."

"One thing no man can lick is death," I commented.

"By God, Cap'n Munck did it!" said Bill savagely. "Soldier of fortune. Not the movie kind, though. He was short and stocky like me, with wide shoulders and no belly, you bet, and kind of steady in the eye when he looked at you. Say, did you read about those brass cannon they dug up at Fort Churchill, on Hudson's Bay?"

"Who dug 'em up?"

"Hudson's Bay Company men, when they founded the post there. Those cannon were stamped with *'C4,'* which means *Christian IV.* He was a king of Denmark, if you recall your history."

"Hold on, now." I laid on the oars, eyed Bill severely, and thought back. "What are you trying to

hand me? Fort Churchill was founded somewhere around 1700. Christian IV of Denmark lived about eighty years before that."

"Correct. The year was 1619. Cap'n Munck had adventured in Brazil and all over the map, joined the Danish navy, took embassies hither and yon, and made quite a name for himself. When King Christian decided to grab North America and get ahead of the Pilgrim Fathers, he sent Cap'n Munck to do the job. Gave him a good stout ship, the *Unicorn,* with a crew of about fifty, and the *Lamprey,* with a crew of sixteen. She was a little cat, the kind I've described; a sloop, if you prefer the word, decked over. About as big as a lifeboat, or maybe two rolled into one."

"For a college professor, you're vague on detail," I observed. Bill grinned at me.

"Boy, you don't know college professors! Well, Cap'n Munck started in May, and in September he was in Hudson's Bay. Storm all the way, and no charts, and storm in the bay itself. And what happened? It blew him slap into the one good harbor there—pure blind luck! Square into a river mouth. And there he was, aiming to start a colony and seize this whole continent for Denmark, and knowing no more about the place than you would if you woke up tomorrow morning in Tibet. The dream in his eyes and the glow in his heart—"

Wrong. The glow was in the eyes of Jens Munck, as he stepped ashore on the river flats under massive pines that grew close down to the water, a forest primeval, a land primeval and empty—his! For the moment, he took no thought to the fury of the September gale blowing snow that stung, blowing in ice that scored great weals along the ships. New land, his land, found and gripped!

Steady eyes, weather-wrinkled, true. Steady hand, that fell on the shoulder of the stout youngster beside him, Erik his nephew, last of the Munck strain.

"My land!" he said in his deep voice. "Our land, Denmark's land! As vast as Russia, it may be, richer than Siberia. Well, enough of dream! Now to work. Ho, John Watson! Move the ships upstream to that cove, away from the ice!"

The English mate fell to work, with the weary men.

All these long weeks they had been battling ice and storm, fighting through the iron straits. Snow was coming in on the east wind, and bitter winter was howling among the deep trees.

The ships were kedged a bit upstream to a cove. On the shore, Munck and his nephew stood, and with them a third. No man, this Biorn, but a mastiff, with eyes steady and true as those of his master. The dog went leaping among the trees for joy of the land, and Erik Munck with him. Smiling a little, Cap'n Munck turned back to his job. Winter ahead, a colony to found, dreams to come true!

But there was no man, no native, not even an Eskimo, to tell them of the winter so close upon them.

All hands pitched in to make the two ships secure from ice. At low tide, logs were hammered into the mud; an ice-jam was made about the hulls, filled with rocks solidly. Chaplain and surgeon and captain labored with the rest. John Watson, the English mate, was a dour, massive man who had the strength of three.

Massive hawsers moored the ships to the trees ashore; the water was pumped out; the bottoms were scraped, the smashed rudders mended. Slow work, all of this, running into weeks.

"And now for the winter that's on us," said Munck, when all hands gathered one cold evening. "Thank God, we've come through all safe; we have stores of all kinds, powder of the best, tools, everything to keep us until spring. Two of us are surgeons, to answer for our health. Shall we winter aboard or ashore?"

They looked ashore at the dark soughing trees and the drifting snow.

"The ship's a house; keep it!" said John Watson. "There's wood for the cutting."

"No lack, lads," assented Munck. "And with the stones about, we can build hearths for fires, here on the decks. Warm clothing, no end of it. Do we stay?"

Stay, they voted gladly, and so fell to work with the stones ready to hand. Three huge fireplaces were built, two on the ship and one on the cat. What better than staying here, close to provisions, and casks of wine and kegs of Danish beer?

The days grew shorter, and the snow piled so thick ashore that none could leave the ship save a few who contrived snowshoes. October passed. Great piles and stacks of logs were cut and laid ready for the fires, but the intense dry cold of the northland was setting in; the frightful frost of the Arctic was at hand, crackling and banging through the forest like great guns at work. On the shore, ice was thundering, piling high.

The men suffered. By night or day, by fire or sunlight, they had no warmth except in bed, and little enough there. The chests of woollens were broken out and clothes were heaped on. They were useless, and worse than useless, hampering the circulation and giving scant protection against such cold as the Danes had never known.

There was none to tell them that in this land men could winter alive in only one way. Biorn alone suffered nothing from the deadly frost.

The others had no furs, and could shoot only a few foxes. One night a fusil banged, and all hands came tumbling on deck. A dog had come up to the ship, and lay dead; the man on guard had taken it for a fox. They did not save the fur.

Lethargy crept upon the men. One of the surgeons was down with some unknown rotting sickness. Captain Munck felt uneasiness and a strange horror growing within him. He gave of his boundless energy keeping the men at work and play, buoyed them up with cheery words and example; yet they drooped. He too was pierced to the heart by the frightful cold; only at night, huddling in the berth he shared with Erik, did he know warmth. The mastiff helped here too, for Biorn had comfort and was never cold.

Suddenly the real frost of November came swooping down, and winter was upon them.

A pistol-shot rang out in the darkness. Munck leaped out of bed and hauled on his clothes and boots. Another shot and another. Men were shouting. Biorn caught the wild contagion, and his deep-lunged barking filled the cabin.

"Indians!" cried Erik. "An attack!"

Munck burst out and stumbled on deck, where one of the fires was flickering. Another shot and another; they sounded from below. Men appeared. Shouts resounded, and dwindled into laughter, as the sick surgeon came dragging himself out in wild fright. No shooting after all, it seemed. Merely the frost, reaching into the surgeon's chest of medicines and exploding the bottles, one after another.

Before day came, not a glass bottle was left aboard.

There was food in plenty—salt meat and fish of the best. The men, however, lost appetite; they complained of nausea, of swelling joints, of loosening teeth. They huddled about the fires, in the grip of lethargy.

Munck worked desperately with them but could spur them into nothing, save the one task of cutting wood. He himself, with Erik or John Watson, braved the terrible frost and ventured out on the ice of the bay, or up the frozen river, but saw no living thing. He would take Biorn, when no one else would go.

December came in. On the tenth, Munck and John Watson and the mastiff took to the ice, but before they had gone a half-mile, a cry of terror broke from the mate.

"Master Munck! The moon—look to the moon!"

Munck peered into the frost-white sky, where a full moon hung; they lived by night now, for daylight was almost gone. And as he peered up, he saw the earth's shadow creeping across the disk. He looked at the mate and laughed.

"An eclipse, John. It's nothing."

They watched, keeping moving for the sake of warmth. A howl broke from Biorn, and Watson uttered a choked cry.

"Nothing, is it? Judgment Day for all of us, that's what it is. Look! For the love of God, master, look at the sign!"

The eclipse was full. About the moon was a large glowing circle of luminous fire, and in the dark round shadow of the earth was a radiant cross.

"I'll come out no more," said Watson in stark terror. "Doom is on us all; keep to the ice if you will, but I'm done."

He went stumbling and slipping back to the river and the ships.

Jens Munck called Biorn to him, hugged the dog for warmth, and watched the eclipse drift past. Gripping his musket, he headed on across the ice-waste, seeking only the exercise he must have, driving his iron will to it. No living creature was in sight.

Judgment Day? Doom? The words of John Watson lingered with him. To his mind came thought of these men whom he had led here, and who depended on him alone. The boy Erik, whom he loved with all his heart, and in whom he saw his own sturdy youth renewed. His second mate, Hans Brock, who had been in bed long weeks, helpless. The priest, the cabin boy, the stout-hearted Danish seamen. Himself, who had slaved in Brazil and coasted the sunny Spanish shores.

The uneasiness, the nameless horror, grew within him. Something was wrong; he knew not what. This land lay outside his experience. And because he was a very brave and simple gentleman, he came to his knees on the ice and prayed to God, for strength and wisdom to accomplish his task and see these others safe home again.

From the heaped ice-masses along the shores of the bay drifted the melancholy and sinister howl of a wolf. A growl broke from Biorn, a growl and a ringing bark of challenge; with a rush, the mastiff went hurtling toward the shore, and was gone from sight.

Later, Biorn came back to the ship, with slashes in his pelt and blood frozen about his jaws, and a look of calm satisfaction in his sad eyes as he dropped down and licked his wounds. He, at least, had not failed.

Two days after, the chief surgeon died. So terrible was the frost that for another two days his body remained unburied; not even Munck could go ashore in this dread cold that bit to the very marrow. The other surgeon was staggering; many of the men were sick, and there was no cure for them.

Munck forced himself to keep up daily entries in his log; writing was lis sole outlet and relief. Watson was muttering about the wrath of heaven, though as yet he remained well and hearty, and his mutterings infected the spirits of the rest. Young Erik whistled up the men to games and skylarking, but soon this fell flat. The frost deepened; wolves howled from the forest; the great trees creaked and banged like devils let loose.

The remaining surgeon could offer little help. He himself was barely keeping his feet, and he showed Munck discolored swollen limbs and teeth falling out.

"Try liquor," he said in desperation. "A pint of whisky, two pints of wine to each man per day."

At first this helped; then nothing helped. Some melted the frozen wine, swigged it down with the whisky, and relaxed in drunken torpor. Others took it more slowly, but only complained the more when it was gone. The priest was sick now; Munck rallied him, however, and rallied the men.

"Christmas is on the way. Up, and moving!" His hearty ringing voice stirred them to life. "Out, Erik, and cut greens! Come along, John."

Watson grumbled, but got his ax and accompanied them ashore. The tireless energy of Munck, the boyish abandon and high courage of Erik, swept through them all, lent them new vigor. Green branches were hung about; frozen kegs of wine and beer were brought up and thawed; the decks were cleared of ice and snow; wood was cut and brought in.

"Thank God, lad, I believe we've turned the corner!" said Munck that night, as he crawled shivering into bed. He pummeled Erik, and Erik lashed

"Master Munck! The moon—look to the moon! Judgment Day for all of us!"

back at him; laughing, panting, they worked each other into a glow, while Biorn leaped on them with furious delighted barking.

"Let's hope we have, Uncle," exclaimed Erik, and said nothing of the lethargy that had been creeping on him these days. "Once this accursed sickness is past, we can make shift to endure the cold. We can't fight both at once."

"Bah! We can fight all hell!" Munck cried cheerfully. "Men were made to fight, lad, and there's no fight unless the enemy is stout. Merry Christmas!"

Christmas Eve brought wine and beer thawed out by the keg, and jollity reigned supreme with song and story. Munck was bubbling over with vigor and good humor. He told them how, at twelve years of age, he swam to the Brazilian coast from a shot-shattered ship, and for a year earned his keep over a cobbler's last. All the fantasy of true adventure, sprinkled with comical interludes that kept everyone in a roar.

A memorable night, a gay night, while the log fires roared high. No fights, no drunken brawl; sober, clear-headed men, these Danes. They could drink or die with a smile and a steady word and a firm handclasp.

With the morrow, the chaplain did his duty right manfully and preached them a fine hearty sermon. According to old Danish custom, all hands chipped in to make the priest a handsome present; little money enough, but some of them had white fox furs, which they gave to line his coat. He, good man, intended missionary to the New World and chaplain of the Danish colony to be, was full of dreams and fervor, and the snowy heathen coasts stirred the heart in him mightily. Yet he was not to go ashore after the manner of his dreams.

The corner was turned; Munck was sure of it, and instilled eager confidence in them from cabin boy to priest. He watched, as day followed day, and kept all hands stirred up joyously, until New Year's day clamped down with frost such as they had never yet felt. It was terrific. It took the heart out of them. It put uneasy fear even into the stout soul of Munck himself.

Then, suddenly, the mysterious rotting sickness ravaged them. The surgeon took to his berth; the priest followed. The chief cook died. Munck, hearing John Watson talk darkly about doom and Judgment Day, flew into a fury but kept himself in hand. He went down into the dark cabin to find Erik there, drooping and smitten; Erik had to tell him the truth at last.

At this, Munck quivered; the blow went deep. A low cry burst from him, and he fled to the cabin where the surgeon lay. He exploded in frantic words:

"Do something—you *must!* Tell me what to do. This is what you're here for. We must do something for these men, make use of every remedy. Tell me what to get from your chest."

"Death, and relieve us all, if you will," mumbled the surgeon from swollen gums. "I've used as many remedies as I can find, and they do no good. If God won't help, there's no remedy."

Day followed day, death followed death; January wore on; coffins were knocked together and buried in the snow ashore. Hans Brock, the second mate, died at last, and Munck stirred up everyone to lay him away as befitted an officer.

The priest was propped up in his berth to mumble a funeral sermon, death in his eyes, and his dreams gone glimmering. The small guns were discharged; the frost had contracted them, and they burst. More men came down, dragged into their berths, and moved not. Munck, tending his brother's son with gentle hand, saw that Erik was going from bad to worse.

Agonized, he sought out the dying surgeon, and berated him with passionate incoherent words, scarce knowing what he said. The living corpse sighed back:

"If God won't help, there's no hope."

"God!" said Munck, clenching his fists. He sought out the priest, who was now almost past speech.

"Help me, help us all!" he said hoarsely. Close to breaking was Jens Munck. "I've prayed—you do it now. There's nothing else. Make Him help, force Him to help—damn it, what good are you if you can't do this? What's faith, to us?"

He stamped up and down the cabin, raving in a burst of wild blasphemy, cursing God and the mystery of this sickness, like a veritable madman. It was love and grief for the boy that tore him asunder, until he had exhausted himself with frantic words. Then he heard the voice of the dying priest.

"Steady, Jens, steady. God knows His business. You're quick at cursing, lad, but you're alive and well. We're dying men. Pray for us."

Pray for us. This was the last word the priest spoke, then or ever. Jens Munck felt all the wild furious rebellion go out of him, and flung himself down

The Norwegian Cat

Munck's iron will fought the deathly lethargy and kept it at bay. He drove himself to labor each hour of each day, living as in some evil dream. Food to fetch, the sick to tend, wood to cut, water to be melted from snow; Erik dying in the cabin, and the dead to be buried.

For the sake of the boy, he lashed himself ever to fresh hopes, to new efforts. He plied what drugs he found in the surgeons' chests; he experimented with new forms of diet; knowing nothing of scurvy, he did not hit the clue. There was no help, from food, from drugs, from heaven.

John Watson was staggering now, doomed, but still putting his brute strength to whatever Munck directed. February passed by, and March came in, dragging its weary course, with frost and blizzard and hammering ice.

Jens Munck fought on, grimly. Like some lonely wild bird, he went on his ever-lengthening rounds, from cabin to forecastle, from dying to dead, with food and drink here, and a prayer there. Even to melt the snow and ice into water became labor of the hardest. Besides, none of them were now able to bring in more fuel. The fires died, but could not be left dead. Munck stirred himself anew, and began to break up the small boats for the flames, and hewed into the bulwarks. Even to swing an ax, however, was nearly impossible.

April came, and Erik smiled and died.

"I'll not shame you, Uncle," he had said at the last. Munck went to pieces then, in the frightful cold solitude of the cabin, clasping the poor dead hand as he knelt; went to pieces and lost his grip, for a little, until the words of the boy came back to him and steeled him.

"God help me, lad, I'll not shame you either," he groaned, and wiped the freezing tears from his shaggy cheeks. It was a vow to be kept.

There was no pause, no rest, no break in the days that dragged on in relentless and unending

beside the berth in a desperate agony of prayer, not for himself but for these dying men.

When he came to rise, it was not easy. He realized suddenly that his knees were swollen, and his fingers. So he knew that it had come to him, as to all the others except the mastiff Biorn. Upon Munck, as upon them, now lay the hand of death. The shock came, and lifted; he went back again to his nephew Erik with the calm and quiet assurance of one who has now passed all fear.

A punishment, he thought, for his wild blasphemy. He made no complaint.

The days wore horribly along, an incredible and intolerable round past all human bearing; yet it was borne. Day followed day, with biting frost and cold beyond endurance. Yet men endured, creeping or staggering about, clinging hard to life. February drew half its span away. John Watson and five others, besides Munck, alone were able to lift hand to any work.

agony; through everything, Jens Munck doggedly forced himself to struggle on against the insuperable. Beyond the mystery of this pestilence which nothing could abate lay death; he fought the one and the other without ceasing.

Among the supplies of the dead surgeons, he came one day on bundles of forgotten herbs. He was grasping at any straw now, quite literally. He dumped the bundles into a cask of melted wine, stirred them together, and summoned all hands to join him. Only four men answered the call.

One by one, each was aided to climb into the cask, there to bathe in the strange mixture. Here was a clue in the right direction, had Munck been able to recognize it, for this bath refreshed and helped all four of them to renewed life.

The next day was Good Friday, and Munck read the sermon for that day to the four. No others were so much as able to sit up and listen.

Day followed day in the Arctic darkness.

Among all his grim duties, Munck managed to keep entries going in his log, thus counting the endless days. April merged into May, and John Watson died, but there was none to bury him.

Munck could only crawl about. Two of the four men had dragged themselves over the side, falling to the snow below, creeping to the shore to die on solid ground. The other two were in their berths, dying. On the decks and in the forecastle, men lay dead.

Spring, and thawing snows, wild geese and other flocks winging overhead, Biorn going ashore on forays, ice drifting out; and the ship a charnel-house of hell. What the little *Lamprey* was like, alongside, Munck did not know; he could no longer reach the rail to look at her. The days and weeks passed. The stench from the rotting ship was past bearing, but the bitter frost had gone.

Here at last was June, and the fight ended. Munck came out of a stupor one morning to hear the wolves howling from the shore, with Biorn answering their challenge from the deck above. Here was the end. He dragged himself out of his berth and back again. There was no strength left in him. There was no food, and he could not reach the galley. On the deck beside his berth, the cabin-boy lay dead. No living soul existed in all the ship now, except the one man here whose will fought on.

Days passed, four of them, with no food. It was the end; with shaking hand Jens Munck opened his logbook for the last time and scrawled words that sprang from a soul of iron:

> *"I now have no more hope of life.... Herewith, good night to all the world, and my soul to God."*

He relapsed into stupor.

Then Biorn came to him. The hot eager tongue licked his hand, licked his bearded matted face, fetched him back to flickering life. The torment of thirst spurred him to one last vital effort. He dragged himself out, gained the ladder, crawled out on deck. A draft of wine gave him a little strength; and hearing voices, he crept to the bulwarks and looked out. There on shore were two ragged scarecrow figures—the two men who had gone ashore to die. Instead, they had lived.

They got aboard, helped him away from the deathly ship, and built a fire to keep animals off. The three of them ate the young grass, sucked the roots of vines and green things. And this green food, like magic, drained the sickness out of them.

"God help me, lad, I'll not shame you either," Munck groaned.

Haggard, shaggy, shadows of men, they yielded to the insensate craving that was more powerful than all their wisdom; and strength returned.

"And now, what?" said Jens Munck. His steady, purposeful eyes looked past the other two, at the big ship and the little cat. "Let's settle it. What's to be done?"

They sucked the broth, made from fish and fresh game shot down, in silence. They were seamen, obedient, able men, but shattered in will and resolve. In Munck alone gathered energy and driving power of decision, as he sat and fondled the ears of the mastiff.

"Stay here? Useless. We must go home, and come back again with fresh crews, make a new start. Furs! We must have furs, to keep out the cold, next time. And herbs of all kinds, green things; yes, we've learned our lesson. The wilderness remains here for us; the dead remain. The land is still ours!"

The other two stared at him stupidly.

"Go home?" said one, and pointed to the two ships, fast in their solid berths. "How can we go? We've no men to work ship, master."

Munck's thin lips twisted under his beard.

"We've ourselves, lads; enough, with a bit of help."

"Help? From whom, master?"

"Kneel down," said Munck, and they obeyed. He looked up to the skies of brief Arctic summer, and spoke to the Great Spirit, somewhat in the simple and quiet fashion of the Indians he had never seen. For when men are reduced to nothing under the wide sky, they come close to the reality of the invisible. Then he rose, and smiled, and held out his hands to them. "Come, lads. Let's to work."

They worked, as their strength lasted and waned and returned again. Not with the ship, for this was beyond them, but with the little *Lamprey*. The rotting corpses were put into the water. The cargo was lifted out of her; even the ballast was cleared, until with a flood tide the cat floated free and came out of the ice-break that had been built about her.

Then the ballast in again, and stores, and casks filled with water from the river; after this, she had to be rigged afresh. Nor was Munck yet satisfied. His vision looked forward until the time when he would return, this year or next, with fresh colonists and other ships. They would have need, then, of all the supplies still aboard the *Unicorn*. So he drove the groaning men to more work, boring holes in the stout oaken planks; and they watched her settle and go down.

"And now, in the name of God, let's start for home!" said Munck.

They went aboard, took Biorn with them, and cast off, on a July Sunday. A full year ago they had entered Hudson Straits, there to fight ice and storm six long weeks ere reaching this spot; and the thought of fighting back through those iron-cliffed straits consumed them with a hopeless terror. They were still weak, emaciated, suffering. The bay before them was strewn with ice-pans and huge floes, hung heavy with ice-mist and fog. Beyond all this horror of the new world lay the Atlantic to be crossed, and three of them only, to do it. It was an utter impossibility.

The two seamen broke. They could not face it. They refused flatly.

"Better to stay here," cried one of them, and covered Munck with his fusil. "Here we have everything; we can live; we can find the Indians, gain strength and life. Out there is only death. We have done enough. Go if you like; we stay here."

Another man would have reached for his pistol. Munck swung an arm about the neck of the big dog, looked at the two panic-stricken men, and smiled.

"Enough? One can never do enough," he said gently. "This is our land, lads, Denmark's land. I'll be back, never, fear, and you with me; but now, home's waiting for us. A stanch little ship, this cat. D'ye mind how our fathers sailed the four seas in ships like this one, opened up Iceland, conquered half the world?"

"Sail her yourself, if you like," said he with the musket. "Not I."

Munck talked on. The two men looked at one another, glanced at the corpses strewn along the shore where snowbanks had melted, eyed the dark silent forest. After all, they were seamen and Danes. So in the end the fusil went down and they sailed out from the river of death and on their way.

As Munck had noted, the drift of the ice was eastward toward the straits. When the mist closed them in, he made fast with a grapnel to a floe, and let the cat drift safely. But now, as though to test utterly his stout heart, the last thing that he loved was stripped from him.

He was sleeping below, when the cries of the men wakened him, and the mad barking of Biorn. He came on deck just in time to see the mastiff go leaping over the rail to the ice, in furious headlong pursuit of a polar bear which had approached closely. In vain Munck whistled him back. Night came down, and a bitter gusty wind, parting the little craft from the floe.

"Head back!" said the men eagerly, for they too loved the dog. "We can find him, master. We can find the floe again."

"Leave the lines alone," Munck said. "Look at the ice there in the darkness—more of it! Wind's coming. We'd waste our strength, and we need every ounce of it. Besides, the search is vain."

"Better to stay here," cried one of the seamen. "Out there is only death!"

Wind and ice smote them. Yet during two whole days they could hear the mastiff's voice from across the floes. The great barks dwindled to faint and dismal howls, and died away; Jens Munck held on grimly. Tempest came down and hit them hard, smashing the rudder and threatening final disaster. Munck grappled another floe and made repairs, with a heart close to breaking.

Once again there settled down a dreary round of intolerable days, tempest and ice and fog, enough to drive them all mad. Weeks of it, a full month of it, before they were across the bay and found the west end of the Straits. Then they drifted with the ice under the iron cliffs.

Out of the Straits at last, smack into the heart of such a storm as even Jens Munck had scarcely seen; but it came from the west. For such weather as this, the stanch little cat had been built; she scudded before it, riding the giant combers like a duck, and so on toward home.

In a bleak September day, a Norwegian bonder saw a boat come in, and went down to the cove to meet it. Then he signed himself and stood all a-stare, in fear and terror, deeming that trolls or devils had come out of the sea. Three gaunt figures came ashore, so shaggy and salt-encrusted and staggering as to seem scarce human. Not until Munck held a pistol to his head, would the peasant lend a hand to make the cat secure.

"And that was the end of it," said Bill Joyce, as we headed in toward the dock.

I rested the oars, staring at him. "But that's no end, Bill! Did Munck go back?"

"He found war had broken out. He was called into the navy again, and died fighting. But man, did you ever clap eye on greater words than those he wrote down in that dreadful cabin?" Bill's eye flashed; his face lighted up, as he quoted them: *"Herewith, good night to all the world, and my soul to God."*

"Where'd you get all this yarn. Bill?" I asked curiously.

"From his own logbook."

"And what became of the ship he sank so safely?"

Bill grinned. "That's funny. The Indians came down to the shore, a couple of weeks after Munck started home, and found the ship. At low tide they started to plunder it, and built fires to dry out the stuff. The fires reached the powder-kegs and blew 'em all to kingdom come. When the Hudson's Bay people started a post there, a hundred years later, the Indian legends led them to the spot, and they dug up those brass cannon. And there's your story—the yarn of the Norway cat. Hey! For the love of Mike, slow up! I've got a fish!"

Not that the fish mattered much, after that story.

PRINCESS OF CALICUT

As *might be expected in the waterfront* section of San Francisco, the waiting-room of Princess Zara was not ornate. Captain Helm was the only person in it.

He was a smallish man with an alert eye; one of those self-contained men who are all the more dangerous for not looking it. He was dressed as an ordinary seaman; the worn cap that he twirled in his fingers did not bear the oak-leaves of a captain, either. When Captain Helm was on the prowl he was not the man for any half measures, and just now he was distinctly on the prowl.

Four days previously, his most cherished possession had been deftly stolen, and now he had run it to earth.

The slatternly maid appeared, holding aside a curtain, and informed him that he could see the Princess. Captain Helm passed into the mystic presence, an expectant glint in his eye. He was suiting his plan of campaign entirely to circumstances, and it mattered very little to him what those circumstances were. Captain Helm had been places.

His eyes swept the room with one glance, and his brain ticketed everything. The skull on the mantel; the exquisite little ship-model with its teakwood stand on the side-table; the astronomical charts on the walls, the Oriental hangings and atmosphere. He sat down at the table, on which were pencils and several small pads of paper, and looked at Princess Zara. She looked at him, and sized him up in one glance. Long custom had made deduction second nature to her.

"What kind of a reading do you want?"

"Why, I dunno," stammered Captain Helm awkwardly. "A dollar one, I guess. I'm sort of given to trances myself, sometimes, and they scare me, so I don't want no trances."

Princess Zara smiled. Her supposedly Oriental costume could have been considerably improved by a trip to the cleaners. She was swarthy, faintly mustached, and much inclined to a middle-age spread. She was, as Captain Helm surmised, a Syrian lady who had removed from Florida to escape the enormous license fees there obtaining.

"I don't give trance readings for a dollar," she said with a touch of contempt. "My spirit guides wouldn't permit it. However," she added briskly, "you'll find a palm and psychic reading satisfactory." A devout expression came into her swarthy features. "My controls are wonderful today—I can feel it; while I relax, you write down your age, name and three questions on one of those pads."

Incredulous joy flashed across Captain Helm's agile brain. He perceived that this woman was a "shut-eye," in the jargon of the profession. That is to say, a medium so apt at tricking others as to have herself gained an unwilling belief in the supernatural powers which she juggled so nimbly. The grim compensation of it is that a "shut-eye" almost invariably ends with suicide.

"But I can tell you them things, Princess!" said Captain Helm huskily.

She leaned back and closed her eyes.

"I don't want you to tell me. My spirit guides must tell me, in order to obtain the psychic results. You must be very certain I don't read what you write. First, light the candle on the side-table, then write what I have told you."

Beside the glorious little ship-model on the side-table stood a candlestick. Captain Helm, careful to let no gleam of wicked joy show in his eye, scratched a match and lit the candle. Then, putting his cap on the table, he took a pencil, drew over one of the small pads, and laboriously began to write with cramped fingers.

"Oh, gosh!" he exclaimed petulantly. "I spoiled that one—"

He tore off the leaf and crumpled it and it fell into his lap. Leaning forward, he wrote as directed. Then he inspected what he had written, in open admiration, his lips moving as he slowly read over the words. His left hand had darted to his lap, and deftly opened the slip of paper there, folded it over once, and over again. Nothing was written on it except the one word "Beware!" in writing apparently that of a woman.

"Have you finished writing?" asked Princess Zara, her eyes still closed. "Now I want you to fold the paper over once, so I can't read it, then fold it over again to be quite sure."

Knowing that he was observed through those supposedly closed lids, Captain Helm was making no mistakes. He folded the slip once, and again. Between the first and second fingers of his left hand was held the folded slip from his lap. As he finished folding the written paper, he deftly replaced it with the other.

Captain Helm, in the good old days, had obtained a round five hundred smackers from many a clairvoyant for the secret of this one-hand switch; and cheap at the price.

"All finished?" Princess Zara opened her eyes, leaned forward, and picked up the folded paper from the table. The sweeping gesture of her hand alone betrayed that she, too, was making the switch for another folded paper between her fingers; Captain Helm admired the superb dexterity of her fingers. She held the folded paper—presumably that on which he had written—to her forehead.

"I want you to hold it like this, against your forehead, and concentrate on your questions," she said, letting it fall to the table. "Then, when the vibrations become strong, burn the paper in the candle. I'll tell you when. Close your eyes and concentrate."

With an expression of awe, Captain Helm obeyed. He did not need to use his eyes to know that her hand, in her lap, was opening the paper on which he had written. He caught a startled grunt from Princess Zara—and his eyes opened.

"It's got me—it's got me!" His voice was hoarse, thick, horrible to hear. His eyes dilated wildly, his respiration became fast; he was panting. "Oh, God! It's got me—it's my punishment for saying it was all a fake—beware, beware—"

A violent shudder passed through his body. His staring eyes were directed at Princess Zara, but were not focused on her. They were focused on the wall behind her, so that he seemed to be looking straight through her.

Those last two words, repeating what was written on the paper in her lap, held the Princess spellbound. She had no suspicion that this ordinary seaman had worked the one-hand switch himself. She, through nearly closed lids, had seen him write out his name and questions—yet the paper now held only the one word *"Beware!"*

"You have compelled me to your presence," said Captain Helm. His voice had changed; now it was a liquid, rolling voice, his words fluent, as though some different person were speaking through his lips. The woman became intent, startled, frightened.

"It was not accident that brought me here—it was destiny," he went on. He sat stiffly; his eyes were

His voice rolled on again, monotonous and hypnotic, richly vibrant.

"It was Da Gama's second voyage; we had six caravels, light fast craft, and twelve great carracks. These were stout, massive ships, built especially to sail around Africa and Cape Tormentoso to the newly found Indian realms. So we had come to Cochin, where the king was most friendly to us, and his daughter Zaminda was the loveliest creature in all the Indies. On the day I first saw her, my heart was laid at her feet. She was exquisite, glorious! I had found my way into the palace gardens, and curiosity led me on until I came upon her and her slave-women; for no guards dared to stop me—"

fixed; only his lips moved. Then his arm lifted. Slowly, his hand went out, as by involuntary motion. The hand pointed directly at the queer but exquisite model of a ship on the side-table, a ship of another day and age. "You do not know what that ship is, but I shall tell you. It is a carrack. It is a copy of my own ship. Look! Upon it is the name, *San Tomas.* She helped to change the history of the world, the whole history of naval design; and I sailed her. I shall tell you the story, for it is my own story. I was a young man when I sailed with Vasco da Gama for India, but already I was captain of my own ship. I, Lorenzo Diaz—"

He was silent for a moment. Princess Zara was horrified but fascinated by this manifestation of the supernatural. The entrance curtain lifted, and the slatternly maid appeared, with a gesture.

"Close the bookstore, and get out. Thirty-eight!" snapped the Princess, and returned her fascinated attention to Captain Helm. The maid, thus apprised that the psychic parlor was to be shut up, a worth-while sucker being in tow, withdrew. But whether Captain Helm or the swarthy princess was the "thirty-eight," remained to be seen.

Under his words, the dingy room seemed to widen and broaden into vast sunlit gardens, where cool fountains played and monkeys swung through the trees. The wondering seaman, young and ardent, steel cap aflash, steely eyes aglint, black-bearded features alive with eager curiosity, paused suddenly upon a scene that set his pulses hammering.

About a shaded pool and fountain lay half a dozen young women, one of whom was reading from an Arabic book and translating into Hindustani as she read, to the delight of the others. Diaz stood gaping at the reader. She was all in white, jewels glittered on her arms, and, unconscious of any strange watcher, her gestures were unrestrained. Black hair, an oval golden face, a golden-tinted skin—she was the most beautiful thing he had ever laid eyes on. And as he stared, she glanced up and saw him there.

She gasped; her women looked around, uttered frightened cries, and plunged away into the garden depths. But she, coming to her feet, stood cool and imperious as Diaz approached, no terror in her lovely gaze. She spoke, in rippling music; he smiled and made reply, and suddenly they both laughed at their mutual inability to understand.

The admiration of Diaz was swift, intense, impulsive. Under his eyes, the girl colored faintly. Then, to his utmost astonishment, she spoke in Portuguese:

"Señor captain, you are welcome."

Almost could Diaz believe in miracles. He burst into impassioned speech, but she laughed gayly.

"Too fast, too fast! I understand only a little. My father is the King."

This checked him, shocked him, startled him. He began to see sudden short shrift for Lorenzo Diaz; then he bade consequences to the devil, and fell to talking with the girl. Gradually her women returned, peering fearfully at the white man.

At first, Diaz was charmed by her mere physical beauty, for she was exquisite past belief, like some golden nymph or dryad caught in the flesh. Then, as he sprawled beside her and they talked together, and he drank the sherbet one of the women shyly proffered, a change came upon him. The King of Cochin was her father, yes; but it was not this that caused the change. To the handsome young Portuguese, arrogant in his pride of race and color, even the daughter of a barbaric king might have seemed no more than the possible plaything of an idle hour.

But this girl was different: Her pride was no less than his own; besides, it was her character that grew upon his astonished gaze, her wisdom, her mental abilities. They were on a par with his own, if not better. Last year, Da Gama's fleet had been here nearly four months, trading, and she had picked up some Portuguese from one of the good monks aboard. Other monks were aboard now, and she was eager for one of them to teach her further.

"Assuredly," replied Diaz, promptly. "It'll give Fray Francisco the greatest of pleasure. I'll inform him within the hour. Your name?"

"Zaminda," she said, and it was music to him. When he realized that the sun was westering, he started up; he was overdue for a meeting of the Admiral and captains. She summoned a guard, who appeared instantly and saluted. Diaz comprehended that he had not gone unwatched, this while. He bowed over her fingers, kissed them gallantly—she laughed gayly at the novel gesture—and was led out of the garden maze by the guard.

He might have known there would be talk; he talked himself, when he came aboard the *San Gabriel,* the flagship, for the conference. He was all in a flame of ecstasy over his adventure. While they awaited the Admiral, he talked to two of the captains who had been here last year.

"By the saints, Diaz, you were in luck," said one of them. "I've heard of this Princess Zaminda, and saw her once or twice last year. She's free of the religious rules of these heathen, it seems; that's why you found her unveiled. They say she speaks many languages, has extraordinary learning, and that her influence over her father has caused his great friendship to us. By the saints, if I had not grandchildren of my own in Lisbon, I'd give you some competition!"

The Admiral appeared, and from laughter they went to sober business.

In all these Malabar coasts the greatest city was Calicut. There, Da Gama and his captains had last year been entrapped, taking vengeance later; indeed, upon arriving on the coast this voyage, the fleet had bombarded Calicut before coming on here to Cochin for settlement and trade. And they had found all the shipping of Calicut gone.

"Gone where? Nobody knows," said Admiral da Gama, eying his captains sternly. "Now, these heathen of Cochin are friends; their King is most cordial. I want strict orders given all your crews that we're to exert every effort to make friends with these heathen. No plundering, no molesting women, no swaggering or drinking; any man who does not conduct himself as a Christian cavalier, whether he be man or officer, will be straightway hanged. Understood? One thing more."

He paused, to drive home his grave words.

"There's some talk of driving us out of India, my captains. We can take our chance by sea. By land, it's different. These native princes fight among themselves; hence, our welcome in this place last year. Let them combine against us and we're lost—they can summon armies of incredible power. The Moslem princes in the north hate us as Christians. These Hindus are our friends. You comprehend? Publish the orders, and have them rigorously obeyed."

That same night, Diaz relayed the request of the princess to good Fray Francisco, who was overjoyed at the prospect of teaching, and of a possible conversion of the King's daughter. The more so, as he had heard great things of Princess Zaminda and her eagerness after all kinds of learning.

Next morning, however, a boat came over from the *San Gabriel,* summoning Captain Diaz to attend

Diaz comprehended that he had not gone unwatched; he bowed over her fingers, kissed them gallantly.

the Admiral instantly. There was no staying ashore for Da Gama or his captains. The traders, the friars, the clerks and merchants might live at the concession, where the huge warehouses were bursting with goods for Portugal, but the crews stayed on duty, except when on leave.

In some perplexity, Diaz rendered himself aboard the Admiral, and was led straight to the grand cabin. Here he found Da Gama, stroking his grizzled beard in evident fury; here, too, were interpreters, and a magnificent knightly figure that drew the eye of Diaz in open admiration. Armed in glittering chain mail from crested helm to foot, of heroic build, here stood a native chieftain whose gems proclaimed his rank, and whose bearded features bespoke his arrogant and indomitable nature.

"Captain Diaz," barked the grim Admiral, "this is the Rajah of Chaul, a state to the north of here. Rajah Singh is a guest of the King, and I am in some hopes of making an alliance with him and opening a trading settlement in his territory. He has, however, laid a most serious charge against you—he states that while you were ashore yesterday you intruded into the privacy of the royal gardens, frightened and molested the women in their reserved section of the gardens, and insulted the King's daughter. What have you to say?"

Diaz looked at Rajah Singh, this time with very different eyes, and read the bitter hatred in the face of the warrior. However, knowing his Admiral well, he did not make the mistake of flying into a rage. Instead, he bowed very coolly and spoke slowly, that the interpreters might translate his words.

"Excellency, before touching upon the truth or falsehood of this charge, should we not consider by what right it is made? So base a violation of royal premises should be resented by the King or one of his court, it seems to me, and not by a visitor."

The Admiral, a glint of appreciation in his eye, turned to the Rajah and waited. In obviously repressed fury, Rajah Singh spat out a curt response. One of the interpreters put it into halting Portuguese.

"Rajah Singh speaks as the betrothed husband of the Princess Zaminda."

"Indeed?" said Captain Diaz. "Apparently she knows nothing of this betrothal, since she did not mention it to me yesterday."

Da Gama eyed his captain keenly, and scenting fire beneath all this smoke, held his peace. Rajah Singh put hand to hilt and spoke again. The interpreter bowed.

"He makes his suit to the King; the Princess does not need to know of it."

"Then," said Diaz promptly, "we deal with jealousy, not with resentment. Excellency, I lost my way yesterday in the palace gardens and chanced upon the Princess. We talked together at some length, and at her request Fray Francisco goes ashore today in order to instruct her further in our tongue; and, I trust, in the true faith. The charge of this heathen is false, and with your permission I challenge him to—"

"Enough," broke in Da Gama quickly. "The affair is in my hands, not yours; in my hands, also, is your honor. Leave it so, and hurl no challenge at a man we seek to win as a friend. I hold you in no blame."

Captain Diaz bowed and withdrew; and never did

man perform wiser, action. Only a man capable of conquering his own anger, the Admiral was wont to say, could overcome the fury of others. So the matter ended, where Diaz was concerned.

He inquired diligently, and learned that Rajah Singh was indeed here to woo the princess, and was like to win her, by all accounts.

Half the crews were put ashore, to prepare the goods in the warehouses for loading into the ships; these carracks were armed with cannon, but were primarily cargo ships. They were bluff, blunt and sturdy, and even with a smacking wind and a bone in the teeth could go no more than five or six knots an hour. Very different were the smaller caravels, fast ships for cruising. The six caravels were sent off up the coast to Cananore, under Commodore Sodrey.

Diaz was among those commanding the work ashore. Thus, it was not long ere he was in touch with Fray Francisco, who heard him out and held up both hands in horror.

"God forbid, my son! If I did this, the Admiral might well clap me in irons and take me back to Portugal, for he is a fierce and terrible man in his wrath."

"You don't need to prate to him about it," said Diaz, laughing. "Ask her if she'll see me; if you don't, I'll seek her another way, for my will is set on it. And find out if she intends to marry this heathen prince."

The upshot of this matter was that when the friar went to teach his pupil, Captain Diaz accompanied him. And having seen Princess Zaminda in company of the friar, Diaz was not long in arranging to see her otherwise.

Now, between the two of them, matters went very swiftly and joyously; for if he was all ardent flame, she had naught wherewith to quench it. Certain of the guards were men devoted to her, and it was no hard thing for Captain Diaz to gain entry to the palace gardens and be led to the spot where she awaited him under the stars. And after this had happened once, the way was open for a dozen meetings.

Swiftly was the burning anxiety of Diaz set aside, for Zaminda told him that she was not minded to wed Rajah Singh, or any other man; and could not be forced to it.

"Our family is not as the common run of folk," she said proudly. "I'm no captive like other women, no animal to be bought and sold like a water-buffalo in the fields! I've set my heart upon knowledge, upon learning and wisdom."

That might be, but, swore Diaz, she would not be the first woman to find something better in the world than wisdom alone. He knew right well that she inclined to him.

These meetings of theirs held no harm. He talked

of western ways; she, of the mighty Moguls and the rich Moslem kingdoms in the north, and the knightly Rajputs, and the far Arab lands, and even of Cathay; though she was not certain just where this land lay. She had great store of practical knowledge as well as mere book learning. She had skill in masonry and the plans for building houses and temples; but it was on the subject of ships that the two of them were on common ground.

Through this Malabar Coast passed all the commerce of the far Indies, meeting here that of the Red Sea and Constantinople and Egypt. Of ships, Zaminda knew much, both of building them and of sailing them. And, on the evening when they met thus for the last time, Diaz found her very sad for his sake. He and his comrades, she said, were doomed.

"I have heard rumors," she said frankly, "and so has my father the King. Where are all the fighting ships of Calicut? They intend to sweep you from the seas. Their Admiral Cassim is a famous fighting captain, and they are not little ships, nor poorly armed. But worse—Kojambar the Admiral of Egypt, I hear, is coming with an enormous fleet of huge armed dhows, ships that carry six hundred men or more each. Where these ships are, no one knows. If they come upon you, then you are all dead men."

"If they came upon us with our caravels away and half our crews ashore," said Diaz, "things might indeed be open to argument. Even so, our carracks are noble ships, and it would be a fight worth seeing."

"Not for me," she said sorrowfully. "Truly I think you are all dead men, and so does my father and his council."

"Men die but once, and it's well to die happy," said Diaz, and caught her to him and kissed her on the lips.

This was a new experience, but it was very nice, and Zaminda admitted as much; yet she was quite determined not to marry anyone, for she had long ago made up her mind to a life of chaste seclusion. To his astonishment and dismay, Diaz found her resolved on this point. Himself madly in love, with vague but honorable proposals of marriage on his lips, he was utterly baffled by her mental inhibitions.

At this moment the two were startled by a clash of arms, an outburst of voices, and as they sprang apart a flood of dark figures invaded their privacy. Diaz found the King before him, with Rajah Singh at one side and guards everywhere. He gripped his sword, only to find himself once more baffled. This was not at all the conventional situation, as he expected it, of the irate father.

Somewhat to his bewilderment, the King showed no anger whatever, nor was his own life in any peril. He was surprised, and the dark-visaged Rajah Singh was openly disappointed, but so it was. As a matter of fact, the King of Cochin was not narrow-minded; he had no race or color prejudice, and he held the white men in immense admiration and liking, as well he might, for their trade was making him rich at the expense of Calicut.

So, far from any anger, he expressed himself as vastly pleased that his daughter had honored Diaz with her affections, and he presented the captain with a very handsome jeweled necklace as a token of his appreciation. He then demanded on the spot whether Zaminda would marry Diaz.

"I don't intend to marry anyone," she returned spiritedly. "I shall devote my whole life to study and philosophy and wisdom."

"Grandchildren are more important to me than philosophy," said the King, who had a very practical nature. "I am glad that you refuse this man; I love him and his friends, but they are doomed men who will very soon go down to death. Their great ships are no more than floating coffins. In any case, you shall end this accursed study and philosophy which has ruined your life. Whether you like it or not, I shall give you in marriage to Rajah Singh."

"If you do that, I'll kill myself!" the girl cried out.

"No fear," said the King placidly. "You might as well be dead as childless, anyway. Guards! Take her away and confine her in the east tower. No books, mind. Beyond keeping her to the tower, no restraints. And if she wants to kill herself, provide her with a dagger and see that it is sharp."

He turned to Captain Diaz, who had understood little or nothing of the conversation, and who, even if he had comprehended its import, would have still found the King's line of reasoning far beyond his Portuguese understanding.

"As for you,"—the King beckoned an interpreter,—"go back and tell your good father the Admiral that I am giving a feast tomorrow for him and for his captains. My heart is very sad for them, and I wish to make them good cheer before they die."

So Captain Diaz departed, with a last vision of the tormented, anguished features of Zaminda, and an utter bewilderment as to what had transpired.

When he got back to his shore quarters by the warehouses, he woke Fray Francisco out of a sound sleep, and set before him as much as he could tell of the situation. The good father was not at all pleased.

"First, my son, you should have postponed the King's invitation a day; tomorrow is a Friday and therefore a day of abstinence, and the feast would have done us all much more good on Saturday. The King has really admirable cooks. Secondly, I've been on the point of converting the princess to the true faith; in fact, only this morning we were discussing baptism and the articles of faith, and she was most receptive. Now you've spoiled everything by wakening more worldly emotions within her, and are guilty of a very great sin—"

"Hold on," broke in Diaz hotly. "The emotions you term worldly have nothing to do with baptism, but they've a lot to do with marriage. It seems to me that if you were to point out that marriage is a sacrament and a most holy estate, whereby Zaminda might attain great wisdom and the very acme of education, you'd be trimming your canvas much closer to the line of duty. She'd listen to you, in such case. Once you baptize her, you can marry us with a good conscience. So, Father, you should really thank me for wakening the proper instincts in her. And you've got me to think of as well. If you can't persuade her to marry me I'll be in a bad way, let me tell you."

The friar admitted that there might be something in the argument, and promised to see the princess in the morning.

Captain Diaz went off to the *San Gabriel* when the sun was high, sought out the Admiral, and very frankly laid the whole adventure before him, also the invitation of the King. Da Gama, stroking his great beard, eyed Diaz at first grimly, then with a twinkle, and then frowned again.

"What was it she said about the Calicut ships, and the Egyptian admiral from the Red Seas?"

Diaz repeated the girl's words.

"By the saints!" mused the Admiral thoughtfully. "This begins to explain why all these people treat us with mingled affection and sorrow. They're not a warlike race here in Cochin. They take for granted we're all doomed to extinction."

"Well, Excellency, if you stop to think of thousands of warriors laying us aboard, of a hundred war galleys from Calicut alone, of these Red Sea ships holding upwards of six hundred men each, you're bound to admit there's something in their viewpoint," Diaz rejoined. "On the other hand, this talk of great fleets combining to exterminate us may be mere gossip. No one has seen any such fleets. No one knows definitely about them."

"True," said the Admiral. "Well, get back to work. I'll issue orders for all the captains to attend me ashore, this afternoon. By the way, do you intend to marry the princess?"

"I love her with my whole heart and soul," Diaz said simply.

"Then good luck to you. I'll countenance no light affair with a lady of her rank; but you're an honorable cavalier, Captain Diaz, and you have my blessing."

Vasco Da Gama was not trifling with destiny by any means. That morning he dealt extensively with spies, with informers, with all the news-mongers he could contact. To his vast relief, he learned that nothing whatever was known of the Calicut fleet under Cassim, except that it was somewhere in the north. The Red Sea dhows under Kojambar were said to be on the way, with the idea of sweeping the Portuguese once and for all from the Indian ocean; but this was highly indefinite.

So, as all threats came from the north, and the six caravels under Sodrey were certain to bring news of any enemy in that direction, Da Gama composed himself for work. Loading the carracks was a business of long weeks, for the monsoon was bringing in the East Indian trade daily now, and the whole commerce of India and the East was being diverted from Arabia and Cairo to the Portuguese establishment here at Cochin.

Before joining the Admiral and the other captains for the palace entertainment that afternoon, Diaz had an interview with Fray Francisco that left him stunned.

The good father had sought the princess as usual, and was summarily sent packing, by orders of the King. He acquainted Diaz, for the first time, with what had actually transpired at that scene in the gardens; with the attitude of the princess and that of her father.

"It's a queer situation," said the priest. "You, my son, are high in favor with the King; but the girl has refused to marry you, and that settles it. He's determined that she shall take Rajah Singh, and that

"We fight: we do not run," said Admiral Da Gama.

man hates you and all of us like the devil hates holy water. She's lost to you, so make up your mind to it."

"I will not," Diaz said gloomily.

"What can you do about it?"

"Nothing, I suppose, for the present."

"Exactly nothing; and if you lose your head, you'll make matters worse for her."

Diaz went to the feast with no joy whatever in his heart....

Like honored guests and friends whose doom was certain, the Portuguese were royally entertained. The King was vastly sorry for Da Gama, and said so frankly, advising him to get the best out of life before he was swept away. Those Calicut galleys alone could smother the Portuguese carracks with fighting-men; and if the huge Red Sea dhows did show up, crowded with savage Moslem warriors, it would be just too bad for Da Gama. At which, the Admiral only stroked his beard and eying the dancing-girls appreciatively, replied that he had every confidence in God and in his stout captains.

He might better have stuck to heaven alone, for his captains were rapidly and joyously getting drunk on palm-wine and arrack, as the King placidly observed. Captain Diaz in particular, who saw no reason to remain sober, indulged in the fast-flowing bowl. However, he and the rest carried their liquor like good cavaliers, and when the feast was finished and the lights expired, got home to their quarters somehow.

Captain Diaz was snoring in the dawn, when two of the seamen pummeled him and shook him into life.

"Here's a native asking for you, Senhor Captain, and speaks right good Portuguese too!" said they. "He gave us a piece of gold to rouse you up. Will you see him?"

"Eh? Yes; what the devil!" stammered Diaz. "Fetch him in. And bring a light."

A man was led in. He wore the steel cap and glittering chain mail of the palace guards, tulwar and dagger at his belt, round target on his arm.

"Senhor Capitan, a word with you alone," said he.

At that voice, Diaz leaped up and sent out the men. He seized the lantern and held it to the laughing golden features of Zaminda.

"You!" he gasped incredulously.

"So it seems, Lorenzo!" And she laughed again, then sobered. "Now take me quickly, on the instant, to your Admiral! I have news for him. This moment, do you hear?.... Well—after all, it is very nice and takes almost no time—"

Diaz, in a delirium of joy and eagerness, could gain no explanation except that she had vitally important news. So, since there was nothing else for it, he called men and escorted her down to the landing. They shoved off a boat, and went to the *San Gabriel.*

There, with lanterns dimming the dawn, Da Gama wrapped a robe about his bony frame and stared at them. Diaz introduced the Princess, and she burst into passionate speech.

"Excellency! A fast-sailing sloop arrived during the night, and went away. With her went Rajah Singh. She brought word that the fleets of Kojambar and of Cassim have joined together—a hundred galleys of Calicut, and seventy great Red Sea dhows. They are in the north. Rajah Singh has gone to bring them upon you while your caravels are gone and half your men ashore. I escaped from the palace that I might warn you—"

Da Gama stroked his beard and looked hard at her.

"I do not think your alarm was for me, Princess; but let that pass. I thank you. I'll have you escorted ashore—"

"No, no!" she broke out with hot words. "Don't you see? I can't go back now; I have taken the arms of a warrior; I have come to join you and die with you! For unless you flee quickly, you are all doomed and cannot escape."

"We fight; we do not run," said the Admiral. "God forbid that good Christian gentlemen and noble cavaliers should turn tail on Moslem ships! Therefore, if you want to go back—"

"I will not. I cannot!" she panted. Coming close to Diaz, she put her arm in his. "My fate is with you; nothing matters now in life, except that I share your fate."

"To which, apparently, Captain Diaz will not say no." And the Admiral smiled. Then he crooked a finger at his lieutenants. "Sound the trumpets. Every man aboard. Dispatch ten men in a fast native craft up the coast to Cananore, to find Sodrey and bid him join us. We sail within the hour, if the ships can be got ready; and we sail north." He looked again at Lorenzo Diaz. "As for you, sir, take her with you if she so desires; and you had best take Fray Francisco as well; heaven forbid that this lady, who has done us so great a service, should not receive at once the benefits of the sacraments!"

Captain Diaz stopped not to debate which sacrament might be in mind, but departed hastily, and the princess with him, to his own ship, where in no long time, the good friar joined them and would have taken Zaminda to the safe seclusion of a cabin. She refused point-blank, between tears and pride. Knowing now that the fleet sailed to meet the enemy, she knew it went to certain death.

"I will keep the deck; I came here to die, and will not sulk in a cabin," she said. "Baptism? Yes; anything you like. My whole life is wiped out now and gone. Nothing but death remains. I will take that by your side, Lorenzo."

"Well, that is true," said Diaz, and winked at the scandalized friar. "We have only death to expect, my heart! Therefore let us greet it like honest Christian folk, with all the sacraments possible. Gird yourself, Fray Francisco, and marry us when we stand out of the harbor. I'll be busy until then."

It was mid-morning when the twelve carracks were ready for sea, and stood out for the north. By that time, the friar had made a right good Christian out of the King's daughter; and the city wharves and shores were lined with sorrowful folk waving farewell to the Portuguese, whom they thought never to see again.

"They are doomed men... their great ships are no more than floating coffins."

Before noon, Fray Francisco said mass in the chapel of the carrack, and so Captain Diaz and the princess were married. Hardly were they wed, however, when the sky grew dark; the monsoon waxed into a gale and the twelve ships scudded north, and there was no going below-decks for all hands. The lovely ex-princess was a very seasick woman.

Next afternoon, the six caravels were sighted, and the fleet was joyful at the reunion; but their joy was short. With next dawn, the fleets of the enemy were sighted, six miles away.

The flagship took the lead as the fleets converged. Admiral da Gama had given his orders, and his captains had only to obey. Madness, it seemed to all of them, as they looked out at the horizon covered with ships—the massive Red Sea dhows, seventy of them, and the hundred war-galleys of Calicut following. Captain Diaz, standing by his helm with his wife beside him, saw that the Moslem fleet was keeping well out from shore.

"The wind's squarely offshore," he said, "on our starboard beam—ha! We have them to leeward, and the Admiral knows it! There go the caravels; watch, watch!"

The six fast caravels drew out in advance, heading straight for the line of dhows in apparent insanity. An hour passed, and still they held on, the heavy carracks following. Kojambar, intent on letting not one of the Portuguese ships escape, was forced farther downwind.

Then, suddenly, the caravels hauled up just beyond range of the Moslem guns, and their broadsides let fly. The Red Sea ships, carrying only light cannon and depending on coming to close quarters, were unable to reach the caravels. One by one, the huge dhows received blasts of heavy shot; one by one they were dismantled or sent in among their consorts, until the entire fleet was in mad confusion.

Da Gama followed with his carracks, shortened sail, and with his heavier guns opened a long-range fire on the disorganized mass of dhows. Like floating castles, those twelve carracks were impervious to the scant return fire. They held the windward gauge, they kept just close enough to pour shot in upon those Moslem ships, hour after hour, as the day wore on. The thunder of the guns sounded unceasingly, until the proud Red Sea fleet was no more than a mass of shattered wreckage, with here and there a dhow beating off to leeward in wild flight.

The caravels kept on, and the hundred war-galleys of Calicut received the fire. Now it was different; these galleys could handle under oars, and handle they did, striving to reach close quarters. The caravels eluded them, the carracks smashed through them, pouring a hail of death into each galley that tried to grapple. Then, as the sun went westward, the galleys broke and fled, but the fast caravels held after them with guns roaring, and gave no mercy. In the sunset, dead men and wreckage strewed the whole ocean.

Thus, once and for all, were the Indies won by caravel and carrack. All the ships of Orient were helpless before those stout Portuguese. The story went through the whole eastern world. Let Mogul and Moslem hold India; the carrack with her great square sails held the seas, and was supreme. With one blow, she had swept away the sea-power of the east, and in reward gained all the rich commerce of India and the lands beyond.

And Lorenzo Diaz took his bride back in triumph to Cochin—princess no longer, but woman now, not regretting that death was some long years deferred. As for Rajah Singh, he came no more into the matter; and in the affair of grandchildren, the king of Cochin was by no means disappointed. But that, of course, is another story.

The tale was finished.

From Captain Helm burst a low, tense groan. Again a shudder ran through his whole body; he moved convulsively. Princess Zara eyed him anxiously. Perspiration was standing out on her forehead. Then Captain Helm stiffened and his lips moved again.

"That is my story, Princess Zara—you who call yourself by that name," came the voice of Lorenzo Diaz. "For you, I have a message. Evil hangs over you; retribution is upon you. From a credulous seaman you took, in payment for false prophecy, the model of my carrack. It stands here on the table in your room. This action is bringing an evil destiny upon you, for the ship-model was stolen. I give you warning; even at this moment, the police are in the street outside, waiting to descend upon you! Yet you have one chance and only one of averting the fate that hangs over your head."

At this instant the curtain was drawn aside, and once more the slatternly maid appeared. She said no words; but with terror, in her face, lifted three fingers of one hand. "Three!" That was the jargon of the profession for a detective.

The sweat gathered and dripped down the swarthy features of Princess Zara. She dismissed the maid with an impatient gesture, and leaned forward.

"Tell me!" she gasped hoarsely. "Tell me! How?"

"Give away this ship-model and you will save yourself. Give it to anyone—to this seaman through whose unconscious lips I am speaking!" said Lorenzo Diaz sternly. "That is the only way—the only—avert—"

The voice died out. Captain Helm shivered again, moved spasmodically, and his eyes jerked open. A cry broke from him, in his own rough seaman's tones.

"Where am I? What's happened? Oh, it's you!" His gaze gripped the Princess Zara, and he heaved up out of his chair. "Lemme out of here! I knew that danged trance would get me, and I'm scared of it—lemme out of here, I tell you!"

Princess Zara was nothing loath.

Five minutes later, Captain Helm descended the front steps of Princess Zara's abode, a large parcel wrapped in newspaper under his arm. Across the street was standing a man whose square-toed boots and general appearance betrayed his profession. Captain Helm made a gesture, and the detective followed him down the street. They met at the corner.

"Well, I didn't need to call you in," said Captain Helm cheerfully. "I got it back myself, and had some fun doing it; so you can tear up that warrant. Here's a five-spot for your trouble."

"Much obliged," said the detective. "How'd you manage to pry that dame loose from it?"

Captain Helm chuckled.

"Oh, that was easy! I used to be in the same business myself, once upon a time, before I took to the sea! So long."

FOR GLORY AND THE MAIN!

"S*porting dolphins and spouting sea-monsters!*" said Cap'n George Dexter. "Want to see 'em? I got me another book today and found something nice in it."

I was visiting aboard his ship; the skipper has a nautical library to knock your eye out. He prowls in every port, for books, and shares his finds with his friends. He laid before me an old French tome on ship-handling, a real old one, and bound in with it was a chart. On the ocean portions appeared not only the usual antique monsters, but also two sailing craft, to indicate deep water.

As a ship-lover I was instantly curious. One of these ships was a true model of the 1665 period, but exaggerated. A blunt three-master with highly steeved bowsprit and sprit boom. At the very tip of the bowsprit was a sprit-topmast, reaching almost as high as the fore yard.

But the other one! There was a ship almost of our own day, a square-rigger with conventional top-hamper. The bowsprit was leveled to an almost straight thrust. In place of the sprit-boom was a spreader and martingale, with the regular bobstays and martingale guys.

"Trying to put something over on me, George?" I asked. "This square-rigger was drawn on the chart a hundred years after the thing was printed!"

My host chuckled. "Want to bet on it?"

I did not. Dexter had been master in sail for thirty years, and was an authority on ships and rigs.

"Look again," he said, and handed me a reading-glass. "Sure it was printed?"

I obeyed, and suddenly got the point—or thought I did. This map was not printed, but drawn. It was an original, a chart of the western coast of Haiti.

Dexter chuckled. "Both ships drawn at the same time, by the same man. This," and he pointed to the apparently modern vessel, "was his conception of how the bows of the future ship would look, in his mind. The other, obviously exaggerated, shows the clumsy bow-rigging, the low sprit or water-sail, of that period."

"And just who was this brilliant genius?" I inquired with some skepticism.

The skipper, with his chart-reader, magnified the signature of the old-time cartographer. The name was Eli Darden; above it was the inscription "Charte of Hispaniola." Name of romance, this!

Darden? It came back to me after a moment. His career had been curiously like that of William Dampier. Unlike Dampier, however, he had never published any "Discourses" of dubious adventure; nor, after abandoning piracy, had he been given the command of a king's ship. Far from it!

Instead, he had been cursed and reviled by those very buccaneers who profited most by his skill in navigation. Finally, as a last gesture of thanks, they "wet-marooned" him between Grand Cayman and Cape Gracias a Dios, and left him to perish.

Somewhere I had read about it. Now the picture came back to me from boyhood's days. I could vision the Caribbean of that fateful August morning, lying flat and glassy. Even the dawn-breeze had failed. The boat, old and battered, drifted with what current there was. The sun lifted in a blinding golden maze, promising intolerable white heat.

Roused by the warmth, the man in the stern sat up, rubbed salt-burned eyes, and blinked dully at the sea. He held a hand up to the fiery disk, measuring by force of habit its height above the horizon; then his hand fell. Half-crazed laughter struggled on his caked and blistered lips.

"No instruments here," he croaked dully. "No nothing. Nothing."

With the hopeless word, he sprawled again, and retrospect overwhelmed him. What a fool he had been to counter the insane ferocity of those buccaneering wolves who had elected him captain!

Against his will, voting him down, they had laid a Portugal aboard in a blustering, futile fight, only to be beaten off as Darden had foreseen. Licking their wounds, frenzied with disaster, blind with rum, they vented their rage on "Mad Eli," as he was too often known, on him who loved beauty in a world of fury. He could still hear the voice of Tighe, Red Tighe with his one eye, the master's mate:

"Cast him loose, wet-maroon him! Let the sun fry the addled brains out of his noggin—the Jonah! It's bad luck to all he does."

Tighe wanted to be captain, yes. That red Hercules had ambition. And now Eli Darden drifted in an empty boat, his beloved papers and instruments lost; another day or two and he would go mad with the dry-flesh prickle of thirst.

He stirred, shook himself, and stood up, a slender wiry man in ragged drawers. His face, bronzed, hawklike, caught the imagination; hard and strong, but the eyes lacked shrewdness. They were wide set, open, the eyes of a dreamer.

Nothing in sight, three ways; the other direction was closed by sun-dazzle and glare. Eli Darden slumped again, staring vacantly at the one other thing in the boat—an empty jug rolling in the bilge. These two days he had stared at nothing else, striving to keep his sanity by fastening attention on the thing—yet it was only now that he noticed the bottom of the jug. He stiffened suddenly, sat up, rubbed his eyes.

Suddenly he reached out, retrieved the jug, and muttered in astonishment. Yes; here were scratches on the bottom of it. He squinted, slack-jawed, at the rude words:

"Yr papers safe. Knife inside. K."

He could not comprehend at once. Papers safe, his beloved papers safe? He must be dreaming. "K." would be Willy Kirk, the cabin boy; yes, the lad could read and write, for a wonder. He held up the unstoppered jug and shook it Something moved. He held it bottom up and shook again. An object protruded and he tugged it out.

A slim, deadly knife, eight inches long, tightly wrapped in torn silk. A grim smile cracked his lips as he fingered it. Bless the lad! A knife to end his thirsty life when he could endure no more, eh? Well, he was not yet at that point.

He thumbed the blade, his brain acrawl with bitter thoughts. Upon what evil days and low estate had he fallen, he who had been a gentleman once! Guide and companion of sea-wolves, lowest of the low, unable to comprehend thought or discretion; mad outcast wreckage of humanity, men who savagely destroyed all society, religion and the lovely things of life in their insensate lust for plunder and women they were not men enough to gain honestly. Aye, there was the simple truth of it.

He sat with head bowed and torment creeping upon him as the sun drew higher. He could hold his own among these wolves. He cherished a snarling hatred of them all, a hand quicker to strike, a brain quicker to grasp; yet here he was, a man doomed. This was the end of things for him, a wasteful end. Ah, with what he knew now, if he could but get out of it all—

"Ahoy the boat!"

The voice reached him, shook him, lifted him erect with ghastly face. Had madness come to him so soon—ah! There against the sun-dazzle was something; or was it a vision come to plague him? No; it must have been there all the time, and he blinded by the sun. Trembling, he caught his breath. A ship, a real ship, drifting down on him, overhauling him with the current.

Even in this desperate moment, Eli Darden could admire her as she crept from the sun-glare into his clearer vision. A ketch, probably some Frenchman from Martinico; a trim and splendid thing, helped along by some faint breath of air that did not touch the sea. Against the vivid blue of the still water, against the sun-filled sky, she stood clearcut and serene. Only one thing to spoil the picture; this was the absurd bowsprit with its sprit-topsail sticking up like a sore thumb.

Voices hailed him in French and Spanish and English. He recoiled as he comprehended; buccaneers! Wolves like those he had left. His own name was uttered. They knew him, some of them. Laughter and jeers and oaths poured at him. A line was flung, and he caught it. All the while, he knew his desperate plight, once he was aboard her. He must think fast, act rapidly, or he was a lost man.

No mercy here; survival of the fittest, and nothing else. No hesitation if he meant to live. Catch at opportunity or perish! His tumultuous, rioting brain was at work as he came alongside, was hauled aboard, was given sips of water. Scavenger wolves, these; not even honest buccaneers. Riffraff buzzards of the sea, hated and despised by the bold blades of Tortuga, stealing women, murdering fishermen.

As they passed him toward the poop he counterfeited a weakness he did not feel. His quick glances appraised everything; a sweet, fast craft, four guns to a side, in hands unspeakably evil. Filthy decks, filthy men. The knife pinned by its own blade under the waistband of his drawers, lent a touch of comfort.

Here on the poop was a moon-faced rascal in bedraggled velvet, Spanish top-boots, and gold-laced hat. Eli Darden knew him: Hog Huber they called him along the Main, and spat upon the name.

"Well, if it ain't Eli Darden!" Huber slapped a fat thigh with a roar of mirth, as he eyed the unshaven gaunt derelict. "Cast adrift by the *Florencia,* eh? That's luck for me, right enough. Glad to have ye, Cap'n. Mind the day in Port Royal when you damned me for a lousy dog and rammed your fist into my belly? Ye don't scorn me this day, eh?"

A vicious glint in those piggish eyes. Leaning against the poop rail in assumed faintness, Eli Darden's brain was racing. Filthy decks and filthy men, below his sight; a crying shame for so splendid a ship to be in the hands of swine. And this man hated him bitterly.

He thought of Willy Kirk, saving his beloved papers, scratching on the jug's bottom, daring greatly. He had cherished that boy like a son. It was Willy Kirk who had given him the knife; and now Eli Darden must have manhood enough to work out his own salvation. But it could be only in one way—such a way as these swine would understand.

All this in a split second, a flash, as Huber took the long pistol from his shoulder-sling and cocked it.

"Now, ye dog," said the jackal, licking his thick lips, "bang goes a ball through your blasted hand! That'll pay you out for the blow at Port Royal. Then I'll have you keel-hauled—you'll scrape the barnacles down below, and come up in ribbons. And all the while, keep Port Royal in mind, and your scorn and your blow. Fine gentleman, huh? There'll be little enough o' that left when you've been hauled under the keel and the barnacles 've slit your blasted skin. Ho—Diego! Lay aft with a pair o' the lads!"

There was the moment. They were alone on the poop; Huber's little eyes flitted to the deck below, and the mate. The instant would never come again—

Darden was suddenly leaping, one hand streaking from his waistband, the other striking the heavy pistol aside. The needle-point of the keen knife sped upward and drove home, pinning the velvet coat to hairy chest. Huber's jaw slacked and his knees buckled; he clawed at the rail, and sank down, death-driven to the heart.

The pistol did not drop from his hand. Darden wrested it away, then leaned forward and plucked its mate clear of the sling He straightened up, a long and heavy weapon in either hand, and faced forward.

Staring bearded faces, eyes rolling at him, a shocked and amazed silence. Then a yell burst from Diego, the mate, and straight for the ladder he came springing, with two men lumbering at his heels. Eli Darden let him come, looked at his olive skin, his gold hoop-earrings, his flashing knife—and fired point-blank. Diego flung out arms and collapsed atop his two men, bearing them back to the deck below.

"Who's captain now?" said Eli Darden through the belch of smoke. "Vote on it, ye scabby dogs! Vote on it—or come get the next bullet!"

Irresolute, they gawked at him, held by the spell of his ringing voice, his personality, his actions. Here was something they could comprehend. One of them swung around; John Oreb, the gunner. His voice broke the silence.

"A good job done seamanlike, says I! Who's for Cap'n Darden, the smartest navigator on the Main?"

Hard eye and hard jaw and pistol-mouth above, unloved men dead, the spur of a voice to prod acceptance—there was no easier way out for any of them. With the gunner's hoarse roar, the crisis was past. A murmur arose, a murmur that lifted into a roaring assent. They stared up at the sun-blackened thing they had saved from the sea and Eli Darden stared back at them, grim and gaunt.

"The vote's took, sir!" bawled John Oreb. "It's you to work ship!"

"More than that," said Eli Darden. "Captain, d'ye understand? And the first man to question an order gets his ear nailed to the mast. Mind that, my bullies! And now look alive—look alive! Brace yards around for the wind!"

Wind? They looked suddenly at sky and sea; a shout arose. Darden's voice stilled it and swung them into action.

"Look alive! A squall's making up. Alow, there!" He drove sharp words at the helmsman in the whipstaff hutch. "Larboard—hard over! Larboard!"

A squall it was, with wind in the sky behind it. Men jumped to stations; Eli Darden had brought them wind and luck, said they. And the wind, Eli Darden knew, had brought *him* luck—if he could keep it.

So the *Claribel,* once the pride of a thrifty French shipmaster, went scudding for Cape Maisi and Nuevitas, the buccaneer keeling grounds on the eastern coast of Cuba. And Mad Eli, the only man aboard who could navigate, ruled her with an iron hand. After two bloody nails in the mainmast, and two men nursing sore ears, his grip was sure.

They had a master, and knew it; strangely enough they came to like it, or most of them did. Too long lazy, idle, rum-sodden, they came to life under Eli Darden's harsh voice. The gunner, John Oreb, aided much in this by example and good will. The ship was cleaned and burnished from stem to sternpost, the rusting guns were furbished, the Irish pennants trimmed away; most astonishing of all, the men smartened up their personal appearance.

A week, two weeks, and never a sail to break the horizon, with Nuevitas still long leagues away. And now the men muttered that Mad Eli was himself again.

He had the long bowsprit sawed off, just abaft the spritsail yard; this did away with the complicated mess of rigging needed to handle the spritsail. Gone was the yard with its dipping water-sail, the gammoning, the spritsail sheets, pendants, lifts, clewlines and halyards.

Next, Darden had the bo'sun bring the foretopmast and foretopgallant stays down to the shortened jib-boom. The head lead thus shortened took practically all the slack from the stays, giving them a steeper angle and forming a stronger brace for the mainmast. From the topgallant stay he then had rigged an old lateen sail for use as a jib, and spent hours teaching his men how it must be handled.

Mad Eli, eh? So they said at first, grinning behind his back; but when he began experiments in tacking, their grins died. He developed a trick of having plenty of way on the ship before easing down the helm and hauling the jib amidships. As the sail stopped driving her, he would ease off on the fore and head sheets, having hauled the weather pennants over the stays. To the utter amazement of the buccaneers, this caused the ship to tack readily, with a minimum of labor.

When he made fast a light boom to the loose foot of the sail, there was even less work. Seldom did the ship miss stays or get in irons, and with the wind on the quarter she was steadier and steered more easily. Their jests changed to cheers, but Eli Darden only smiled thinly and went back to his figures and sketches below. When the pinch came, it might be otherwise. He had called one Shark Haslam to be mate under him, a man rough with authority who could make himself obeyed. The new rig, vowed Haslam, would sweep the old out of existence when news of it spread abroad. Darden but nodded, and hoped luck would stay with him.

To Nuevitas for overhaul, eh? The ship careened for scraping, one-eyed Tighe and all hands drunk, and Eli Darden walking in on them! This was the purpose flaming in all Darden did, these days. Take off Willy Kirk, get his instruments and papers all back, make the rogues pay up a bit for their fun—and then what?

"Why, out of it!" said Eli Darden to the silence of his cabin. "A gentleman adventurer once more, away from this muck and blood and fury! I'll back to Bristol town and take Willy Kirk with me. We'll put our brains to use for honest mariners, egad!"

Thus ran ambition and desire; but crop-eared Shark Haslam and his mates were to be reckoned with, if one ran afoul of destiny.

Fair winds, good winds; another three days, Darden calculated, and they would make their landfall. And then, in the sunrise, a barking hail from the maintop:

"A sail! Sail ho, bullies!"

Eli Darden had dreaded such a cry. The stamping, the wild voices, brought him on deck with pistols in their sling and a cold despair in his heart. He joined Haslam on the poop, and the mate bawled gleefully at him:

"A galleon as ever was, cap'n! A triple-cursed Spanisher, aye!"

The men were at work, snatching tampions from gun-muzzles and weather cloths from priming-pans, fetching powder and ball, loading muskets. But Eli Darden lifted his spy-glass and gazed in long silence on the cloud of sail to the northward.

Something queer about her—aye, he had the focus now! A galleon, sure enough, with one mast knocked away and a jury rig in its place, with holes gaping along her high bulwarks, with things that had been men dangling from her yards. These, as he looked, were cut away. Metal flashed aboard her; soldiers. And beyond her, a farther shred of sail just breaking the horizon.

"Get them swabs and rammers ready!" Haslam roared. "John Oreb, look to the slack in your gun-tackles!"

"Look to the Spaniard," and Eli Darden handed over the glass. "Ports triced up, soldiers aboard, and a second ship off to the north'ard of her. Look well."

Haslam looked, and cursed savagely. "Aye, she's been in a scrimmage, too. Be damned to her! We can lay her aboard afore t'other can come up."

Darden called the men together. No force would avail him here; only the vote, by buccaneer custom.

The instant would never come again—Darden was suddenly leaping.

He looked down at them from the head of the poop ladder. Whites, negroes, swarthy Latins, Frenchmen; hard-bitten rogues, all, living for but one thing ere their tarred carcasses swung high above Execution Dock. A little loot, a little rum, the smiles of soiled women. He felt a queer compassion for these hopeless men, wolves though they might be. Thieves, and worse than beasts. Yet Eli Darden would swing as high as Shark Haslam if it came to capture.

"Vote, bullies," he said, running his eye over the upturned faces. "I say to hold our course and leave her be. Two of'em there. Soldiers aboard, guns ready; and by her course she's outward bound from Spain, with no gold aboard—"

"She has women, right enough!" yelled Haslam in sudden fury. "I've heard ye called a bloody coward afore now, Mad Eli, but I didn't believe it of you! Lay off like cowardly sculpins and let her pass, you say? I say no!"

"You'll say too much one of these days," Eli Darden told him coldly. "Lads! By the rules, it's your say. Vote on it! If you say fight, I'll fight; but I advise you to lay off. We've got Nuevitas ahead. Here's hard knocks and no gold—"

"Gold be damned, where there's women!" howled someone.

"And two Spaniards," went on Darden. "Mind that, lads! What's the other one hanging off for, if not to trap us when it's too late?"

"Put it to the vote!" Haslam shoved him aside in a stark rage. "You're no cap'n here, Mad Eli. I say fight, and I'm the man to take your place—"

The pistol in Darden's hand thudded down across

his skull and dropped him in his tracks. Over him stood Eli Darden, smiling thinly.

"Aye, vote!" he said to the staring men. "While I'm cap'n here, none of you dogs dare say me nay. Now vote—fight or run?"

"Fight!" shrilled up the wild, fierce cry, and not a voice to oppose. Eli Darden knew they would rush him did he go against the vote. He had no recourse.

"Fight it is, then, and God help the lot of you!" he said grimly. And true too, he thought; if ever a man got anything away from the upper dog, he must fight for it. "Stand by to wear! Jump to it, bullies! Up wi' the mainsail; brail the jib! At the helm, there, luff ship!"

Smoke belched from that high stern, and Darden felt his ship reel.

A yell, a chorus of oaths, and they were about their work with a will. Darden cast off restraint, thrilled to the tingle of it all, gave himself up to it since he must. A strange, furious stimulus gripped him as he ranged the poop.

"Hard up the helm! Brace the main yards in—lively about it!"

As if the devil himself had taken a hand, the breeze suddenly freshened. The *Claribel* had luffed around until the leaches of the topsails began to sing and shake. The Spaniard was drawing close, and Darden eyed the high-castled poop with two stern gun-ports beneath.

"Hoist fore tacks! Shift head sheets over!" rang his voice. "Haul in your main braces—look alive, blast you!"

He had forgotten Willy Kirk now. He remembered rescued galley slaves, their backs a mass of livid scars. He recalled a fellow Englishman who had escaped from Cartagena. The man had been a walking skeleton, all enlarged joints and pulled tendons; a living symbol of the rack.

"Where'll you have me, Cap'n?"

Haslam was up and at his side, eager now to obey, unmindful of the blow that had felled him.

Eli Darden gave him a glance.

"Take charge for'ard. All hands below except men to work the lines, and John Oreb's gun-crews. We've but sixty men and none to waste."

Haslam grinned, touched his forelock, and leaped for the maindeck. Gun-crews labored with tallow kegs, powder-kegs, canvas bags of bullets and scrap-iron. Others broke out the devil's claws-grapnels, bending on chain. Pistols and cutlasses were being passed around.

Some of the men were got below under cover. Gunner Oreb came aft at Darden's hail and squinted up at the poop.

"Starboard guns, Oreb," said Darden calmly. "Load with ball; plant every shot at her rudder-post. Then stand by the larboard guns when we tack. Same load."

Gunner Oreb darted away. Yelps of delight broke from the men; there was the cap'n for you! The same old trick—lay under her stern, smash her rudder, cripple her, then board at will!

Eli Darden paid no heed to the cheers, but surveyed the galleon with sardonic eye. These tactics were the only ones possible; the ketch, scarcely larger than the pinnace towing under the galleon's stern, could not dare venture within range of these heavy broadside guns. Those little stern guns would do her scant damage, however. She could cripple the proud Spaniard and then finish her with impunity.

"Ready about—stations for stays! Weather sheets to windward! Ease down helm—"

Darden's orders rang along the deck. He glanced at the second Spaniard; she was coming, but without haste. He wondered about those men who had been hanging at the yardarms, about the signs of battle the galleon showed; but she plowed along her stately course as though disdainful of the trim little ketch.

dream of swift seamanship, swift tacking, sharp and brainy fighting. The women on the galleon's deck had become men, gay dresses flung overboard and floating. A trap, a trap! And now the Spaniard was luffing, to get her broadside to bear.

From up forward came one wild yell:

"The bow's stove in! She's going down by the head—"

Darden left the poop in one leap, came down on the quarterdeck by the whip-staff, gave his weight to the helm. Another man rushed to help—the helmsman was dead. Only one chance now.

"Lay her aboard, get into her!" his voice lifted. "All hands stand by—"

They knew it as well as he. Water was pouring into her. The broadside from her little guns had not failed, however; all that splendid galleon's stern was a splintered ruin, gun-ports knocked into one gaping hole splashed with blood. No fear of those big guns now. No fear of the galleon, with her rudder-post smashed; but under their feet was a sinking ship.

Darden knew now what those hanging figures had meant: Some other buccaneer had fallen into the Spaniard's trap.

No time to think, no time to give orders. Gallant to the last, the little ketch came slogging sluggishly under that towering stern. Already she was down by the head as water poured into her broken bows.

A staggering crash. Grapnels were flung, caught, made fast. A storm of shot poured down from above. Pistols answered it. Like cats, like madmen, the buccaneers went pouring aboard—up the carved and gilded work, in at the wrecked ports, up to the stern walk. Most of them, however, streamed in by those smashed lower ports. The trap of the Spaniard had become his ruin.

Not a soul was left aboard the doomed ketch, save the dying.

Darden, stripped to the waist, sword aswing, went in with the first of the boarders—a lean, tanned devil, apparently immune to bullets. With his men, he had at first a clean sweep. From those lower stern cabins, the buccaneers hewed into the bowels of the huge craft before the Spaniards really knew they were there.

With Shark Haslam and a dozen men sticking close, Eli Darden fought his way through the cabins that gave egress on the main deck below the poop. And these Spanish men fought; there was no panic, no surrender. With each passing instant, the dread certainty clutched cold at Darden's heart. None of the usual luxury here in the cabin quarters. This ship was meant for business, and those aboard her—a trap, a trap!

A wild lurch of the decks, a burst of voices; that was the ketch plunging under. Haslam went down, a dozen bullets through him as a number of Spaniards loosed pistols. Eli Darden was into them before they could reload. Cold steel clicked. Pikes lunged and tore. The fury of the buccaneers burst the way clear. Sunlight ahead, and the open deck!

Five men behind him, Eli Darden emerged, and halted. He blinked in the sudden glare of light, blinked at the sight ahead. Here, a wild tumult of fighting figures, a swirling chaos of men; but beyond, rank upon rank, glittering soldiers of Spain! A volley crashed out. Three of his five men went down. The other two leaped into the thick of the fury. The poop was won, the cabins were won, but beyond lay the whole deck and the forecastle untouched.

All this at a glance—and the curl of smoke coming from the main hatch, which was open. Smoke, a sudden mushrooming burst of it; a low, muffled roar as powder let loose below. The decks heaved. The Spanish ranks recoiled into the bows. A few of them darted into the chaos. Morions gleamed, breast-plates flashed through the smoke. They struck upon Darden and passed over him. One of them pitched on top of him; with the shock he lay senseless.

"Fire!"

The loose powder, the kegs below decks, had gone up in smoke, making all the waist a blackened ruin. Panic seized the Spaniards now. Those of them who remained aft, finished the remnants of the buccaneers, struck down the wounded with point or butt, and went scrambling forward. The other galleon was bearing close.

Fight the fire? Not they; not with powder everywhere about the decks, with a magazine of it aft in the stern! Their work was done, the buccaneers were finished to a man, and flames were licking through the open hatch. A few of their own wounded were hastily rescued as the flames drove them forward again. There were no boats—only the little pinnace towing under the quarter, and they could not get to it now. Nor was there any need; the companion ship was almost aboard, lines were being flung. Presently was a crash, a rocking lurch, as the two ships touched and clung, and the Spaniards went aboard their consort in frantic haste.

She sheered off, set her canvas to the wind, and went booming away from the doomed galleon.

Eli Darden, blood-smeared from the dead Spaniard atop him, moved and stirred and writhed clear of that dead weight. He sat up, rubbed his eyes clear of smoke, and looked at the decks where only dead men lay. Smoke was pouring from the main hatch, and the red glint of flames pierced through it. A wounded man, caught there, screamed for a moment and then died.

Coming to his feet, Darden found himself unhurt, save for that blow over the head. There was the other galleon, standing away and pausing not. A yard away one of his own men, a brawny Scot, was gasping out his life.

"They dirked me, Cap'n, they dirked me!" he cried out, and sank on his face.

Aye, the wounded had been dirked or battered down. Darden, blood-covered and hidden, had escaped. He caught up his sword from the deck and darted back into the cabins. Dead men here, one or two dying; that was all. Only a mortal hurt could stretch those sea-wolves on the deck. The cabins and passages were a reek of smoke.

Darden plunged through it. He came into the main cabin. Not even a corpse was here. The table was set for a meal, jugs of wine stood racked and ready. Darden caught at one of them and quaffed deeply. The wine revived him. Then he checked himself, his head cocked, his eyes glinting about. Somewhere a voice.

"Help! Help! Brethren of the Coast!" A voice and muffled pounding—where?

A bolt in the deck—ah! The lazaret!

Darden flung himself at it, and lifted the hatch, after loosing the heavy bolt. As it swung up and back, he recoiled with eyes bulging. A monstrous red thatch of hair, a face scarred, one-eyed, set in ferocity—Tighe!

If Darden was stupefied by this apparition, no

less astounded was Tighe the one-eyed, at sight of Darden. A roar burst from him.

"You! Mad Eli! In the devil's name, out o' my way—"

He roared and rushed, and Eli Darden stood aside to let him pass. Then a second figure came up through the trapdoor, and with a shrill cry hurled itself at Darden.

"Kirk! Willy Kirk!" gasped the amazed Eli, "Are ye real? How came you here, lad?"

"Oh, sir! They took the ship and sunk her—killed all of us! They kept me for a slave, and Tighe for hanging at Cartagena—and—I hoped you'd come to rescue—"

Eli Darden folded the boy in his arms, convulsively.

"Praise God!" said he slowly. "Rescue you? Poor lad, take heart! My ship's gone, my men are gone, we're afire—"

A gush of smoke came swirling through the passages, half filling the cabin. With it, like a furious demon, came Tighe, a Spanish rapier in his grip, his eyes wild.

"Fire!" he roared. "Oh, ye damned Jonah, if water can't hurt you, then fire will, or I will—"

"Quiet, you fool!" barked Eli Darden, but his voice was unheard. Big Tighe was upon him with a rush and a torrent of oaths, and the rapier driving in; frenzied, a mad-dog froth on his lips, Tighe wanted only to kill this slim man whom he hated.

He was close to doing it. Darden backed and backed, frantically parrying that long Spanish steel; only his agility saved him now, and all the while his harried brain was playing with the thought of fire and the powder magazine below. Of a sudden, through the smoke he saw the figure of Willy Kirk appear, shrilling something at them that went unheard.

The blades clashed anew. Coughing sobbing for breath, Darden backed into a corner. Then, like a flash, his chance came. His wiry body uncoiled—his sword, like a prolongation of his arm and hand, shot to the mark. Tighe took one staggering backward step, clutched at his throat, and went to the deck with a crash.

"Quick, quick!" Darden, in a red haze, felt Willy Kirk tugging at his arm. "A boat! A pinnace under the quarter, sir—*quick!* I know the way—I saw her—"

Darden coughed and stumbled after.

They came out at the smashed and crimsoned after ports where men lay staring dead. The fresh live air revived Eli Darden on the moment. He clambered along the stern walk after the boy, and dropped into the pinnace, and fell exhausted.

After a moment he staggered up. Willy Kirk, in a blaze of excitement, had cast off the line. The galleon was surging away from them under such of her canvas as still remained. A column of flame and sparking smoke was belching up from her 'midships into the sunlit heavens.

"Saved!" And Darden caught his breath. "Saved, by the love o' God! Lad, we're two poor creatures to have such work done for us."

Willy Kirk looked up at him, the boyish cheeks pinched and wan.

"I'm sorry, sir. About your papers and instruments, I mean. If—"

A huge laugh broke from Eli Darden, as his arm went about the boy.

"All's well over the horizon, lad! We're but fifty leagues south o' Pinos, and I've friends there. England beckons us, and Bristol town, where the ships come up among the houses with the tide."

The thought of the old story, the memory of it, faded out of my mind. I looked at Cap'n Dexter and his book, the reading-glass in his hand, the chart under his finger. How long had I been standing here adream—half a day? No. The brass clock screwed to the cabin bulkhead told me the truth. Only a minute or a trifle more. A dream in sober truth, when half a lifetime passes in the flash of a split second.

"You seem interested." Cap'n Dexter chuckled. "Aye, you well may be. You know, this Eli Darden is said to have invented the bow rig that the buccaneers used, which replaced the old spritsail and all that mess—"

"When did Darden die?" I asked abruptly.

"Can't say." Dexter shook his head. "The last heard of him was somewhere in the Caribbean in 1672. But he certainly drew this chart. And just as certainly he drew this sketch—look at it!"

He turned over the chart. On the other side was a sketch, a ship stern-to in perspective, sailing away before a breeze. He held the glass over it; there, magnified, I could read the legend on the ship's counter:

WILL KIRK
Bristol, 1678

WE MUST FIGURE ON DEATH

The advertising business, these days, runs into some strange by-paths. A friend of mine, Tony Lawrence, who handles a lot of advertising problems for a citrus fruit concern, dropped in at the house one night when Captain Corbely was there, and started an argument. Tony had been working up an entire library for his company, on the subject of citrus juice being used at sea as a preventive against scurvy, and claimed it had first been done about 1800.

"You're a couple of centuries off," said Cap'n Corbely, who had brought over some books to show me. He picked up one of them. "The year is 1600, my friend."

Tony waved his hand. "I'm not talking about some chance shot in the dark. All the old seamen were trying to prevent scurvy, and couldn't do it. I'm talking about the first deliberate use of citrus juice for that purpose."

"So am I," said the skipper grimly. "And it's all in 'Purchas His Pilgrimes' for you landlubbers to read, only you spend your time on scientific rot instead of old sea-captains' reports."

Tony Lawrence got excited about it, and Corbely lugged out some of the East India Company's reports, and they went to bat. Scurvy was one of the great scourges of the world, which according to Tony had been set to rest by science. It had been probably the greatest factor in sea life, in trade and commerce, wiping out ships and entire expeditions. When the period of discovery opened up distant sea-lanes, and voyages lasted for months and years, scurvy got in its mysterious work. It had to be fought, guarded against, at huge cost and effort. Not until science finally tracked it down and beat it, did the Seven Seas become a safe place for mankind.

Corbely sniffed at all that. "Science, my eye! A seaman beat it, long ago. A housewife in Woolwich tracked it down three hundred years before your land-sharks and doctors did. And they didn't have sense enough to make use of her wisdom, that's all!"

We dug into it to learn the truth. One had to get acquainted with the men of that day, with what it meant to go to sea in that period. Our present era of charted seas and scientific precision had to be swept clear away.

So it was that we came upon the four men in Woolwich....

Of a bitter January night, they sat about a blazing fire in the Red Rose tavern, and over their sack and mulled ale discoursed of the death that lay ahead. All four were master seamen, but chief of them was James Lancaster, bluff and bronzed, with wide blue eyes set above his short curly beard.

Lancaster pulled at his long-stemmed pipe and listened thoughtfully while Middleton barked away:

"I've the Dutch charts for you, James, aye; and Linschoten was dead right in every word he said o' winds and tides. But we must figure four months to the Cape, and ye all know what that means,"

Lancaster nodded. It was the first voyage of the East India merchants, and he was the general in command, and his high ship the *Dragon* was admiral of the four. In those days a ship, and not a man, bore this title.

"That's why we're taking along the little *Guest,*

John. Before we reach the Cape, we'll refill our water-butts and our supplies from her, and cast her adrift. And our dead men will be replaced by her crew. Aye, lad; for we must figure on death."

All four nodded gravely. Death by sea and wind and unknown shores, death from shot and ball, death from scurvy—grimmest and surest of all.

"Tell me something, Lancaster," spoke out Master Heyward of the *Susan.* "I've run into you during long voyages, and after 'em. Ye've never been took sick a day. When your men were rotten and you couldn't muster a boat's crew, you were always hale and hearty. Why?"

Lancaster chuckled in his beard. "My wife has a remedy against all disorder, or so she thinks. It's the grace o' God, not her sovereign remedy, that's kept me well. But I'm a man o' my word, as she knows, and she gives me a store of the stuff, and I take it on my promise. Think no more of it. Aye, lads, it's a fearsome and terrible reflection, that when we get to the Cape with its winds and storms, when we need every man on the lines, we're certain to have two-thirds of our crews wi' their teeth rotting out and their bodies swollen and helpless!"

"We'll revictual and refit at Saldanha Bay, north o' the Cape," put in William Brand, drawing down his shaggy brows. He captained the *Ascension,* a dour, hard man. "But that won't save us from the scurvy. One says one thing about it, another says another; every man to his own theory, and surgeons be damned! Eat salt meat, as we must, and there's no escaping it. Well, then, face it with a good heart!"

"Better still, find a way to avoid it," Lancaster said. "We'll have two hundred men aboard the *Dragon.* If we reach the Moluccas with a hundred and fifty, we'll be in luck. That's heavy odds o' death, lads. However, we'll make it if the Dutchmen can! We're carrying twenty-seven thousand pounds in cargo and money, and the company's spending forty-five thousand on the ships and men; we've the best of everything, and by heaven we'll prove that the fleet's not lacking in the best o' men to do the work! Well, I must home. Good night to you all."

He tucked his cloak about him and stamped home through the snow, thoughtful enough, the problem of death still weighing on his mind. Much to his relief, his good wife was in bed and sleeping, so he turned in without waking her.

*Next morning, however, Mistress Lancaster cor*nered him. She was a plain, hearty, sensible woman, and if she had a tongue in her head, she used it for love's sake and not for shrewish byplay.

"Now, James, where are those bottles?"

"Bottles?" he repeated blankly. He was checking over a Dutchman's pilotage for the journey home around the Cape. "What bottles?"

"For the remedy," said she with tart tongue. "As you know well. Out with 'ee, and fetch me home bottles and jugs!"

Lancaster frowned. "The remedy be hanged, woman. Now, look you! Homeward bound about the Cape, if a man hath no weather for observation, he can safely keep in sixty fathom water while the ground be shelly; but if it be oozy, he'll know he's near Cape Agulhas—there's a valuable point to note. And you prate of bottles!"

"Aye," said she. "Bottles and jugs. I'm making up enough o' the lemon juice for your whole crew, James, and I'll need a plenty of containers."

He shoved aside his work, in dismay. "Nell, there's not a lass in England who's your equal—but pause a bit. In our ship, for such a cruise, every bit o' space is precious. You can well enough put up a few bottles o' the juice for my use, but for two hundred men—Lord save us all! There's no room for it."

"You'll make room," she said firmly. "If it hadn't been for my remedy, you'd be a dead man this day, or the life would be rotted out of you, as it is out o' many an old seaman. And now you go on an important voyage, wi' letters from Her Majesty, and you general in command, to the far Indies. And think ye I'll see you go unprepared? Not I. The lemons are bought and ready, and I'll have you get the bottles."

"It's absurd!" Lancaster broke out. "Why, my men won't stand such treatment! I'll be the laughing-stock o' London."

"You'll do what I say, James Lancaster; else you don't go to sea—general or no general!" his wife declared, and meant her words. "Scurvy, say most, do come from sea air and eating salt meat. I know better. I've talked wi' many a seaman, and one and all tell me the same thing; the craving for green stuff, for acid tang i' the blood. You've said it yourself."

"Listen, my precious lass," said Lancaster earnestly. "Ye know nothing about it. The great men of science, the royal societies, the queen's own physicians, ha' looked into this, and they be wiser than you. Fresh meat, they say, will cure it—"

Mistress Lancaster shook her finger at him.

"You'll do what I say, or another man goes master o' the *Dragon,* if I must to London and see Her Majesty myself! Now, is it yes or no?"

Lancaster suppressed a groan. "Aye, if you're set on it," he said sourly.

"And ye'll ladle out each man two spoons per day, of a morning—on an empty stomach? Your word of honor?"

He swallowed hard. "Aye, if you'd make a fool of me."

"Better a live fool than a dead lion, my man; and you mind it," she retorted. "I be none o' your

wiseacre scientists, but I know that when a body craves something, that's what a body needs. And lemon juice hath kept you in health these many years, so to the Indies it goes with you. And your word of honor, mind!"

"Aye," grunted Master Lancaster unhappily. "But lemons cost good round money, lass, and—"

"And I've spoke wi' Sir John Hart yesternight, when he was watching the lading of the ships, and got his warrant for the lemons as part of the expenses of your ship," she broke in. "So ha' done with your objections."

Lancaster got her the bottles; but soon enough he began to hear from the matter. Sir John Hart, one of the associated backers of the venture, held his sides when he told about it—and he told the tale everywhere.

When it first reached Lancaster's ears, he was arguing with the chief rigger about the price of a main topsail, holding that twelve pound twelve shillings was too high. "Not so high as delicacies like lemons for common seamen," said the other with a grin. And they began to call him "Lemon" Lancaster; but not to his face.

Visitors were coming down from London in flocks. The new company was sinking its whole subscribed capital, over seventy thousand pounds, in this venture; a tremendous sum to gamble on spice from the Moluccas. Among the visitors was many a learned man. The physicians talked at length with Lancaster, trying to show him the folly of this wasteful notion. For lemons were expensive as the devil.

Each wise man had a different theory about the scurvy, and a different remedy. The other captains harkened. Heyward took aboard a great quantity of fowl; hen's blood being a sure remedy, according to him. Middleton laded chests of purgatives. Brand damned the lot of them for fools, but saw to his salt meat casks with careful eye. And Lancaster, stowing the jugs and bottles that his wife sent down, was the butt of many a joke.

The surgeon appointed to the *Dragon* strove with him earnestly. A dour and opinionated man, this surgeon held all acids in abomination. One night he came to Lancaster's house and expounded his own theories about the scurvy. Claimed he, if enough saltpeter were fed all hands, the scurvy would be warded off, since it was but the restrained humors of the body seeking escape through the tissues.

"Stuff and nonsense!" said Mistress Lancaster, and the argument waxed hot. In the midst of it, in walked Martin Hearne, who was nephew to the good lady. He bussed her roundly and shook hands with Lancaster, who gave him curt greeting.

A dark, lean man was Hearne, with clever eyes and the name if not the spirit of a gentleman. He was learned in clerkly things, had killed two men in duels, and to Lancaster he was a bird of ill omen. As a matter of fact, some queer things were said of Martin Hearne. He had the gift of second sight, went the word. Not that it brought him any great luck. Like all such folk, he might foretell the fate of other men, but his own he could not see.

He listened to the argument with his thin-lipped, twisted smile, and then put in a word or two of his own.

"You need not argue the matter, for three reasons," he said to the surgeon. "The first is Master Lancaster, who listens to no reason. The second is Mistress Lancaster, who will hear no reason. The third, my good sir, is that you'll be dead of the scurvy yourself within the six-month."

The surgeon, having already perceived the folly of argument, took his leave.

Hearne, smiling, turned to Lancaster.

"Uncle James, I've good news for you. I'm going on the voyage. What's more, I'm appointed to your own ship, the admiral."

"You?" said Lancaster. "God save us all!"

His wife hugged young Hearne. She had a leaning to such evil, ruffling blades, as most good women have. He explained to them, briefly.

Aboard each of the ships went a merchant, to handle trading and all business of the company. Since death was ever close in such a voyage, each merchant had an associate and each associate a substitute. If two died, one would live to keep the books. Martin Hearne was third aboard the *Dragon.*

Lancaster, looking into that dark face, shook his head.

"Best be frank about it, lad," said he, wasting no words. "I like you not, nor you me. But God forbid that I do you a wrong in my heart, so come and welcome! But mind well, there's discipline aboard."

"And lemon juice," said Hearne, with a smile. "Neither one nor the other will cause me any loss o' sleep, I promise you!"

Later, Lancaster frowned at his good wife when she bade him take care of Hearne.

"Martin's got the makings of a great man, husband," said she. "He's never been out of England afore now; a bit wild, maybe, but worth the right guidance."

"I doubt it," Lancaster said bluntly. "He's the kind to explode when pent up on shipboard. But for your sake, lass, I'll be easy with him."

It was the middle of February when the ships dropped down the river, and two months more when they left England; in those days, men waited for a wind. And almost before the anchors were hoysed and stowed, Lancaster had trouble on his hands.

His surgeon was stubborn in his refusal to countenance lemon juice, little dreaming that Hearne's prediction was safe enough to come true. There were some aboard glad to adopt his advice, if so they might escape that sour morning draft on an empty stomach. The ship's company had its share of malcontents and trouble-breeders, and the scoffing at Lemon Lancaster had spread among the crew. So the surgeon, with the master gunner and a round score besides, flatly refused the lemon juice. In this, Martin Hearne took a leading part.

Lancaster had been out to the Indies ere this, and knew the vital need of discipline. Now he saw it ebbing away rapidly, with Hearne egging on the others. As they sailed to the southward, he spoke once and again with the young man, but had no luck.

It was the seventh of May, the day they left the Grand Canary behind, that he summoned Hearne into his cabin.

"You're a sullen dog, Martin," said he, being a man of plain speech. "I've tried kindness with you, and to small avail. You're the one man from whom I'd expect full backing, but you only provoke trouble daily. What's the answer?"

Middleton barked: "Four months to the Cape, and ya all know what that means!" And Lancaster nodded. "Aye, lad... we must figure on death."

Hearne regarded him with a thin, bitter smile, his dark eyes smoldering. Wine was in him now, as it was often.

"I'll not lick your boots, Uncle James," said he, "nor any other man's boots. You're too high and mighty for my taste, as you know well. You can shift me into another ship, as you know well also."

Lancaster frowned at him.

"I will not. Pass on to others a drunken wastrel and admit I can't handle him? Not me, lad. You know the rules about liquor. The next time you're drunk, you'll get a dozen lashes."

"Flog me like one of your seamen? If you do, so help me, I'll kill you!" cried Hearne. "I'm a gentleman!"

"I'm not," said Lancaster, fingering his brown beard. "I'm general of this fleet, lad. What's more, I've a commission of martial law from the hands of Her Majesty, God bless her! And I'll have you triced up quicker than any other man aboard, for the simple reason that you're known to be my nephew."

"Not yours, thank heaven!" sneered Hearne.

"My wife; poor lass!" and Lancaster sighed a little. "For her sake I've been patient, Martin; but I'll stand little more of your nonsense. You're infecting this whole crew with discontent. You're endangering the venture. I'm warning you with a kind heart, as bidden by Holy Writ; but some day you'll go too far."

Hearne's thin lip curled.

"You're a simple dolt in your way, Uncle James," said he with contempt. "You and your Bible reading every day—ha! This venture needs a man of spirit. Now, look you! I'm none of your crew, to be sodden with your sickly sour juice and doltish notions. I'm not responsible to you, but to the company. I'll drink what I damned please."

"I've said my say, Martin," Lancaster replied calmly. "God help me, I'm responsible for every ship and every soul in this command. My wife gave you into my care, but four hundred and eighty other men are in my care, and seventy thousand pounds, and the trust of my friends and my queen. Dolt? Aye, I'm no very great commander, God wot, but I do my best. And it's only a very wise man, Martin, or a very simple man like me, who reads Holy Writ—the one because he understands it, the other because he needs it. And you, Martin, are neither. No more warnings. Clear out."

Martin Hearne swaggered out with a twist to his lip. James Lancaster sat there with his hands clenched before him, as the ship swayed and the timbers creaked, and his eyes were troubled.

It was a week later that Hearne, drinking, ruffling

and dicing, drew his dirk and would have killed the chief merchant but that men fell on him and held him fast. Lancaster strode into the cabin, and gave quiet orders—and Hearne was taken out to the deck and spread over a gun-carriage, and was given a dozen with the cat.

When they had washed the blood off his back with brine, he stood up. He was sobered, and he looked Lancaster in the eye as he spoke.

"You'll mind what I promised if ye did this."

Lancaster said nothing, and Hearne went below with a red devil in his eyes.

Meantime, each morning, the lemon juice was ladled out, and those who would have none of it began to swell in the joints and move listlessly about the decks. The surgeon worked with them mightily, and talked much with the master gunner and with Hearne, and there was great murmuring against Lancaster for his iron hand and his grim discipline. But the ships sailed on.

One night there was a crossbow loosed, none knew where or by whom. The bolt missed Lancaster by two fingers' breadth, as he stood on the poop conning the stars. He said nothing of it, but the wind of death had fanned his cheek closely that night. If he could prove nothing, he knew all he needed to know. And was helpless.

The Master's Mate came to him another night, and told of mutterings and dark words among the men alow and aloft. Hearne was in the thick of it, but nothing could be proven against him. Many of them feared the man.

"He's fey at times," said the Master's Mate as they talked. "Why, sir, what d'ye think he told me but this morning? He looked at me hard, and said he, I'd die and have honors at my burial, in a far place; and the guns of this same ship would be fired to do me honor, and would kill better men than me. Sir, he's daft!"

Daft or not, he was dangerous. And in a later day, Lancaster was to remember that queer saying, when the shotted guns of the *Dragon* roared over the watery grave of this same Master's Mate, and slew Master Brand and others of his crew from the *Ascension* in their boat.

Fear and terror of Martin Hearne spread through the ship. He had a swaggering masterful way with him, but after that one flogging he refrained from liquor, though hatred sat in his eyes when he looked at Lancaster. There began to rise talk of mutiny, and what could be done by lusty men if they took the ship and set out to seek plunder; it came to Lancaster's ears, and he knew Hearne was behind it, and he was helpless.

Night after night he sat in his cabin, the weather being good, and conned the big Bible with its heavy black type. Night after night he lay in his berth, or knelt beside it if the seas were not strong, and wrestled in prayer for guidance from aloft. He was a simple man, with a strange simple faith and simple iron will, the sort of man to do great things and do them quietly, or do terrible things and do them sternly, or do little things and do them nobly. But here he did not know what to do. Hearne was too clever for him, would give him no handle, and that was the truth of it.

Take care of the lad, Mistress Lancaster had said; little did Hearne need any care-taking! It was not this that troubled James Lancaster one whit. But he realized that, first, his life was in danger night and day from this man, and much depended on his life. Further, and more important to his mind, the entire voyage was in danger.

Here was a festering sore rapidly infecting the whole ship. This one shrewd and unscrupulous man menaced everything. Talk of mutiny and piracy, of gold and riches and women, was enough to set all hands stark mad; and backed up by Hearne, by the master gunner, by the dour surgeon, it would lead to wreckage, unless checked. How to check it?

Lancaster, helpless, sought higher help, and knew not that it was already within his heart and soul. For, like many another man, he sought the voice of God from the tempest and the earthquake; and recognized the still small sound only after it had come....

On the twentieth of June, the ship's boy came to him, whimpering, with a queer story of voices heard that evening on the stern walk—a gallery above the rudder, around the square stern. The boy was scared stiff. Men's voices, he said, talking of mutiny and powder and killing in cold blood. He knew nothing definite, but he told enough to send a cold chill through Lancaster's very soul. So it had come to crisis! And not a shadow of excuse to clap Hearne into irons—even if that would do any good, which was doubtful.

That night, Lancaster read in his Bible with agony of soul, and knelt in prayer, for the ship was on a steady keel. Two degrees north of the Line, with calms and much contrary wind, and all the ships keeping well in company.

He fell asleep at last—and wakened to shouts and trampling feet. Horror seized on him. He reached for sword and pistols. Mutiny, then? The sun was up, and he broke for the deck hurriedly.

No mutiny. Instead, a great proud Portugal bellying out of the north, a carrack deep-laden for the Indies. Alert and joyous, Lancaster sent his roar along the deck, ordered out signal for the other ships to follow, and sent the *Dragon* booming along with every scrap of sail set to the steady light air.

The other ships fell behind. The morning waxed and heatened to noon, over a glassy sea with hardly even a ground-swell, and still the *Dragon* leaned to the spread of canvas. Mile by mile, she crept up on that big Portugal until, by noon, the carrack was desperately and frantically loosing the cannon from her high stern, to no avail.

Lancaster bore on. His men were armed and ready. Sink her? Not he, by heaven! She was deep-laden, and a prize worth the having. He paced the poop deck, in his gleaming steel cap and breastplate; his men had matches alight, he had his pistols ready. Muskets and crossbows and swords, as the two ships crept closer, until a spattering fire broke out, and the grapnels were poised for flinging.

And there was Hearne, in steel cap and breastplate likewise, the first man over her rail as the ships staggered and crashed and swung—the first man, after Lancaster himself. A quick, brief breaking of battle

The men of the *Dragon*, hale and hearty, stared amazedly at the men of the other ships. The scurvy had laid upon them all.

there, and the Portugal fled for it, and Hearne after them into the cabins with a wild yell on his lips.

And after Hearne, James Lancaster.

He came on the man in the big after-cabin, came upon him striking down a poor devil and stripping him of jeweled gauds. Beyond a swinging door was an empty cabin. Lancaster came up to Hearne, mindful of a pistol-ball that had glinted off his breastplate a moment earlier; and Hearne swung around, his dark lean face aglow with devil's light.

"So it was your pistol, Martin?" said Lancaster. "And it failed, as your crossbow failed!"

Hearne gripped at his empty pistol and cursed, hotly. Lancaster, his own pistol cocked and ready, nodded at the empty cabin.

"I'd have a word with you—in there," said he. His eyes were wide and cold as ice, but very steady.

"Have it here, damn you," said Hearne.

"In there, I said. What!"—and Lancaster laughed with no mirth at all. "You and your precious mutiny—you'd not talk it over with me, man? What if I'd be willing to join you and navigate the ship—eh?"

"You? You'd join—plague take you!" Hearne's eyes widened for an instant; then he smiled his twisted smile. "Join us, eh? No chance of that. Trying one of your tricks on me, eh?"

Lancaster nodded, but his eyes were more than ever like ice.

"Aye, lad, and it worked. I've heard enough. In there, for a private word in your ear—quick about it!"

The sharp command, the knife-edge of the voice, sent Hearne into the cabin. After him went in Lancaster, and closed the door.

The Portugal was taken, and not a man lost in the taking, despite all the shooting and conflict; or so it was thought, indeed. But when the other three ships came up and their crews came swarming aboard to join in the looting, sad word arose and was brought to James Lancaster, as he stood in the late afternoon sunlight directing the work.

In a cabin had been found Martin Hearne, with a pistol-ball between his eyes. And below, with a sword-stroke through his heart, the master gunner was dead. Hearing this, Lancaster nodded.

"It is the will of God," said he in his quiet way.

The matter was passed over as of small account, before greater things. The lading of the carrack was easily shipped out and divided, in that quiet sea; but here was something else. The men of the *Dragon* were hale and hearty, for the most part, and finding themselves suddenly cheek to jowl with men from the other three ships, stared amazedly. For those men were pallid and like lead in color, and moved heavily, and were broken out with sores and swellings. The scurvy had laid hold upon them all.

"And not upon us?" said Lancaster, when he heard about it. "Well, then, let's give thanks to God, where it belongs."

"And not forget the lemon juice," said some one. Bluff Middleton of the *Hector* let out a snort and a scoffing laugh.

"Nonsense! It's but a touch that comes wi' the salt meat. I've got it well in hand with medicines. When we touch at Saldanha Bay, ye'll see my crew sound and hearty. But you and your lemon juice, James—ah!" He shook his head sagely. "Ye know well that it comes quickly to some ships, slow to others; and when it comes, it's with a rush. I feel sorry for your poor men, James Lancaster."

"They'll come through," said Lancaster. Middleton gave him a sharp look.

"What's wrong with you? By God, here's a fat prize, hardly a man lost, weather good—and damme if you ain't got the look of a man in torment! What's wrong?"

"Nothing's wrong, John," and Lancaster smiled. The deep strong gravity of his eyes was returning slowly; it was true, his face had worn a queer haunted look—but his smile banished it.

"No, nothing's wrong," he went on, and glanced about. "At least, nothing's wrong with my ship. Better look to your own, for I don't like the faces of your men by half."

Middleton clapped him on the shoulder and laughed jovially.

When they had shared everything out of the Portuguese ship, they let her go her ways, and the wind shot them down across the Line.

Here they took all the victuals out of the little *Guest,* stripped her clean, divided her men among the four tall ships, took her spars and broke her upper works asunder for firewood, and cast her adrift.

On into July and through August, ever to the south and eastward, with the winds fair enough on the whole. And as the four ships drove, Lancaster made out queer things aboard the other three; staggering skeleton men about the decks, the merchants taking turns at the helm or up aloft, and fewer and fewer persons in sight at all. Aboard the *Dragon,* however, all was well enough, and there was no more muttering or discontent.

It was the ninth of September when they raised Saldanha Bay. Lancaster came first into the bight, and cast anchor. The other three ships were standing in, but as he watched them come and saw how they handled, his face whitened.

"Out wi' the boats," he ordered. "All hands! And God preserve us all this day, for we'll have need of it."

A true word and a bitter one.

The three ships came staggering in. Aboard each of them nothing moved. A few poor feeble things crawled about the anchors and managed to let go; that was all. Not a boat was hoisted out, not a sail was taken in, not a line touched. When Lancaster stepped aboard the vice-admiral, it was like a ship of the dead. Sodden things lay about the decks, rotting shapes crawled and moaned, bluff Middleton was himself like a scarecrow. Swollen, dying creatures, every one of them. And so with the other two ships as well—down to the last man.

A hundred and five died there, and the others were little better, until rest and proper diet set them afoot again. But not in James Lancaster's ship.

"And that," said Captain Corbely, as he thumbed over his books and drew down his brows at us, "is all of the yarn to the point. Lancaster went on to success and knighthood—"

"But hang it, wait!" broke in Tony Lawrence excitedly. "Why, if that yarn is true, cap'n, the greatest scourge of the sea was licked right there! Then why wasn't it made public? Why wasn't it known?"

Corbely gave me a wink.

"They didn't have radio back in those days, that's why! And no joke about it, either. That's a fact. Lancaster knew, sure enough, what he'd discovered; but people laughed at him all the same. It wasn't followed up."

"Why," gasped Lawrence, "it's an amazing story! It's magnificent!"

"So it is," said Cap'n Corbely, "but I don't mean what you mean. I mean this seaman Lancaster, who could do things the way he did; he went on—he walked with kings, as the poet feller said; but the big thing in this yarn, to my mind, is how he made everything right aboard that ship of his."

"Oh, nonsense," Tony Lawrence put in. "That's all right, sure; but good Lord, man! The big thing is in the discovery about citrus juice—"

"That's because you work for citrus juice," said Captain Corbely gravely, "and I'm a master in sail, like James Lancaster. Maybe, after all, that's why he didn't think the lemon-juice business very important. He probably remembered what one of them Bible chaps said about putting first things first."

But Tony failed to get the point.

FLYING DUTCHMAN

W*e were talking about the Flying* Dutchman, three or four of us, in the Seamen's Institute, which overlooks the wharves and the East River, across to Brooklyn. It started with an old woodcut of the caravel, the ship that served Columbus and Vasco da Gama.

Cap'n Frazier, stroking his long white whiskers, declared she looked like a sea-going wooden shoe with a chicken coop perched on the stern.

Billings, the Cunarder chief steward, stuck up for her lines, however, and the old skipper nodded judicially.

"In a way, yes. No other type of ship is so peculiarly charged with the poetry of the sea, with that weird and grotesque quality which, by moonlight or day distance, comes so near to perfect beauty. We couldn't possibly manufacture the Flying Dutchman out of anything that was launched in the Nineteenth Century."

"Ever see her, Frazier?" asked somebody. "Ever see Vanderdecken?"

Frazier, who looked like Vanderdecken himself, grunted harshly.

"Don't be absurd. Nobody's ever seen that ship. It's just a myth—one of those things that can't be explained."

"It can be explained," said Billings quietly.

Like many of these Cunarders, Billings had a lot of war decorations, a thirst, and a hard practical eye. There was a burst of laughter at his statement, which no one took seriously. Talk of the Flying Dutchman filled the air for a space.

Vanderdecken.... Accursed. Doomed to an eternity of sailing, forever baffled by gales and headwinds that kept him from rounding the Cape, never to know peace or security; and all because of a burst of profanity when the elements perversely turned against him.

There'd be many another like Vanderdecken if profanity could do it, said somebody; and we all laughed. Old Frazier, on occasion, could blast forth a salvo of salt-water language fit to curl the very rope-ends.

Vanderdecken.... Never beating to the northward of 34° South, but eternally there, and visible on misty moonlit nights, or the specter of his ship gliding along under a driving wind and fog. A fabric with high, stairlike poop, a shape flying over mountainous seas, leaping from some ghostly foam-squall, dissolving again like a flash from the swelling spray under her bluff bows.

"Bosh!" snorted old Cap'n Frazier. "She's never been actually seen."

"She has," said Billings in his quiet way. Frazier ignored him.

"Her type of ship did great things—discovered America, discovered the Indies, or rather opened up the road to 'em. Little ships, we'd call 'em; maybe some o' you saw the model that lay so long in the Chicago lagoons? Aye; but big, back in them days. Slow and steady. Built to take battering seas for months on end, and to be pulled up somewhere on shore and careened, and scraped clean. Handmade, you bet. Not machine-made like these blasted craft—"

And he let loose a broadside of censure anent modern shipbuilding.

"Gun stations, and stand by!"

Everyone had heard of that spot, or had been there. Not so far from the Cape; it was and still is an excellent haven for ships requiring repairs, water or re-victualing. Wild cattle and goats range the granite hills above the bay, and there is good water. From the earliest times, this was the halting-place of the English bound for India, as it had been of the Dutchmen before them.

Captain Webb of the *Sussex,* outward bound on the long voyage for the East India establishments in the year 1665, was more than glad to drop his hook in the bay. Half his men were down with scurvy, and his water had gone bad. A stout, hardy man was John Webb, and thankful to find no other ship in the bay, and no Dutchmen here either.

He had crept to rest with the sunset, and dawn came up misty, with promise of squall and fog. Wind and fog together were no strange thing in these parts on the tip of Africa, and when Webb came on deck, he was thankful to be berthed snugly.

"Cattle, aye!" After scrutinizing the shore, he handed his glass to Hopkins, the mate. "Look at the fresh meat for the having! We'll have to trade with the blacks, o' course. There's a cairn up on the shore; that'll be letters from some other ships; if by the grace o' God they've left some fruit and greens, we'll round the Cape happy."

"If we don't meet head winds," growled the mate, "or anything worse—Lor' love us all, sir! Look at her! *Look at her!*"

Webb snatched the glass from him and focused it. Sure enough, the dim object enveloped by the opaque vapors was the outline of a ship. Something queer about the vessel, something ghastly strange; but Webb did not wait to see further. He sent a sharp bark along the deck.

"Gunner! Cast loose and provide. All hands! Gun-stations, and stand by!"

The mate, squinting through the swirls of fog, shook his head.

"Look again, sir. Better belay; she's harmless as a

"Did you ever hear," Billings asked, "of 'The Vision of Captain Webb?' An old book published about 1680?… No? Well, you've missed something. It was taken to be a lie at the time, but it was true as Gospel. Cap'n Webb saw Vanderdecken, in a way. His yarn explains how others have seen him. It explains Vanderdecken entirely."

"Stuff and nonsense," sniffed old Frazier. "You can't explain away a myth."

"I'm talking about Vanderdecken, not a myth."

"Do you have the gall to claim that yarn is actually true?"

Billings gestured with his pipe.

"True, in a way, yes, like any other product of the human brain, from logarithms to deep-sea soundings. You'd have a devil of a time proving they exist; but there they are, just the same. Would you care to have me give you Cap'n Webb's yarn? I know it pretty well by heart…. I suppose you've heard of Saldanha Bay?"

"Your destiny lies with me!"

toothless hag. Has a look of the derelict to me—look there, how she yaws wi' the wind!"

Captain Webb took another look. He was not the man to strike fire at the sight of a strange ship; but he had a heavy lading and was responsible for it. A thrill shot through him as he examined that ghostly ship. Her sails were untrimmed, untended. She had a queer uncanny look about her. But her ports were triced up, and he could take no chances.

"Out tampions!" rang his order, as the men thudded along the deck. "Shot the guns, light your matches."

A growl came from Hopkins. The two of them stood staring. Instead of making in for the anchorage, the stranger was standing dead toward a reef, plainly visible under her bluff larboard bow.

"The fool! Is he daft?" exclaimed Webb, startled. "Look at that rig—look at the lines of her!"

"Out o' control and adrift," commented Hopkins.

The sea was like oiled lead; the fog was lightly drifting, the sky unbroken gray. Any seaman could sense wind and squalls coming down. Indeed, clouds of uneasy seafowl were wheeling about as though in warning; and Webb noted the sinister nimbus bank whose sudden appearance at the Cape always presaged a storm of great violence.

The strange ship showed no colors or signals, indicated no life aboard. There would be sun, as the east indicated, and there would be wind, as all else indicated; but now there was nothing except a light air and coastal currents. Webb took the glass again, trying to pierce the vapors that furred the stranger. His eyes narrowed abruptly as he stared.

"By the Lord Harry, a Dutchman!" he muttered. "An old, old ship—look at that crazy rig! Look at that poop! One o' them old caravels."

As a powder-monkey under Blake in '53, when the doughty Tromp had swept the English from the seas, John Webb had learned to hate Dutchmen. And now the vicious trade war in these seas and farther east had increased and embittered the feeling. The Flemings, as English seamen termed these cross-Channel neighbors, had pride of their own, gave blow for blow, and had something of a monopoly on the spice trade.

"She'll be stranded in less'n half a glass," said Hopkins, dourly gloating. The seaman in him, however, fetched a frown. "Blast it! Why don't she luff? Current's taking her, more'n the air."

"Bo'sun!" Webb's voice barked again. "Rig out the longboat!" He turned to the mate. "I'll get a brace o' pistols and lay aboard her. She's been long off soundings, by her look. Keep matches alight, and a sharp eye on her, Hopkins."

He went below, presently coming on deck again with pistols in a sling. The mist was by this time thinning overhead, but the eerie vapor persistently clung to the other ship. A strange chill seemed to accompany her into the harbor. Hopkins, eying her through the glass, growled oaths beneath his breath. Uneasiness lay upon him and upon all the men, watching that queer old ship.

Webb clambered down into the longboat. "Way together!" he commanded. The crew dipped oars and lay back. Webb, at the tiller, stared fixedly at the growing shape ahead. It was brighter now, and the light airs had freshened.

"Oars!" he snapped suddenly. The men stopped pulling and glanced over their shoulders, startled by what they read in Webb's face.

For without warning, without a soul appearing aboard her to haul on tack or sheet, the strange ship luffed. She went into stays, then sluggishly came about on the larboard tack, and slowly forged away from the threatening reef. Either she had worked herself around by sheer luck, or else men were concealed behind her bulwarks in ambush.

The first lances of the sun began to pierce the haze enveloping the ship. A mutter broke from Webb's lips: "A Hollander of a hundred years ago, or I'm a Fleming myself!" She was a queer, stubby craft of caravel build, with a triple slanting poop, short 'midships, and a long upcurving beak. The seamen began to mutter.

A derelict? Apparently; and Webb's eyes grew bright at the thought. Here along the tip of Africa ships had disappeared by the dozen, Portuguese and Dutch and English, driven ashore or foundering—ships laden with all the wealth of Ind. Many a ship had been picked up adrift, with no human soul aboard, her decks abandoned to seafowl.

"Give way!" barked Webb, and the men obeyed.

The longer he watched the Dutchman, the more singular appeared her maneuvers. She seemed unable to decide whether to come into the bight or run to sea again. A look astern showed him that Hopkins was heaving short and making sail. A signal burst from the monkey-gaff of the *Sussex;* the mate was following with the ship. Webb smiled grimly.

The freshening air was now filling the tattered canvas of the old hulk, and she was heading for the open sea; but the longboat was overhauling her. On this closer approach Webb, studying her, had a glimpse of her open ports; some triced up, some sagging crazily. He could swear that he saw faces there through the wisps of fog. A thrill of superstitious fear ran icy fingers down his spine, and the hair on his neck uplifted.

For an instant he thought of turning about and regaining the ship, but he could envision the sardonic grin of Hopkins, and set his hard jaw stubbornly.

Within hailing distance now, Webb let out a roar. He had no response whatever. The uncanny silence of the derelict was heartening, for it tokened that she was indeed a derelict. Her appearance fascinated Webb.

Now he could see the reason for her peculiar fuzzy look from a distance. It was due to nothing save long neglect. The spars, cordage, a great part of her bulwarks, were rotted and green from a total lack of scraping or tar-brush. The grotesque tops, extra large in all ships of her period, were sagging gloomily, and the rope nets that railed them were in ribbons.

Battered and moldy, the queer castellated forecastle seemed caving in from sheer decay, and was white with the rime of countless boarding combers. Toward the high stern with its three superimposed quarter galleries, everything was covered with sea-moss; the broken carved work was a roost for row upon row of solemn white noddies. And what was worse,—what was fearful to see in its ghastly incredibility,—plants and creepers were actually growing out of her, here and there.

In the water alongside, as Webb steered to make her low waist, appeared monster trailing weed; and her scarred, moss-grown planks showed monster barnacles. Although he eyed the portholes sharply, no more faces appeared there. Some of her cannon were in place, but lashed fast and closed with tampions. Others were clear gone. He hailed again, and received no answer.

"She's a drifting hulk, lads," he said to hearten the straining-eyed oarsmen. "And ours for the taking."

The men made no response. They were frightened.

Webb looked up, as the boat drew under her counter, and quick chill gripped him. There, peering over her rail, was a face. A white-bearded, clay-hued face, the eyes looking glassily down at him. It vanished so abruptly that he wondered if he had imagined it, and quickly let out another hail. No answer.

Over her side lay a crazy gangway, lashed fast; a gangway of rotting old boards and cross-pieces made of sticks with the bark on. The bowman hooked fast. Webb beckoned to the stroke.

"Take the tiller." His gruff tones sounded flat and forced. He did not half like this business himself. "If I'm not back in five minutes and you hear nothing from me, pull for the ship and tell Master Hopkins to lay her aboard."

He scrambled up the shaky gangway, which fell to pieces under his weight, flung himself across the bulwarks, and was on the deck of the Dutchman.

He stood blinking, all astare. A deck with gaping holes, a deck that sprouted green things; woodwork molded and mossy, cannon actually green with verdigris, everything in sight rotten and decayed.

"Ahoy below!" he called. "Anyone aboard here?"

"Who be you?" came a quavering voice. "Be you pirates?"

"Pirates? Lord love you! Cap'n Webb of the *Sussex.*"

A murmur of voices. Then a queer old figure appeared, clad in rags and tatters, a figure white-bearded, skinny, peering at him.

"We be all Dutch but me, master," said the apparition. "What's left o' two hundred souls cast ashore fifteen year ago. We found this old hulk on a reef and put her in shape—"

"He's lying to you!" burst out a roaring, bellowing voice. A huge gaunt man came from aft, a man who was a veritable giant, with shaggy white hair and a massive white beard. His voice lifted again, in mingled Dutch and English. "I'm master here, Vanderdecken by name. Here, everybody! Seize this accursed Englishman!"

Webb first thought that he was dealing with a madman; but he changed his mind about that. Out on deck, from aft and forward, poured some forty scarecrow shapes—withered, sea-twisted old men, most of them, armed with everything from belaying pins to rusted pikes.

"Overboard with this Englishman!" roared the giant Vanderdecken. "He's an enemy; we're at war with his country—"

"You fool, we haven't been at war with Holland for a generation!" broke out Webb. "Listen to me, you pack of old nitwits!" He shouted in Dutch, which he spoke fluently. "I came aboard to do you a service, not to harm you. There's my ship yonder; and if ye do me any hurt, she'll lay you aboard!"

He might as well have shouted at the wind. The pack of old scarecrows, mewing and cawing like a flock of enraged gulls about a scavenger shark, closed in with a rush. Webb backed away, lashing out with heavy fists as they bore down upon him, but their attack was sudden and sweeping. A skinny claw whipped in under his gullet, and as he staggered, something crashed on his head from behind. He caught at the moldy rail, then sagged to the deck as they closed over him. The last thing he heard was that wild frenzied voice of Vanderdecken:

"Overboard with him! *Overboard!*"

When Webb returned to consciousness, he was sitting in a huge straight-backed chair at the head of an enormous carven table; it was bolted to the deck in the center of a triangular cabin. Some dingy oil portraits and tatters of tapestry decked the paneled walls. Overhead guttered a storm-lantern, whose spirals of acrid smoke mingled with the overburdened air of the closed cabin.

Webb looked down at himself, flexed his bruised knuckles, looked up. Opposite, at the other end of the table, grimly eying him, and puffing at a pipe, was the giant Vanderdecken. Above his patriarchal beard were parchmenty features. The broad, bony forehead was indented by skeleton sockets from which gleamed the man's blue eyes. Wild eyes, yes, but dreadfully sane.

"Vanderdecken's just a legend—"

"So, you are awake! And now your destiny lies with Vanderdecken," said this gaunt specter.

Vanderdecken! The name smote into Webb with sudden significance. A sudden chill of superstitious fear assailed him. He remembered seamen's wild yarns about this Flying Dutchman, as they called him—the Vanderdecken who, for his tremendous profanity, was supposedly condemned to spend eternity beating about the Cape. Many a seaman swore to having seen his ghostly ship scudding in storm. Until this moment, Webb had not recalled the fantastic stories, current in shipping circles during the past sixty years.

"Destiny?" he exclaimed frowningly. "What fool's talk is this?"

Vanderdecken grinned at him, puffing at his pipe. Webb went on hotly:

"You ordered your mummy crew to heave me overboard. What am I doing here in your cabin? This is a fine return, for coming aboard to offer assistance!"

"Assistance!" Astonishingly, the bearded giant became solemn, sober, gravely intent. "Aye. You've said it yourself. Assistance! So the Lord has relented at last, after the weary years I've waited. Today you pilot me around the Cape, master Englishman. And then the curse is lifted."

"Vanderdecken—bah!" exploded Webb. "That fellow's just a legend, he and his blasted curse—"

"And Vanderdecken I am!" The old man lifted a skinny hand and pointed. "Captain Vanderdecken, bound for the Ind and the Moluccas, bound to get there despite hell or heaven! Now that you've offered your assistance, the curse is lifted."

"Be damned to you!" flamed out Webb angrily. "I've offered no such assistance. You're mad as a March hare!"

His superstition was crushed now. Here was no specter after all, but an old demented shipmaster who imagined things. Blown south of his reckoning, perhaps shipwrecked along the coast and picking up an old hulk, just as that doddering Englishman had told him; and this old giant with the ghastly claw simply was gone daft. Nothing else for it—unless he were indeed Vanderdecken.

Webb shivered a little at this thought. He caught a thin, high moaning sound, and started up in alarm. Wind, by heavens!

"Mad, am I?" roared Vanderdecken, and ripped out a blast of oaths that startled the listener. "Hark'ee—I'll beat around. In spite of the devil, high water, all the head-winds in creation, I'll beat around! And you'll pilot me, you Englishman! Mad, eh? I'll show you how sane I am."

He leaned forward, and again shook that pallid claw at Webb.

*"Show me what's new in seamanship, English*man! In these past years, there's been many an improvement in ships and sailing, in knowledge of currents and winds and of the coast itself, and the Cape. Many's the ship I've followed, trying to watch the cut and handling of her canvas. Many's the ship I've spoken, trying to get a pilot. Thirty years ago one came aboard, but dropped dead as he stepped over the rail. Always failure, failure! But now you've offered assistance, and I'll hold you to it. You'll give me your skill and knowledge. You'll pilot me, master, you'll pilot me!"

"Be damned if I do!" shot out the furious Webb. "Either I'm out of my head, or you are. But my own ship lies waiting, and devil fly away with me if—"

His hot-tumbling words were cut short. The smoky cabin reeled; the lantern swayed wildly on creaking gimbals; and Vanderdecken's pipe went crashing to the deck. So did Vanderdecken, with Webb almost on top of him. The ancient tub heeled nearly on her beam ends, under a hissing onrush of wind and water.

Slowly, while the storm-racked ancient timbers groaned and creaked, the ship righted herself. Webb was frightened now, actually in panic. He no longer doubted that this white-haired giant was really Vanderdecken.

"The storm! The unending storm!" boomed out the gaunt Dutchman, as he staggered up. "On deck, Englishman! Show me your skill now, for the curse is lifted!"

He caught Webb by the arms and propelled him. The master of the *Sussex* struggled, but was like a child in the grip of those huge bony hands. Cold as ice they seemed, even through his stout woolens, cold, as the fear in his heart.

Presently Webb found himself shoved out on the lower of the stairlike poops, while the ship listed over, buffeted by a gale the like of which he had never before encountered, even off the Cape. The morning had darkened, the sky blackened; the air was almost like night. To his appalled gaze, his own ship had vanished, and so had the bay and the shore and the hills—everything.

From the deck before him came a moaning and screaming that froze his heart. The old scarecrow seamen were howling in thin voices:

"The curse is upon us! The wrath of God again—"

"All hands!" roared Vanderdecken. "Here, Englishman—take charge!"

Webb did so, his voice ringing down the decks, and the blaring boom of the Dutchman seconding his orders. Vanderdecken stood erect, fearless, beard flying like wild mares'-tails. From the ominous black clouds ripped out a blue-white streak of lightning. Webb had a frightful vision of those gnarled, dead-faced old men scuttling about like crippled crabs amongst a tangle of running gear, hauling frantically on tacks, sheets and brails, struggling to trim ragged sails to the whooping gale, while spume burst high in a cloud above the ship of the dead.

"Alow there on deck!" Webb's voice cried. "Take in all the light sails—jump!" The gibbering bearded shapes sprang to work with amazing agility.

Vanderdecken volleyed a sudden storm of oaths. To Webb's astounded wonder, the wind perversely veered about, and with a wild shriek swung to dead ahead. Another thin, terrible lament rose from the old men. In a lingering lightning-flare, Webb caught a glint of rolling, accusing eyes cast on Vanderdecken. A sail blew from its bolt-ropes with a tremendous report. Vanderdecken, staggering to the poop rail, flung skinny arms aloft, fists shaking, and from his bearded lips volleyed a torrent of blasphemy.

Lightning ripped and cracked. Webb was certain the bolt had hit the crumbling forecastle; he could smell the sulphur, could feel the old ship reel and shudder to the crash. It was like a reply to Vanderdecken's frightful oaths. Again the wind lifted and veered. The ship buried her beak under tons of black water. Sails slatted; blocks screamed as in mortal agony; and rigging thrummed like the strings of a giant harp.

Cursing the crazy Dutchman, his own luck, and the scene around, John Webb hurled himself at the wraithlike old men. Whether corpses or specters, he got them to work with his furious energy. Men swung on the tiller; others fell to on the lines. The slow old tub paid off, filled, and forged ahead. The wind died out. Almost instantly, it came sweeping and howling down—from dead ahead.

In vain Webb tried to tell himself that this was no more than the furious winds of the vicinity always did; he could not repress the superstitious panic that seized on him. Then came reality, with a bellow from Vanderdecken, another lightning-flash that cracked open the whole heavens, and sight of his own ship barely a cable's-length away. She was ploughing along under treble-reefed main topsail and fore t'gallant. She was real; she was tangible; and a load dropped from his soul. She must have left the shelter of the bay, and have been caught in this wild erratic blow.

"There sails a ship!" blared out Vanderdecken. "There sails a ship around the Cape! Follow her, Englishman. Watch her, follow her!"

Webb sent the old bearded ghosts to the maze of ropes leading aloft. The gale was increasing in violence. Rain began to lash down in sheets, and there was no standing against the wind—though Vanderdecken stood against it. Webb took shelter

under the weather bulwarks, and after a moment fisted on to a backstay. He knew what was needed to bring order out of this chaos. Sight of his own ship had stabilized him, given him new heart.

"Alow there on deck!" Webb's voice carried. "Take in all light sails—jump! Brail in the lateen—lower tops'l yards! Brace in lower yards!"

The gibbering bearded shapes stared at him, then moved obediently, sprang to work with amazing agility. The tattered, rotten canvas, what remained of it, was got in and the yards were braced.

"Helm, there!" Webb yelled to the men at the helm, who were heaving in and checking the relieving tackles, as the old ship yawed and plunged. "Put it up—helm up! We'll bring the wind around and take it over our quarter—"

Sluggishly, the caravel went around. The wind came roaring over the starboard quarter, and Vanderdecken, with a ghastly grin on his face, clapped Webb on the shoulder.

"Well done, Cap'n! We'll beat around in spite of hell and the devil— Ho!"

The words were cut off by a thunderpeal. Again the wild lamenting shriek went up from the seamen, as the wind swooped and hauled again, and roared down from dead ahead. Again the sails were aback, tautened to the bursting point. Vanderdecken, shaking his fist at the sky, stood at the rail, raving curses.

A terrific lightning-bolt ripped down. The heavens were split in a blaze of light—light that endured steadily, in a blinding glare. Webb felt the ship shake and shiver, felt her reel and go heeling as an enormous comber swept her in a thundering deluge of spray—felt himself caught up and carried over, washed clear of her deck, felt the strangling gag of the salt water as he went down and down.

Webb opened his eyes. The glare, indeed; the glare of sunlight now. He was retching the salt water out of his system, as two of the seamen held him in the longboat. He sat up, all astare, like a man gone daft. He was in the longboat, yes. The sun had come out, scattering the fog. There was no storm whatever.

His dilated eyes fastened on the Dutch derelict. She was running away down the wind, away into the fog that ran with her. The *Sussex* was back there in the bay, the signal still flying from her monkey-gaff. Webb knuckled the salt water out of his eyes and blinked at the seamen around.

"What is it, lads—what happened?" he blurted, trying to wrench himself back to where he actually and undeniably was. "The storm—"

"You got a crack over the head, master," said one of the men. "A big fellow came to the rail and threw you over. A man with a long white beard, he was. We hauled you into the boat—that's all."

Webb, warming to the sunlight, tried to get the kinks out of his tangled brain. That's all—aye! And that was all. There was no storm, never had been any. When he struck the water, it had brought him to life. The men had hauled him in. Gradually the wonder of it, the comprehension of it, grew upon him.

All that had happened aboard that spectral Dutchman, everything he had witnessed and heard and done, had occurred in his own brain, And all of it, within the spanking moment of time when he was picked up and dropped over the side.

This was the sober truth; yet to believe this truth, was a rank impossibility.

Such was the yarn that Billings of the Cunard outfit told us, as we sat listening to him in the Seamen's Institute. He sucked at his pipe and concluded it, solemnly:

"Poor Webb never did get the right of it through his head. He published his story and elaborated on it a bit, with details I've passed over. He was called a fool and a liar for his pains, and lost his master's berth, and went out with some other ship—Lancaster's squadron, I think—that was never heard of again."

Old Cap'n Frazier pawed his long white whiskers, and snorted thoughtfully.

"There's something to it," he pronounced. "Aye, there's a lot to it! Like the life we can live over in a flash of drowning, or the hours and days that can pass in thirty seconds of a dream!"

"Well, just what was that Dutch ship, then?" asked somebody curiously. "There was a fairly logical explanation of her, until the supposed Vanderdecken appeared!"

Billings shook his head, and glanced around with that hard, practical eye of his.

"Supposed Vanderdecken?" he repeated. "No, mates; that was the real Vanderdecken, and his ship was the real Flying Dutchman—my word on it! It's hard to grasp, I grant you. It'd take one of these psycho-analyst chaps to get the rights of it, but there it is. And it explains the whole Vanderdecken story from start to finish."

"Huh!" Cap'n Frazier snorted in his whiskers. "Ye mean to say it's all real?"

"Suit yourself, sir," said Billings, with a noisy suck at his pipe. "As for me, I have my own opinion. Good night to you!"

And he walked out, leaving us staring after him in vain speculation.

ROGUE'S YARN

One astonishing thing in this life is that you never know what's in the past of a man, even if he be your best friend, until somehow it leaps out to give you a shock of surprise.

One evening in a famous Los Angeles cafe I was talking with John Oakledge, who runs the place, and watching the floor-show. He was a hard-jawed West of England man, with a cold eye for any question of business, like all these hotel autocrats. Somehow there was mention of sailing-ship days, and Oakledge let slip a word or two.

"And what would you be knowing about square-riggers?" I asked, smiling.

"I was around the Horn aboard one at fifteen," said he. "And a cadet aboard the old training-ship *Mersey.* And I saw the last keelhauling that ever took place on her, when one of the lads was put down one side of the ship and hauled under and pulled up dead from the barnacles that caught and held him there."

Before I had recovered from this shock, he fished in the pocket of his Tuxedo and held out something to me. It was a bit of sisal hemp with a bright scarlet thread centered in the twist.

"No," I answered his query. "How would I know what it is?"

"There's a story in it," he said thoughtfully, and his eyes lifted to the girl who was doing a torch song with the band. "The story of the greatest private navy the world ever saw; and Dan Curlew, who got it a-going; and what reward he had for his genius. But no magazine would ever print it."

"Why not?"

"Because it's a tale of hard bitter life and reality, not of young love and kisses." Oakledge nodded at the orchestra. The red lights were flashing, a sign that the broadcast radio hook-up was about to begin. "Those lads play hot music—because it's what the people like. Classical stuff—bah! There's real life in the hot music."

"Your argument is involved," I said, "and isn't consistent. Any other reason why your story wouldn't get printed?"

"Yes. Because it goes back to old days and times, back to Bombay of the 1680 period, when the city was being built, and the seven little islands that formed it made up the worst plague-ridden spot in the world."

"And the East India Company," I said, "was the most romantic private venture the world has known."

"There's no romance in Dan Curlew's story," he rejoined. "Except, maybe, that it answers a question. There's a lot of questions about ships that have no answer. Who rigged the first wheel? Nobody knows. Who built the first teak ship? You seek in vain, unless you ask me.

"I'm asking you," I said. Oakledge looked up at the dials in the broadcast-room. He spoke softly, reflectively.

The East India Company was stingy in those days, too niggardly to employ any engineers; so Bombay was built by rule of thumb. The island channels were silting up, turning the place into a pestilential hell-hole. Men sickened one day, and were buried the next. Promotion was rapid but few men waited for it. John Company's rule was absolute, cruel and sordid. So everybody, from officials to cabin-boys, went out for what we'd call graft today. They looted everybody, from natives to the Company itself. This was natural; it was get out quick, or die if you stayed.... The Company itself looted where it could. The coast was a pirates' paradise. Dutch and Portuguese and English looted one another. Moral sense was at its low ebb. Life had no value, especially at Bombay. The government of the Company was established at Surat in those days.

There's the setting for Dan Curlew, clerk. You must see him as no brawling braggart, but a slim, quiet man, lean of face and deep of eye, holding a circumspect course through the troubled waters. Tyranny, disease and greed passed him by; perhaps he seemed of no importance. He watched the Company's troops mutiny, heard men talk in barracks and bazaars, saw fellow-humans hanged for little and clapped into a death-cell for less—and held his peace.

One day he was invited to Government House for dinner, perchance by some mistake. He went, dressed in his sober best. On his left hand sat Captain Keigwin, who had done notable things at sea, a hard but impulsive man; on his right hand was Edmund Yates, a Member in Council who had a hand in many things, a soft-spoken, shrewd-lidded man of tremendous influence and some wealth.

Dan Curlew made no mistakes. When the cloth was removed and the wine passed, he filled only one of his two glasses, for the King's health. He listened much, applauded the beefy, truculent Governor, ventured no stories. But he heard Keigwin mutter at some of the things said, and caught the low words:

"Egad, the right man could end all this tyranny and seize India!"

"It could be done," said Curlew calmly. Keigwin's head jerked around.

"Sir? Are you addressing me?"

"No sir—myself. It could be done, by taking the right measures."

The eyes of the two men held for an instant, questioning, answering. On the other side of him, Curlew heard Edmund Yates addressing him, and turned.

"I think you said, Mr. Curlew, that it could be done? I was speaking of vastly increasing the Company's fleet, and stopping the leaks of treasure."

Dan Curlew smiled slightly as the humor of it struck him—his one remark so differently interpreted on either side.

"Oh, very readily, Mr. Yates," he replied. "The type of ships employed are at fault. Some day I'll draw up a memorial pointing out the needed improvements. And as for the leaks, that's fairly simple."

"I haven't found it so," Yates observed sharply.

The most quiet and reserved of men may talk too much, when the chance and listener appear. This is a failing of human nature; and for all his caution, despite all his wary aloofness, Dan Curlew was human enough.

"Take one thing alone—cordage," said he. "The losses in this department are enormous. Why? Because the Company's cordage is pilfered right and left."

He did not say what was in his mind; that not only was it pilfered, but that officials sold it wholesale to native shipowners and pocketed the money.

"And how might that be stopped, sir?" inquired Yates.

"We have a shipyard here; we have a rope-walk at Madras. Most of our rope is made here; we send the hemp home to the Blackwall yards to make the rest. What simpler than to weave a colored yarn in all Company cordage—and if it's found elsewhere, we have proof positive whence it came!"

"Oh!" said Yates, and extended his snuff-box. "You interest me, sir; damme, but you interest me! If you have the same excellent notions in regard to other matters—for example, ships—I'd like to hear them."

Dan Curlew smiled.

"Notions, Mr. Yates? I've more than that. Plans and figures—but this is no place for such technical discourse."

"You say well. Dine with me tomorrow evening, sir, at my house, if you'll do me the honor. I'd be vastly gratified to learn your mind on such matters."

When the Governor, after two hours of wine and talk, lifted his glass and gave the toast, "A good afternoon!" as a signal to break up, Dan Curlew went away walking on air, his thoughts in the clouds. A mere clerk, to dine with a Member in Council? A humble nobody, to be entertained by one of these moguls who ruled the fringe of India with more than despotic power?

There was fortune made, if rightly handled. Promotion, favor, and inside of five years enough wealth to go home for life. When a ship captain could count, what with legal and illegal fees and graft, on from ten thousand to thirty thousand pounds' profit in a round voyage, even a minor official could ask no more than five years in which to thrive on India takings!

But that same evening, in the factor's house where he lodged, Dan Curlew had a visitor, who came in palanquin and with servants, but sat alone with him in the big cool room overlooking the factor's garden.

"I'm no man to mince words, Master Curlew," said the bluff and hard-eyed Captain Richard Keigwin. "What I saw in your eyes today, what I heard on your lips, brought me here tonight."

Curlew's brows lifted.

"There must be some mistake, sir," he said quietly.

"Don't get off soundings, now; and don't let go your kites and jump at things," Keigwin replied grimly. "It could be done, says you. Come, let's out with it! This place, like the other factories of the Company, is a hell-hole of injustice, misrule and oppression."

"I'm a clerk of the Company, sir."

"Thank God I'm not! I'm an officer in His Majesty's navy—or was, and may be again. Come, sir! No evasion. What I've seen in this city makes my blood boil. You know India better than I do. I read the truth in your face today."

Dan Curlew yielded.

"And I heard the truth on your lips," he said. "The right man? Why, yes. But who's the right man?"

"I am," Keigwin said abruptly, a hidden flame in his eyes. "And others are with me in a pinch. The Company has ships and troops and power—all of it rotted through. You've dreamed a dream or two, else I miss my guess."

"I think your brains are touched by the sun; but then, so are mine." And Dan Curlew smiled whimsically. "The right man, if he seized all India, would find things ripe. The Company's troops are mutinous to the core. Their servants, from governor down to clerks, are inefficient, covetous, selfish. Bombay might be seized at one stroke, if the fort were grasped. But then what?"

"That's what I'm asking." Keigwin relaxed, with a gesture. "Go on. Talk."

Curlew shrugged. "The first thing—could the right man seize Bombay for himself? No. But for the King, yes! If the Governor were clapped into irons and the right man voted into power, he'd get the votes of the Council—by force, if needful. Then, if he acted in the King's name, he'd have everyone behind him."

"But after that?" queried Keigwin. "Trade and commerce would fall off—"

"No. Company trade be hanged! Throw open the port to interlopers, as they're called—free traders. Abolish the monopoly of John Company! Keep the judges in power, but moderate all penalties. Reform the taxes that grind down the natives. Three things, and no more."

"By heavens!" exclaimed the other, a flush in his sun-bronzed cheeks. "You've hit the nail on the head, sir! I'll not withhold the truth. There's a movement afoot, and I've been asked to lead it."

"That's taking your life in your hands," said Curlew slowly.

"That's what my life's for," was the brusque response. "And now I put it to you straight: Will ye join us? First Bombay, then Surat and the governing

Arrest for theft? Why, it was absurd! He burst into a passionate resistance.

headquarters of the Company, then Madras and the rest. There's a place for you, a big place."

Caution gripped Dan Curlew: caution, and honesty.

"I can dream such things, for there's no lock and bar on a man's thoughts," he said. "But I'm a Company servant, sir. And while the Company pays me, I'll not share in any plot against it. Very simple."

Captain Keigwin grimaced.

"Zounds, sir! I'm offering you fortune and position!"

"Indeed? The gallows offers the same things, in another meaning." Curlew shook his head. "No; a good servant doesn't betray his master, right or wrong."

"Men higher placed than you think otherwise about it."

"I'm answerable only for my own actions, sir. We've talked in confidence. I'd not betray honor in one respect or in another, so have no fear that I'll tell any tales of what has been said here. But I'm a Company servant."

And with this response, Keigwin had to be content, if not satisfied....

Dan Curlew—like many another honest man—could keep his mouth shut, but not at the proper moment most to further his own interests. After the mutinies, the general dissatisfaction with Company rule, the executions, he was not astonished that rebellion was rife, even in high places.

"Men higher placed than you—" Aye, Keigwin had backing in his amazing audacity, no doubt of it; and strong backing. As Dan Curlew went about his work next day, the words recurred to him many a time. He could almost put his finger on some of those men. He himself was a fool; his blood tingled to think what a chance he had passed up, but there was no help for it. Better an honest fool than a rascally wise man, he told himself with a shrug.

And tonight he was dining with Edmund Yates. Once he had interested Yates in his proposed memorial to the Company, his fortune would be made, and he could look himself in the eye with a clear conscience to boot. So reflecting, Curlew went about his work with an energy and vim that made his lackluster fellows regard him in slack-jawed wonder. He even neglected the customary siesta in the heat of the day, to wander down by the waterfront and look at the Company ships in harbor, sleek black ships with a white ribbon along their sides, and dream of vastly different ships.

These were good bottoms, stout bottoms of English oak; but he knew a better wood and a better ship for the purpose.

Evening at last. Not for his slender purse the palanquin and servants and other luxurious adjuncts of the officials of John Company; he walked, and dignity mattered no whit. Like a fairy palace was the glittering establishment of Edmund Yates; just the two of them at dinner, and that dinner of the finest.

Then the cloth was removed, the glasses and decanters set forth, and they were alone. Yates, his shrewd eyes and soft tones all most courteous, had played the perfect host. Curlew felt at ease by this time, felt assured.

"Y' know, Curlew, your words of yesterday were devilish interesting," Yates drawled lazily. There was no laziness in his glinting eyes, however. "So our Company ships are at fault, eh? Our India-men aren't better than the Dutchmen?"

"They may be that, but still at fault." And Curlew smiled a little. "They're good cargo-ships or good fighting-ships; they should be both, and passenger-ships to boot. Think of the Company servants crowded into each ship that comes, penned in like

"Zounds, sir! I'm offering you fortune and position!"

sheep! Think of the invaluable cargo space that must be used for provisions and guns and stores of every kind! Not to mention the safety of the return voyage."

Yates drew down his brows.

"Egad, man, I don't get your drift! They're good ships. Our Blackwall designers have built 'em for speed—"

"We don't want speed; we want comfort and safety," Curlew broke in. "Here; let me show you this sketch I brought along." And he spread a sheet of paper on the table. "Here's our present Indiaman, adapted to the purpose. Here beside it is a different design, built for the purpose. Built to batter storms around the Cape, built to carry cargo without leakage or spoiling, and also built to fight. A massive, stately ship that can carry the Company's flag proudly. Built with passenger quarters on the orlop deck, room and to spare."

The bilious features of Yates lit up. "Ha! Now I begin to get your notion, Curlew; and you're right. You spoke of figures. I see none."

"All in my head." Curlew began to reel them off, making swift approximate comparisons between the two types of ship. Yates listened, staring thoughtfully at the paper, and finally nodded.

"Damme, sir, you have something well worth while here!" he said at length. "But you mentioned a better wood than oak? There's none in England."

"There is here. Teak wood," Curley said quickly. "A thousand times better. And out here it's dirt cheap. The oil in it makes it last forever against worms and the sea. We'd have to bring out shipwrights and lay down a shipyard here; later we could ship the wood back home to Blackwall. Look at the native craft along the coast—you know how stout they are. A teak ship could stand any battering sea. Instead of losing one ship in every three, we'd not lose one in ten. And besides all this, the design allows for gun space. There's a ship both for fighting and for cargo."

Yates drew a deep breath, his jaundiced eye kindling.

"A noble thought, 'pon my word, Curlew! Magnificent, all of it. But look you. By the time your memorial reached England and got consideration, think of the time that would pass—months, years! It should go first to Surat, be passed on by the Company's officials out here; and with their approval, go to the governors of the Company at home. It should include all figures, all facts, even to the comparative cost of teak and oak."

"I have everything in my head," said Curlew. "If you would do me the honor of furthering such a memorial—"

"Why, damme, I'll back it with every bit of influence I have!" exclaimed Yates with enthusiasm. "I'll get it approved by the governors here and at Madras, before it goes to headquarters at Surat; and from there straight back to London town. Eh? Why, it'll cause a revolution in the Company's management and business! And for the man whose brain conceived it, there's fame and fortune."

"I hadn't thought of that primarily—"

"But ye must. Fortune, Dan Curlew! That's the greatest thing in life. Gold means power. Here's gold for the having—promotion, rewards, a title. Aye! It'll be Sir Daniel Curlew, I'll stake my oath upon it!" His flush died out. He bent glittering eyes on his guest. "Come! When can you supply all facts and figures?

Down to the last detail, remember. You must show the Company where such a scheme will increase their profits, mind. Cursed stingy devils, they are."

"That's the easiest thing of all," Curlew responded. "The facts are eloquent; the figures prove themselves. When? Ah, there's the rub! I've small time for it after working-hours—"

Yates gestured brusquely. "I'll have you relieved of all clerkly duties in the morning, assigned a room in the factory for working, and left alone. When can you produce the finished results?"

Curlew thought swiftly. "A fortnight."

"Then account it done. We'll have a fancy scrivener write up the memorial in a good fist. The *Guzerat* will be leaving for home in six weeks, when the monsoon breaks; by then, I'll have the approval of the officials out here, and send back the papers by her, direct to the governors of the Company. To work, lad! Five years from now, Sir Daniel Curlew will be getting his nine-gun salute when he comes sailing in, and here's to the wish!"

The glasses clinked. Presently Curlew rose and took his leave.

"Have you thought," he asked, "about any plan such as the one I suggested, to help stop thievery and looting?"

Yates gave him a queer sharp glance.

"No. That's a petty thing. Here's the big thing to put our brains upon! Let the other wait its time."

Again Curlew was walking on air as he started homeward. Thought of Keigwin and any plot dropped back and was lost before greater things. Only, there lingered with him the memory of that queer glance Yates had darted at him, when they parted. At times, it worried him. Something in those sharp, glinting eyes disquieted him; but he put away the faint worry. A man's not responsible for his looks, always.

In the days that followed, Curlew lived as in a dream. A work-room to himself, his plans and figures and estimates to be labored into definite shape—oh, it was a great thing!

A week passed, and another. He was ahead of his promise by two days, finally. Everything was here, even to rough sketches of the new type of ship, detailed drafts of her layout and rig. All his estimates were checked over and verified to the last farthing. He himself was amazed by these estimates, by the savings and profits they revealed; no sane Company official, he thought, but must see instantly what a tremendous thing this would be in a financial sense alone.

Captain Keigwin, he understood, had gone to Madras on some personal errand. He could guess dimly what it must be: more men and backing. He was doubly thankful now that he himself had held aloof from that plot. The unrest, the discontent, were increasing here in Bombay. Harsher and harsher measures were being employed by the judges to crush it down; no man, white or brown, had any rights. But gripped now by his own vision and work, Dan Curlew gave little heed to such matters.

He took the finished work to Edmund Yates, who went over every figure with him and gave minute care to the whole.

"Superb!" exclaimed Yates at last, in a glow of admiration. "Curlew, you've done a magnificent job of it. Why, these estimates will sweep those crusty old moguls in London off their feet! As soon as it's copied, I'll get the governor's approval and then be off with it to Surat myself. We must catch the *Guzerat* with the papers. I'll not bother about Madras. Government House at Surat is the important thing."

As Dan Curlew went back to his own lodgings in a glow, he passed an execution-squad of sepoys, taking to the gibbet a poor shrinking devil of a seaman who had been condemned to the noose for stealing a gill of rum. Another man might have read an ill omen in this meeting, but Dan Curlew's eyes were on the horizon, and his hopes and all ambition.

More days passed.

One morning Curlew heard that Edmund Yates had departed for Surat in a Company barge. He looked out at the harbor and the proud *Guzerat,* outfitting for the voyage home, and his heart leaped. She would carry all his future this trip; when she came back again, there would be news from his memorial. Long months away; well, the months would pass swiftly now!

A bit odd, he thought, that Yates had sent him no further word.

Suddenly, with a rush, destiny was upon him. A scrivener's clerk came for some papers that must be copied fair. Curlew turned them over to him, and the clerk gave them a sharp glance.

"Eh? Why, Master Curlew, these figures be in the same hand! Only last week we completed a task for Mr. Yates—"

"Oh!" Curlew smiled. "My memorial, eh? Yes; he was assisting me in preparing a memorial. So you did the work!"

"Aye, but your name was not in it." And the clerk gave him a curious glance. "Have a care of your tongue, I warn you! It may be you drew up figures and estimates for him; but steal no credit there, or you'll kiss the whippingpost."

A chill touched Dan Curlew's brain.

For an instant everything went black before him. Then he sat clutching the edge of his desk, his face drawn and white.

"Fortune! That's the great thing in life. Gold means power." The words of Yates sang at him in memory; the queer glint in the shrewd eyes came back to him. Stolen, stolen! His name not in it at all! Like a fool, he had turned over everything to that fine gentleman. He had turned over fame, fortune, credit, rewards, a title—everything. His vision was thieved; his dream was stolen.

And he, mere petty clerk that he was, could do nothing, dared do nothing. If he so much as breathed an accusation against such a man, he would get a flogging or worse. A shiver took him. Helpless, helpless! Loyalty to the Company—and this his reward!

For hours he sat stupefied, immobile. He still sat there when an officer walked in with a file of sepoys, read a document which he scarcely heard, and walked him out of the factory under arrest.

Desperately, then, he wakened. Arrest? Arrest for theft, for sale of the Company's stores? Why, it was absurd, ridiculous! He burst into a passionate resistance. A gun-butt hammered on his head, and he dropped to the flagging.

Dazed, hurt, bewildered. Curlew found himself before the judge and the packed court. Men he knew, men who knew him; and no mercy in them. He heard the lengthy addresses; necessity of stamping out theft and disloyalty, new regulations in force. Absurd, all of it! He broke out hotly, and was knocked back into his seat in the dock.

His brain ceased to function. There was the evidence; here were the witnesses: natives, caught with Company cordage aboard their craft. They confessed to everything. They identified Dan Curlew as the man who had sold it them. Damnation heaped upon damnation. The Company prosecutor was speaking.

"If it please the court, this cordage can be readily identified by a secret mark now being employed for the first time. At the suggestion of Mr. Edmund Yates, a scarlet thread is being woven into the cordage made for the Company. This is the first occasion when the value of such an idea becomes evident—"

Curlew burst into a fit of wild, hysterical laughter, so horrible to hear that the court broke into commotion. He saw everything now, everything! His ideas stolen, with which to close his mouth; his memorial stolen, with which to enrich his betters. False witnesses, false testimony—his laughter went into bitter oaths. He lost his head completely. He cursed Yates; he cursed the court, the injustice around him.

A blow stretched him out, quivering. He heard the sentence, and was dragged off to a cell and manacled. He sat broken, bruised, lost to all hope, crushed by the most bitter possible torment of thought before which his very brain reeled.... And there he fades from our sight.

Oakledge had finished his story. A burst of applause rocketed through the café and I looked up, startled. The applause was not for him, however. It was for the dancer who had just finished her number.

"Well," I exclaimed impatiently, "go on with the rest of it!"

"Yes?" Oakledge's eyes flickered to me with their touch of blasé and sardonic weariness. "You could put an end to the tale yourself, no doubt."

"Of course; it's a natural!" was my warm response. "Keigwin came back from Madras, seized Bombay, and saved Dan Curlew's life. Eh? That is, if the story of the plot is historical."

"Oh, it's historical," said Oakledge. "Keigwin did seize Bombay and held it for the Crown, but his plan to seize the other settlements failed. And when orders came from the King to turn Bombay back to the Company, he complied. He was given command of a frigate in the royal navy, and was later killed in action. All that his revolt did, was to bring some sadly needed reforms into the rule of the Company."

"But Dan Curlew?" I asked abruptly.

"I was back in England a couple of years ago, back in Devon." Oakledge fingered the twist of hemp with the scarlet thread in the middle. "I found this among some of the family heirlooms. Rogue's yarn, they called it. This was brought home from India by one of my ancestors who served the Company."

"What's that got to do with Curlew?" I said. "Evidently his memorial went through. The teak Indiamen became famous—"

"Aye," said Oakledge, a thin and bitter twist to his lips. "But Dan Curlew didn't. I told you this was real life, and not romance. The reason this little twist of rogue's yarn was brought back from India as a memento, was because it was cut from the rope that hanged Curlew."

CORSAIR OF CANADA

The noon express out of New York for Washington usually affords a fascinating group of travelers, lobbyists, diplomats, earnest revolutionaries and whatnot. I was in the observation-car, comfortably planted in one of the swivel-chairs by the table at the extreme rear.

People do not usually fall into casual conversation on this run; it is not long enough. So I was mildly surprised when the other man, across the table from me, looked over and addressed me apologetically.

"Pardon me, sir, but is your name O'Brien?"

"It isn't," I said gratefully.

He looked puzzled. He was a massive fellow, elderly but with a spry and fantastic look in his eye. At my scrutiny, he sighed.

"Stung again! I see you're wearing a gold seal ring with the crest of the O'Brien family. I'd wager the motto reads, in Gaelic: *'Lamh laidir an uachtar.'* "

I broke into a laugh. "Meaning, *'The Strong Hand Above.'* Correct. You're Irish?"

"Oh, no!" he said. "My name's Smith."

"Well, I don't like the Irish, myself," I confided. "My people were Irish, and I inherited this ring from them, that's all."

"My family's Irish too. You're wrong not to like them, my friend," he contended. "I study the old histories and such. It's all very thrilling."

We had an argument, friendly and good-humored, and the steward fetched drinks.

Smith tapped a book which he had in his lap, fixed me with his alert, glittering eye, and asked a question which seemed to mean a lot to him.

"What ship was it that for three hundred years revictualed half Europe and changed the eating habits of the world?"

"What ship?" I repeated. "Rather, what fish? The codfish would answer your query."

He positively beamed. "But to catch cod, you must have a ship, a thousand ships, fleets of'em from France and Portugal and everywhere!"

"Granted!" And I laughed. "Now I'll give you one: Suppose you tell me when the inhabitants of Canada were first called Canadians!"

That would settle him, I thought. The Canada Club in our city had for the past year been trying to resolve this problem with the help of all the learned minds north and south of the border. All we could find was that the word *Canadian* had come into existence about the year 1800.

He beamed at me again and tapped his book, an ancient volume bound in brown calf.

"That's easy; about the year 1650," he said promptly. He became even more intent upon me, and his eyes gleamed. Tumultuous words rushed out of him.

"In fact, your question ties up with mine! By that same year, a new type of ship had come into use, evolved by the seamen of Brittany—a ship they called a *terra-nueva,* or Newfoundlander. And it's curious that both your question and mine tie up with Irishmen. The chain is complete. Codfish—ships—Canadians—Irishmen! You see?"

"No, hanged if I can see!" was my response. "It looks rather insane to me."

He laughed, his brown face aglow. I began to think that my friend Smith, like his words, might be a bit balmy. Then he showed me my mistake.

"Under Cromwell, the Irish royalists were shipped

to the plantations abroad as slaves. Many of them were sent to Newfoundland. Wonderful things happened all up and down those coasts," he went on with enthusiasm, with a relish in his words. "Battle and murder and sudden death were everywhere; pirates ravaged; broken men set themselves up as wilderness kings. Why, a town in Maine is named after Baron de St. Castine, who married an Indian princess and became a savage lord!"

"Which," I said, "has nothing to do with ships and codfish."

"It has everything to do with them! Let me give you a story out of La Potherie!" And he fondled the book in his lap. "Never been translated, almost unknown, yet Parkman called it the only source for certain portions of Canadian history. Documents, memoirs, and treaties otherwise lost to the world are preserved in these pages!"

True enough; I had heard of this book he had; it was, indeed, one of the curiosities of literature.

"Like Dumas, it has suffered from translation," I observed. "Do you remember how, in 'The Three Musketeers,' the word *canot* is translated to mean *canoe?* A canoe on the English Channel!"

"Do you want to hear my story or not?" demanded Smith.

"Not particularly," I said frankly. "There's nothing interesting in codfish or Newfoundlanders or Irish slaves."

He blazed up. "Nothing interesting! Romance, courage, indomitable spirits, blood on every page! Here, take a look at the bleak, savage coast of Newfoundland—the deep bays dotted with struggling, isolated settlements, the inner island unknown and savage; the hostile redskins, the intense privations, the day-and-night battle to keep alive! And set down in all this, branded and lashed and made a slave of the rude settlers, a man who had been a gentleman, who had talked with kings—"

Gentleman? There was nothing to tell of it, in the appearance of the man thus forcibly presented to me. Shaggy with long hair and beard, clad in rags and skins knotted around his body, thin hawk-nose, and untamed eyes shining, Sir Phelim Burke was now only a slave. The slave Burke, a beast of burden for his masters.

Only the fierce eyes told of the unbroken spirit within him, as he peered forth from the rocky shore at the battered ship lying in the little harbor. She must have come in for shelter from the storm, before

Transfixed, the man went over into the icy water, and his cries ended abruptly.

day broke. Back at the settlement, around the crook of the bay, her presence was unknown and unguessed. Burke had discovered her just now, in his search for firewood.

His gaze devoured her with swift hope—here, perhaps, was escape! The hope died. She was a three-masted fishing craft, high of stern and bow, square sails on her fore and main, a lateen on her mizzen. Rigging riven and hull battered, she lay anchored while her crew made repairs; a small boat on her midships deck was being patched up for landing, and water-casks were being floated. The voices told Burke that she was French. French cod-fishers, then, they would be, coming ashore to water; he must give the news to the settlers, who might otherwise make discovery themselves and set muskets to work. He drew back from his covert, under the great trees. He tramped back to where the huddle of houses and the stockade stood beside the creek. Boats and nets and gear were being overhauled under the stockade; these settlers, too, were making ready for the spring runs of cod.

They were rugged West of England men, these who broke off work to stare at Burke and hear his news; men made savage by their environment here, by their endless struggle.

"Ye dog, we sent ye for wood, not news," said one, and struck Burke heavily across the face. "News o' Frenchmen, above all! Snarl at me, and I'll have ye laid across a stump and given three-score lashes. I'm sick of your damned insolence. Ho, mates! Break out the powder and muskets!"

Gaunt-eyed women made haste with weapons; the stockade was closed; two scouts went forth to spy upon the harbor beyond the turn; muskets were loaded. Danger from the sea was a new peril. Inland were only trackless forests and brute savages. These outflung settlements existed for the sealing and fishing alone, which promised wealth. If the Frenchmen brought trouble from the sea, it would be a bad thing.

No trouble, however. The scouts brought in word of friendliness. The smallboat, towing roped casks behind, came toiling up the harbor reach; two Frenchmen landed, laughing and babbling broken English, with gifts of tobacco and cognac. The first ship out from France for the season, said they, only to reach the Banks with bitter storm, and run on here for shelter.

Arms were laid aside. Brandy flowed; tobacco burned; tongues ranted away. But the slave Burke, waiting on his masters, fetching and hauling, the butt of every abuse and oath, guarded careful silence. More of the French came ashore toward evening. There was music and dancing; wine and cognac flowed again. Their repairs completed, the French were sailing on the daylight tide. Now, for the evening, they were devoted to joyous gayety.

Through it all moved the slave Burke, buffeted and kicked, yet resenting nothing. Resentment, he knew sadly, meant a flogging; he was not a man but a beast. The only one of them all who spared a kindly word, a kindly look for him, was the young Priscilla. She was eldest daughter of Bentham, the chief settler here, and promised in marriage to the youngest of these dour men. Much against her will, as Burke well knew.

Caribou meat was roasted; the precious stores of provender were broken into recklessly, and Burke was kept sweating at work with the women, some of whom danced not at all. What began in gayety passed into riotous drunken uproar. Burke, dragging in a log for the fire, was met in the doorway by the girl Priscilla, panting and disheveled.

"I'm afraid!" she broke out, white-faced. "Help me, Burke, help me! I can't stay here. Can we go out in a boat until they stop drinking?"

"No," said Burke. "They're roaring for you now. Give me a hand with this log, girl. Then wait and take things easy. We can slip away when the time comes."

"But they'll flog you tomorrow," she said, hesitating. "And—"

"There may be no tomorrow," Burke broke in grimly. "Lend a hand!"

She stooped to the weight. They bore in the log and cast it on the fire, where more meat was sizzling. The puncheon floor quivered to the stamp of sealskin boots and sea-boots. Breton bagpipes were skirling madly, and a maudlin chorus was being roared forth. Men and bedraggled women alike were excited, shouting and laughing, wrought to a high pitch.

A dozen fishermen—no, sixteen, as Burke counted them. Fourteen English settlers, and the women. These were rough, homely country folk, no more than brutes at the best except for their leader Bentham; they were fired now with unaccustomed liquor and the mad contagion of high spirits, of boisterous revelry let wild and loosed from all restraint. A spark amiss, Burke thought grimly as he

crouched to one side of the fireplace; there would be the devil to pay. He looked at the unsheathed sword lying on the mantel-shelf, Bentham's sword, and his palm itched for the feel of the hilt.

Suddenly came the igniting spark: A wild dance began. The girl Priscilla was drawn into it, taken whirling about, passed from hand to hand. Flushed and terrified, she struggled to get free. Amid a roar of laughter, some one caught her into the whirl again.

A Frenchman seized her, held her close, and kissed her ravenously. Bentham, with a hot oath, plunged for the man and knocked him sprawling. A yell, a chorus of snarls, and a knife went smack into Bentham's heart.

Phelim Burke came out of his crouch, and with a leap had the sword and was to one side of the fireplace again. None noted him. The tumult swelled into a roar of fury.

Knives were out; fists were in; women were screaming or fighting, with wild shapes reeling or grappling. Some one found a musket and let fly. In the murk of powder-smoke, Burke found the girl Priscilla and drew her out of the riot. A Frenchman, with reddened knife, hurled himself after her, and Burke ran him through the throat very neatly.

A louder yell, and two others were driving at him; his teeth flashed through his shaggy beard as he held their knives in play, lunged at them, sent them dancing and sliding.

"Out the back way, lass!" he called sharply, and the girl heard him.

One of the two Frenchmen was down. Another musket roared, and a hail of slugs flew through the room, and men screamed. Burke fought his way to the door, after the girl. One of the settlers plunged for him, with a sharp yelp at sight of his sword, and Burke killed that man deliberately. He owed him for a flogging at his first arrival.

To the open now, the girl's hand dragging at his arm. Another musket banged away inside; the fighting and uproar had redoubled; men were struggling like wild beasts. Something was afire; a flicker of flame glinted redly. Then Burke swung the sobbing, terrified girl toward the shore below.

"The boats! Get to the boats!"

They ran panting down the slope and reached the lonely shore together. The first boat was heavy, but they tugged in unison, and ran her by degrees over the shingle. A stout lass was Priscilla Bentham, strong as any man. Burke scrambled in after her, shoved an oar into her hands, and took another himself.

"Now row," he commanded. She obeyed him in wild gasping panic, without question. The boat surged out, the tide being already on the ebb and helping them. The tumult of fighting lessened with the distance as they rowed on. They came to the turn of the bay, and a light glimmered ahead, where the ship lay at anchor.

"Lead on, now; my pistol's ready too, if ye show no gold!"

Once near her, and Burke sent a hail aboard in French. A man answered him.

"Give us a hand!" cried Burke. "Is your ladder down? Good."

"What was the shooting about?" demanded a seaman at the rail.

"Fighting, between your comrades and the Englishmen. We got away from it."

Somehow, Burke forced the girl up the rope ladder, and followed her. The half dozen men on deck crowded around in wild excitement. It flamed up into hot flaring oaths; then of a sudden there was a rush. The Frenchmen were tumbling into the boat alongside, scrambling for the oars, frantic to be ashore and helping their comrades; another musket-shot and another came faintly across the night.

The girl clung to Burke, trembling, and he soothed her. They were alone here on the dark deck.

"Come below," he said. "You're done up, poor lass. I'll put you in a warm bunk and leave you. All safe now."

She yielded dumbly to his will, all resistance stricken out of her. He picked up the lantern from the waist and led her below, aft, to the deserted cabins. In one of these he left her, gasping with dry sobs, and went back on deck.

She too had been plucked out of a living hell. He thought back across that winter of horror—of dirt and filth, of crowded humans worse than animals. This girl was far above all that; she had fine things in her. She too had been little better than a slave even to her own family. A pallid, unlovely thing, frightened of the present and the more terrible future—Burke pitied her profoundly. No fate could be worse than leaving her here among these people and their appalling living conditions.

"And now she's free," he said to the stars, and a laugh broke from him. "She's free. And I'm free—*free!*"

With this, he set about what he had to do. Few other men would have dared it, but Phelim Burke was past caring.

When the girl came on deck again, the sun was shining warmly, the sea was glinting and sparkling; it was mid-morning. A queer little frightened sound escaped her lips, as she stared around. Blue crags to the west and the south, blocking the horizon; all the rest was ocean. The harbor was gone; the cliffs were gone—the ship was at sea!

She swung around, searching the decks, her lips white with swift panic. A single figure was visible by the tiller aft. A stranger, a tall, straight man smoking a pipe. He wore a somewhat frayed suit of brown velvet; he had a neatly pointed beard; his hair was clipped—

"You! Oh, what has happened, Burke!" She ran to him, in sudden recognition. "Where are we? Where is everyone?"

"In hell, I trust, my dear Priscilla." And Burke waved his pipe at the horizon. "French and English alike. I cut the cable last night, and here we are. D'ye like my new beard, lass? Faith, it hides the branding mark on my cheek, anyhow! But, my lass—Lord, what a fright you look! Run down into the big cabin. You'll find an open chest there. I got these clothes from it, and there's some woman's gear in it—plunder, perhaps. A wash, and a comb in your hair, and—"

"But where are we?" she broke in with a frantic wail. "Where are we going?"

"Upon my word, I haven't the faintest idea," said Burke, chuckling. "And I don't care a tinker's dam. And there's food on the cabin table, so help yourself. It'll put heart into you. You do look terrible, my dear."

"Oh!" she cried out. "My father—I remember now—"

"He's dead; your past is dead. You've a new future; it's what you make it. Below!"

She stared wide-eyed at him, then turned and went below with a choked sob. Burke smiled at the glinting sea, cocked his eye at the square sail forward he had half loosed from its brails, and puffed at his pipe contentedly. She would get over it.

So, indeed, she did, for she had sense enough and to spare. Facts were facts; when she came on deck, later, she was in new garments, with her hair neat and tidied, with the salt sea air bringing the red blood to her cheeks.

"But you're a lovely thing!" cried Burke, taking her hands and looking into her face. "You were always a lovely kind thing in my eyes, Priscilla; now you've blossomed from the child that you were, into a sweet woman. To the devil with all dirt henceforth! The sea's clean and sweet like yourself; the sky's no bluer than your eyes—"

"Why, Burke! You talk like poetry," she said, and blushed happily.

With such a beginning, the day's end was sure. Sunset found them dining royally while the ship drifted before a light breeze, the shore a dozen miles distant. She was facing the future more calmly now, accepting the present gladly, unregretting the past; for her mother, poor thing, had died this past winter.

So night came down upon the quiet sea; and Phelim Burke made his bed on deck near the tiller and sent the girl below again. He must steer the ship, and her, and himself, he mused bitterly as he lay under the stars; and the gray that streaked his clipped hair and beard must keep him as a father to her.

In the dawn, came a voice up out of the sea, and other voices. Burke started up and leaped to the bulwarks. At first he thought the crew had come again, for the voices were French that hailed, and in the night the ship had drifted near islands that lay off the mainland shore. A black mass lay in the water, and the voices came from this. He perceived it to be a shapeless sort of raft, and many persons upon it. He flung a line, and in the dawnlight a tall agile figure was first on deck, saluting him joyously. Priscilla, wakened by the voices and the stamp of feet, came hurriedly from below. Thus together they met these famished and weary men, who wore woolen garments and huge black hats. Their leader bowed gallantly upon seeing the girl.

"I am the Sieur de Montrouge," said he. "And I thank you in God's name for this rescue. If you have food, give it to us. We've lived two weeks on shellfish and birds' eggs while this raft was building—"

A scream of fury came from the girl; she snatched a belaying-pin and hurled it.

Food there was, and to spare. Canadians, they called themselves, twenty of them in all; and Montrouge was a hearty, lean-jawed, laughing blade. Rovers, all of them, young woods-runners who had been down the St. Lawrence with a trading-sloop. Swept out to sea by a two-day gale, dismasted and wrecked on one of the islets off the Newfoundland shore, they had built a raft to reach the coast, and in this calm night had set forth, only to be carried off by tidal currents and then to sight the ship.

They feasted into the full daylight, scraped their faces clean, filled the ship with strange oaths and laughter and Mohawk words, for most of them had spent much time among the Indians. They listened to

Burke's story, embraced him, promised him freedom and a future in Canada, and then, rather blankly, considered the present. None of them were seamen.

"I am," said Burke. "Or was. Which way lies the St. Lawrence?"

"God knows, not I!" And Montrouge chuckled. "Bah! Follow the coast. We can't miss the river. And by the looks of the red sky, we'll not miss storm either."

Burke glanced at the ominous morning, and nodded.

"With twenty of you to work ship, we'll weather anything in this craft. To the lines!"

They fell to the task, got sail on the ship, and surged westward under a moaning wind.

To Priscilla, these joyous, care-free Canadians were like beings from another world. They treated her like a great lady; they sang and laughed and brought the color to her cheeks; and when the wind swooped down and sent the ship staggering, they worked like devils. In Montrouge, Burke found a kindred soul, and took counsel with him as the gale drove them toward the iron coast.

"You played those French fishermen a scurvy trick, but they deserved it," Montrouge chuckled. "We who are Canadian-born don't think so much of the French. You shall have a home with us, my friend—but first to reach Canada! Why not make shelter along the coast yonder? If we can find an Indian or two, we'll learn where we are."

"And if we run afoul of some English ship?"

"The devil! We have muskets, tomahawks, knives—and tongues. What better?"

Burke shrugged and assented. As an escaped slave, he had little to expect if he fell into English hands again.

So they bore for the coast, scudding close-reefed, the stout little ship a marvel to them all. Even Burke, who knew the sea well, and had himself owned ships out of Galway in the old days, had never seen one of her build or rig.

From papers in the cabin, however, they learned that she was owned in St. Malo, and had been built by riggers there as an experiment for the Banks fisheries, designed in all ways for just that work, both by winter and summer. The *Hirondelle,* she was named.

With afternoon, the wind and currents took them past rugged cliffs and into a deeply indented bay. Whether it were the north of Newfoundland, or New Scotland, or some other land, Burke had not the faintest idea. With headsail spread to the wind, they forged down the apparently endless bay while the gale screeched overhead. The shores were rocky and savage; and having no smallboat and but one remaining anchor, Burke was minded to take no chances. Besides, most of the Canadians were seasick and helpless.

Then a little open cove beckoned and they made for it, surged into it, and down splashed the anchor in five fathom, and good holding-ground. Sunset was not far off and it was too late now to do any woods-running, so all hands stayed aboard to recover from the tossing sea-sickness. Priscilla, who had suffered little, cooked a meal and Montrouge acted as cabin boy, with many a gay jest. Burke, regarding the two of them, smiled in his beard....

"Over with you!" Burke exclaimed. "Over—and swim, if you want your lives! The captain is dead, and you follow him!"

With daylight, every man of them plunged overboard and swam ashore, regardless of the icy water. The powder-horns and muskets were floated ashore.' Ten minutes later, the dark masses of trees had swallowed them all up. Burke, alone with Priscilla, stuffed his pipe and stretched out comfortably on the forward deck. The sky was a gray scud of cloud, but the cove, while open to the bay, was well sheltered.

"Strange happy men!" said the girl, her eyes ashine as she stared at the empty woods. "Will they come back?"

"Aye, and with fresh meat too," Burke replied lazily. "Will you like Canada?"

"I think so." She reddened a little. "Will it like me?"

"When you learn French, aye. Montrouge seems to be teaching you the language fast."

"And do you mind?" she said, looking at him.

Burke shrugged.

"I? Lass you've no master in me; a father, if you like, but what you do is your own concern. Life is opening to you, so make the most of it."

She looked at him again and turned away, a shadow in her eyes.

Mid-morning came, and no sign nor sound from the dark shrouded forests or the sandy beach of the cove. Burke did not expect to hear from Montrouge or the others until toward evening. He was unhurried, luxuriating in freedom and mastery. No hurry any more, ever, he told himself. Then, suddenly, he heard the girl's urgent voice.

"Burke! Look! *Look!*"

Burke sprang up. She was at the rail amidships, pointing. Out in the bay beyond the cove he saw a small, slatternly ship heading seaward; she must have been somewhere up at the head of the bay. As he looked, she swung about and pointed in for the cove. She had sighted the *Hirondelle* and was heading for her.

Priscilla came running forward, eagerly asking: "Who is she, Burke? What is she?"

In dismay and consternation, his slitted eyes probed this apparition. A small ship, bluff-bowed, wallowing; two guns to a side. No fishermen. Her decks were thick with men.

"English," said Burke in a dull voice. "Or worse."

The heart was stricken out of him suddenly. Seek safety ashore? He could not swim. Hails came in English and French from the other ship, as she stood into the cove. The girl, in realization, stared blankly at him.

"Oh, Burke! For you it means—"

He smiled wryly. "Never mind. Pretend to be French; don't talk. Keep busy in the galley. These look to be more wolves than men."

The other craft dropped anchor and a boat. Hails came in English and French; Burke responded, and dropped the ladder. The men, their ship, their leader, told him all too much. Some French, mostly English; no pretense would go with these ruffians. The big black-bearded leader swung over the rail pistol in hand, swept the empty deck with his eye, and stared hard at Burke.

"Well, and you? My name's Hurd, o' Boston town."

"And mine is Burke, of St. Malo; you're welcome," said Burke. But he had heard of this fellow. The settlers talked of him in winter nights. The Bostonnais, he was called. A beast who ravaged pitilessly; fur-pirate and freebooter—no man, but a monster.

"Where are your men?"

"Ashore," said Burke. They had ringed him in, staring curiously, fingering weapons. "There's naught here to plunder, my friends."

"Friends be damned!" said the Bostonnais. "Truss him up, two of you. Where's that woman we saw aboard? We'll have her, and what provender ye have.... Off with the hatches, lads! Ashore, says he? A liar, then. There's no boat ashore. Just the two of 'em, unless more be hiding below-decks. Look for the brandy and wine, all of you."

Fight? As well might a cornered rat try to fight a dog-pack. Burke was tied up and made fast to the mainmast. The Bostonnais routed out Priscilla himself, kissed her most heartily, and set her to work in the galley with two of his men helping her. Half starved were all these sea-wolves. They had been at the head of the bay, watering, had found no fresh meat, and their stores had run out. They ravened through the ship, broke out the liquor, and another boat brought the rest of their crew aboard. Priscilla and her two lusty helpers got the salt meat and fish and bread to cooking, and at the dire threats of the Bostonnais, not a man dared so much as touch her.

Of the silent, captive Burke they took no heed as they drank, waiting for the food to be ready; but presently the Bostonnais came swaggering up to him, and spat in his face with a laugh.

"There for you! What's to prevent stringing you up and done with it, eh?"

"What I have to tell you," said Burke in a low voice. "About the gold."

The bloodshot eyes widened into his steady gaze.

"What's this? Gold, did ye say?"

"Softly, softly," cautioned Burke. "D'ye want these fools to hear? Give me my life, Master Hurd, and I'll show you where the gold's hid. There's only a small box of it, not enough for all your men to share."

The other's eyes flamed with avidity.

"So that's it, eh?" muttered the Bostonnais. He swung around suddenly, and let out a roar that swept down the deck. "All hands! No drinking and setting fire to the ship. Take the food and a keg ashore, and guzzle your bellies full if ye will! L'Etoile, you and five men stop aboard here for a bit. Ashore with you, ye dogs!"

The men yelled lusty assent to this order. L'Etoile was a Frenchman with one eye and a hideous scar where the other had been; he, Burke judged, was the mate of the rover, lieutenant to the Bostonnais. He swiftly picked five other men to remain aboard. A brandy-keg was slung over into one boat and it started ashore, crowded. The rest of the men, with the other boat, waited until the cooking food was nigh ready, then impatiently lowered it, kettle and all, into their craft. Await the bread they would not, but seized biscuit and tumbled down, and sent the boat ashore with a will.

The Bostonnais came up to Burke and flourished a knife, laughing.

"Gold and a wench and liquor—what's more to be asked?" he growled out, as he cut Burke free. "Lead on, now; my pistol's ready too, if ye show no gold, ye damned rogue! Ho, L'Etoile! Keep the deck. And if ye touch the wench, I'll split your skull, d'ye mind?"

Burke, chafing his numbed wrists and hands, cowered in assumed fear.

"It's below in the cabin, master," he whimpered. "And remember, you promised me my life for showing you!"

"You'll have it, craven," snapped the Bostonnais, pistol in hand. "Lead the way!"

So Burke went to the after companion, and on down the ladder—and as he went glanced shoreward, hoping for some sign of Montrouge; but there was only the sand-beach, and halfway to the fringing dark forest the sprawling men, guzzling food and drink, some twenty-five of them spread over the place.

Phelim Burke's heart fell. Desperate, he went on, and turned from the passage below into one of the stern cabins which he remembered clearly. Despite the dirty stern window, the light here was dim, the cabin obscure. And behind him, as he went, the Bostonnais followed with heavy pistol leveled, heavy flint and hammer back-cocked.

Burke's eyes darted about frantically. He was staking everything on one flashing instant. If he failed to stop that pistol's explosion, he was lost, for the other six would be down at the sound of it. If he missed his plunging grasp—but he must not miss!

"Where is it?" growled the Bostonnais. Burke halted, swung around toward the dark corner, and then came to one knee before the black chest standing there.

"Here," he said. "It's hidden, a secret place—"

He threw up the lid. Hurd was close beside him now, craning forward. There under the lid of the chest were the knives Burke had seen—the big curved-bladed knives for cleaning cod. And on the instant, Burke flashed into motion.

His left hand went to the pistol-pan; his right swooped at a knife; and with the action he was rising. The cocked flint came down cruelly on his hand; but the knife drove up and thudded home; the game was won.

A bursting gasp escaped the Bostonnais. He staggered, loosed the pistol; clenched on Burke's hand, it hung pendulous. The stricken man put both huge paws to the knife-haft, then suddenly doubled up and pitched forward on his face.

Burke stepped nimbly aside. Agonized, he freed his hand from the pistol, and sucked at the torn flesh in relief. He frowned down at the heavy, clumsy weapons, shook his head, and stepped out of the cabin into the one adjoining. Here he had left the sword that he had fetched aboard. He secured it, and then went to the ladder and mounted.

*Head and shoulders protruding from the com-*panion-way, he halted and called to the knot of men in the waist.

"L'Etoile! The cap'n says to come below."

The lithe one-eyed rascal came quickly enough, and Burke descended.

"What is it?" demanded L'Etoile from the head of the ladder.

"He's found something here; he wants you."

The Frenchman stumbled down, but came with a knife in his hand and his one eye probing ahead.

"Cap'n! Where are you?" he called sharply, and halted on the bottom step. A laugh broke from Phelim Burke as he lunged out of the obscurity, and his blade went home.

L'Etoile dived headlong, and his knife stabbed into the deck; but he did not pull it free.... His greasy knitted cap fell off.

Burke picked up the cap, wiped his sword on it, then went up the ladder. On deck, he stood drinking in the clean crisp air. The sky was gray with storm-scud, but it was as yet little past mid-morning. In the waist, the five men stood at the rail, watching the swilling crew ashore with eager eyes, and bolting the food Priscilla had provided.

One look at the dark and silent forest; then Burke laid his sword and the cap on the after hatch, and sauntered forward. The men turned to eye him curiously, and he gave them an affable nod; two English, two French, and a negro with gold rings in his ears.

"Good news, lads," he said. "The Cap'n is plundering below with L'Etoile. He says you're free to drink, so fall to."

"Who says so?" growled one of the Englishmen. Burke laughed lightly.

"Oh, I'm one of you now," he said, and went on to the galley with careless air. The five men broke for a wine-keg that had been fetched on deck, and smashed into it.

Priscilla, her arms bare to the elbow, flushed with the fire-heat, regarded him with startled wonder and relief.

"Then it's all right?" she broke out. "You're free?"

"So far," said Burke cheerfully. "If trouble starts, go below forward; not to the cabins. The Bostonnais is done for, and his lieutenant; but I'm playing for time, until those Canadians show up."

He turned away and went aft. The men ashore were bawling forth a drunken tune; the five amidships were tight around the wine-keg. Burke reached the after hatch, sat down, lit his pipe, and began to polish his sword-blade with the cap of L'Etoile, He kept an eye on the line of forest, but saw no indication of the Canadians returning. The two boats on the shore were being left high and dry by the ebbing tide.

Suddenly the party of carousing men fell silent and then scattered. Some went for their weapons; a number leaped up and dashed into the cover of the trees. They came back with one of the Canadians in their midst. Voices broke out; the Canadian tried to get away from the men around him; there was a swirl of figures, a flash of knives. The Canadian lay on the sand, still struggling, until other knives finished him.

From somewhere among the trees pealed up a sharp, shrill war-whoop. That Canadian, trusting these strangers too easily, had not been alone.

The two Englishmen at the wine-keg came staggering aft, as the men ashore broke into shouts for the captain; they came to where Burke sat, and halted.

"Where be Cap'n?" demanded one. Burke merely pointed below. The other man uttered a quick cry, his eyes dilating on the cloth.

"Why, that be L'Etoile's cap!"

"So it is, so it is," Burke assented cheerfully. "He has no more use for it, lads,"

His words, his manner, bewildered their fuddled wits, as he went on polishing the sword. Fresh calls came from shore. The two men went to the companionway and started down the ladder. Burke rose and followed them, as far as the hatch.

There he heard oaths as they stumbled over the body of L'Etoile. Their voices were drowned as Burke slammed shut the storm-doors and shot the bolts. Then, sword in hand, he turned down the deck toward the two Frenchmen and the negro, who were gawking at the doings ashore. There a shot burst forth, yells were rising; but Burke looked only at the three around the wine-keg, by the shoreward rail.

"Over with you!" he exclaimed in French. "Over—and swim, if you want your lives! The captain is dead, and you follow him."

They swung around, gaped at him, heard the frantic hammering of the trapped pair, and broke into sudden savage motion. An oath and a yell, a flash of steel; the three of them spread out and then drove at him. Burke evaded with one swift leap, and his point lunged in under the arm of the nearer Frenchman. That man dropped and lay kicking for a little while. But the negro flung a knife, and Burke felt his left arm pinned to his body by the blade as he staggered back against the rail.

The two were upon him like dogs on the kill, but this was the death of them both. The long steel slipped in over their knives, drove into the Frenchman's throat, and the hilt smashed the negro in the face. He fell back a pace, and this gave Burke time for a second lunge that slid home.

Meantime, tumult heightened ashore; but Burke, clinging to the rail, had no eyes for it. With a rush, Priscilla was coming across the deck, catching at him, supporting him, seizing the knife and wrenching it free of arm-flesh and ribs. She was no wench to flinch at the sight of blood.

"Off with your shirt—here, hold to the rail!" she cried. "Give me the shirt for a bandage; that's right. Oh, Burke, I thought you dead! But it's not so deep, not so bad. Steady, now—"

Stripped to the waist, he hung on the rail while she bandaged him, then fetched him a cup of the wine. This cleared his head, and just in time. For the negro was on one knee, shaking his head so that the gold ear-rings dangled and jumped, plunging up with a knife in hand. Burke kicked out at his face, caught up his sword again; and this time the black lay quiet with the others.

Ashore, wild whoops were rising from the trees; men were dying on the beach, muskets were pluming the wind with powder-smoke. Montrouge was avenging his murdered comrade in ghastly fashion,—tomahawk and scalping-knife at work,—and had cut off the raiders from their two boats, driving them to the shelter of the trees. Some of the Canadians were tugging one of the boats into the water, flinging in oars, scrambling aboard. It was a wild and furious mêlée; and in the midst, Burke heard a cry of alarm from the girl. He swung about.

The two Englishmen he had barricaded below were on the poop. They must have smashed through a stern window and climbed up over the quarter-rail, Now, with Hurd's pistols, they headed forward. Burke felt the girl tug at his wounded arm.

"This way—quickly!" she gasped. "Oh, don't stand there like a ninny—"

He laughed a little and stumbled after her, wondering at his own weakness; he must have lost much blood! He could scarce hold his sword. Yells and oaths of fury were coming from the two Englishmen as they ran forward to get at him. He could not reach the galley with Priscilla; he came to a dead halt as the strength went out of him. He swayed, caught himself, and went to one knee. There, leaning on the sword so hard the blade quivered, he stayed himself. It was the end. His eyes darkened. He was conscious of the rush and swoop of the gale overhead; then voices reached him.

"Ye damned murdering rogue!" one of the two raiders brayed. They had stopped, had swung up the heavy pistols to bear on him. Burke's head jerked up, and a smile touched his lips.

Then something whirled in air. A scream of dismay and fury came from the girl. She had snatched a belaying-pin from the rack and hurled it; now she hurled a second, with true aim, at the two men. One pistol exploded, wild; but not the second. Its owner fired deliberately, and the girl crumpled.

Madness flamed in Burke; his brain afire, an access of spasmodic rage lending him strength, he was up and hurling himself at the two of them. An empty pistol hurtled at him. He met it with his wounded arm, and felt no pain, for his sword was plunging home and wrenching out again. One man down. The other turned, and with a scream of terror leaped for the rail, but Burke was upon him like a whirlwind, and the thirsty steel darted up.... Transfixed, twisting the blade from Burke's fingers, that man went screaming over into the icy water, and his cries ended abruptly.

"My poor lass, my poor lass!"

Burke staggered back across the deck. He dropped, and tears were on his bearded cheeks as he drew the girl's head into his lap, and wiped the blood from her brow. Her eyes came open. A quick delirium of joy seized upon him as he looked at the wound and saw that the ball had only furrowed her skull. She smiled up at him, and her hand crept to his with a firm, strong grasp.

They were still quiet, there, when a boat crashed alongside, and up over the rail flooded the Canadians. Not all of them; and of these who came, some were sore hurt; but Montrouge headed them with a laugh and a wild oath at sight of the red decks.

"There's your man, my lass," muttered Burke. "On your feet, now, and welcome him! And a brave fellow he is."

"No, no," she said, coming to her knees and drawing at him to rise. "No, Burke! It's you, now and always; you and no other!"

He stared at her for a moment, while the Canadians came crowding around them; then he suddenly caught and held her close to him, and kissed her.

"Cut the cable!" His head came up, his orders

flamed at Montrouge. "Out with the tide, out with the gale, lads—to sea! And when we reach Canada, we'll send this ship back to St. Malo with our thanks and our blessing. Have you found where we are?"

"North bay of Newfoundland," replied Montrouge. "And the way clear before us."

Thus, in the end, the *Hirondelle* came back to France again; and others were built in her likeness, and the "Newfoundlanders" came presently to the Grand Banks by the hundreds. So stout and well-suited for the work were they, that they came even in winter fleets to dare ice and storm, changing in rig and build down the centuries, but ever stout and hardy beyond all compare.

So the story came to a close, with Washington's outskirts greeting us. I looked at my friend Smith, met his penetrating eye, and shook my head.

"All very well," I said, "but what about my question? The first Canadians?"

"I've told you," he replied, and tapped the little old book in his hand. "It's all here in La Potherie. The French settled Canada; their children, born there, called themselves Canadians. The first dated mention of the name, here in the book, goes back to 1697, but it was in use long before that. And here you can find about the Irish slaves, and how Burke helped Perrot discover the Sioux in the West, in 1660, and where the first white child was born in Newfoundland, and—"

The train squealed to a halt. We were in. Smith was cut short; we shook hands and parted....

The noonday run to Washington is nearly always interesting.

SATAN SAILS THE SHIP

Old Frazier, our third mate, came up to me one morning with a startling query.

"Sir, would ye like to clap eyes on the first wheel ever to sail the sea?"

"Very much indeed," I said dryly. "So would many a man."

"Then call out the work-boat, and I'll show it to you," said he.

Wherever and whenever seamen get to gamming, one argument is left eternally unsettled. The question of the first fore-and-aft rig, the evolution of the schooner, can be run down to the early years of the Eighteenth Century and the New England trade with the West Indies. Ship's bell, customs of all kinds—these things can be traced back. But never the invention of the steering-wheel.

We were lying in St. Thomas with some extensive repairs under way, early in the prohibition period. Old Frazier poked a thumb over the rail at an arrowy schooner of two hundred tons, probably a rum-runner. She lay at anchor under shadow of Bluebeard Hill and the pirate castle three hundred feet above the sea.

"Two hundred year old, she be," said Frazier.

I laughed at that.

"Yeah? Ships don't serve that long, my bucko."

"And what about *Old Ironsides?*" said he. "Or the *Constellation* at Newport? Or the *Worcester* off Greenhithe, the *Conway* in the Mersey?"

I piped down. Frazier had a short, bulging white beard, and he was old. He admitted to sixty years; my idea was that he was nearer eighty.

"Yonder is the *Hawk,*" said he. *"El Halcon,* in Spanish, and I once sailed in her. I'll show you where my name's cut. And the first steering-wheel ever used."

He was in dead earnest, and that was enough for me. We got away in the work-boat and white-ashed it over to the schooner and aboard her scarred decks. And if ever there was a first schooner to skim the seas, I judge she was it.

Frazier hustled me into the fo'c'stle, and sure enough, there was his name carved over one of the bunks, with a hundred others. By this time the old rascal had me just where he wanted me. He took me to the cabin; here, on a black oaken deck-beam forward of the mizzen, he showed me the carven figures *1713.*

Anybody could have carved that, and I said so. Frazier led me around to the after side of the mizzen-mast. There, between the deck-head and the cabin mess table, were the names of the masters who had sailed the *Hawk,* done in polished copper tacks. Near the top was the name *Patrick Martin.*

Frazier peered at me in the semi-gloom, his bronze features crinkled up, his wise, sea-faded eyes twinkling.

"Does that mean anything to a Johnny-come-lately like you?"

I shook my head, and Frazier snorted.

"You've been in Tacon Theater in Havana? Aye. Know who built that gingerbread show-house?"

"Yes," I said. "It was Marti, the smuggler chief. He struck a deal with Tacon, the Governor-general, became the exclusive purveyor of fish to Havana, and thereby Cuba's first millionaire."

"And Marti was really one Martin," said Frazier,

"a rascal who sold out his brother rogues to the Spanish garroters at El Morro. His grandfather was the Patrick Martin whose name ye see here. Ah, what a man he was, what a sailor-man! Ye know, when he sailed the *Hawk,* she was called the devil's ship. Why? Because she was a schooner, for one thing, a new rig in these waters, with speed none could touch; further, she'd been seen to maneuver with never a man on her deck. And once they killed the man at the helm, yet she sailed on and handled neatly. Why, those *guardia costas* knew for sure the devil was aboard her!"

As a matter of fact (he went on) Patrick Martin used to run contraband New Bedford rum into Santiago harbor—aye, rum-running is two hundred years old, and older! But in those days the order was reversed; American rum to Cuba. And he did a bit of smuggling and free trading to boot, as who didn't in those days? He was a fine upstanding man, with blue eyes and black hair, a laugh in his eye, and a tongue that could manage stately Castilian or honest New England sea-oaths with equal facility.

He knew Havana intimately; he was a friend of the Captain General; he was on the inside of the game; and he knew just whose itching palms to grease in the *aduana.* So all was smooth for Patrick Martin, up to the day he ran down from New England into Santiago harbor. No one came out to meet him; no one warned him. News was slow, those days.

He did not know that there had been a sudden and drastic shift of officials, from the Captain General down. He sailed the *Hawk* in under Estrella Castle, through the narrow channel into the harbor; and four *guardia costa* craft closed in around him. Ten minutes later Patrick Martin learned that graft was out—and he was in.

The *cuartel* held him tight, and a dozen more as well—some of his men, some of his friends, and chief among them young Juan Cardenas. Patrick Martin loved that youngster, and in the two days he dwelt within the *cuartel* cell, grieved for him. Cardenas had been taken to Morro Castle in Havana, he learned. This meant the garrote, sooner or later—probably sooner. Cardenas was, in plain terms, a revolutionist.

Yes, Patrick Martin had walked into a fine trap; and two nights later he walked out of it, with the help of his mate Gomez and the giant black, José. And the *Hawk* walked out of the harbor, with grape and musket-balls whistling across her deck, and never a man at the tiller. Satan sailed her, true enough!

And straight as a homing bird could make the course, the *Hawk* headed for Havana.

It was the beginning of the hurricane season, and the night they raised Morro Castle's lights, the sky was overcast and bleak squalls were howling down. A

"Raise tacks and sheets!" Martin jammed the wheel hard alee. "Watch ho!"

black ghost with all lights doused and running-gear greased, the *Hawk* eased into the harbor, headed into the wind and anchored stealthily.

Gomez came boring aft through the driving rain to Patrick Martin's side.

"I say again you're crazed to try it!" he growled. "We're rats in a trap with El Morro's guns to starboard and La Punta's to larboard; and there's probably a round dozen *guardias* inside ready to slip the leash and come after us!"

"True enough!" And Martin clapped him on the shoulder, with a gay laugh. "But you'll be out and away when day breaks."

"Away? One of us is a fool, and it's not me. However will we work out of here against a dead muzzler?"

"Get it through your head, once and for all! A hurricane's making up. At the start it comes from west-sou'-west; but by morning the wind will haul east-sou'-east, traveling counter-clockwise and drawing to the north'ard. Before dawn it'll strike from the east—and then you can beat to sea."

"And you, Cap'n?"

"I'll be where I said I would. It's one night's work, all of it—and hardly that. If I fail, back you go with the *Hawk* to the rendezvous."

"Fool's errand," grumbled Gomez. "Señor Garrote has cracked the neck of young Cardenas long ere this. If you ever see him, it'll be in the Shark's Hole, along with the bones of other rebels."

"Bah! We don't live forever. Get the pumpkin-seed ready."

"Silence, Excellency!" said Patrick Martin.

Martin went below. When he came back on deck, he was wearing a Spanish naval officer's uniform and cape.

The pumpkin-seed, a dinghy with extra large beam, was put over. Into it stepped Patrick Martin, and with him the giant black. Once a slave in the Captain General's palace, José knew every nook and corner of the place, and its secrets. Martin had freed him, with many another slave; and the giant loved Patrick Martin with the utter devotion of a dog.

The two of them laid to the oars, and the pumpkin-seed vanished in the darkness, toward the great star-shaped bastion of La Punta de la San Salvador.

That evening, the Captain General returned early from the artillery officers' *baile* at Fort Cabañas, on the upper bay; he was no man for balls and merrymakings. At the great desk in his library he sat in a thronelike chair, his tall, spare form rigidly encased in its uniform. Decorations starred his chest. He was lean and ascetic in face, bitter and proud of eye, and of heart.

His quill scratched busily. The shutters rattled in the moaning grip of the rising hurricane outside; but neither scratching nor moan drowned the squeak of the sliding panel in the wall that slipped open. The Captain General looked up at the officer who stood there—piercing blue eyes, wide-set, a lean shaven mouth and chin—and with a pistol in his hand.

"Silence, Excellency!" said Patrick Martin, stepping to the floor. He stood for a moment, swiftly appraising this lean, hard old man with the bitter face. With sudden decision he uncocked his pistol and put it away. He swept off his hat and bowed.

"Who are you?" snapped the Captain General. "You're no officer of mine?"

"Correct. I've come with information not intended for eavesdropping ears. You, I think, are Señor de la Vega, or you'd not be sitting here."

The Captain General studied his visitor in turn. An assassin? Very probably; he knew of this secret passage, knew the other end was guarded. Therefore his soldier must have been killed. But he replied in precise, cold tones:

"I am Captain General Don Diego de Cordoba Lazo de la Vega, Governor-general of the island of Cuba by grace of his most Catholic Majesty. What is your business here?"

Martin had, after one glance, discarded any idea of force. With such a man, it would be useless. Now he bowed again, sweeping the floor with his tricorne hat.

"Excellency, I understand you have offered a reward of twenty thousand reales for information leading to the capture of the Gulf smuggler, one Patricio Marti, who was recently captured at Santiago, but escaped."

The cold eyes of Don Diego flashed.

"Ah! So that explains your presence! How did you learn of this secret passage?"

"From this Patrick Martin himself, Excellency. He was a great friend of your predecessor in office."

"Who is now on his way to Spain, to answer for his crimes," said Don Diego. "Yes; this Martin or Marti is known to be in open alliance with Satan. This was proved at Santiago, where his accursed ship disappeared without a man on deck, with the tiller moving, guided by an invisible hand." The Captain General crossed himself swiftly. "I am waiting. What have you to say?"

"I offer to put this Martin in your hands, Excellency—on conditions."

"You're one of his men, eh? I don't make conditions with traitorous dogs."

"But they make conditions with you!" And Patrick Martin's white teeth flashed in a smile. "I don't want your promised reward. I offer to put this man into your hands this very night; I ask only your sworn oath on two points."

And there Patrick Martin overshot the mark. He had judged his man aright; force would accomplish nothing here; honor would accomplish anything. But he had missed the cue, in his eagerness.

"No reward, eh? It is possible," said Don Diego slowly, "to replace the offered reward with something else, assuredly. What do you want?"

"First, the release of Juan Cardenas. Second, your oath to clap this Martin into the Shark's Hole, the instant you have him prisoner; at once, do you comprehend? If he remains alive until daybreak, even if he's in your deepest dungeon, my life will not be safe."

This was clear enough, and logical.

"I'd prefer to hang him as an example," said Don Diego. "However, I agree with pleasure to your request, señor. I appreciate your point of view."

"You'll give Cardenas a pardon and freedom, with permission to leave Cuba?"

"Yes. When you have put this Marti in my hands."

"Swear it."

Angry color rose in the lean features.

"So, senior, the word of an hidalgo of Spain does not content you? Very well.

I swear by these orders of knighthood,"—Don Diego touched the decorations and crosses on his breast,—"by this cross under my hand. Are you now satisfied?" he added with a sneer in his eyes.

Martin inclined his head. "Cardenas is in the Royal Prison?"

"No; in Morro Castle."

"Then suppose we go and see him released, you and I. And remember your oath."

"An oath," said Don Diego with contempt, "is so unusual a matter with me that I am not likely to forget it. It is you, señor, who forget your share of the bargain. You have yet to deliver this Patricio Marti to me."

"On the contrary. I am Patrick Martin."

Don Diego met the bold blue eyes with his chill gaze, and nodded slowly.

"I suspected as much. Evidently my predecessor taught you some of the secrets of this place. Will you have the kindness to call my guards, señor?"

"No. We go together, alone." Martin gestured toward the opening of the secret passage. "My boat should be waiting. We go to the castle; I remain in your hands while Cardenas goes free."

A thin smile curved the ironic lips.

"What? You would trade yourself for this young fool?"

"I owe him much," said Martin quietly. "I love him. He's been like a son to me. His life's worth more than mine."

"So? And you demand the Shark's Hole—why?"

"I prefer that to the garrote or a rope, Excellency. I'm sure of a quick death and an easy one. I don't care to be tortured."

"If you prefer the Shark's Hole, I shall accommodate you. Or I'll give you a firing-squad if you say the word."

Martin knew this was kindly meant, if such a dour man could mean anything kindly. That underground chute in the castle, El Hoyo Tiburon, the Shark's Hole, was a thing of ghastly fame; a foul tunneled incline that led to a tide-washed cavern under the limestone foundation of the fortress. Here went garbage and refuse, the bodies of the condemned, whatever was destined to disappear forever in the maws of avid sharks. Men who went that way alive had a quick death, indeed, but no pleasant one.

Martin shivered slightly—for effect. He was not the fool he seemed, by far.

"Excellency, one thing frightens me, and one alone: the thought of torture. Bullets may bring lingering death. I prefer certainty."

"As you wish." Don Diego surveyed him keenly. "You appeared with a pistol; you put it away again. Why?"

Martin smiled. "Because my first intention was to lead you out of here a captive, and so affect the release of Cardenas. After seeing you, I understood that force would serve me poorly."

"You are right." Don Diego rose. "It must be close to midnight. Señor, I am at your service. I shall, I warn you, take you into the castle as a prisoner."

"That is understood," Martin said coolly. "I trust to your oath for the rest of it. An hidalgo of Spain does not break his oath."

Don Diego reached for his cloak and hat, and the movement concealed the angry color that again rushed into his stony features.

Martin took a light from the silver candelabrum on the table, and ushered Don Diego into the opening. A narrow corridor, steep steps that seemed to wind interminably ahead; they went along in silence, the flickering candle lighting their way. A faint harsh clangor of bells reached them: the bronze tongues in San Francisco tower were hailing midnight.

Don Diego laughed curtly. "My celebrated Guardia Civil seems not to have hindered your entry, Señor Martin; let us trust they'll not hinder our departure."

Martin made no response. The exit lay ahead of them; a massive iron-bound door that opened into

the courtyard. José should be waiting there. He handed the candle to Don Diego, removed the heavy bar of the door, and swung it open. In the gust of cold rainy wind, the light was extinguished instantly.

Martin followed outside and peered at the sentry-box near by.

"José!" he said sharply. "Quickly!"

"Muy bien, señor," came muffled response. Figures moved; a dark lantern was unmasked from a cloak; of a sudden, Patrick Martin was aware of bayonets and uniforms around him. He stood stupefied, pinned in by the sharp steel. The officer who held the lantern played it over him.

"So? And whom have we here?"

The harsh cackle of Don Diego broke in, drew the light, drew instant consternation and apologies.

"So it appears we have one officer on the alert," said Don Diego. "I supposed the entire garrison was asleep from here to Cabañas. *Teniente,* how came you here?"

The lieutenant stammered: "Excellency, in making my rounds I found the sentry here dead. We caught a giant negro, but he escaped us by the help of Satan; he had the strength of ten men! So I waited here, to see who came by the door—"

"You did well, and you are promoted one rank," said Don Diego crisply. He turned to Martin. "Your pistol, señor! You are my prisoner, as I think you agreed. Tie this man's hands, lieutenant; use a belt, anything! Then send and make ready a boat. We go to El Morro."

Patrick Martin submitted in silence. It was not the first time he had been tied up. When one of the soldiers produced a belt, he smiled to himself and held out his arms. In that dim lantern-glow, it was no trick to hold his crossed wrists so that the leather belt, however tight, could be made to give slightly when he relaxed his posture. And the rain was coming down in sweeps, now.

Two of the soldiers had darted off to make ready a boat. Bayonets around him, Martin strode away, the lieutenant and Don Diego going ahead with the lantern.

Evidently José had been caught, had escaped! Well, things might be worse, Martin thought. After all, he had chosen to gamble with death.

They followed the Paseo Ysabel, in those days named the Reale, which led to the Boca and the La Punta fortress landing. The Royal Prison was dark and silent as they passed, in the moaning wind and the rain-gusts. When they came to the landing, a barge with boatmen was on hand.

The chill eye of Don Diego saw his captive in. He followed with four soldiers, and they were off across the tossing channel. With a wry grimace, Martin acknowledged that here was a Captain General who did things; a man of very different stripe from his predecessors in office.

They fetched alongside Morro landing, No sentries were out, and Don Diego disembarked with a grim air. The prisoner was led up the long causeway, protected on either hand by ten-foot walls; and passing the ramp, they halted before the iron-bound gate of the fortress. It was a gate of the dead, deaf to all hails, until the angry Don Diego fired a pistol in the air. Then sentinels appeared.

"Open, you dogs! Open to the Captain General!"

Now befell wild dismay, consternation, frantic haste. Lights fluttered. A half-dressed officer appeared; the gates opened. Don Diego strode in, eyed the guard falling into ranks abreast the *cuartel,* and barked a curt command:

"Bring a prisoner named Juan Cardenas. Quick about it!"

Martin eased his wrists. With the rain, the water in the boat, the belt-fibers were well soaked, and gave readily to his straining muscles. Satisfied, he then stood quiet and awaited whatever might come.

"Will you not come inside, Excellency?" pleaded an officer.

"When I come inside, you'll regret it," snapped Don Diego. "I'll finish with other matters before taking up the question of discipline here. Close the gates, fool!"

The gates were closed.

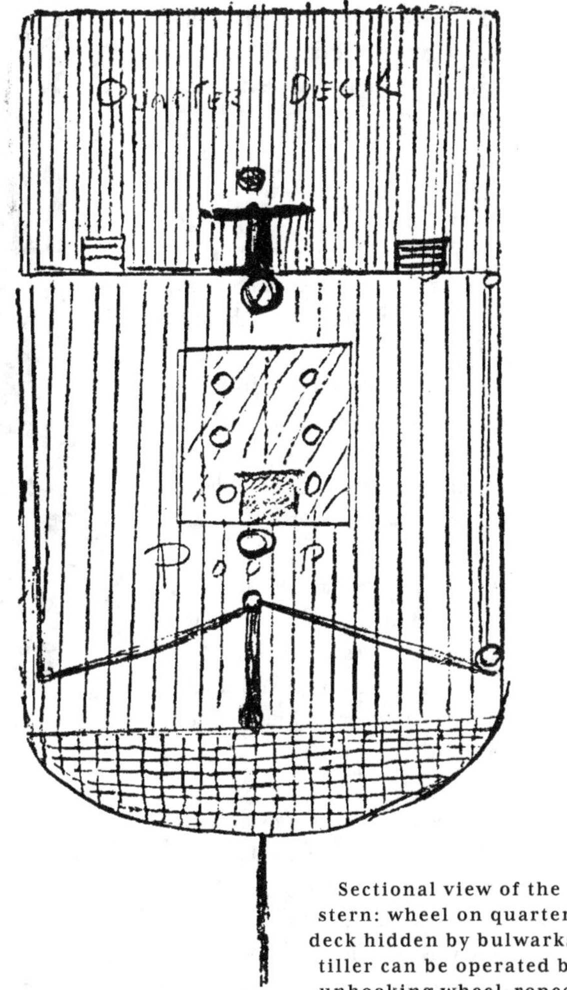

Sectional view of the stern: wheel on quarter-deck hidden by bulwarks—tiller can be operated by unhooking wheel-ropes.

Martin eyed the steep stone bridge that led to the dreaded "Door to Death." Beyond that narrow opening was the execution-yard; inside of it reposed the infamous *silla,* the rude chair of wood and iron with its steel collar, worked by a set-screw from behind.... This neck-cracking, strangling garrote was no chair for Patrick Martin. Better by far the Shark's Hole—especially with his secret knowledge of the latter. At that, he might be wrong—he swallowed hard at the thought. Well, it was a gamble!

A commotion arose. Martin turned, and saw lanterns bobbing, a group approaching, and amid the group Cardenas, unbound. A handsome fellow, this Cardenas, who held his head high despite his prison rags. His gaze fell on Patrick Martin, on Don Diego; but beyond a quick nod of recognition he gave no sign.

Don Diego glanced from one to the other, and beckoned an officer.

"Have these two prisoners ironed together," he directed crisply. "Then have them hanged—also together."

Martin started. He swung around, and his voice leaped out.

"Excellency! You cannot do this—your oath! You swore to me Cardenas would be released! You, a hidalgo of Spain, to break your word—"

Don Diego wiped rain from his lean cheek, and bowed slightly in icy irony.

"Señor, you mistake. A hidalgo does not break his word. I offered you my honor, and you scorned it. You demanded an oath. Well, señor, an oath obtained by force, an oath given under duress to a spy and an enemy, is not binding. And may I add, an oath given to one in open alliance with Satan—"

"It's past daylight now," said the burly mate. "Douse that torch, José! Lay over those oars!"

With a muffled oath Patrick Martin slipped his bonds. One instant he poised, and his voice rang clear.

"To me, Cardenas! Come on!"

He was into the soldiers about him, fists lashing out. He broke them, sent them reeling, wrenched a musket from the nearest man and flailed with it. Cardenas struck aside his guards and with a leap was at Martin's side.

"With me, now—with me!"

Men ran in. The muskets hammered at them, smote them, crashed on them. The iron barrel in his hands, Martin was leaping for the stone bridge and what lay beyond; and Cardenas was at his heels.

The tumult swelled in yells of shrill mockery. All knew this narrow way ended at the Door to Death—which gave upon the Shark's Hole. Cardenas knew it too, and gasped out a quick word of warning.

Patrick Martin laughed.

"Gomez is waiting below with a boat. There's a way in, a way out. The tide's at flood—it's safe enough, if Gomez is there. Chance it! On with you!"

Cardenas fled on. Martin swung the iron musket-barrel as the tide of yelling men swept up at him in the squally rain. Powder was wet; guns were useless. Steel flashed. But groans and screams went up as the desperate Martin swept down crushing blows. The tide broke and fell back, leaving dragging figures behind.

And Martin, turning, fled after his companion.

Once in that dread dark tunnel, a chill took him. The concave roof was so low he had to bend almost double; the platform underfoot, before the plunge, was slippery with slime. A stench arose from far below—and here was Cardenas gripping at him in the blackness.

"Jump for it, blast you!" cried Martin furiously.

"I cannot! My friend, I cannot. The sharks—"

In his heart, Martin could not blame the man; he felt the same way, now that the pinch was here. But light struck in upon them, voices sounded. Guards were hot after them. With a quick hot oath, Martin caught the clutching figure.

"Go with God, old fellow! I'll be after you—"

A scream burst from Cardenas as he swung up and dropped. The scream died away in a descending wail. The light came forward, faces a-snarl, bayonets flicking out—then a musket banged, the pan kept dry by some miracle.

Patrick Martin felt a stunning smash, and was knocked backward—then darkness enfolded him mercifully.

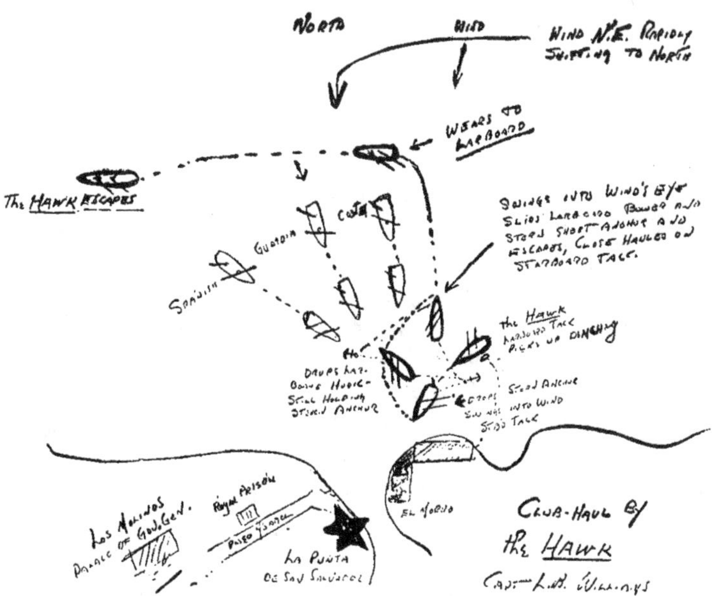

When Martin wakened, he thought he was in hell; and the bullet-furrow across his scalp backed up the thought.

Ruddy torchlight streamed redly around him, reflecting from a cavern roof; the torch was held by a naked black demon of gigantic size, who looked curiously like José.

Finding himself in a boat, Martin sat up and stared into the bearded face of another apparition.

"Gomez!" Suddenly his brain jerked to life. He was covered with slime and mud, and beside him in the boat was another figure, unmoving: Cardenas. "You, Gomez?"

"Aye. We've had the devil's own time bringing you two around," said the burly mate. "Had to work over Cardenas; but he's alive. And it's past daylight now. Douse that torch, José! Lay over those oars! Take the tiller, Cap'n. I'll take the stroke."

Martin struggled to the tiller. The noisome stench around was terrible. As the torch plunged out, he had a glimpse of a huge whitish body alongside, and shivered. He wanted to know nothing more about that long plunge from the castle above.

The boat stole out from the opening beneath the castle, out into a windy gray dawn and a nasty cross-chop. Patrick Martin's heart leaped. There, as he peered through the spoon-drift, he could see the trim outline of the *Hawk,* hove to under jib-staysail and treble-reefed mainsail.

"Pull, bullies, pull!" he cried jubilantly. "Once aboard, and a dash of rum—"

"Look to seaward, Cap'n," grunted Gomez. "They've caught us."

Caught—aye, caught! For there plunged three *queches de bombe,* queer ketch-rigged Coast Guard craft, under straining double-reefed mainsail and a small triangle of lateen. And the schooner was caught between them and Havana harbor, with the wind piling down out of the northeast in shrieks.

"Caught? Not yet!" rang out Martin's voice eagerly. "Aboard, lay us aboard, and we'll give 'em a run for their money yet!"

The stout ash bent. The boat crawled out; the second mate of the *Hawk* brought her around to form a lee. The groaning but alive Cardenas was hoisted up, Martin and the others followed to the plunging deck.

Martin stumbled aft, his gaze sweeping ships and shore and sea. A shot puffed from the leading guard-ship. The three had the *Hawk* hemmed in now; there was only one way she could run, apparently—straight into Havana harbor. Obviously, those Spaniards were seamen—but before they got through, Patrick Martin thought grimly, they were going to need all their seamanship.

Two men were at the tiller, on the poop above Martin. He shouted at them to lay below, shouted quick orders at Gomez, and disappeared. He was under the break of the poop now, and hidden from sight by the schooner's high bulwarks.

Here stood a crude wheel, made fast at the forward end of a long round timber. This timber revolved on a sawhorse frame securely bolted to the deck, and was grooved to hold the tiller-ropes that wound about it. These ropes led to blocks in the starboard and larboard waterways, and from there aft through the main cabin to an auxiliary tiller that projected from the rudder post.

Martin jerked the canvas covering off his wheel, as another gun boomed. Here a man might stand and steer, invisible. He glanced at Morro Castle—they lay just off that towering mass. Gomez came with a wild yell.

"You can't do it! You can't club-haul here!"

"Get for'ard! Get that lee anchor aft!" blared Martin. "Quick, blast you!"

Gomez pounded off to obey. As the clarion voice broke across the wind, the men leaped to the lines. The *Hawk* wore and headed off on the larboard tack, straight past El Morro for the harbor mouth.

*Martin's eyes stabbed across the larboard bul-*warks. Blocks were screaming, cordage strumming; the lee shore was not a thousand yards away. He had one swift vision of the three guard-ships, and a wild laugh burst from him. They had forced the *Hawk* into a trap, and had fallen into it themselves. They were coming about on the larboard tack, and well did Patrick Martin know what would happen to the clumsy craft with their square rig forward. They went into irons, missed stays, and began drifting to leeward.

"Raise tacks and sheets!" Martin suddenly jammed the wheel hard alee; it was do or die now. His men darted through the dawn-spray. "Watch ho! Let go the lee hook!"

Gomez had worked like mad. The lee sheet-anchor, ranged aft to the larboard quarter and suspended on a slip-stopper, was let go. It caught ground almost instantly, and the *Hawk's* head reached north into the wind.

"Watch ho, watch! Gomez! Let go the lee bower!"

The bursting voice reached. Gomez tripped the lee bower anchor, while men aft checked the taut sheet-anchor cable that led directly astern. The ship's head pointed directly into the wind's eye.

"Watch!" Martin lifted up for a glance astern at the giant breakers lashing the angry rocks below El Morro. "Cut the spring line! Let go and haul, *haul!* When the bower is slipped, take cover—"

An ax-stroke hewed the taut line; the sheet-anchor was forever lost. Men forward labored at the capstan; others hauled the booms over. Instantly the canvas filled; the larboard bower was cut away—they were off, off, slowly clawing off the lee shore!

Upon the *Hawk* burst a storm of lead. Bullets, grape, everything the three guard-ships could bring to bear; but the decks were clear of men, the tiller swung on the poop and held steady as though by an invisible hand. And off into the hurricane mist and rain plunged the *Hawk,* apparently steered by no mortal hand, and was gone to sight.

But those three guard-ships drifted to their doom on the rocks of El Morro.

Old Man Frazier tucked a pipe into the corner of his mouth, held a match to it, and wagged his head at me.

"Schooner rig, and the first wheel," said he positively. "There ye have it, sir! Now come along to the break of the poop for the proof of it. There's no wheel on the poop, as ye may have noticed already."

He showed it to me there under the poop. The original log was replaced by a steel drum, and the wheel-ropes were pliable steel cable; but there stood Patrick Martin's rig on its hardwood horse. Frazier chuckled as I examined it.

"The Spaniards were ten years solving the mystery of the devil's ship," said he; "but some lime-juicer carried word of it home to England, and the wheel came into use. And there's history for you, sir!"

So it was indeed—if it was true. And I'm rather tempted to think that old Frazier told the truth.

HERO IN DEFEAT

In most of us beefy he-men there's a queer strain of sentiment for some school-teacher out of the past; and I don't mean any Freudian yearnings, either—but ordinary respect....

After twenty years of wandering, in passing through Columbus, I looked up Miss Noble. She was older, retired, living in a little dream of a cottage; otherwise just the same. With the same gentle confidence in what she knew and was, the same understanding smile and wise, aloof heart. We went out for dinner, and came back to her cottage and talked, and she unfolded a map before me.

"Here's something that should interest you, since you're so fond of ships," she said. "It's intimately connected with the greatest development ever made in that field."

At first glance, the map was a crude affair such as a child might have drawn from memory, showing the "northwest parts of the United States" in 1785, from the Ohio to the Canadian border. Then I saw it was engraved. It was dotted with queer comments on places and things, and had been made by one John Fitch.

"What on earth has it to do with ships?" I demanded.

Miss Noble smiled.

"So I can still teach you something. Did you never hear of this man Fitch?"

"Never."

A faint color rose in her cheeks.

"Oh! You've missed something really great!" she said earnestly. "He made the map from his own surveys along the frontier. He learned to engrave by doing powder-horns for Indians, and brass buttons for British soldiers, when he was a Revolutionary prisoner. But the greatest thing of all—"

She paused, a trifle embarrassed by her own enthusiasm. Then:

"Fitch was the kind of man you read about in ancient sagas, the primitive hero type, who fights an eternally losing battle with destiny, yet clings to his ideal and struggles on, rising superior to disaster. At every turn of his life, a malign fate smote him in the very instant of success; but how he fought back! It's a story that ought to be in every schoolbook. He was a plain, hard, uncouth Yankee, rugged as an oak, with a smattering of education."

"I thought you said it had to do with ships?" And I tapped the old engraved map.

"It has everything to do with them! You'll see. And his story is the most American thing I know, in its ingenuity and indomitable resolution. You see, I must make you visualize the man himself.... But are you interested?"

"Very much," I replied. She drew a deep breath, smiled again, and smoothed out her skirts with the old prim gesture I remembered from twenty years back.

"It grips me, the story of that man," she went on slowly. "He had great expectations, when he made that map. He had every reason to think he would be appointed surveyor to the new Northwest Territory, which not only carried a salary, but meant that his land-grant to thousands of acres would be confirmed. Politicians got ahead of him, and another man was appointed surveyor. At one blow he had lost everything. But I do want to make you see what was in the man himself—"

And she did. A man held by a single flaming purpose, who just missed wealth as he missed everything else. A shrewd Indian-fighter, a surveyor of the frontier rivers and forests. A man struggling, and daily trampling down impossibility. A man all alone, but hardy, with queer gifts both of brain and of fingers, trudging the frontier traces and the streets of cities; a man presenting immortality to Benjamin Franklin—who, possessing it already, ignored the gift.

A man with the spark of vision in his brain, the vision of a boat propelled by steam power. A man otherwise empty-handed, but far from empty-headed. In that day, before railroads were known, the future of America seemed to lie in its waterways, in its canals and rivers and ports.

"Y' know, Cobe,"—and Fitch scratched that long nose of his, as he sat in the wheelwright's log shop which he called home, down in Bucks County, Pennsylvania,—"if Congress had app'inted me surveyor to the Northwest and upheld my land-grant, I'd be a rich man today! But it just ain't so. And times has changed. You got to have money to get anywhere, these days."

"Well, you got the map, John," said Cobe Scout, the wheelwright. "It'd ought to do right well. Folks going into the territories need a man, and yours is the thing to sarve 'em proper."

"Aye, it'll do, but it won't make me rich."

Fitch went on with his labor. Here was the sheet of copper; he had hammered it out and polished it himself. Now, with his sole tool a graver, he was engraving upon it his own map of the Northwest, fruit of his wanderings and surveys. The Northwest was being opened, and people had need of such a map, and there was none to serve their purpose. He was doing a beautifully precise job of it, too.

"I seen Charley Garrison today," said the wheelwright. "He says, sure, you can use his cider-press to print your map on. Only you got to clean it up afterward."

So the map was born, beyond civilization and printing-presses.

Fitch was fired to the task, the horizon opening to his vision of a boat not driven by hands. It was nothing to him that never before had one man conceived, engraved and printed a map; John Fitch could do it, and did.

Then he set forth to sell his map for bread, and to sell his vision to those who might forward it. He knew nothing about steam or engines, but he learned. There were, indeed, only three engines in America at the time, and these were for pumping water.

So, that summer, he moved in upon Philadelphia with his maps and model boat and his wild, fierce hopes—a man bent upon conquest. Selling his maps on the way, he fought doggedly on to Trenton and on to the seat of government in New York itself, interviewing man after man of prominence, displaying plans and sketches and boat model. Man after man approved it, somewhat blankly, and gave him letters to the next.

In New York, a petition to Congress went into a committee waste-basket. But the Spanish minister met this wild-eyed, hard-jawed man and caught fire from his vision, shared his enthusiasm, and approved his designs. Here was a definite offer. Money? It would be supplied for experiments, by

all waters of the State. Recognition! No money, but that would come, and meantime the maps sold well. Now back to Philadelphia, where he knew many prominent men, to form a stock-company. Fitch went at it with feverish energy, and after a week of hard work he had the job completed. Four hundred dollars was subscribed. Better still, three hundred was paid down on the nail—with which to build the first steamboat.

The hard-jawed, hard-handed trudger had never so much as seen a steam engine. With the horizon of his vision overpassed, he was now face to face with cold reality; being the man he was, he pitched at it headlong....

Over a dram in a tavern, he met Henry Voigt, the clockmaker of Second Street, a handsome, stubborn Dutchman. The story was told; there was a quick glow of hot eyes, a swift exchange of words, a flying of sparks. The two men somehow clicked. It was an electric meeting.

"My hand on it!" Voigt stretched his arm across the table, gripped the hard bony fingers of Fitch, and rolled forth a joyous oath: "Be damned to the lot of'em—we'll show them! You and I can do it, man, and do it we will. You've got a workshop?"

"Well," Finch grinned happily, "there's an old warehouse down on the shore that can be rented. I reckon we can have the place to ourselves. I've got an idea about working the side paddles by a shaft and chain, like I said. If you and I can build the engine—"

"Build it? We can build a dozen!" cried Voigt. "We'll have to make a model, to be sure of it. Meantime, we can try out your chain-and-paddle contraption, to see if it works all right. Bring your designs and plans over to the shop, right now."

Fitch was all in a glow, inspired by achievement and a new horizon. Late into the night the two men talked, and with every moment grew more sure of one another. They separated with rum-fumes and vision sadly intermingled, but with the design of the engine somehow worked out and settled.

Now the old warehouse by the Delaware took

all means; and in return, naturally, exclusive rights must go to Spain.

"Not by a long shot!" declared John Fitch, folding up his designs. "Not while I'm an American!" He never thought again of the Spanish offer; not even with a regretful twinge in dark days.

Back he wandered to Philadelphia, with his horse-cart; there he saw the aged Ben Franklin, and presented his model and plans to that gentleman's Philosophical Society. Then on back to Bucks County again, serenely confident that Franklin was behind him and would see him through. Vain confidence! His wakening was bitter.

More tramping and map-selling. Now to Mount Vernon, to see General Washington, and another blank draw; the old General was not interested in steamboats. On to Richmond and to Patrick Henry—a great name. The same dogged presentation of letters, the same eager argument; and, in a sudden blaze, encouragement from the Virginia Assembly. No money, true, but many promises.

Heartened by this, the gaunt, rugged figure trudged on into Maryland and on into New Jersey, and here the spark struck fire. In March, 1786, the legislature gave him exclusive steamboat-rights on on life and hummed with frenzied activity. When Fitch flung himself into an enterprise, he went at it full vigor and energy, and Henry Voigt was like him. The two men moved in, working early and late, and to Fitch's vast delight, he discovered in Voigt a genius for mechanics, that could translate his somewhat chimerical notions into hard fact. They were a perfect team, each complementing the other.

The model steam engine, with a one-inch cylinder, progressed under their combined efforts; if it proved feasible, the next step would be one with a three-inch cylinder to be installed in a skiff. But first came the mechanism that was to be worked by this power of steam, and Voigt was keenly impressed by the importance of this point.

Before the model was completed, Fitch had the paddle mechanism with its endless chain in shape. To make sure this would propel a boat, they decided to give it a trial by hand. Fitch began to realize this was, indeed, the crucial point of the whole affair. Unless the boat was sent forward, the engine would be useless.

So the mechanism was installed in a light skiff; and out of the water it worked like a charm. On the afternoon of July 20th, they launched the skiff with its apparatus in place, and Fitch went to work at the shaft.

In no time at all, a crowd gathered along the wharves to observe the operation. Boatmen and roustabouts, loungers and townfolk, to whom Voigt was a well-known and highly respected tradesman. Fitch worked away; he stared at Voigt, mopped his face, fell to labor again. The machinery moved, but the boat did not. A few jeering cries came from the crowd, quickly taken up and increased by other voices.

"No go, Harry," said Fitch despondently. Voigt flushed under the storm of catcalls and jeering remarks, then turned white as a sheet.

"For God's sake, get out of this, then," he snapped. "I've let myself in for this tomfoolishness—it'll ruin me. Take the oars! Let me out of this accursed skiff!"

Fitch fell to work at the oars, and rowed ashore, stunned and heartbroken. As the skiff touched, Voigt jumped to the landing stairs and departed without a word. Fitch put away the boat, and made no response to the free-and-easy remarks hurled after him; but as he walked up the street his spare, lean frame drooped. He stopped in at a tavern and called for rum, and more rum.

Next day he wakened sick and despondent, courage gone out of him. No work this day; no word from Voigt. Everything was ended. His great hope had been that the steam-engine would work his chain-and-paddle mechanism; now it was smashed. The very foundation of his whole work was gone.

A heartsick, terrible day. Night came at last; he had not left his boarding-house. He lay awake, staring into the darkness as the hours sounded. Midnight came and went. One o'clock—suddenly it flashed into his mind. He leaped out of bed, trembling with eagerness as the vision took hold. He saw the thing in a split second, lit a candle, sat down to table and made a rough draft. Cranks, of course! Cranks and paddles—why, there was the answer!

In the cold dawn he went to Voigt's house on Second Street, called Voigt down in nightcap and gown, and spread the diagram before him with excited words. Voigt eyed it sleepily; his face cleared; suddenly he took Fitch by the shoulders.

"You've got it!" he cried, his eyes ablaze. "You've *got* it, John! Come on down to the shop—wait till I get some clothes—"

They went back to work together.

Once more they were united in a common vision, and the weather mattered not at all to them; they labored on through the hot sweating days, the steaming nights. The tiny engine model was completed, and it worked admirably.

Now came the three-inch cylinder, and this moved on apace, while the cranks and paddles were brought to proper adjustment and tested. Money ran low, but what of that? Success meant that further funds would be provided. In a frenzy of enthusiasm, the larger engine was finished up and tried, and found perfect enough, it seemed. Now for the boat, and no public test this time, with half the town looking on!

Quietly, without a word to anyone, the two men shoved out into the river on a warm summer's morning. They crammed the firebox. They watched the machine anxiously. Steam mounted, and more wood was shoved in. Before their intent gaze, the piston began to chug bravely away. The cranks and paddles fell to work. The skiff moved. It moved upstream! It kept on moving, and it gained speed.

"Done it!" An exultant yell burst from Voigt as he clapped Fitch on the shoulder. "It works, John, it works! Look at her go!"

The haggard, lined features of John Fitch warmed and relaxed. A glow came into his deep eyes; here,

After all, there was no monopoly on the thing except in New Jersey waters. Anybody could steal the idea. Fewer stockholders appeared. Commercial profits? Perhaps; but they were not visible.

Grim and sunken-eyed, his lips compressed, John Fitch stared across the tavern table at Henry Voigt. Success had come and gone. The fight had to be waged all over again. Fitch flew into a rage with the blind fools who could not see his own vision.

"But I'll manage the money somehow!" he swore. "Sell the model, seek capital elsewhere, sell my own stock if needs must—but I'll do it!"

"We'll do it," corrected Voigt. The company had magnanimously voted him two shares of the stock to recompense his labors.

Letters, appeals, frantic cries to the Pennsylvania Assembly; the result was nil. Weeks passed into months. The stockholders lost interest.

Suddenly Voigt had an idea. The New Jersey monopoly was bootless, but with similar patents from other legislators, interest would spring up. More documents would bring in more money. Why not try?

Fitch tried, but Pennsylvania remained chill to his pleas. Then, in February of 1787, the tide turned. The Delaware Assembly granted the requested monopoly there. Flushed with this success, Fitch went to New York. He interested Alexander Hamilton, and in March an act was passed; with this monopoly in his pocket, Fitch found Pennsylvania suddenly inclined to favor him. Another monopoly there. Everything was coming now!

And Voigt was correct. Documents drew money; the stockholders woke up, the cash was voted, the large boat was ordered.

for the first time, all his labor and vision and dream were justified. He said nothing; but as he watched the shores flit past at a good six miles per hour, the cup of his happiness brimmed to the full. The impossible had come true; his faith had borne fruit. Words, at such a time, were such little things!

The news was broken to the stockholders next day.

Dr. Say the philosopher, the baker, the butcher, the merchants and others, were all assembled. The tale of success was told, the skiff was put to work. All the money had been used up, but here was success undoubted! The company was amazed, exultant, grateful.

Now to make the thing commercially profitable. A forty-five-foot boat would be required, and must be constructed at once. Fitch calculated that an engine with a twelve-inch cylinder would furnish sufficient power.

No one, however, would put up the additional capital.

At this and further meetings, new questions arose.

The boat was built. Once more the old warehouse saw Fitch and Voigt hard at it, day and night, laboring over the large engine. Day after day, week after week, until June wore on again and all Philadelphia jeered at the inventors. After repeated and heartbreaking efforts, Voigt's genius at last brought the large engine to passable perfection.

And the boat worked! Once again, success!

It worked, but imperfectly. Fitch, however, learned by the failings of this engine. He saw that the cylinder must be larger, the entire style of the job must be recast. There was no money in the thing yet; it must be made right. No money? The stockholders sat aghast when he told them the blunt truth. Ye gods! The man was mad!

Not mad, but destitute.

Sacrifices were made; stock was sold; and after grim hard months of labor, a new engine sat in the now battered hull. A public trial was made now. Fitch and Voigt were confident that no weak spot had been overlooked. Exultant triumph was ahead this time!

In 1787 the tide turned... Fitch went to New York—interested Alexander Hamilton. Everything was coming now!

And they were right. Triumph indeed! Crowds were everywhere to see the sight. The paddles chunked merrily, the boat walked up the current at a fair speed. A delegation from Bucks County was on hand to applaud success, boats and ships sent cheers of amazement and delight across the water. The roar of cannon sounded in congratulation.

The chugging craft bore on upstream to Burlington, where a tremendous crowd waited. She was headed in for the Burlington Landing and the ovation there—and without warning the boiler blew out. Destiny had struck in the very instant of acclaim.

With it, the hearts of two men were close to breaking.

However, the boiler was replaced, and the boat began to make trips on schedule with gratifying regularity. At this point it developed that the craft was too slow for commercial use on the Delaware. She was losing money. A new hull must be had to give the proper speed. This discouraged the stockholders; many of them backed out altogether.

Voigt, facing stark poverty, took to drink and became quarrelsome, and withdrew from the whole thing.

Fitch, leaner and grimmer than ever, drove doggedly ahead. He made new gains, brought fresh men into the company, once more forged upstream. Money was put up and a new boat was built. Voigt was drawn in to work on the engine.

At last came the great day when it was tried out. The two friends looked on as the test was made, and words failed them. Here was perfection, absolute perfection! The engine was superb. The boat had speed, room, everything! At last, after so many failures, success was absolutely certain.

That night, malign fate struck again. The new boat took fire, burned, sank.

John Fitch gave up, momentarily. He trudged home to Bucks County in rags, cleaning and repairing clocks for a living. He had not a cent to his name. His vision had proven empty and barren. His stock in the company was gone. His maps no longer sold.

Yet the company, without him, made some headway. When he slogged back to Philadelphia, a gaunt and grim figure, to live on charity, the company was flourishing and at work on another and better steamboat. Fitch looked on and perceived mistakes, and voiced

That night, malign fate struck again: the new boat took fire, burned, sank.

his thoughts. Mistakes, one after another. This engine would not work, and he told them why. The stockholders, grudgingly, took him back into the company.

They were well repaid for the deed. The new craft was tried out. She worked to a charm, an accomplished success at last. In 1790 she covered nearly three thousand miles, running on a regular schedule. The ragged scarecrow was full fed and clothed now. One day a fine gentleman came and watched the boat running. Aaron Vail was this man's name—he was newly appointed a consul in a French port.

"Come to France with me," he said to John Fitch. "I'll pay all expenses, and I'll get a patent from the king for your steamboat there—the French will be wild about this invention!"

And so John Fitch, a success at last, a tricolored cockade in his hat, backing and fame assured him, stepped aboard a packet and sailed away.

I looked up in surprise as Miss Noble ceased speaking. She seemed to have forgotten me; she had fallen into thoughtful, half-puzzled reflection.

"Well?" I prompted her, and at sound of my voice she started slightly and turned to me. "Well? So we leave your hero there, with fame and success ahead?"

She smiled slightly.

"Oh, that's not quite the end, you know! The boat was built in France; patents were granted; everything was lovely—and then the Revolution broke, and the whole thing fell like a house of cards. Fitch came home. His boat here had not made money. Litigation arose, bickering, and struggles. The invention worked perfectly, but there was no profit in it. Fitch, a spectral figure, disappeared into the backwoods whence he had come. He was still unbowed by destiny. The last we hear of him, he was hoping to get a steamboat built on the Ohio. And there the curtain falls."

I drew a deep breath.

"At least, the man lives again in your words, Miss Noble! The man, struck down time after time at the very moment of success—still struggling on! Heroic in his failure—is that what you meant by your primitive type of hero?"

"No," she said rather tartly, "it's not. Heroic failure, indeed! Can't you see that it was a heroic success—that this man, breasting a continual evil destiny, was himself a great figure, a great emblem of success?"

"Success?" I shrugged. "Hardly success, as the world understands the word."

"Doesn't success mean anything higher to you?" she broke in. "Doesn't it mean anything nobler or finer than the worldly hope men set their heart upon? If Fitch's plans and designs were stolen and used by others, if he died poor, like Christ—can you call it failure? Then look at this." She flung down a postcard before me. "Look at this, and think of John Fitch every time you see it."

The postcard held a colored view of a great ocean liner.

LONG TOM O' DEVON

Kenny halted the car and turned to me.

"Get out," he said abruptly. "This is one of the most remarkable places in America."

I got out, gaping around. Nothing seemed unique about it to my eyes; the shore curved in below the road with a snug strip of yellow beach. For an hour Kenny had been driving in a mad maze of New York suburbs, highly confusing to a foreigner from California; whether this was New Rochelle or Larchmont, I had no clear idea.

Kenny led me down to the beach. He's one of those men with what might be called a well-rounded education, rarely found these days when education seems an angular, highly specialized affair. Kenny knows something about everything, and a lot about some things.

"Run that sand between your fingers," he said, squatting down. "It's an experience you'll never have again, unless you return here."

I obeyed, puzzled. It looked like sand; it felt like sand: it was sand.

"What's the catch?" I demanded.

Kenny drew a letter *A* in the sand, with his finger; from this he extended a wriggly line to a second point, *B;* from this a long straight line to a third point, which he marked *C.*

"This is where we are now," he said. "This letter *C.* Get it?"

"I see, yes," was my reply.

Kenny frowned slightly; he dislikes levity when he's serious. He pointed to a building.

"That house, we'll call *X,*" he observed. "It doesn't look up to much. It's old. It was built a long time ago out of ship's timbers, according to local report. The ship's timbers are still in it, though it's been modernized and made into a swell house. Now, you keep running that sand through your fingers. Does it feel queer?"

"No," I declared. "It's just like any other sand."

Kenny shook his head. "It is not. No other sand in America is like it. Now, this,"—and he indicated his sand-drawings,—"is a diagram which symbolizes one of the most pronounced and dramatic advances in shipping which has ever taken place. Sailing-ship design, you know, has exerted a profound influence on commerce and history—"

"What the devil are you driving at?" I demanded. "What has the history of sailing-vessels got to do with your normal flair for letting blood?"

He grinned. "Boy, this is a story fairly smoking with hot blood! That's a fact. Long Tom o' Devon knocked 'em off hard and fast, believe me; he had to do it, in his business. He had to do it if he wanted to go on living—and not living alone, either. She was a squire's daughter, you see."

I blinked at him. "This time I don't see. You and your diagram and your squire's daughter—are you gone daft? Not to mention sailing-ship design."

"Oh, that's really the nub of the whole thing!" he rejoined. "You see, in the latter part of the Eighteenth Century, the south coast of England did a roaring trade in smuggled goods otherwise highly dutiable—spirits, tobacco, and so forth. Half the fishermen were really smugglers, and everyone sympathized with them. The gentry put up money for the traffic, and many a fine big house in those parts today was built on the proceeds. The penalties were heavy, and the smugglers did not hesitate to put up a stiff fight if caught in the act. There's your background, with half the British Navy trying to stop the business and failing. The smugglers had guns too, and used them in a pinch. Long Tom o' Devon got that name because of the Long Tom mounted aboard his lugger—a long twenty-four.

"That craft of his was big, and she was fast as the devil. A lugger; the type had come in for cross-Channel work—"

"Luggers be hanged! Who was this Long Tom o' Devon?" I inquired.

Kenny gave me a pained glance, and then shrugged slightly.

"I was getting to that. He was just a name; a mystery, to people in general. Some said he was a Frenchman who had made himself into a great smuggler; some said he was a fine gentleman from London who had gone broke and turned to smuggling; his crew must have known, but did not talk. He flitted about, landed his tubs of spirits and tobacco of a dark night, and was gone. He seemed to have an uncanny knowledge of all the traps set to catch him. Twice he was nabbed, and fought his way clear, with a desperate ferocity that made an impression, even in those desperate days.

"No one could catch up with him. His lugger had the heels of anything afloat; she was a three-master, and had a dipping lug with topsail on the foremast, which was in the very eyes of the vessel. So with the mainmast, while the mizzen set a lug with outrigger and topsail. So much for Long Tom's darling. As for Long Tom himself, only one person in the world knew or suspected that he was Geoffry Craven."

With all his skipping about from diagrams to shipping rigs, Kenny had reduced me to utter bewilderment, and I said so. He merely grinned, and retorted that the prologue was necessary, and that I'd get the hang of it all in good time. With this, he launched into the yarn of Geoffry Craven and what happened at Squire Cardigan's fine old house on the Devon coast.

Craven came swinging up to the house all unsuspecting, a fine figure of a man as he crunched the gravel of the drive. He was looking forward to seeing Alice Cardigan, but what he saw was one of the grooms coming on the run to warn him. Perhaps the grooms, like the country people, suspected a little about Long Tom o' Devon.

"What's wrong?" asked Craven, his gray eyes sharp and alert.

"Visitors, sir," and the groom touched his forelock. "I thought best to tell 'ee a coach is here, wi' Sir John Hardesty and another officer, up from Plymouth on business wi' the squire."

"Oh, Hardesty! He's the captain of that new cutter they've been outfitting, eh?" Craven nodded, and his gay smile came out again as he tossed a coin to the groom. "Here's a lucky piece for you, my lad, and thanks. Miss Alice is at home?"

"Aye, sir—in the garden, all of 'em."

To the garden Craven went, bold as you please, though there was no love between him and his cousin Sir John. His arrival created something of a sensation. Bluff Cardigan met him with surprise and chill formality, but welcomed him. Alice regarded him with wide eyes of alarm. Hardesty, precise and aquiline and savagely cynical, did not dissemble his dislike. The other officer, a young lieutenant, perceived nothing wrong at all and shook hands heartily.

"We've met ere this," snapped Hardesty, at the introduction.

Craven chuckled.

"Aye, cousin John, long ere this! And you're still a fine gentleman in His Majesty's service, with your stiff collar and cold eye. And, God help me, I'm still a graceless runagate who prefers country to town, honest fishermen to honeyed courtiers, a good horse and a hard morning's run to lolling about a coffee-house or wasting my earnings at high stakes."

"Earnings!" repeated Hardesty with contempt. "Earnings, indeed! Are you in trade, that you should talk of earning money?"

"Aye, in trade, and a disgrace to the family," Craven said cheerfully, tipping Alice a wink. "But don't let me interrupt, gentlemen. A drink and a pipe—I have my own pipe, with your permission.... Good tobacco you have, Cardigan. Smuggled stuff, I'll warrant you!"

He made himself breezily at home, disregarding the anxious glances of Alice, who was in talk with the lieutenant.

Sir John Hardesty rather stiffly went on with his business. This was to urge Squire Cardigan, as a magistrate and man of position, to cooperate in putting down smuggling hereabouts. Cardigan evaded, up to a certain point, but was pressed into consenting. Craven put in a word now and then, slyly, which increased Cardigan's embarrassment. Far from having any sympathy with the coastguard, Cardigan had many a tub of tobacco and spirits in his cellar at this moment.

"However," he said at length, "if you have any scheme for catching this fellow they call Long Tom o' Devon, I'm with you on it."

"That's the nub of the whole affair," said Hardesty, eying Craven. "But I've no mind to speak too far in the presence of others. This precious cousin of mine would be only too glad to tip off a ruffian like Long Tom."

"True for you," said Craven, beaming. "However, cousin John, I'd hate to spoil the sport. I'll inform nobody—you have my word on it."

Hardesty nodded stiffly. "And your daughter, sir?"

Cardigan turned to Alice, who laughed and promised secrecy. In that day, when a man's word meant more than any bond, Hardesty might well be satisfied.

"Very well, Cardigan," said the officer. "You'll see why I need your help. This rascal Long Tom has a remarkably fast lugger, but I think I've ended her glory and that of all other smuggling craft of the kind. I've a cutter outfitting at Plymouth, and finished, which embodies some new principles. To cope with these luggers, the ordinary cutter won't do. We need a craft heavy enough to carry guns, stout enough to keep the sea at all times, and speedy enough to run down a lugger."

"No small order!" Craven chuckled. "I'd love to see one of your cutters trying to overhaul a lugger on a reach!"

"You'll see it, sir," snapped Hardesty. "Now, I shan't go into details, but I've fitted my craft with a new rig—it will set a precedent for the Royal Navy, I believe. The Admiralty is already studying the plans. I've learned a bit about this Long Tom, who usually lands his cargoes along the coast. In fact, his last cargo was landed a week ago at Tor Bay, two miles from here. He's expected back in about three weeks from today, and if you'll lend a hand, we'll nip the rascal for good."

Craven puffed hard at his pipe and avoided the glance of Alice. Good Lord! The man had everything exact. Somebody must have played Judas.

"Very well, sir," Cardigan said with energy. "Count me with you. I'd indeed be glad to make sure that this rascal would never land another cargo! My tenants have been demoralized by his goings-on. Only three months past, he fought his way out of a trap, killed half a dozen men, and emptied his guns into a brig that tried to halt him. Why, the fellow's no better than a pirate!"

Hardesty warmed. "Egad, sir, I'm glad to hear such sentiments from you! Then it's agreed. On Monday, I'm taking out my cutter for trials. Three weeks from tonight, I'll have twenty coastguards here under your orders to block the paths up the cliffs. The lugger usually runs in after dark, on a signal from the shore folk that all's clear. Let the signal be made on this occasion; keep your men hidden. I'll arrange with a second cutter to show up an hour after dark and scare our man off—slap into my hands. I'll be hanging off and on to await him. This, of course, depends on the weather being fine. If otherwise, it'll be the next night, or the first fine one. You understand?"

So taken and accepted. Sir John Hardesty refused to stay the night, having a dinner engagement at Plymouth. He made his farewells, bowed stiffly to Craven, and departed with his lieutenant.

When their coach had left, Cardigan returned to Craven, who was standing deep in talk with Alice. He went up to them, took Craven by the shoulder, and looked into his eyes.

"Now, Geoffry Craven, it's no time for slippery words," he said grimly. "We've been friends, we've done business together, I've made you welcome here. That's ended. You got my letter, requesting you not to enter this house again?"

"I got it. That's why I came," said Craven steadily. "Such discourtesy must have a reason, I think?"

Cardigan glanced at his daughter and ordered her out of the room. Craven nodded slightly, and she departed. The bluff squire turned to his visitor again, and indulged in no weasel words. He was a blunt man.

"Craven, I'm no fool. I can guess that either you're one of Long Tom's agents, or his lieutenant; for all I know, you may be the rogue himself! That's neither here nor there, for our relations are ended."

"Out of this, and for good!" he ordered. "Don't attempt to see my daughter or I'll pistol you!"

"Why?" asked Craven coolly.

"Gad, sir! I've waked up to your impudence, that's why—you're daring to lift your eyes to my daughter!"

"What of it?" Craven smiled a little. "Come, come, man! I'm of good birth. I've made money in the game. My name's not clouded; and, if you consent to the match, I'll quit the trade entirely."

"You infernal scoundrel!" snapped Cardigan. "Why, damme, sir, have you the insolence to suggest that you'd ask my daughter to live on money earned in such fashion?"

"I fail to see the distinction, since you've certainly pocketed enough by your own dealings with Long Tom—"

Cardigan flew into a rage, having no answer to this truth.

"Out of this, and for good!" he ordered. "Don't come into this house again. Don't attempt to see my daughter, or I'll pistol you! It's too much to expect that you'll keep your word about warning this rogue of what you've overheard today—"

Geoffry Craven bowed slightly. "Since you think so ill of my honor, sir, I suppose I should bluster and call you out and so forth. I prefer to leave you to your own sad ignominy. A man so utterly illogical as you are, creates his own hell. Good day, sir."

He departed, humming a gay tune; but this was more affectation than reality.

As he passed the stables, he encountered the groom who had warned him. Beckoning the man. Craven handed him another coin—a yellow one.

"Now, Tom, listen well," said he. "The squire and I are no longer friends, but I'd have you get a word to Miss Alice for me—it'll be the last time. Tell her it's for Tuesday night, and to take no chances."

He stepped briskly away down the drive. At the corner of the house, he heard a little voice call his name, and glanced up. At the window of her room was Alice. He blew her a kiss, flung her a smile and a wave of the hand, and went his way.

In the fishing village under the cliffs, Craven came to the tavern and found there a dark, merry, foreign man whose teeth flashed in a smile of greeting.

"The horses, Pierre!" he said shortly. "And quick about it. No talk. We must get back to the lugger and away before dawn."

Two good horses were brought out and saddled. A bite and a tankard, and the two men rode away together. Once at the top of the cliffs and on their road, Craven reined in.

"Pierre, somebody's blown the works," he observed. "Everything's known, about the next cargo; even to the very spot and the time."

"So! Then you'll change the plans?" asked the Frenchman.

"I will not!"—and Craven laughed. "I may advance them a trifle, but I'll not change them. All I'll change is the future. On Monday, lad, we'll discover just what the Royal Navy has up its sleeve. Cousin John's a canny seaman; if he's done what he says, the next cargo will be the last for me. I'll take that cargo of wines for Alexandria that the Bordeaux Merchants have offered, and become an honest trader."

"Alexandria! In the Levant?" gasped Pierre. "But, m'sieu, one cannot make money by being honest!"

Craven laughed heartily at this philosophy. "I've other plans, lad," he said.

On Monday, with a spanking breeze out of the west, Captain Sir John Hardesty took his newfangled navy cutter out of Plymouth and set to work testing her paces. She was like nothing ever seen, and good to look upon. Of big displacement, with her greatest draft at the heel, she was sturdily built and amazingly strong aloft, with lofty topmasts, long yards, long bowsprit and booms, with extra stout shrouds, backstays and runners, and with canvas to make any seaman stare.

Sir John Hardesty

The lugger that swaggered insolently along certainly stared, as did Geoffry Craven aboard her, and Pierre and all his foreign crew. Being well to leeward of the cutter, up went her canvas in no time. Pierre grinned.

"We'll run from her quick enough, m'sieur! You'll see."

"I don't like what I see, Pierre." Craven lowered his glass, then lifted it again, as he stood beside the Frenchman. "Take a look. My good cousin has done something that may prove original. In fact, the British Navy should make him an admiral—"

An exclamation broke from Pierre. The cutter, hauling about to overtake the lugger, was suddenly crowding on unsuspected sail, her yards spotted with men at work. Craven, watching, began to count the canvas aloud.

"Jib, fore staysail, and she's got a square-sail for'ard, topsail and square t'gallant sail—look at it bloom out! Square stunsails on either side of the topsail. What's that triangular canvas above the yard of the lower course? Oh, I get it! The thing fills the gap left by the goreing of the topsail—then her mainsail, and a ringtail set abaft the leach—good Lord!"

"And every one of them drawing," groaned Pierre. "She has the legs of us, m'sieu. She can sail circles around us!"

"Not quite; but that's all I want to know. Now try her out—take the helm!"

Two hours, three hours, the lugger maneuvered as though trying frantically to escape from this towering mass of canvas. Speedy as she was, the cutter was faster. On the wind, into the wind, the cutter had the advantage any way the game was played.

Craven, watching narrowly, could give his cousin full credit. Here, he knew, was an evolution in rigging which bade fair to change all seamanship. With cutters like this, the King's men could sweep the comparatively clumsy luggers off the seas—that is, in theory?

"One thing they don't count on," he asserted, as he prepared to duck below. "Everything shipshape, Pierre? Yes, I see it is. Take the deck, then."

He vanished, as a gun sounded from the cutter and the shot dropped in the ocean ahead.

Sail fell off. A boat came aboard, with Hardesty in person. An armed lugger? But yes, m'sieu. Why not? France and England were not at war just now. An honest ship laden with wines. Papers in order, cargo in order. Suspect as he might, Hardesty had no proof. Craven was stowed snugly away below. The boat pulled back at last, and the lugger set her course again for Bristol—supposedly.

When night drew on, a small boat set Craven ashore.

"Get across to Cherbourg, load your cargo, and come back on schedule," he told Pierre at parting. "Send this letter to the Bordeaux Merchants for me. You know where to pick me up when you return. Leave the landing details to me. And, mind you, it may mean trouble! They're out to nip us this trip."

Pierre showed his white teeth. "Give the orders, m'sieu—we obey!"

"Then have the guns loaded and shotted when you pick me up; double-shotted, with bags of bullets," said Craven, and went down into the boat that was to land him.

On Tuesday, as sunset deepened into dusk, he was riding along a dale, half a mile from the Cardigan manor. He came to a bridge crossing the rivulet, and there a horse was waiting; and beside the horse, stood Alice.

They met in silence—in a long embrace, a long look, a swift happy smile.

"Your father?" asked Craven.

"In Plymouth. I'm afraid, my dear, he's in earnest."

"Faith, so am I in earnest!" and the gray eyes twinkled at her. Then they sobered. "My dear, will you marry me despite him?"

"Of course," she said simply. "But it can't be done in England."

"Then it'll be done out of England, if you'll trust me," he said gravely, holding her two hands, looking into her eyes. "If you'll trust me, and trust the future. It needs so much trusting, my heart! It's enough to frighten any woman—"

"Devon women aren't cowards," she said quietly. "Listen, dear. He suspects that you're Tom o' Devon himself. Somebody must have talked."

"Somebody has talked—we've some traitor in the crew," said Craven. "No matter. I can't ask you to marry Long Tom o' Devon; but will you come with me when Long Tom makes his last landing? Will you come to France, and marry Geoffry Craven there?"

"I will, as you know," she replied, and gripped his fingers hard. "What's in the future, that I must trust so hard?"

"All of life, and a new world," he said. "We land our tubs here; I'm committed to putting this cargo ashore. It'll make me absolute owner of the lugger, with money enough besides. We go back to Bordeaux, and from there take an honest freight to Alexandria, with good pay. And from Egypt, we make a long traverse for America. Can you face that, my heart? All the chances of sea and of life, for the two of us?"

Her face lit up suddenly. She was a deep-eyed, deep-bosomed young woman, with red roses in her cheeks, quiet measuring gaze, and none too ready words. But now her words came suddenly, to second the swift springing glory and love in her eyes.

"Oh, my dear! All the chances of sea and life—why, what more could I ask than such a honeymoon?"

"You'll not regret to leave your father?"

"Yes," she said honestly. "But I'd regret more to leave you and all the rest of life, my dear. Kiss me."

Craven stooped to her lips. Then she drew away, still holding his hands.

"I must tell you—they know exactly when and where you're going to land!" she exclaimed.

He laughed lightly.

"They think so. No one knows that except Tom Long—and you. Instead of Tor Bay, it's the cove ten miles east. Instead of after dark, it's in broad daylight—in the middle of the afternoon. Should weather or aught else spoil the landing, it'll be the next day."

"But—the shore folk will have to be told about the change in plans!" she exclaimed. "Somebody will have to know in advance. And if anyone knows, someone may tell. They've put a reward of a hundred guineas for your capture."

"Too cheap by far!" And Craven broke into an amused chuckle. "What you say is true. The Sunday before the landing, tell that groom of yours about the change. He'll spread the word to the right people. We'll be met—and no one will blab."

She stared. "Our groom—then he's one of your men! All right. But, my dear, think of the risks! Sir John's new cutter, and the other one—"

"You'll share the risks," said Craven gravely. "Two days before the landing, I'll pick you up. A boat takes us west along the coast—the lugger picks us up there."

"West?" she questioned. "But your lugger comes from France!"

"Precisely," he said, smiling. "No one suspects we'd come from the west, but thus it is. Are you content to share the risks? If caught, it means everything to you—"

"If not caught, it means everything!" She dimpled suddenly. "Ah, my dear, but you're a man to face the world with, for good or ill!"

He took her in his arms, kissed her.

"And you," he said huskily, "you're a woman to live and die with, my dear; God bless the two of us! Now, then, you know the landing's on a Tuesday. I'll come to the door of your house on Sunday evening at seven, with an extra horse ready. You'll have to leave behind everything except what you can carry."

"No loss," said she, and laughed. "You'll come to the house itself?"

"I'm no sneak," he replied with a touch of anger. "Aye! Let your father ride after us and be damned to him! I know the roads. I'll take you from the door of your own house, for your pride and mine—"

As, in fact, he did when the day came. Alice had not forgotten the message through the groom, and next night the message went out to the right people.

On the Monday, a blunt-bowed fishing craft went dancing to the westward along the Cornish coast, to meet the lugger coming in from her wide sea-sweep—if indeed she came.

"Why not? The weather's good, and will hold good," said Craven to the woman beside him, as the fishermen scanned the horizon for the expected sail, and the little boat bowled along. "We gamble on Pierre—a good man. We gamble on life and wits and brawn, and on destiny."

"Perhaps on God," she said softly, and pressed his hand. A woman does not shrink from voicing what a man thinks only in his heart.

And while they gambled, the country folk gambled also. On the Tuesday morning, carts and men converged on a barren cove, ten miles west of Tor Bay. A daylight landing was something bold and rare, but they took no chances. In a dingle above the cliffs, the carts were hidden, and men let down lines, and other men were posted out every way as guards, and on the shingle below the boldest of them waited.

From the cliffs, lookouts scanned the sea. Off to the eastward, near Tor Bay, flashed the glint of canvas where the smaller cutter was taking her position. Off to the south, every now and then a fleck of white showed on the horizon, where Sir John Hardesty's new craft stood off and on.

Then, creeping in from the Cornish coast, came the old brown lugger with the weathered sails that did not show at a great distance, and her topsails doused. She came unhurriedly, and was hauling in almost before she was recognized.

She hove to off the shallows, and her hook dropped, and her canvas fell, and her boats were out. Men trooped aboard her in all haste to aid the crew, and stared at the cloaked woman who stood beside Long Tom o' Devon; and many a man recognized her and touched his forelock, but said no word.

Now the tubs went ashore—cognac and spirits of all kinds, tobacco, a bit of lace and other things. Ashore with them, any way at all, with a rush and a thump; ashore, and up the steep cliff paths, and away to the waiting carts. The Devon men joked in their uncouth jargon, the Frenchmen of the crew laughed and jabbered in their lilting bird-talk, Craven smiled and watched the tubs go ashore and up the cliffside.

"We're really doing it!" said the woman beside him, a thrill in her voice.

"Why not?" His gray eyes danced. "We've cleaned out most of it already. Another ten minutes, and we're off. If we—"

"Ahoy, below!" A thin voice came down from the top of the cliffs. Men paused, staring up. "Ahoy there! Cutter to the south'ard reaching in!"

Pierre came up on the jump. "M'sieur! She's bound to see us—we have no shelter—"

Craven's voice blared in fluent French and English, now at the seamen, now at the shore folk. The tubs were put over with a rush, the hatches were clapped on, the country folk went hurriedly ashore, the anchor came up. Canvas fluttered and lifted.

"Enough has gone ashore to win the game," said Craven. "But enough's under the hatches to damn us if caught. We can't get rid of it until night—"

"Looks like she's made us out!" hailed a man from aloft.

The brown sails were peaked to the wind, Pierre himself took the tiller, Craven beside him. The Frenchman indicated Alice at the rail, with an inquiring gesture.

"She stays," said Craven shortly.

A breeze rippled over the water. The lugger paid off by aid of her jib, and stood out. The cutter had changed course slightly, and with all canvas bellying, stood toward the lugger. At sight of her sailspread, the Frenchman pointed and talked excitedly. Pierre shook his head.

"Look how she cuts the water, m'sieu! No need to give her a race to tell that she has the heels of us," he said, and emitted a growl of oaths. "What can we do?"

Craven uttered a quick, ringing laugh.

"Do? Use our heads of course, until we must use our hands! Keep near shoal water, run along the shore; and keep that blasted cutter sailing on the wind. The breeze is freshening. This craft is new, her

"You," he said huskily, "you're a woman to live with and die with, my dear!"

evident that the cutter held command. Anxiety grew in her eyes.

"My dear, Sir John was right," she said quietly to the man beside her.

"Only too right," said he. "And your father the magistrate—is that what's in your mind?"

She searched his face. "You're still hopeful?"

"Faith, I don't hope; I know!" and as he spoke, his laugh rang out. "Look—look! Pierre! She's done it!"

Shouts arose from the men. Sure enough, the cutter's main boom had been topped, the sail bellying forward of the mast, the boom slapping up against it. Pierre's orders bellowed down the deck, and barely in time. The lugger, still dangerously wing-and-wing, was nearing a jutting point of rocks. The cutter's crew muzzled the mainsail, wrestled the boom amidships, and brailed up until the wind was on a safe quarter, then began to draw swiftly offshore.

"Shift over the sheets!" bawled Pierre. "Stand by to haul aft starboard—down mainsail—set mainsail—haul aft the main sheet—"

crew aren't used to her yet; sure as fate, she'll jibe! She won't sail by the wind while we're on the wind or she'd lose too much ground in tacking. If she jibes once, we'll have our chance to tack offshore—they'll be paying more attention to all that spread of canvas than to the ship—"

Pierre grasped the idea, and his voice blared out joyously.

"Look alive for'ard! Haul the foresail over—wing-and-wing!"

So they were off on what was to prove no short chase or merry jaunt, but a grim matching of wits and wits, ship and ship, hunter and hunted, with flame and death at the run's end.

Pierre knew by heart every reef and corner of this rocky coast. As the craft slipped through the water, as the time passed, even to Alice Cardigan it became

The lugger had come by the wind on the new tack. Craven watched as the minutes fled, as the afternoon wore. Always it was the same. The lugger would tack offshore, then square away, while the cutter had to duplicate every move—and sailed faster. But, being forced to go on the wind most of the time, Hardesty was cautious. To keep from jibing, she must continually brail up her mainsail before letting the wind shift, and so she lost precious way.

The thing could not last, however. Eventually, as the sun wore westward, the heading-off tactics of the cutter began to tell.

"We're losing," said the girl quietly.

Craven nodded, biting his lip.

"Aye. My worthy cousin is playing cat-and-mouse; he's got us, and knows it. He must know you're aboard, too. Clever fellow! And if he respects you, I must respect him and not play my one last card—"

A groan escaped him, then a shout of warning to Pierre. Too late.

Caught in a shallow bight with small room to maneuver, Pierre tried to come about, missed stays, and fell in irons. Desperately Pierre endeavored to send her around on her heel and let her fill, but under the lee of towering cliffs, the lugger had not enough way.

The cutter bore down. An officer leaped into the hammock nettings with a trumpet.

"Lugger, ahoy! Put down your helm and ease off on your main sheet. Fetch to, or I'll fire into you!"

"If you do, take the consequences!" shouted Craven furiously.

Pierre put down helm, eased his main sheet—just enough to pass under the stern of the cutter. A little gust of wind came off the land. The foresail and square topsail shivered. Pierre's voice lifted again. The lugger put her nose into the wind and shot ahead, clearing the cutter by a cable-length. The breeze picked up. She filled away on the larboard tack. But Craven, seeing the sudden stir aboard the cutter, seeing her swing around, seeing her ports fall, caught Alice about the waist.

"Down with you! Below! Pierre—get the cover off the Long Tom. By the Lord, the last card gets played—"

He had her below, on the ladder, when the broadside crashed from the cutter, when men shrieked along the lugger's deck, when the ship reeled to the belching rattle of iron. He shoved her down, ordered her to stay there, and was up again with a leap and a roar of gusty orders.

The Long Tom swung and lifted. Craven pointed the gun himself as the lugger rose and dipped and rose again. Once more—then match clapped to linstock, and the long gun boomed and the lugger reeled to the shock of her recoil.

A wild yell burst from the dark foreign men. The bags of bullets had gone slap into that towering mass of canvas, slap into the broadside below. And as the lugger fell away and went slipping through the water, picking up the wind and racing like a hound dog for the horizon and the coming night, behind her the cutter was a mass of fluttering canvas and severed lines, one spar carrying away and then another, a ruin of majesty....

"For France, my dear, for France!" And Craven brought the girl on deck again to point back at the hapless wounded thing behind. "For France and the new life, and the new world!"

"And for us," she said....

Kenny had finished his story; he made it quite obvious that he had finished. We were again looking out across Long Island Sound, and I discovered that I was still running that yellow sand through my fingers.

"So," I observed with sarcasm, "they just sailed away and lived happily ever after, huh? Is that your idea of a story?"

He looked up at me with his quick, flashing smile.

"You miss the whole point, with your impatience! Of course they went on and on, to Alexandria and finally over to—here." He waved his hand at the houses behind us, then jabbed down his finger on the spot marked *C.* "From *A,* on the Devon coast, to *B* at Alexandria, then here. Get it? The house I was talking about, back yonder, was built from the timbers of that lugger, years later."

"Do you call that the point of the story?"

"Not at all," he rejoined, with a sigh. "The point is, that Craven was dead right. There was only one answer to the cutter rig Hardesty had evolved—guns. Craven gave that answer and got away. Others didn't. That rig went into the Royal Navy and practically drove the smuggling luggers off the sea. Some smugglers even copied it and used the rig themselves. It became an integral part of sea lore. And Craven never knew it, probably, but that one blast from his Long Tom not only cut the rigging of Hardesty's ship to pieces, but it killed Hardesty."

"Oh!" I said thoughtfully. "That's not so bad for a kick-back. But what's all that yarn got to do with this sand? And why is this plain, ordinary sand so darned peculiar, anyhow?"

"It's not plain, ordinary sand!" And Kenny chuckled. "It's sand from the shores of the Nile—Egyptian sand, a whole shipload of it! Craven couldn't get any cargo from there for America, so he filled up with sand ballast and dumped it here. Any how, that's the local tradition, and local tradition is usually right. Now are you satisfied?"

HANGING JOHNNY

The Inner Harbor yacht anchorage is the place for curiosity-seekers who know a thing or two about sailing-ship rigs, old and new. There, rubbing strakes with the more modern craft, may be seen Chesapeake Bay bugeyes, Bahama spongers, Grand Bank codfishers, Down East fore-and-afters, and even South Sea outrigger war-canoes. For the movies and those who make them gather rigs from all the world over.

Some of the older wind-ships sail only for the movies. Some are still owned by die-hard masters, and still make a living for their owners. A crowd of us were watching one day when a tall-sparred skysail-yarder stood up for the anchorage behind a tug. Her patched canvas was harbor-furled. She was weathered and salt-crusted as if from a stormy voyage. When she swung, we saw between her crude quarter-davits the legend: *Sharon, New Bedford.*

"An old-time whaler!" exclaimed somebody.

"Whaler, nothing!" snorted old Cap'n Tucker, master-rigger in the shipyards. "It's Cap'n Charley Guntert's schooner *Lottie Carson* with a new dress. I set up them topmasts myself and rigged her square for the movies. And rigged her wrong, for whalers of her day."

"Another fake," said one of the yacht-club boat-keepers. "Well, she looks like a whaler, anyhow."

"She don't, neither," growled Cap'n Tucker. "I just told you I rigged her wrong. Them davits swung overside—whalers of the early period didn't have boat-davits."

Boat-davits! I had searched a hundred books on the sea without success, for certain information covering those two words; luckily, I kept silent. For Captain Tucker was a crusty soul, and only diplomacy would make him talk.

The others, too, eyed him warily. Cap'n Tucker was famous for his love of fiery Barbados rum, his crotchety temper and his tales of the sea.

"The movie people," I ventured, just to guide the matter aright, "must have known what they were about when they ordered those davits rigged. These days they're careful about ships and rigs in the pictures."

Cap'n Tucker snorted, thereby disposing of moving-picture research. One of the others, with a wink at me, put in a barb and prodded it.

"I suppose New Bedford whalers, like every other rag-wagon that ever sailed the ocean, are just nuts for you. Of course you know all about 'em."

The old skipper rose to the bait of sarcasm.

"I do!" he asserted, bridling. "If you Johnny-come-lately seamen knew as much about the gingerbread gas-barges you shine bright-work on, it'd be better for your owners."

"Sure, sure," agreed the heckler. "But that fake you rigged there—where'd you get the notion of a whaler with skysails? Was it from some ship named *Sharon* you shipped aboard when you were a lad, maybe?"

"Mebbe it was," snapped Cap'n Tucker. He fished out a blackened clay pipe and stuffed it with whittled navy plug, as though he had said his say.

I struck in promptly:

"Was there ever a New Bedford whaler of that name, I wonder?"

"There was," blurted the skipper. "And with a woman skipper. I got the log she kept; it's a hundred and seventeen year' old."

"Then she didn't have boat-davits on her ship," I said with an air of finality.

"She bad the first there ever was!" snapped Cap'n Tucker, with a glare at me. And then he was off, full steam. He began to talk as he puffed his clay pipe alight, and he kept right on talking; while we gazed out as the fake whaler came to anchor, he broke out the coil and unwound his yarn fathom by fathom.

Not that the Sharon left New Bedford with a woman skipper; not likely! As though we stood on her swaying poop, we could see Cap'n David Davids in the dawn, asleep in his canvas-backed chair cleated to the deck in the lee of the wheelhouse. The skipper always kept the deck, first night out, so the mates, who had set all the canvas and worked out the ship, could get some rest. Utility, not kindness; there was no kindness in Cap'n David Davids. Despite the potted flowers below, and the window-curtains, and the wife who sailed with him, he was the best-hated skipper, and the *Sharon* the worst hellship, afloat.

A frowsy seaman, one bleary eye cocked at the shivering main-topsail leach, held the *Sharon* before a stiff nor'wester. He cursed the ship and the skipper impartially, but his weary spirits lifted as a dark form padded forward on silent feet. It was the mate going to break out the drunks. Soon he would be relieved. The mate, aye, and a bucko! Johnny Carver, and a devil if there ever was one.

The whaler made dogged headway under bellying courses, huge single topsails, topgallants and royals. The dark eastern horizon began to light up faintly as Johnny Carver paused by the main fife-rail, then went on forward. A lean man, with eyes like the following sharks when the try-works were sooting up the heavens. If David Davids was the most cruel and rapacious of all skippers who sailed after oil, Johnny Carver was the best brutal driver in the fleet. A good pair, said sullen-eyed men.

With boot and a hardwood heaver used for beating down ice-stiffened sails, Johnny hazed the drunken crew up the orlop companion, just as the first reflections of the sun touched the royals with a rosy glow. They rubbed bleary eyes and stared dazedly, as he produced a greasy piece of paper.

"Line up there by the main hatch," he growled. "Answer to your names as you've marked 'em on the articles.... John Kane, A.B.!"

"Here, sir! But I didn't sign on—"

"Pipe down! You all signed for a three-year voyage after sperm. Robert Stone—Tom Avery—Philo Ramsgate—"

No answer to this last. Johnny Carver swept the motley file with challenging eyes, then looked to where a big-boned blond man sat in the lee of the forward house, cynically watching proceedings. A dirty, disheveled man in white shirt and trousers and silk stockings, obviously a gentleman in distress.

"You, Philo Ramsgate! On your pins! Aft here for muster."

The other never budged, and Johnny Carver started for him.

Lieutenant Philip Rand of the U.S.S. *Ranger* surveyed the mate with his cynical gaze, and laughed harshly as Johnny Carver halted before him.

"Now I know why I'm aboard Cap'n David's old fish-barge!" he observed. "I met you somewhere last night and stood you a drink, eh? That's all I remember. Shanghaied me, did you? Stripped me and shanghaied me! That's a joke, all right; but it's on you."

Johnny Carver glowered, and hefted the hardwood heaver.

"None of your fine airs with me, you thick-headed swab! I never clapped eyes on you before. The runner delivered you with the others, and all drunk."

"You lie," said Rand flatly.

"What? Look here, blast you! Signed on as Philo Ramsgate, you are—"

"Have it your own way," broke in Rand, with a shrug. "Cap'n Davids happens to be a friend of mine, my fine bucko."

"Oh!" said Johnny Carver with a sneer. "And I suppose the Missus is baking cakes for you right now, huh?"

"If you refer to Mrs. Davids, I don't know her, but I've heard a lot of her," Rand rejoined, with an air of casual chatting; but his eye was alert, for he guessed what was coming.

Swift as a striking snake, Johnny Carver lashed out with no warning at all. To his intense disgust, Rand not only dodged the heaver, but was up and on his feet, his own arm lashing out in return. The crack of the blow was sweet and clean, and the force of it sent Johnny Carver staggering back.

"Assault a United States officer, will you?" rasped Rand. "Try again if you want more of the same, my bucko."

Carver, his thin features contorted by a blaze of fury, clapped hand to pocket; a cry of warning came from the other men as he whipped out a little brass pistol. He had been struck and shamed before the men, and there was but one answer.

"Officer be damned!" said he, as he cocked the pistol. "There's no officers aboard this ship but me—"

Then came a paralyzing sound that halted everything, that unnerved both men and all who heard; the sound that brought every man aboard plunging to the windswept deck pellmell. A woman's scream of mortal anguish, so blood-chilling, lifting so eerily on the wings of the wind from aft, that it went through Rand like a knife.

Johnny Carver turned a pallid face, swung around, went aft at a run. Rand joined him. The other men trailed after. They halted beside the booby hatch at the break of the poop, staring up at the woman there. She was in seaman's trousers and boots, watch-cap and faded pilot jacket, her hair flying, and a look in her face of such frozen horror that it hit them like a blow.

"The Cap'n's dead," she said jerkily. "Dead. Stabbed while he slept in his chair. A knife in him. Lay up here, Mister. The rest of you scum, stay for'ard. Break out the mates and boat-steerers. Mister, do you know an order when you hear one?"

Johnny Carver wakened, and moved to the ladder obediently. The woman stood there, staring down at the rest of them.

Rand knew that she was the Captain's wife. He had heard of her. Davids had spoken of her only yesterday; she sailed with him, and her flower-pots and curtains made the *Sharon* a ship to talk about. She had a hard, bony face, a glitter in her eyes, a grim mouth.

It was not a good moment to choose, but Rand chose it. He saluted her and spoke.

"Lieutenant Rand of the Navy, ma'am. I was talking with your husband yesterday; I've known him on and off for some time. I was shanghaied aboard here—"

"Lay for'ard and clap a stopper on your jaw," she broke in. "I don't know you and never heard of you. Stow it."

She swung around, ignoring him, a woman of cold indomitable fury. The body of Cap'n Davids was stiffening in his chair; she ignored that, too, and fastened her eyes on the mustering afterguard. She listened as Johnny Carver questioned the frowsy helmsman.

"I dunno, sir," came the response. "I seen you go for'ard; it was too dark to see anything. I ain't even sure it was you. I hadn't no time to stare about the deck."

Mrs. Davids eyed them with that frozen glitter: Johnny Carver and the other two mates—the Dubois twins, Cain and Abel, Maine Indian halfbreeds, infamous rogues but peerless whalers and harpooners; alike and ugly as two cutting spades, their beady eyes were the only signs of life in their wooden brown faces. A little apart stood the three Portuguese boat-steerers from Santiago, rolling yellowish eyeballs.

"Since I'm in command now," spoke up Johnny Carver, "I'll call all hands and get to investigating—"

"You're not in command," spoke up Mrs. Davids. "The Cap'n is dead, but that doesn't make you master. You'll stay in your place, Mister. As owner, I appoint myself master for the rest o' this cruise."

Johnny Carver's lean jaw dropped. The two Indian brethren regarded her impassively. She dismissed the boat-steerers from suspicion; they were not the men to have knifed David Davids, She eyed the three mates with bitter gaze.

"Rogues for'ard and rogues aft, as usual," she rasped uncompromisingly. "You've all sailed with us before. You all hated him— Shut up! None of your back-talk," she broke out, as the three mates stirred angrily. "Any man for'ard might ha' done it, or you."

The mate, Johnny Carver—a devil if there ever was one.

Johnny Carver cleared his throat. "Ma'am, if I was you, I'd go back to port and let proper authority handle this."

"If I were you, I would," she said scathingly, regarding him with cold fury. "But thank God, I'm not you! You three mates have made us plenty of trouble; he's held you in your place, and you've hated him for it. Now I'm holding you in your place, and I can do it. I'll have none of your bewigged shysters and drooling juries covering up this crime. It'll come out who did it. Murder always comes out."

One of the Portuguese boat-steerers, stealing a glance at the corpse, looked back to her and bobbed his head, the gold rings in his ears shaking in the sunrise light.

"Missee, how you find out?" he asked, like a child.

"The black-hearted Judas who did this can't escape," she said. "I don't know who did it; but he knows, and God knows. I don't believe in taking justice into my own hands when the course ain't clear. I'm leaving it to a higher power, and we're cruising after sperm till our bar'ls get filled. Mr. Carver, you and the mates take Cap'n Davids, below. José Santos, go fetch Sails with his ditty-bag and a new bolt of canvas. We bury the Cap'n at meridian, this date."

A practical woman, Mrs. Davids.

As day drew into day, and days into weeks, the smirks and grins forward died out. From officers to cook, the crew stood in a deadly fear of the woman skipper which was hard to understand. Rand, who never ventured again to intrude himself upon her, and who found Johnny Carver avoiding him somewhat gingerly, accepted his situation with the best possible grace; there was no help for it, and he was not the man to make a fool of himself.

He could understand this cold, grim woman who shared her bitter hatred among all hands as she waited to learn who had murdered her husband. He could understand the stark and uncompromising personality of her. The men would have cursed and feared Davids, for his harsh fist and flailing boots; but they feared her tongue tenfold more, and the hard spirit of her. A woman skipper was new and incredible to them.

Ever stony of face as a granite image, she did the master's work, but she kept her distance and also kept to herself. She played no favorites and asked no favors; that she actually hated every man aboard, was plain enough. She made it plain the day the whaleboats were overhauled. Those gimlet eyes of hers missed nothing, and she let out burning words at Johnny Carver.

"You're slack, Mister," she said caustically. "You let the hands shirk, and you shirk as well. Smarten up, if you ever expect to fill those bar'ls below. Get the try-works cleaned up, and put the cooper to work on his job. And send up a hand to cut adrift that Irish pennant on the fore royal lift. Next time I see one, you'll lay aloft."

"I'm an officer, remember," growled Johnny Carver.

"And I'm master." She turned her back and paced up and down, and finally came to a halt beside the helmsman.

"What was that song-and-dance you tried to give me the day Cap'n Davids was killed? About being a friend of his? A Navy officer?"

Rand gave her a glance, with a sense of shock at her words, at the fact that she remembered what he had said that day.

"It was so," he rejoined calmly. "I had met your husband several times. I'm an officer, yes. I had a few drinks the night you sailed, and was shanghaied."

She eyed him coldly. "You don't seem het up about it."

"I've got over that," said Rand. "Wouldn't do any good to rant and rave. Besides, there'll come a reckoning later, if I want it; and I'm not sure that I shall. I'm rather enjoying myself, Cap'n. That is, except for your abominable food."

She grunted. "The food's all right. You're the one man aboard who knows his job. Can you navigate?"

"Naturally."

With this, she turned away and did not speak to him again.

She hazed Johnny Carver, however, with the natural result; Johnny Carver took it out on the others. The food got bad and the water worse; no sperm were raised, and they lacked the relief of violent action to work off spleen.

There was no further word of Captain Davids' murder; not a word, except among the men forward. Rand had been keeping his ears open, and learned nothing at all. Gamming in the fo'c'stle gave him no information. He could well believe that any one of a dozen men aboard had given that deathly thrust, but he co'uld suspect no particular man.

The skipper saw everything, yet she seemed to notice nothing. She paced the deck endlessly, her stony features masking unshared thoughts. She had grown gaunt and hollow of cheek, and had become a sexless creature devoid of femininity. Her hair was shorn close; in her rough garb, she could have passed easily for a man....

Abruptly, they sighted a school of blackfish one morning, and the boats were put out for harpoon drill. Rand, to his surprise, was ordered to take part as boat-steerer. When the day was over, he stood out as the only promising harpooner among the hands forward. That evening, at change of watches, Johnny Carver curtly addressed him.

"Stow your dunnage in the for'ard cabin, Ramsgate. Skipper's promoted you to boat-steerer. You can mug up with the Portygees and learn your business. Officer, you are."

Rand met his surly, biting gaze and managed a smile.

"No thanks to you. Who shanghaied me aboard here?"

"Blast you!" snarled Johnny Carver. "Damned fine gentleman still, huh?"

"Assault a United States officer, will you?" rasped Rand. "Try again!"

The voice of Mrs. Davids suddenly lashed out; she had approached them unobserved.

"Belay it! I'll have no bickering aft. Instead of quarreling and cursing, you two might find some means of launching the boats faster. This morning you looked like bumboats going after garbage."

She turned away and was gone, with no more words.

There was dark talk forward; the gloomy Finn carpenter started it, when some one mentioned the sooty gull hovering overhead when Cap'n Davids was buried. Meantime, the *Sharon* sailed south and ever south, bootlessly, raising Tristan d'Acunha in Latitude 37 and passing under a t'gallant breeze in her way to Mozambique.

A legendary bird, said the Finn, an omen of ill-fortune. Into that sooty flying bird had gone the spirit of Cap'n Davids, and one day he would return to perch on the main truck. When that happened, death would again come to the ship.

An ominous cloud that no amount of brilliant sunshine could dispel, settled upon the men forward. Instead of occupying their spare time with model-making and scrimshaw work, they sat around grumbling, cursing. With the passing of Cap'n Davids, they said, luck had deserted the ship. And so it seemed, for never a whale was raised....

One evening in the doldrums, an insufferably hot evening, Rand had the deck watch. Mrs. Davids—now "Cap'n" to all hands—was below as usual when not on duty. The three Portuguese boat-steerers sat on the booby-hatch whispering mysteriously in the darkness. Johnny Carver and the half-Indian Dubois twins sat playing cards in the forward cabin, where the reeking oil lamp, slung in gimbals, lent odor to the discomfort.

Rand went down to the cabin in search of his tobacco pouch. No thought of eavesdropping occurred to him, nor did he attempt to silence his approach; but outside the half-open door, the voice of Johnny Carver checked him abruptly.

"A fine cruise this is!" The mate flung down his cards with an obscene oath. "No sign o' fish, not a barrel coopered yet. The damned tub's jinxed, like that horse-faced Finn says."

"Your fault," said Abel Dubois.

Rand peered in. Johnny Carver was staring up at a calendar on the bulkhead. Along with a ship under sail and the usual chandler's advertising, was the hurricane verse:

June, too soon.
July, stand by!
August, look out you must;
September, remember!
October—all over.

As the dour halfbreed spoke, Johnny Carver jerked his head around. The two dark men sat watching him like a pair of lynxes, unblinking, impassive.

"What d'ye mean by that?" he snapped with a growl of challenge, his shark's eyes alert and dangerous.

"Stow it," said Cain Dubois laconically. "I saw you. That morning."

The lean face of Johnny Carver tautened into gray flint.

"What d'ye mean?" he repeated.

"Nothing." Abel Dubois reached for the cards. "Ain't our business. Forget it. My deal, ain't it?"

The game went on. Rand waited, but caught nothing further than growling oaths, and went back on deck—quietly, this time.

So there the truth had come out; Johnny Carver had done the trick. And what of it? Rand knew those two half-breeds would never talk; they had hated Cap'n Davids virulently, as most others had hated him. Still thinking of the secret he had thus surprised, but which occasioned him no surprise, he was aware of the skipper's gaunt shape, and her voice.

"Come down to the cabin at eight bells, Ramsgate."

He assented mechanically. He had accepted the name with the situation; Ramsgate or Rand, it was all one.

When he went into the cabin, Mrs. Davids was sitting over the log-book. She looked up at him, her face stony.

"Gallows," she said abruptly. "What does that make you think of?"

Rand barked out a laugh of exasperation at her cryptic, inhuman manner. He felt the force of her, as everyone felt it: a hard, driving force of character that was beyond a woman's nature.

"Makes me think of your mate, for one thing," he snapped.

Instantly she came alive. Her eyes flashed. Her face changed; a spot of color rushed into her weathered cheeks.

"Out with it!" she said in a low, tense voice. "Out with it!"

"Nothing to prove it," he answered. "I heard a bit o' talk; enough to make me think who killed your husband. Those that know, won't talk."

For a moment she regarded him steadily, searchingly, and then nodded.

"Aye; Johnny Carver did it. I've thought as much all the time. Others won't talk, eh? They'll be punished for that. Wait and see. I've nothing to do but sail the ship until God takes action. Never fear, it'll come! And I stay at sea till it does come, if the stores turn to solid weevils and the water to sour vinegar; we put into no port till the punishment has come from above."

Mentally, Rand recoiled from her; she was mad, insane upon her fixed idea, he thought.

"Was that what you called me down here for?" he demanded.

"I called you down on ship's business," she rapped out in her coldly hostile way. Shoving back her chair, she rose. "Come here."

Rand turned with her to the stern port with its curtains and potted flowers. On a shelf stood a model of the *Sharon,* a neat bit of work. From the model's deck she picked up two tiny L-shaped bits of wood. She inserted each one upside down in holes just abaft the miniature lazaret hatch, so that the arms protruded over the rail.

"You're slack, Mister," she said caustically. "You let the hands shirk and you shirk as well."

"This is the gallows I had in mind," she said.

Rand was positive now that she was daft. A moment later he revised his opinion.

*Through holes drilled at the end of each protrud*ing arm, she inserted lengths of twine, which were made fast to a miniature whaleboat. With these, she hoisted the little boat until it hung beneath the counter of the model ship. A sharp exclamation broke from Rand.

"Hello! Upon my word, Mrs. Davids—a hoist for boats!"

"Appears to surprise you that a woman could use her brains," she rejoined acidly. "I worked this out last year, and Cap'n Davids laughed at me. Yes, it's a hoist, to lower away fast and hoist fast. And I got the idea," she added grimly, "by thinking about how Johnny Carver would look when he trips the gallows. You've got more brains than anyone else aboard. Get to work with the Finn; he's a right good smith. Set a fire in the try-works and have him beat out a metal gallows like this, a pair of 'em."

"You compliment me," Rand said ironically; then his enthusiasm broke down the bars. "Why, Cap'n, this is a great notion, positively great! Do you know what it'll mean to ships, if it works—to all ships alike? Not alone speed in hoisting boats out and in, but safety and convenience—"

"If it works?" broke in Mrs. Davids with caustic energy. "You fool, there's nothing to make it work except a block rove at the end of each gallows! Nothing else to keep it from working, if a body has common sense. A man on each lift to haul away, and what more d'ye want?"

"We'd better put in at Ascension Island for fresh water," blurted Rand.

"I've told you once, and you can pass on the word to the scum for'ard, we'll put in nowhere till the murderer of Cap'n Davids has received punishment!"

From that wildly glaring eye and harsh voice, Rand fled.

He took with him, however, the idea of the gallows; a very simple thing. And with next morning, he was at work upon it with the Finn. He told no one at all what the thing was, except that it was a contraption of the skipper's implying that he himself did not know; and for the next three or four days he was hard at work.

Meantime, all hands muttered blackly, realizing that the ship was not putting in at Ascension. There was talk of lofty Green Mountain, and the eleven-fathom anchorage off Plymouth Point, and the wonders that a run ashore might do for everyone; hatred and a vicious spirit grew both forward and aft.

Never in all these weeks had Rand run foul again of Johnny Carver. A dark, quick look like a stab, a curl of the thin lip, a rasp of the voice—nothing more. But now Rand discovered a change in the man, a more open hostility, a meaningless but challenging oath when they met. Rand refused the challenge. Queerly enough, the secret knowledge that this man was the murderer of Cap'n Davids steadied him. He remained cool, alert, wary, and thereby irritated Johnny Carver the more.

At sunset, the day the job was finished, Carver stood by the rail, watching with a sneer as Rand completed the rigging. He had improved upon the skipper's crude idea by reeving an upper and lower block; and in each lower block was securely fastened an enormous iron hook, to make fast to a boat.

"Fine job you're doing," said Johnny Carver. "Aiming to hoist blubber on deck so's you won't get your fine gentleman's skin oily?"

"No." And Rand gave him a look. "One of these is a gallows to hang Cap'n Davids' murderer on. The other's for the man who knows and won't tell."

The gloomy Finn, working on the iron standard, cackled out a laugh. But Johnny Carver went livid. His shark's eyes gave Rand one frightful, murderous look; then he turned and walked away; but that expression in his face had spoken for him.

The last bit of the job finished, the lines running freely, Rand went down to the after cabin. The sun was just dipping under the horizon.

"If you want to bend on a whaleboat and try the contraption out," he said, after telling the skipper the work was done, "we can do it now."

"Wait till morning," she rejoined. "Getting dark now. Have them lookouts aloft and spry with dawn; I smell whale tonight."

Rand departed, laughing softly to himself. Smell whale, indeed! But—

"She blows, she blows!" came the yell whipping down in the sunrise. The magic words brought all hands tumbling on deck like mad. "She blows! Thar she blows ag'in! Four p'ints off the sta'board bow—and a blow ag'in! And a blow!"

There was a rush for the boats, nested snugly forward. A joyous yell and a wild cheer went up; not one whale, but half a dozen, a whole school of them! Now Mrs. Davids came charging down the deck, long spyglass under arm.

"How many boats you aimin' to take out, Mister?" she snapped.

"Three, ma'am," said Johnny Carver.

"Three!" The word fairly blazed out of her. "I s'pose you'd be plumb satisfied to lay one fish alongside and get a bare smell of ile, huh? And a fair day, no sea to speak of, and the breeze falling. All boats, all hands—every man jack of you! That's sperm over yonder, not blackfish. All hands away! I'll tend ship. Play loose boats!"

Her scorn and derision sent the lean face of the mate red and redder still. He was off in his own boat a moment later; after all, Johnny Carver was a peerless harpooner.

The Dubois twins, dark Indian features all aglow, took a boat together. The Portuguese were off. Rand was off—all hands, cooper and cook, tugging at the oars.

Canvas was got up; the oars came in temporarily; and fanlike, the boats headed for the spurts of white froth that broke the horizon.

With an old New Bedford veteran steering, Rand stood in the bow, harpoon ready, lances ready, tubs and line all clear, his knee braced against the lubber's chock.

The Dubois boat was fairly close; they were holding almost together, while the others had separated.

Close and closer came the jetting froth. The huge black bulks broke the surface, blew, forged under again in majestic slow procession. Abel Dubois, poised in the bow of his boat, took in sail, and Rand followed suit. Oars out now, the boats drove in silently to bisect the course of the leviathans.

Suddenly the Dubois boat swung, as the steering sweep tugged it around at right angles. The cunning Indians had guessed aright—a black hulk was coming up almost alongside. Rand saw Abel hurl the iron; there was a wild flurry of flukes.

"Starn all!" yelled Abel. "Haul the warp—he's not sounding!"

He and his brother both had lances out of their beckets and on the rests, as the boat backed. Rand heard one of his own men vent an awesome oath, heard another cry out, saw the black shape rising beneath the other boat—saw the broad black tail whip into air, come down with a slapping crash, and sweep the water into a smother of foam. From that welter of spume came the faint anguished cries of dying men.

A hit! Rand sprang aft. As he did so, Johnny Carver's harpoon flashed.

"Hit her square, by God!" yelled the bow oar, next to Rand. "Hey, *look!* There's the mate's boat!"

"Give way, all!" rasped out Rand. "Pull, you bullies, pull! Bring her in close, steersman. Two of you look after those men in the water—"

Suddenly, between water and vast sky, there was a fury of haste. Johnny Carver's boat had appeared, unobserved; now it was heading slap for the whale. The boat of the twin brethren had disappeared. Abel was gone, his brother was gone. That huge black tail was still lashing, slapping to and fro in frantic fury. Two men from the wrecked boat swam among the floating tubs and oars, no others.

Rand's boat cut in between Johnny Carver's boat and the threshing animal, and then swung, so close to the frenzied tail that Rand caught his breath. His men were pulling in the two survivors of the other boat. He had one flashing glimpse of Johnny Carver himself, poised, harpoon in palm, as the mate's boat rose on a wave.

Then his own shaft drove home, and drove deep. A hit! Rand sprang aft, and snatched the steering-sweep from the veteran. As he did so, Johnny Carver's harpoon flashed above him.

The mate was an old hand at "pitch-poling," the trick of heaving a harpoon high above a rival boat, to strike the whale first and give his ship prior claim to the booty. This time, Rand had beaten him, but his harpoon went home. Instantly the whale turned tail up and sounded, down and down until the line had to be wetted as it ran sizzling from the tubs.

A frightful cry went up from the men; they fell over one another in confusion. Rand saw the cause, and a wild yell of wrath burst from him. The boat was being held down, was being dragged under. Johnny Carver had belayed his warp. Another instant, and the taut line, going down with the sounding whale, would have sent Rand's boat under—but Rand had already acted. His knife was out, was whipping at the other warp. One of the men had caught up a hatchet, ready for such use, and was cutting at it. The line parted.

The two boats were close. Johnny Carver's lean and fury-filled face showed, high above as a wave lifted his boat.

"You damned Judas!" shouted Rand. "Murderer! Wait till we get back—"

The words were swept away, but Carver had heard. Now everything was swept away, with a rising wall of spray and water on either side the bows, as the boat leaped off and was gone. The bow oar had belayed the warp on the bitts; the run of line was stopped, and the boat was off at terrific speed in tow of the wounded whale.

The other boat, the wreckage, were gone in an instant.

"He done it deliberate!" An oarsman shook his fist back at Carver; other men sent up a chorus of oaths and curses. "Tried to drag us under, he did!"

"Steady, men." Rand, white with anger and peril,

got himself in hand. "Our job's to kill this fish. I'll settle later with Johnny Carver, blast him! We may have an all-day run ahead of us—"

He broke off to check on the position of the *Sharon.* A yell went up from the men. An all-day run? No chance of that. The whale was sounding again. The boat eased down in speed. The smoking line ran out and out, then ceased. The men brought it in and flaked it down hurriedly, staring at the water, fearful and tense; suspense shook them all. The whale might repeat, might come up beneath them as it had done with the Dubois boat.

When the whale broke water a hundred yards away, there was a general sigh of quick relief. The oars went out; the boat started forward. Rand had had a couple of old hands aboard to set him aright if he went wrong.

Lances ready, they crept up on the wounded beast. Close and closer, almost upon that black mass. The first lance went in; the second followed. Up tail, and the whale was gone again, but this time with blood streaking the water; and not gone for long.

A kill! Cheers broke out; the boat was baled clear; the canvas was hoisted, and she leaned over to the breeze. Chancy work, this handling a whaleboat under canvas, but that was Rand's business, and he carried it out in true Navy style....

It was mid-afternoon when they came alongside the *Sharon,* which was slowly forging toward the kill, and took a line. A few men were aboard; Johnny Carver's boat had come back to the ship empty-handed.

"You men keep your mouths shut," he ordered. "I'll handle this thing with Carver."

He was up and over the 'midships rail, inwardly seething with fury. His eagerness was checked abruptly; he found himself face to face with Mrs. Davids, and something in that grim, stony expression of hers chilled his blood. Bony, gaunt, terrible, she stood impassive.

"Congratulations," she said. "Your first fish."

"Never mind." Rand was glancing about. He saw a couple of men from Carver's boat, slinking, furtive, white-faced. "Where's Johnny Carver? I want a word with him."

"Do you?" said she, in a tone of hideous mockery. "You come too late. Didn't I tell you things would happen when a Higher Power got ready? I seen what took the two Dubois brothers. I said punishment would come. Mister, where you heading for?"

Rand did not notice the title. He wanted to get away from her insane voice.

"Get out of the way," he rasped. "I want to find Carver. Where is he?"

"Aft," she said, and stood aside.

Rand strode aft, and she followed him. The man at the wheel, white of face and wild of eye, shrank and cowered away. Rand came to a halt, staring at the thing dangling on the standard he had rigged—the starboard standard.

Johnny Carver was dangling there, and one look was enough to tell he was dead. Rand swung around and met the stony eyes of the woman. Suddenly he knew that she was sane, dreadfully sane. She had been alone here when Carver came back aboard, too.

"How did this happen?"he demanded.

"It's already wrote down in the log," she said impassively. "He jumped at that rope, Mister, and the lower block overhauled. His weight took him down. The block came up, and the hook catched him under the chin."

He looked at her, steadily, and she met his gaze without flinching. Rand knew perfectly well that the mate had not jumped; he read in her eyes that something else had happened here—something he did not know about, did not want to know about.

"Accident, was it?" he said.

"No," she rejoined. "No accident, Mister. I told you how I got the idea for that there gallows, didn't I? Punishment, that's what it was. Now, Mister, you'd better take charge of the ship and look alive. We got three fish to get alongside, and there's no time to lose if we're going to get to work cutting in."

Rand swallowed hard. Mister? That meant he was mate. And there was work to do. He glanced up suddenly, at a singsong, bawling voice. The men were tailing on the lines; one of them, a chantey-man, was lifting his ringing, doggerel words to an old tune:

Oh, they call me hanging Johnny,
Hurray, hurray!
Because I hang for money—
So hang, boys, hang!
Oh, first I hung my mother,
And then I hung my brother;
Oh, hang and haul together,
Oh, hang for better weather—
So hang, boys, hang!

With a shiver coursing up his spine, Rand looked at the woman's stony face, then turned and went to work.

The story was ended, and upon a somewhat ghastly note. Old Cap'n Tucker knocked the dottle out of his clay pipe. He filled it up again and scratched a match. As he puffed, he darted a glance at me beneath his shaggy gray brows.

"What was you wanting to know about boat-davits?" he asked. "How they started? Well, you know now."

Somebody else, quicker of wit than I, caught at the name and let out a whoop.

"Davits! Boat-davits! Say, is that how they came by the name? *Cap'n Davids—Mrs. Davids—davits!* Is that it, Cap'n Tucker?"

"Sure; ain't it plain enough?" affirmed the old skipper. "Why not? A knot was named after Matthew Walker, and a bend after Carrick."

"And a sail after Bentincks," I put in. "And a boat after Berthon and Hampton."

"And, if I'm not mistaken, a locker after Davy Jones!" said somebody else, with a laugh. "Cap'n, I'd be the last man in the world to contradict you. It was a swell yarn. It almost sounded as if it had really happened."

Cap'n Tucker eyed the speaker for a moment, then emitted a loud, unholy snort of scorn that included all of us in its scope, and went stalking away.

BLACK CARGO

Captain Trumbull scowled across the table. "What's the mother of invention?" he demanded truculently.

"Prevarication," said Mr. Miles, the first officer. There was a laugh, in which Captain Trumbull did not join. He was not a man who laughed very often; life had been grim to him, and he looked it.

"I'm not joking," he proclaimed dourly. "The barkentine rig always was half flesh, half fowl. Hermaphrodite was the old name for it. When you get through with all your silly pawking drivel, and Mr. Miles here has finished cutting his jokes, I'll give you the facts in the case. Get it all off your chests while I'm finding the sort of cigar I want."

He rose and stamped away toward the bar and the cigar-counter.

"I'll bet it's a long black one that'd choke a mule," said Mr. Miles.

We were sitting around a table in downtown San Francisco, talking about the new bridges and one thing and another. We had drifted together for dinner by sheer chance, but the presence of Captain Trumbull was no delight.

It was a hard, rocky presence, a strong one that made itself felt. You've met men like that—so uncompromising, so gaunt and rock-ribbed against the world, that they provoke instant dislike. Their very gaze is a challenge. The queer thing is that you may hate such a man at sight, yet you respect him. And so it was with Captain Trumbull.

"If you get a yarn out of that old shellback," said somebody, "it'll be all blood and rum—or worse!"

There was a laugh, and the talk went back to barkentines. It was the general opinion that this rig had come into being as a result of the greatest shipping depression ever known, caused by the French and British embargoes during the first ten years of the past century, when England and Napoleon between them nearly ruined American shipping.

"Some Yankee skipper by the name o' Fallon invented the rig, I hear tell," said one voice. Captain Trumbull, who had returned to his seat at the table, heard this with a grunt. He had a long black cigar, sure enough.

"Why any Yankee coasting skipper would want square canvas for'ard," spoke up Mr. Miles, "I dunno. Or rather, how he'd learn that it could be used on a three-mast schooner. Schooner men love their little fore-and-afters and swear by 'em."

"Aye," said another. "And there's no better rig for beating up and down coast, and in narrow rivers with short tacking to do. Back in them days, the fast American schooners were about the only craft that could outsail the privateers and pirates that infested the whole coast. So why try out a new rig?"

"Probably," came a suggestion, "some fore-and-aft skipper, Fallon or another, got into some jam where nothing but square canvas on the foremast would do him any good. A matter of life and death, maybe—"

"Where Necessity became the mother of Invention," barked Captain Trumbull all of a sudden. "That's what happened, too. Fallon was the man, Cap'n Tom Fallon. There's a yarn back of it to curl your hair."

Mr. Miles laughed. "Curl away, Cap'n! We've been around some. After a chap has looked into the waterfront situation from Suez to Shanghai, not to mention such places as Havre, his hair needs a lot to curl it."

Captain Trumbull regarded him with a severe eye, and replied without diplomacy:

"You, huh? You or me, we're babies compared to those Yankee skippers of around 1800. If we kill a man, we've got courts and unions and God knows what to reckon with; but they killed 'em regardless, and no questions asked. They had to contend with pirates, slavers, all sorts of rascals—and with each other. Saints? Not by a danged sight! They were hard-fisted men, dealing in rum and slaves and human misery, and you bet there were rascals among 'em. Why, the oldtime bucko mates were just a mere hangover of brutality from those days! A skipper like Fallon had to fight fire with fire or go under; he had to be worse than the worst, and a little bit better than the best. He was all man, if he wanted to keep his ticket. A skipper in those times had to do things, and think nothing of it, that today would make newspaper headlines all over the world and land him behind the bars."

Glynn caught him off-balance, rushed him off his feet.

"Give us the yarn, Trumbull," spoke up a skipper from down the table. "Do you know how Fallon came to invent the barkentine rig?"

"I do," asserted Captain Trumbull truculently. "It all came about because Tom Fallon got knocked overboard and drowned, off the Florida cays. That is, he was supposed to've drowned, only he didn't. Glynn, Butcher Glynn, boarded him and looted his schooner; that's how he got overboard. The *Betty Cross* was the fastest, liveliest thing under canvas; there was bad blood between the two men; and Glynn just laid aboard and grabbed. Glynn, mind you, was a respectable skipper out o' New York. He was in the slave trade, running blacks from the west coast of Africa over to Cuba or Charlestown, from time to time. He was a member of a shipping-firm in New York, too."

"Members of the firm usually are slavers," said some one, and there was a laugh. Captain Trumbull glared around for silence—and got it.

"Fallon had a half-brother," he went on. "Nobody knew about it; the name was John Martin, and he was no angel, but sometimes brothers stick together. Martin was an A.B. aboard Glynn's vessel when Tom Fallon came back to New York, with not another soul knowing him to be alive. He had lost everything with his schooner; nobody knew what had become of the *Betty Cross;* and there was just one thing Tom Fallon wanted-to get even with Butcher Glynn. So he met his half-brother in a groggery, and then he went walking in the bitter winter weather, and it was a walk worth describing to you."

Well, no one would have dreamed that old Captain Trumbull had it in him, but he pitched into a masterly description of Fallon's walk, that bitter night.

He brought up out of nothing the old Battery as it had once been, with the waterfront around it and along the East River—streets all a-smell with tar and hemp and molasses and rum, streets ranged with lofty square-riggers, squat New England coasters, rakish deepwater schooners that plied to the Caribbees and Mexico and Africa and farther.

A chill wind was whipping down from the north that gray cold evening; the frowsy waterfront was deserted. Trade and commerce seemed dead. Fallon could not hope to get a ship or a job, even were his identity known; none the less, he was on the prowl this night for a ship and a job together. Ship, job, money—everything staked on one desperate lone-hand play.

Leaning against the biting norther that searched through his ragged garments, Fallon passed beneath the trellis formed by the bowsprits of a hundred laid-up ships, a wilderness of stripped spars and weather-cracked masts reaching into the dark sky. He cursed it—everything included: The English, who had stopped American ships with their refusal to permit European trade; the French for the same reason; the President and a craven Congress who, in a super-anxiety to avoid disputes and war, allowed all commerce to sicken and die.

Tom Fallon had revolted against the law, against his own evil destiny, against the smug rascality whose "pull" protected Butcher Glynn. Thanks to John Martin, opportunity was in his grasp; and his grasp was strong enough, desperate enough, to grip and hold....

A drift of fine rain and sleet needled through his rags and whetted his resolve. He slipped across the frozen mud of Governor's Alley, passed Fly-market slip, and so reached Burling Slip at the foot of John Street. And there, close-warped as his brother had informed him, lay the craft he was seeking.

Covered by the obscuring haze, Fallon walked to the edge of the dock and looked the *Lively* squarely between the eyes; that sea-squinting gaze of his needed no daylight to discern the facts. Two hundred tons, he appraised her, with a knifelike bow and a run that wouldn't draw a bucketful of dead water after her in a twenty-four-hour cruise. By her waterline, she was laden for a long voyage—cleared for Mexico, John Martin had said. Yes, Butcher Glynn was likely to head for Mexico! Once past the blockade, it was haul up for Africa and black ivory, and British frigates be damned!

No one was visible along her decks. All working canvas had been bent, and the kedges were astern in the stream, ready for a quick offshore haul. So Glynn was signing on a skipper this night to take her out, eh? Glynn, acting for that smug John Street firm of his. Glynn, who handled the details of the dirty work while he was ashore, between his own runs. Well, Glynn would get a skipper this night he was not bargaining for!

Fallon turned away, numb with cold, and his wind-burned eyes shifted from stream to streets. He gained the lee of a warehouse door and settled himself to wait in the shadows. If Martin were right, Glynn would be coming aboard after his drunken splurge, ready to await his skipper.

Glynn, with liquor in his belly and gold weighting his pockets! But more important than gold were the

Custom House clearances and the bills-of-lading. Glynn would come with visions of a warm cabin, final arrangements, a last bottle of rum—and the *Lively* slipping out into the darkness.

Fallon smiled grimly. A new ship, Martin had told him; a fine new craft Glynn had fetched in and put to register. He peered out at the dark-rimmed lines of her, and a queer fluttering stirred in him, a stir of excitement. He could not account for it, and his smile died in a frown. Where was Glynn's fast-driving *Salem Lass?* Where was his own lost *Betty Cross?* No telling....

Sleet drove thicker and faster; the warehouse doorway was colder than an ice-cavern. Presently the click of heels echoed down the empty street. Head down against the wind, snorting and splashing through the icy slush, appeared a tall figure.... Glynn, and alone! On came the man, until he was passing the very doorway. Then Fallon stepped out.

Stepped out, head bare, a jaunty greeting on his lips. Glynn halted, peered at him in the obscurity, recognized his voice, recognized him. An oath of wild alarm and terror broke from him:

"Fallon—Tom Fallon's ghost—get away from me—"

The belaying-pin whipped out, and the crack of it was heard across the wind as it smacked home.

Fallon's fist landed, thudded home savagely, thudded again. Another blow, this time a crusher for the belt; but as it snapped home, Fallon's foot slipped on the cobbles.

He went sprawling. As he scrambled up, Glynn had all the recovery needed, and met him with a bellow. The two men hammered and slogged over the treacherous cobblestones, while the laid-up ships, groaning under dock-fetters, stared with stoppered eyes at these twisting, fighting shapes in the obscurity.

Fallon knew he had failed of his attempt. He had counted on surprise and the first driving blows to end things quickly, and he had failed. Unless he did end the matter swiftly, his whole plan must go overboard. He could hope for no more than the satisfaction of hammering Butcher Glynn to a finish....

Again he slipped—his boots were sodden things. This time Glynn was upon him before he could recover, caught him off balance, rushed him off his feet. As Fallon came half erect, Glynn's hobnailed boot went into him, low and foul; but that cursed sodden footgear of his had settled his hash. He writhed up, got in one savage crack, then sprawled face down on the stones, senseless.

Glynn staggered, straightened up, gasped out wild curses. That one final blow had all but finished him. As he stood, catching his breath, a lantern bobbed and a form came on the run from the schooner—a man holding a lantern in one hand, long horse-pistol in the other.

"Ahoy! That you, Cap'n Glynn?" sounded his hoarse voice. "Need help?"

"Help?" grunted Glynn, wiping blood from his lips as he swung around, glaring at the man. "Ye cowardly skulker, I could ha' done with a hand, aye! So it's you, John Martin! Lay hold o' this blasted—"

Desperately, Martin acted, foreseeing everything lost. Glynn was caught unawares by the swift, unsuspected attack. The pistol-barrel whaled him over the head, and without a sound, he crumpled beside the figure of Tom Fallon....

As for Fallon, he had only dazed memories of what followed, until he found himself in the warm cabin of the schooner, Martin pouring rum down his throat. He stared around; then his jaw fell and his eyes widened incredulously.

The cabin of the *Lively?* No, not a bit of it. Here was a cabin glistening with bird's-eye maple, polished copper, hand-rubbed mahogany; the transom seats covered with leather, every nook and corner and scar and timber well remembered. Fallon passed a hand across his eyes, stared again. He was in his own cabin, aboard the *Betty Cross!*

Suddenly it all flashed on him. His amazed brain leaped at the truth. His own ship, of course! Glynn had made a few changes, altered the paint and so forth, had put her under some foreign registry by dint of a bribe to Mexican or Cuban officials—and this was the *Lively.* With Tom Fallon, master and owner of the vanished schooner supposedly dead and gone, it was safe enough.

Martin had left the cabin, and now came back with an armful of clothes—good sturdy garments.

The dazed Fallon looked up at him.

"Did you—did you know this was my old schooner, under a new name?"

Martin's long, narrow face was shot with astonishment.

"The *Betty Cross?* Why, no! Glynn's firm bought this hooker from some Cuban owner. He's been refitting her here. Good Lord, Tom! Then we can get the law on him—"

"The law be damned!" In a gust of anger, Tom Fallon came to his feet and began to strip off his rags. "What've we got to expect from the law? Months of delay, argument, law-sharks nipping us, trickery of all kinds—be damned to it! We'll go ahead as planned, or I will. Thanks for the clothes. I need 'em. So you fetched me aboard, eh? Good man! Where's Glynn?"

"Tied up and gagged, in that doorway. He'll keep."

Fallon got into the garments, brass buttons and all: Glynn's outfit, no doubt.

Martin looked a lot like his tall half-brother. The same narrow features, the same high-bridged nose and crisp jaw. Only the eyes differed. Martin's were dark and eager, younger. Those of Fallon were stone-gray, cold, bitter hard, older.

"I'd like to lay that rogue aboard and take him to sea," said Fallon. "And by heaven, I'll do it—"

"You won't if you're wise," broke in John Martin. "Forget the past, Tom; you've got your ship again. You can change her back to the *Betty Cross* later. Some of your old crew will turn up, and then you can go to law if you like. Besides, don't chance it with Glynn aboard. The mate is Murphy, his old rascally standby. You've got to work and work fast if you're going to make sure of the ship this night."

Fallon compressed his lips; then the harsh lines of his features relaxed.

"You're right. What's that you've got? —Oh, I see! I clear forgot about anything except what ship this was."

He watched as Martin emptied his pockets of the loot taken from Glynn. Two small leather sacks of coin; keys, no doubt of the lockers aboard here; the ship's papers, all duly signed and sealed; and last, Glynn's watch and heavy gold fob-seal, the official seal of the shipping firm in which Butcher Glynn was a silent but important partner. With this seal, Fallon knew, he would be recognized and accredited in Africa or elsewhere.

Two hundred tons, Fallon appraised her, with a knifelike bow and a run that wouldn't draw a bucketful of water after her in a twenty-four-hour cruise.

"Me the master mariner and you the foremast hand, brother," he observed. "That's strange, when you've got all the brains: You always did have."

Martin grinned. "Nope; you're the leader, Tom. I rigged this deal, but it takes you to put it over. Everything's here. Since we parted at the tavern, I've heard from Murphy that Glynn is sailing tomorrow or next day himself, in the *Salem Lass.* And here,"—he paused to grab a scrap of paper,—"here's his rendezvous with whomever he got to captain this ship. Sierra Leone—ha! We've got everything, Tom!"

"Aye," said Fallon, thrilling to the sheer exultation of it. "But regardless of moral right, it's piracy. We'll get a tail-block at the yardarm, and the two of us hanging betwixt high and low, if we're caught. You take this money and slip ashore. Leave me to handle—"

"Like hell!" flashed Martin. "I rigged this deal, and I'm putting it through with you. That goes!"

"All right, brother, have it your own way. You

always were obstinate. Where's this Murphy, the mate?"

"Drinking with the rest of the swine, for'ard. I'm supposed to be lookout."

Fallon nodded, and thankfully put down what was left of the rum.

Even while his hand moved, while he swallowed, the hard facts rushed through his brain: it must be a one-man job, and a quick one. For the sake of their old mother back at Stonington, he could not risk the two of them swinging for piracy, or worse. He must knock John Martin on the head, put the money in his pocket, and leave him ashore.

As for himself—well, a dozen courses were open to him. The quickest and simplest was to play lone-hand bucko skipper, and sharp about it. One man could cow the score up forward into obedience; he had done it before now. Reefer Murphy was a good seaman, a vindictive little devil; well, Reefer could be handled.

"Let's go," said Fallon. "Rout Murphy out and send him aft."

He paced the after-deck. The night was black, but the rain had turned to snow, and this lightened things. Forward, a light showed briefly as the cuddy opened and closed again; a burst of raucous voices sounded and was silenced. Murphy came to the poop and passed the lantern in the mizzen rigging. A sharp, wide-shouldered little man, with a nose like a Cape pigeon.

"New cap'n aboard, sir?" he sang out. "That ain't you, Cap'n Glynn—"

"New master, Mr. Murphy," said Fallon, coming closer to him. "Nip for'ard and break out the crew. We're in a hurry."

"Aye?" said the mate. "That's funny. Cap'n Glynn said you'd not be aboard until after he had transferred the gold to his own ship. I ain't turning a hand until Cap'n Glynn changes the orders—"

Fallon hit him twice; no slipping sodden boots this time. Murphy collapsed in the scuppers. Fallon called sharply:

"John! Come and give me a hand with him. To the dock."

They took Murphy over the side and stowed him safely on the wharf. Presently Tom Fallon came back. He came back alone, breathing hard; the snow was heavier. The waterfront, with its dim occasional street lights, was silent.

Fallon went forward and broke out the dazed and drunken crew. His boots and fists stirred them into activity. There was Manuel, the Portygee second mate, and the rest were like unto him; all brown men, the whole eighteen, Cuban and Spanish and Verde Islander.

Upon a snowy drift of gale, the Lively *was out* and away to sea. There would be no trouble; these men would not begin to think, until next day. Fallon turned in and got some sleep. He could risk it now better than later; the one crisis, he knew, would settle things.

He came on deck in the morning, sent the steward for his breakfast, and ate it at the rail, swigging down the hot coffee. All blockading ships had been eluded in the night and the snowy gale, but the wind was howling down out of the northwest. Fallon gave his orders. He caught the stare of Manuel, the staring eyes of the other men as they obeyed; they had small time to think, none to talk. Fallon got the schooner treble-reefed on fore and main, with the mizzen-sail stowed and gasketed. Then, pacing the heaving poop, he waited for the inevitable, alone except for the vague, well-wrapped figure of the man at the wheel.

His own ship under him again—still he could scarcely believe it. This, more than anything else, brought the old spring into his muscles, the old light into his gray eyes. His glance roved the decks eagerly enough. They were talking below, now, putting two and two together; perhaps some of them had recognized him. Another half-hour, and they'd be coming for an explanation. Fallon squeezed the belaying-pin stuck in his jacket pocket, and grinned frostily.

Gold aboard—Glynn's gold, to buy black ivory on the West Coast. Well, why not? A cargo of slaves meant big profits. They would be waiting there for delivery to Glynn, and with Glynn's seal and money, he would take the cargo himself. He might even see Butcher Glynn there, since the *Salem Lass* was bound on the same errand. He could get rid of these rats and ship a new crew there, too, Kroomen and a few whites. Then, the slaves sold, he could go back to his old West India trade, his ship under her own name again—

Fallon stopped short, staring at the helmsman. The latter looked up, grinned at him, and spoke.

"I've a hard head, Tom. Thought you were rid of me, eh?"

"Good Lord—*you!*" grunted Fallon. "Why, you fool, how did you get here? I thought I'd saved you from hanging for piracy, let alone being shot by the British for a slaver!"

"You always did send me home to Mother, but I'm a big boy now." And John Martin grinned joyously. "Didn't work, huh? I found a wherry, and barely got out in time to catch your fore-chains as you got up canvas."

"The devil's luck, brother!" said Fallon. "The *Salem Lass* and Glynn!"

"Well, you're here now, and I'm damned glad of it." Fallon broke into a laugh. "Hell's rising from below—and here it comes! You hold her steady and leave the heavy work to me."

"Look out for Frenchy," spoke up John Martin quickly. "He's the worst, and got a knife like a needle."

Fallon grunted, and moved toward the quarter-deck rail. Men were clustering in the waist, staring up; Manuel and two others were climbing the ladder. Fallon eyed them in grim frozen silence as they came. Frenchy, with the long mustaches and the sly glint of intelligence, was not hard to identify.

The three stopped short before his cold stare. They glowered at him, their hands already raw from fisting in ice-hard canvas.

"Where's Cap'n Glynn, sir?" demanded Manuel without any preamble. "And Mr. Murphy? And who are you—"

The second mate held an eighteen-inch fid in his hairy, swarthy fist; he was ready for business, but Tom Fallon was a trifle readier. The belaying-pin whipped out, and the crack of it was heard across the wind as it smacked home.

The second man took a boot under the belt that laid him gasping and sprawling beside Manuel; but in came Frenchy with an oath and a sliver of steel. Warned of it, Fallon hit the arm with his belaying-pin, hit the man with his fist, and then started to take the deviltry out of him. He did it grimly, efficiently, and then booted the bleeding, whining man aft.

"Go take the helm, Mr. Martin! Come here."

Fallon lifted Manuel, kicked him back to life, and followed him down the ladder with the other man; then he stood grimly, John Martin beside him.

"I'm master here," he said, "Mr. Martin is mate. Who's the carpenter? Get below and sound the well. All hands, shake out a reef on the fore and main, and stand by to the handy-billies. Move, damn you, or I'll move you!"

Their staring hostility broke. That one brutal lesson of blood was enough; they obeyed quickly, if with curses.

Fallon kept them at it, that day, the next day, the day after, alternating watches with the one man he could trust. He knew exactly how much he could do with this ship of his, and did it to the limit, the pumps going steadily, the exhausted men moving about like shadows.

The schooner sped on before the gale, black hull sleek as an oiled eel, slashing through graybacks that ran sometimes as high as the caps. Storm-trysail after trysail blew out of the bolt-ropes and went skittering to leeward over the raging seas, but new canvas went up, hauled aloft by bloody, half-frozen fingers.

Fallon was on deck day and night, a lean tireless phantom, savage of voice and fist. He was making no time, for he must drive far to the south to save his ship; and if it were any race, Glynn would have the advantage of him by waiting for the gale to blow out and then hauling a straight course; but what he wanted was to break those men, and he broke them.

Eight days the gale lasted; and when they ran out of it, all hands were worn to the bone, pale staggering men with no fight or mutiny left in them, and barely life itself; of Fallon they stood in mortal terror, as well they might.

Forty-six days the run stood, when they raised the green Sierra Leone hills. In those days Fallon had become convinced that Glynn would lose no time getting after him; the gold was aboard, plenty of it, and trade goods. He had ripped the very heart out of Butcher Glynn when he walked off with this ship and what was in her. And now it was Glynn who would pay the freight, but it was Tom Fallon who would load the slaves and sell them, and then head up for New York with the *Lively* washed out of existence, and his own schooner in her place again. A fine prospect, a fat prospect—if he made it.

They stood in to the coast, hunting for that secret river-mouth laid down in the private charts. Manuel had come to the fore these last few days; the swarthy man knew the coast dialects and every trick of the slave trade, and Fallon had need of him. Manuel bobbed his head, shook his gold earrings, and promised everything.

The river opened. A black pilot came aboard, and Fallon plied him with gin and questions. Captain Glynn? Not arrived, but expected; the barracoons were filled with prime Pangives, ready for him at thirty dollars a head. Fallon showed the gold fob-seal, and nothing more was needed. The slaves were his. But what about the British?

A frigate and a corvette had showed up a week ago, but had gone off toward the Rio Pongo. All was well. So the schooner stood in, crossed the bar safely and headed up between the verdant river banks for the anchorage. John Martin was driving the men, breaking out guns from the hold, rigging the slave deck. Six long nines, and a gleaming brass thirty-two, for mounting on its pivot carriage.

Fallon watched Manuel, gabbling with the pilot and his helper, and frowned. How far this Portygee could be trusted—well, time would show. First came the palaver ashore, the trade goods and the bright gold coins. John Martin could handle all that.

He handled it to perfection, with Manuel helping him, while the schooner lay moored to the long palm-log jetty. With a curl of his lip, Fallon let the men have their run ashore. They were no better than the blacks there, or the blackleg whites who came thronging to the gangway, begging for rum or clothes. A sorry mongrel lot, deserters from other slavers or from King's ships; most of them served the black king, manned his guns or trained his soldiers. Tom Fallon talked with them, gave them rum, and bided his time. One or two among them had been good men once.

John Martin handled the palaver, yes; within two days the slaves began to come aboard. Manuel, under Fallon's watchful eye, paid out the trade goods and coin. Manuel was for packing in the poor wretches like smoked haddock, but Tom Fallon would have none of that. He took only half the cargo Glynn would have crammed below-deck; and to himself he cursed that his schooner should acquire the slave-reek. It would wash out of her when her honest name came back, he vowed.

The days fled with never a hint of alarm from the lookout on the hill, who searched the sea for any sail. The ballast of palm oil went in; white ivory was stowed away. The last of the slaves were aboard. The water-butts were filled of a late night, and the pilot ordered for the dawn.

To Fallon, it was all like magic. Magic had laid hold of him from that moment in the cold and frozen night when he clapped eyes on the *Lively* and felt a shiver and stir of recognition in his heart—though he had not known what it was. Point to point, everything after that moment had gone without a hitch. Now the guns were in place, all was stowed, the hatches ready to clap on, the schooner ready to fight or run as needed. The job was done.

John Martin summoned him in the dawn—summoned him to giant Pongo Jim, the most famous pilot of the coast, who regarded Fallon with his usual wide grin.

"Damned niggers desert last night," he said. "Boat-crew gone. Must get new crew before I take you out. No good!"

He waved his hand, touched his cocked hat, and strutted off the schooner. Tom Fallon looked at Martin, and what he read in the latter's face startled him.

"Well, John? What's wrong?"

"His boys aren't the only deserters," said John Martin. "Tom, the ship's empty. They're all gone!"

Empty it was. Not a man remained aboard. From Manuel to the cook, every man jack had taken his bag and decamped during the night.

"If you want 'em back," went on Martin, "I'll see the king and hold a palaver, and he'll send 'em back quick enough—"

"No," said Fallon. "Wait—let's see what the rats stole!"

They took a quick look all around. Strange to say, nothing of account was gone with the missing men. It was clear that Manuel had arranged matters with Pongo Jim. Glynn was expected daily; if the schooner could be held here until the *Salem Lass* arrived, Tom Fallon was in the soup.

"Pilot be damned!" he said cheerfully. "I can take her across the bar myself—high water at sunset.... Yes, it'll work out fine."

"But you can't sail her home with me to hand the lines and feed the slaves," said John Martin, as he prepared a hasty breakfast of fruit. Fallon gave him a look and a grin.

"You stop aboard, brother. Leave the crew to me. We sail at sunset."

He went down to the cabin, filled his pockets with Glynn's gold, or what was left of it, and then strode ashore. Far from being cast down, he was hugely relieved by this desertion; he had foreseen some such trick. He had his own ship, and now he was able to have his own crew. He asked nothing better of fate.

In the blinding heat of noonday he came back to the schooner, wilted with sweat, and behind him trailed ten men. And such men! Three were blackish Verde Islanders; the others were riffraff of various bloods—all of them men who had gone native and had their fill of it, and were glad enough now to head back to the open world again.

"Here's ten," said Fallon to John Martin. "Break 'em in. Before sunset, we'll have a dozen more. Abel Stone, who was a Nantucket man once, will show up with four British deserters from down the beach, and six or seven Kroo boys who want to see the world. Now I'm ready for a bath and a bit of sleep. Work ahead tonight, brother!"

There was more work ahead that night than he dreamed.

Abel Stone showed up, with fourteen more men instead of eleven, and Fallon was well content. The Nantucket man was a wreck, but Fallon appointed him second mate, and before the offshore breeze sprang up with sunset, the *Lively* was ringing with laughter and eager voices, the shaggy desolate beachcombers were transformed into naked devils ready to work their hearts out, and the chained rows of slaves below decks had been fed and watered and tended.

"Let's go," said Tom Fallon, and ordered out the boats.

They towed the schooner downstream until she could catch the breeze in her upper canvas; then Fallon took the helm and held her for the bar. He had marked that channel carefully at their entry, and in the last flickering daylight the schooner slipped across with never a scrape.

Most of those men who had come aboard, seizing the chance of escape back to the larger life they had once cast aside, knew their business; by this time every man of them knew the ship. Fallon's heart thrilled to the work of them as the stars glimmered out and the canvas went up, the greased blocks offering no whine of complaint. Away and away, with a long reach across the Middle Passage—

"Sail ho-o-o!" floated down a call from aloft.

Fallon leaped to the rail.

"Where away?"

"Four points on the larboard bow, sir. Just outside the cape."

John Martin darted below and returned with the night-glass. Daylight enough was left. Fallon picked up the vessel that had so suddenly showed up around the cape, and then lowered the glass.

"The devil's luck, brother!" said he quietly. "The *Salem Lass* and Glynn—and we had to pop out slap into his arms! He's hauling about."

"Run for it," said Martin—but Fallon shook his head.

"I tried that once before; the *Lass* has the heels of us. This means business. Go for'ard and load the guns. Abel Stone's a gunner, or was; give him the long gun."

No King's ship at any rate—the men cheered, and fell to work with a will. The wind was freshening fast. Tom Fallon eyed the water, the shores, the starlit sea. The moon would be up in an hour, in a clear sky. Down to the southward, another long cape fell away to seaward—long rolling headlands down there, with deep water close in. All in a moment, this swift appraisal of his keen gray eyes; then his course was decided, his resolve taken. Fight, if fight he must, but first run for it. And his only chance to outrun Glynn lay dead before the wind.

"Helm down, there!" rang his voice. "Ease off fore-sheets!"

Men went leaping. The weather pennants were hauled over the stays; Fallon, displaying the strength of three men, hauled the spanker boom amidships alone. "Let go and haul!"—and the *Lively* came around quickly. Now she was heading south and west, away from Glynn's sail, toward those capes jutting afar.

The minutes passed. Fallon studied the other craft, a scant mile distant, and his heart sank. Aye, Glynn had overhauled him once before, and he remembered the bitter moment. The same now; he was certain of it. So intent was he, that he failed to note the outburst of voices forward, the furious storm of curses, the hot words.

"Tom!" John Martin came on the jump, panting and dismayed. "That damned slimy Manuel—the powder—every keg's been stove open and wet down!"

Fallon said nothing for a moment. Tricked! His chance of fighting Glynn was gone now. If he could not run or fight, he must give in, hand over everything.

"Break open the kegs," he said at last. "It's not so easy to flood a keg of powder. There'll be a little dry left, at the bottom of each keg. Give Abel that job, then you stand by with all hands."

Despair? No. He studied the other craft again. Glynn was overhauling him, no doubt about it. As though in answer to his thoughts, a spurt of flame leaped from the other ship, a dull roar; Glynn had a pivot gun mounted. The shot fell short.

Now Fallon thought fast. Often and often had he recalled that bitter moment when Glynn overhauled him off the Florida cays; that had been on a wind, as now. A vague notion had come to him once or twice—now he pinned it down in his mind. He was thinking of just what might be done, of just what must be done now, in a pinch. Every detail must be right. A slip would mean disaster.... What? Disaster? Why, disaster was already upon him, overhauling him fast!

A little laugh broke from him. The moon was trembling above the African hills. Another ten minutes and the sea would be a flood of molten silver. He went to John Martin and touched him on the shoulder.

"You stay here, brother, and don't let her jibe. I'm going forward."

"Can you do anything?"

"Make a spoon or spoil a horn," said Fallon grimly, and went forward. The men grouped around him, and he spoke quietly. "Break out the spare flying-jib boom."

The long, tapering spar was broken from its lashings. Fallon, with a rope's end, skinned aloft and directed the work from there. The rope was rove through the jib-boom sheave, and the heavy spar was parbuckled aloft. Three more sailors hurried aloft and aided Fallon to square the makeshift yard across the mast. Working with the sure rapidity of old seamen, they made a temporary truss and bibb. The yard was then swung free, and halyards and downhauls rove off.

All this in a few moments of time. Once Fallon's idea was grasped, the men threw themselves into the job heartily. Spare jibs were sent aloft, foot up, and seized to the spar; the head of the sail was hauled down and made fast to the main boom end, the leech of the upended jib paralleling the tack of the mainsail.

The new canvas thus rigged formed a crude but effective square-sail, and at once the schooner felt the drive of it. She went leaping ahead, but Fallon was not satisfied. He had the working-jib boom unshipped, and the men wrestled the tugging foresail across the deck, putting the schooner on the wind wing-and-wing.

Again came the work of sending up a temporary yard, reeving halyards, tacks and downhauls. More canvas was broken up and bent on. Now a balanced rig was gained; the schooner came more to an even keel. Fallon, coming down from aloft, was met by Abel Stone, who touched his forelock.

"Got a little dry powder out o' them kags, sir," he reported. "Enough to make one likely charge for the long tom."

"Load and stand by," said Fallon, and hastened aft. John Martin was yelling at him, the men were shouting and cheering—he thought it was for the obvious success of this rig. The moon was up now, and the *Lively* was dancing the other schooner behind as she raced.

The moon was up, yes; that was why Martin was shouting his throat out. He caught Fallon by the arm and swung him around, pointing frantically. The men forward had sighted those white splotches, and had suddenly fallen silent now. Fallon glimpsed them. He had no need of the night-glass Martin thrust at him. Once more his heart sank.

"Corvette and a frigate," he said dully.

The moon had pricked them out, as they stood in from seaward. They had rounded the capes from the south, and then cut in for the river mouth, standing close-hauled, leaning towers of shimmering canvas.

The frigate was drawing away to cut off Glynn's schooner, a lovely thing with all sail from courses to st'unsails glinting. But the other, the corvette—

"She's got us, Tom," said John Martin. "We can't outrun her."

True enough. The corvette was standing in to cut the schooner's course. Fallon saw instantly that she had him cut off from seaward flight. He might head on for the south and west to clear the capes, but then she would have him.

"Steady as she is," said Fallon, with the calm of desperation. "I'm going for'ard again."

"Look out you don't sp'il a horn this time," said Martin.

"Liable to make another spoon," flung back Tom Fallon, and was gone.

He came to where Abel Stone was working. The long thirty-two was loaded and swinging on its pivot.

"Enough powder for one charge, sir," said Abel. "That's a King's ship."

A flash of red, pale in the moonlight, broke from the corvette to point the words. The round-shot spurted, well ahead of the *Lively;* they were in range.

"Chance it," said Fallon curtly. "Even keel. If you miss, we swing for it."

"We swing anyhow, with them blacks below," said Abel Stone. "You'd best take the match, sir. Quill's all set and ready. I'll give the word."

Fallon took the glowing match. The quill, with its charge of powder, was set in the touch-hole, the end broken off and ready. He waited while Abel Stone directed the men, while the long gun swung and steadied. One look back; the frigate was fluttering away after Glynn's ship, detonations were drifting down the wind, red flashes spurting; Butcher Glynn was done for, this night.

"Now, sir, *now!*"

Fallon brought down the match. Flame spurted from the touch-hole; the long gun reeled and thundered in a vomit of white smoke. The schooner shivered; the blacks down below lifted thin and dreadful screams of terror.

A yell burst along the deck, a frenzied yell of incredulous joy. That lovely pyramid of white was shattered in the moonlight. Not badly, but still shattered.

"I loaded wi' grape, sir!" croaked Abel Stone. "Grape, to cut up her rigging. Got some of her top-hamper, anyhow."

"Down!" shouted Fallon suddenly, as the corvette swung. "Down, all hands!"

Too late. The red spurts blasted out as the corvette's broadside let go. The schooner raced on like a deer, almost lifted out of the water by that spread of canvas. Balls whistled and screamed in air. Splinters flew from the bulwarks; the little craft shivered again as the iron thudded into her.

Then it was done. The crisis was past, and she was racing on, unharmed. All safe aloft, and out of range before the stricken corvette could wear and fire again. All safe aloft—but on the deck beside the gleaming brass gun lay Abel Stone, a smile on his freshly shaven face, and death triumphant in his heart.

And the *Lively* raced on—on for the Middle Passage, on for the free seas and her own good name again, and a new rig to increase the story of ships and men.

Captain Trumbull ceased to speak. He struck a match and held it to his dead cigar-butt. There was a stir of relaxation around the table.

"So that's how it was!" said somebody. "All I got to say is, it's a darned good yarn, even if it ain't true."

"Ain't true?" roared out Captain Trumbull abruptly. "It's true, every word of it! That's how Fallon invented the rig. And inside o' five years, it was being copied on every sea. Every word of it is true!"

Mr. Miles leaned forward. "You say it's true, Captain Trumbull," he observed. "You may even think it's true. But—how do you know?"

Captain Trumbull looked at him for a moment, then turned fiery red.

"None of your damned business," he said, and stamped away.

THE FIRST CLIPPER

Years ago, in an uptown New York shop near One Hundredth Street, I bought a ship in a bottle. I took it home and gave it to my son. He still has it.

Last week Dr. Kung, a Chinese scholar sufficiently cultured to lecture in this country, was visiting me. He happened to see the bottle with the miniature ship, studied it a moment, and turned to me.

"Do you know the name of that ship?"

"It has none," I said carelessly. "It's just one of those things made by seamen to kill time."

"You mistake," he replied. "I think it's a model of the first genuine clipper ship, the *Rainbow,* built in New York in 1845. How do I know? That is very simple, my friend. As *Sherlock Holmes* would say, it is elementary. When we return to my hotel, I'll show you something."

Later, in his hotel room, he produced a small old book, the size of an autograph album.

This book was full of sketches. He turned to one page bearing the design of a full-rigged ship. Other pages showed various details, not of rigs, but of the ship—the stern, the bows and so forth. Coming back to the sketch of the ship herself, I found that it did look oddly like that model in the bottle. However, it was certain that this sketch had not been done by any seafaring man; that it had been made by some Chinese artist was equally certain.

"This looks like a sketch made by a Chinese, back in clipper-ship days," I observed. "It isn't like any clipper ship I ever saw pictured, however, in some of its details."

Dr. Kung smiled in his gentle way.

"Oh, it was made before there were any clipper ships."

"What?" I gave him a sharp glance, wondering if he realized just what he was saying. "Is it that old?"

"Nearly a hundred years old," he rejoined. "The story is not what you, perhaps, would term a happy one. In those sketches are contained the life and death and ambition and struggles of men; all very curious. And that is how the American clipper ships came to be built."

"Eh? You're wrong there," I said in my positive Occidental fashion. "They were due to a draftsman named Griffith, who invented them. The *Rainbow* was built from his designs. So—"

My eye fell upon the designs of the Chinese artist. One of them bore a date: *Canton, 1841.* As I fell silent, Dr. Kung smiled again.

"It might be argued," he said, "that no one ever really invented anything—except God. However, that has nothing to do with the matter in hand. I might tell you that the earliest printed book extant is a Chinese work whose printing was finished in May, 864 A.D.—but it would leave you cold. But were I to tell you the famous American clipper ships, which changed the history of seafaring, commerce and shipbuilding, came from China, you would prick up your ears."

"Decidedly," I assured him. "Their origin is too well known. Why, the giant airliners of today are known as China Clippers, after the old tea-ships!"

Dr. Kung positively beamed. He touched the date on the design.

"Precisely, my friend. At this date, American commerce was well established in Canton; European commerce had a quarter to itself, the East

India Company predominating. These factories or *hongs* handled their China trade through immensely wealthy Chinese merchants, and these *hong* merchants were great gentlemen. There were thirteen of them; and they had a monopoly on all foreign trade in Canton.

"One of these merchants was Tan E, who had purchased the blue button of a third-grade mandarin, and who dealt very largely with the American *hong*. His son, also known as Tan E, was a particular friend of Bob Clark; so, it might be said, was his daughter Chu or Pearl, an independent young lady who had imbibed heavily of foreign ways. This was a great scandal to poor old Tan E, but there was nothing he could do about it; he was that kind of a man. After all, he had many children. He could well spare one.

"Clark had been out here two years, and so far had not made his fortune. I wonder how to make you realize what sort of young man he was? Shall I say, like one white peony in a field of red ones?"

Dr. Kung's similes, while no doubt charming to an Oriental mind, had an unfortunate effect on the Occidental ear. However, he elucidated the matter, and conjured up a very satisfactory portrait of Bob Clark—a thoughtful dreamer lost in a world of frenzied business activity. A slender, dark man, sensitive and aloof, with no leaning toward bawdy stories or singsong girls; a student who had mastered the Canton dialect in six months and was of such inestimable value to his firm that they overlooked all his eccentricities—even his friendship with the Tan E family.

Clark was out of the hong more often than in it, and spent more time on the river in his skiff than at his desk; his very absences were of tremendous importance to his firm, for just then everything was changing, and he picked up information or even trade, where none else could.

The East India Company had lost their monopoly on English trade; the Opium War of 1840 had opened up other treaty ports; and American business was rushing out in cutthroat competition. Clark might have set up on his own and made a fortune, but that was not his way. He was content, and his firm was content. It was in the spring of 1841 that Clark went to his boss, hard-jawed old Abner Perkins, about tea-ships.

"Mr. Perkins, I've been thinking it might be a good thing if we abandoned the practice of sending home mixed cargo, and sent some entire tea cargoes for a change."

"Brilliant idea, Mr. Clark," said old Abner with sarcasm. "Has it occurred to you that teas are shipped down to us from the interior between August and November; that just so much tea and no more is in the market; and that as no ships can leave before November, owing to the monsoon, and can make only one round trip a year—"

"Excuse me." Clark disdained the sarcasm fired at him. "I happen to know that more and more tea is coming down from the interior, as new plantations come into bearing, and new treaty ports are open. Now, if we had ships that cut off a month from the passage home, and another month from the out passage, we'd have something."

"We would," said Abner Perkins. He rose and took Clark's arm, and led him to the window. Before them the terrace of the American factory extended to the river, and at the anchorage were grouped a dozen ships in plain sight.

"Look at 'em," said old Abner. Clark obeyed. They were "country ships," East India Company's bottoms, broadly built, with full bluff bows; beautiful ships of teak, glistening like men of war.

"The finest ships in the world, Bob," said Abner Perkins. "And ours are modeled on them. The finest, safest, stoutest ships in the world."

"And the slowest," said Clark. "I'd like to see a ship built to carry tea only—a ship that could make the passage home in ninety days or less."

Abner Perkins snorted. "Neither you nor I nor our children or grandchildren will ever see such a miracle as that, my boy. By the way, we've been offered some large quantities of the very best Campoi, Bohea and Young Hyson by an outside merchant named Hung Qua—a stranger around here. Do you know anything about him?"

Bob Clark turned. "Yes; he comes from Fukien. I heard some interesting gossip about him last night. If I were you, I'd let his stuff alone."

Old Abner frowned, and scratched his grizzled beard.

"I'm about to bid against the Dutch company for the whole lot."

Clark smiled. "This fellow has something new, I understand. You've seen the samples, even some of the chests, eh? He faces the chests with blue and yellow paper, which heightens the brilliance of the tea; and I believe you'd find a lot of chopped

"You said once that gold and jade together were unlucky."

They passed among foreign ships, Clark exchanging greetings with many a seaman he knew. Often he had talked with these men, always on the one subject, so that good-natured jests were flung at him from more than one ship.

"Hello, there! Found what'll make a ship go faster yet?"

Crack-brained, many of them called him—these bronzed and bearded seamen who had sailed the world. Nothing could cut time from a ship's voyage except more and more canvas, which was an impossibility; most of these ships carried all they could bear.

Tan listened to him, pointed out various kinds of junks, and made absolutely futile suggestions. Finally they landed at the *hong* merchant's residence, three or four miles west. Clark was spending the evening with Tan and his sister.

elm-leaves mixed with the tea, not to mention iron filings in the powder at the bottom."

"Great heavens!" exclaimed Abner, staring. "Why, Bob, such things have never been heard of! Such dishonesty is impossible."

"That's why this Hung Qua isn't a *hong* merchant and never will be," said Clark. "You deal with our regular merchants, and you know what you're getting—on their word alone. Well, some of the lads from elsewhere are cutting into a good thing, and they're going to spoil it, that's all. Times are changing."

"If—if that's the case," grunted Abner, "you've done me a good day's turn. I'll look into it."

He looked into it, and did no business with the gentleman from Fukien.

*Bob Clark picked up young Tan E late that af*ternoon, took him into his skiff, and they ran about the river hither and yon.

Young Tan was a bright fellow, quick to learn, eager to absorb foreign ways and things. Educated in the classical Chinese style, he was an expert draftsman, an artist with pen or brush. Bob Clark could not draw even a caricature, and regretted keenly his lack of talent.

Like the residences of all such merchants, this was a veritable palace—an enormous estate comprising gardens, small lakes, a dozen buildings of various kinds, servants innumerable. Since the fortune of such a trader often ran into the scores of millions of dollars, this imperial luxury was to be expected. The unusual feature here was that a foreign devil from the land of the flowery flag was taken in practically as a member of the family.

Chu met them—a glimmering, agile girl whose feet were disgracefully large to native eyes; a girl delicate and eager, aflame with the joy of life. She welcomed them with mock formality, burst into a peal of laughter, and escorted them to a tea-house overlooking the river and the sunset. Here servants had brought pillows and gay mats, trays of food and sweetmeats, charcoal pots to keep the wine and tea hot. The three settled down to a leisurely meal that would last for hours, while servants came from time to time with fresh courses.

To Clark, it was all like some dream of restful paradise. These two were his friends; this shimmering Pearl, this girl beside him, was even more. All the poetry of his nature leaped out at her and around her, and he knew that she loved him—and that it was all impossible. Not from his standpoint, perhaps, but from hers. Marriage to a foreign devil was simply out of all reckoning.

As they talked, Tan told of the jests flung at Clark from foreign ships; and amid their laughter, Pearl gave him a puzzled look.

"Make a ship go faster? How?"

"That's the question," Clark said ruefully. "I don't know how. But there must be a way. There must be a reason behind it all. More canvas? That's given me many a headache; no hope there, I fear."

Pearl reached out for the hot wine, and poured it anew into the tiny cups of mottled jade. As she replaced it, something fell from her robes with a tinkle. She went white; for an instant her eyes met those of her brother in a swift, silent exchange of glances.

Bob Clark, oblivious to all this, leaned forward and picked up the knife—a pretty little knife with a handle of gold and green jade.

"I thought you said once," he observed, "that gold and jade together were most unlucky."

"Only if one thinks so." And the girl forced a laugh.

Clark played with the knife abstractedly, thumbing the keen sliver of steel. Almost at their feet was an arm of water, a little reach of the lake, in which gold and silver fish darted about. The girl, turning from the probing glances of Tan, took a stick and swished it through the water idly. Suddenly she turned to Clark.

"The knife—give me the knife! Now, look!"

She cut the water with the blade, and met his puzzled frown.

"Well?" he said, smiling.

"Look!" She took the stick, swished it, then followed suit with the knife. "You see? Water holds anything back. The knife cuts through it faster than the stick—it is sharp! If a ship had a prow like a knife—"

A sharp exclamation burst from Clark. In this instant the clipper ship had been born.

The thought burned in his brain. Even while the moon slipped up the sky and he sat there with Pearl beside him and his friend Tan kindly oblivious, Clark could not forget that flash of conception, of inspiration. A prow like a knife!

It did not occur to him to wonder why Pearl should be carrying that slim blade.

The night was magic, the moon glinting across the rippling river, a drift of song coming from the flower-boats; the three of them lost in the immensity of the stars and each other. Bob Clark felt this girl wakening in his brain, as always, the kindling spark of impulse, of dreams, of things vaguely glimpsed. He who so hated the harsh world around, could find peace here with her.

Bob Clark went home again. For two days he worked furiously in the office, more furiously in his private quarters; he hardly slept, but slaved far into each night, carving and cutting, shaving away at a tiny boat-hull.

On the third morning he was summoned to the hong of Tan E; the merchant wanted to speak with him. He went to the office on the creek and found his friend Tan, who admitted him.

"This afternoon, Tan!" he exclaimed eagerly. "I want you to help me."

"Gladly; we shall dine again at the tea-house," the young Chinese replied, but more gravely than usual. "My honorable father is expecting you."

Clark greeted the old man with polite formulas. A weak man in many ways, though shrewd in business,

Tan E was not unsuited to his name, which meant *Solitary Idea.* He questioned the young foreign devil pleasantly about business, about his personal affairs, and finally asked whether Clark did not want to go back home.

"Of course, some day," said Clark. "First I must make my fortune."

"How much money would that require?" asked Tan E, and Clark laughed.

"Oh, hard to say—fifty thousand dollars, perhaps!"

"I will place it to your credit today," said Tan E gravely. "You may leave on the ship which departs day after tomorrow. It will give me great pleasure."

Clark, dumfounded, could not believe his senses.

"I have learned of your honorable ambition to build a new type of ship," said Tan E. "All is settled."

Yet it was true; the blank yellow features twitched nervously before his gaze, his astonished questions. Such generosity was not unknown among the *hong* merchants. One of them, not long before, had torn up promissory notes amounting to seventy thousand dollars, in order that an American merchant might return home with a clear slate.

"I have learned of your honorable ambition to build a new type of ship," said Tan E. "Now it is accomplished. All is settled. We are friends."

Clark went back to his own factory as in a dream, walking on air. He burst in upon old Abner Perkins with his amazing news; words bubbled from him.

"It's incredible!" he concluded. "Fifty thousand dollars, sir—mine! Think of what it means. I can clear out, I can go to work on my ideas for a ship; I've just got them in shape, I'm going to see about the sketches with Tan today. He can put what I have in mind into concrete designs. And I can leave with the *Eagle* day after tomorrow!"

"Aye, and a good thing," grunted old Abner.

Clark stared at him.

"Why, sir, what do you mean?"

"I've been aiming for a word or two with you, Bob," said the other grimly. "No need of it now."

"Let's have it, sir. Have I done anything amiss in the office?"

"No, but plenty out of it. Tan E is being disgraced far and wide by your idling with his daughter. The same dalliance is disgracing this factory, your own name, and the good fame of all Americans. The Chinese don't care for any foreign alliance; and we don't either. Is that plain?"

White to the lips, Bob Clark kept his temper.

"Very plain, sir. I sha'n't argue the matter—"

"There's no argument," said Abner Perkins. "You're relieved of duties, lad. I'll take passage aboard the *Eagle* for you; enjoy yourself tomorrow—your last day in Canton. And by the way, I'll have private letters home to entrust to you."

Clark went to his own quarters and sank into a seat, staring blankly before him. Fifty thousand dollars—not from friendship or benevolence; he was being bought off and sent home by Tan E. Marriage? Devil take marriage! The New England conscience and the Chinese instinct alike would repudiate such a marriage; a love-affair might be endured, but marriage was absurd to contemplate.

This afternoon, then, would be the last time. But Tan would advise him; if appeal to the old merchant were possible, Tan would know. And there was always the chance of stealing Pearl away, of taking her with him. Captain Grimsby of the *Eagle* was a good old scout. A word with him might settle everything.

Take the money of Tan E—and steal his daughter too? That was not the Chinese notion of honor. The money was being given him to avert disgrace, in native eyes.

With an oath, Clark shoved the whole problem aside for the moment and went back to his toy ship-hull. He had the thing more or less the way he wanted it, and now he made some crude sketches, to help guide Tan's pen and brush.

At lunch he found himself the envy of everyone in the factory; word of his good luck had spread like wildfire, and congratulations overwhelmed him. The irony of it left him grim-eyed and bitter.

When he picked up his friend Tan that afternoon, the two sat in silence while Clark sent the skiff upstream. He avoided the ships at anchor, avoided the other skiffs and boats of the merchants who were airing themselves on the water. As they drew near their destination, Clark suddenly broke out in an explosion of all his pent-up emotions, desperately seeking advice and help from his friend.

Tan listened to him gravely, and at length shook his head.

"You should know better," he replied. "What you ask is impossible; it is contrary to the rites, to the customs of our people and of yours. Already my father has lost much face. He will not even discuss the matter with you."

"But—but Pearl loves me!" exclaimed Clark.

"That may be; but she is going to marry Li Han the merchant. It was arranged this morning; as soon as a favorable day is set, the betrothal will take place."

Clark stared at him, read something inflexible in the saffron features, and with a little groan said no more.

They landed and went up to the summer-house where Chu had everything ready. At the first glance Clark saw that she knew everything; her gayety was only a brave shadow of itself, and her wan pallor betrayed the inner ache and emptiness. When he told how her suggestion had given him the idea he needed, she wakened into a little flutter of joy and eagerness, for a moment. Then she drooped again, pathetically.

Clark turned to his friend. Before Tan he laid his crude sketches, the model of his ship's hull; he explained everything in detail. Tan, who had ink and brushes and bamboo pens at hand, began to make sketches with a clever hand. Clark corrected them, and pointed out the details he desired changed, while the sunset flamed and died. At length Tan had everything in his head and on paper.

"Tonight," he said, "I will make proper sketches, my friend. I'll send them to you in the morning. Let me borrow this model ship until then. The sails will be like those of the *Eagle,* you say? I'll copy them and make a picture of the ship as she will look under sail."

For two days Clark worked furiously, carving a tiny boat-hull.

So the matter was laid aside.

Pearl touched the strings of her lute and sang them fragments of song, but the songs were sad things, and lifeless. Thin clouds veiled the high moon, and the oppression that weighed upon all three left them listless and silent, ill at ease, dispirited. Clark at length stirred and rose to depart. Tan went down to the boat; it was his one chance for a word with Pearl. He caught her hand, slipped his arm about her shoulders, felt her yield to his embrace, and spoke softly.

"Tomorrow night, half an hour after sunset, I'll come for you. Be here, beside the little lake."

He could feel her trembling to his words, caught a half-choked murmur, and so went down to his skiff and departed down the darkling river. He had drawn blank here; now to see whether Grimsby would help him out. If not—well, that contingency spelled only frantic desperation. Grimsby must!

Luck favored him. He was in his own quarters at the factory. A package had just come; opening it, he found his ship model and half a dozen sketches Tan had made. Beautiful things, showing; exactly what Clark wanted shown, with one of a full-rigged ship which would have made any seaman smile, but which pointed the changes in hull construction excellently. These were spread over his bed when one of the clerks came to tell him that Captain Grimsby was below.

Clark hurried down to the main office, found Grimsby with Abner Perkins, and discovered that his passage was all arranged. Grimsby was rather a young man, still in his thirties, with a salt-bitten countenance and a twinkling eye. Two of his men had just deposited a huge and heavy mail-sack near old Abner's desk, and there was much joking about it as the two men sipped their rum and invited Clark to join them. Before night, all the mail that the *Eagle* had brought out would be distributed.

This mail-sack had been carefully held up ever since her arrival, as was customary. Each skipper bringing out mail from home, guarded it jealously until the hour of departure, lest rival agents and merchants receive orders or instructions should spoil his chances of a cargo; also, his own agent must get home news first and ahead of all rivals.

When Captain Grimsby departed, Clark went from the office with him.

"Captain, will you come to my room for a few moments?" he asked. "I want to speak with you privately—as man to man."

"Aye, with a will," said Grimsby heartily, and winked. "Some private commercial venture that'll need my help to squeeze past the Imperial customs people downriver, eh?"

"A venture, yes, but not a commercial one."

They came to Clark's room. Captain Grimsby took a seat, lit his pipe, and listened to what Bob Clark had to say. Then a slow frown gathered in his keen eyes.

"A risky business—for me," he said finally. "If it were learned that I slid your lass out of here, I'd run into hot water next voyage. I fear—"

"Ten thousand dollars, Captain," said Clark quietly. Grimsby's eyes widened. "Ten thousand, before we sail. I'll have Mr. Perkins make out the papers. Does that cover your risk?"

Grimsby put out his horny paw.

"Done with you—and be damned if I'll take your money in such a cause! I'll do it and run my own risk. Get her aboard tonight after dark, and leave the rest to me. I know that mandarin downriver who handles the customs; I'll slip him a hundred dollars, and you can pay that back to me, and passage for the lass—no more.... Hello! What's all this?"

Grimsby had caught sight of the model and sketches spread over the bed. In a glow of excitement, gratitude, eagerness, Bob Clark broke into quick explanations of his great idea. The skipper listened at first with keen interest.

"Look at the model, now," and Clark continued, as he showed the shape of the hull. "Designed to cut through the water like a knife—you see? None of your bluff bows that beat the waves, shaped like a barrel, but concave bows and a sharp stem. This carries her breadth of beam farther aft than is usual, but you see how the quarters and stern are lightened by rounding up the ends of the main transom—"

He was interrupted by an explosion, a gale of laughter. Captain Grimsby fairly held his sides, until able to speak.

"Man, man, it's a madman's dream! Forget it, or you're liable to be clapped into jail as a lunatic. Concave bows, says you? Why, she's a ship turned inside out, clear against the laws of nature! She looks pretty, I grant you; but take a seaman's word for it, such lines would never do in practice. Why, such a vessel would have a tremendous dead-rise, tremendous! And she's positively wall-sided. Your proportions are all off, too. That amount of beam to her length would never be safe. Speed? Aye; she'd take herself and her crew to hell faster than any craft ever yet built! No, no, Clark; you're no seaman. Stick to your last, my friend, and don't play with such crazy notions as this. Get your duffel sent aboard, and I'll expect you tonight."

Left alone, Clark sat disconcerted and appalled. Arguments would not have shaken him, but ridicule shattered all his hopes. Grimsby was a friend, risking everything to help him; and yet Grimsby had roared with laughter. This great idea of his—why, all it evoked from a man who knew, was mirth!

Well, his dreams had failed; what of it? His life remained to live. With an oath of irritation, he stuffed the plans and the model into his duffel-bag. Now he had something more important to think about. A few more hours, and the broad horizon of life would open to him and the woman he loved! And Grimsby would marry them, had already consented to do it. Everything was turning out simply and beautifully for them.

He forgot only one thing—the deep and terrible filial piety in which the Chinese were reared.

When the sun that evening dipped down to

the horizon, Bob Clark was idly rowing his skiff on the river. When the sun had disappeared, he made a cautious approach to the grounds of the far-reaching residence of Tan E; with darkness, he came quietly to the shore. The sky was deepening into full darkness; the pale stars were gleaming and winking, as he drew near to the little summer-house beside the artificial lake.

But Chu was not here.

"Pearl!" he called softly. There was no reply; she was not here at all. He peered to see her shape glimmering across the gardens, but there was no sign of her. As he looked about, his eye caught something white beside the pool. He picked it up—a strip of white paper, the color of sadness and mourning, on which were drawn Chinese characters. The paper had been weighted down.

Clark took a box of phosphorus matches from his pocket and struck one. Having a fair knowledge of Chinese, he could read the characters; in fact, he knew this quotation from the classics:

A Lifetime of Remorse cannot be called Happiness

The flare of the match died out. Clark repeated the words over; he realized this was a message intended for him. He stooped and picked up the object that had held down the paper. It was smooth and slippery to his hand; it was the gold and jade sheath of the little knife Chu had carried.

Then she had refused to cover her father and her family with disgrace. This was what the message meant. Never could she have forgiven herself, trained as she was in filial piety, for the shame her flight would bring upon Tan E in native eyes.

Clark turned away, in mad passionate impulse to seek out Chu and plunge into swift argument, convince her, show her how the truth lay as he saw it. He took a few steps—and came to a halt. His heart leaped. There beneath a drooping willow was a figure, sitting motionless, head bowed.

"Pearl!" The word broke from him. He hastened forward, but had no response. He parted the light drooping branches of the willow and fell on his knees beside her. His hand went out—

His fingers touched the jade haft of a little knife protruding from her bosom.

"I warned you." The voice of Dr. Kung roused me again to reality with' its gentle, almost mournful insistence. "I warned you that the story was not what

"Tomorrow night, half an hour after sunset, I'll come for you. Be here."

you would term a happy one; although to a Chinese it is very beautiful and ends as it should end. Indeed, the story of the girl Chu is still told in Canton as a model of filial piety."

I stirred uneasily. That was one way of looking at it, of course; it reminded me of sly old Brantome's argument as to whether maid, wife or widow were best fitted to enjoy love.

"But what about Clark?" I asked. "What became of him?"

"Nobody knows. He did not, however, go aboard the *Eagle.* When that ship passed down the river in the morning, she sighted his skiff floating empty, with the bows stove in. Whether he committed suicide, or while rowing in mad blind grief was run down by some junk, was never known....

"It is not hard to imagine," he went on reflectively, "that his effects were unclaimed when the ship got home, perhaps were sold, and came into the hands of others. Perhaps the model and sketches came into the hands of the man Griffith, who is said to have designed and built the first clipper ship, four years later. I do not know. One can never be certain about such things. But it is plausible."

Plausible, yes; it all depended on how much truth lay in this story he had been telling me. I challenged him.

"How do you know what happened a hundred

years ago in Canton? And what are those sketches of yours—they're certainly not the ones made for Clark?"

Dr. Kung smiled. "No; these are copies that Tan made for himself at the time."

"How did you get them?" I demanded.

"In the most logical way possible," he said. "You see, it was not customary for an honorable family to use the family name in commercial affairs. The commercial name of Tan E, the *hong* merchant, was very famous; but few people among the foreign devils knew his family name."

"And that was—"

"Kung," said my friend, with his beatific smile. "Kung. He was my great-grandfather. That is how I know what happened a hundred years ago in Canton, and how the first clipper ship came to be dreamed about."

SKIPPER OF THE GREYHOUND

Captain Rawlins snorted down his bushy whiskers and glared at us.

"Seamanship! Ships! Why, blast it all, what does it take to be a skipper in steam? Nothing. Less than nothing. Any lubber who can lean on the Hydrographic Office and the radio and all them gadgets, can get his job done for him gratis. Steam killed the old-time skipper."

"No," said Captain Merriam gently. He was a little old man, a great student of sea lore; we were sitting in his cabin and sampling his Demerara rum.

"Nothing of the sort, Rawlins," he went on, thoughtfully squeezing a drop of juice from a green lime into his rum. "You're like all these chaps who think there was a sudden jump from sail to steam; but there wasn't. It was a gradual transition. Steam put an end to the clipper ships, yes."

"Far from it," I put in, brashly venturing to splinter lances with these two old seadogs. "What about the Black Ball Line?"

"Whoosh!" Captain Rawlins snorted again. "Damned steam packets!"

"No, no," said Merriam. "Let's talk about the Dramatic Line instead—the old Dramatic of Boston, and E.K. Collins, and his shore-skipper Cap'n Stout, and how the transition from the old clippers really took place. You know, that first voyage of the *Greyhound* was an epic, seen through the eyes of Cap'n Wallace, who took her across the Atlantic. Conflict? Rascality? Tough work? Why, Wallace had everything to beat on that voyage, and a thousand times everything—including the Cunarders and the Atlantic and the blackest sort of treachery. The clipper ships were dead; the Britishers were sweeping everything before them—and it was Collins who had the vision to build up the American steam packets, as an evolution of clipper ships."

"Evolution?" demanded Captain Rawlins sharply, pawing at his red whiskers. "Evolution?"

"Aye. Collins had everything against him, too. Before he could get any mail contract, the Government stipulated that his ships must be at least two thousand tons' burthen, and must prove their worth before any talk of contract and subsidy. And he turned out the best steamships ever built for their size, to this very day. But when it came to the first one heading out across the ocean, there was hell to pay and no pitch hot."

"I've heard o' them ships," said Rawlins. "No bowsprits, but a straight stem, a wedge-shaped bow, and a long, easy run curving to a graceful stern; and so high out o' the water, they were dry and comfortable. Three-masters, aye. I remember; the Dramatic Line, it was, sure enough. What's it about the first one to sail?"

"Wasn't settled until the last minute who'd go master," Merriam responded. "There'd been trouble; dirty work and plenty of it. A lot of people didn't want to see the new American packet go through. Collins had enemies. Jealousy was rampant. Commercial interests had a finger in the pie. And when the *Greyhound* was loaded and ready, her passengers all aboard, within an hour of sailing-time, what happened?"

We stared at him as he paused, and I spoke up impatiently.

"Well, I'll bite. What happened?"

"Her master up and disappeared; bought off, likely. Something had to be done, and done fast; and in the Collins office you can bet there was a hot scene. Picture Collins himself there, a genius in his way, but caught all unprepared, and with him old Cap'n Stout, his shore-skipper. And outside, the wind was blowing off the hinges of hell—"

A gusty scene outdoors and in, with the history of transatlantic shipping hanging in the balance, with success or failure staring Collins in the face. He could trust old Stout, and not another soul. He had suddenly realized that treachery, sabotage and worse lay aboard the *Greyhound* waiting to snare him, and this shook the very heart in him.

"Bully Cowles could take her out," he observed.

Cap'n Stout spat an oath.

"Be damned to him! I tell you, Cowles is crooked from stem to stern! Because his family has influence, because he's good in his way, you've got faith in him; but you don't know him the way I do. No! If anyone takes out the *Greyhound* this day, it must be a man who knows how to look slap into hell. We've a dozen prime masters at hand, but—"

"But they know nothing about steam," said Collins.

"Right. Give me the say and ask no questions—and I'll guarantee she sails on the nick and wins the Liverpool race. Yes or no?"

Collins looked with haunted eyes at the bluff, savage old master.

"You're the one man I'd trust to Halifax and back, Stout," he said simply. "It's your say, old friend; go ahead. I'll stand back of anything you do. Who's the man?"

Cap'n Stout struggled into his coat, caught up his hat, opened the door, and then paused briefly to make reply.

"Robbie Wallace," he snapped, and slammed the door shut on any protest.

Through windswept streets he made his way; twenty minutes later he was clawing over the gangway of the three-sky-sail-yarder *Black Eagle,* moored with other tall clippers at India Docks. Since morning the wind had been whipping over the crowded basin and the craft moored there. Shore-fasts had been doubled and even trebled; worried mates drove seamen almost as hard as though they were at sea. The mates were wise. The wind was increasing, and it would be no joke if a ship came adrift in the basin while the great steam-packet *Greyhound* was beating to sea.

Halting at the clipper's galley, Stout sent a stentorian shout forward to where Wallace was getting out spring lines, and turned in. Five minutes after, Wallace stamped into the galley, wiping rain out of his eyes. A young fellow, Wallace, master of this clipper only for the past year: young, trim, hard of eye and mouth and hand, and the very apple of Cap'n Stout's eye.

"I'm shifting you today." Stout had a mug of coffee in one hand and a cruller in the other, and spoke from a full mouth. "Right now. Pack your gear and get aboard the *Greyhound.* Move lively! She's to sail in an hour."

"The *Greyhound?"* said Wallace, staring at him. "Why, I was to keep this ship! And I thought—"

"You thought?" Cap'n Stout emitted a roar and a spatter of cruller crumbs. "Thought you were a fixture here with your loblolly seamen! Well, you're not."

"So that's it!" The face of Wallace flamed brick red. "Sending me aboard her as second or third, eh? Well, I'm for steam; it's the coming thing. But you can give E.K. my compliments and both of you go to hell! I'll ship as cook in a coaster before I'll step down from master to be mate of that paddle-wheel tub."

Wallace checked himself, catching a twinkle in Stout's eye.

"You're taking command, Robbie."

"Command? Me?" Wallace could feel the heart-leap register in his eyes and voice. "Command of a steamer? Of all the luck! Why, there's gray-beards in port who commanded ships when I was a pup—"

"Graybeards and mossbacks who can't get sail out of their eyes." Stout abandoned his brusque, blowing manner and became confidential. "It's your job, if you can handle it. Her skipper disappeared; you're master now. They'll know better than to try to buy you out, you that's been like my own son to me; but they'll try other tricks. There's deviltry aboard."

"What sort?" snapped Wallace.

Stout grunted into his coffee. If I knew, would I be worried? Well, get started! E.K. wants a word with you, and there's plenty of important matters to look after."

"You're not sending her out in this blow?" Wallace said. "This will turn into a duster before dark; it'll be dangerous work beating out."

"You mossback sailing-ship master!" sneered the older man. "Come snow, come blow, the cursed British are sailing a steam-packet tonight from New

York. You must beat 'em across, for the mail contracts. That's the orders. The whole future existence of the line depends on it."

He gulped his coffee, slammed down the mug, and clamped on his hat.

"It's no bed o' roses, Cap'n Wallace," he rumbled grimly. "You're the one man we can trust; you know a bit about work in steam; you make or break with us, and you do it now. And God help you! Plenty of people want to stop us. It's like every new thing; all the world's ag'in' it; there's more enemies than we know. There's one man aboard the *Greyhound* to rejoice your heart—and a score who won't. No help for it. You've got to take the mess and handle it man style."

"My job," Wallace said curtly, to hide the springing exultation of his heart. "I'll do it."

*His ship, his ship! He scarcely knew what inter-*vened, realized not at all the few words with E.K. Collins, until he was standing on her deck at last, with Cap'n Stout at his side. His ship! The first of the Yankee line to battle storm and British and monopoly; and himself to make or break with her.

His ship! His crew, his passengers, his risk, his responsibility; and back of him, standing or falling with him, the Dramatic Line, the dreams of Collins, the new vista of shipping and commerce across the world. Standing on the windy quarterdeck, he went hot and cold by turns. The whitecaps whipping over the water, the swaying masts of the tall clippers moored inside the basin; storm and stress against him, and worse—

"I think you've been shipmates before, gentlemen," Captain Stout was saying.

Wallace looked at the massive, round-shouldered man, twenty years his senior, and shook hands mechanically, with a downthrust of his heart. Bully Cowles, yes; saturnine, vindictive, and competent. An unloved man, with powerful influence ashore, and hatred in his eyes for this younger officer stepped up over his head.

"Aye," said Cowles, without enthusiasm. "I think you sailed under me as third, some time back."

"Right. I hope we hit it off in this smoke-pot," Wallace rejoined. "I've sailed a bit in steam, but I'm still green at it. I hope we can pull together, Mister."

"I'll do my job, sir." Cowles touched the peak of his sou'wester and somehow made the respectful gesture an insult. "Wish ye luck, Cap'n!" he growled, and returned to his work forward.

"Wishes ye in Tophet, rather!" Cap'n Stout emitted a snort. "Twenty year with Collins and the Dramatic Line; two master's jobs blowed to hell; and himself as well, if I had my say. Now he hates the sight of you. How soon can you pull out?"

"When everything's made fast. I have twenty minutes' leeway; going below for a pipe. Will you come?"

"No; I'll say good-by now." Stout put out his hand. "Make or break, Robbie, and God bless you!"

Down in the cabin, Wallace laid aside the coat and plug hat, symbol of a captain in that day, and got his oilskins ready to don once more. He disregarded the gold-braided uniform laid out for him, and with his

pipe alight began to pace up and down the cabin. So Cowles was aboard! That meant trouble....

A loud, hard knock at the door. The man outside jerked it open and stepped in without awaiting an invitation. A stout, heavily muscled man with broad red face and ginger hair, who stood unsmiling at the new skipper. He had a streak of yellow grease across his broken nose, and was redolent of oil and cinders.

"Jerry!" Wallace caught his breath. "Jerry O'Dowd, or I'm a Dutchman! Are you the engineer aboard this tub?"

O'Dowd gripped hands with him, and the red face suddenly grinned widely.

"So Robbie Wallace it is, and now a master—oh, it's good to find you here, Robbie! Cap'n Stout, the old rascal, told me to take a look at the new skipper, and never a word that it was you. I'm glad to see you, lad."

Wallace drew a deep breath. So this was what Stout had meant by one man aboard to rejoice his heart!

"Not as glad as I am to see you, Jerry; not by half," he said gravely. "How are your coffee-grinders?"

"Ready to go at the first jangle o' the bell," said the chief briskly. "And the black gang's with you, even if the deck swabs ain't."

"So that's the ticket, eh?" Wallace puffed at his pipe, as he met the shrewd little eyes. "How about the mates?"

"Well, the third might stand by you, in a pinch." O'Dowd wrinkled up his nose. "If you ask me, there's a gang o' Liverpool rats aboard to curl your hair!"

"I see. Cowles would have a crowd of his own choosing. Look here, Jerry! Is Bully Cowles the rascal back of whatever's going on here?"

"Nothing so easy as that, Robbie." It came hard to O'Dowd, who had known this young man from the cradle, who had loved his mother and lost her—it came hard to put on the "sir," here in private. He, like Cap'n Stout, had watched this seaman grow to full size, and hoped for greater stature yet.

"Them as pays the coin, stops safe ashore," he went on, wrinkling up his nose again—an unlovely habit, but denoting thought on his part. "Them as takes the coin, does the job. Who? I dunno. I've picked up talk. One or two in the passenger-cabins, I'd say."

Gusty anger seized Wallace. "It's a dirty business, all of it! A damned dirty business. To hell with steam packets!"

"Easy, now," cautioned the other gently, shrewdly. "It's a new business, Robbie; it's got to be broke in. You're the man to break it in; master it! When ye got your ticket, it was as master—mind that. *Master!* That's the proper word. Cowles and his rats won't start anything below decks, take my word for it. See to the decks yourself. Agreed?"

Wallace seized the big, hard fist. "Agreed, Jerry. We'll break—or make!"

When Wallace took his place on the quarterdeck, it was with a queer sense of desertion. The crowd on the dock, the blaring brass band, had all gone; the gusty squalls of rain had wiped them all into cover. Only Cap'n Stout stood there, alone, resolute, his arm waving. Wallace answered the wave, and turned forward.

Having none too much confidence in the steam power, he had ordered the yards braced around, the jibs, and fore and main topstails set. He picked up his trumpet and ordered the shore-fasts off, and spoke to the third officer.

"Slow speed ahead, both engines." Then, glancing at the pilot, who stood before the helmsman: "I'll take her out, Cap'n Downs, with your permission."

The special Collins pilot, a grizzled Cape Codder, met his eyes and nodded, and stepped to leeward. The mist and gusty rain obscured everything. The wind, pushing lustily against the braced yards and jibs, was shoving them broadside away from the pier. The huge side-paddles were threshing the water now. Under both steam and sail, the *Greyhound* approached the narrow entrance of the basin.

Then, just as the fairway opened, a British three-sticker popped her shore-fasts with explosions like cannon-shots. Like a wind-blown chip, her towering spars caught the gusts; she drifted out into the fairway, squarely athwart the *Greyhound's* course.

"Full speed astern!" lashed out Wallace's voice. "For'ard, there! Back topsails, down jibs. You at the wheel—port helm, hard a-weather! Into the wind with her—smartly, you ship-keepers, smartly! Jump alive there, Mister!"

He had a swift vision of Cowles, up forward, moving leisurely about. His voice lashed the men; they jumped to the work.

Through the windswept streets old Stout made his way to the India Docks.

Only the swiftness of those orders saved the day. Wallace could not credit the thing as an accident; yet he could not make himself believe it was deliberate. He rapped a torrent of oaths through his trumpet at the limeys, as the steam packet slid past her; then they were safely out of the basin and clear of the inside hazards.

He ordered more sail spread. Again he saw Cowles, up forward, noted his slack obedience; but held his peace. He kept his ship close to the East Boston side, recklessly skirting the shore, and caught up his trumpet again.

"Mister! Unfurl courses. Pile on that canvas, you lubbers—smartly!"

He turned to the watchful, concerned pilot, as the ship heeled under the press of taut canvas, and laughed.

"She may be a paddle-wheeler, but it takes canvas to beat out in this duster, Cap'n Downs! Tell that to E.K. when you see him. Without sail, we'd have piled her on Noddles, there to leeward— Mind your helm, you blasted packet-rat!" His blare leaped at the helmsman. "That's Bird Island ahead. Shiver that topsail just once, and I'll brain you!"

Out and away from sprawling Boston town, past Noddles Island to the north and Governor's to the south, dimly seen through the storm-wrack, the *Greyhound* ratched her way with sail bulging and inky smoke trailing from her tall funnel.

A good ship, Wallace thought; a stout ship, but a smart sailer. A little stiff as yet; that was to be expected. He nodded with satisfaction and faced forward, his keen eye searching out the bulky figure of the mate, watchfully. He spoke over his shoulder to the third mate, at the telegraphs.

"Give her all she'll take—full ahead with both engines."

Past Apple Island, close-hauled on the starboard tack; then Deer Island, a biscuit-toss under his lee. Now his voice harried the mate and the hands forward, until they toiled like devils to brace around; and off rushed the ship past Deer Island, through Necks Mate and outside.

"Well done, lad!" The old pilot clapped him on the arm. "Good luck to you, and to hell with the others! You'll make it."

He was gone with the pilot-boat, a dancing chip on the waters. Cowles headed aft, and with a careless word to Wallace took his position deliberately to windward, the undisputed post for a skipper under way.

"I'll watch her," he growled, hunching his bulky

said the man. "They think maybe we shouldn't ha' put to sea in this blow."

"I'm running the ship," Wallace said curtly. "Clear out. I want some sleep. Waken me at eight bells."

The passengers! He remembered what Jerry O'Dowd had said; no, Cowles was only a part of the whole thing. As later he lay in his heaving berth and tried to sleep, he felt an access of disgust and horror and incredulity. This treachery and intrigue, this fog of distrust, this atmosphere of unreliable officers and men—why, it was an unheard-of condition! It was not the sea as he knew it, or as he wanted to know it.

"Steam packets be damned!" he said to the darkness. "And yet—I took it with my eyes open. Stout warned me. Commercialism, eh? If we win clear, it's a new epoch for new ships, the dawn of a new day for shipping and commerce. Aye, it's worth fighting all the devils to put over such a thing! I'm the one to break the way, that's all. Ten years from now, a new code of ethics, new customs, new ways, will crystallize around this new type of ship. Sail's passing out. Like breaking a trail in deep snow—the man who does it catches all the hell. Take it on the chin, Robbie Wallace, and stand up to it!"

He fell asleep smiling.

All night he drove the Greyhound under both sail and steam, savagely resolved to take the lead from that British packet which had sailed from New York at the same hour. But by morning the gale had increased to such violence that he bent his will to it, hove to under the main-topsail alone and shut down the thrashing engines to save the paddles. The wind had hauled around to the northeast with full gale force; the ship rolled and tossed and plunged in the frantic sea like a mad thing.

Scarcely had he got things shipshape, when a palpably frightened delegation of four passengers sought him out on the quarterdeck. They protested his driving the ship in such fashion. Below, they said, all was hell let loose; cabin furniture was splintered; water had flooded the saloons; ports were smashed;

shoulders aggressively. "You can go below and accept the congratulations of the passengers, sir."

Wallace stepped up to him, and caught a whiff of liquor. He took Cowles by the shoulder and suddenly clamped it in his iron fingers until the man winced and swung about.

"You're the one to go below, Mister, and do it in a hurry," he said, loudly enough for the helmsman and third officer to hear. "And stay there until you sober up. No officer of mine comes on duty drunk. The next offense will put you in your cabin until the voyage ends. That's the last word on it. Get!"

For a long minute Cowles stood facing the skipper, his lips a thin red gash of fury, his eyes ablaze. Then he wilted.

"Aye, sir," he said, and obeyed.

The second mate, having finished his duties, came aft and reported, offering to take over the watch in the mate's place. Wallace studied him briefly, and with a curt nod of assent, yielded the deck. The second was a tall Bluenose with narrow features and cold gray eyes. There was little love or fidelity in that man.

Nor in the obsequious steward who brought him a meal in his own cabin.

"Some o' the passengers are asking for you, sir,"

the women were terrorized. Wallace regarded them with a flinty eye. Then, as they went on to repeat what the mate had said, he stiffened, his lips white-ringed.

"Thank you, gentlemen," he said quietly. "I trust that there'll be no further cause for alarm. That's all."

He sent for the chief mate. Presently Cowles came clawing aft, and one glance into the man's face was enough.

"Still drinking, are you?" he lashed out. "Now, you yellow dog, you've overstepped yourself. You've belittled the master's ability and judgment before the passengers. You told 'em this was my first command in steam, that I was green and—"

Cowles erupted in a passionate rage.

"Aye, so I did, and would again, ye blasted upstart! You're sailin' us all to hell; passengers sick and scared to death, the hands for'ard on the edge of mutiny from your slave-driving—"

Wallace struck without warning, but he had timed the blow to the thrust of the reeling deck. It seemed no more than a flick of his arm; no display about it. To the smack of the hard fist, Cowles looked astonished, and then collapsed in his tracks. Wallace had been raised in a one-blow school, and had made the most of his teaching.

"Mr. Fletcher!" Wallace swung to the second officer, who clung to the weather stays. "Lug this mutinous dog below and lock him in his cabin; I'll log charges against him. Have we any irons aboard?"

"Irons, sir?" The Bluenose stared. "But Mr. Cowles wasn't responsible. You hit him."

Wallace stepped toward him. "You too, eh? So you're working against Collins instead of for him also, eh?"

The second sprang back, his long face a mask of snarling hatred.

"Hands off me, Cap'n! I'm already witness to your striking the chief officer. It'll mean your ticket and your job together!"

"That's as it may be, when we learn who's paying you," rasped Wallace. "Lug that drunkard below and bring me the key of his cabin. Any talk out of you to the passengers, and you'll go the same way. Move, you swine!"

The Bluenose obeyed.

Wallace paced the heaving deck, slowly, methodically. To himself he cursed the Dramatic Line and all in it. The insolence of Cowles was explained; a deliberate attempt to make him lose his temper and strike. He had done it—harder than Cowles had anticipated. He would do it again if necessary. Job be damned, and ticket to boot! He was master here. The Shipmasters' Association would uphold him in it. Why had old Stout put this ship in his hands? Because no other master in the line would be willing to make or break! That was it—make or break! He was one man who would forget all except the basic fact; he was master here. Old Jerry had hit the nail on the head.

"Master, aye! And by God, they'll learn it!" muttered Wallace, and felt power grow in him. Forget everything else; rules be damned! He was master of his ship.

Yet as the day advanced and drew toward night, he realized what madness it had been to sail in this weather. Before evening the wind was blowing a ninety-mile gale, the ship straining alow and aloft in every timber. At four bells in the first watch, two cargo hatches were stove by boarding combers. The cotton bales stored there, a trans-shipment from Charlestown, were wet.

Wallace watched, grimly delighted, as Mr. Fletcher drove the men; Bluenose was working for his own life now. The sodden, half-frozen seamen labored in the icy spume and got new battens and hatch-covers rigged.

Below-decks, O'Dowd was having trouble. Although the engines were stopped, the engineers remained at work, knee-deep on the swishing floorplates; water was in the wells, and steam had to be kept up, to drive the pumps. In this stress Wallace was forced to rescind his orders; a penitent, respectful message from Cowles, the need of having every officer on hand, impelled him to restore the mate to duty. Sober enough now was Cowles; his lesson was learned, thought Wallace....

All storms, though, must end; another day found the *Greyhound* swinging along over the green rollers, her paddles slapping the water, her canvas drawing to a fair southeast wind. Wallace, with an eight-hour sleep behind him, received with frozen features the compliments of his passengers. He himself had little to say, but wondered which of these men were really friends, and which were hidden enemies.

His first elation on finding the ship had sustained no great damage, had died away. Mr. Cowles was respectful and subdued—too subdued. Mr. Fletcher was subservient—too much so. The entire ship was shaken down into smooth-running perfection, all too perfect. Not reason, but instinct, told Wallace to look out for unsuspected squalls. The days flitted finely—all too finely.

Jerry O'Dowd stalked into his cabin one night.

"Three days to the Fastnets, I hear," said he abruptly. "And you walking up Mersey Docks in your fine gold-braided cutaway and your stovepipe hat—is that what's in your mind the night, Robbie Wallace?"

Wallace gave the chief his keen, searching glance.

"You had best think twice afore you act, Robbie, I tell you the crew's ugly!"

"You're not a good mind-reader, Jerry. Three more days to raise the Fastnets, aye; but the glass is dropping fast."

"And you'll need hot pitch to pay the Old Nick," said O'Dowd darkly.

"What's up?"

"Ye've made a damned fast passage; it'll be a record. What would your mate and your second be doing in the fore-peak wi' the men? Why would one or the other be walking the deck with passengers and talking in odd corners? Why would these packet-rats up for'ard all of a sudden have secrets? Something's brewing."

"So I've felt, without knowing why." And Wallace frowned. "You and your gang have kept an eye open, eh?"

"Both eyes, Robbie. It's proud I am to see you a real ship's master."

"That'll come in good time, maybe," said Wallace; and each understood the other....

An icy blast from the North Sea, and the glass falling, and the engines shut down to save the racing paddles. Wallace pacing the deck for a day and a night, seizing a bit of sleep when he might. Storm staysails set, and an inky, wind-swept day that kept the sick passengers praying in their bunks....

Another dawn, with the scud low-flying and the gray combers racing and bursting. Wallace had turned in a bit after midnight. He was wakened to the gray light By Jerry O'Dowd stalking into his cabin and shaking him.

"It's come, lad. Wake up to it."

"Eh?" Wallace hung over the weatherboard of his berth, staring. "What's up?"

"Plenty, or I miss my guess. Mr. Cowles has the deck, and we've passed a ship to windward, showing distress signals."

Wallace looked at the tell-tale, the big course-needle on the ceiling of his cabin, and leaped to the deck.

"Is Cowles heading up for her? Is that why we're off our course? And he didn't send word to me?"

"No," said O'Dowd. "He's passed her, I tell you. Half an hour or more ago."

Wallace stood staring for a moment. Passed a ship with distress signals, and no word sent to the captain! With a rush, he jerked on his clothes and went to his desk, and flung it open. He took two pistols from their case, examined the loads, and thrust them into his pockets.

"Did you see the ship yourself?" he demanded.

"Aye," said O'Dowd grimly. "A steamer, looked like: hard to tell. She'd lost a lot of top-hamper. You'd best think twice afore you act, Robbie. I tell you, the crew's ugly, and—"

"Stand by if you like, Jerry," said Wallace. "If this is the pinch, I'll play it for all it's worth."

Cowles was at the weather side of the quarterdeck, chewing tobacco and perversely spitting to windward. He halted at sight of Wallace, and his eyes hardened into slits.

"Why did you change course without orders,

Mister?" Wallace asked quietly.

"Thought we'd better bear up a point or two to windward, sir; making enough leeway—"

"Why didn't you report sighting and passing a ship, Mister?"

"Not worth while, sir."

"A ship, flying distress signals?"

"Flyin' a hoist o' some kind," growled Cowles. "Couldn't make out the flags, but I took it to be a greeting—"

"You lie," said Wallace. "You've deliberately violated the most sacred code of the sea, and disgraced this ship and the line, by refusing help to a distressed ship. All hands, Mister, and make sail!" He turned to the helmsman. "Down helm. Steer nor'-nor'-west."

The man obeyed. Wallace caught a stir and a faint cry from forward. Mr. Fletcher and half a dozen men were clambering out of the Number Two hold, their faces streaked and blackened. Behind them a tendril of smoke was issuing from the open hatchway. They came piling aft, all of them.

As Fletcher swung around, he was met by a crushing blow that sent him reeling against the rail.

Her paddles threshing the water, the *Greyhound* pointed into the wind and methodically climbed the green rollers. The icy wind sang through the rigging; the ship rolled and creaked, the tall black stack spouting smoke and cinders which whipped about the silent gathering on the quarterdeck.

Make sail, Mister!" The voice of Wallace was like a saw rasping iron. "Put everything on her but the royals and brace around on the starboard tack. We're going back to that distressed ship."

"You can't do that, sir," burst forth Cowles furiously. "We couldn't risk a boat in this sea; the passengers won't stand for it! And the hands won't lay aloft and break ice from the lines—"

"Right, sir." Mr. Fletcher took a step forward. "The ship's afire, Cap'n, and making water below. To go back now would endanger the lives of every man aboard. We've got to think of the passengers, sir! We must hold our course and try to make port—"

Wallace ignored the second mate. "Make sail, Mr. Cowles. Everything but the royals."

"You fool!" Cowles whirled suddenly. "Mr. Fletcher! Men! You're here as witnesses the master's gone crazy! I'm taking over command for the sake o' the ship, the passengers and all hands. Do ye stand by me or not?"

"Aye!" exclaimed Fletcher. "We're with you!"

From the seamen broke quick assent. A sudden burst of smoke erupted from the open hatchway forward. Others of the crew appeared there, the third officer frantically calling all hands.

"Your last chance to avoid the charge of mutiny, Mister," said Wallace. "Make sail."

Cowles turned toward him. "All right, men. Come on, subdue him! I'm in command now, and—"

Wallace took one pistol from his pocket as the mate approached, and deliberately shot him through the head. Cowles fell forward, and slid toward the scuppers. For a long moment there was stark staring silence.

"Mr. Fletcher!" Wallace brought out the other pistol. "Make sail. Everything but the royals, and brace around on the starboard tack. Lively, Mister—lively!"

Bluenose stood rooted, his face ghastly. Then he took a step backward.

"Aye, sir," he croaked. "Hands, aloft!"

The body of Cowles rolled and rolled as the ship came around, gathered into a lump and lay in the scuppers like a bundle of old clothes. Only then did Wallace see Jerry O'Dowd coming, with blackened stokers at his back, and he smiled grimly at the excited engineer.

"Too late, Jerry," he said. "The game's played out now. Come on below."

Fifteen minutes later Wallace crawled from the hatchway, with O'Dowd close behind. He went directly aft to where Mr. Fletcher stood, and halted before the second officer.

"Mr. Fletcher, it was a smart trick to touch off a bale of cotton soaked in oil, eh? You're going into irons here and now, you and your friends among the men; but before you're laid up to answer to charges ashore, I'll give you my opinion of you."

Fletcher looked at his men, lifted his voice to them—but the third officer was among them with furious oaths, the black gang and O'Dowd were among them. And as Fletcher swung around, he was met by a crushing blow that sent him staggering and reeling back against the rail. He plunged forward, only to run into another that knocked him sprawling down the deck.

"Take him below, Jerry," and Captain Wallace felt his knuckles. "Too bad; they say it does take two good ones to put a Bluenose under, though. Better get down to your engines, Jerry—I'll be needing all you've got, pretty soon. Mr. Graham! You're acting mate now. Put those passengers below and keep 'em there."

Several protesting, obstreperous passengers were bundled back whence they had come; and the third officer, now mate, returned to salute Wallace briskly. From some of the men forward came a cheer, a ragged cheer that told its own story.

"Trouble's ended, sir!" Mr. Graham grinned happily.

"Just begun, rather." Wallace pointed to a heaving speck on the water. "Stand by with all hands, now."

"But sir—shall I have Mr. Cowles carried below?"

"Leave him where he is," said Wallace, "so he can see what it's like to be a ship's master. We'll bury him when we've less work on hand. Lively!"

And there was the first rescue of steam by steam in the long Atlantic lanes, and the work done by steam to boot....

Old Cap'n Merriam ceased to speak, and stared down speculatively into his glass of good Demerara, and stirred it about meditatively as though he saw us not. Captain Rawlins waited for an instant, then emitted a snort and pawed at his red whiskers.

"Well?" he exploded. "Well? I don't believe a word of it. The work done by steam, ye say? Not wi' the best bronze propellers going! Not in any such sea! By steam?"

Old Cap'n Merriam looked up, and smiled faintly.

"They didn't have propellers in the eighteen-forties; they had side paddles," he said mildly. "And what's more, they had canvas on spars, and masters who knew tricks o' the sea that's forgot nowadays, Cap'n. How d'ye think Wallace sent a line aboard that disabled craft, eh?"

"That's what I'm asking you," snapped Rawlins in irritation.

"Why, he stood up to windward of the other ship and sent adrift a spar to carry a line. Then another spar, with a running bowline bent to the bight of the towline between the spars, and—"

"And the bowline on a bight acting as a lead for the bridle between 'em, of course!" burst out Rawlins. "Drifted the line-carrying spars down on each side of the derelict, sure. Any fool would know that!"

"And steam holding his ship steady," said Cap'n Merriam. "It took a good deal to be master back in those days, Cap'n—back before there were customs and ethics and whatnot. A man had to be a real master to deserve the name, then."

"Well, that's what I claimed in the first place!" declared Captain Rawlins stoutly, and reached for the Demerara bottle. "Nowadays, what does it take to be a master in steam? Less'n nothing. Just a bunch of Hydrographic bulletins, weather reports by radio, automatic gyro-pilots and gyro-compasses, sonic sounding-machines and a lot o' other gadgets to turn with your thumb and finger. Harrumph! Here's to your health."

Cap'n Merriam only gave me a look and his gentle, wise old smile.

MEN OF THE RIVER

There are two places where the old Mississippi packet-boats were and are to be found, and I was in the other place, talking with Dan Fletcher and watching the shooting of some scenes of a movie, supposedly located at Natchez.

Dan Fletcher has some job in Sacramento, when he works at it. Like most people in California, he comes from somewhere else; in his case, it is Baton Rouge. As we sat watching the reaches of the Sacramento River, with the imitation cotton-pickers on the bank and the gorgeous old river packet-boat puffing, Fletcher laughed suddenly.

"Funny thing," he observed, "how all the Mississippi River pictures are made right here on the old Sacramento! And why not? I guess folks back East don't know that we have packet-boats here, and had them, for that matter, back before Civil War days."

"They didn't start here, however," I put in.

He nodded. "That's right." Producing a queer kind of knife, he began to sharpen a pencil with it. I have seen all kinds of knives in my time, but never one like this, before—and I said so.

"Curious, isn't it, why we do things?" Fletcher said. "Seeing that packet, made you say river packets didn't start here. That made me think of a yarn Cap'n Roche told me once, and thinking of him made me get out the dirk. He gave it to me, you see. He was the last of the old river captains—I mean the old breed. This was a knife he got when he was a youngster on the river, when fighting meant dirt."

It was a sturdy, viciously shaped little stabbing blade, the haft riveted through the center of a curved piece of ebony. It fitted into the hand like an invitation to murder.

"When you think of all those floating palaces in the old days," went on Fletcher in his easy Southern drawl, "it's hard to realize that the Mississippi is pretty empty now. Quality folks don't travel by packet; they have autos, and they're in a rush. My dad was a river pilot—"

"But who started that peculiar type of craft in the first place?" I asked.

"Steve Campbell started them," he said, staring out at the water and the puffing packet. "That's the story Cap'n Roche told me, the yarn I mentioned. It goes away back—a hundred years ago and over—when steamboats were new, just taking hold everywhere, and often burning up or meeting with disaster."

"Steve Campbell, eh?" I said, and shook my head. "Never heard of him. Some lawyer who formed a company and made a snug fortune?"

He gave me a pained look.

"You ought to know better. Things weren't done that way in America, back in those days; at least, not out West on the frontier. Campbell was an illiterate flatboatman. He used to take rafts of logs and trading goods down the Ohio, on down to New Orleans, and hoof it back. But he wasn't satisfied with that."

He went on to picture this Campbell, and the man took shape before me. Young, shock-headed, a hard drinker and a ready fighter, but with a streak of canny Scotch thrift and a devouring ambition. Back from New Orleans, the last trip of the year, he landed in Shippingport in the early winter.

Just below the rapids of Louisville, the thriving Shippingport was the outlet for all the waters above, and for Kentucky and Ohio to boot. It was busy and bustling, even now; rope-walks, sawmills, timber-yards, and warehouses filling with winter goods to go down-river with the spring thaw. Boats with boatmen of all kinds, fur-traders, Indians, half-breeds, harpies, gamblers, and slick Easterners.

During two whole weeks Steve Campbell looked around in silence, spending most of his time just looking, and occasionally listening. Then one day he went over to the port where the flat-boats and barges were drawn up from the ice, and looked them over. There he met Dave Blaney, and fell into talk.

Blaney was a little man, with a chip on his shoulder, and a quick eye and a whisky mouth; however, he knew ship engines—and he was out of work.

"I hear Squire Naylor had bad luck with his steamboat he built for river trade," said Campbell cautiously.

Blaney sniffed.

"Good boat, good engine in her too; but she smashed her paddles on logs and went ashore, wrecked."

"Her engine could be bought cheap," said Campbell. "Other men are building steamboats."

"They'll never work on the river," Blaney said in his cocksure way. "Look yonder, where Squire Naylor is building his new boat: Got bigger engines for her, but they're no better than the old ones, if you ask me."

"I've been looking at her," Campbell replied. "She'll carry a sight o' freight."

Blaney erupted in raucous laughter. "Sure, sure! She's built deep and heavy; a good job, but a poor craft. Steamboats won't never do anything on the river. Can't clear the bars; too many deadheads to stove 'em in; they can't turn quick. Load 'em down, and they draw too much water; can't get upriver against the current."

"Aye," said Campbell. "I've been thinking about that. Anybody who invents a boat that can break down them objections, will have something. Anybody who can fetch a load upriver will have something. Anyone can get down; it's getting back that'd be worth while. What do you know about engines?"

"Everything," said Blaney.

"Have you any money to invest?"

"A little." Blaney gave him a sharp look, and Campbell nodded.

"Meet me at ten in the morning, if you're interested, right here," he said, and walked away.

He investigated Blaney, as far as possible. The man had been discharged by Squire Naylor, who blamed him, wrongly, for the loss of his new boat. The Squire was a truculent, domineering, not-too-scrupulous man who had grown rich in one way and another. He had bought out the Frenchman's rope-walk and he meant to grow even richer in river trade.

Blaney was no angel, but there was nothing bad against him except that he had ideas. Campbell had ideas too; he meant to get ahead. Here in Louisville he discarded all his river ways. He dressed passably; he carefully patterned his speech on that of people who had schooling; and if he swigged a glass or two of raw whisky with his meals, this was only because it was customary. He did no drinking, as the river knew it. Both in Shippingport and in Louisville he was regarded as a canny Scot.

Next morning he tramped out in the snow and found Blaney waiting by the acres of drawn-up boats and rafts.

"If you'd hitch an engine to a flatboat," said Campbell, as they talked, "you'd be on the right track. Look at that barge yonder; she's from up the Allegheny."

They looked at the barge. Shallow draft, wide as sin, stoutly built.

"You want to build an engine boat for the river?" Blaney asked bluntly.

"Aye," said Campbell. "No need of building her; that long barge has the hull, and she's sound as a dollar."

"No cargo space, if you put engines in her and use her as a hull."

"I don't want cargo space," said Campbell. "People will pay money to travel down-river. They'll pay bigger money and lots of it to travel upriver. I want no more cargo space than will do for a deck-load, with wood for the engines. Take that hull, put in the engine from Naylor's wrecked boat, build a superstructure on most of the deck for cabins."

"Hm!" said Blaney. "That's a new idea. It'll weight the hull down almost to the waterline."

"Why not?" asked Campbell. "River waves aren't big. Can it be done by the time the ice goes out?"

"It can, if we both pitch in."

They repaired to the nearest of the many Shippingport taverns and settled down with paper and quills and ink. Blaney had a little money; not much, but a little hard cash went surprisingly far on the frontier. Campbell had more.

"Two thirds to me, one third to you," he said, as he wrote out an agreement. "Is that fair?"

"More than fair," said Blaney, and right he was.

The agreement signed, they fell to figuring on loads and weights. With all allowances, they finished by estimating that the deck-line of the barge, when the engine was in and all else done, and men aboard, would come within a foot of the water.

"Plenty and to spare," said Campbell with a nod of satisfaction. "We can take a small load of fast freight and put a high price on it. Money's in passengers. Now get the engine bought, and keep a close tongue; I'll buy the barge, and we'll get to work on it. A rough job, no paint, no trimmings, no cabins, till we see how she handles. Agreed?"

Blaney was filled with wild enthusiasm, and it did not die down with time. He went off to see about the engine, and Steve Campbell bought the barge and had it taken to the shipyard opposite Sandy Island. With this began incessant labor, day in and day out.

Until the engine was installed and the decking built in, Campbell scarcely had time to do any more looking around; but he kept his eyes open none the less. Squire Naylor's new craft was building close by, and a beauty she was, the finest ever to be launched on the Ohio.

Campbell got the job done, got the paddles in, and went to work on the boxes. On the day he finished the paddle-boxes, he noticed Squire Naylor inspecting the other boat. Naylor had come down from Louisville with a jingling sleigh and a spanking team of horses. He was a tall, lean, dark man, affable enough, but with a glinting hard eye. Presently he came strolling over to where Campbell was at work.

"Queer contraption you're working on," said he.

"Aye," rejoined Campbell.

The Squire laughed. "So that's where the engine went out of my old boat, eh? Well, my man, I wish you joy of it, and of that rascal Blaney. I hear he's your partner."

"Aye," said Campbell, and glanced around in search of Blaney. But the little man had gone uptown.

Naylor laughed again, raspingly,

"This thing is a sheer waste of good money. Why, you've no cargo-space at all here! You might better have put your money into my enterprise."

Campbell caught a distinct note of hostility, and straightened up.

"Your enterprise, as ye call it, isn't worth a penny; like your boat."

"What?" Squire Naylor flushed darkly. "What's wrong with my boat?"

"Everything," said Campbell. "You've forgot to allow for cargo and crew weight; she'll draw too much water and can make no speed against the current. This boat o' mine will go over sandbars that'll hold yours fast."

"Bosh!" snapped the Squire angrily. "Everything about my boat has been figured out from a scientific standpoint."

Campbell grinned. "Then figure out how to keep logs from breaking your paddles."

"How do you aim to do it?"

"That's my business." Campbell turned his back and went on with his work. Naylor swore, and departed.

Bad blood there, hostility; but why? There must be a reason. He learned the reason later, when gossip and laughter came to him: Blaney had been talking. Blaney, after a drink or so, had been boasting that Campbell's new boat would run the Naylor craft off the river.

With morning, Campbell picked his time to remonstrate. He was showing Blaney just what the latter was to get made, in Louisville, to fend logs and snags from the paddles on either side of the craft.

"Any pilot can see a swimming log," he said. "The sunken ones won't damage; we'll slide over 'em, but they'd smash the wheels to kindling, as they did in Naylor's first boat. Get these steel guards made, at exactly the angle marked here."

"Why the angle?" demanded Blaney, scowling. "Why not straight?"

"A deadhead would break 'em off. We must aim to deflect a log, that's all—send it down under or sideways. By the way, Naylor was here yesterday. Acted sort of ugly. You've been doing some talking, I hear. That won't do. We don't want to make enemies."

Blaney flared up hotly. "A lot you should care—the toughest flatboatman on the river, and afraid of making enemies! You don't expect Squire Naylor's going to be a friend, do you?"

"Keep your shirt on, little man—" began Campbell good-humoredly.

Blaney gave him a torrid oath.

"Little man, huh? I'm as good as you any day, Steve Campbell, you big hulking lump! Off with your coat. I'll wrassle you here and now!"

had it in his heart a long spell.... Here, here, blast it, get civilized!"

He had been muttering in the shiftless river-speech. With an effort he forced himself to a different level of talk.

"I can spill words as good as Squire Naylor, I reckon; and I'd better stick to it. Now, then, what about Blaney? Hanged if I know. Most likely he's got some grouch against me. Doesn't like my advice, says he. Do nothing, then; wait and see. He was right in one way, though: Squire Naylor won't be any friend in need."

It did not trouble Campbell that the Squire was said to be a bad enemy, with business interests up and down river, and no lack of men at his beck and call, from the courts down to the tavern-keepers. Campbell worried only about Blaney's attitude. For Blaney was his partner.

That same night they met face to face in the street, and Blaney apologized with warmth and frankness.

"You r'iled me, Steve; and I was full of liquor. Forget it all, will you?"

"Sure, sure," Campbell returned amiably. "Bad thing to fill up with liquor for breakfast. Lots of the boys do it, and—oh, Lord, I forgot you didn't want any advice."

Blaney grinned, and the spat was mentioned no more. But Campbell remembered. Every now and again he caught a glance, a word, a gesture. He knew that Blaney was an enemy, and he was helpless to do anything about it; he could not understand it....

However, there was more than Blaney to worry him. With the thaws ahead and the boat just where he wanted her, the money ran out, as money will. Both he and Blaney were down to their last dollar, and this put an ugly glint in Blaney's eyes, as he sat with Campbell and figured on their needs.

"As soon as the ice goes out of the port," said Campbell, "we can try her out and make sure everything is right; until then, we don't need to spend a cent more. The lumber for the cabins, the furnishings, the paint, and a stove and dishes—I make it three hundred dollars to finish. But we don't need that now."

Campbell laughed, and sent him staggering away with a shove.

"Get gone, get on your way, get those guards made!"

The little man swung around, half crouched, hand at his belt; at the look of vicious hatred in his eyes Campbell's laugh died in shocked incredulity.

"Yah! Lord it over me, would you?" spat Blaney. "I've had enough of your blasted arrogance, and of your damned advice as well. Always know best, don't you? Think that because you're bigger'n me, you can come the river bully over me! For two cents I'd let the worthless life out of you!"

Then, as Campbell did nothing and said nothing at all, Blaney mouthed another sullen oath and went off.

Campbell sat down, bit off a hunk of prime twist, worked it between his jaws, spat, and stared over across the river past Rock Island—No. 63 in the river charts—at Clarksville on the opposite bank.

"This is bad," he muttered. "The little feller is always sp'iling to show he's better'n the big feller; maybe I said a word too much! But it ain't natural for him to show murder-sign like that, without he's

"We have to eat, don't we?" snarled Blaney.

"Charge it, the way I do." Campbell grinned. "You're known as my partner, so your credit's good."

"It's good enough on my own hook," snapped Blaney. "How'll you live for the next two or three weeks, till the ice goes out?"

"I've got a job at the yard, building log rafts. There's one for you if you'll take it."

"Thanks." The little man's tone was venomous with sarcasm. "Don't bother; I'll get along without slaving up to my knees in slush. Where do you aim to get three hundred dollars?"

"Borrow it," said Campbell cheerfully.

The other grunted, filled his pipe, and sat back with a scowl.

"I wish to hell I had my money out of this fool business!" he burst out suddenly. "It's crazy nonsense; I've found that out. There's no such thing as passenger traffic down or up. Government men or soldiers go by barge. Settlers and such couldn't afford to pay high fares; they can go free by raft or flatboat."

"There'll be a tremendous passenger business, quick as we start."

"All nonsense," snapped Blaney. "I tell you, I want my money out of it!"

"You're in, sink or swim," said Campbell with a dour look. Anger stirred in him. "You stay in. I need some one to handle that engine; you have to do it."

"All right," rejoined Blaney curtly, and departed.

Campbell went to Berthoud, the merchant whose big warehouse was already crammed with goods waiting to go downriver when the thaw came. He knew the Frenchman well, had dealt often with him—knew him for a cautious, kindly, able man.

Berthoud puffed at his pipe and heard Campbell out, with occasional nods.

"You should have started your enterprise at New Orleans," said he at last. "There's no travel, no paying travel, from this point down; there may be some day, I grant you. But from New Orleans up, there'll be plenty. Get what you want at the shipyard, Steve, have it charged to me, and I'll carry you for it. They owe me a large bill anyway, and I've put money into Tarascon's rope-walk without much luck so far.... No, wait!"

He cut short Campbell's quick thanks.

"Wait. I'm doing this because I know you to be as honest as I am, maybe more so," he continued. "Not because I expect you'll succeed. I'm practically

certain you'll fail, Steve, for two reasons: There's been a lot of talk; some of the Louisville pilots say your newfangled ideas may be right. Suppose they are? Suppose your boat works well? What will happen? You'll lose her. I'm not mentioning any names; but it's easy for a boat to burn, for instance."

Campbell's lean face hardened. "You mean Squire Naylor?"

"Lord, man!" Berthoud looked horrified. "No names, I said! Well, that's one reason anyhow. The second is that your partner, Blaney, is pretty thick with the Squire; and in my belief, that man Blaney is a thorough rascal."

"You're mistaken." Campbell frowned. "He may be a rascal, but Squire Naylor and he aren't friends. He used to work for the Squire and got fired."

Berthoud shrugged widely in typical French manner.

"Maybe; but my negroes know a thing or two. They've seen the two of them together lately, several times, in friendly talk. Earnest talk, too. Steve, you watch out for tricks! I don't want to make an enemy of Naylor. I do a lot of business with him. Don't say I'm lending you the money; just go ahead, and your credit's good with me. But watch out for tricks."

"Thanks," said Campbell. "Maybe you're right. There won't be no tricks, lemme tell you, if I'm sleepin' aboard that boat! Let 'em try any, and I'll show 'em what it means to be sired by an alligator and weaned by a streak o' lightning—"

River talk, blast it! But he went away grinning happily, with a warm spot in his heart for old Berthoud. And he said nothing, even to Blaney, about where the money was to come from if his boat succeeded.

Blaney became friendly, sneakily friendly; this was a bad sign, for he cursed Squire Naylor lustily; and Campbell read treachery here, but held his peace. He needed Blaney desperately on that engine. He began to be aware that men talked of him behind his back, eyed him in passing, shook their heads after him. It got on his nerves. He felt himself surrounded by vague, indefinite enmity on all sides. But he worked away, earned his keep, and handed over his tools with a heart-leap when the rain came.

Two days of it, warm and drenching rain that cleared the snow down to black ground and sent all hands frantically to work, striving to get the big boats into the water while there was ice on which to slide them out. Campbell, drenched to the skin, saw his boat go out, and leaped aboard as she went. She rode steady and dry, the engine housed; he slept beside the engine that night as she lay moored, a rifle close at hand.

Afternoon—sunlight and flood-waters. He hazed Blaney aboard, got two black men at work with firewood, and steam began to rise. Finally he cast off and headed out, with a small crowd of men thronged along the shore to watch. The paddle-wheels churned nobly; and as the channel here followed the Kentucky shore, they were out past Sandy Island in no time, swept along on the rain-swelled flood.

Campbell was at the helm, trying with delight and a fierce exultation how she answered to the rudder, when Blaney came scrambling to his side.

"We've got to go back, Steve! Packing's worked loose around the shafts, and water's coming in!"

Campbell reached out one long arm, caught the little man by the shirt, and jerked him close. He glared into Blaney's face with red-rimmed, terrible eyes.

"How'd it get loose? You don't fool me, you fish-eyed swipe! If we go to the bottom, you'll go with her, lashed to the engine! Now we're heading back upstream, and you keep that water out of her if you have to stick your thumb in the hole!"

He shook Blaney once and cast him loose. In the little man's gray face, the glinting eyes were positively murderous; but Blaney, after one look, went scuttling back to his engines. Campbell laughed and swung the craft around, and headed back against the current.

His heart was high. The boat almost skimmed the water; she answered like a witch to the helm; she was perfect! And when he saw how she walked upstream against that flood tide, joy leaped again in him. What a boat to take upriver from New Orleans! Why, those river merchants and planters would pay any price for such passage!

When they nosed in again and moored, Campbell caught Blaney's arm, clapped him on the back, and spoke in a surge of generous spirit.

"Forget everything between us, Blaney! The

world's ours, I tell you! From now on, remember we're friends; both of us remember. To hell with the Squire! What say?"

"Done," said Blaney, grinning widely. But his eyes gave Campbell a shock, for in them was a lie, and vindictive enmity. He knew suddenly, in this moment, that he could expect no friendship from this man; and it sobered him. But he made no comment.

"Carpenters in the morning; three days of work, and she'll be ready enough for our purposes," he exclaimed. "A day to paint her, three more days to dry and put aboard cargo, and we're off for St. Louis and New Orleans!"

Next day Squire Naylor and his friends came down from Louisville to see how their new boat, launched and readied, would behave. Campbell, furiously at work, watched her chug and puff away with the party aboard; a fine, sturdy boat, built like other boats, solid and substantial. He saw her come back after an hour, and saw the party disembark with much cheering and jollity. He saw Squire Naylor striding over to where he was working with the lumber gang, and broke off to receive the visit.

"What d'you think of my craft now, eh?" said the Squire, a glow in his face.

"She's fine," said Campbell. "A grand boat, heavy and deep in the water; she'll lose money hand over fist for you."

Naylor's face darkened. "Why, confound you! D'you know I've got all the freight chartered that she'll hold, clear to New Orleans?"

"It's getting there that counts," said Campbell. "I'll be there and back before your craft passes Baton Rouge, if she gets that far."

The Squire made a furious gesture. Campbell, anticipating a blow, threw out his arm to ward it off. Naylor's stick struck the arm; his other arm went out, and his fist sent the Squire sprawling in the mud. Campbell laughed at him as he scrambled up and departed, cursing and furious.

"Guess he didn't mean to fight after all," he said to Blaney, as the little man came running up. "I thought he aimed to hit me; he thought I aimed to hit him; and I did hit him. Come on, let's get this lumber aboard."

He slept on the boat, and nothing happened. Superstructure and rough cabins were going up fast. Next day toward noon, Berthoud came strolling down, and Campbell went to meet him, beyond earshot of the Workers.

"Steve, there's a lot of talk about people in Louisville wanting to take passage with you," said the old merchant. "Looks like there may be something in this passenger game, after all. I hear a party are coming out this afternoon to see you."

"No passengers," said Campbell firmly. "I want to make the downriver run with the boat, first, and get to know her. Passengers mean responsibility.... Besides, spring waters are in; it may be a dangerous trip. I'll take all the cargo I can stow and be content."

"All right. I'll give you all the barrels of whisky you can take down," Berthoud rejoined. "It's cheap, and it's insured, and if you get to New Orleans, it's a quick sale."

"Done," said Campbell. "Send word to town, will you—no passengers."

Blaney, when informed of this decision, scowled but made no comment. That afternoon half a dozen men showed up, asking about passage; Campbell, to save time, scrawled a sign to the effect that no passengers would be taken this trip, and stuck it up. He was knocking off work for the day, when a man on horseback rode up, dismounted, asked for him, and shoved a paper at him.

"Court order, Mr. Campbell; you're forbidden to take any passengers on your new boat until the proper officials have passed on her safety."

Campbell laughed, tore up the order, and tossed it into the river.

"Squire Naylor's been at work, has he? Well, look at that sign. I'm taking no passengers. To hell with the court and you likewise! I'll start to work from New Orleans; and when I get back here, I'll take all the passengers I please, and Squire Naylor can stew in his own juice. Good day to you."

Too late, the truth burst upon Campbell, as they closed around him.

He strode off, straight up to Berthoud's office, and found the merchant worried.

Berthoud listened to his story, then nodded.

"I understand things are in a turmoil, Steve. It suddenly appears that there is a demand, after all, for passenger service, and people will pay for it. It seems to have thrown confusion into the enemy ranks. Squire Naylor's associates complain that you've got the jump on him. If I were you, I'd get out of here at once; your idea of going to New Orleans and arranging with the authorities there, is excellent. How soon can you go?"

"Well," figured Campbell, "I can let the paint job

wait till I get there. We'll have the necessary work done tomorrow. I can get off at sunset."

"What?" Berthoud was startled, for night travel on the river was unheard-of until now. "You'll not tie up at night?"

"Not much, if the night's clear! Get your load of whisky aboard tomorrow afternoon, and I'll cast off and be on my way. Agreed?"

"Agreed."

That night Campbell slept out on deck. Near midnight he was wakened by a slight thump. Roused,

he caught a mutter of voices alongside, and sat up, throwing off the covering of his rifle. He felt the jar of bare feet on the planking, and stared aft. There, in the starlight, he caught the flashes of a hooded lantern. A boat had stolen upon him, and men had come aboard. Next instant, from the lantern, he saw a flame springing into a pile of paper and chips.

He drew a bead and pressed the trigger; to the rifle-crack, there was a yell, a heavy splash overside; at his rush, the dark figures vanished, and the boat pulled away hurriedly. He scattered the fire, kicked the lantern overboard, and went grimly back to his post. Nothing else happened that night.

"One of 'em paid in full, anyhow!" he said with some satisfaction.

With morning, he rushed the work. Noon came, and he sighted the first wagonload of whisky coming. He called Blaney and broke the news.

"Get uptown and engage six men for New Orleans. We're putting off as soon as our load comes aboard."

Blaney goggled at him, jaw fallen. "What? But the job ain't finished, Steve! The paint—"

"Can wait for New Orleans. Get going! We're taking down a load of whisky. I've got firewood coming aboard in an hour. All we need is the men."

"It's flood-water, Steve. Flatboatmen won't go; too dangerous."

"They'll go with me!" said Campbell. And he was right. "I'll take you all down safe—don't worry; I know the river. Have 'em aboard at four o'clock."

At four o'clock they came rolling aboard, roaring drunk. Campbell answered their loud, maudlin greetings and shrugged; they were not men he knew, but they were rivermen, and he set them to work. The casks were in place and lashed down; steam was up. Campbell ordered the lines cast off, waved farewell to Berthoud, who had come down to see them off, and the boat moved out into the channel. The six men stood around Campbell, swigging whisky and watching the wheel with curiosity.

"Ain't much like a flatboat steering-sweep!" said one, with a guffaw. "Steve, what's the boat's name?"

He looked at them, with a dawning grin.

"Boys, I've been so busy I hadn't thought of naming her! *River Packet*—that's her name. Break a whisky-bottle over the bow."

They did it, with a whoop.

At sunset Campbell got an hour's sleep. To the awe of the men, they were off Blue River, a good twenty miles—making ten miles an hour with the current, and the engine barely at half speed. When Campbell wakened, the negro cook had supper ready, and all nine of them sat around the board, black and white. Then, with dusk, Campbell took the wheel.

"Moonlight," he said. "Good night. I'll keep her going. Blaney, pick out two men to stand watch and keep the fires stoked; relieve 'em at midnight."

He caught an exchange of looks, a grin that swept the rough faces, and went off exultantly to his post. Behind, Blaney and the men talked long, before turning in.

The river was swollen, empty, majestic. All cares left behind, Campbell kept the craft steady; there would be no need of worrying about the course until they reached Flint Island and Harden's creek, and by that time the moon should be up, full and strong.

A bad place, at Flint Island. One had to hug the island shore close on the left, then make a quick pull out toward the right shore, to avoid an ugly sandbar below the island. Campbell had done it a score of times, and could do it even in the darkness; but moonlight would help.

The island grew, a black mass in the starlight. Behind, the first moonrise was trembling along the water. Suddenly he caught voices; the men were awake and up. One voice, thick with liquor, lifted and the words reached him hoarse and raucous.

"I tell you, he shot my brother last night! Now's the time."

Campbell twisted around, abruptly startled. One of the men on watch came to him with a quick cry.

"Steve! Look out for a deadhead—you're bearing down on her!"

Campbell strained to see. The man moved swiftly, caught up his rifle standing close by, and sent it flying overboard. Then came a rush.

It was unexpected, swift, deadly—all planned ahead. Too late, the frightful truth burst upon Campbell, as they closed around him, bore him off his feet, carried him aft. He loosed a roar of utter fury as he broke clear, got his back against the engine-house, and whipped out his knife. Then they were on him again.

Foremost was Blaney, cursing like a madman, shoved in by the others. A glitter in his hand: a knife, a queer sort of knife, a blade that issued from his clenched fist. Campbell hammered him, but he felt the blade bite into him, and again. With this, he cut loose. Blaney went down; another man went down. Campbell staggered, and a pole hit him over the head. He went to his knees on top of Blaney, and the latter stabbed up. With a groan, Campbell seized the little man, felt the knife go in again, caught Blaney up and hurled him overboard, screaming.

Then a rifle-barrel whaled him above the ear. He staggered, lost balance, and went toppling overboard, with shrill whoops of exultation ringing behind him.

Not long after this, from a sandbar on the Kentucky shore, a pillar of fire shot up into the moonlit sky, as the barrels of whisky took the flames and fed them. The ruddy glare spread across the river. On the Indiana shore a dripping, hurt figure crawled out of the water on hands and knees, looked back at the spouting glare, and shook a weak fist; then crumpled and lay still.

A settler found him there unconscious, the next morning....

Campbell opened his eyes to find himself lying in the settler's cabin. Above him was the sweet face of a girl, merry-eyed but now pitying. She had finished bandaging his hurts, and held a reddened knife in her hand—a queer sort of blade, riveted to a black, semicircular piece of wood.

"Hello!" said Campbell. "Alive, am I? Where'd you get the dirk?"

"It was sticking in you." And the girl shuddered. "My father had to pull it out. Here, take this hoe-cake and this milk—don't talk, yet. You're all right."

"But the boat isn't," said Campbell. "What's it worth, to be alive?"

"Worth a lot," said she, looking at him. "Maybe!"

There Dan Fletcher's voice trailed off; his story came to a conclusion, and the world of a hundred-odd years back died away. Once more we were looking out at the reaches of the Sacramento, and the movie crowd, and the paddle-wheeler churning up the water.

"That," I said in disappointment, "is a typical example of what might have been a good story! To finish it there is a crime, with your hero wiped out financially, and stranded."

He gave me an odd look, then laughed softly.

"We were talking of the first river packet, not of heroes," said he. "Don't many and many human stories finish on the coasts of disaster? Steve Campbell—but here, take a look at this bit of ebony."

He passed me the queer knife again, pointing to the ebony handle. I looked at the spot indicated. Cut neatly into the black wood, but not deeply, since it is difficult to cut ebony, were the letters *S. C.*

"Campbell's story didn't finish there; he married the farmer's daughter." And Fletcher chuckled as he spoke. "Then he went on with her to New Orleans, and ended up with a whole fleet of river packets. He had one child, a daughter; she was my grandmother. That's how I got the knife—it's Blaney's deadly little dirk."

"Oh!" I said, and closed my fist about the thing. "I thought you said you got it, and the yarn as well, from old Cap'n Roche?"

"I did," replied Fletcher, smiling. "He was my grandfather."

STORMALONG

Jack Rankin was a hard man, tall, frosty-eyed and short-tempered. "Stormalong" Rankin, they called him, and for reason aplenty. He drove his ship by the shortest distance between two points, and be damned to wind, weather or human life; but that made owners' profits and his own. Under him the *Naiad* was the fastest ship afloat, on the long haul.

In those days men swore by all sorts of things, for the new things were unproven, and the old things wore well; Stormalong Rankin swore by sail and oaken bottom and clipper bow and a crew worked to the bone. He had no use for steam and paddles, for newfangled iron ships; and a large share of the world agreed with him. He could outsail any steamer going, and was not alone in that. Any good clipper ship could do the same.

Stormalong was no man to love, but he was a man who did things. When he walked into the Tontine House bar and found that Tommy Lund was made captain of the *Porpoise* and was posting a notice about letters for Canton,—all mail went from the Tontine House in those days,—he laughed long and loud.

"Why, Tommy was mate under me, and no damned good!" says he. "So it's Cap'n Lund now, is it? Master of the *Porpoise* hybrid—square rig and paddle-boxes! Lord save us, what does he want with mail for Canton and the China Seas? Those new ships of iron can make no speed either by canvas or by steam! Knock a hole in 'em, and it's like knocking a hole in a crockery teapot afloat in a tub! When's Tommy pulling out?"

Somebody told him; they were crowded about him thick as flies, every one with an ax to grind, for Stormalong was a great man among shipping-men. Here in New York, where shipping was growing more important than along the New England coast, he could grant many a favor or pull many a rope.

"What?" he rapped out. "Two days ahead o' me? Why, I'll beat him to China and meet him outbound before he drops his Foochow pilot!"

Just then, in came Cap'n Lund. The two shook hands, with a deal of apparently good-natured talk and hearty words and back-slapping; and indeed Lund was a man of great good humor. A big fellow, unruffled and easy in his ways, with a wide, generous mouth and a cautious eye. None of your dandies like Stormalong; no attempt to impress the world with his explosive energy, by dint of heady oaths and hot barking words.

He leaned over the bar, and the two had a drink together; and he shook his head slowly when Stormalong rallied him about his hybrid tub on a China voyage.

"True enough," said he in his calm way. "But you and I are different, Cap'n Rankin; and owners are different, and ships are different. You're running for tea and a record passage and crack on everything! Quick results and quick profits."

"Aye, and results show," said Stormalong.

"My owners are a new outfit," went on Lund. "No tea for us, no racing and killing crews; make haste slowly—that's the word. Cargo space and safety. And at that, we'll make a fast passage."

"With engines and coal to lug, and an iron bottom?" The derisive laughter of Stormalong lifted high and sharp. "Not a chance, Cap'n Lund, not a chance!"

"Would you come along to the Brooklyn yards and look over the *Porpoise?*" Lund rolled an inquiring, amiable eye. "There's a new idea or two going into her."

Stormalong looked at his fat gold watch, and nodded; and they went off together. The men at the bar looked after them, and one nudged another:

"There goes the devil, and polite as could be!"

"Ah, but Tommy Lund's no fool," said the other....

He was no fool, indeed; still, he scarcely reckoned what evil could fill a man's heart, himself being without envy and malice. Captain Rankin had discharged him as mate, railing at him for a slow stick and a softy unable to work the crew properly; and any man who wrongs another comes to hate that other. Lund was, in reality, anxious to win the esteem and admiration of Stormalong; but when they came to look over the rebuilt *Porpoise* as she took in cargo, even his well-argued convictions were shaken by the positive, aggressive derision of Rankin.

"Nothing new about iron ships," he said. "They've been tried out for years, and they're coming into use more and more—"

"Ha!" broke in Stormalong. "They have their points, but they're no good. Too heavy. Sails can't drive 'em; your dinky engines can't drive 'em. Takes too much coal to drive the blasted engines, and coal costs money. That eats up the profits. It's been demonstrated over and over."

"Sure," admitted Cap'n Lund, rubbing his broad, smooth chin uneasily. "Sure. But this is different. She's barque-rigged; we'll use the paddle-wheels only to increase her speed and in emergencies."

"Barque-rigged she is," Stormalong agreed contemptuously. "Think of the *Naiad* with her canvas rising to heaven! Think of how she foams along! You'll never equal her speed with this barque. Besides, what have you got under your feet? An iron pot, that's all. Strike a spike of coral, and she'll sink before you can get your pumps greased!"

"No, no, Stormalong!" protested Cap'n Lund, and pointed to the ship, whose holds were fast filling. "Something new there. A double bottom, against just such an emergency; more, the holds are divided off into compartments by bulkheads."

"What?" rasped Stormalong. "Bulkheads? Never heard of such a thing!"

"You will in future. Suppose the worst happens, a hole punched in her side or even an outbreak of fire. That compartment is closed off by iron doors. The water can't spread. The fire can't spread. Why, it'll change all shipbuilding!"

Stormalong uttered a roaring laugh.

"Hark, my lad! Theories are all very fine, and not worth a damn. Double bulkheads and a double hull—that'd be better yet, eh? Weight! There's your answer. To make this weight forge through the water at even six knots, you'd need double engines and ten times the canvas!"

Lund's blue eyes took on an anxious, doubtful look. Cap'n Rankin pointed now to the forward deck with its pronounced camber, with its iron rails instead of the usual bulwarks.

"Look there! Your hands will be awash like a half tide rock all the time!" he exclaimed in scorn. "No bulwarks at all to fend off the seas!"

"Nor to hold 'em aboard." Lund brightened a trifle. "There's no earthly reason for bulwarks, except old custom. And there's every reason against them. Think of your own *Naiad!* Her deck's like a swimming-pool half the time; when she gets a bit of a list, the load of water tends to keep her from righting. But here—well, the *Porpoise* will deserve her name in heavy weather. The water will be gone as soon as it comes aboard."

"And your men washed away with it," Stormalong rasped. "No, no! You've got a crazy thing here. Not to mention the compass trouble in an iron ship."

"That'll be taken care of, never fear."

"Aye, I've been aboard iron ships before this, my lad; I know all about your deviation figuring and so forth," stormed on Cap'n Rankin contemptuously. (And months later, Lund was to recall this remark at a bad moment.) "What's this I hear about you being bound for Chefoo? Thought it was Canton?"

"No; the orders are to make Chefoo first," said Lund. "A lot of coal to unload there."

"Why, I'm making Chefoo first myself!" Rankin exclaimed, staring.

Lund broke into a hearty laugh.

"Not first, Cap'n! Not ahead of me, anyhow."

"You don't seriously expect to equal my time outward bound?"

"No; I should beat it easily," Lund said amiably. "Your fastest day's run isn't your average, by a good deal; but my average will be brought up to a steady mark, thanks to the engines. You know the old fable about the tortoise and the hare."

"Aye, and I know the sea, and I know folly from wisdom, and I'll put a thousand dollars on it!" Rankin cried. "A thousand or ten thousand on clipper bow against straight stem, on fact against untried theory!"

Tommy Lund was easy-going, slow to wrath, never a man to wager; but the rasping voice and the edged words got under his skin. It is a hard thing to chart a clear course against headwinds of derision.

Hot words went to worse, and caution plunged overboard. There on the wharf the bets were made—money in the bank, master's share of the forthcoming voyage, credit pledged and reputation at stake. Old Israel Long, one of Cap'n Lund's owners, came up in time to write down and witness the bets. He pleaded against the folly, but it was hot blue eyes against lurid black ones, with hatches ripped off old dislikes, a crowd ringing in the two captains and eager voices whooping up the bets. No backing out now, and devil take the loser!

"It's her! It's her!" And the *Naiad* it was.

Both ships were to sail in two days. The two captains, impressive in their blue broadcloth, their stovepipe hats, calmed down and shook hands and smiled at parting. Old Israel Long, standing at Cap'n Lund's elbow and watching Stormalong stride off with a gang of admirers at his heels, groaned under his breath.

"Thomas, Thomas, you're a terrible fool for taking chances!" said he, shaking his head anxiously. "There's many a mishap in a long voyage."

"Poor seamanship, many mishaps," said Cap'n Lund tersely.

"Tut-tut! The point is, man, your ship's not proven. Stormalong may be right about the weight; if so, where are you?" Old Israel wagged his head again. "Proud of your iron ships and engines, aye! But pride's a mortal bad thing at times."

Damn all croaking! Lund tried desperately to forget the words, and could not.

The two craft got away the second morning at ebb-tide, with a brisk sou'wester blowing. This meant head-winds for the sailing-vessel; but the *Porpoise,* spouting black smoke, paddled out into the East River and headed for the Narrows. As she passed Gibbet Island, where pirates had once hung in chains, the foremast lookout reported the *Naiad* under way, but not following the steamer.

Stormalong Rankin, instead, was heading through Hell Gate with everything set to the sou'-wester.

Lund, pacing the quarterdeck, felt a thrill of admiration for the man. Only supreme seamanship could work such a large vessel safely through Hell Gate; even the Sound was not exactly comfortable for a square-rigger in a gale. But he knew Rankin would win to sea around Block Island, and be on equal terms when they started the long leg down to Rio.

Holding within sight of each other almost every day, the two ships made good runs to the equator, crossed, and picked up the fresh southeast trades. Neither skipper was doing any pushing. Lund spent long days getting his deviation-card in shape, with scrupulous exactness.

With a hull and engines of iron, which readily take on magnetism and themselves become magnets, every projecting point about the vessel became a pole of these projected magnets. He knew the danger here. On the different directions of the ship's head, these various projections changed position relative to the compass needle, which was affected by the dominant force. Thus, for each heading, was a different deviation.

Determining these deviations by observations, tabulating them, testing them repeatedly, Lund finally finished the job. With a deep breath of relief, he at last tacked his deviation-card to the inside of the chart locker door, handy for applying the readings when he laid off his course. It was done, and well done!

So was the first leg of the voyage. Almost neck and neck, they raised the bold headland of Cape Frio, forty-four days from New York; then it was crack on all sail, stoke the fireboxes, and race for the entrance!

The sea breeze ended with ebbing day, however. When Lund made the entrance islands of Pai and Mai, the *Naiad* was far to the rear, her canvas flapping dismally; and there she was forced to anchor all night. The *Porpoise,* her paddles threshing mightily, churned past Sugar Loaf to port, answered the hails of Fort Santa Cruz to starboard, and dropped anchor below Cobras Isle, where the port doctor came aboard. The first leg was won.

With daybreak, the land breeze was striking off with strong gusts, with squalls of wind and rain and peals of thunder. Half an hour passed, then an hour; and out of the storm-wrack loomed a tall ship coming in under topsails and reefed foresail. Word of the race and the wagers had by this time spread through all the assembled ships and along the waterfront; when Stormalong brought his vessel to anchor, a burst of cheers from the *Porpoise* was echoed from the harbor.

Nothing lost, nothing won; after four days the anchors were weighed together, and both ships passed out to sea and headed on down the long reach south.

Off the Plate River they ran into a strong pampero. Severely battered, and pushed far out to sea, they were separated and lost to sight of each other. After passing the parallel of 40 S., however, Lund one morning picked up the *Naiad's* canvas. He laughed softly to himself, and served out extra grog with a glad hand. He had not pushed things a bit, but he had picked up that lordly craft handily; this told him all he needed to know.

They hung in company now, preparing for heavy weather off the Cape; the best canvas was bent; new running-gear was rove; thick clothing was broken out. And ahead was coming the first test. Lund made ready for it coolly, methodically.

They had a brush with a twister off Patagonia, but stayed together to the Falklands, and thence to Staten Island, lying east of Tierra del Fuego. And there came separation; the *Porpoise,* under easy canvas and spouting smoke, steamed boldly for the strait of Le Maire.

Stormalong Rankin luffed up and hesitated, as he

watched his rival head for the inward passage. For once, however, prudence ruled his action. Baffling winds, treacherous currents, tremendous rises and falls of tide, denied those iron straits to him. With an oath he filled away and headed around the Cape.

Before evening he caught it, as mist raced down from the southwest. All hands were frantically summoned, light sails clewed up and handed, topsail halyards let to by the run, reef tackles hauled out, buntlines and spilling-lines bowsed tight. With a blast of sleet like grapeshot, the gale burst.

Gale followed gale as the days passed. It was three full weeks ere Rankin could work up into the meridian of 80 W. and into fair winds. Then, with all the canvas she could stagger under, the *Naiad* bore for Valparaiso.

And all this while the *Porpoise* had been aground off Punta Arenas.

The deviation-card was gone! Lund darted for the deck.

When Lund came into Valparaiso harbor, he was in despair, had completely given up hope. When he learned, from the bumboatmen who came aboard, that the *Naiad* had left port a fortnight earlier, he plucked up heart. A lead of two weeks was bad, yes, but he knew his Pacific; he had been all the while gambling on the Pacific, and the long stretch to the Sandwich Islands, and the longer one beyond. Many a time had he made the run to Chefoo and Canton, and only once had he gone bowling ahead with never a bad break to stay his ship. This time he was prepared for breaks.

He put in to anchorage and began to discharge mails and cargo. Going ashore with the port doctor, Lund was greeted on the pier by a smiling Chileño who announced himself as a runner from the Old House at Home, a sailors' boarding-house at the foot of Maintop Hill, close to the waterfront.

"What's this?" growled Lund as the man handed him a dirty envelope.

"It's known you were coming, Cap'n Lund. Two men have been in jail for the past few days; they paid me to watch for you."

Lund tore open the envelope and took out a letter, crudely scrawled in pencil:

Captain Lund of the Porpose.

Sir and good friend to sailermen:

We be two hands in Jale here. The sojers treat us terble. Work all day and bean soup with no beans. Black bred and coffee which aint coffee. We be starving and dying from hard work and no food. We skipped from the Rainbow *ship but we beg to God that Captain Lund will bale us out and will work our heads off if he helps us leeve this dam hole which ain't fitten for american sailer men. Respkfuly,*

Sam Peak
Hook Avery.

Lund smiled grimly as he stuffed the letter into a pocket. He had been a foremast hand; he knew how easy it was for a seaman to get into jail in South American ports. And several men were sick aboard, too weak to work; he could use two good hands.

He went about his shore business, taking no end of chaffing from the consul and others. Stormalong Rankin had done a lot of bragging upon unexpectedly finding himself ahead of the *Porpoise* after all; and news of the sail-steam race was everywhere. Upon learning from a consul that the *Rainbow,* a Canton-bound clipper, had actually been here and gone a few days since, Lund arranged for the release of the two seamen in question, conditional on his getting them out of Valparaiso at once.

He went to the *carcel* and was admitted by a surly police official. In the patio of the jail he halted to await his men. They were in plain sight. At the far end of the rectangular jail yard was a medieval treadmill. Working this full steam, pumping water for the day's use, were a score of seamen.

The officer rapped out an order and the mill

stopped turning. Twenty ragged, emaciated, woebegone seamen of all colors and nationalities stared hopefully; two names were called; and two men, bearded and unkempt, stepped down from the torture-wheel. Another order, and the others resumed their weary journey to nowhere.

The two half-starved figures stumbled forward with wild words of rejoicing. Lund broke in upon them gruffly.

"Get your gear, if you have any, and report aboard the *Porpoise.* Never mind any thanks. Get going."

It was evening before he came aboard himself, and spoke with the mate.

"Did those two rascals come aboard?"

"Aye, sir. Reg'lar packet-rats and no mistake. Scum, but they work willing."

"Give 'em slops and put 'em at easy work. When they get some meat on their bones, turn 'em over to the engineer; he needs some more help in the stokehole."

The two were fed and clothed from the slop-chest and set to work. They worked with pathetic eagerness; and presently Captain Lund forgot the whole matter.

Now, heading north, he drove the Porpoise for all she was worth. Next port of call was Acapulco, the galleon port of Manila ships. Ten days behind, there; he was gaining a bit, better than he had expected.

Off again in record time, every man aboard throwing himself into the work with vim and energy. On across the Pacific, with the northeast trades blowing them toward the Sandwich Islands. Not until Honolulu, which although not the capital of the islands was the harbor most frequented by ships, would they know how far behind they were.

The morning they stood in past Diamond Head, Lund was nervously pacing the deck; and the crew was on high tension. And there, slap before them, was the *Naiad* at anchor. One almost incredulous look, a yell from the man aloft, and then wild cheers burst from the whole ship. Lund flushed happily, exultation in his heart. Caught her, by the Eternal! But the strain had told on him, and he was weary of it.

Ashore, the two skippers met, shook hands, laughed together.

"What happened to you?" inquired Lund. "You led me handsomely at Valparaiso."

Stormalong, who was immaculately tricked out in his best shore rig, grimaced but seemed not at all cast down.

"Head-winds, where the trades should have been, for one thing," he rejoined philosophically. "A touch of bad luck, that's all. I haven't begun to fight yet, Cap'n. The pull will come from here on to Chefoo."

Lund nodded.

"If you want it so, yes. But it's my race. Say the word, and we'll call off the bets. I've proved my points; my ship's got the heels of you; and when we strike the China sea it'll be typhoon season. Say the word, and the race is off."

Rankin's face darkened ominously under a rush of blood.

"Whining, are you?" he rapped out. "Trying to crawl out of it, you dog! Not much; save your fine words for the owners. I'll beat you and your misbegotten iron pot to Chefoo, and you'll pay through the nail. Good-by, and bad luck to you!"

He swung off and away, leaving Lund astounded by this revelation of snarling hostility. Until this moment, he had never regarded Stormalong as an actual enemy; he had never thought Stormalong so regarded him. He had not viewed the race, indeed, in any light of personal vindictiveness. But now his eyes were open.

He went back to the ship with a blaze in his heart and a blaze in his face and summoned the mate, an

"I've wished for this day!" said Lund... and smacked his fist into the dark face.

angular Yankee with a reputation as tough as his hardbitten features.

"Push everything," he said savagely. "No shore leave!"

"Aye?" said the mate in sour surprise. "By rights we'd be here a week at the least, with the gear to overhaul—"

"You heard me, Mister!" snapped Lund. "When does the *Naiad* pull out?"

"Day after tomorrow, I hear."

"Then we sail the morning after she does. See to it."

As ordered, so done. The men grumbled, cursed; but the driving mate got his overhaul done, preparing for the long beat to the China coast. Lund himself inspected the hatches and holds where the coal and the cargo for Chefoo and Shanghai was stowed; the possibility of fire by spontaneous combustion was always a specter to dread. All was well; the hatches were battened, and the *Porpoise* put to sea one day behind Rankin in the *Naiad.*

And now it was drive with a vengeance, and a thousand leagues passing under the forefoot—with never a sign of the towering windjammer. Outwardly calm, Lund paced the quarterdeck with uneasy heart. The weather was too steady altogether. If Rankin were bowling along day after day with all canvas drawing, he would walk away with the race. Yet this was unlikely: some days were fast; some were slow; some would be sheer exasperation of light shifting winds, if the average held true. But to the slower *Porpoise* the long run should mean victory, with the paddles to churn where the wind failed, as now and then it did.

The long leagues slid away with the passing days. And then suddenly, unexpectedly, as Lund and the mate were coming up to take noon sights, with the dangerous Chusan archipelago ahead, a cry droned down from the man aloft:

"Sa-a-il ho! Sail ho! A point off the sta'board bow!"

Lund seized his glass and leaped for the mizzen shrouds. From aloft, came an excited yell, even before he was sure of the white dot breaking the horizon.

"It's her! It's her!"

The *Naiad* it was, with the wind failing to light, baffling airs; and Lund's heart hammered to the cheers of the men.

But the wind picked up, and the tall clipper clung like a leech now, sometimes hull down, sometimes with her courses rising, sometimes out of sight but ever forging into view again. It was going to be a finish fight; this was certain. And then, hauling up for the northeast promontory of Shantung,—the finish almost in view,—came the final gamble.

Since early morning a half-gale had been blowing. Lund, impelled to caution in these waters, furled everything but jibs and upper topsails. About meridian the *Naiad* began to walk up; with every stitch of canvas bellying taut, she drew up and passed the *Porpoise* at a good fifteen-knot clip. Lund nodded to the pleading look of the Yankee mate, and the lower topsails were spread; but Stormalong was in the lead now.

Thus, with night and the gale blowing up fresher, they drove in upon the fabled Wohushih, a snarling stretch of rocks and reefs lying off the promontory and stretching far out. The Tiger's Tail, it was called in general. Tiger's Tail Rock itself lay eight hundred yards off the head of the promontory; since it was awash at low water and clearly visible in a heavy sea, he had no misgivings. Junks beating up the coast for Chefoo and beyond never used the treacherous inside passage, for evil spirits dwelt there, and no sane seaman would tread upon the Tiger's Tail, as the proverb had it. A proverb as old as China itself, and this name was probably as ancient too. Evil mists and sudden, unexplainable fogs imperiled all this place, and many a good ship's bones had been picked by the slavering fangs of the Tiger Rocks.

Stormalong Rankin bore straight on, and Lund grimly followed. There were no lights in those days, warding every headland and reef and danger-point on the coast; no warnings at all, but Rankin knew the passage, and so did Lund.

His last fix had shown him he should pass safely to the south of Heilu Tao and Kwa Shih, another nest of reefs and shoals stretching northwestward beyond the Tiger's Tail.

"Are ye going to chance it?" asked the mate, as Lund came from looking at the compass. "A tricky place, with false channels and overfalls and God knows what!"

Lund stopped before the wheel and stared straight ahead. The moon had risen, a pale disk affording just enough light to see surf breaking over a reef.

"Aye," he said. "If Stormalong gets through, we

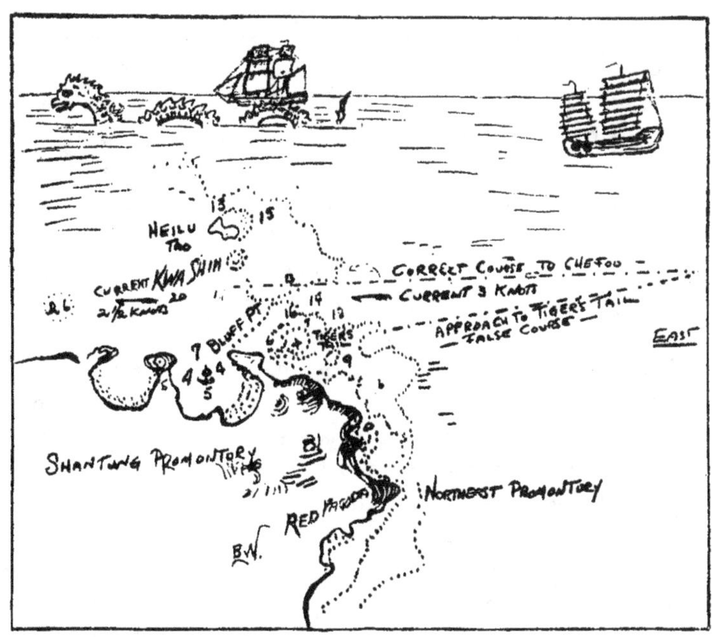

can. It'll save hours of sailing. It means winning or losing."

The mate muttered and went forward. Lund resumed pacing, now and again halting to take a bearing on the black bulk of the promontory looming off to port. At regular intervals the masthead lookout reported the position of the *Naiad,* and Lund altered course to keep in her track. Northeast Promontory appeared a little closer than it should be; but if Rankin could risk being set in close, so could he.

"What are ye getting for'ard?" sang out Lund to the leadsman, who had been taking a breather in the chains. The man took a cast, and cried out:

"Quarter less three, sir, and shoaling fast!"

Lund sprang to the bell-cord that signaled the engines, and jerked it. The paddles ceased slapping; straining forward, Lund stood listening intently. He knew the locality, knew the chart by heart, and was sure he could peg his position within a few hundred yards.

This, at sea, is plenty of room, but can mean tragedy in narrow waters. Lund turned and leaped suddenly for the chart-room. The devil! He had forgotten—

At the chart locker, he groped blindly. Struck a match, looked, groped again. No sign of it. The tack was gone; the deviation-card was gone! With one wild oath, Lund darted for the deck again. The mate had set the course here—

"Mister! Ah, here you are!" he broke out, as the gangling figure loomed. "When you set this course did you check by the deviation-card?"

"No! The card was plumb gone—I thought you had it."

Then came the lookout's stunning cry:

"Breakers ahead! Breakers!"

"All hands, Mister."

The moment bulked long; an eternity. Lund realized that he had been led into a trap. Off somewhere to starboard in the mist sounded the slatting of canvas, the clattering of yards and blocks, the unmistakable thunder of backed topsails, hoarse orders to let go both anchors, and the heavy splashes as they fell.

Lund cursed hotly, striving to keep panic from his voice, lifted a shout at the mate, who was getting the anchors cleared forward.

"Let go both anchors when you're ready! Bear a hand!"

Getting out those heavy hooks was no simple task. The men labored mightily, but there was scant time. Lund gritted his teeth. Stormalong had rigged his anchors out long ago—had schemed all this!

All in a moment, a long, long moment; the gale was high, but the mists were thinning in the wind. Suddenly off to starboard loomed a small, flat-topped island. Lund choked on the recognition. They were inside Heilu Tao, a mile north of Bluff Point—actually treading on the Tiger's Tail!

Worried, incredulous and puzzled, Lund glanced into the binnacle. Then the dreaded cry from both masthead and the mate on the fo'c'sle head:

"Breakers ahead and on the port bow!"

It all cleared, windy sea and brain together, at the tag end of that frightful moment. The mists vanished. There was the *Naiad,* long bowsprit pointed in the opposite direction, heading into the wind, breasting the tide and overfalls with both anchor-cables taut as bars. Trap or not, Stormalong had come within a hair's-breadth of putting his own ship on the rocks, for the tide raced at full flood.

Lund, aware of his ship being pushed relentlessly, went forward on the jump. He had clear vision now;

one glance from the knighthead, and he swung around.

"Belay the anchors but stand by," he ordered the mate, and lifted his speaking trumpet at the second officer, aft.

"Hard up the helm! Port—hard over!"

Here, providentially, was a channel opening—a close shave, but it could be done. He ordered full speed, the paddles began thrashing; to his horror, the *Naiad* was blotted out again as the mist came swirling down. He raced aft.

The *Porpoise,* her stack emitting black streamers of smoke that were whipped to ribbons in the wind, thrashed into the narrow gut. She made it, with only feet to spare; the mist whirled thick and thicker. Then a wild cry from the mate.

"Breakers ahead and on the sta'board bow!"

The ship was flying with wind and sea dead astern. There was no sea-room to go about. Astern, the surf thundered.

"Full speed astern! Let go both anchors!" roared Lund, and groaned to himself.

A booming swell rolled up and lifted the vessel like a chip. She struck, she staggered; even the roar of surf was drowned by the grinding of the reef against her iron bottom. Another swell—the screech of scraping iron sounded anew. Then she was floating, listless, all way stopped. The anchors plunged down.

The second mate, the hands who had been working sail and tending yards, left the rigging and gathered in a mute group on the halfdeck. The mate came aft. Lund was calm now, despite the cold sweat on his forehead.

"Furl all sail," he ordered. "Where's Chips? Sound the well. Unlimber the pumps."

He waited, watching the drift of mist all around, until the carpenter came with his soundings.

"Wells are dry, sir!"

Lund, with one deep breath, relaxed.

"Your watch, Mister," he said to the mate. "That double bottom may have weight, but it's proved its worth once more. Wake me up at any alarm."

He went below. Nothing to do now until daylight, when he could determine how completely he was trapped. He could not understand it. His bearings were all off—the mist had ruined his perception, and loss of the deviation-card when it was most needed had put the skids under him completely. To remember the deviations offhand was impossible. He searched the chart locker again, searched everywhere, and found no card. Weary and dismal of heart, he turned in to await daylight.

Morning showed the ship lying among rocks, anchored and riding safely; but one look at the gut through which he had come, and Lund swallowed hard. It was incredible that he should have made that narrow passage in safety. By daylight, he never would have attempted it; last night, he had thought he was on a clear course. There was no clear course at all, in sight. Northward, the surf broke over a curving reef that completely cut him off from the open sea beyond.

Around the end of the Tiger's Tail the Naiad was ratching by means of kedges. Lund watched her, too thankful that his ship was saved, to think about losing the game. Then he turned his glass to the reef on the north side, and examined it with attention. The tide was coming in heavily. He knew where he was, now; he knew every depth of water, even the depth over that reef. If he went at it, the double bottom would be torn clean out of his ship—and he had almost gone at it last night.

"Nothing to do," he said to the mate, "except to work back through the gut and take the long way around. You haven't found that deviation-card?"

The mate worked his lean jaws on a twist of tobacco.

"Well," he said, "I've got my suspicions, and they ain't nice. If you was to tell me to foller my own nose—"

"Run 'em down, Mister." Lund gave him a sharp glance. "If you think there was anything— Hello! What's Stormalong up to?"

His attention was suddenly diverted. Under light, uneven airs the *Naiad* had worked around the island and the reef, but instead of bearing up for Chefoo, had rounded up and was dropping her longboat. Cap'n Rankin, resplendent in blue broadcloth and glossy high-topped beaver, descended into the boat and headed her in among the reef channels.

Lund watched the boat pull in. Presently Stormalong waved his hand, hailed them in greeting, and came in under the side. He clambered up to the deck, and stood looking around, saturnine, darkly handsome, powerful. The Yankee mate, who should have met him at the rail, had vanished completely. He strode aft to Lund, and with a grin shook hands.

"Well, well, Cap'n! You'll have a few days to study

the Tiger's Tail, looks like. Maybe you can win back through the gut when the spring rise starts—it comes to seven and a half feet hereabouts. I thought I'd relieve you of the mails and anything else you might have to jettison to lighten ship."

Lund merely laughed slightly.

"Last time we met, Stormalong, I offered to cry quits on the wager. Now I'll offer to double it. Yes or no?"

Rankin shook his head, smiling shrewdly. "Tall talk, tall talk!" he said. "I suppose you'll be sailing right out?"

"Within the hour," said Lund. "And in Chefoo ahead of you."

"Right out, against the wind, eh?" Stormalong chuckled. "Paddles won't do it, Cap'n. You're too low in the water."

"Might be, if you were master," said Lund slowly. "That's the difference between us, Cap'n. Hello!"

The two men swung around. The Yankee mate was coming on the run. He was breathing hard, his eye was alight, and his skinned knuckles were bleeding. He paused to clutch the man Avery from amid a group of watching seamen, and shove him aft.

Stormalong Rankin stiffened a little.

"I got it!" panted the mate, bringing Avery to a halt.

Lund's brows lifted.

"What's the meaning of this, Mister? What have you got?"

"A confession out o' that blighter Sam Peak, what come aboard at Valparaiso! And here's the other blighter. —You, Avery! Hand over that deviation-card! Quick, you dog, or I'll put you in the sickbay!"

Avery shrank suddenly, white with panic. The angry mate reached for him, but with a subdued squawk, he produced the missing deviation-card.

"I found it, sir,"—and he shoved it at Lund. "I found it laying—"

"You lie!" roared the mate. "Cap'n Rankin give you money to lay for us and come aboard and rob us in a pinch! Sam Peak told the whole thing! Git! Down into Cap'n Rankin's boat or I'll take a rope to you!"

Lund fingered the card.

"Well, well! Mighty queer," he said affably, "how things do come out—"

"What d'ye mean?" rapped out Stormalong suddenly. "I warn you, pay no attention to this outrageous lie! Don't dare accuse me of trying to wreck your ship. Tell that to a Board of Inspectors back home, and they'll snatch your ticket!"

Cap'n Tommy Lund smiled.

"I'm not telling anyone anything, Cap'n Rankin," he answered cheerfully. "You're a fine, clever, upstanding man, and many's the time, aboard your ship, I've wished for this day to come."

"What d'ye mean?" demanded Rankin truculently.

"Why, just this!" said Lund, and smacked his fist into the dark face.

Tommy Lund knew better than to bother hitting for the face if he meant to kill, but he just could not help it. Next instant, he regretted his mistake.

His regret did not last longer than it takes to get a black eye and a split lip, for he rallied and tore into Stormalong with both fists, while the yelling men formed a delighted roaring circle. True, Lund drew another black eye to match the first, but that was nothing at all to what Stormalong Rankin drew—absolutely nothing at all.

Ten minutes later, beaver gone, blue coat in shreds, and a blob of gore where his handsome face had been, the sorry remains of Stormalong were handed down into his waiting boat, where his two jackals now crouched.

"A pleasant riddance to the lot of you," sang out Lund from the rail. "Douse some water over your skipper and tell him to watch our smoke. Engineer! Steam up?"

"Aye, sir," said the joyful engineer.

"Get below and give us a full head. Mister Mate! Get in them anchors—all hands to stations! Make sail!"

One and all thought for certain that Tommy Lund had gone stark raving mad, but they yelped and obeyed him, swarming aloft. Steam or not, Cap'n Lund had never neglected sail drill; and together, precisely, the topsails were shaken out, then the t'gallants and the courses. Navy style, and a sight to see!

Smoke poured from the stack of the *Porpoise,* for she had kept up full steam. The anchors were cat-headed, her canvas filled away, and with her twin paddles churning like mad, she presented her broad quarter to the breeze. Like mad, aye; Lund was at the helm, and a madman they all knew him.

For, with every stitch of canvas spread and the engines boiling, the *Porpoise* was heading slap for the reef across the bight.

"God help us!" said the mate, looking at Lund with stricken eyes. "There's not above twelve feet o' water yonder, and it's steep-to both sides!"

"That's what I figure," said Lund, eyes bright on the reef. His voice blared, and the mate sprang to obey.

Men leaped to tacks and sheets and braces, and the yards were sharply braced. The port, or lee, braces were hauled flat aft and bowsed taut. Then, at the very risk of taking the sticks out of her, Lund put his helm hard up, with the reef almost under her forefoot and men braced against the shock.

With the wind almost dead on the starboard beam, the pressure of wind was suddenly so tremendous that the *Porpoise* either had to spill her sails, carry them away, or lay over on her beam ends with shattered masts. But the straining rig and canvas held under the thrust of wind; the ship canted over on her side, with the weather paddles stopped, the lee paddles wildly thrashing the water.

And thus, drawing on her beam ends not half the water she would when on an even keel, the despised hybrid eased across the reef with feet to spare.

Shrill yelps of incredulity, then cheers of wild amazed delight, burst from the crew. Lund, battered but grinning, left the wheel and was caught in the rush and hug of the Yankee mate.

"You did it, you did it, sir! By the horns o' Moses, you did it!"

"Just the old pilot-boat trick, Mister," said Lund, still grinning. "What one can do, another can try. By the way, you and I will have a bit of a celebration in Chefoo. I'm not forgetting that I owe you something."

He went to the companionway and there paused, to look back across the water at the *Naiad,* and the boat pulling for her through the reef-passages, and the soggy unkempt figure in the stern-sheets. Cap'n Lund waved his hand.

"Smart fellow, Stormalong!" he muttered—and with a twinkle in his blackened eye, he headed below.

THE YELLOW SHIP

We had been talking of queer ships; rattan ships, concrete ships, and some one even mentioned the old Chinese Navy *guardo* built of red brick, that used to be moored off the Shanghai Bund.

"Queerest of all was the Yellow Ship," said the Professor; he had thick lenses, a shock of rope-yarn hair, and a positive way of speech. "That is, if you look at what's inside of a ship, not outside. There's a great yarn in her last voyage."

"Never heard of her," grunted Cap'n Fitzmaurice, the hydrographer.

"It's not a nice story, some ways," the Professor said, hesitating. He drew an old, tattered book from his pocket and thumbed it. "All dead true, but strong. A bit too strong, I expect."

Cap'n Dahl, the local steamboat inspector, who had commanded his own brig at twenty-one, let out a booming laugh.

"What d'ye think we are, Professor? Kids in school?"

The Professor frowned, screwing up his face and thumbing his bit of a book.

"Well, not that. It's the sort of thing people shrink from facing, nowadays; they like to say it never existed." He glanced at Cap'n Birchwood, the big Britisher. "I'm talking about convict ships, which had a definite place in sea history; but I don't want to offend anybody, and—"

"Yoicks! Don't mind me!" bawled out the husky Birchwood. "You Yanks still have your chain-gangs, not to mention sweat-boxes where you burn prisoners alive. Strong stuff, is it? Then let's have it! Yellow ship and the broad arrow, I suppose. Eh? If you can get any worth-while yarn out of a convict ship, you have my leave!"

"You can get a worth-while story out of anything," said the Professor, holding up the old book. "It's all here, printed in 1827, set down by James Conroy; but I warn you, it's—well, it's a thing to shy at, if you're afraid of the truth. It's none of your la-de-da yarns about nice people and perfumed ladies and polished gentlemen."

"Thank God for that!" exclaimed Cap'n Dahl fervently. "If it's the real stuff I'll cry amen! I'm mortal sick of the sort of tripe that uses cusswords just to make an impression, like some men I know."

The Professor smiled. "All right, you asked for it. It's real, too; all eye-witness stuff. We're dealing with criminals, remember. Felons. None of your hero-falsely-accused lemonade, but honest rum with a kick to it."

"One o' the best men I know," said Cap'n Fitzmaurice, "is in Sing Sing today, and deserves to be there. Heave ahead! Where do we start?"

"At Spithead, year not specified, but around 1800," the Professor rejoined. "The *Phœnix* sailed in convoy with four other convict ships. She was Moulmein built, of solid teak; like the others, she was painted a bright yellow and blazingly marked with the mark of Crown property, the broad arrow. Being the largest and best equipped of the whole felon fleet, she was designated as a women's ship; that is, given over to female prisoners alone. You'll have to understand conditions—"

Hard enough in all conscience—for felons were not human but mere beasts, so far as treatment went.

Crowds of wretched females, all ages from twelve years to sixty, were jammed into the narrow cells, with no ventilation and only occasional supervision by the convict guards. One may well shrink from the facts.

Captain Ronson, in command, was a gross hulk whose life had been spent in the meanest of all ships, the coasting colliers. His mate was one Ned Wolf; his second, a furtive gallows-bird named Spink. Captain Halter, officer of the hangdog soldiers who served as convict guards, had graduated from the prison docks at Portsmouth. No worse, or better, scoundrels could have been chosen by the contractors whose wolfish greed crowded the vessels to slave-ship capacity. The contractors received sixpence per day for each convict's food; the longer the voyage, the more they received from the Government....

With all hands drunk or recovering from shore debauches the first few days out, little heed was paid the prisoners. Then Ronson sobered up, to find the ship bowling along on a fair wind and all well. He sent the cabin-boy for the mate, poured himself a round of grog with shaking fingers, and downed it.

Taking a long clay pipe from the rack, he filled and lit it, and eased himself into the big chair under the stern-window of the cabin. He was a coarse, bloated hulk, with a vile fury of temper when crossed, and at sea was a tyrant dreaded by men and officers alike. Hanging under the window, close to his hand, was a sling that carried two brass pistols. As he waited, he primed them afresh, then let them be and went on smoking. Another drop of rum, and he felt quite himself once more. He had been in a drunken stupor since yesterday.

Ned Wolf appeared, a lean, powerful man with boldly aggressive eye and truculent mien. The skipper surveyed him without love, and sneered at sight of a fresh bruise on the mate's upper cheek.

"So ye've been at the lasses already, Ned? And got something for your pains. Serves ye right for a scurvy rogue! Well, I suppose we got to sea without the smith and armorer we lacked?"

"We did not," said Ned Wolf without respect. "You signed him on yourself, with Blowsy Fanny on one knee and her holding the quill."

"Say ye so?" Ronson chuckled. "Is the fellow good?"

"Too blasted good," growled Wolf. "A damned impudent rascal who needs a flogging. His name's Connell. He knows his business, though."

"Then all's easy." The skipper laid aside his churchwarden. "Come! Out wi' the prisoner list, and God help you if you've laid a finger on one of 'em!"

Glowering, the surly mate produced a sheaf of papers. Ronson took them and scanned them quickly, and a contented chuckle shook him.

"Four hundred and thirty-one!" he exclaimed. "Happen there'll be a few pearls among hell's sweepings; there always are. Eh? Speak up, speak up!"

"Aye." The mate grinned faintly, but his eyes remained dark and evil and alert.

Ronson grunted and poured another drop of rum into his mug.

"Fetch 'em in for inspection. And mind this, ye blackguard! Any cheating, and I'll have ye triced up and given three dozen of the cat! That's a promise."

Wolf shot him one hard glance of bitter fury and disappeared.

Presently he was back, and Spink with him, and they ushered in six young girls, transported for offenses as monstrous as filching a comb from Madam's dressing-table or mayhap stealing a loaf to avoid earning it less honestly. Half-clad, bedraggled and dirty and seasick, all six were weeping bitterly.

Before any could speak, however, a new sound came through the quarterdeck passage, a sound of thin wild cries and screaming.

"Zounds!" A bellowing oath escaped Ronson, and his empty mug slammed down on the table. "Spink! Find Halter and get below—jump! Any man who touches a lass now gets a dozen of the cat. Below, ye rogue! See to it!"

Spink darted away. Ronson sat back, muttering about the impudence of the rascals. His eyes scanned the six girls, and settled on one of them.

"Ha! You by the door—what's your name?"

The one addressed, a pretty country chit of fourteen, could only stare at him, speechless, frightened, shivering.

"Speak up, speak up, lass!" said Ronson. "Passage aft, good bunks, good food, and naught to be afeared of, besides a chance of reaching Botany Bay alive and hearty, which is more than all those below can hope for. What's your name?"

The girl burst into violent sobs. Ronson came to his feet, but at this moment came quick, heavy steps in the passage, and the door swung open. From the mate broke one low and vicious oath of rage.

Spink, now returned, was ushering in, with his crafty grin, a young woman and a tall, muscled figure of a man.

"This is one on the list but not below, Cap'n," he exclaimed. "And here's the smith and armorer likewise, who'll have a word with ye."

The skipper looked at the powerful features of the armorer, uncomprehending; then at the young woman.

No country girl, this, no sorry scum of the London streets, but a tall, darkly handsome lass who stood the deck like a seaman, and met his questing look with an eye of scorn. Well clad, brown of cheek, capable and alert, she was beautiful by any standard.

"Cap'n, this is Nell Bently of Devon," said Spink, a malicious glitter in his eye as he caught the furious look of Ned Wolf. "Took for a smuggler and transported. Cap'n Nell, she's called, having her own ketch and being a good seaman by all accounts. You'll find her on the list all shipshape, but I found her locked in the mate's cabin and fetched her along. All's quiet down below for the present, Cap'n."

The armorer, Connell, stood with arms folded across his chest, appraising the men and the scene before him. He had direct, unflinching eyes beneath straight black brows.

"So that's it, is it?" mouthed Cap'n Ronson, fastening a deadly stare on the mate. "Holding out on the cap'n again! What, Ned, you'd cheat the master as loves you?"

His voice was deadly as his eye. Wolf rolled out a curse.

"Nothing of the sort! I tell you—"

"And she gave you that bruise on the cheek, Ned?" went on the master.

"I tell you, you don't understand!" rasped Ned Wolf furiously. "Why, damme if I so much as knew she was aboard—"

"Belay," came a new voice. Connell had suddenly broken silence, his tones ringing and vibrant with angry scorn. "No lies, no lies! Everyone knows Cap'n Nell was convicted and sent to the *Phoenix.* And she paid the mate well to keep her out o' the cells and put her in peace."

"Aye, aye," spoke up the second officer craftily, a viciousness in his manner. He hated the mate bitterly. "It was her as give 'un the mark, Cap'n. He wanted her for hisself, but I fetched her aft. 'Twas me duty and no more."

Ronson, finally comprehending things, was glaring at the mate, a purplish flush stealing into his gross features. He gently tucked one hand behind him to the sling hanging on the wall.

"Remember what I promised you, Ned," said he. "You damned double-dealing rogue! Triced up to a grating at sunset, and three dozen of the cat crisscrossing your back, and a dose o' salt rubbed in for good measure. I'll learn ye to hold out on the ship's master— 'Ware, you fool! Hand away from that knife—"

"Damn you, 'ware yourself!" screamed Wolf shrilly, suddenly, and his hand flickered up and down. With that sudden scream, all hell was loosed.

The skipper's hand leaped into sight, the brass pistol roared; the women shrieked wildly and powder-smoke rolled through the cabin. That heavy ball went true. With the blue mark of it between his eyes, the mate lay in a huddle. Ronson let fall the pistol and plucked at his fat throat with both hands. Ned Wolf's knife had likewise driven true. Ronson plucked it out with a rush of blood, fell back against the wall, and slid down out of sight behind the table. He groaned once, then was still forever.

The girls were clinging to one another as the smoke cleared. Spink had retreated to the door; he stood against it, with a small pistol in either hand, his crafty, high-boned features alert and excited. Nell Bently was standing now within the arm of Connell, who craned over for a glance at the skipper, and then straightened up and met the gaze of the second mate. The women calmed down.

"Well," said Connell curtly, "you're in command."

"Done, is he? Good riddance," shrilled Spink. "And now what, Cap'n?"

"Eh?" Connell frowned, and the other laughed harshly.

"Oh, I twigged you the minute ye come aboard! Cap'n Connell, Cap'n Tom Connell o' the *Devon Maid!* The shrewdest, boldest smuggler 'twixt Tilbury and Penzance, shipping as armorer aboard a yellow ship—ha-ha! The reason's plain to see, in the bend of your arm."

Connell's eyes flashed cold and challenging. He abandoned all pretense.

"Aye, Cap'n Nell and I hang together," he said curtly. "Do you turn back and ship other officers, or do you play out the game yourself?"

The excitement deepened in the pinched, bony features.

"Aye, that's it!" Spink said quickly. "Cap'n, is it? Master of the ship, by God! A rare stroke of luck, and I'd be a fool to miss it. And yet—"

Connell's laugh rang out sardonically.

"It'd make your reputation! Aye, Master Spink! To navigate the ship to Botany Bay would be the makin's of you for life—if you knew how to do it! But your duty is to signal the convoy and take a master aboard."

"Damn the convoy!" cried Spink. "I get what you're driving at. You're a captain and a famous one—the greatest blackguard on all the south coast to boot, and a reward on your head. King's money for your capture. Ha! You risked a lot for the sake of a lass, you fool! Do we talk proper, or not?"

"Why not?" said Connell, relaxing. "Clear out these women and the two bodies, and then we'll talk—you and I and Cap'n Nell."

"Right," said Spink, and cocked an eye at the window. "Sunset coming, and the night ahead—right! Stay here, the both of you. We'll talk, over a bit o' supper."

So they did, and came finally to agreement on a basis of mutual understanding. Nell Bently said little, but used her eyes; she was used to dealing with men, and knew a bad one when she saw him.

Not that Spink seemed overtly a bad one. Connell read him for a cunning and cowardly rat—and was dead right. However, the man was affable, friendly, driven by a sudden ambition to seize destiny, by the forelock; he demanded that Connell teach him navigation and other duties of a master, stand behind him and coach him, and when needful fight for him.

To all of which Connell readily agreed, being himself eager to seize the great chance offered him. He was to become first officer, and Cap'n Nell would perforce share his cabin, space being cramped aboard. The women were not to be molested, and those in irons were to be loosed, confirmed criminals or not.

Spink protested, but gave in.

"You're asking for trouble," he said. "It's custom for the men; full half the crowd are criminals or worse, anyhow. Well, have it your own way! There'll be ructions in the morning."

Connell bared his teeth, a way he had.

"Back me up with pistols, and I'll handle these scum alone. We'll give 'em no time to think of women, after tomorrow! There's work enough to keep all hands slaving. And before we sight Botany Bay, you'll set me and Cap'n Nell ashore."

Spink promised readily. "What about taking a few more with you?" he said, laughing. "There's half a hundred would follow at your word, and you might set yourself up like a Grand Turk."

"I can't save 'em all from hell," said Connell, "though there's many of 'em might be worth the effort. Now, we're faster than the other ships. Stay you with them?"

"Damme if I will!" exclaimed Spink. "I'll crack on all sail tonight, and they'll be under the horizon with morning. Agreed, then! And here's my hand on it."

Later, alone together, Connell took Cap'n Nell by the shoulders and met her brave steady eyes, gravely.

"Lass, from the day ye gave me your love, I've looked at no other woman, nor ever will. I shipped aboard here in hopes to save ye from hell; belike, it's done. And for me, a new life and a new name, somewhere in a new country. We'll share the future. Content?"

She laughed softly, richly. "My dear, I've been

content from the day I first met you! But have a care. Don't take too much for granted. Spink is cunning, crafty, playing for his own hand. He'll stab you in the back if he gets a chance."

"You watch my back; I'll answer for the front," said Connell. "Besides, he's tied to us, now."

"He's not one to let the women alone," said she bluntly.

Connell nodded. "Like enough. None shall be forced, at least; there's plenty of them to consent willingly, and we'll let it go at that. But the young lasses sha'n't be molested. And there's Cap'n Halter to be reckoned with, too, with his sojers; but he's dead drunk now, and won't sober up till sometime tomorrow, so time enough to think of him."

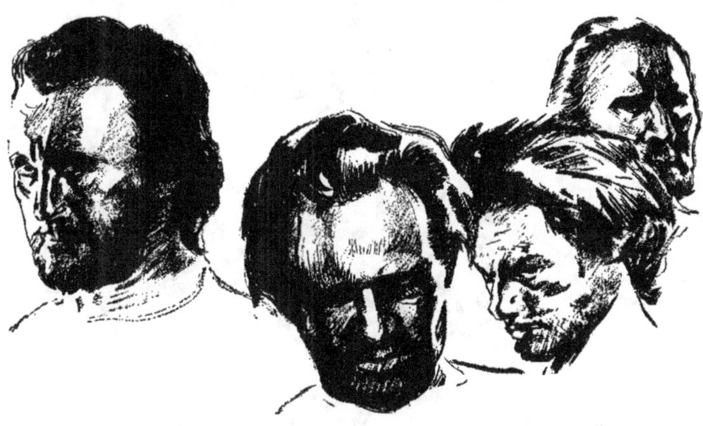

Morning, he knew, would bring crisis, and he was ready to meet it with brutal efficiency. It was stay on top or go under, and he had no notion of going under. Luckily, Spink must stand or fall with him; he would have needed support here.

By morning, indeed, the ship was in ferment, for the convoy was out of sight, and it was known that captain and mate were dead. Connell was privately picked out the best man in the crew, one Jem Hanaker, to act as second mate. A husky giant, approved by Spink, Hanaker moved aft and could be relied upon for backing. Also, Captain Halter remained in a drunken stupor, which was lucky, for there was trouble in the man.

The men trooped aft to the quarter-rail where Spink and his new officers stood, to the shrill of the bosun's pipe. They had arms, open or concealed; but they also had an innate, panicky fear of authority, as Connell well knew. Navy deserters, offscourings of waterfront jails, short-term felons, they were an evil lot, and they meant trouble.

Spink, with a ruffling swagger, pointed to the shrouded forms of Ronson and Ned Wolf, announced their decease, announced the new officers.

There was a surly growl, and one of the hands let out a shout.

"How about the wenches?"

"No," said Connell, at the ladder. "Not now nor later, you scum! That's all ended."

A yell went up, a surge forward; threats and imprecations and fury filled the air, and they went at the ladder.

Connell, with one leap, was down among them, sending two men sprawling. Then the heavy teak belaying-pin in his hand began to crack out mercilessly. For thirty seconds they fought him viciously, but his silent, grim ferocity overawed them; he lashed, clubbed, kicked with all the power of his two hundred pounds.

Then Jem Hanaker joined in; and Spink, his brass pistols glinting in the sun, stood at the rail above. The throng broke, with wild cries. One man, drawing aside, whipped out a pistol, but Connell saw the weapon in time. His bloody belaying-pin shot through the air like a bullet, with perfect aim; the fellow dropped with his skull crushed in, and the fight was over.

"All hands! Line up, line up," commanded Connell. "Come along, Cap'n Spink. They want to turn over all weapons to you."

A shrewd move, he thought, to gratify Spink's new authority, but Spink was the shrewd man here. While the two mates stood off, he moved among the cowed and bloody crew, taking a weapon here and another there, but not all. Those knocked out and agroan on deck were disarmed. The dead man was ordered flung over, and the two former officers with him.

"There ye be," said Spink, with a spiteful disdain as he eyed the fifty-odd men. "Not a weapon left among the lot, as is proper. And any man who growls at orders from aft, gets a dozen lashes. I should give most of you rogues a touch of the cat now, but bein' a humane and kind-hearted master, I'll give the warning instead. And any man complained against by one o' the women below, gets three dozen on the spot. Mind that! Get to your quarters. Mr. Hanaker, keep your watch on the run, clean up these decks, get started on the brasses. You dogs will work from now on."

Cap'n Nell spoke with Connell later.

"Spink has friends amongst 'em," she said briefly. "Three or four he passed up, with a wink and a look, when he was searching."

Connell shrugged. "Let be, lass; the main thing is that we're on top, and Spink has need of us. Besides, we've got Halter to reckon with yet."

This reckoning came at noon, when Connell was making his observations on the poop. In his capacity of armorer, he had gone the rounds below, freeing the poor shackled women from their irons, and had heard that the guard captain was up and stirring. Now he saw Halter approaching in a fury, two pistols protruding from his belt.

A loose-lipped hulk of a man, all in disarray from his carouse, Halter was typical of the bullying, brutal convict guards. As he came, he hailed Connell in accents redolent of Bow Bells.

"I sye, you! What the bloody 'ell d'ye mean by tykin' the basils off my prisoners? I'll 'ave ye triced up for it!"

Connell set down his octant on the cabin scuttle and picked up the belaying-pin placed for ready use. He regarded Captain Halter with assumed surprise, and the other came close with beefy fist shaking.

"Speak up, ye dog!" he roared. "I'll 'ave the flesh off your back for this! Let my prisoners loose? S'elp me, I'll 'ave your bloody life—"

Silently, Connell smashed him fair between the eyes with the cruel teak, and Halter went to the deck. Before he had done quivering, Connell leaned over him and took away the pistols, then returned to his observation.

Presently Halter shambled and stumbled to his feet, gripped a backstay, and wiped away the blood. Connell turned:

"I took the irons off the prisoners because they're not needed. And you'll not need pistols to bully women prisoners. You have iron gratings over the hatches, and that's enough to keep the poor wretches in their pig-sty."

"I'll be the judge o' that," fumed the other. "Who the bloody 'ell are you?"

Connell laughed thinly. "I'm the man who'll have you triced up and given three dozen of the cat you talk so much about, if you lay hand on one of the women below. Now get back to your duties, ye rogue, and be thankful I don't have ye stripped and flung below amongst the prisoners."

Halter let out a bellow at the half-deck, where a number of his soldiers were lounging.

"Lay aft 'ere! Guards! Up 'ere and clap this blackguard in irons!"

The men snickered among themselves and remained deaf to his commands. He fell silent, wiped the blood from his eyes again, and fear took hold of him, as he met the gaze of Connell.

"Stay off this deck, officer or not, unless you're bid," the latter said coldly. "Now get for'ard among the other swine where you belong. Get!"

He took one step. Captain Halter turned and hastily decamped.

A hard eye, a hard fist, and merciless punishment was what these men understood best; and they got it in plenty. The cat-o'-nine tails was bloody more than once thereafter; the men were hazed and slaved and driven like dogs, and Captain Spink made them like it.

Spink, somewhat to the surprise of Connell, pursued his ambition hard, drank not at all, worked long and steadily at navigation lessons, and took a crafty, gleeful pride in the role of ship's master, and in enforcing Connell's advice. Also, he remained affable and friendly, and it was settled that after rounding the Cape, Cap'n Nell and Connell should be set ashore at St. Mary's of Madagascar.

"But I distrust him," said Cap'n Nell, a glint in her dark eyes. "Mark my words, Tom, he'll cheat us yet!"

"If he does, I'll kill him; and he knows it," Connell said grimly. "I doubt if he'll risk it."

He forgot that Spink was learning, more fully with each day, the duties and the responsibility of a master, and was building a new and glorious future on the outcome of this voyage.

A month ran on, two months, well into the third; the *Phœnix* was making good time and a speedy run. She was across the Line well ahead of schedule, with never another glimpse of her consorts. Other sail were sighted, but the yellow sides and the broad arrows blossoming on the canvas made her shunned like the plague.

At last they drew in at the old watering-place of the East Indiamen, Saldanha Bay, north of the bleak Cape. Here they found no other vessel, and remained for three days, all hands and prisoners taking trips ashore and stretching legs on land, or bartering with the fierce blacks who brought down wild cattle, and filling water-casks anew for the long voyage ahead.

"Why not leave her here?" demanded Cap'n Nell, as she and Connell walked ashore. "We may never get another chance. Here's our time, Tom!"

Connell laughed harshly, as he pointed to the black warriors and their spears.

"Aye, time to die quickly! I've heard tales o' this end of creation. To jump ship here, means sudden death amongst the blacks, or what's worse, slow death. Nowhere to go here; huge deserts, barren uplands, black savages who kill anyone—"

"Is that worse than prison and slavery?" she demanded.

"It is," said he. "For at worst, one has hope. Here there's none. At St. Mary's of Madagascar, we'll be among friendly, pleasant natives who like whites."

"And if we don't get put ashore there, Tom?"

"Why, then, make the best of it and fight on!" said he, smiling. For he did not share her distrust of Cap'n Spink—at least, did not share it sufficiently.

Off again, rewatered and refreshed, and around the Cape with a tall wind—not halting there, for the yellow ship got scant welcome. Connell was in high spirits, with only another day or two before freedom; but now fate closed in....

"I'll not do it," said Cap'n Spink bluntly. His shifty eyes went from Connell to Cap'n Nell.

"You'll not set us ashore?" gasped Nell Bently. "But you promised!"

"Aye, and I'll do it later." Spink leaned forward. "Look'ee, Connell! I don't dare, and that's the truth, my davy on it! Think o' the thousands of miles ahead, and me alone! I need ye, man; I have need of your navigation."

"Yours is good now," snapped Connell.

"Not good enough." Spink wagged his head doubtfully. "Not for what's facing us. The chart puts fright into me."

"You damned coward!"

"Aye, like enough," admitted Spink. "Once acrost the Indian Ocean, there's time and places enough. I'll need you till then."

Connell assented, not with good grace, but helpless. And two mornings later he found the brace of brass pistols clean vanished from the cabin.

"I told you so!" exclaimed Cap'n Nell.

"Aye," said Connell, his oaths done. "You were right," he added bitterly. "And there's not a man of all aboard who'll lend me a hand. Not Hanaker; he's turned surly. The rest hate me."

"They don't hate me," said Cap'n Nell frowningly. "Put a good face on it, see it through; and where would ye land if all went well?"

"Melville Island," replied Connell. "What's in your mind?"

"A boat, and men to lower it," said she. "I can manage that, never fear. That is, if he still refuses then."

So Connell put a good face on it, and spoke Cap'n Spink fair. All this while, Spink touched no liquor; he aimed to sail into Botany Bay as master.

"Not that anybody except Connell stands in the way," said Jem Hanaker darkly.

"I'll take no chances," snapped Spink. "A carouse, and I might well lose the ship, for he'd have to be killed first. Cap'n Halter's getting out of hand too; you bid him wait till the time's ripe."

Connell found, as the long days wore drearily, that he was being watched—watched everywhere and in everything he did. Four of the crew proved ever more friendly with Spink, backed up his orders, served as his spies and men forward—the same four who had not been disarmed at the start. Bullies, they were, and proper bullies. They watched, and the soldiers watched, and Jem Hanaker watched. Cap'n Spink, affable and friendly, did no watching at all, but the crafty glint in his eyes got ever deeper.

And for lack of pistols, Connell had to temporize. Nor could he get any, as the ship sped down across the Indian Ocean; he was watched at all times, as Cap'n Nell was watched; and the men she thought to bribe could get her nothing. They did promise, however, about the boat—because they also wanted to skip the ship. So there was hope.

The misery of the sweltering holds brought many a death below. Then came the hurricane which swept and battered the ship for six days, with only the superb handling of Connell pulling her through at all. When the battened hatches were lifted at last, even the callous Captain Halter could not bear the sight below. They sent over fifty bodies of women to feed the sharks that day.

On through the Arafura Sea, on to Melville Island, Cap'n Nell scheming well with the two men forward. Every detail was set and ready for the next night. But in the morning, topsails were sighted. Spink ran up a signal; for once, the other craft did not run from the yellow ship, but stood straight for them.

And upon Connell grew the awful realization. A sloop of war, the Union Jack, and the end of hope. She drew in close, luffed, and hailed. She would convoy them to Botany Bay. Haul away and remain in company!

He went down to his own cabin and found Cap'n Nell shaken with sobs. She turned to him fiercely.

"And now what's the end of it all? Botany Bay, and me a felon, and you with a price on your head, a wanted man, as Spink well knows! He'll turn you in. They'll laugh at the marriage he performed as captain, though it's legal enough."

"Aye," said Spink, opening the door quietly and stepping in. Outside were two soldiers with muskets.

"Aye, like enough," Spink went on, as the two of them stared at him. He grinned faintly. "No more need of your navigation now, Connell, with a King's ship to guide and stand by us. And me being master, every female on the books will count. You go in as a felon, Nell, and your man gets turned in. The reward's fat."

A whiff of rum came from him. Connell started up, but Spink whipped out a pistol, one of the fine brass pistols that had vanished.

"Stay you here, and break out if you want," said he, backing through the open doorway. "There's loaded guns and heavy butts, if you want to show fight; if not, stay you here, and the door's barred."

Barred it was, and full welcome. For all restraint was off now, rum was broken out, and with only a guard at Connell's cabin and a man to tend the helm and keep the ship within sight of the sloop of war, all hell was let loose on the yellow ship.

The days passed in a riot, as the two vessels crossed the Bay of Carpenteria and passed Cape York. Spink played his rôle of master with a brave swagger when sober, with crafty brutality when drunk. A true hell-ship now, the *Phœnix* bore on, with Connell and Cap'n Nell prisoners and desperately guarded in the cabin, and with her convoy sloop stood well off the coast to avoid the Great Barrier and other reef-perils.

Then excitement thrilled through the decks, with the word that next morning would see them safe anchored in Botany Bay and the voyage ended. Spink made a maudlin effort to get his ship straightened up and his men sober. Just at sunset, the two ships altered course and land was raised. Spink went aloft with the glass, and sighted the high bluish bluffs that marked the entrance to Botany Bay. He sent down a jubilant shout to announce the news—and with its accustomed lack of warning, the dread southeasterly "buster" of the South Austral waters leaped down from a clear sky.

The hurricane-squall struck from dead astern. By the time Spink regained the deck, the topsails had been ripped from the bolt-ropes. The huge fore-courser, which had been sharp-braced on the larboard tack, held the wind, and the ship lay almost on her beam ends.

The entire deck was plunged into chaos, with shrieking women fighting to get up from the holds, and men running frantically to clap the hatches shut. Spink, in an access of terror, caught hold of Captain Halter.

"Get Connell! Get that damned Connell before we're sunk!"

Himself in a frenzy of fear, the guard captain went below on the run.

Connell came on deck to find men milling around the fife-and pin-rails in a tangle of buntlines, reef-tackles, down-hauls and other gear. He leaped among them, and the confusion subsided.

"All hands shorten sail! Larboard watch for'ard, sta'board at the main!"

The men took stations, frenziedly readying the gear, while Spink clutched a back stay on the poop. Obeying Connell's roar, the man at the wheel got the helm down, two more men came to aid him, and the ship headed away before the gale.

For the moment, safe; but whole water was slopping over the bulwarks, and the following seas rocketed spray over the high poop. Gaining power every moment, the buster harped through the rigging until its wild howls drowned the wailing shrieks from the battened cell-holds below.

Connell swung on a weather stay and peered into the storm-wrack. Darkness had come full down; the land was completely blotted from sight; there was no mark, no light by which to con the ship to safety. He found Hanaker at his side, as the ship rolled high on a towering wave.

"Come along! All hands at it—must get that foresail reefed. Can ye do it?"

"Aye," responded Hanaker, and they clawed forward together, driving the men cruelly. Connell saw to the passing of the lazy tack and the casting adrift of the chain fore-tack, belayed to the capstan where it had been hove down before.

"Furl the weather and loose the lee!" lifted his roar through the speaking-trumpet Spink had shoved into his hand." Stand by weather clew-garnet—man weather gear—"

Hanaker eased off the tack as the men took a strain, then let it fly; and with thundering claps the great canvas was snugged to the yard.

"Lee gear, stand by!" Up went the lee-side, and the thunder aloft subsided. Every man was working like a frenzied fiend now. "Up and reef it!"

Hanaker led the way. The men clambered up and laid out on the jolting yard. Reef cringles were picked up, reef-earrings passed; the reef-bands stretched along the iron jackstays; the reef-points were knotted—the job was done.

"Down with ye! Down and set it!"

The lee-sheet was dragged home, the tack bowsed down; the reduced sail took the wind, and with fiercely exultant relief, Connell found the ship steadying. Aft, now, to get the yards squared, and he loomed up before the men straining at the huge double wheel.

"Keep her before it!" he shouted. "If she jibes, you drown, you dogs!"

A wind-torn figure came to him in the obscurity, staggering through the spray and clutching at him. It was Cap'n Nell, and he drew her to the rail, placing her arms around the backstay.

"We'll weather it!" he shouted to her.

"What for? To rot in a prison ashore?" She put her face close to his, in the wet roaring darkness. "No, no! Why save the ship, Tom? Let her sink! Let's go with her!"

Connell held her close, and her words stabbed into his brain. A cold hand gripped at his heart. Save the yellow ship—why? For whom? Better die with the ship, as Nell said, than save it and be plunged into living hell ashore! Die with it, go down with one

"I shipped aboard here in hopes to save ye from hell, lass. We'll share the future. Content?"

"Get for'ard among the other swine, where you belong," said Connell. "Get!"

Connell had glimpsed them for himself, the dull white loom of thunderous waters beating on a lee shore. His trumpet came up. If that were South Head—

"At the helm! Larboard! Hard larboard!" He turned. "Hanaker! Larboard the fore braces!"

Hanaker's voice responded. Men were buffeted about the decks, but the yards jolted forward. The ship reeled.

"Keep her hard down!" shouted Connell. "Sta'board main braces—let 'em run!"

Moments, endless moments, dragging at eternity. Then, as Connell's arm held Cap'n Nell close, lightning crackled and crashed anew; a gasp broke from him. A maelstrom of tossing, foaming waters, dashing against towering cliffs close at hand. No salvation now; nothing would avail, nothing!

She struck; and so passed the *Phœnix,* within sight of the bay called Botany.

roaring whirlwind of death and destruction—aye, why not? Die, with Nell in his arms, die and end it all happily, fearlessly!

Hanaker came clawing along the rail.

"We ain't far off'n the Heads!" he shouted. "We'd better wear, unless we want to pile up!"

A hoarse, wild laugh burst from Connell. Save a reeking hell-ship so she might carry more wretches to a living death? He stared into the swirling blackness, the instinct to live numbed in him.

A sudden glare of lightning leaped white across the sky and was gone. Connell's trumpet lifted; he sent a roar down the deck, to the lookouts.

"Watch sharp for North Head! Next flash!"

Cap'n Nell cried again, despairingly: "Let her go, Tom! We'll go together—"

"Aye, but not to hell," he cried. Temptation was done. "I'll not have the blood of all hands on my head, and you in my arms before God! Let be, lass!"

Another crashing blare of fire across the sky. A terror-stricken shriek from the men forward.

"*Breakers!* Breakers ahead!"

The voice of the Professor ceased. His story was ended. As though in emphatic confirmation came the voice of a tug with a freighter in tow, whistling across the harbor for the drawbridge.

"Well," said somebody, with a sigh, "I suppose it's the proper ending for a yarn of that kind—all hands perished."

The Professor smiled, and thumbed his old book lovingly.

"In that case," he said, "who wrote this eyewitness account—some twenty years later—of what happened aboard the *Phœnix?*"

"Fiddlesticks and fisheyes!" snorted Cap'n Dahl. "No living thing could've got ashore. I've been in Sydney many a time. I've seen the bones of good ships on North Head, where the worst man-eating sharks in the world—"

"Belay!" roared out Cap'n Birchwood suddenly. "Ever hear o' the *Duncan Dunbar?* She was wrecked off North Head, and able seaman Johnstone survived. A matter of record, me lad!"

"Now, hold on, hold on," intervened the Professor gently. "I didn't say the story was ended. I didn't say a man wrote this book. As a matter of fact, a woman wrote it—a woman who lived in old Hobart Town, with a raft of kids fathered by a sealing-skipper whose rightful name might have been Connell instead of Conroy. Satisfied, gentlemen?"

The question was needless.

DEATH GAVE HIM HIS CHANCE

The tale is to tell of Dan Lowry and the steam propeller. . . . Dr. Franklin fathered the idea of propelling ships by pumping water in at the bow and out at the stern, and the Royal Navy made good use of it later, but Dan Lowry did even better.

For, when death gave him his chance, he leaped at the opportunity.

He was designer and builder for old Jock Cummins, down the Thames below Greenhithe. Today it is practically all London Docks, but a hundred years ago it had green fields and country lanes and cows and river-pirates. Cummins had a little struggling shipyard of sorts, stubborn backward brain, and no family except some distant relatives with some sort of title. He was a hard and ugly old man.

The works had built a paddle-wheel collier for one firm, and they had ordered a duplicate ship built. Dan Lowry's work was good, and Lowry was the man who did the actual work. He tried to induce Cummins to install a propeller instead of paddles; Cummins laughed and sneered at propellers, which he had never heard of, and swore at Lowry.

In the upshot, they had a terrific scene. Cummins told Lowry he was being fired in the morning, and meant it. An hour later, old Jock Cummins toppled over in the street, dead from heart-failure.

Now, Dan Lowry was a bit under thirty, and intelligent. He was powerfully built and could use his fists, for he had worked up from nothing; but when he went back to his lodgings on this late afternoon, he had lost hope and ambition together. Unaware that Cummins was dead, the future looked dark to him.

When he climbed to his own rooms, he flung down his things and sank into a chair, bitter-eyed. The strong bony lines of his face set hard. He was a man beset by the devil, if ever one was!

Rather, beset by a dozen devils. Fired in the morning, eh? Old Cummins had meant those words, too. His position was gone, and his future was gone with it. Debt held him enchained; debt and a lost dream. He had no family, no prospects, no influence; without these, his common origin damned him in the London of a hundred years ago.

Rising at last, he went to the cupboard and flung open the door. The fading daylight glinted on metal, on glistening brass: the flanges of a huge propeller that stood there; it was his own design, though not his invention, for the propeller had broken the hearts of many an inventor ere now, and had come to no good.

"Your chance is gone, and mine as well," said Lowry in despondent gloom. He kicked moodily at the shining brass. "For a year past, I've sunk every farthing I could rake and scrape, to get you made. On your account, I'm deep in debt to boot. And now I'm discharged! Back to the gutter that spawned me, says he; and the bitter old man said a true word there. The only friends I know are in the gutter—I'm off for the same place, here and now!"

He caught up his cap, and departed.

In his morose mood he wronged himself. He had made friends, plenty of them, in the office and in the little shipyard, with men who knew Cummins, with the shipping firm that had ordered the new collier. But, at the moment, the words of that bitter old man burned like fire, for Jock Cummins had ever a harsh tongue.

Along the river, in those days, was no lack of gutter, from Limehouse to Rotherhithe; packet-rats, foreigners, thieves, river-pirates galore.

Hungry and tired and savage, Dan Lowry stumbled into what, long ago, had been the Bellerophon public-house; now it was the Bell & Ruffian, and deserved the second part of the name. He plumped himself down and called for supper.

"Dan Lowry's back! Lowry, lads!" went up the word.

Hard drinks and a hard world, but loyal in its own fashion. Years ago, Dan Lowry had left off all drinking but tonight he had left off all hope. Now he drank deep to banish the misery of broken ambition, and full well he banished it!

An hour later you might have seen him at it, hammer and tongs, with the Lime-house Killer. Both men were stripped to the waist under the glaring gaslights, bare-knuckled, and ten quid to the one who could last the longer. All the aristocracy of the river-scum were gathered thickly, obscene jests flew fast, cruelty was uppermost; men and women alike had the tongues and faces of hell.

*Lowry, scarcely marked at all, took the ten gold-*pieces and looked down. The Killer lay stretched out on the bloody canvas, an old woman hugging his head and moaning at his ear, and not a soul noticing them. All tongues were for Dan Lowry, slaps on the back, drinks proffered, eager hearts swelling to him. He shoved them roughly aside and went to the old woman, and pressed the gold-pieces into her hand.

"Take what your lad fought to earn, granny," said he. "You need it sore, and I don't."

He had been fuddled enough when the fight began, but his head was clear now. As he headed out for the street, sickened by the sight and smells and sounds of the place, a tap came at his shoulder. He turned to see Slasher Grimes.

"I'll walk with you, lad," said the Slasher, "and we'll finish our bit of business."

Dan Lowry, only vaguely recalling their conversation, growled something as Grimes fell into step with him.

He knew that Slasher Grimes, who had made a name and many a golden guinea fighting, was now the biggest man along the river, drawing tribute from all the dark sources that hid in dark places from the law. To those in the know, Slasher Grimes had a gang of river-pirates that laughed at the Thames police. Sometimes the laughter turned sour—and of late the police had done a lot of damage among the liberty-loving heroes of the docks.

Grimes aped the gentleman in dress and speech; perhaps he had once been a gentleman at some time. He was dark and sinewy and strong as an ox.

"One minute, my lad," he said, pausing, as they came to the dark and empty docks. "For a hundred quid, says you, I could have the secret of a snug river craft that'd show her heels to any police boat on the river. Here's your money."

Dan Lowry looked at the extended notes, then at Grimes. It all rushed back on him; he had told the Slasher the truth. That propeller in his room, or a smaller one like it, fitted to a tiny steam-launch, would turn the trick.

Aye, he had poured it all out, thanks to the liquor and his mood, though he had not told the exact secret. Now it was different. He had recoiled before the filth of the ghastly gutter; the fight, the night air, had cleared his head.

"Sorry, Slasher," said he, refusing the money. "It was the drink in me talking."

"Don't lie," rejoined Grimes harshly, tapping Dan Lowry's chest with his gold-headed stick. "Liquor doesn't lie. If ye have what ye say, lad, this hundred is only a starter; it means wealth, to you and me both. Come, out with it!"

Wealth? With everything lost as it was, Lowry was tempted by the word, and had the temptation come earlier, he might have yielded; but his little dip into the life of the gutter had caused revolt to rise in him. He saw things as they were, now; he saw from what he had arisen in these years, knew he had worked himself up to a new and totally different level. He was no longer a creature of the gutter.

"No," said he, and turned. The hand of Grimes clutched at him. He struck it away. The stick belted him over the skull in fury; then he let Slasher Grimes have it right and left, to go sprawling and slithering in the slime of the street.

"You'll hear from this," gasped the voice of Grimes, with a volley of oaths.

Not unlikely, he thought, as he went to his lodgings. Despair settled upon him again, because he had reverted for this little hour or two into the old life. The one decent thing he had won in these long years, was sullied and tarnished. Was he, after all, doomed to gin and tatters and sordid filth for the rest of life?

"By heavens, no!" he told himself savagely. "It's a good thing, perhaps, that I took the dip tonight; it's made me realize what I am and might have been. Good! We'll start fresh from the bottom tomorrow."

But, getting home, he heard that old Cummins was dead.

And he had not been fired. Instead, he was now the unquestioned head and authority in the struggling little shipyard with its one boat a-building, its little offices and its three accountants and boy. Across the desk of old Jock Cummins, which was now his desk, the lawyer told him so; the dry, precise Queen's Counsel, an eminent man and well tailored.

"For the present, Lowry, carry on in full charge; it's the wish of the heirs," said he. "I talked with them this morning. They're highly placed and titled, though lacking in money. They can't afford to have the name linked with this place, or to have it known that they own it. At least, such are the orders for the present."

"Too blue-blooded to be in trade, eh?" commented Dan Lowry. "Thank God, I'm not! Will they put money into the business, perhaps?"

"They need what the business earns for them, in order to live," said the lawyer. "Can you carry on this ship to completion?"

Dan Lowry laughed harshly. "More than that. If Cummins had listened to me, I'd have made money steadily for him. Give me the authority to buy those barges tied up at the next dock. I can repair 'em in the spare time of the hands, and sell 'em in a fortnight. Give me authority to do a dozen things that need doing—"

He named them. The eminent lawyer departed somewhat dubiously, but returned that same afternoon, bringing a young woman with him, a Miss Colson.

"You shall have full authority," said he, "provided you give Miss Colson a place in the office, to handle all accounts on behalf of the heirs. I don't think you will regret it."

Regret? Dan Lowry wanted to kick the man out and then laugh in his face. What—set a woman to spy and interfere? Put a woman into a business office? It was unheard of, and an absurdity! Suddenly he recalled that Cummins had used those same words about his propeller.

She was a quiet but capable young woman, and her shy smile conquered his instinctive dislike. He agreed, since he must. Miss Colson went down to the waiting cab, and the lawyer paused for a word regarding her.

"You'll find her rather exceptional, Lowry, in that she has a gift for business. I might add that she comes of a very good family; a gentlewoman in distress, if I may say so, who is compelled to support herself."

Dan Lowry merely grunted, being skeptical of gentlewomen, especially in distress....

To his astonishment, he discovered that Miss Colson was not only intelligent in business ways, but had a swift comprehension of what it was all about. She interfered not at all. She assented to all the reforms and changes he had vainly urged on old Cummins, and even suggested a couple herself. Their relations were not inimical, but friendly.

When she vetoed his proposed contract with a supply firm at Limehouse, he was furious, but assented with a growl. A week later, he found the firm was in trouble with the Admiralty. She only nodded when he told her. She had known this all along.

"And how, may I inquire?" he demanded.

"That I can't tell you, Mr. Lowry. I have family connections, and I use them."

"Well, you were dead right!"

He came to have a vast admiration for her ability, in fact. So did the clerks. The dingy old office became clean, and even took on an air of well-being. The hands always had a smile and a touch of the forelock when she hove in sight. Dan Lowry learned very little about her personally, and was too busy to try: besides, she had an air that discouraged any curiosity. A lady, as the clerks said; the word spoke volumes.

Meantime, two things pended: the ship on the ways, and Slasher Grimes.

With the ship, things had come to a point of decision; for here, Dan Lowry trembled under a temptation that was tremendous and overpowering. Either he was to put in the paddle-wheels, as Cummins had planned, or he was to put in the new propeller—as he had it planned. He could go ahead and do this, and say no word about it to Miss Colson; but he scorned the evasion. But he had to do something, and do it immediately. The audacity of his temptation, the audacity of what he planned, did not occur to him as such. He had even brought the big brass propeller up to a corner of the office, pending decision.

While it pended, Slasher Grimes walked in on him one noonday. He was alone in the office with Miss Colson, who was eating her luncheon in the inner room. Grimes strode in and came up to his desk, hard-eyed, and extended a sheaf of banknotes.

"Well, Dan Lowry? Here's your hundred quid. Do you keep your promise or not?"

"I thought you'd forgotten all that," said Lowry.

"I forget nothing, my lad—nothing!" was the significant reply. "Yes or no?"

"And supposing it's no?"

"You'll have the week-end to ponder, this being Friday. Bright and early on the Monday morning," said Slasher Grimes cheerfully, "I'll offer you the hundred quid for the third and last time. If ye say no, I blow my whistle, and up pops the devil! In other words, gents with a warrant for your apprehension. No doubt you've forgotten the little matter of Magistrate Herriott and the case o' schnapps. But the law, my lad, never forgets. Like me—never! Think it over, till the Monday morning; it's friends or enemies, your own choice."

And, cocking his beaver over one ear, he walked out.

Lowery, scarcely marked, looked down at the killer.

Dan Lowry sat, white to the lips, eyes blazing, a sick dismay in his heart. He looked up to see Miss Colson staring at him from the doorway of the inner office.

"Who was that man, Mr. Lowry?" she asked. "What did he mean, about the schnapps?"

Lowry swallowed hard, and drew a deep breath.

"God help me!" he said, then squared his shoulders and smiled into her eyes. "I can't tell you now; there are feet on the stairs—the clerks are returning. I'll tell you later, this evening. Perhaps you'll have supper with me. But it's a dismal tale—nothing for a fine lady like you to hear from a gutter-rat like me."

His bitter words belied his smile.

She nodded slowly.

"I'll be very glad to have dinner with you, Mr. Lowry. But that's not what's been worrying you all day, and yesterday too?"

"No," said Lowry, as the two accountants reentered. With an effort, he put away all thought of Slasher Grimes, for the moment. The dikes were broken, now; out poured all the flood of his perplexities, which had suddenly taken second place. A warrant, and jail!

"Draw up your chair, Miss Colson; rather, let me draw it up for you," said he, and suited action to words. Then he produced a portfolio of diagrams, designs, figures, and spread them all out; and with them, his dreams.

He talked to her, low-voiced, quietly, steadily, for an hour or more. His enthusiasm was quenched, now; nothing mattered, for a man who was going to prison on the Monday.

There in the corner was his propeller—his own, for which he was still heavily in debt. He showed her the calculations, the theories; he showed her the proofs gained by other propellers, and discarded; he showed her letters, his rebuffs from the Admiralty, from ship-owners, from builders. He showed her the comparative costs, the cheapness of the propeller as opposed to paddle-wheels.

"I talked with the firm who ordered this collier from us," he said. "They agreed that if Cummins, meaning this firm of ours, wanted to install the propeller instead of paddles, they'd accept the craft subject to its efficiency. Cummins is dead. I'm in charge."

"The contract covers such substitution?" she asked. He nodded. "And you could do it?"

"Not honestly, Miss Colson, without your consent. I believe there's no risk at all, but the owners of this business depend upon it, I understand; if anything went wrong—well, you see what it would mean. Monday morning, we have to know whether the propeller is to be installed or not; the work now depends on this."

"It would cost no more; it might mean a tremendous improvement. Hm! If it's as you say, the Royal Navy should use propellers instead of paddles."

Lowry laughed. "Admiralty clerks laugh at innovations, as you should know."

"Indeed I do," she agreed. "But if I authorize the substitution—"

"Then we'll go ahead."

She hesitated. "Let me borrow all these papers until Monday. I'll not be down in the morning; I'm spending the week-end with relatives at Richmond. Monday morning, I'll give you my ideas about it. Yes?"

"Yes, by all means," he agreed. Leaning forward, he picked out one of the papers and showed it to her. "There are figures covering two craft of approximately equal tonnage. They're correct. They prove that this ship on the ways, when finished, could actually tow backward any equal ship equipped with paddle-wheels! That is, with my propeller."

"Oh!" A trace of color leaped in her cheeks, and her eyes danced. "What an idea! I'd love to see it tried out here in the Thames!"

"But,"—and his face darkened with sudden recollection,—"be here early Monday morning, please. If you're late, I may be gone."

"Where?" she asked in surprise.

"To prison," he curtly rejoined, and walked out of the office to oversee the yard work. But her eyes followed him in memory—her eyes, wondering, incredulous and hurt.

They bore the same hurt look that evening, as they faced him across the dinner table. He spoke with plain blunt words, not bitter, but strong and forthright as his strong face and level eyes.

"I'm no genius, Miss Colson. I didn't invent that propeller, as I told you today; but I've perfected it, and I've perfected the engine connections, as I've perfected a lot of things, including this little shipyard; but I can't perfect myself—that is, in eyes like yours."

She regarded him steadily, as if searching the meaning behind his words.

"Do you think it necessary?" she asked in her cool way, which might have meant anything.

"Perhaps not. My father was a ship captain; I grew up along the wharves of this river. I was left alone when young, and went with the only crowd I knew. I forged ahead little by little; meantime, I had to live. I did odd bits of thieving at times."

"Who hasn't?" she asked idly. "I stole apples, once, and got a sound birching."

His eyes darkened impatiently. "I don't mean childish things; I mean actual theft. Once, with some river-pirates, I broke into a warehouse. A case of schnapps was stolen; we were caught; because I was no more than a boy, Magistrate Herriott gave me only five years in prison, instead of life. I never reached prison—I got away."

"Oh!" Her eyes dilated upon him. "So that was it! How long ago?"

"Nine years, when I was eighteen. It was nothing of great account, perhaps; still, the whole thing taught me what I needed. I went in for fighting, boxing, and broke away from the river gangs. I made a little money, and went to work, leaving fighting behind me. Step by step, you see. Every step meant cruel work."

would have been helpless before any thieving launch so equipped. He told about the fight, and then, hesitant, skipped to his interview with the Slasher.

"Wait." She checked him. "Where are the ten sovereigns?"

"I—well, I gave them away," he said lamely, and told how. Her eyes warmed, and she nodded. He finished his story, and told just what Grimes had said this morning, and there it was all out.

"You see," he concluded, "the rascal thinks he has me in a cleft stick."

"Hasn't he?"

"Devil a bit of it. I'll take my medicine, though it'll be hard. The law has no mercy, and I've no influence."

"You have what's better," said she. His brows went up inquiringly, and she smiled. "I don't think there's anything so terrible in all you've said, really."

"You? A lady?" He threw out his hand. "Me—a product of the gutter?"

"Well," she observed with staggering perception of values, "until the present reign, our royal family has been remarkably content to remain lower than the gutter; and if you knew the origin of our noble families, you'd realize that some of them have come far, very far, from the accident of birth! You shouldn't be so conscious of inferiority that does not exist."

"I'm not!" he disclaimed swiftly. "It's not that; it's only that there's no chance for me. Now I'll be a prison bird, and down goes Dan Lowry for good. I'm telling you all this because it's your due. You can take proper action on behalf of the owners, when I'm gone."

"Is that the only reason?" she asked, looking at him.

He flushed slowly.

"No, by God!" he began impulsively, and flushed more deeply. "No. But it's all I can say now, except that—well, we've been friends."

He traced those steps for her, sparing himself nothing in the accounting, spurred on by her interest and attention. Then he came to the evening when old Jock Cummins had fired him, and told her what had been said.

She nodded.

"I know. He left a memorandum to discharge you in the morning. I found it among his papers one day."

"What? And you said nothing?"

"Don't be silly." She smiled slightly; and not for the first time, he noted how a smile transfigured her whole face and lighted it. "Go on, please."

"All right." With that, he plunged, and did not spare himself here, either. That wild idea of turning over his propeller, or one like it, to the river-pirates, was not so wild as appeared; the Thames police

"No," he said, and turned.... The stick belted him over the head in fury.

"Not have been, but are," she said, and smiled again. "Now, let's forget the whole thing, please. What shall you be doing between now and Monday?"

"Completing plans and designs for the work, if you decide to go ahead with my scheme. There's a lot to do on them. Then, my plans for the shipyard. If this collier succeeds, I'd thought of taking on the adjacent land and going in for larger operations."

"Tell me about it," she begged, and he complied.

When Dan Lowry went home that night, he found himself light-hearted despite the doom that overhung him.

Monday dawned ominously, with a drizzle of rain; and there was no Miss Colson at the office. Instead, a messenger boy arrived, bringing the portfolio of plans and a note.

Dear Mr. Lowry;

I am not returning to the office at once. You have my authority to install your propeller in the new craft, and the owners have also consented. I wish you the best of luck.

Cecily Colson.

Dan Lowry swallowed hard.

The best of luck! And prison facing him. And she was not returning at once. She, a fine lady, had heard a bit too much of his story. When he was safely stowed away, and gone from the place, she would show up again; or the owners would come and take over, noble name and all. And they would profit by his work, if this propeller did its work.

With a harsh laugh, he gave the orders, and sent the foreman his designs.

The office was bleak without her. When he told the clerks she was not coming back at once, their faces fell; a feeling of absence was upon the whole place. And then came a tread of heavy feet upon the stairs, and Dan Lowry faced about with heavier heart. As he feared, it was the Slasher. Into the office came Grimes, and smiled wickedly at him.

"Ready, my lad? It's touch and go, so speak up prompt. Is it yes?"

Dan Lowry came up to him. "Slasher, you wouldn't do it? You wouldn't turn me in?"

"Like a shot, my lad, if you don't come across—"

"Then do it and be damned to you!" said Dan Lowry, and cut loose.

Grimes did have a whistle, and blew it shrilly, before Lowry knocked it down his throat. The Slasher put up a creditable fight, but it did him no good at all; the ferocity with which Lowry tore into him was something unholy to watch.

The whistle brought no runners or constables. It did bring a tall, elegantly attired gentleman with chiseled features and an air of authority, who came into the doorway and stood leaning on his stick with an air of keen enjoyment as he watched proceedings. He even lifted his voice in delight, as the Slasher went staggering.

"Well hit, well hit! A noble right, man! Again!"

Lowry flung him a glance and continued, hoping to get his money's worth before he was torn off. And he got it. Grimes was no coward, but not the bravest could stand long to the fearful punishment he took. As he went down for the last time and tried unavailingly to get on his feet again, the stranger stepped forward.

"Mr. Daniel Lowry, I believe?"

"I've no time for business now." Lowry turned to him. "Who are you?"

"Patrick Lowther." The stranger gestured at Grimes. "Have your clerks throw this rascal out."

"Eh? He has men downstairs—"

"I've dismissed them, Lowry."

Then, suddenly, Dan Lowry felt that name crash through his brain. Patrick Lowther! The famed jurist, of course—Lord Durwent, Lord Chancellor of the Queen's Bench, one of the greatest men in London! While the two clerks hustled the Slasher out and away, Dan Lowry stood staring. Then the visitor smiled.

"Very well done, Lowry; I follow the fancy a bit myself, or used to do so in my younger days. Rather lucky that I showed up, what? This business of yours—Magistrate Herriott and the case of schnapps, you know. It's been brought to my attention."

"It's—what?" stammered Dan Lowry. "Your attention—you—Lord Durwent? Your attention, My Lord?"

The other chuckled. "Yes, I understand that one of your people here brought it to the right quarter, and I was asked to handle the matter. I have done so. In due course, the entire affair will be written off and the case closed, though it may be necessary to obtain a pardon from the Crown. You may rest assured, Mr. Lowry, that you have nothing more to fear. By the way, my men below will hold that rascal; you may care to prosecute him for attacking you."

"He didn't," Dan Lowry said dazedly. "He didn't. I attacked him."

The visitor laughed heartily, bowed, and departed, still laughing. When Dan Lowry rushed to the stairs, wakening from his daze, he reached the bottom to see a dispersing crowd and a coach vanishing down the street.

He shut himself in the private office and sat staring at nothing. *"One of your people."* The phrase buzzed in his head. Miss Colson, of course. She must have acted quickly. She had reached the owners; even though impoverished, the nobility could work wonders. And they had somehow reached Lord Durwent.

In a glow, Lowry reached for pen and paper, and wrote her a letter of thanks. He wrote a long, long letter, and poured out a great deal of himself in the words; he begged her to return, and gave her a dozen excellent reasons why she should return. He wrote so much, in fact, that the penny post would not serve and to send the letter cost him thrippence.

Then he went down to the shipyard and hurled himself into the job there.

Three days later came a short reply; she was detained by illness and would come back to the office when and if possible. It was a curt and formal note, but had a postscript of a few words: *"Your letters are lovely. Write again."*

"Monday morning," he told her, "I may be gone—to prison."

He read that, grunted to himself, and went back to work. These days, work absorbed and swallowed him; he was rushing the collier to completion as fast as possible; and he was a new man. The past had been wiped away by a word from her. He wanted to rush up to the City, see the estate lawyers, and find her; half a dozen times he even started, only to come back and hang up his hat with a grim shake of the head....

They launched the craft, with no ceremony at all, and began to finish the job and get the engines installed. Dan Lowry was with the work day and night. He could not wait to get those engines turning over and make sure how his propeller worked. One night he made a try of it, in secret, with three of the hands whom he could trust. They got a fire going, got steam up—enough to run her for two minutes. When she nearly tore her cable out of the riverbed, he knew all was well; and he raked out the fires. The propeller worked. The real tests would come in another fortnight.

But before they came, arrived a hansom at the street door, and a tall, weather-eyed gentleman whose card said he was Captain Sir Adolphus Brett, R.N., of the Admiralty.

"We've heard something about this craft you're building, Mr. Lowry," said Brett very pleasantly. "In fact, I have copies of your correspondence with the Admiralty, sometime in the past, regarding a proposed propeller."

Dan Lowry eyed him in bewilderment.

"I never got to dock-ends with your Admiralty clerks," said he.

"I am not an Admiralty clerk," Brett rejoined. "In fact, I've been ordered to handle this matter and propose to you a certain test. We're much interested in this steam propeller. The First Lord of the Admiralty himself, I may say, has it under advisement."

"My God!" said Dan Lowry. "It's like a fairy tale!"

He could not realize it, even when Brett broke out laughing and informed him that while the Admiralty was slow, it was after all sure. It let nothing escape its eagle eye, and so forth—an affable and quite convincing speech.

"The test," said he, "should be very simple. Out here in the reach of the river. A cutter with paddles will pass a hawser to your craft; they'll be of approximate tonnage; they'll pull in opposite directions. I warn you, sir, that the general opinion is that the cutter will pull your craft very easily, which will mean the end of your steam propeller."

A spark leaped in Dan Lowry.

"Very well, Captain Brett," said he, and named a day for the test. "Do your best, and it'll mean the end of paddle-wheels in the Royal Navy!"

It was arranged as simply as that, Dan Lowry plunged back into his work, carried on from day to day by a heart-hurried smother of eagerness. The craft was finished, her engines were tested, all worked like a charm. And then came the day.

To Dan Lowry, it was like a dream. He could not believe it was actually happening to him, out there in the long reach of the river. He was aboard the craft himself; so was a party of Admiralty men. An Admiralty launch hovered near with gold lace showing on a uniformed figure: old Admiral Duckworth, they said, the First Lord himself.

The hawser was passed, the trim navy cutter churned and churned, her paddles slapping the water. Dan Lowry shouted at his engineer. The hawser tautened, grew rigid as steel; a huge fourteen-inch hemp, brand new. An inch or two, a foot or two—slowly, puffing and churning, the Navy cutter moved astern. The collier moved forward, gained speed and power and momentum, and dragged the trim cutter a half-mile before the hawser broke asunder. No more was needed....

An hour later, Dan Lowry sat in his private office, alone. The day was dying. The clerks had gone. He was trying to scratch a letter to Miss Colson. For the whole future had burst gloriously open, and he could hardly realize it.

A light, quick step on the stairs. He looked up, startled. The door opened, and she stood there, smiling at him.

He leaped to his feet.

"You! You! I was just writing you," he cried. "It's really you!"

"Really me, Dan Lowry," she said, and laughed as

she gave him her hand. "Oh, it was a grand sight to see! I was watching it all. You've won, you've won!"

Before he knew it, he had won more than he had ever dreamed. Somehow, it happened they were clinging together, looking at one another hungrily.

"I can't realize this crowning marvel!" he said huskily. "That you should care—"

"A lot, Dan Lowry," she broke in upon him. "Don't you?"

"Don't I? With every breath in me, with everything that I am and have!"

"That's plenty," she said. "And will be more, before long. Fame and wealth and new horizons—all ahead of us, Dan Lowry. Agreed?"

"With all my heart," said he, and met her lips with his.

Then she drew back.

"You're no longer worried because—because I'm a lady, as you used to say?"

"Lady be damned!" said Lowry fervently. "You'll be my wife."

"Praise God," she said softly. "And you'll be my husband.... Now—I'll have to tell you something—a confession. It's hard to make. I fear you'll hate me for it; I do indeed." She eyed him anxiously. "I've never lied to you, Dan, but I have deceived you a little, and now I'm in fear to tell you of it, lest you resent it."

He broke into a great laugh.

"Hate you? Resent it? My lass, my lass, I love you with my whole heart! Nothing you could say or do, nothing now or in the past or in the future, could waken any such feeling within me!"

"Swear it!" she said, doubtingly. "Hold up your hand and swear it, Dan!"

He did so, smiling and yet deeply earnest. She drew a long breath.

"Very well; then you'd best have everything at one blow. I'm Cecily Colson; I needed the money that I earned here, it's true. I'm also Lady Cecily Colson; except for this place, I was dependent on the charity of my uncle, Admiral Duckworth, the First Lord. That's how I was able to help you, in one way or another. I did it because I knew you loved me, Dan Lowry, and because I loved you. And now don't you dare to jilt me!"

Dan Lowry came out of his daze to find her in his arms. And, as he should very properly have done—he kept her there.

TRAMPS OF THE SEA

C*ap'n Herrick sat in the Liverpool* headquarters of Lorrins & Co., swallowing a bitter pill. The general manager was a supercilious London cockney, acid-tongued, who joyed in humbling the once proud master of clipper ships.

"Mind you, 'Errick," said he, "we're signing you on only because we must. You're known for a drunken dreamer. You laid the *Morning Star* ashore, and should never 'ave another berth by rights, but this is an emergency."

"I'd like to talk with the owner," said Herrick, a spark in his eye.

"I represent 'im," rejoined the other importantly. "As a matter o' fact, 'e ain't abaht much. Just inherited the line, 'e did, and 'as other interests. Mr. Lorrins leaves the business to me, so to speak. First of the year, 'e tykes active charge himself. Now let's see abaht the papers and so forth."

Herrick settled back in his chair, shoulders sagging. He was a man of fifty, sturdy, rugged of face, with a hard but somewhat wistful eye.

"Before I lost the *Star* and was lied out of a berth by those rascally officers, I never drank," said he. "Since then, I have. Now—not again."

The cockney sneered. "Like enough. Mr. Lorrins 'as no use for drinking men, 'Errick, and you're being taken on because we can't get better."

Herrick listened, a grimly sardonic twist to his lips. Up and down the Mersey docks, he was known for his prophecies of what the commerce of the seas was coming to; and here, by a stroke of luck, he saw the truth of them fulfilled, in a small way. For the propeller had come in at last; the steam-propeller, whose invention would do away with paddle-wheels....

The Lorrins Line was old, solid; the Lorrins barques and square-riggers had run for generations between English ports and those of Spain and the Mediterranean. The last owner, now dead, had grudgingly invested in one of the new steam-propeller colliers, to haul coals from the Welsh ports to London.

With an emergency cargo of machinery and small stuff for Bilbao, the towering three-master to carry it had caught fire; the damage would lay her up for weeks. Not another Lorrins keel would be here for more weeks. The new owner had ordered the collier pressed into service for the run. She was downstream off Bootle docks, loaded and ready; a crew had to be found in haste, and officers for a steamship were not easily picked up. Hence, Captain Herrick gained a berth.

"Papers all clear? Aye. Off wi' the morning tide," said Herrick, fumbling over the papers. "Half a dozen more men needed, eh? I'll have 'em aboard tonight. Trust me."

"We'll trust you not to drink on duty," said the London cockney with asperity. Herrick flung him a snarl and walked out.

"It's come true, this proves it!" he muttered, pausing out in the wet street. "And no reaching that lunkhead of an owner to make him see it. Hm! I'll pay my debts, get my duffle, and catch a coach to Bootle this evening."

He found that a coach to Bootle, Waterloo, and beyond, would leave at seven, booked a place, and went about his own affairs.

It had come true, yes, but after the fashion of many a dream—not at all in the way he had imagined it. He talked about it that evening, bitterly enough, as a sort of grousing farewell to British soil.

The coach to Bootle was late, a horse was lame, there was only one other passenger inside, the rain pitched down in torrents. The other passenger was a man of thirty, all in gray—gray eye, gray gloves and suit and greatcoat. Herrick surveyed him, in the passing dim gaslights, with a somewhat jaundiced eye.

"Nice send-off for Al Gorta!" he said. "I'm taking out a damned Lorrins Line tub."

"Where, may I inquire, is Al Gorta?" asked the other, a bit condescendingly.

"Port o' Bilbao. You're no seaman, I take it."

"I am not," said the other curtly.

Herrick grunted, and lit his pipe.

"Might do you good. Time was when Englishmen were in the front of everything to do wi' the sea; not any more. Now every shipping firm hears me out and shows me the door. 'Good day to you, Cap'n Herrick, and we'll think it over.' Arrgh! And this damned Lorrins Line—the wind blows opportunity into their lap, and they don't know it! The owner's some jackanapes who's fallen heir to the line. I offer him a fortune, and he won't take it."

"Are you, perhaps, the shipmaster they call Tramp Herrick?" asked the other.

"I am, and proud of the name!"

"I've heard of you, it seems. A singular and rather amusing prediction—that all sailing vessels will be swept off the seas, that the commerce and trade of England will pass to tramps—isn't that your word for it? An odd term for ships, I must say."

Herrick puffed his pipe, while the coach rattled on over wet cobbles.

"An appropriate term," he rejoined. "A ship—in the seaman's sense of square-rigger—follows the winds and currents, makes a voyage to a certain definite port and back again. I hold that the time's at hand when this will be changed. The steam propeller will do it; a proven success, it's going to cast a tremendous influence. The whole world's commerce and trade will be altered, in another ten or twenty years."

"What has that to do with the odd appellation of 'tramps' to ships?"

"A steamer that's like an aimless tramp wandering the lanes—the coming carrier of commerce. She can cruise anywhere, vagrant; to one port, on to another, picking up cargo here, cargo there. The telegraph, that magnificent invention, will assist her. None of the slow voyages, delays, accidents, that impede a sailing vessel."

"An impractical vision, sir," said the other. "I know something of trade. The commerce of the world is adjusted to the sailing ship. It would have to be completely readjusted for your journeying tramps. It would be thrown off balance entirely by your petty notion-cart peddling wares from port to port. You command a Lorrins Line ship, sir?"

"A collier, a steamship, the *Limerick;* switched to a Bilbao run to do what no sailing ship can do—a quick run across Biscay in stormy weather. Notion-cart, eh?" Herrick grunted again. "A shipping firm is in business to make money, isn't it? Aye. This run will make quicker money in a fortnight for Lorrins than a square-rigger would make in two months. Will they see the light? Not much. Same old way—it's good enough. Commerce would be thrown off balance—of course it would! And high time it was. The world changes. Why, I can see where, twenty years from now, these notion-carts, these commerce tramps, will be going up and down the world, the trade of the Seven Seas readjusted and balanced again to suit; and who'll profit? Not our stodgy English firms, content to do as their grandfathers did, but the French and Americans and Germans, who have vision!"

"Truly, you speak as a dreamer," said the other man slowly. "But a shipowner must have a care. Innovations are dangerous. He must be guided by experience. Stout oak ships are Britain's walls; they're the backbone of commerce and wealth."

"Bah! They're building better ships of iron right now," retorted Herrick. "This collier is one. But you talk like all the other Liverpool merchants. Not a damned one of you knows the sea; have a care, says you! That's just it. Any man who breaks old chains must fling caution overboard. I was brought up in canvas: Bully Waterman, Martin, Forbes—I've sailed rings around 'em. But I know steam's got the future by the neck, and I'm for it. Lost my ship, aye; juniors ganged up and lied, to make me a scapegoat. And now I'm taking the *Limerick* to Bilbao for fools who won't see the fortune in their hand!"

"Perhaps your dream is not concrete enough," commented the other.

"Bosh! Details are simple. The first shipping firm

to put a dozen screw steamers into this business will make a fortune. First contacts are the most important; prestige means a lot to Latin and Levantine and Greek merchants. Drop off a cargo agent at every big port, and the thing is done; look where there's a telegraph line, and use it. That's all."

The other was silent for a space.

"I fear, sir, you're lost in dream," said he at last, as though with regret. "The consensus in the shipping world is that these iron steamers are very good for coastal work, but for nothing else. Merchants will fear to ship goods in them. Once away from home, they could not be repaired in case of breakdown. Above all, there's the irregularity of their schedule."

"Which could be very regular. Like everyone else who knows nothing about the sea," declared Cap'n Herrick, "you're a fool."

Which, not unnaturally, put an end to the conversation.

Arrived at Bootle, then a town to itself, the two passengers alighted. Herrick left his companion without a farewell, and sought a certain boarding-house proprietor. He wanted six men aboard the *Limerick,* which was laden and ready to be off.

"Have 'em aboard before three," said he. "I sail wi' the tide at four."

The crimp grinned. "You'll have 'em long ere that, Cap'n, though there's not many folks abroad this dirty night."

Herrick shrugged and went his way. Crimps, and a drop of dope or even a bash over the head, and the law be damned! It was the custom, and the bad luck of those on the short end. Crimps had been known to ship a corpse, now and then; or perhaps the persuader was too heavy for a thin skull.

A boat took Herrick out to the *Limerick.* All was clear; he got acquainted with the chief officer and the second, and heard the surprising information that the owner, Lorrins, was coming aboard to see them off that evening. So, at least, said the chief engineer, the only soul aboard to have had a glimpse of the owner.

"Show up on a night like this? Not likely," growled Cap'n Herrick. "If he's aboard by eight bells, midnight, rouse me up to meet him. If not, to hell with him! Tide's on ebb and we're off, at eight bells sharp. Mister, six men coming aboard—"

A hail from the water. Here were the six now, and the runner to collect his money. The mate attended to it, and had the six rain-sodden, senseless lumps of clay handed below to get over their liquor, dope or bumps by morning. No questions asked, none wanted.

No Lorrins showed up. Eight bells; in a squall of rain, the *Limerick* headed down Crosby Channel, and the Rock Light was lost behind. In the gray dawn, she smashed through heavy seas, making dirty weather of it with her flush decks; but Herrick was delighted by her speed and handling.

Hand-lines were rigged and a canvas dodger, for the bridge was low in those days and the storm-apron was needed. Herrick, booted and oilskinned, was

"Mister, six men coming aboard—" Here were the six now—rain-sodden, senseless lumps of clay.

staring intently into the wrack when he caught a gasping voice beside him, and took it to be the mate.

"What's the meaning of this?"

"I changed course a point to the sou'-ard. She rides better heading into 'em." He glanced around, then straightened. "Hello! Who are you? Get your oilskins if you're the wheel relief—"

"I demand you put me ashore!" broke in the other, shivering and gasping.

Herrick stared.

The man was coatless, in rags, and green with seasickness; over his head was jammed a broken, shapeless hat, wild hair sticking out from beneath it. A trickle of blood had run down over one cheek, he had a black eye to boot, and a pair of cut and puffed lips.

"Ashore, I say!" he repeated. "Or I'll have you in jail!"

The bosun appeared. Herrick turned to him. "Who's this man?"

"One o' the hands come aboard last night, sir." The bosun knuckled his brow. "Had a time of it rousin' him, sir. Bound to speak to the cap'n, says he, and no stoppin' of him."

"You're Captain Herrick?" cried out the hapless wretch, lips blue with cold. "Yes, I recognize you. I'm the owner of this ship, do you hear? I want the ship put about at once for Liverpool. At once! I demand you do it!"

"Oh, ye do!" Herrick slipped the grinning bosun a wink. "So you're the owner, are you? You look the sort of ragpicker would be a Liverpool shipowner—"

"Confound your impudence!" screamed out the man, coming closer and shaking a fist under Herrick's nose. "Lorrins is my name, d'ye hear? You know me well enough! Put this ship about and get back to Liverpool—"

Herrick's fist took him squarely between wind and water, and doubled him up.

"Take him for'ard, bosun, and teach him his place."

The bosun obeyed promptly. But, as the man was hustled away, his voice came back on the wind in a gasping cry:

"Jail for this! You know me. I was in the coach with you!"

Cap'n Herrick squinted into the scud and wrack again, a cold chill running down his backbone. The man from the coach! And Lorrins had not shown

"Craft like that are doomed—the day will come when canvas will be a rarity."

up. Could that man have been Lorrins, the owner? A sudden gusty oath broke on Herrick's lips.

"By the Lord Harry! If it was, then he let me talk on about Lorrins and the Line, and never peeped—a damned dirty trick! Knew who I was, and kept a tight tongue. The blasted desk-warmer! He deserves nothing from me; he'll get nothing."

Presently he went below, located the chief engineer, and talked earnestly with him for a time. The chief scratched his nose doubtfully, but finally gave in.

"Ah weel, ye ha' the richt of it, nae doot! I'll not recognize the lad if I see him."

After which, encountering the bosun, Herrick stopped him and asked about the man.

"Jem Carlock, sir, is his name on the articles. He made a bit o' trouble."

"Is he still pricked by that fool notion about being the owner?"

"I think he's forgot it, sir. I gave him some good advice with my boot; he's been bad beat up, sir. Probably addled his head."

"If he makes more trouble, haze him. Better haze him anyway, after he has a chance to get his sea legs."

As for Jem Carlock, he lay retching on his thin straw mat with the rest of the larboard watch, most of them dead to the world and the others wishing they were likewise.

Jem Carlock! The name was drilled into his brain; he was Jem Carlock, nothing else. The bosun's advice had been imperative and brutal. Being actually a man of intelligence, Jem Carlock saw clearly that if he claimed to be anyone else, he would be met by jeers and taunts and disbelief. He had taken one look at his face in a broken mirror, and it lent sickening disillusion. No wonder the captain disbelieved him.

Shanghaied! He knew what it meant; he had been a fool to come down to Bootle after dark and alone. Now, to the tossing of the *Limerick,* he was utterly sick of body and mind alike, appalled and hopeless by the filth and brutality surrounding him. The fury of the gale grew. The sea smote the little vessel in a series of violent surges that set her groaning; sea water seeped into the fo'c's'le through the hawse-holes, as it swept the flush decks.

Men wedged in their bunks, seasick, groaning, cursing. The ship was pounding down the Irish Sea. He slept or dozed fitfully, with fever and wetness and pain goading him, until the hatch opened to admit a burst of spray, and a man who yelled:

"Larboard watch! On deck, watch!"

Those who could not, did; by boot and fist they got to the deck. Jem Carlock went with the others, at peril of being washed clean off the flush deck, to the little galley. A copper kettle was in a rack, holding steaming liquid. The men, securing hook-pots, ladled out some of the stuff.

"Arf!" exploded one, spewing a mouthful on the greasy deck. "Rank poison!"

"Bilge, it is," growled another. "B.&H.—*bilge water and holystones*—that's what ye get in a Lorrins packet. We were a pack o' fools."

"Not me!" cried another in profane rage. "Shanghaied, me and Bill were! Warn't we, Bill? Bloody shanghaied! I've sailed in B.&H. ships o' this bloody Line afore now. Lorrins knows how to starve a crew without actual murder; that's how they make money, blast 'em! I'd like to have me hands on this here Lorrins!"

"D'ye know him?" asked Jem Carlock, managing to down some of the slime from the kettle.

"Do I! Toff, that's what he is. Fine bloody gentleman. And a proper belly-robber, too. Skin a louse for its taller, he would!"

Salty conversation flowed over the hook-pots, unthinkable curses and filthy speech, and if ever the owner of the Lorrins Line was blasted in words, it was here. Jem Carlock listened and learned many things not taught in schools or city trade. Because he had intelligence, he kept his mouth tight; and because he kept his mouth tight and was so obviously a poor devil of a landsman knocked on the head and shipped by the crimps, a brawny big Donegal man took a liking to him, with rough kindness.

The talk fell on Captain Herrick.

"He's a proper little bully," observed the Donegal man, "but a grand master, and fair with the hands. No danger of him getting walked on, neither, afloat nor ashore! He takes care of his hands, mind you; nobody walks over Tom Herrick's crew."

"Aw, he's crazy," said somebody. "No secret. Lost his ship and took to liquor, and now he's a ravin' madman."

"Tell him so," said the Donegal man, with a grin.

Eight bells struck. The men went out, stokers dodging down the fiddley, seamen making oilskins fast. The Donegal man got oilskins for Jem Carlock from the slop-chest, and took him to the wind-swept bridge, proclaiming that they were watchmates.

"I'm bridge lookout and lee helmsman. Your first wheel, matey."

Carlock went to the wheel, with only a hazy idea of what he was doing, and the man there gave over with a snort of relief.

"Sou'-sou'east, and nothing to the east. She's steerin' main 'ard, too."

The vessel climbed a giant comber, and Jem

Carlock, knowing little or nothing of what he was about, was off his course on the instant. He was knocked sprawling, kicked to his feet; boots and fists thudded into him right and left, while the Donegal man was put at the wheel. Brutality, sickening him, leaving him spent and gasping and bruised to stand watch; the fury and everything else knocked slam out of him, with only the will to live still in his heart.

He glared at Captain Herrick, who glanced at him and ignored him, obviously with no recognition whatever. He thought of himself as he had been last night, passed a hand over his beard-sprouting, bruised face, and kept his mouth shut.

The hours passed, the mate came to take over. Carlock heard them talking.

"This blow will be over before we reach the Scillys, but we'll hit it again in the bay," said Herrick. "How are the engineers making it, mister?"

"Tired out from throttle watches," the mate said. "Trouble with the coal; chief says they must clean fires twice a watch to keep the grates clear. Damned Lorrins stinginess; coal's no better'n slag, they say. The new owner pocketing his money and us slaving for him."

"That's what owners are for," said Herrick grimly. "Maybe he knows nothing. That blasted cockney office-manager pockets the swag—grafts on grub and coal and all else. What d'ye expect from a louse of an owner who keeps his chair warm and never sees the ocean?"

The watch changed, and Jem Carlock dragged himself below, fell on the sodden straw, and slept for two hours till somebody fell against him and sent pain through his aching body.

He struggled up and got on deck. No one noticed him. At the galley, a cup of alleged tea gave him heart, and he descended the fiddley. Here was warmth; for a time he watched the sweating stokers bailing coal into the fireboxes. Then, with an air of determination, he went into the engine-room.

He stared around, marveling that men could move and work with any safety amid the complicated mechanisms. By the vague light of smoky lanterns, the greasy, half naked figures slipped between the steampipes of copper that wound like vast serpents around and above them. The greasers, with their swabs of grease, dodged the giant side-levers of the engine. At the throttle stood the assistant engineer, feeding steam when the ship squattered, easing the engines when she took a dive. He had just relieved the chief, who was turning to go above.

Jem Carlock halted him, hand to sleeve, under a lantern.

"Mr. McLeod! You'll remember me. We met in the Line office last Monday; you wanted special grease for the engines, if you mind."

For a long moment the chief stared him in the face blankly, then vented an oath.

"Oot o' my way, ye crazy loon! I'm at wor-r-rk, not raising blisters in an office chair. Oot o' here! On deck where ye belong!"

A heavy boot gave the words emphasis. Jem Carlock recovered balance, face contorted with pain, dodged a second kick, and went on deck with agility. He ran slap into Captain Herrick, and started back.

"Oh, it's you!" he burst out. "You'll suffer for this, Cap'n Herrick! By God, sir, you can maltreat and torture me as you will, while you have the chance; but my turn will come soon. This is your last voyage, understand? Your last! I'll not only have you in jail, but I'll see to it that you never get another berth—never!"

"Oh! You're the fellow with delusions." Herrick looked hard at him. "Haven't come to your senses yet, eh?"

"Have your joke while you may," cried Jem Carlock, bitter hatred in his eyes. "Your last voyage, Tramp Herrick; that's a promise! Your last—"

The bosun appeared, and Jem Carlock fled, dribbling oaths on the wind. After that, he labored on the brass-work, while the wind died to a whisper as they neared the Scillys. Land's End behind, they shaped a course for Ushant, off the coast of France, then southeastward toward Bilbao.

The mate was the one person to whom Cap'n Herrick could talk freely. A disappointed and therefore understanding soul, the mate showed a certain grasp of the possibilities, and was naturally agreeable to whatever the captain said was so.

Paying no heed whatever to the deck hand scouring away on the brasses, Cap'n Herrick unbosomed himself.

"They've all laughed at me, Mister; these pursy city shipowners nowadays take the advice of their clerks, instead of knocking about the world and doing things—but look how this voyage proves all I've claimed! It'll take us four days, maybe five against weather, to Bilbao. How long would a square-rigger

"I demand you put me ashore!" cried the hapless wretch. "I'm the owner of this ship—I want the ship put about at once for Liverpool!"

be beating and tacking about? Two weeks or three, wi' twice the crew and double expense. Coal's dirt cheap, and will be cheap for years to come. I'll put this craft against the proudest ship in the Lorrins Line, and deliver freights in a fourth of the time, at a third o' the cost—aye, less! Quick ships will produce quick cargoes, with short runs, port to port."

"It do stand to reason, sir," acknowledged the mate. "Why won't they see it?"

"They'll not listen," the captain said bitterly. "They won't listen, damn 'em! Ten years from now, the Yankees will have us off the seas, unless they do listen. Canvas is all very well for transatlantic work, for the wool trade, for the China trade; long runs and costly cargoes. But it's sheer waste for runs like this."

"Aye, sir," said the mate dutifully.

Toward eight bells of the afternoon, with Bilbao due in the morning, the skipper was at it again. The *Limerick* was churning along under a gray and threatening sky. The mate, with change of watches about due, sucked an empty pipe and listened. Jem Carlock, on an endless task of scrubbing and polishing, had to hear whether he liked or not.

"I'm surprised, sir," the mate said, with one eye on a Bristol barque that headed north against the horizon, "that you could get no one to listen."

"I'd like to throttle a few owners and make 'em listen!" Herrick said grimly. "And especially the city prig who's owner of this line now. Ye'd think such men would have foresight, breadth of vision, daring! But no. They sit on their hams in carpeted rooms and count their siller, and never had the feel of a ship in their fat lives. Look!"

He flung out a hand at the barque making for Bristol.

"Craft like that are doomed. Wines from Spain for Bristol cellars—they'll come cheaper and in a fraction of the time they come now. If I had my way and a fortune, I'd contract to deliver wines from Lisbon and Cadiz to Marseilles, Leghorn, Corinth, Alexandria; this craft under us would make the round trip with freights in every port, while yonder barque was outward bound!

"Doomed, aye," he went on. "The day will come when canvas will be a rarity. Ye needn't smile, Mister; you'll see the day, and die in some old sailors' home for lack of a berth, unless you stick to steam. And all up and down the seas, commerce tramps will carry the heavy freights of the world—I can vision it as though it were now!"

He turned and strode away. The second officer came to the bridge.

"Old Man ranting again?" said he.

The mate nodded gloomily.

"Worse'n a fishwife," he stated, sucking at his pipe.

"Crazy as ever?" asked the junior, with a grin.

"No-o, not by half," the mate delivered slow-considered judgment. "If you ask me, he's got more sense than any of 'em. It's natural he can't get his mind off'n them tramp ships he talks about, but by gorry, what he says makes sense; more he talks, the harder sense it makes. A seaman can see it. These blokes ashore can't. And when it comes to that, nobody ever sailed with a better seaman than him."

"That's true enough," agreed the second mate.

Jem Carlock straightened up his weary back, staring at them.

Eight bells struck. He was free, and went. The mate went also.

Twenty minutes later, Cap'n Herrick came up to the bridge on the jump.

"Glass is down to twenty-seven!" he exclaimed. "We're in for it—"

A lightning-bolt split the sky and sea, drowning his voice. Biscay had struck. With a roar, the wind hit them; the ship went over almost on her beam ends. Herrick sprang to aid the helmsman; he was cool, able, unhurried. With full speed ahead, the ship gradually righted, heading into the wind, answering the frantic propeller at last.

After that first flurried moment, the fight began. Herrick was everywhere, seeing to everything, yet leaving the bridge only briefly. When the boats stove, he was there and then back to the bridge; when men were hurt, he saw to them and was back aloft to keep control of everything.

Jem Carlock, caught on that perilous flush deck by a smashing green billow, was going overboard when a powerful hand jerked him back and held him. The water drained, and he blinked into the savage features of Herrick.

"You! Should ha' let you go," said the skipper. "Keep to the hand-lines after this."

The Donegal man came along and took Carlock in charge, chuckling.

"All's well, matey! Every block and tackle, so to speak, running smooth; but Gawd help us wi' some skippers I know! Get along for'ard."

The afternoon wore on into black night; the night dragged toward dawn. With the morning watch, Jem Carlock and the Donegal man took the thrashing wheel; Cap'n Herrick was there—red of eye, face crusted with salt rime, but still cool. The mate spoke, and the skipper nodded.

"Take a sounding. We've made stern-way and have probably drifted into the bight. Bear a hand wi' that sounding!"

The mate returned, presently, reporting eight fathom.

"Both anchors!" roared Herrick. "Let go when you're ready!"

To Carlock, it seemed rank madness, but the Donegal man explained, by fits and starts:

Between Villano Island and Rabanal Point, thirteen miles to the westward, the coast formed a bight four miles deep, with Bilbao in the middle. In that dangerous bight with an onshore wind, a ship was lost—unless the anchors held. And they certainly would not hold—nothing would hold, if anything happened to the engines.

The engines held. The ship labored heavily, continually taking seas over the bows, all boats stove or swept away; but, with the engines to ease the strain on the anchors, she continued her wild pitching and budged not.

"One weak link in the anchor-chain, and we're done," said the Donegal man to Jem Carlock, as the day passed and the night came. "D'ye mind, second day out, how the Old Man inspected them cables, and half the watch cussing him for a fool? Proper seaman, he is. One weak link—that's the sea, matey. Weak foot-rope on a r'yal yard, weak link in a cable; that's death. Master walks the deck and takes his salute; but if he's a proper seaman, he does a lot more. That's the differ' between a wise man and a fool, matey."

Toward midnight, the wind had died down to fitful squalls.

With morning, Jem Carlock wakened. He was stiff and sore and bearded, but he was ravenous. The ship was moving; a pilot was aboard and she was making for the quay at Portugalete, six miles below Bilbao. Most of the crew were still dead to the world, but Jem Carlock drank great gulps of

Jem Carlock, caught by a smashing billow, was going overboard when a powerful hand jerked him back. Then— "You! Should ha' let you go," said the skipper.

the morning air into his lungs, and knew he was alive.

He swigged tea at the galley, and smacked his lips heartily over it. Some one said the agent of the Line had come aboard with the pilot. Jem Carlock grimly headed for the chartroom.

The door was ajar, and he paused there, unobserved. Captain Herrick, red-eyed, salt-rimed and unshaven, was talking with the Spaniard who looked after the affairs of the Lorrins Line.

"The cargo's all in good shape: machinery, cotton and woolen goods. Not a parcel shifted; my first officer's good at stowage."

"You did wonders, Captain, to get here so well," said the sleek Spaniard. "It is too bad you go back to England. We have much cargo; a cargo of pig-iron, flour, wine and skins for Marseilles. A Todd Line three-master should take it, but the telegraph says she put back to Bordeaux because of the gale."

A harsh burst of laughter, quite mirthless, came from Herrick.

"If I had my way, we'd take it. Ten years from now, we'd take it. But no; our confounded owner would have a fit if I made money for him. Sorry."

He glanced up, saw the figure in the doorway, and rose.

"So, it's you!"

"I suppose," said Jem Carlock, coming forward, "you'll not attempt to prevent me going ashore here?"

"I will not," Cap'n Herrick said grimly. "I could, but I will not. My last voyage, eh? All right. You can pay me off here, and ship another master, and be damned to you and yours! I've done one thing anyhow—damned well made you listen to me!"

The Spanish agent stared from the Captain to the ragged scarecrow.

"Who is this man?" he asked in surprise.

"This," said Cap'n Herrick, elaborately sardonic, "is Mr. Lorrins, owner of the Line, by his own say; he shipped aboard us this voyage, to get a taste of the sea. And by God, he got it!"

"Quite so," said Jem Carlock, who was now Lorrins. "I'll establish my identity very easily, once ashore. So, Cap'n Herrick, you still have your vision of the sailing ships swept off the sea and doomed, and the cargoes of the world carried hither and yon in commerce tramps—tramp ships, like tramp men, vagrant from port to port?"

"I have," Captain Herrick said defiantly. "And the likes of you will know in days to come that it's a true vision!"

Lorrins eyed him coldly. "How soon can you get off this ship, sir?"

"At once," snapped Herrick, a flame in his eye. "At once! The sooner, the better."

"I agree with you. This is your last voyage, sir."

Herrick scowled.

"You needn't remind me of it."

"I think it's necessary. You'll arrange with our agent, here, to ship the cargo for Marseilles; the *Limerick* will go on, with the first officer as acting master. I believe he's competent, and fully acquainted with the procedure. You'll join me ashore at the hotel. After a bit of sleep, we'll have much to talk over and arrange, before getting under way for Liverpool."

"Eh? *We?*" said Herrick, his brows beetling as he stared.

"Certainly. I did a good job of listening, Cap'n Herrick. The Lorrins Line is going to sell its canvas ships while prices are good, and is going in for commerce tramps, as you call them. Not a bad name at all. You, by the way, will be general manager of the Line, with *carte blanche* to handle matters as your experience suggests. We'll arrange details of salary and so forth over dinner and a bottle of wine this evening. Good day to you, gentlemen."

The sun glinted upon Bilbao and the long docks; and they faded, faded into a vista of little ships like the *Limerick*—little ships with steam propellers, scuttling from port to port. Little ships with no lordly cargoes of Ind and Cathay, but with loads of machinery and the less romantic things of life, readjusting the commerce of the world; little ships going up and down the Seven Seas like vagrant tramps in English lanes, replacing, the towering canvas of the square-riggers and clippers with the smoke of cheap coal—the humdrum and prosaic symbols of progress, with all the business of the earth under their hatches.

And there, in a thousand ports, was the last voyage of Cap'n Herrick written.

A LARGE-OUTPUT WRITER TALKS

M*onday morning's mail brought* a hearty response to my request for an interview with H. Bedford Jones.

"Sure!" he wrote. "Time and questions as you like. Say, Tuesday morning, any time until eleven."

So bright and early Tuesday morning—if ten o'clock could possibly be called bright and early—I walked up the steps of his residence in Michigan's university city and rang the bell. Mrs. Bedford-Jones was just going shopping, but she ushered me into the hallway and called: "Henry!"

The author himself, a tall handsome man with a decidedly distinguished appearance, came lightly down a stairway. I introduced myself and he shook hands with a comradely smile which I was soon to learn was usually near the surface.

"Take off your hat and coat," he said cordially. He took them from me and hung them up. Then he led the way into the parlor.

I settled myself in the comfortable chair he drew up for me, while he lolled indolently on a sofa.

"I've been told that you are the most prolific of present-day American writers," I smilingly hazarded, by way of a beginning. "Do you agree with such a statement?"

"Well, no," he laughed. "That might have been true a few years ago, but William Wallace Cook turns out more and better stuff than I do. I was once able to write a 25,000 word novelette in a day. Takes me a week now. Getting old, I guess."

Mr. Bedford-Jones certainly did not appear to be very old. He scarcely looked his thirty-nine years, though to be sure there were a few gray hairs to be seen on his head. His figure was slender and straight, almost military.

"But twenty-five thousand words a day!" I marveled. "Do you mean that you got your plot-ideas and everything, and wrote the entire story in a single day?"

He nodded smilingly.

"What is your opinion of the use of 'rules' in story writing?" I went on, feverishly taking notes.

"Of course we may be said to have certain rules," he replied. "And yet, in writing, even in commercial writing—by which I mean large-production writing for the fiction markets—there are no rules whatever. A story may be written that breaks every rule in the game—and still be a world-beater. After all, principles and not rules are the lasting things. Learning rules can never be more than a beginning; we can learn not to make mistakes only by making them. Get the rules down pat, if you will, but then forget them. Sit down and write your story with all restrictions, relegated to the subconscious mind. Otherwise, what chance have you for originality?"

Just then the mail man came and Mr. Bedford-Jones excused himself for a moment. I was glad of the diversion, for it enabled me to catch up on my notes.

It was apparent that the author held refreshingly "unorthodox" views on certain points of writing—at least from the viewpoint of academic theorists. But, as the inimitable Ring Lardner impertinently remarks, what of it? Surely the writer who has some forty published books to his credit, a hundred or so book-length novels, as many novelettes, and several hundred short stories in addition, is entitled to his own theories and a disregard for rules.

Consider also, as a case in point, that ninety-nine percent of Bedford-Jones' written work has sold. Just how many hundreds of thousands of words he turns out each year he was unable to say offhand, yet the total must be enormous.

"How do you get the material for your stories?" I resumed when the author again entered the room. "For instance, how did you get the material for Rodomont?"

The story I mentioned was of olden France, laid around a monastery on an island which, at low tide, could be reached via dry land. The tale had appeared serially in *Adventure,* and has since been published in book form.

"I've been in France for the past two years," the author answered. "I visited the place, an odd enough island off the French coast and imagination did the rest."

Travel is a great aid to the writer, Mr. Bedford-Jones believes. Not very long ago he could be found one day in a little mountain village in the West; the next sunrise saw him on his way with a little caravan of two automobiles, and darkness would find him miles distant, busy with the inevitable typewriter.

"What is your opinion of 'hack' writing?" I ventured. "Do you think the beginning writer should take it up or not?"

His ready smile flashed again.

"That depends upon whether the writer wants money or art. You hear the lament raised that there is too much commercialism in writing. Some writers have plenty of money and do not need pay for their work. But most of us must earn our living, and what better way for an author than by writing? Let the young writers write to sell; get themselves firmly established in 'hack writing,' or whatever you chose to call it. Then, if they feel the urge to turn out masterpieces they at least will not starve."

Mr. Bedford-Jones has a distinct aversion to sex stories, and also to the use of profane language. He holds that in the majority of cases proper effects can be obtained without the use of oaths at all, recourse to them implies inartistry.

"I don't believe I've seen any of your short stories lately," I next said.

"I've written few in the past five years. My work now is novels and novelettes."

"Do you find the longer type of story easier to write?"

"Much easier. In the short story everything must be condensed into as few words as possible. In the novelette you can expand. It's harder to boil down than to expand, you know."

"Most authors," I continued, scribbling hurriedly, "have a long struggle to win recognition—"

He guessed what I had intended saying.

"I had the same trouble. At first I worked on small newspapers, then wrote juvenile tales. It was 'Uncle Bill' Cook who got me to writing for the fiction magazines."

He was not at all hesitant in acclaiming the man who had helped him over the bumps at the beginning of the road. It developed that William Wallace Cook had met him while he was working on a newspaper, and for some years had encouraged him, showing him what to do and what not to do in the construction of stories. Finally Mr. Cook sent one of his pupil's stories to a magazine and it was promptly accepted. Later, Mr. Fred Moore of *The Argosy* featured Mr. Bedford-Jones' work, and he found himself firmly established as a fiction writer.

"What is the source of your story or plot ideas?" I inquired. "Observation, reading, inspiration, or just plain imagination?"

"Imagination and reading, mostly," he replied. "Observation, of course, is of great importance not only to the writer who travels much but to the one who must find his material in his own neighborhood. By observation we learn how people act, and how they react to the situations into which they are drawn.

"But imagination exceeds all others in importance. One doesn't have to travel extensively if he can imagine correctly the places he wishes to write about. I once sent a long story laid in Algiers to an editor who had lived there. The story was accepted and the editor has ever since refused to believe I had never been in Algiers at all!

"Imagination, plus accuracy, will carry the writer a long way. Naturally, one must be very accurate with place names, with dates, or with fact in any story; for readers like to 'come back at' authors who do not adhere closely to actualities. It pays to he accurate, deadly accurate!"

I did not dispute that last statement. Rather, I had every reason to concur, for only the day before I had received a letter from an irate reader who declared that an article of mine was all wrong. I managed to convince him that it was he who was on the wrong side of the fence, but the controversy convinced me, in turn, that it does indeed pay to be deadly accurate, if only to retain the confidence of the editors.

Asked how he went about writing his stories, Mr. Bedford-Jones replied smilingly:

"Just put a sheet of paper in the machine and write. An interesting situation or a good bit of dialogue serves for an introduction. After a few pages I stop and study the characters. Then, when they are clearly in mind—or perhaps they will develop later on, if intricate—I write on, page after page, letting the plot form itself."

He did not by any means advocate such a formula for the beginning writer, save as an experiment. I suggested that he had written so many stories that their construction was now second nature to him. He refused to commit himself, and I had to be content with a smile and "Probably."

I asked him if he had any other remarks to make. "Yes, I have," he answered. "Let the young writer depend more on hard work than on the fine inspiration he is hopefully waiting for. Inspiration, we might say, is just another name for experience or, as someone has termed it, perspiration.

"William Wallace Cook has more plots mapped out than he will ever write. And, unlike most writers, he can turn out any type of story desired; be it an historical tale, a Western action story, a wild, Jules Verne novel, or a humorously sentimental yarn that will make you cry and laugh at once. How does he do it? By inspiration, of course—about thirty years of it!"

I glanced at my watch and rose to go. As the genial author helped me into my overcoat he averred:

"That old admonition to write and keep on writing still holds true. Write at every opportunity. And don't mind the taunts against 'commercialism.' Remember, we may be too proud to fight—but we can't be too proud to write!"

www.ingramcontent.com/pod-product-compliance
Lightning Source LLC
Chambersburg PA
CBHW081132300726
48982CB00005B/942
* 9 7 8 1 6 1 8 2 7 4 0 1 4 *